GW00393783

ACKNOWLEDGMENTS

I would like to thank Paddy Mary Stentiford who, from the other side of the world, painstakingly edited my novel with me through all its myriad drafts. I would also like to thank my sister Wendy Ealey who produced the cover design and interior typesetting, Rebecca Singh and my son Burnham Arlidge for painting the mountains and eerie moon and my father, Tim Ealey, for painting the moonlit forest. The front cover is a true family affair.

THE WIZARD'S CURSE

THE SORCERER'S OATH – BOOK TWO

JENNY EALEY

Copyright (C) 2015 Jenny Ealey

Layout design and Copyright (C) 2019 by Next Chapter

Published 2021 by Next Chapter

Edited by Elizabeth N. Love

Cover art by Cover Mint

For all those children who fight to defy disability or trauma in their quest for happiness.

CHARACTERS

SORCERERS

Tamadil Royal Family:
King Markazon (deceased)
Queen, Markazon's wife
King Kosar, eldest son of King Markazon
Prince Jarand, second son of King Markazon
Prince Tarkyn, third son of King Markazon

Courtiers:
Danton Patronell, Lord of Sachmore, Tarkyn's friend from childhood
Andoran and Sargon, friends of Tarkyn at court.
Stormaway Treemaster, wizard for Prince Tarkyn and King Markazon
Journeyman Cloudmaker, Prince Jarand's wizard
Sergeant Torgan

Trappers:
String
Bean

WOODFOLK

Wanderers:
Waterstone
Sparrow, Waterstone's daughter
Autumn Leaves
Thunder Storm
Creaking Bough, Thunder Storm's wife

Rain on Water, Thunder Storm's son
Rustling Leaves
Grass Wind
Lapping Water
Summer Rain, healer
Falling Rain, Summer Rain's exiled brother

Forestals:
Raging water
Falling Branch, his son
Sun Shower, Falling Branch's wife
Rainstorm, Falling Branch's son
Gatherers:
Ancient Oak
Tree Wind
North Wind
Running feet

Mountainfolk:
Dry Berry
Woodfolk near Tormadell
Ancient Elm
Dripping Rock
Sighing Wind
Blizzard
Cavern
Hail

Captured Woodfolk:
Golden Toad
Rushwind
Ibis Wings

THE STORY SO FAR

*"Even with the oath, one man against a nation is poor
odds."*

In Eskuzor, land of sorcerers, nineteen-year-old Prince Tarkyn
faces unjust charges by his brother the king and the king's twin
brother Prince Jarand. He escapes, leaving a trail of death and
destruction behind him. As he flees the city of Tormadell, a
family of thieves first try to rob him then aid him to evade
pursuit.

After days on the run, he wanders into the woodlands in
the company of an old wizard, Stormaway Treemaster, only to
find himself unable to leave. Woodfolk attack him, and he
retaliates with threatening displays of magic. But then Tarkyn
is horrified to discover that he is the unwelcome, bitterly
resented liege lord of these elusive people who fear sorcerers
and whose oath to 'protect, honour and serve him' has been
spellbound to the welfare of their forest. The prince is shocked
by the woodfolk's behaviour in the presence of royalty and
clashes with Ancient Oak and several others.

Before the woodfolk have taken adequate measures to
protect him, bounty hunters capture Tarkyn. A
misunderstanding of the prince's magic by the woodfolk lead to
him being severely injured during his escape. While Tarkyn
lies unconscious, Stormaway, disguised as the prince, draws the
bounty hunters far from the forest.

For more than a week, the prince lies unconscious, while
one woodman, Waterstone, stays by his side talking quietly to
him and bringing him back to an awareness of his surroundings.

As he recovers, Tarkyn, raw from his brothers' betrayal and wary of the woodfolk's resentment, gradually develops an uneasy friendship with Waterstone.

Woodfolk can hold conversations and send images mentally to each other. Sorcerers and wizards don't have these special powers, but gradually, Tarkyn discovers that he can receive and send images and feelings, but not words. In fact, Tarkyn's strong feelings sometimes transmit to other people without his knowledge or control.

When a hunting party of the king and his brother enter the woods, Tarkyn's reaction to seeing his brothers overwhelms Waterstone's daughter, Sparrow, and she blacks out. Although Tarkyn looks after her as she recovers, Waterstone is furious, hurling threats at the prince and trying to attack him. This flouting of the oath causes an area of forest to be seriously damaged before Tarkyn finds a way to curtail the destruction by actually giving Waterstone permission to attack him.

Summer Rain, the healer, tells Tarkyn that her brother, Falling Rain, had been exiled twelve years ago by the woodfolk for revealing their presence to the king and that the woodfolk are divided on whether he should ever be allowed to return.

Struggling with the politics surrounding the prince and the potential damage his own anger could cause, Waterstone almost abandons his friendship with Tarkyn, but decides to persevere.

Tarkyn offers to help to repair the forest, amazing Waterstone that sorcery could have more than martial uses. While Tarkyn is holding up branches for woodfolk to bind into place, Stormaway returns and rails at the prince for not behaving in a manner due to his station, until Tarkyn treats him to a dose of royal hauteur. Later that evening, Stormaway tells him that the bounty hunters had been Andoran and Sargon, Tarkyn's erstwhile friends. As Tarkyn wanders down near the river thinking about this further betrayal, an attacking wolf is stopped by Waterstone's arrow. Then, from a viewing point above him in the trees, Tarkyn sees another wolf approaching behind the woodman. Tarkyn shouts a warning and uses shafts of magic to kill the wolf.

Tarkyn's ability to trust has been so badly damaged by his brothers' and friends' betrayals that Waterstone allows Tarkyn free access to his memories to establish his own trustworthiness. However, Tarkyn delves too far, causing Waterstone to flee. He is confronted by Autumn Leaves who intervenes angrily on his friend Waterstone's behalf.

Stormaway lets slip that he had used mind power on Falling Rain, which then expiates Falling Rain's guilt. As reparation for a wrong done by sorcerers, Tarkyn resolves to trek across the mountains to find Falling Rain and bring him back to the fold.

Tarkyn discovers that, unlike the woodfolk, he can also share images and emotions with birds and animals and uses this discovery as a reason to approach Waterstone and repair the rift between them. As he talks with Waterstone and Autumn Leaves, it becomes increasingly obvious to Tarkyn that the egalitarian woodfolk have a very different concept of service from him and that he must work out how much to modify his expectations.

While he is mulling this over, an eagle gives him its view over the forest of an impending, large-scale wolf attack. Tarkyn warns the woodfolk and allows them the use of his powers.

Soon after the wolf attack has been averted, Stormaway notices green shoots appearing on Tarkyn's walking staff and, upon investigation, finds that the trees Tarkyn helped to repair have recovered unnaturally fast. Much to his embarrassment, Tarkyn learns that his newly discovered powers of healing and communing with animals define him as a legend in the woodfolk lore: the guardian of the forest, who appears among the woodfolk to aid them in times of great strife.

The celebrations of the advent of the Forest Guardian go late into the night, but the next morning, Tarkyn and the woodfolk consider where the source of the danger might be. The survival of the woodfolk depends on their ability to stay hidden. They work out that a hunting party will be coming to find the wolves they killed but instead, will find the dismembered, cleaned wolf carcases that will betray the woodfolk's existence.

As they prepare to face this threat, Waterstone's resentment of the oath surges up, leading to a fight between Tarkyn and himself. As a result, one of Tarkyn's previously broken ribs punctures his lung and only his healing powers as Guardian of the Forest, supplemented by the life force of the woodfolk, save him. Tarkyn then realises that he can also draw on the power of the forest through the trees to heal himself.

After helping the woodfolk to avoid a hunting party of wolves and armed men on horseback, Tarkyn then discovers that the woodfolk he is with have been concealing the existence of others of their kin from him. He feels betrayed, especially by Waterstone and, using an owl as a guide, leaves them to find his way to a community of oathless woodfolk.

He offers this community of woodfolk, the forestals, the opportunity to kill him, to release their kin from the oath and to ensure that oathbound woodfolk do not have to fight oathless woodfolk to protect him. The forestals are suspicious and hostile but decide their honour will not allow them to help their kin to betray their oath. So, they cannot kill the prince. During this process, Tarkyn finds a feisty ally in a rebellious young woodman, Rainstorm.

Autumn Leaves trudges into the forestal's firesite and, with Rainstorm's help, faces a resistant Tarkyn. When Autumn

Leaves explains that all woodfolk are sworn to conceal their kin, Tarkyn accepts the need for their duplicity, but is left feeling separate from them.

His resigned acceptance of his ongoing isolation, unbeknownst to Tarkyn, rolls around the woodfolk camp, causing the forestals to reconsider their attitude toward him. During the following week, woodfolk gather from all parts of the forest to discuss the unknown threat. In recognition of his demonstrated commitment to them, the woodfolk decide to make Tarkyn a member of the woodfolk nation in a ceremony in which Waterstone and Tarkyn become blood brothers. Tarkyn discovers that this also makes him Ancient Oak's brother and Sparrow's uncle.

Tarkyn's unreserved acceptance by the woodfolk is short lived. The next day, when another group of oathbound woodfolk arrive who have not spent any time with Tarkyn, the resentment against him surges up again. Eventually, the prince decides to assert his authority temporarily but unequivocally in the interests of protecting the woodfolk in the face of the impending threat, reasoning that he intends to leave the next day anyway so it won't matter if he upsets a few people temporarily.

However, the next morning, an enormous magic-driven storm threatens to cause widespread flooding and to force the woodfolk onto the open higher ground. Tarkyn harnesses the power of the forest to channel magic into Stormaway who orchestrates the dissipation of the storm.

Using Tarkyn's suggestions from the night before, the woodfolk discover that three of their kin are missing and are possibly being held prisoner by sorcerers. A power play amongst rival factions ensues where decisions are being made more on the basis of whether they support Tarkyn rather than on the issues themselves. Tarkyn confronts the worst of the factions and neutralises their antagonism.

Once the course of action had been decided, Tarkyn uses a mind link with a mouse to reconnoitre the sorcerer's encampment. The woodfolk are gravely shaken when he discovers that the woodfolk are indeed being held at the encampment and at least some people from outside the forest know of their existence.

Meanwhile, a strong sense of unease prompts Tarkyn to link up with an eagle owl, which spots a shadowy figure skulking in the woods near the firesite. Tarkyn recognises the figure as a palace guard. The woodfolk capture the guard, who turns out to be Danton, Tarkyn's erstwhile friend. But having been betrayed before, the prince is wary of trusting him. Tarkyn, the wizard and the woodfolk work together through a night of vigilance to confirm the guard's loyalty to the prince. When they are satisfied, the woodfolk allow him to stay in the woods with them, but Danton brings the expectations and protocols of the Royal Court with him, leading to disputes between several woodfolk and himself and causing Tarkyn to re-evaluate his relationships with the woodfolk.

When the prince stops a fight between Danton and Rainstorm, the young woodman turns his attack on Tarkyn. The wind thrashing through the trees makes Tarkyn realise that Rainstorm and the oathless woodfolk have somehow become subject to the sorcerous oath. Despite their friendship with Tarkyn, Rainstorm and Waterstone are both horrified when they find out that the oath has spread, and it is decided to keep it from the others until after the rescue of the imprisoned woodfolk.

The woodfolk all insist that Tarkyn should not take part in the rescue because they must ensure they protect him. Since Tarkyn has also vowed to protect the forest, he cannot risk them refusing his orders and destroying the forest. So, he does not insist on going with them but agrees to take part from a distance.

Danton and Stormaway infiltrate the sorcerers' camp, in preparation for the woodfolk mounting a rescue. They run into Sargon and Andoran, and Danton is forced to assume a disloyalty to Tarkyn to maintain his role in the rescue plot. Firstly, Stormaway, and then Tarkyn and the woodfolk, suspect Danton of duplicity. Once Stormaway is reassured, the wizard and Danton concoct a series of unpleasant revenges on Sargon and Andoran, involving hallucinogens, itching powders, and slow-working, non-lethal poisons.

During the lead up to the raid, Tarkyn discovers that Waterstone's objections to using horses stems from a fear he has of them. In the ensuing discussion, it becomes apparent that Danton's possible betrayal and accumulation of people's adverse reactions to the oath have distressed Tarkyn. Waterstone gives Tarkyn an unequivocal assurance of his enduring commitment to him, as both friend and brother, and Rainstorm bravely goes swimming with him in an icy creek to cheer him up.

Using their own deadly accurate hunting skills and Tarkyn's abilities to guide animals from a distance, the woodfolk knock out the boundary guards and throw the chained woodfolk onto remotely guided horses that carry them safely in the woods. But while everyone else has escaped, Tarkyn receives a strong, fear-filled image that makes him realise that Autumn Leaves has been captured by Andoran and Sargon. Tarkyn translocates into the sorcerer's encampment to rescue him. When he returns, he faces the woodfolk's ire for putting himself at risk but makes it clear to them that he will no longer allow them to dictate to him.

Because Danton has been so convincing in playing his part

as friend of Andoran and Sargon, Tarkyn and the woodfolk lose faith in him and take him captive. Danton refuses to defend himself and insists that they trust him. Tarkyn relents and Danton then avers that Tarkyn is the only true hope for the future of Eskuzor, a sentiment that Stormaway reiterates.

I

THE INFESTATION

"And yet, my lord..." Low and intense, Stormaway's voice came from behind him as it reverberated around the gathering. "Your destiny is written in the stars and lives deep inside the trees of the forest. It has been clear from the day of your birth for all who have knowledge of such things to see. Your father and I always knew. That's why you had to be protected. You are not only the Guardian of the Forest. You are the one true hope for the future of all Eskuzor."

1

---

arkyn whirled around to face the wizard, his long, black hair flying out behind him. "No, Stormaway. I can't be."

When the wizard made no reply, the prince pressed home his point. "I will not pit myself against the king. I have never wanted the throne. You know that. The intrigue would be more than I could stand." He glanced around at the woodfolk who stood silently watching him. "Besides, I would not ask these people to go to war against my own brothers, especially when the countryside is littered with people who would turn me in for the price on my head." Tarkyn scowled. "The whole concept is preposterous."

The wizard shrugged. "I did not say you had to wrest the throne from your brother. I said you were the one true hope for Eskuzor. I do not know how the prophecy will evince itself. But in the life of a prince, your own wishes are not always paramount. If, one day, you had to assume the monarchy, I know you would put your personal preferences aside for the sake of your people."

"But not at the expense of my people." Tarkyn swept an

arm around him. "Anyway, I cannot see how having me on the throne would do anything to forward the welfare of the woodfolk, except perhaps to relieve them of my presence." He gave a wry smile. "But I am vain enough at this point to think that they no longer have a vested interest in getting rid of me."

Waterstone watched this interchange with some satisfaction from the periphery, pleased that Tarkyn no longer felt so alienated from them. His attention was drawn to North Wind who glanced at Waterstone as he stepped forward to speak.

Before he could say anything though, Danton placed his hand on the prince's shoulder and said in a tight voice, "Sire, the woodfolk are not your only people. Don't forget the rest of us."

Watertsone smothered a smile as he saw Tarkyn stiffen under the unaccustomed familiarity from Danton.

However, since it was Tarkyn himself who had granted Danton permission to behave less formally with him in line with the woodfolk's behaviour, Tarkyn could do nothing but suppress his automatic response and relax his shoulder muscles under Danton's hand. As he turned slowly back to look at Danton, his liegeman's hand dropped from his shoulder.

"Sire," Danton glanced around the gathered woodfolk, "I mean no disrespect to the woodfolk, and I know you have a special bond with them. But you are also a prince of sorcerers and wizards in the world outside these forests. And those people may need you every bit as much as the woodfolk do."

Tarkyn stood silently considering him for several long seconds, "Danton," he said finally, "I am guardian of these forests and all who live in them. That is not the case with the sorcerers and wizards. My brother is their sovereign. Since his betrayal of me, I have foresworn my allegiance to him but that is no reason for me to challenge him and bring civil war to Eskuzor."

Stormaway shook his head. "I am afraid civil war is brewing, even as we speak, Sire. Conversations around the firesides in the encampment were all of unrest and revenge."

Danton pressed home his point. "According to Sargon and Andoran, the encampment itself is a marshalling point for vigilantes waiting to take the law into their own hands because King Kosar is failing to protect his people."

"I didn't realise that, Danton. This is grave news." Tarkyn looked around the gathered woodfolk. "I think we had better sit down, have some breakfast and hear everything you and Stormaway have to tell us. Perhaps this will also shed some light on how and why woodfolk are being hunted."

As they headed back to the firesite, Tarkyn manoeuvred himself so that he was walking next to North Wind. "So. What did you wish to say to me?"

The woodman glanced up at him. "I didn't think you'd noticed."

Tarkyn merely nodded.

North Wind drew a short breath. "I wanted to say that even though your death would mean we were freed from the oath, I wouldn't want you to die."

A puzzled frown creased Tarkyn's brow. He shook his head slightly. "I see...Thank you, North Wind, I think...actually, no. I don't see at all. Why are you suddenly telling me this? I thought we were already friends."

"We are. That is, we were...and we still are. It's just that..." North Wind stopped walking, in a total fluster. The people behind them nearly bumped into them. "Tarkyn, when I first got to know you, when we were helping Rain Storm, well, it was more that I thought you were better than I expected, given that I had to put up with you as our imposed liege, if you see what I mean."

Tarkyn looked at him quizzically. "More or less."

North Wind took another breath. "So now, I would choose to put up with you, even if I could choose not to."

Tarkyn laughed and clapped North Wind on the shoulder as they set off once more. "I do see what you mean, and I thank you for it. It is high praise indeed if my company is worth your freedom."

"Yes, it is high praise," said North Wind stiffly. "And although I may not have expressed myself very well, I did not come to this view lightly."

"I beg your pardon, North Wind. I hope my laughter did not offend you. It was pleased laughter, not derisory." Tarkyn glanced down at the young woodman. "I hope you weren't bullied into your new viewpoint. I know Waterstone can be a little feisty at times...and I couldn't help noticing your bruised jaw."

North Wind gave a reluctant smile as he shook his head. "No. Woodfolk don't work like that. Waterstone wouldn't bully me into submission. He just belted me because he was angry about something I said. I make my own decisions. That's why I didn't come straight over and talk to you. I needed time to think."

"I see." Tarkyn did not tell him how much anxiety the woodman's reticence had caused him. As they reached the firesite, Tarkyn headed straight over to where Autumn Leaves was sitting, propped up against a tree with a blanket over his legs.

"How are you?" asked Tarkyn as he sat down beside him.

Autumn Leaves glanced at him. "Not too bad. My face is still sore where they slammed me with the knife hilt." He shrugged and gave a wan smile. "I guess it could have been worse. They could have used the sharp end."

"It feels horrible, doesn't it? Being treated like that. I hated that a lot more than the pain."

The woodman nodded miserably. "Yes. Much worse. I felt as if I were some sort of contemptible, curious beetle they had found. I still feel now as though my very soul has been jarred."

Tarkyn grimaced, "And what's worse, now you'll have an even poorer opinion of sorcerers than you did before."

"No, I won't," said Autumn Leaves firmly. "Not when you put yourself in danger to rescue me. I already knew Sargon and Andoran were amoral bastards." He nodded across at Danton. "And it looks as if your friend there maintained his loyalty in the midst of the enemy. So, the score still stands at two good sorcerers, a few known bad ones and thousands still awaiting my judgement." He looked at the sorcerer beside him. "Tarkyn, thanks for what you did. I know you said you weren't at risk, but we both know you were."

Tarkyn shrugged. "Well, I wasn't in as much danger as everyone assumed I would be. I did have help from my little mouse scout. I was very careful, for your sake as well as mine."

"And you knew you would have to face everyone's displeasure when you returned."

"If you can risk being burnt to a crisp to support your friend, I think I can risk a small argument... But seriously, Autumn Leaves, no one is going to stop me from helping my friends if they are in trouble."

The woodman gave a little smile. "Do I gather from your tone that you gave them one of your supercilious set-downs?"

Tarkyn nodded. "Yes. I'm afraid poor Thunder Storm drew the worst of my fire. He made the mistake of demanding that I should not place myself in danger again."

"I wondered how long you would meekly accept everyone's overprotectiveness."

Tarkyn raised his eyebrows. "Did you? You didn't say so."

"No. That would have diverted the focus away from rescuing Golden Toad and his family. I knew you'd assert yourself when you needed to." Autumn Leaves gave a reluctant smile. "You do, after all, hold the balance of power."

As he finished speaking, Danton handed them each a bowl of porridge and sat down on the other side of Autumn Leaves, "I hear you had a bad time at the hands of Andoran and Sargon. They are utter bastards, those two. Although it is not appreciated," he added with heavy irony, "I had to endure hours of their company. True, I wasn't being battered about like you two. But I did have my senses assailed by their opinions, and it tested me sorely to listen to them running you down, Sire, without retaliating."

Tarkyn gave a rueful smile. "I'm sorry we doubted you, Danton. If it's any consolation, I banged their heads together very hard. So they should at least have bad headaches this morning."

"Oh, Stormaway and I have done worse than that. We spiked their water and wine and rubbed crushed nettles and poison ivy in their bedclothes. It won't kill them, but it will make them very sick and uncomfortable!"

Waterstone chuckled, "Danton, you were cross, weren't you?"

"Unfortunately, the hallucinogens in the wine kept Sargon and Andoran awake and I spent the evening of the rescue trying to distract their attention from the sounds outside." He shrugged. "Only partially successful, I'm afraid. At least they didn't rush outside at the first sounds they heard. I managed to hold them until right near the end. I'm sorry I didn't do better, Autumn Leaves, but of course I was in no position to help you after that because this suspicious lot kidnapped me about then."

By this time, Stormaway and the other woodfolk were seated around the fire, listening to Danton.

"You're right, of course," said Waterstone. "The outcome would have been better if we'd trusted you."

"Yes, possibly. I may have been able to save Autumn Leaves straight away which would have saved him from having to endure all that unpleasantness. But, despite what I said earlier, I'm not sure that I could have maintained my role with Andoran and Sargon. When they thought back over the evening, I think they may have realised that I had been consistently trying to dismiss their suspicions. It depends largely on how confused they were as a result of the drugged wine. You probably did me a favour getting me out of there."

Tarkyn was watching Danton, a small crease between his brows. "Danton, what are you up to? You can't possibly be grateful to us for knocking you out and keeping you tied up for hours."

Danton's eyebrows snapped together, and he spoke with a formality that barely covered his impatience. "I am not up to anything, Your Highness. I didn't say I was pleased with being knocked out *again* and tied up *again*." He drew a breath to reign in his temper. "But it might actually have been a good time to leave anyway. I certainly didn't want to stay. Ask Stormaway. I hated having to spend that time with Sargon and Andoran."

"Sire, Danton acted tirelessly on your behalf even though it clearly distressed him. He knew he risked arousing your suspicions but took that chance in support of your cause."

Danton sighed, "I was not particularly surprised to find myself back in the forest under guard. I was annoyed, but I was also relieved that I wasn't in the same predicament somewhere in the sorcerer's encampment."

"You have been playing a dangerous game, haven't you, Danton? Made all the more dangerous by having an uncertain liege." Tarkyn accepted a cup of tea from Lapping Water who came to sit beside them. He blew on it and took a sip before saying quietly, "I apologise for my lack of faith and applaud your courage, my friend. It is one thing to risk physical danger but quite another to risk alienation from people you care about."

Waterstone watched the colour in Danton's cheeks heighten as the passionate young sorcerer murmured gruffly, "Thank you, Sire."

There was a short silence. Finally, Waterstone broached the subject that was on everyone's minds.

"Stormaway, Danton, how many people know about the captured woodfolk that we rescued?"

The two men looked at each other, then Stormaway shrugged. "We can't say for sure. But my impression is – not many. No one mentioned woodfolk or anyone bearing any resemblance to you in the conversations around the fire. Sargon and Andoran didn't mention them as far as I know. Danton?" When the blonde sorcerer shook his head, Stormaway continued, "Golden Toad and his family were kept concealed in a tent that had a magically warded entrance. And people we spoke to thought there was a sick wolf chained up in there."

There was a collective sigh of relief.

"So, who does know?" asked Waterstone.

"Whoever was feeding the wolves knows," said Tarkyn unexpectedly. "I saw him through the raven's eyes when I was watching the encampment. He's the young man who led the hunting party after we foiled the wolf attack."

"Is he? I wish I'd known." Stormaway frowned. "It is very

frustrating to be unable to pick up images like you and the woodfolk. I could have told you who he was when you showed everyone the image of the hunt more than a week ago."

Tarkyn raised his eyebrows. "And?"

"And what?"

"And so, who is he?"

"Oh, sorry. He's my old apprentice, Journeyman Cloudmaker. And unless I'm much mistaken, he will also have been behind that storm we dissipated last week."

Thunder Storm looked from one to the other of them. "So, is this Journeyman the driving force behind the search for us? Why would he be looking for us?"

Stormaway shook his head. "No. He is not a leader. He will be acting under orders."

"Andoran and Sargon told me that the encampment was a gathering for forces who are being financed by some lord, Davorad of Stansbeck. Apparently, he is concerned that brigands are mounting constant attacks on farmers and travellers and has decided to address it himself." Danton looked at Tarkyn. "Do you know him?"

"I have met him at court. He is a thickset bullish sort of man, not that I suppose that's relevant. He didn't strike me as a philanthropist. In fact, I would have said he is the classic sort of parasite that revels in the games of power that are rife at court." Tarkyn scraped out the last of his porridge and set the bowl down on the ground. "So. I can think of three reasons that he might be doing this. He might be supporting the king by clearing up the countryside on his behalf. He might be supporting Jarand by gathering resistance against Kosar, or he might be planning to overthrow both of them."

"No," said Danton firmly. "Your family has held the monarchy for over a thousand years. The populace would not contemplate an outsider usurping the throne."

"I think you're right, Danton," put in Stormaway. "From the discontent I heard around the campfires, I would say that Davorad is marshalling a vigilante force to show up King Kosar's shortcomings. It remains to be seen whether it is a political ploy to embarrass the king or the beginnings of a civil war."

"Oh stars above! My bloody brothers!" exclaimed Tarkyn. "Why can't they learn to work together? They look so alike they could take turns at being king if they wanted to and no one would know the difference – Well, maybe my mother would, but she'd never go against their wishes anyway." Tarkyn ran his hand through his long, black hair. "But no! Kosar neglects the protection of his people while he fights off power plays, and Jarand, instead of supporting Kosar to refocus his energy, grasps the opportunity to undermine him."

"Which leaves you," concluded Danton.

"Oh no, it doesn't!" countered Tarkyn swiftly. "What are you thinking? That I choose which one of my brothers to support? Or that I take them both on and divide the country into three factions?"

"I think you should concentrate on being our forest guardian and protecting us against whoever is hunting us," said Autumn Leaves, entering the fray. "Perhaps the meaning of the prophecy will become clearer over time. You don't have to change what you're doing to make a prophecy come true. It's not a script. It's a future reality."

Everyone stopped and stared at him. Waterstone raised his eyebrows and remarked, "That was remarkably profound, Autumn Leaves. I'm impressed."

"Although I agree in principle with Autumn Leaves," said Stormaway, "I should point out that being the hope for the future of Eskuzor is a present reality and an uncertain future"

"Even more profound," Waterstone nodded approvingly, a

twinkle in his eyes, "and so early in the day. We haven't even finished breakfast yet."

The wizard scowled. "Waterstone! Will you take this seriously?"

Waterstone suddenly became stern. "And will you take seriously that you are trying to lay an enormous burden on one young man's shoulders? I remember, if you do not, how hard it was for Tarkyn to come to terms with being our forest guardian. Let us just bring our planning back into the present and stop demanding the impossible from Tarkyn."

"Easy for you to say," grumbled Danton. "He's already supporting you. What about all those poor sorcerers and wizards who are being attacked with no one to defend them?"

Thunder Storm's deep, rolling voice made itself heard, "Ah, but didn't you say they are organising themselves to defend against marauders?"

So intent were they all on this discussion that they took a while to notice that Tarkyn had quietly stood up and walked away.

—————————

2

Tarkyn wandered down through the golden leaved trees until he reached the stream. Here, he found a comfortable rock to lean against and sat staring out across the sparkling, rippling water. He let his mind roam out through the surrounding trees and bushes, tuning into the birds and animals around him. He reflected with a small, inward smile that there was nowhere he could go where he was really alone. He tuned into a little field mouse that was snuffling around under a nearby bush and asked her to come over to him. The little mouse scurried over the few feet of open ground and scuttled up his leg to sit, quivering slightly, on his knee. Tarkyn sent her waves of reassurance and friendship until she became still and calm. Very slowly, Tarkyn reached into a nearby bush and pulled off a small bunch of dark red berries. He had no idea what they were but hoped that the mouse might like them. He offered one to the mouse who grasped the berry between her front paws and, after giving it a careful sniff, began to nibble it. Tarkyn received a little wave of thanks.

Suddenly, Rainstorm and Ancient Oak were standing in

front of him. The mouse jerked with fright, but a calming message from Tarkyn kept her from scurrying off. Tarkyn looked up at the two of them and smiled. "Hello, you two. Have a seat."

They both dropped into cross-legged sitting positions.

"Hi, Prince," said Rainstorm. "Just thought we'd come down and see what you're up to."

Tarkyn smiled broadly at them, "Thanks. I'm fine," he said, correctly interpreting what Rainstorm meant.

Ancient Oak frowned a little. "You're not angry at them all for talking about you, are you?"

Tarkyn spread his hands slowly, careful not to frighten the mouse. "Do I look angry? No. I just got a bit tired of it all and needed a break...and a bit of time to think. I'm sure I'll pick up the thread of the discussion when I go back." He shrugged and said cheerily, "I've already decided what I'm going to do. So, I'll let them know when they've had time to talk over all the angles."

"So, what happened to consultation? Aren't you going to consider anyone's views?" asked Ancient Oak with a slight frown. "You're not coming over all autocratic again, are you?"

"Big brother, I never stopped being autocratic. I just try to act as though I'm not, most of the time. By the way, thanks for supporting me against the others over my rescue of Autumn Leaves. I suspect I did not appear particularly grateful to you at the time."

Ancient Oak's cheek tinged with pink. "No, not really. But like you, I didn't stick up for you for your gratitude. I did it because it was just."

Tarkyn glanced at him before offering the mouse another berry. When it was happily nibbling again, he looked up and smiled in satisfaction. "I'm developing quite a fondness for mice after my brave little friend in the encampment helped me in my rescue of Autumn Leaves." He gave a slight smile. "Did you have to endure a tongue-lashing, Rainstorm, for helping me to translocate and put myself at risk?"

Rainstorm grinned. "Ooh, just a bit. Nothing I'm not used to, though. Poor old Thunder Storm was beside himself. He felt he'd let everybody down, letting you get away into danger."

"Oh dear. And then I snapped his head off when I got back. I'd better have a chat with him at some stage. He rubs me up the wrong way sometimes, but he really cares about doing the right thing, doesn't he?"

"And he cares about you," added Rainstorm.

Tarkyn smiled. "Yes, I know he does. And I have come to care about him too. So, I'll make sure I sort it out with him." Tarkyn fed the mouse another berry and gave it a gentle stroke with one finger.

"Right, then," said Rainstorm impatiently. "So don't keep us in suspense. What have you decided? And why aren't you consulting anyone?"

Tarkyn looked from one to the other of them in an effort to build the suspense then grinned. "I'm going down into the southwest to find Falling Rain and bring him back into the fold, for his sake and for ours. For some reason, I think he's going to be important to our plans. The home guard, and whoever else wants to, can come with me. We'll leave some people near here, keeping an eye on the encampment, and some people should watch the main road through the forest and gather information on these bandits that keep attacking the travellers. When we get back with Falling Rain, we'll decide what to do next, based on the information gathered. How does that sound?"

Ancient Oak raised his eyebrows sceptically. "You're asking us?"

Laughter lit Tarkyn's eyes. "Oh yes. I'm asking. I just may not listen."

"Very funny," scowled Ancient Oak.

"Oh, come on, Ancient Oak. Of course I'll listen. Anyway, there is nothing new in these plans. They are still the same plans we all decided on, the day before the storm. Remember?"

Ancient Oak nodded reluctantly.

"So? Are you happy with them or do you have other suggestions?"

The woodman thought for a moment. "What about this business about being Eskuzor's hope for the future? Doesn't that change things?"

A shadow passed over Tarkyn's face. "I don't know. Stormaway is right. As a prince of Eskuzor, my life is not just my own to do with as I please. The same is true of being your forest guardian and liege lord. But Waterstone and Autumn Leaves are also right. We can't achieve the impossible overnight. So, let's take it one step at a time. First, we'll gather information and work out how to deal with the crisis facing the woodfolk. Only when that is sorted out and we are clearer about what else is happening can we begin to consider wider issues outside the forest and whether I should have any involvement in them."

"And what about the oath and the forestals?" asked Rainstorm.

Ancient Oak frowned. "What about it?"

Tarkyn raised his eyebrows at Rainstorm.

"Oops. Sorry." Rainstorm did not actually appear to be very contrite. "Well, now I've gone this far, you'll have to tell him. He is your brother after all. You shouldn't be keeping things from him, anyway."

"Rainstorm, considering who my other brothers are, that is probably one of your less well considered remarks." There was an edge to Tarkyn's voice as he said, "And I think it is my business, not yours, how I behave with my brothers."

Rainstorm was not so easily intimidated. "Oh, get that supercilious tone out of your voice. For heaven's sake, can't a person have a simple conversation without you getting on your high horse? If I can't express my opinion, there's no point in talking to you. You can disagree with it if you like. That's up to you. But lay off with the superior tone."

Tarkyn stared at him, white faced with anger. A wave of outrage rolled out from him and rocked the two woodmen. The mouse on his knee froze. After what seemed like an eternity, Tarkyn turned his gaze to Ancient Oak and, pointedly ignoring Rainstorm, said in coolly polite voice, "Ancient Oak, I did not intend to exclude you. It appears that Rainstorm and, presumably, the rest of the forestals, in fact possibly all woodfolk, have become subject to the oath and its sorcery, not just those who swore it originally. Rainstorm and North Wind were there when we made the discovery, and I have only told Waterstone about it subsequently. I didn't want the controversy it would cause to distract us from the rescue of Golden Toad and his family."

Ancient Oak's eyes narrowed. He went to speak but then said nothing. The mouse, seizing its opportunity, scuttled off, having decided that the atmosphere was not worth the berries.

Still in the same unnerving voice, Tarkyn said, "No. I didn't do it. And yes, I know you're upset about having more of your kindred subject to the oath, and I'm sorry. I promise you I did not engineer it."

"I didn't think you would have. I would have liked to be included, though."

Tarkyn unbent enough to give a small rueful smile. "You're much more contained than Waterstone, aren't you? He acted as though the world had fallen in when I told him."

Ancient Oak smiled back. "No wonder you weren't anxious to tell anyone else."

Tarkyn shook his head. "That's no excuse. I should have told you too. But, to tell you the truth, it's a long time since I trusted my sorcerer brothers. So, for me, it does not naturally follow that because you're my brother, I include you in everything."

Ancient Oak looked down at his hands for a moment then glanced back up at Tarkyn. "Well, just remember that a family is there for you to call on in times of need. That is our code. You don't have to, but I'm here if you need me."

"Thanks, Ancient Oak." Tarkyn smiled warmly at him. "I will remember."

Rainstorm swallowed nervously and said in a small, strained voice, "I'm here too, you know."

Tarkyn's face hardened as he swept his eyes around to look at the younger woodman. Before he could speak, Rainstorm spoke more formally than either of them had ever heard him speak before, "I am sorry, Your Highness. I can see I've overstepped another of your boundaries. I beg your pardon. I shouldn't have spoken to you like that."

Tarkyn's tone was equally formal. "Rainstorm, not only were you unacceptably rude to me, you also broke my trust." He was still clearly angry. "I would suggest that you do not try to force my hand again if you wish to retain my friendship. I will think twice before including you in my confidence in future."

So saying, he stood up and walked back up the track, leaving two shaken woodmen behind him. He had only gone a little way when he heard hurried footsteps coming up behind him. Tarkyn stopped and waited, arms folded, knowing that whoever was approaching was carefully warning him of his arrival since normally a woodman's footsteps made no sound. Ancient Oak appeared beside him.

"Well?" asked Tarkyn with raised eyebrows.

"Tarkyn, remember when we were talking up in that old oak on the day the crowd was arguing about how you should behave?"

Tarkyn nodded.

Ancient Oak took a breath. "Well, you said to feel free to pull you up if you became too arrogant or dismissive."

Tarkyn waited.

"So, I've come to say that I think you were too harsh with Rainstorm."

"Do you? And is he a particular friend of yours that you stand up for him like this?"

Ancient Oak shook his head and smiled. "No. But he's a particular friend of yours, and he just gave you the most handsome apology I've ever heard him give anyone and you rejected it."

Tarkyn frowned. "He made me very angry. I have never had anyone speak to me like that in my entire life...and I have no intention of allowing it to continue." His mouth twitched in a half smile. "There is only so much familiarity I can handle. No matter how close people come to me, they must still treat me with respect." Seeing Ancient Oak's face tense, he added, "I expect myself to treat people around me with respect too. It is not a one-way expectation."

"You could argue that he's treating you with respect because he treated you as he would one of his other friends."

The prince shrugged. "Yes. You could argue that and you might be right. And yet, I'm afraid I cannot tolerate that level of familiarity. But I am also angry that he told you about the oath when we had agreed to tell no one."

"Apparently, you told him it would be time to tell everyone soon. So, he didn't think it mattered as much, now the rescue was over."

"And do you think he should have told you as he did?"

Ancient Oak shook his head reluctantly. "No. He was definitely being cheeky to tell me like that. It should have been left up to you."

Tarkyn gave a slow smile. "But he's young, impetuous, passionate, and it is second nature to him to push the boundaries. And I guess that's why I like him. After all, he defied all his elders to untie me when I first met the forestals." Tarkyn turned on his heel. "Very well. I'll go back down and put him out of his misery."

When they arrived back at the stream, Rainstorm was sitting where Tarkyn had left him, methodically breaking bits off the end of a stick, just as Tarkyn always did. As they approached, he looked up and Tarkyn could see the strain on his face.

"I'm really sorry, Tarkyn..." he began.

Tarkyn waved a hand. "You have already apologised. Once is enough. I accept your apology."

Rainstorm let out a sigh of relief. "And are we still friends?"

"Yes. We are still friends." It looked as though he would say more but then changed his mind and said, "What needed to be said has been said. Let's leave it behind us."

"But will you trust me to keep your confidence next time?"

Tarkyn looked at him for a moment. "Probably. I don't think you'll pull a stunt like this again, but you might blurt something out if you were angry. So, it would depend what it was."

Surprisingly, Rainstorm took this in good part. "Fair enough, Your Highness."

Tarkyn's eyebrows twitched a little at Rainstorm's use of his title. It suggested a certain distance in their relationship that had not been there before. But Tarkyn did not comment on it, deciding to give things time to repair. After all, he couldn't berate Rainstorm one minute for being too familiar and then criticise him for being too formal the next.

"Come on," said Tarkyn, offering his hand. He pulled Rainstorm to his feet. "Let's go back and plan our next moves." He gave a little smile. "While we're walking back, you can put their minds at rest about my wellbeing, if you like. You could also let them know my suggestions for future actions. That will give them time to think about it."

While Ancient Oak went out of focus to mindtalk with the others, Rainstorm frowned suspiciously at Tarkyn and asked, "What are you smiling at?"

Tarkyn's smile broadened. "Having all of you looking after me. It's quite nice in its way."

"Haven't you always had people looking after you?"

Tarkyn considered for a moment before replying. "I suppose so. Certainly, in a practical or material sense. But most people looked after me as part of their role. Looking after my needs was the job that they were paid for."

"What?" Rainstorm looked profoundly shocked. "Did none of them genuinely care for you at all, Your Highness? I can't believe that."

Tarkyn gave a rueful smile. "I'm sure some of them did, but they would always have had the ulterior motive of making sure they kept their position in the Royal household."

"What about Danton? He seems to care about you."

Tarkyn put his head on one side. "You know, it has only been since he came to find me that I have really understood how much." He shrugged. "The trouble with being a prince is that you just don't know who would still be there if you didn't have the power, money and influence."

"So, why is it any different with us?" asked Ancient Oak, joining the conversation.

Tarkyn was a little taken aback but made a recovery after a few moments' thought.

"It *feels* different. You two came to see if I was all right, not because I was in danger or because the oath required it. Waterstone spent hours, days, looking after me when I was recovering when there was no payment or requirement to." He nodded at Rainstorm. "You came swimming with me in that freezing stream yesterday because you knew I'd been upset. You didn't have to. You could have stood on the bank or not come down to the stream with me at all."

"Well, obviously, we're not interested in money, but maybe we just want to share your power and influence," suggested Ancient Oak, playing devil's advocate.

Now, a hint of uncertainty passed over Tarkyn's face.

"Stop it!" Rainstorm intervened firmly, "Tarkyn is only just learning to trust us, or anybody for that matter. Don't confuse him." He glanced up at the prince. "You were right the first time. We do care about you, above and beyond the oath. You know for a fact that I do because I wasn't even under the oath to begin with. And I couldn't give a toss for power and influence."

"I'm sorry, Tarkyn. I was just teasing," said Ancient Oak, giving his adoptive brother a pat on the back. "I care no more for power and influence than I do for money. Woodfolk are used to having a fair say in things that matter. It's usually a given, so it's not something we hanker after."

Tarkyn's face relaxed into a smile, but Ancient Oaks' last words had given him food for thought. As long as the woodfolk had a fair say, they wouldn't be angling for power; but if he upset their traditional decision-making too much, he would become the focus for power and attract the same sort of conniving attention that he had been the target for at court. So far, he had insisted that the woodfolk keep their decision-making capacity, but the urgency of recent events had meant that he had taken the lead on planning out their activities. With a jolt, he realised that he was quickly slipping back into his more accustomed role of being dictatorial.

"Ancient Oak, you'd better send everyone another message asking them for any other better ideas, if they have them, about what we should be doing."

Ancient Oak regarded him quizzically for a moment before going out of focus to relay the message. When he had finished, he said, "I wasn't trying to make a point, you know."

"I didn't think you were. I just suddenly realised the dangers of assuming too much authority. I can do it, but it will have consequences for me as well as for everyone else." Suddenly Tarkyn grinned. "I can remember when Waterstone first offered me his friendship, I told him I couldn't be sure he wasn't just using me for his own ends. That's the problem with wielding too much power. You can't be sure of anyone."

Ancient Oak boggled at him. "You said that to *Waterstone?* He must have been livid!"

Tarkyn chortled. "He was. He was furious!" Then his face fell. "But soon after that, the controversy over Falling Rain's exile reared its head and he began to realise why I was so circumspect about professed friendships. In fact, when he realised the complications, he nearly retracted his offer of friendship to me altogether."

"Wolf's teeth, Tarkyn. That was a bit rough." Ancient Oak frowned. "I'm surprised at Waterstone. You can't just be a person's friend one day and then change your mind when it gets a bit difficult. True friendship is not like that."

Tarkyn gave a slight smile. "Don't judge him too harshly. He was the first woodman to risk getting to know me. Neither of us knew at that stage how we were going to co-exist under the oath. Neither of us knew that I wasn't going to assume total control. If I had done so, his friendship with me would have made him a target for woodfolk seeking to influence my decisions, just as I had been a target for those seeking influence with my brothers at court. He wasn't sure that he would know how to manage that...and on top of everything, I still didn't fully trust him at that stage."

"Still..."

Tarkyn shook his head. "No, not still. It was really just Waterstone's way of saying he didn't know how to cope with the challenge of being around me. He'd just wrecked part of the forest with his temper too. So, he was feeling very bad about that and was worried about it happening again." Tarkyn shrugged. "That's the main reason I maintain my permission for him to attack me if he needs to, and why I have given it to you two and a couple of others, as well. Damage to the forest is too wicked a consequence for a temper outburst, especially when I am perfectly capable of defending myself."

"I didn't realise he'd damaged the forest," mused Ancient Oak. "He hasn't told me any of this."

"Hasn't he?" Tarkyn grimaced. "Maybe I shouldn't be telling you either, then." He thought for a moment. "But all the home guard know about the damage to the forest. We all worked on repairing it together. So, it's not really a secret, is it?"

"So, what decided you to trust him in the end?" asked Rainstorm.

Tarkyn glanced at him. "Trust you to be the one to ask the awkward question." He shook his head. "Now, that really would be breaking Waterstone's confidence to tell you that. You will have to ask him and see whether he will tell you. I don't feel that I can. However, I can tell you that it was an act of extreme courage on his part that decided the issue."

"What? Did he save your life?"

"Rainstorm, I'm not going to tell you. So stop guessing. He

did save my life at one time but that could just have been the oath, so it proved nothing. You will have to ask Waterstone. And don't say I asked him to tell you, because it is totally up to him. Clear?"

"Yes, Your Highness," replied Rainstorm meekly.

Tarkyn gave a short laugh. "And I think we have had quite enough of the 'Yes, Your Highness,' 'No Your Highness.' You can go back to calling me Prince or Tarkyn anytime you're ready."

Rainstorm grinned. "Thanks, Prince. If you're sure that's not being too familiar."

"Don't push your luck, Rainstorm."

The young woodman sighed. "I can see why Waterstone thought it was a challenge being around you. It really is quite tricky trying to figure out how to act with you."

"Oh, good," replied Tarkyn, completely unfazed by this little gambit. "The world is back on its axis then. It's well-known that I'm difficult to be around. Ask anyone. So, if you're finding that too, everything must be back to normal."

Rainstorm subsided with a little huff, and they walked in silence for a few minutes. Then Tarkyn ruffled Rainstorm's hair and gave him a couple of hearty thumps on the back. "Come on, Rainstorm. We'll sort it out. We've only had one run-in with each other, so far, not counting your fight with Danton. Considering how much you like to rub people up the wrong way and how difficult I am to figure out, I'd say we're doing pretty well."

Rainstorm pushed his arm away but gave a reluctant smile. "I guess we are, if you put it like that."

As they approached the firesite, Summer Rain came down to meet them.

Tarkyn frowned in sudden anxiety. "Is Autumn Leaves all right?"

The healer smiled reassuringly. "Yes. He's fine. I wanted to talk to you about Golden Toad, Rushwind and Ibis Wings, the woodfolk we rescued."

"Go on." As he spoke with Summer Rain, Tarkyn noticed with some trepidation that his two companions were making a beeline for Waterstone. However, as his attention was being firmly claimed by Summer Rain, there wasn't much he could do but leave Waterstone to his fate.

"You know that Golden Toad and his family contracted an infection some time ago that robbed them of their mindtalking abilities?" asked Summer Rain. When Tarkyn nodded, she continued, "I was wondering whether you, as forest guardian, could use your esse to restore their mindtalking. They would be much safer if they could keep in contact with everyone else."

"Yes, they would. I would be pleased to help them if I can," replied Tarkyn, "provided, of course, that they feel ready to trust me. I will discuss it with them after we have decided what we are all doing."

Meanwhile, Ancient Oak was reproaching his brother. "How could you threaten to withdraw your friendship from Tarkyn? What sort of friendship is that?"

Waterstone looked bewildered. "What are you talking about? I'm still Tarkyn's friend. At least I am, as far as I know."

Ancient Oak frowned impatiently. "I don't mean now. I mean back when you first knew him."

Waterstone's brow cleared. "Oh then." He smiled a little ruefully. "Yes, it was a bit mean, I suppose. But everything was very new and strange then. All this business about power games and not being trusted. Poor Tarkyn was very kind about it when I said I wouldn't be able to stay around him. That's what made me stay, actually."

"And what made him trust you?" asked Rainstorm.

Waterstone glanced at him then looked away. After a

moment, he looked back at him and asked, "I gather Tarkyn didn't tell you why. Did he say that it would be better coming from me?"

Rainstorm shook his head and replied faithfully, "No. He said you didn't have to tell us."

"But," added Ancient Oak, "he said that it was extremely courageous, and we're both dying to know."

Waterstone laughed. "Another classic example of Tarkyn manoeuvring people."

Ancient Oak smiled. "No. In fairness, I don't think it is. We were pressing him hard, and he refused to budge."

Waterstone looked around to check who was nearby. "I don't want everyone knowing about this. Some people may think it was foolish or excessive, and I don't want judgements being passed on my actions. So, if I tell you, it goes no further. Agreed?"

The two woodmen nodded solemnly.

"I gave Tarkyn free rein with my memories without any veto," Waterstone said shortly.

"Oh." Rainstorm sounded deflated. Then he thought about it a bit more and his eyes widened. "Oh! Stars above, Waterstone! Tarkyn was right. That was excessively brave."

Ancient Oak regarded him thoughtfully. "You really have put yourself on the line for him, haven't you? Over and over again. And you invited him into our family in front of a full assembly of woodfolk without even being sure he would accept. That would have been horrendously embarrassing if he had refused."

Waterstone smiled. "Yes. It certainly would have been. For a heartbeat of time, I thought he was going to. After all, it was a huge commitment for him to get his head around with only a few seconds' warning; choosing whether to become part of what, from his perspective, is a commoner's family."

"So why did you do it?"

"Which one?"

"Both."

Waterstone shrugged. "Lots of reasons. He accused me at one point of having him as a pet project. That was partly true. I saw how damaged he had been by the betrayals he had suffered and I wanted to help him to recover. As I have come to know him, it has been intriguing to watch him digest our culture and change his behaviour and expectations to accommodate us. I suppose the fact that he was able to shift his thinking so fast that he could accept joining our family on a moment's thought sums it up, really. He's amazing, the way he can change his preconceptions."

"Huh! I just had a dressing down for being too familiar with him. So, I'm not sure I agree with that one."

Waterstone smiled. "But I bet that was more because Tarkyn has thought out how far he wants to go and has drawn a line in the sand. Whereas, you see, most people just stay as they are, without question. If he had done that, we'd all be bowing and scraping to him by now, just as Danton did when he first arrived."

Rainstorm looked much struck. "You're right. I keep forgetting where he's come from. Hmph. I suppose it's reasonable that he doesn't want to go all the way to being the same as us."

"No. He is, after all, from a completely different culture, not to mention being a prince. He's never going to be the same as us, but that doesn't mean we can't get on with him." Waterstone grinned. "And he's always made it perfectly clear that he can't go as far as considering himself equal with everyone else."

"Which makes it all the more amazing that he joined our family."

"Yes. It does, doesn't it?" Waterstone thought for a minute. "Oh no. I know how he's thought his way around that. In his birth family, different people have different ranks. His brothers are both more highly ranked than he. So Tarkyn can easily be a member of our family and have a higher rank than us. He doesn't have to consider himself as equal at all, does he?"

Ancient Oak shook his head in bemusement. "No, I suppose not. What a peculiar system they have."

"Besides, he's the only member of your family who has everyone beholden to him under the oath," added Rainstorm.

"True."

Waterstone put his head on one side and considered his brother. "I don't think I told you this, Ancient Oak, but he felt genuinely honoured to be asked to join our family."

"I think you're right. I'm sure when he said it to me that he wasn't just saying it to be polite."

Waterstone shook his head and smiled. "Tarkyn would not be polite at the expense of truth. Because of all the betrayals and our resentment about the oath, he is very unsure of himself in some ways. He is very strange mixture of vulnerability and strength." He shrugged. "Anyway, despite or maybe because of that, he has managed to pull something workable out of the hideous reality of us having to accept him as our liege lord."

Ancient Oak gave his brother a slow smile. "I think he might have struggled more if he hadn't had your support."

"I think we all might have struggled more if he hadn't had your support," added Rainstorm.

Waterstone nodded. "Possibly. But I try not to use my friendship with him to manipulate his attitudes. Looking back, I can see that things I've said, and Autumn Leaves has said, have changed his views, but that was mostly because it gave him new information. If I wanted him to change his attitude about something, I would say so to him directly."

"Oh, for heaven's sake, Waterstone! You don't have to tell us that," exclaimed his brother. "We know you. You have all the subtlety of a rock."

"Thanks very much," replied Waterstone dryly. As he spoke, he saw Tarkyn on the other side of the clearing raise his eyebrows in query. The woodman raised his own eyebrows and nodded in response. Tarkyn let out a guffaw of laughter that made Summer Rain frown at him. As Waterstone looked away, Tarkyn was trying to explain to the humourless Summer Rain what he had been laughing at.

3

I t wasn't until the evening that Tarkyn had a chance to address the issue of the freed woodfolk's lack of mindtalking. During the day, they had discussed and endorsed Tarkyn's plan of action, acknowledging that it was what they had all previously decided upon anyway. Everyone, even Danton, agreed with the premise that the prophecy should be ignored until the threat facing the woodfolk had been investigated and dealt with.

When they had settled down after dinner and everyone was sitting back around the fire, drinks in hands, Tarkyn spoke diffidently to Rushwind, "I understand you have lost your mindtalking ability. Is that right?"

Rushwind nodded unhappily. "It makes us feel cut off from everyone."

"I know just how you feel," said Tarkyn dryly. "I am also unable to mindtalk." He leaned forward. "However, Summer Rain and I were thinking that I might be able to repair your ability. If you would trust me and let me try. I can't promise, but it might work. What do you think?" Seeing Rushwind hesitate, he threw up a hand and said hastily, "Perhaps it's too soon just yet. Think about it. Maybe later when you get to know me better."

Rushwind glanced at Golden Toad and little Ibis Wings. Then she smiled and looked at Tarkyn. "Although my experience of sorcerers to date has not been pleasant, I believe I can trust you. All my kin seem to trust you, and you were very careful when you removed the chains. Yes. I believe I can trust you and I would like to try."

"I can promise I'll do my best, but I can't guarantee success." He looked across the fire. "Summer Rain, do you think you could assist us please? Are you sure this idea is safe?"

Summer Rain walked around to sit beside Tarkyn. She considered her answer carefully. "Yes. I think it will be safe. I know little about this type of infection and even less about your power, but it is a healing power. I can't see that it could do any harm. I will stand by to help you if you need it."

"Thanks." Tarkyn refocused on Rushwind. "You will need to close your eyes and concentrate. Do you want to do that here or go somewhere quieter?"

A tiny flicker of uncertainty betrayed the limit of her trust.

"Fine," said Tarkyn dryly as though she had spoken. "We'll do it here." He placed his hand firmly on her shoulder and instructed, "Now, close your eyes and focus on your centre. Feel around with your mind and look for the place where your thoughts are blocked. Even if you can't really see it, imagine what it must look like and where it is and what it is made of." He waited. When she didn't respond, he asked, "Can you do that?"

She shook her head. "Everywhere I go, there are patches of scarring and bits of foreign matter, small grey globules, drifting around in my blood."

Tarkyn frowned. "I am going to send some of my life force

into your body. You must direct it to repair the damaged areas and to rid your blood of those foreign particles. You will feel it entering your body through my hand...now."

Rushwind went rigid under his hand. Her face paled and beads of sweat appeared on her brow. She frowned fiercely with concentration and grimaced from time to time as waves of pain swept through her. Tarkyn held his hand steady on her shoulder, although he sent the occasional anxious glance at Summer Rain. Suddenly, Rushwind cried out, "The grey things are getting stronger and multiplying."

Tarkyn threw a frightened glance at Summer Rain. "I'm going in," he said.

"How?"

"I don't know but I am." He shut his eyes and followed his own power along his arm and down through Rushwind's shoulder into her blood stream. He found himself assailed on all sides by grey globules that rushed at him and sucked at his power. Before his very eyes, they expanded and solidified and came back for more. He drew on more power, but they just absorbed it all the faster. With a sense of panic, he felt his strength fading and felt himself being swept through Rushwind's blood stream, his very essence dissipating into the grey parasites around him. Far outside in the world around the firesite, he managed to whisper, "Tree." As he started to lose consciousness, he thought of Waterstone and Rainstorm and the faith they had in him. Sometime later, a steady stream of energy began to seep into him, but this time he harnessed it and didn't let it go beyond his boundaries. Once he had accumulated enough power, he raged in anger at these beings that were trying to destroy him when he had at last found a way to live. He brought centuries of royal arrogance to bear and dared them to assail him. Then he struck out with a mind blast of wrath that tore down the byways of Rushwind's bloodstream burning away any grey parasites in its path with a massive overload of energy.

When that terrible barrage of wrathful power had burnt its way into every corner of Rushwind's being, Tarkyn pulled the power back in and waited in fear that Rushwind might be too damaged. She was certainly unconscious. He sent a gentle exploratory trickle of healing power coursing through her bloodstream to soothe the aggravated interiors of her veins and arteries. All the surfaces were raw and burnt. There were small tears in some places. He increased the flow and gradually repaired all the damage. He found her heart and felt that it was still beating strongly. He flowed into her lungs and felt the rise and fall around him. Slowly, with a sense of dread, he worked his way up towards her brain. He nudged against its borders but felt a firm resistance. He nudged harder and was pushed firmly backwards. Then he sensed Rushwind's voice saying, "Keep out. This is mine." Tarkyn let himself go and flowed backwards towards Rushwind's shoulder, back along his arm and into his own body. Then he drifted away completely.

He opened his eyes to see a ring of anxious faces bending over him. He was nowhere near the fire. He was lying with his palm placed against a large oak. There were other, bigger trees nearby, but Tarkyn suspected that Waterstone knew he liked oaks best. He remembered his ordeal, and his eyes widened in panic. "Rushwind. Is she all right?"

For an answer, Autumn Leaves went briefly out of focus and reported, "She says she's fine."

Tarkyn let out a long breath, "She can mindtalk again? Oh good. I'm glad it was worth it. I nearly died in there and so did she. And I think she went through a lot of pain." He looked around himself. "Thanks for moving me here. You saved my life and hers by doing that."

"Are you right to get up yet?" asked Waterstone.

Tarkyn lifted his head then let it drop back down. "Hmm. Maybe not quite yet. I am really thirsty though. It was an inferno in there for a while." He lifted his other hand and inspected it. "I haven't gone green yet. Just shows I haven't overdone the power refill yet."

It was quite some time before Tarkyn felt strong enough to move. Even then, he wavered when he stood up and had to be supported down to the firesite. As he was lowered carefully to sit with his back against a log, he became aware that Rushwind had scuttled away from him around to the other side of the fire. He frowned and asked Rainstorm, "What was that all about?"

Rainstorm grimaced. "I don't quite understand but it has something to do with a wave of your anger."

"I didn't get angry with her," replied Tarkyn in a puzzled voice.

"I don't know. She said you sent a huge mind blast of rage and, I don't know, hauteur? arrogance? through her. And she said she was afraid of anyone who had that in them." Rainstorm met Tarkyn's eyes reluctantly. "Something like that," he finished lamely.

Tarkyn's amber eyes glinted in the firelight. "It was that rage and arrogance that saved her life and mine." He crossed his arms. "Blast her. She's a sanctimonious little pond dweller! Would she have preferred me to politely allow those grey bloodsuckers to annihilate us both?" He glared at her across the fire. Suddenly she rose and came around to stand before him, clearly quaking.

"Rushwind, I am offended by your behaviour. Yes. I have rage and arrogance within me, as we all do. If I hadn't harnessed mine to attack those foreign bodies in your blood, you would be dead by now. Your ingratitude and lack of civility sorely tempt me to unleash my anger on you and really show you what you have to fear. But you have suffered enough at the

36

hands of sorcerers. I will not add to it. You can think on this, though. My rage was not ungoverned nor was it directed against you. It was harnessed for your protection." He glared up at her. "I hope that if you ever entrust someone with your dark side, they do not reject you as summarily as you have rejected me." He waved a dismissive hand. "Please feel free to return to the other side of the fire safely away from me, the person who just saved your life."

If this last remark sounded petulant, Rushwind didn't notice. She just turned and fled.

Autumn Leaves wandered over and sat down. He frowned at Tarkyn. "I caught the edge of that summons you just sent her. I gather it was followed up by a salutary dressing down."

Tarkyn nodded shortly.

"So, well done on welcoming her back so warmly from the arms of imprisonment. You showed great understanding of her fear, considering she has been at the mercy of sorcerers like you for the past several weeks."

Tarkyn scowled. "Oh, you totally mistake the case. It is for that very reason that she didn't receive worse treatment from me."

Autumn Leaves frowned at him in some concern. "Are you sure you've put all that rage back where it belongs? You seem to be pretty feisty at the moment."

Tarkyn ran his hand through his hair. "I don't know. Maybe not. You have no idea what I've just endured. It was horrifying and terrifying, and I nearly lost everything. Then to find that the person I laid everything on the line to save has decided I'm some sort of monster is pretty hard to take. She was there. She knew why I had to do it."

"So, what about Golden Toad and his daughter? Are you going to help them?" asked Autumn Leaves.

Tarkyn stared at him in disbelief. "You must be mad. I'm

not going near any of them. They've had enough of me, and I've had enough of them. Fine. If they're scared of me, be scared. They can all go and huddle in a corner and whisper monster stories about me. Blast them all! I did my best by them and got kicked in the teeth."

"You are still angry, aren't you," said Autumn Leaves, stating the obvious.

"Yes. I bloody am."

"Would it interest you to know that Golden Toad is sitting right behind you waiting to thank you for what you did for Rushwind?" asked Autumn Leaves innocently.

Tarkyn stared at him as he digested this, then rolled his eyes. "Oh stars! Now I've done it." He looked sideways at Rainstorm who was grinning hugely. "Quick. What bad things did I just say about Golden Toad?" he asked in a quiet undertone.

Rainstorm chortled, "Nothing really. You had more to say about Rushwind."

"All right then. Bring him on," said Tarkyn. When nothing happened, Tarkyn called quietly, "Golden Toad? Are you there somewhere? Come round to the front where I can see you. I'm not strong enough to get up yet."

Golden Toad walked haltingly around from the back of the log and stood in front of Tarkyn, looking down uncertainly. Tarkyn waved a hand and sighed. "Golden Toad, I'm sorry if I said anything unkind. Please sit down and talk to me. I promise I won't bite."

"You know, sir, for a while there, it looked like you were killing my wife," said Golden Toad, as he sat down a circumspect distance away.

Tarkyn looked at him. "We've both been through the mill then, haven't we? For a while there, your wife actually *was* killing me." He paused, "And in order to save her, I had to come close to killing her too."

"Well, I gather from listening to you and others that you came very close to dying to save my wife, and I would like to thank you." Golden Toad began to relax. "I'm sorry Rushwind has behaved so badly to you. I hope she'll get over it. She's been through a lot, you know. We all have. I didn't think anyone would ever notice we were missing. No communication, you see." He gave a sad little smile. "Well, at least Rushwind can mindtalk again. She'll be able to keep us up to date with other woodfolk even if we can't do it ourselves."

"I'm sorry, Golden Toad. I didn't mean what I said. I was angry. I will help you and Ibis Wings, if you want me to. I know what to do next time to keep us safe." Tarkyn smiled tiredly. "But I'm afraid I can't do it until tomorrow. I am too drained." He looked into the fire for a while then said, "You realise I will probably have to unleash some of that rage that upset Rushwind so much?"

Golden Toad nodded. "I heard what you said. If it's under your control, it should be all right."

Tarkyn turned his head to look at him. "You'd better go first so you can decide whether your daughter should be exposed to it."

"I think she'll be fine," chuckled Golden Toad. "She has a fiendish temper herself. You might teach her a thing or two about controlling it."

Tarkyn looked at Rainstorm. "I was going to ask if you could help me back to the oak tree. And could you organise it so I can sleep next to the oak tree tonight? Someone will have to keep guard. Don't make it you for the whole night. See if you can get Waterstone to help you organise a roster. I'm feeling pretty bad and I need the oak. Can you do that for me?"

Rainstorm smiled. "Sure, Prince. Hang on. I'll get Ancient Oak to help me."

As they supported Tarkyn back up the slope to the old oak, Rainstorm reflected that if that was as close as Tarkyn ever came to ordering him around, the oath would be no problem at all.

4

In the darkness of his shelter, Waterstone lay asleep, his daughter Sparrow a short distance away from him. Outside, the wind was picking up. Within minutes, the trees were thrashing under an ever-increasing gale. Suddenly, an intense wave of fear slammed into Waterstone's mind, followed almost instantaneously by a peremptory summons. Sparrow woke crying.

Waterstone had no time to comfort her. "Stay here," he said urgently as he quickly pulled on his boots. "Whatever you do, don't leave the shelter until I call you. I'll be back as soon as I can."

Sparrow nodded bravely. "Go on. I'll be all right. Tarkyn's in trouble, isn't he?"

Waterstone answered over his shoulder as he left, "Something is wrong, badly wrong. Stay here until you hear from me."

Once outside, the woodman was buffeted by the strong winds that were now shrieking through the trees. He could hear branches breaking and the air was filled with flying leaves and twigs. Eerily, he could see the stars shining peacefully above him in a cloudless sky.

"Oh no." Waterstone said to himself in horror. "It's not a storm. Someone is betraying the oath. The forest is being destroyed."

He ran to the oak where they had left Tarkyn for the night. As he arrived, woodfolk converged on the scene from all directions. Tarkyn was still there lying with his palm against the oak. Rushwind was leaning over him, her hand on his shoulder. Suddenly his mind was filled with an image of Rushwind being struck down with a slingshot. Waterstone didn't hesitate. He drew out his slingshot in one fluid movement and fired. Rushwind dropped like a stone. As her contact with Tarkyn broke, the wind died down. Another image appeared of Rushwind with a barrier around her. Where she lay, the grass and moss beneath curled up and died as they watched.

"Don't touch her," yelled Waterstone.

He looked up into the oak and realised that its branches had dried and withered. His gaze travelled out to its extremities. Where the oak touched other trees, they too were shrivelling.

As the woodfolk ran towards Tarkyn, they received another image, telling them not to touch him either. As they watched, he took his hand away from the tree trunk. Other than that, he was lying motionless, his face pale but sweat beading on his forehead. They stood around him and looked at one another in bewilderment and alarm. "How can we help if we can't touch him?" and fast upon that thought, "How can we help even if we can touch him?"

Waterstone sent an urgent message to Sparrow, "Get Stormaway. Quickly!" He leant over Tarkyn. "We're here. What's happening? What can we do?"

Beneath him, Tarkyn opened his eyes. The whites of his eyes burned bright red and his irises glowed fiery orange. Waterstone had to stop himself from reeling back in horror.

"The infection," croaked Tarkyn. He took a shuddering breath and managed to get out, "I... need... rage," before his eyes snapped shut and his whole body contorted.

Stormaway appeared at a flat run. "What's happening?" he asked shortly.

"I think Rushwind has re-infected Tarkyn. It has spread from him to the trees and I think it will spread through the forest unless we can find a way to stop it."

"Did he say anything?"

"He said, 'I need rage.'"

Stormaway nodded decisively. "Then that's what we'll do. We'll send him anger. Come on, you lot. I can't do it. I'll instruct you though."

"We can't send feelings, only words and images,"

He looked around at the crowd of anxious woodfolk. "You can't send feelings to each other, but Tarkyn can pick them up. Remember? He picked up Autumn Leaves' fear. So, focus on images that will ignite your anger. Stand firmly. Close your eyes. Now think of the outrage of having the forest damaged. Think of those greedy grey parasites killing that old oak and then destroying each tree, one after the other. Think how that infestation nearly destroyed the forest in one fell swoop by making Rushwind hurt Tarkyn. Feed your anger into your images and then throw it all at him. Send him a view of you all working with him against these parasites."

On the ground below them, Tarkyn's body was awash with grey parasites. With a sickening lurch, the sorcerer realised they were changing direction and were slowly but surely converging on his brain. Tarkyn threw up a small magical barrier inside himself at the base of his skull but didn't know whether, or for how long, it would hold. The thought of having his mind taken over filled him with fear, which almost instantly converted to outrage. He steadied his inner core then slammed outwards along his own blood vessels in rage at the grey parasites. His anger-driven life force picked them off one by one. But there were so many of them. He could feel his power holding its own, but the mental energy it was taking to maintain the anger was beginning to tell.

Suddenly, an incoming wave of horror-filled, angry images assailed him, igniting a deep fury within him. Tarkyn's face contorted as the visions of the forest's demise reached him. He dug deep and, reacting to the woodfolk's images of destruction with every ounce of his strength, thrust a blast of power through himself that fried every parasite in its path. As his blood literally boiled under the attack, he screamed in pain, writhing on the ground before the eyes of the horrified woodfolk.

He had no strength left to heal the burning. He lay curled up in agony. He opened glazed eyes and struggled to form the words against the pain of his muscles, "Waterstone. Help me. I need a tree. A healthy one." Then he closed his eyes and surrendered to the pain.

The woodfolk looked at each other uncertainly.

"I thought we couldn't touch him," said Falling Bough.

"He wouldn't ask us to do it if it wasn't safe. Something must have changed," replied Waterstone firmly. "Let's go."

But when they touched him, the contact with him burned their hands. The woodfolk stripped off shirts and, wrapping them around their hands for protection, raised his contorting body.

Tarkyn didn't feel them lift him and carry him to a tree, well away from the spreading infection. He didn't feel his palm being placed against the trunk of a healthy tree and he was unaware of the worried faces above him. All he could feel was the pain of the burning in every part of his body. After a while, he began to shudder uncontrollably as his body went into shock.

"Quickly," shouted Stormaway. "Get water. We have to cool him down."

"But he's already shivering," objected North Wind.

"That's shock. Not cold. You feel him. He's burning up." Stormaway looked down on the suffering young sorcerer who lay juddering against the trunk of another oak. He frowned. "He's beginning to go into spasm. Some of you get water. The rest of you, gather around him. We'll have to feed him some of our life force. He can't focus enough to draw on the tree's strength quickly enough. Someone will have to put their hand on his shoulder. It will hurt, I'm afraid."

"I will do it," said Summer Rain in a voice that brooked no argument. "It is my fault he is in this predicament. I told him it was safe."

She placed her hand firmly on his shoulder, ignoring the slight hiss as it touched his skin. Her mouth tightened, but other than that, she gave no indication of the pain she was enduring to keep her hand in place. The other woodfolk placed their hands on her shoulder and, under instruction from Stormaway, closed their eyes and reached down into their very essence to bring forth the stream of their life force. They channelled their combined strength through Summer Rain into their suffering forest guardian. A green vortex of power swirled lazily in the air above Tarkyn, then slowly drifted down into him.

Tarkyn just endured and waited. There was nothing he could do. He felt his body rebelling against the burning. It felt as though he was trying to run away inside himself. He started to go out of rhythm with himself, different parts of him fighting against others. His mind drifted down into helpless misery with no strength left to draw on. Then through the haze of pain, Tarkyn first felt a strong, steady trickle of strength winding its way through him from his hand. He became vaguely aware that his whole body was jerking, but it was beyond his ability to control it. Then a large, slow wave of gentle life force surged through him from his shoulder. He imagined a cool, clear stream and let it wash through his scorched blood vessels. He could vaguely feel coldness on the outside of him. Gradually, his body stopped fighting itself as the burning was soothed and his temperature dropped. Suddenly, he was freezing cold. He shivered uncontrollably, his teeth chattering in his head.

"Oh no," said Stormaway. "His temperature is dropping too fast. Get those wet clothes off him. Someone, get a rug. We have to keep him warm until he adjusts to the lower temperature."

Rainstorm touched Tarkyn's shaking arm. "He still feels hot."

Stormaway nodded. "He is, but he is a lot colder than he was and his temperature needs to go down more slowly now that we've stopped the burning. Give the wet clothes to Summer Rain. She can wrap her hand in them. That will help to soothe it."

This time, Tarkyn was aware of the blanket being wrapped around him. His mind and body had regained their connection with the outside world. He opened his eyes. They smarted and were bloodshot but were no longer the ghastly red that the woodfolk had seen previously.

"Thanks, everyone," he said between chattering teeth, clutching the blanket around him.

Stormaway frowned down at him. "Lie still. You're not out of the woods yet."

Tarkyn managed a shaking smile. "Very funny."

"Hi, Prince. Good to see you back in the land of the living. You gave us an almighty scare." Rainstorm squatted down next to him. "I hate to bother you, but what do you want us to do about Rushwind?"

Tarkyn's eyes widened in alarm. "Whatever you do, don't touch her." He gave another big shudder. When it had passed, he said, "She has to be quarantined from all life forms: people, plants, animals." He lay panting for a minute with the effort of talking before adding, "Keep her knocked out. Maybe dig a trench around her so the infection can't spread from the plants she's lying on. Make sure you put any tools you use inside the circle with her. Otherwise they may transmit the infection too."

Tarkyn forced his hand up out of the blanket. "I have to get strength from the tree," he said as he replaced his palm against the oak. "I have to fight the infection before it destroys the forest."

The woodfolk looked at each other.

"You're not strong enough," objected Waterstone.

Tarkyn nodded, "I know. I have to become strong enough, as soon as possible." A shadow of fear passed over his face. "And then I have to go back and do battle with those parasites." He shivered again. "No chance of a fire, is there? Somewhere close to this tree so I can stay here and get back my strength and keep warm."

"You are warm, Prince."

"Well, I don't feel warm. It's freezing out here."

"Get him his fire," instructed Stormaway. He turned to Tarkyn. "Your temperature is all over the place at the moment. Actually, it's not your temperature. It's your perception of it. Your actual body temperature is gradually coming down, but it's still too high." He shrugged. "Still, if you want a fire, you shall have a fire. We don't want your temperature to drop too fast."

Tarkyn gave a few shivers before asking, "Is there anything to drink? I'm unbelievably thirsty. I think half my body fluid must have evaporated in the heat."

"Yes. You're probably right." Even as Stormaway replied, Waterstone held a stone mug full of cold water up to Tarkyn's mouth and lifted him up so that he could drink.

After a few minutes, Summer Rain came over and sat down next to him. "I'm sorry, Your Highness. I was incorrect in my surmises. I am sorry you had to go through all of this."

"Not your fault. How were you to know?" Tarkyn frowned. "What's wrong with your hand?"

Summer Rain gave a little shake of her head but didn't answer.

"She burnt herself on your shoulder, sending you the life force," said Rainstorm over his shoulder from where he was setting the fire.

Tarkyn pulled his other hand out from within the blanket. "Give me your hand," he instructed.

"No, my lord. You are not strong enough."

"Summer Rain, give me your hand."

The healer stared mutinously at him for a moment before reluctantly unwrapping her hand and placing it in his.

Tarkyn's eyes widened. "My shoulder did that? Wow! I must have been hot!" He looked up at her. "Thank you, Summer Rain. It must have taken great determination to hold your hand there when it was burning. Now, close your eyes, and I will send you through some *esse*. Don't worry. It will make little difference to my recovery. Ready?" When she nodded, Tarkyn closed his eyes and directed a small wave of power into her hand. "Better?" he asked.

Summer Rain breathed a sigh of relief. When she looked down at her hand, the blisters had gone and the skin was already only slightly pinker than the rest of her hand. "Thank you. That is a great relief."

"Good. The least I could do." Tarkyn looked around at Stormaway and the woodfolk standing around him. "I suppose it's the middle of the night and you want to get back to bed but..."

Looks of surprise on the woodfolk's faces told him that returning to bed hadn't crossed their minds.

"I think we're all a bit too shaken to go back to bed yet, Tarkyn," said Waterstone dryly, shaking his head. "If you were about to say we need to sort a few things out first, I couldn't agree more."

"Oh. Good." Tarkyn raised his eyebrows. "So, it's not just me who's a bit wound up at the moment."

A ripple of laughter greeted this remark.

Waterstone smiled grimly at him. "Tarkyn, the forest has been badly damaged again by the oath's vengeance. We have an unconscious, infectious woodwoman lying over there, under guard. Golden Toad and Ibis Wings are also being held under guard in their shelter until this is sorted out. And the forest is slowly dying around us as we speak. I don't think any of us has any plans for sleep."

"Your Highness, you must explain to us what happened so we know what we're dealing with," said Stormaway.

Tarkyn rubbed his hand over his brow. "I don't know for sure. I think perhaps my power mutated the parasites. They certainly became stronger and larger when they fed on my power. When I cleared them out of Rushwind, I checked all through her body for damage and found none. But she wouldn't let me into her brain. I accepted that because of her privacy, but now I think a small colony of parasites must have escaped into her brain and warped her thinking, maybe even taken over completely. Just before you people helped me get rid of the parasites in me, they were heading towards *my* brain."

Tree Wind frowned. "How do we know they didn't get there or that there weren't already some in your brain and that you're not acting under their influence?"

Tarkyn didn't take Tree Wind's question amiss even though in the past she had been one of his severest critics. His eyes narrowed as he thought about it. "That is a scary question. When I realised what was happening, I did put up a shield, which Rushwind couldn't have done. But what if some were already in there?" He shook his head. "How can we tell?"

"How would we have been able to tell with Rushwind?" asked Summer Rain.

"If you had stayed tuned into her thoughts, you would have been able to tell," answered Tarkyn. "When you think about it, she acted unexpectedly, straight after my attempt at healing her. When she attacked me, I couldn't tell her thoughts, of course, but the images coming through from her were hideous." He looked at Waterstone. "I think it's time to even up the score. Waterstone, I give you permission to have free access to my memories and any images and feelings you can access."

A babble of consternation broke out at this announcement, some of it surmising Waterstone's past actions and some of it in reaction to Tarkyn's offer.

"Sire, that is asking too much of yourself," objected Falling Branch. "Can we not just trust you if you reassure us?"

Tarkyn shook his head. "Not if I am not acting under my own volition. I won't know. I will think I am being honest and so will you, when I may not be. Someone outside me has to scan my thoughts and feelings."

"But isn't the very fact you're offering proof enough?" he persisted.

"I don't know, maybe, but we can't afford to take the risk."

He looked back at Waterstone and gave a wry smile. "Sorry, Waterstone, I dumped you in it, didn't I? I'm not thinking too straight at the moment. Are you willing to do this?"

"I am willing, but could it be dangerous?"

Tarkyn shook his head. "I wouldn't think so, as long as someone is nearby to pull you out of my thoughts. But again, don't rely on what I say until we know whether I am to be trusted. Ask Stormaway."

Stormaway frowned down at him. "Tarkyn, this is very uncomfortable. And can I just point out that if you are indeed still infected, then the tree's power will be feeding the parasites and strengthening them?"

Tarkyn whipped his hand away from the tree trunk. "Oh my stars, Stormaway. You're right. How could I have been so stupid?"

"I think it is encouraging that you do not yet appear to have been overrun when we all sent you that life force earlier on to heal the burning," pointed out Summer Rain.

Tarkyn breathed a sigh of relief. "True. That is encouraging." He gave a little shiver. "Come on, Waterstone. I feel as though I'm going mad here, not knowing whether I am truly myself or not."

Waterstone frowned. "Are you sure?"

Tarkyn smiled. "Yes, my friend. I am sure. I trust you with my memories and images. Go ahead."

"I can't see that I need to go very far back." Waterstone looked around for confirmation and saw several people shaking their heads. "Show me your memory of earlier this evening after you thought you'd healed Rushwind."

Tarkyn's memories did not have words attached to them, only images and feelings. *Rainstorm embarrassed. Rushwind looking askance at me. Outrage and hurt at her behaviour. Autumn Leaves angry with me. Golden Toad nervous but kind. Feeling raw, shaken, frightened by intensity of feelings, tired.*

Waterstone pulled out. "Hmm. I think we could have looked after you a bit better after that first run-in with Rushwind. You seemed to have scored a lot of criticism when you were least able to deal with it. Still, so far so good," he reported with a reassuring smile at Tarkyn. He took a breath. "Right. I suppose I'd better see what happened when Rushwind came to see you tonight.

Rushwind bending over me. I feel mildly friendly. Rushwind's face fills with hatred. Eyes burning red. I'm watchful not frightened. Rushwind puts her hand on my shoulder. Searing pain. Raging wind above me. Everyone, come! Waterstone could feel an echo of the pain from the image, but he persevered. *Parasites pouring into me through my shoulder. Flooding everywhere. Flowing out through my hand up into the tree. Now, grey globules change direction. Moving towards my head. Shield goes up. Fear. Outrage. Power now destroying parasites. Anger and terrible images of forest dying flood in. Unleashed rage. Fiery blast through my all my blood vessels. Blinding, burning pain.*

Waterstone pulled out, sweat beading on his forehead. "Stars above, Tarkyn! You poor bastard! You've been through the wringer."

"But what do you think? Did my shield stop them getting to my brain?"

Waterstone nodded. "I think so. There were parasites in you for some time before you put up the shield, but they seemed intent on flowing into the poor old oak tree at the start. Even if your shield didn't work, your outrage at their intention to enter your mind was what triggered your successful attack on them. So, I think you are not infected." The woodman regarded Tarkyn thoughtfully for a moment. "Do you think you can manage one more? I'll scan your images now. Agreed?"

Tarkyn took a deep breath, let it out and nodded. "Fine. Away you go."

Waterstone looking intently at me. Kind, strong, dependable, clever. I feel strung out and battered but safe and cared for by all around me. Affection. Warmth. Worry. Waterstone going pink. Amusement.

Waterstone pulled out and laughed, still pink with embarrassment. "Very bloody funny! You're fine. Not a nasty thought in you."

Tarkyn grinned. "Now you know what I think of you, don't you?"

"What?" asked Rainstorm from the side.

Tarkyn laughed. "He's easily embarrassed. That's what."

This time, Rainstorm knew when to stop pushing. "So. What are we going to do?" he asked instead.

Tarkyn gave a deep sigh. "Now that I know I don't have any parasites left in me, I can continue to draw power from this uninfected tree. As soon as I've recovered, I will have to whip up my rage again and channel it through my power into the infected trees to destroy the infestation. You can help me with images and anger again. As I get used to the concept of the parasites, it is harder to reach and maintain the same level of outrage."

"What about Rushwind? And Golden Toad and Ibis Wings?" asked Lapping Water.

Stormaway shook his head. "They will have to wait. At least in them, the infection is contained at the moment. In the forest, it is spreading as we speak."

"And," added Tarkyn, "Rushwind must be kept unconscious because, if she runs amok, no one can touch her to contain her." He looked around at the sombre faces. "Is everyone in agreement with that plan of action?"

"I don't see what else we can do," said Autumn Leaves.

Waterstone frowned. "It puts a heavy load on you, Tarkyn, if you have to relive that same hideous experience."

"One more thing we have to be careful of," put in Stormaway. "If the parasites should spread to this tree while Tarkyn is still drawing power from it, he will become re-infected. Even if we move him further away from the infected trees, we will still have to keep an eye on the progress of the infection through the forest. I'm not sure that he would survive another roasting like that."

"I hate to sound pessimistic," said Thunder Storm, "but how can we expect Tarkyn to battle this infestation that is feeding on the might of the forest? His rage was only just strong enough to cure himself, even with the help of our images."

Tarkyn shook his head. "No, it wasn't. There was plenty of energy. Once your images ignited my rage, the infection was burnt out almost instantaneously. It was my recovery from the scalding that took all the time and power. Saying that, it's not going to be easy."

"How long will you need to recover?"

Tarkyn shrugged. "I don't know. Not too much longer, I hope. We can't afford the time. Until I start to turn green. Then we'll know I have as much energy stored in me as possible."

Stormaway had a sudden thought. "Running Feet, would you check whether the infected trees are still alive, please? Don't touch them though."

Running Feet returned a few minutes later to report that the trees were dead or dying fast, as far as he could see.

"Why don't we burn them down then?" asked Stormaway. "It will take much less effort to create a fireball and burn down the whole tree. And then we will have destroyed the bulk of the infected trees, and we can concentrate on burning out the parasites around the edge of the infected area."

"Will fire work in the same way as rage?" asked Summer Rain.

"Combined with my power, the rage does seem to burn the parasites up. So, I think it might work." Tarkyn smiled at Stormaway. "Brilliant idea. You and Danton can get on with that, while I recover. Then I'll mop up the periphery with the woodfolk when you've finished."

Thunder Storm raised another objection, "I'm sorry for being such a pain, my lord, but what about the encampment? Will they not see the trees burning?"

"Of course! They well might." Tarkyn looked around. "It has to be done, though. We'll just have to be ready to move in a hurry, if need be."

"And what about Rushwind? We can't carry her." Thunder Storm sounded apologetic.

"Good point," said Tarkyn patiently. "Either Danton or Stormaway can carry her using levitation so we don't come into direct contact with her."

"And Golden Toad and Ibis Wings?" Thunder Storm was almost flinching now.

Tarkyn smiled at him. "Come and sit down here next to me, Thunder Storm. You and I can iron out all the problems while everyone else gets on with the preparations. How does that sound?"

Thunder Storm nodded in relief and sat down with a sigh.

"In answer to your question, Thunder Storm, I think Golden Toad and Ibis Wings can probably go free. The sickness in them has not been mutated by my power so I think they are safe enough, provided someone keeps an eye on them and they know that they mustn't go near Rushwind. Do you agree?"

Thunder Storm nodded and then went briefly out of focus to relay this, "Good. I think that covers most things. Although I don't see how we can stay and destroy the infestation on the periphery if soldiers come from the encampment."

Tarkyn raised his eyebrows. "If I didn't know you better, Thunder Storm, I would say you were deliberately teasing me. Every answer I come up with, you come up with a new question."

Thunder Storm looked apprehensive. "No, my lord. I wouldn't dream of teasing you."

"Thunder Storm, I'm sorry I bit your head off the other day when I returned from rescuing Autumn Leaves. You were just the unlucky one who said what everyone else was thinking. I know you were only trying to look after me. Please stop looking like a frightened mouse every time you talk to me. You're only asking sensible questions. It's only when you start trying to order me around that we strike problems."

Thunder Storm relaxed slightly.

"I don't mind you teasing me or making suggestions, Thunder Storm; just don't tell me what to do and then we'll be fine. So, how *are* we going to attack the residual parasites if the soldiers come out to investigate the fire? Come on, Thunder Storm. My turn to ask. Your turn to answer."

Thunder Storm gave a faint smile of acknowledgement. "Well, I suggest that if the soldiers arrive quickly, we hide ourselves up in trees before we attempt to destroy the rest of the infestation."

"Can we get close enough together?" asked Tarkyn.

"I think so. We can share thoughts across reasonable distances."

"No one will fall out of a tree while they're concentrating, will they?"

"No. We are, after all, quite adept in trees."

"And should we take up snacks, do you think?"

Thunder Storms eyes narrowed in sudden suspicion. He turned to find Tarkyn grinning at him.

Tarkyn shrugged. "Well, if you won't tease me, I'll just have to tease you, won't I."

"Your Highness, we are in the middle of a crisis, and you're playing games."

"Yep. That about sums it up." Tarkyn smiled ruefully. "I need a bit of light entertainment after that hideous experience. Think of it as helping me to carry out a public duty."

"Oh. Well, as long as there is a reasonable justification for your hilarity, I expect I can bring myself to accept it," replied Thunder Storm in a serious tone of voice.

Tarkyn was halfway through a small sigh of disappointment when he realised he was being wound up in return. He looked at the woodman and laughed. "Very droll. Sometimes you are quite unexpected, Thunder Storm."

Thunder Storm smiled. "We're not all Summer Rain, you know. Hmm. You'll be happy to know you're starting to turn green."

Tarkyn gave a wry smile. "It's a mixed blessing, this green business." He had a sudden thought which he voiced before he had time to stop himself. "Where's Lapping Water?"

Thunder Storm gave what could only be described a smirk. "She is taking Ibis Wings over to be with Sparrow and my two kids." After a tiny pause, he asked casually, "Would you like me to call her over?"

Tarkyn frowned ferociously. "No. I would not. No. Just wondering."

"I see," said Thunder Storm with a slight, infinitely irritating smile.

Tarkyn looked sideways at him and gave a wry smile. "I'm

sick of her seeing me looking like some monster from the deep. I probably look bad enough as it is, in her eyes."

Thunder Storm put his head on one side, a twinkle in his eye, as he studied the prince. "Well, I don't know. You are excessively large, and your black hair and amber eyes are strange but quite striking. On balance, I don't think you look bad. I think you are quite good-looking in your way, especially when you're being funny." He shrugged. "To be honest, it's a bit hard to get past the fact that you look like you, which is very different from us. Probably a bit of green is neither here nor there."

Tarkyn frowned and smiled all at once. "I wasn't actually asking for a critique. And I don't think I'm all that reassured if a delicate tinge of green doesn't make me appear noticeably worse."

"Not so delicate, actually. You're becoming greener by the second."

Tarkyn quickly pulled his hand away from the tree. "Fine. Enough is enough. Now if we can get into position as soon as the trees are alight, we can get this whole thing sorted before any soldiers have time to react to seeing a fire on the horizon. Now I won't have to concentrate up in a tree and that will suit me better because, unlike you, I am not so used to hanging around in trees." Another thought struck him. "How are we going to stop the fire spreading right through the forest?"

Thunder Storm smiled without persuasion this time. "You could use your shields."

"Good idea. Actually, I think Stormaway and Danton can use their shields and I'll save my energy for fighting the infection."

"How are we going to know when we have destroyed all the parasites?" asked Thunder Storm.

Tarkyn frowned. "How did it suddenly become your turn to ask questions again?"

Thunder Storm smiled and shrugged.

"Fine. I don't know is the simple answer to that. I guess we'll just have to inspect the surrounding trees for shrivelled leaves. Might have to have Stormaway floating around so he can take a closer look without touching the trees that might be infected."

5

A loud whumph made them whirl around. The fine old oak was ablaze, and the fire was spreading through its branches into neighbouring trees.

"Aargh!" cried out Tarkyn, his face tightening with shock as he ducked his head down and wrapped his arms protectively around his head.

"What's wrong?" asked Thunder Storm, horrified by the prince's reaction.

"Oh, for pity's sake! The birds, the animals are burning. I can feel their anguish, feel their agony. Oh no!" Tarkyn was rocking back and forth, trying in vain to escape the overwhelming reactions of the burning animals. "I should have thought. I should have warned them. Oh, save me. How could I have been so thoughtless?"

Thunder Storm shook his head. "No one else thought of it either. You are not the only one to blame."

"Aargh. Oh, the pain they're in. I can't stand it. How could I have let this happen? I am their forest guardian, and I stood by and let them all die."

Thunder Storm put his arm around the prince's shoulder. "Your Highness, I think they had to die. If they had travelled from the infected trees, they may have spread the sickness."

Tarkyn raised anguished eyes and gasped, "Thunder Storm, the shields. Make sure they put the shields up." For a few moments, Tarkyn was swamped by the suffering of the living creatures being burnt in the fire. Their agony was short-lived and soon, grim-faced, he was able to straighten up, as though pushing against a heavy weight. He shuddered, "I have to block them out. There's nothing I can do to save them but at least I can make sure the rest of the forest is kept safe.

Tarkyn shed his blanket and shivered right up and down his body as the night air touched his bare skin. "Quick, where's my shirt?" he demanded, keeping his mind firmly on the upcoming task.

"It's wet, Prince," said Rainstorm, arriving with a cloak. "Here. Put this on until the fire dries your shirt."

"Thanks." Tarkyn drew himself up and unconsciously squared his shoulders as he prepared himself to face once more the horror of the grey parasites. Ripples of trepidation, quickly swamped by a wave of determination, flowed out across the clearing. The woodfolk all stopped what they were doing to look across at their Forest Guardian. They called out words of encouragement and several came to pat him on the shoulder and reassure him. Tarkyn frowned a little at this flurry of reactions. Then he looked sideways at Rainstorm and raised his eyebrows in query.

Rainstorm laughed. "Yep, Prince. You've done it again."

Tarkyn rolled his eyes and shook his head, even though his face was still drawn. "Oh my stars! I'd have been laughed out of court if this had happened in Tormadell. I am a constant embarrassment to myself."

"I don't think so, my lord," said Thunder Storm kindly. "Only a fool would face this threat without fear."

"Thank you, Thunder Storm," the prince responded gravely even though a faint smile lurked at the back of his eyes. He took a deep breath. "So. Now that the core of the infected trees is burning, we'd better get started. Perhaps I can send my attack in a circle around the burning trees from one position. I'll try that. It will be quicker."

Tarkyn walked over to an elm whose branches were withering on the side nearest the fire. He looked around. "Right. Everyone who is helping with this, stand around close to me but don't touch me in case something goes wrong and I become re-infected. Do the same as before. Think about the destruction and your anger about it." He waited for everyone to prepare themselves. "Ready? Here goes."

Tarkyn drew up a barrier around himself and then placed his palm on the trunk of the ailing tree. Immediately, he tuned into the tree's suffering and felt the parasites swarming from the branches towards the centre of the tree. As his power connected with the tree, the parasites changed course and headed down towards him. Drawing in the woodfolks' and his own rage at the destruction that was being wrought, Tarkyn gathered his strength into an unassailable ball of fury. When the kernel of his rage was quivering with contained energy, he unleashed it into the tree against the waves of grey parasites. His released power tore through the branches of the elm, frying the formless grey invaders as it passed. He tuned into the parasites and followed their trail out along the elm's branches in to the next tree. His fury sought them out and obliterated them as it swept through tree after tree in the circle around the fire. Where his power met the fire burning in the dead trees in the centre, huge fountains of bronze sparks sprayed up into the air. Those woodfolk watching from further away could see the progress of the purging; the forest guardian's power spitting against the fire as it sizzled its way around its periphery, showering them with flashes of bronze light. A short time later, the bronze fountain had made a full circumference and fizzled out above the damaged elm where it has started.

Still, Tarkyn remained in position. Without opening his eyes, he said, "Thanks everyone. Enough."

Now he sent out a wave of healing through the damaged trees. Tarkyn did not have the reservoir of strength needed to repair so many trees, but he could at least ease their suffering and cool their burning. In time, they would heal themselves.

As the fire raged in the central cluster of trees, Stormaway threw up a curved green shield around the core of burning trees and nodded to Danton to do the same. A sheet of aqua rose on the other side of the fire and between them, the wizard and the sorcerer contained the fire as it burned itself out.

When the last flames had died away, the woodfolk, the wizard, and the two sorcerers stood looking at the black, smoking ruins of a full copse of old trees. Beyond the black ring, many trees were half-burnt and many more had lost branches or had been smashed by the wrathful winds of the oath's betrayal. Everyone's faces were bleak with loss.

6

S uddenly Tarkyn and the woodfolk raised their heads in alarm as urgent messages came through from the lookouts.

"Men on horseback coming this way fast. The wolves are with them," reported Waterstone. "We have to go. Hurry!"

While the silence of mindlinked organising ensued amongst the woodfolk, Tarkyn gave out his own instructions. "Danton, Stormaway. You will have to transport Rushwind. Go now. Head south. Don't let her touch anything living: trees, people, animals or bushes. If you have to, take it in turns to hold her up so that you can levitate yourselves up off the ground. Then raise her above the height of the trees out of sight. Don't worry about getting far away. Just make sure you're hidden. We need one of the woodfolk to go with you to hit her with a slingshot if she starts coming to. Otherwise she may give away your position to the soldiers."

"I'll go," offered Lapping Water as she swung herself into a tree.

"Thanks. *Maya liefka.*" Tarkyn levitated himself for several hundred yards and then found a large, well-covered pine to hide in. When he was settled, he sent a request for Waterstone to join him. When the woodman arrived, he had brought Sparrow and Autumn Leaves with him.

"Good. Now you can tell me what all the woodfolk are doing."

"Might I suggest, Tarkyn, that you hide on the side of the tree facing away from the fire. It's more important to be hidden than to see what the soldiers are doing when they arrive."

Tarkyn gave a wry smile as he nodded agreement and moved his position accordingly. When he was re-settled, he leaned forward and whispered, "Hi, Sparrow. Are you all right?"

Although the little girl nodded, one look at her face was enough to tell him she wasn't.

"Hug?" he asked. She nodded and he wrapped his arm around her as she snuggled up against him in the crook of the tree's branches. "And you, Autumn Leaves? How are you?"

In contrast to Waterstone and Sparrow, the heavy woodman was puffing, and beads of sweat were dripping from his forehead. He grimaced, "I've been better. My head is not taking kindly to me swinging through the branches and jumping from one tree to the next."

"Come here then. Let me give you a bit of life force. We need you well enough to evade these huntsmen."

Autumn Leaves frowned and stayed out of reach. "I can't let you do that. You're too drained yourself."

"No, I'm not. I didn't use that much power, you know. It's just that what I did use was very concentrated."

"What about healing the trees afterwards?"

Tarkyn shrugged. "I did use some then but not all of it. It would have been pointless to try to heal them. I don't have enough power for so many trees. So, I did what I could to soothe the trees and then pulled out. Anyway, I can just draw straight from this tree now. So, it's not going to drain me, is it?"

Autumn Leaves shook his head reluctantly. "No. I suppose not."

Tarkyn frowned and asked gently, "What's wrong? You don't want me to do it, do you." When Autumn Leaves didn't answer, Tarkyn glanced across at Waterstone.

Waterstone went out of focus, as did Autumn Leaves. After a couple of minutes, neither of them had spoken out loud, but Autumn Leaves had turned red and was looking angry. Waterstone wasn't looking much calmer.

"Wonderful!" said Tarkyn quietly to Sparrow. "A completely silent argument. How very novel."

Sparrow smiled and rolled her eyes in response. "Trust them to get into an argument right now when we need them."

"Yes. Quite." Tarkyn leaned forward. "Ahem... In case you'd forgotten, any minute, the ground below us will be littered with huntsmen and wolves. Autumn Leaves, if you don't want my help, don't have it. But just make sure you can keep up. I don't want you endangering yourself or anyone else for whatever reason is holding you back."

Autumn Leaves let out a sigh of relief. "Thanks, Tarkyn. I will take it now, if you don't mind."

"Sorry?" Tarkyn was totally confused.

"When you were so determined to help me, I suddenly got worried that it might be the illness trying to infect me through you. And also, well, to be honest, the intense way you've been throwing your power around is a bit unnerving."

A little wave of irritation leaked from Tarkyn, even though he produced a wry smile. "Horses for courses, Autumn Leaves. You yourself can be gentle or strong, depending on the need. So too can my power." He shrugged. "And in case you hadn't noticed, it takes me a greater effort to come up with an intense blast of power. So, you'd know if one was coming."

Autumn Leaves raised his eyebrows and nodded. "Good point."

Now they could hear hoofbeats and the sounds of people or animals crashing through the undergrowth.

"Just a minute," said Tarkyn. "Protect my back while I concentrate for a few minutes. Autumn Leaves, you'll have to wait." So saying, Tarkyn closed his eyes and let his mind roam through the pathways below until he contacted the lead horse. He nudged against her mind until she let him in. He filled her mind with images of arrows coming at the horses and fire licking at them as they entered the clearing below. He inserted another image of the horses wheeling and heading back to the encampment.

Below, a little way off in the woods, pandemonium broke out. The horsemen began to shout and curse in frustration as their mounts suddenly slid to a halt and began to plunge and buck, wheeling around against the pull of their reins to head homewards. Despite the determined and even cruel efforts of the riders, the horses would not go any further. The wolves slunk around them, whining and snarling, confused and frightened by the behaviour of the horses, occasionally yelping as one of them was slashed by a horse's hoof.

"Good start!" said Tarkyn with some satisfaction. "Everyone managing all right? Good. Back in a minute." He closed his eyes again, and this time sent his mind looking for the dominant, harsh mind of the lead wolf. Tarkyn nudged at the lead wolf's mind but was thrown back by a savage thrust. Up in the branches, Tarkyn slewed sideways and nearly fell out of the tree.

"Hold me," he ordered peremptorily and returned to his self-appointed task without waiting for compliance. The Forest

Guardian drew together his power and his belief in himself as sovereign lord of the forests and tried again, this time demanding entry into the wolf's mind. The wolf brought his head around to stare at the distant presence, amber eyes meeting amber. This was not the gentle co-operation that Tarkyn requested of birds and other animals. This was one dominant male outfacing another. Tarkyn glared at the wolf, bringing to bear all the arrogance bequeathed to him by generations of rulers until the wolf whined and backed down, acknowledging Tarkyn's power and his right to dominion as guardian of the forest. Still, Tarkyn did not relent. He sent an image to the wolf of the wizard's apprentice and pictured Journeyman lying on the ground with Tarkyn's foot on his neck. Then he sent another image of the wolves turning tail and fleeing through the forest until they were far from the encampment and the wiles of men.

Tarkyn was brought back to his perch in the pine tree by an urgent tug on his cloak. "Tarkyn. The wolves are right under us," whispered Waterstone.

Tarkyn gave a relaxed, rather self-satisfied smile. "So they are. You can bid them farewell, if you like. They won't be troubling us again for a while." He sent out a wave of approval to the wolves as they loped underneath. The largest of them, a huge, shaggy male, lagged behind and when the others were out of sight, waited at the bottom of their pine tree, taking short paces back and forth beneath them. Autumn Leaves drew his bow.

"No. Tell everyone. Don't shoot. I'm going down." He disentangled himself from Sparrow and floated gently down to land before the wolf.

The wolf stopped pacing and stood staring up at him. After a moment, he sat down. In response, Tarkyn squatted down in front of him and held out his hand. The wolf sniffed it carefully. Almost experimentally, a deep growl emanated from the wolf, and he bared his teeth. Without even tensing, Tarkyn quietly incanted, "*Shturrum.*" The frozen wolf then had to endure while Tarkyn stroked him gently but firmly. Somehow, although it was gentle, the stroking was filled with menace. When the sorcerer waved his hand and released the spell, the wolf no longer growled but trembled under Tarkyn's hand. Two pairs of amber eyes met and held, but the wolf looked away first.

The sorcerer stood up. "You may go," he said, but it was the wave of his hand and the transmitted image that gave the wolf his orders. The wolf turned and loped quickly off down the trail of his companions, tail held low against his legs.

Tarkyn looked up into the tree. "You can come down now."

In true woodfolk fashion, woodfolk appeared around him almost instantaneously from every direction. There was an awed silence.

Eventually, Rainstorm cleared his throat and said, "Now, let me see if I have this right? You have just single-handedly thrust the entire hunting party into mayhem and overturned the trainer's control of the wolves. You then released the wolves back into the wild.... and, unless I'm much mistaken, completely subjugated their leader. Does that sum it up?"

Tarkyn nodded with a smile. "I thought it might be worth trying to control the animals to prevent the sorcerers from attacking us. And I think fighting those parasites has given me practice in making use of that natural arrogance of mine that you all love so much. That lead wolf was no pushover, you know. That was our second confrontation when he came and waited for me under the pine."

"What happened in the first? Did you win?"

"Yes, the first was a battle of the minds. But obviously he needed to check me out in person." Tarkyn gave a little shrug.

"I think he understands now that he lives or dies by my grace."

"Stars above, Tarkyn!" Rainstorm looked a bit sick. "I didn't realise you were so ruthless."

Unconsciously, the woodfolk had all drawn back from him. Tarkyn flicked a glance around them all. "No. Please don't do this. Don't withdraw. I'm not that ruthless. He is. He only understands things in black and white. There are no half measures. Either I totally dominate him or vice versa. Nothing in between. One of us has to hold the other's life in his hands. That's how he works. If it had been the other way around, he would either have killed me or mauled me so badly that I could no longer pose a threat."

Waterstone nodded and said spuriously, "You're absolutely right. He got off lightly, didn't he, only having his spirit broken?"

Tarkyn shot him a hurt look, but Waterstone was carefully looking elsewhere. It was fast dawning on Tarkyn that unbridled displays of his power were isolating him from the woodfolk, even though he was using his power for their benefit. First Autumn Leaves. Now Rainstorm and Waterstone. He thought over the tasks ahead of him; healing Golden Toad and Ibis Winds and then trying to find a way to salvage Rushwind. He wondered whether, if Rushwind should die, the woodfolk would lay the blame at his door. On the whole, he was inclined to think they would. Tarkyn decided to sort out the infection as quickly as possible and then withdraw for a while.

Tarkyn gave a mental shrug and asked in a business-like tone of voice, "Golden Toad, could you come with me please? I need to speak with you alone."

Throwing an anxious glance over his shoulder, Golden Toad followed the prince. Once they were out of earshot but not out of sight, Tarkyn turned and said, his voice edged with bitterness, "I won't take you right away from everyone because I would not wish to frighten you."

Golden Toad put his head on one side and regarded the prince for a few quiet moments. "They've upset you, haven't they?"

"Yes," replied Tarkyn, remorselessly honest, "but I can't see that it is any concern of yours. It is just something I have to live with."

"I think it is every concern of mine. None of this would have happened if you hadn't been trying to help me and my family."

Tarkyn eyed him. "It's not your fault. The same thing would have happened sooner or later. Everyone is scared of my power and, consequently, of me. When I don't use it, they gradually forget about it. But I've used it excessively tonight, firstly against the infection and then against the wolves and huntsmen." Tarkyn turned and slammed the heel of his hand into the nearest tree. "Blast them all! If I wasn't trying to protect them, I wouldn't have to use it in the first place. Once I have sorted out this infection, I'll leave them to protect themselves for a while. They have managed without me for hundreds of years. I'm probably taking too much upon myself."

"Perhaps you are. After all, woodfolk have been hiding from hunters for centuries. You may have seen it as more of a crisis than they did." Golden Toad smiled. "But personally, I think it was a good move to take the wolves out of the equation." The woodman looked as though he were about to say something but then refrained.

Tarkyn's eyes narrowed. "Come on. Out with it. Whatever you were going to say."

Golden Toad's eyes met the prince's squarely. "Hmm. I was thinking of saying, before wisdom became the better part of valour, that you could possibly have found a less inflammatory turn of phrase for describing your subjugation of the wolf."

Suddenly Tarkyn smiled. "You know, Golden Toad, I think I will have to make you an honorary member of the home guard if anyone else is still in it after tonight. You combine honesty and courage in full measure, especially after your experiences." The prince ran his hand through his hair. "You're right, of course. The feeling wasn't good from the beginning but things took a notable turn for the worse after that, despite my efforts to explain."

Golden Toad grimaced. "You see, the uncomfortable truth is that we all live or die by your grace. And somehow that statement made it all too obvious."

"No. That's not true," protested Tarkyn vehemently.

The woodman gave a sad little smile. "But it is, you see. Your father knew that. Remember? He said the basic premise protecting any sovereignty is 'submit or die.'"

"But no. My father made the punishment for betrayal of the oath damage to the forest, not death to the oathbreaker."

Golden Toad looked at him, not unsympathetically. "But he knew that if the forest perishes, we perish. And if, for some reason, you insisted that we put to death one of our number, we would have to do it to preserve the forest and the rest of us."

Tarkyn looked around wildly. "Where is all this coming from, suddenly? I thought we were all getting on. Why would anyone think I would do something like that?"

"What about Rushwind? She has destroyed a swathe of forest and betrayed the oath."

"So did Waterstone. And he's not dead. He had less excuse than she did. Her actions were not under her control. In fact, I think it is grossly unjust that the forest was damaged when it was the parasites, not her, that instigated her actions against me." Tarkyn frowned. "What? Does everyone think I'm going to have Rushwind killed? Do you think that?"

Golden Toad evaded answering and asked instead, "What if she cannot be cured? What then?"

Tarkyn shook his head. "If you think I am going to decide her fate, you are sadly mistaken. It is up to the woodfolk to make that difficult decision, should it arise. No one is going to thrust it onto my shoulders. All I am going to do is try my utmost to cure her and avoid the necessity of such a decision."

"I see. I didn't realise that you were going to try again with her. That is most kind of you, since I know you will be placing yourself at serious risk." The woodman added slowly, "In fact, so much so that I'm not sure that you should do it."

Tarkyn glanced up at him and spoke severely. "I have had this discussion with the other woodfolk. I will not brook being prevented from helping any of my people, even if it does mean putting myself at risk. If it is my will, it overrides your oath to protect me."

Golden Toad put his head on one side and considered the prince. After a moment, he said mildly, "Your Highness, do you realise that you offend both yourself and me when you assume that any concern I may have for your welfare springs from the oath?"

Tarkyn blinked as though he had been struck. There was a short silence before he replied stiffly, "I beg your pardon, Golden Toad. You are right, but I do indeed find it difficult to believe that you, who have known me for such a short while, could actually care about my welfare." When the woodman began to expostulate, Tarkyn held up his hand and continued in a warmer tone of voice, "I'm not saying I *don't* believe you. But if you ask Waterstone, he will tell you that I struggle with this whole concept, even with woodfolk I have known for much longer than you." A slight smile dawned. "So, instead, I will say thank you for your concern, but tell you that I couldn't live with myself if I didn't make some attempt to repair the damage I have wrought in Rushwind. Is that better?"

The woodman smiled and shook his head. "You're a funny one, aren't you."

"Sorry?"

Golden Toad waved a dismissive hand, not realising how much he was pushing the boundaries. "Don't worry. Let's leave it for the time being. Now, what did you want to talk to me about?"

The prince managed to contain the instinctive offence he felt at someone else redirecting the conversation and refocused on the task at hand. "Two things. I want to heal you and Ibis Wings first, just in case I don't survive my effort with Rushwind." Golden Toad made to interrupt but the prince held up his hand. "Secondly, if I work with you to heal you, you will have to grant me access into your brain. I don't actually think it affects your privacy because it is your physical mind not your thoughts or memories *per se*. But even if it did invade your privacy, I would still have to insist on full access."

"Agreed, but..."

"And now we come to the warnings. I don't know what effect my accessing your brain will have on your mental powers. It may lead to some sort of brain damage, especially if the parasites are more concentrated there." Tarkyn shrugged. "My feeling is that it won't, but I can by no means guarantee it. And the final warning. If I try to cure Rushwind, I will have to gain access to her brain too. She was resistant the first time and will be even more so now that the parasites have mutated and are rife inside her. I think there is a very high possibility that she will end up with some brain damage, if she hasn't already, even if I can save her."

Goolden Toad shook his head. "I can see that we will have

to take the chance with Rushwind, but maybe Ibis Wings and I should just learn to live without mindtalking."

"By all means, discuss it with each other and with the other woodfolk. My opinion, for what it's worth, is that one day the parasites within you may mutate as a result of something other than my *esse*. If that happens before anyone realises, half the forest and scores of woodfolk could be dead before it is stopped." Tarkyn waved a hand. "Go away and think about it. Come back and tell me what you want to do, as soon as you have decided." As Golden Toad turned to leave, he added, "And could you make sure that Danton and Stormaway know that they can bring Rushwind back please? They must be tiring of holding her up in the air. I think the safest place to put her would be where we had her before or in the centre of the burnt-out circle."

"Are you not coming back with me?" asked the woodman.

"No. I think I have had enough for the time being. I'll just stay here and use this tree to recoup my energy... And Golden Toad, if anyone looks like coming over here, could you please dissuade them? I don't think I could stomach any pseudo-kindness at the moment."

Golden Toad flicked a worried glance over his shoulder but returned to the other woodfolk without further comment.

It was not long before he returned, with Stormaway trailing in his wake. Tarkyn watched them approach through narrowed eyes, waiting for some comment from the wizard. None came. Stormaway merely asked him whether he was ready to proceed with Golden Toad.

Tarkyn nodded. "If you don't mind, I will concentrate better if we are tucked away somewhere out of sight. I really don't want everyone watching me use my power again unless it's necessary."

"You don't need anyone to help you create angry thoughts,

do you?" asked Stormaway anxiously.

"No, they have already done a good job," replied Tarkyn ambiguously, throwing a dry look in Golden Toad's direction. "Besides, these are not mutated parasites we're dealing with here. So now that I know to contain my energy, it should be quite straightforward."

As indeed turned out to be the case. A short-lived, intense ball of power stormed through Golden Toad's blood vessels, frying every parasite in its path and meeting minimal resistance even as it entered the woodman's brain. Because it was so short-lived, there was less burning, and Tarkyn was easily able to soothe and repair any residual scalding before leaving the woodman. The same process was equally successful on Ibis Wings, although the resistance to Tarkyn entering her brain was noticeably stronger, despite her previous assurances that she would give him access.

Tarkyn had a short encounter with her fiery temper but overrode her with a neat, sharp jab of irritation. Sure enough, behind her resistance was hiding a small huddle of parasites near the base of her skull.

As soon as he had finished with father and daughter, Tarkyn spent a few minutes replenishing his strength then moved straight on to deal with Rushwind. He remembered how hideous it had felt when the mutated parasites had coursed through him for the few short minutes he had had to endure them. Rushwind had been living with them for hours. Tarkyn overrode his present disenchantment with the woodfolk to ensure that several were standing nearby in case he needed their input. He left it to Stormaway to choose who should accompany him, but in the end, much to Tarkyn's irritation, they all came, either to watch or to help. He did not think it did much for his cause to have them watching him summon the type of rage and hauteur required to assail the parasites.

Against all expectation, the purging of Rushwind went without a hitch. Without needing recourse to the woodfolk, Tarkyn used the same technique as he had for the trees. He summoned his rage at the parasites and struck out aggressively from the split-second his power entered her bloodstream. He burned out the parasites almost instantaneously but stayed in Rushwind much longer, checking everywhere for lurking parasites and soothing and repairing the burning until she was free of pain and back to her normal temperature. When he left her, she was still unconscious but seemed to be healed. Only time would tell whether she had sustained any lasting damage. Tarkyn had not noticed anything obviously amiss but on the other hand, he knew next to nothing about anatomy.

When he had finished, Tarkyn opened his eyes, and took his hand from her shoulder. As he rose to his feet, he looked around the assembled woodfolk and said tiredly, "I think she is all right. And I hope now, we have seen the last of that infection." He ran his hand through his hair. "I'm going to bed. I've had enough for one night."

"My lord," said Running Feet, "the lookouts have reported that, as the men on horseback passed below them on their way back to the encampment, they heard them discussing your magic. We fear that the people at the encampment now know you are here."

Tarkyn waved a tired hand. "And yet I am still going to bed. I will leave it to you to ensure my safety. As I understand it, you have centuries of evading detection behind you. So you won't need me to help you."

Golden Toad gave a slight smile but the rest of the woodfolk looked stunned that Tarkyn was taking no interest in dealing with the new threat. Without another word, the exhausted sorcerer threaded his way through them and headed off to his shelter.

II

DANTON'S TRIAL

7

T arkyn slept for more than twenty-four hours. Drumming rain on the roof of his shelter finally woke him. He lay in the semi-darkness remembering where he was and what had happened. He wondered how Rushwind was, but not enough to venture into the rain to find out. Tarkyn thought about Autumn Leaves telling him he was unnerving, Rainstorm calling him ruthless, and all the woodfolk backing away from him. Most unkind of all was Waterstone's remark about the wolf's spirit being broken. Tarkyn hadn't broken his spirit. He may have mastered the wolf but that same wolf was still lord of the wolf pack. Even at the end, the wolf had met his eyes for some time before acknowledging Tarkyn as his packleader. On balance, Tarkyn decided to roll over and go back to sleep.

When he next awoke, the rain had stopped and he could see tiny pinpricks of sunlight through the entwined branches of his ceiling. He thought about going outside. How would the woodfolk treat him? Would they all pretend everything was all right? Would someone come up and apologise? Would they avoid him? Tarkyn shook his head. He couldn't think of any scenario he could look forward to with any pleasure. On balance, he decided to roll over and go back to sleep.

By mid-afternoon, going back to sleep was no longer an option. Physical needs were demanding attention. He pulled on his boots, reached for his cloak and made his way quietly outside. There was no one was around. After he had relieved himself, he wandered around the area looking at the devastation wrought by the infestation and the oath. The acrid smell of old smoke and wet charred wood still hung in the air. It didn't cross his mind to think how much worse it could have been if he hadn't intervened. He only thought about the fact that it was his power that had triggered the mutation of the parasites in the first place. Tarkyn wandered further afield beyond the burnt area where fallen trees and smashed branches littering the ground marked the vengeance of the oath. Never having considered that a woodman or woman might attack in an act beyond their volition, he had not foreseen this danger. He realised he had become complacent about the viciousness of the oath and had not maintained his campaign with Stormaway to change it.

He wished he knew which way to go to start the journey to find Falling Rain. Then he could just pack up and leave. The others would have no trouble following his tracks and catching him up. Perhaps he could use a bird to guide him. He knew they were heading for the mountains in the south so he could use the mountains as an image

He frowned as it was borne in upon him that there was actually no one around anywhere. This was the first time he had been on his own since the first morning he had awoken in the forest. Even then, the woodfolk had been watching him. Presumably someone was watching him now, but it was strange that everyone was keeping out of sight. He heard footsteps crunching over the tree debris and turned to see Danton coming towards him.

As he neared the prince, Danton gave a slight bow. "Good afternoon, my lord. Are you feeling better after your long sleep?"

Tarkyn shrugged. "I have had enough sleep, if that's what you mean. But I feel quite heartsick about the forest. And I seem to have misplaced an entire nation of people while I slept."

Danton smiled. "Your woodfolk are not far away. They could not bear to face this devastation while they waited for you. So, I have been keeping guard until such time as you felt ready to rejoin them. I think you'll find some packages of food and a waterbag waiting for you outside your shelter."

"Hmph." Tarkyn glanced at his liegeman. "And what is the mood among them? In what light do they see me at the moment?"

Danton raised his eyebrows. "Why do you ask? They seem much the same as always."

"They weren't, I can assure you. After I disbanded the wolves and the huntsmen, they were clearly unnerved by what I had done."

"Were they?" asked Danton. "I missed that bit. Well, you can't blame them. Every day you perform some new magic that has never been tried before. You astonish me, a sorcerer, let alone them."

Tarkyn gave a wry smile. "I don't mind astonishing them. But I do mind when they start to shy away from me." He shrugged despondently. "Still, who can blame them? Look at this mess I've wrought."

Danton waved his arm around. "What? This? You aren't responsible for this. Without you, the whole forest would be like this."

"Without me, Rushwind wouldn't be able to mindtalk, but the forest would be undamaged. It is only because the parasites fed on my power that the infection became so strong."

Danton kicked a bit of wood aside and bent down to pick up a tiny broken egg shell. He looked at Tarkyn for a moment before replying. "I can see what you mean, but I don't think the woodfolk are holding you responsible."

"Perhaps not. I don't know. But I am holding me responsible." Tarkyn swept his hand through his hair. "Maybe my brothers were right, after all. Maybe I am not safe with this power."

"Don't be so hard on yourself. Anyway, you know perfectly well your brothers were only using that as an excuse to disarm you. They didn't really think your power was dangerous." Danton gave a wry smile. "At least, not when they had you arrested. Maybe afterwards they did." He shrugged. "Still, at least no one was killed this time."

Tarkyn glared at him. "No people were killed. But many birds and animals were killed, not to mention all these trees." He sighed. "I can see why the woodfolk couldn't bear to stay here looking at all of this."

"Tarkyn, neither time did you intend to hurt anyone," said Danton gently.

"Tell that to the families of the palace guards I inadvertently killed. I'm sure that will make them feel better."

Danton put his arm across the prince's shoulder. He could feel the tension under his hand but ignored it as he began to guide the prince towards his shelter. "Come on. You need some food. You had a tough time fighting that infection. You need to look after yourself."

Tarkyn's eyebrows twitched together as he looked in surprise at his liegeman. "When did you become a mother hen?"

Danton smiled reluctantly. "If you must know, I am under strict orders from Summer Rain and Stormaway."

"Neither of whom care enough to be here in person."

Silence greeted this remark.

"What?" demanded Tarkyn.

Now that they were walking back towards the shelter, Danton let his arm drop from Tarkyn's shoulders. He glanced at the prince and gave a slow smile. "I couldn't think of a response to that remark that wouldn't sound cheeky or disrespectful. So, I didn't say anything."

"So, you think I'm being petulant, do you?"

"Something like that. Perhaps you don't realise that the woodfolk were actually feeling physically ill from the distress of having their forest so badly damaged. Stormaway has been coming down from time to time, but he's just not here at the moment."

"Hmph. Fine. So, I jumped to the worst conclusion. I admit it."

Danton looked sideways at him. "Do I detect a note of anger in your tone?"

"Of course you bloody do. I'm angry with myself for destroying the forest. I'm angry with Stormaway for the blasted oath. I'm angry at the woodfolk for reacting as they did. I'm angry about the whole stinking mess." He glanced at his friend and gave a wry smile. "And I suppose I'm also embarrassed that I made an idiot of myself running around rescuing everyone from the huntsmen when they were perfectly capable of looking after themselves." He sighed, "All in all, it has been an inauspicious couple of days."

"Just remember how much worse it could have been."

"Cold comfort, I'm afraid."

8

A s prince and liegeman neared the woodfolk's new firesite, a delegation came forward to greet him. He glanced with some trepidation at Danton, thinking that the woodfolk were about to remonstrate with him. But no. As soon as he was close enough, they brought forth a huge bunch of wild flowers and a stone flask of their finest wine.

"Tarkyn, this is to say thank you to you for saving our forest," said Tree Wind with a big smile. "You are a true Guardian of the Forest, and we would all like to thank you for the enormous effort and courage you showed in fighting those ghastly parasites."

All the surrounding woodfolk smiled and murmured agreement.

For once, Tarkyn's court training completely deserted him. He stood there, stunned. Danton's finger giving him a gentle prod in the ribs brought him to a realisation that some words were required from him.

He gave a dazed smile. "Thank you. Thank you very much. As

you can probably tell, I am absolutely astonished. I thought you would be angry with me. I feel I have done much that is wrong and little that is right in the last few days." He took a deep breath and made a better effort to rise to the occasion. "In return, I would like to thank all of you for saving me and helping me when I was infected and for helping me to destroy that terrible threat to the forest."

The woodfolk parted and Golden Toad, Ibis Wings, and Rushwind came to stand before him.

"Your Highness," said Golden Toad, "we cannot begin to express the depths of our gratitude to you, especially when I saw the terrible suffering you went through as a result of your efforts to help us."

Rushwind took a step forward. "My lord, would you mind bending down a little?"

Tarkyn looked slightly puzzled but complied, nevertheless. Rushwind leant forward and gave him a kiss on the cheek. He promptly turned pink.

Rushwind laughed kindly. "That is to say thank you and to show you that I am no longer frightened of you. Although my memory is not too clear about that time, I believe I behaved very badly towards you when those parasites were still in me. I can only say I am sorry. Nothing you have done deserved that reaction."

Tarkyn straightened up smiling and looked into her eyes. "Rushwind, you and I have been through a lot together over these last two days. Only you and I know what it feels like to have those virulent mutated parasites coursing through our veins. I hope you don't remember too much of it."

A shadow passed across the woodwoman's face. "I remember enough. I am so sorry I infected you," there was a hitch in her voice as she added, "and damaged the forest. From what Golden Toad tells me, you never once thought of leaving me to my fate even though I had betrayed my oath to you and tried to kill you."

Tarkyn frowned at this. He glanced around the assembled woodfolk before returning his gaze to Rushwind. "I don't know where the idea came from that I would pass judgement on you. I could hardly condemn you for causing damage unintentionally when I myself have done the same thing on a grander and, one might say, more reprehensible scale." Once more he scanned the crowd. "I suppose there are one or two things I would like to apologise for while I have your attention. Firstly, I am so sorry about the forest. If my power hadn't affected those parasites, none of this would have happened. And secondly, I apologise for interfering when the hunting party was coming. I realised afterwards, with a little help from Golden Toad," he added with a wry smile in that woodman's direction, "that, of course, you are all perfectly capable of dealing with a hunting party and, as I recall, we had an agreement to consult with each other in such situations that I completely forgot." He smiled and waved his stone flask of wine in an arc around himself. "You have obviously forgiven me for which I thank you. I will try not to do it again."

Tree Wind shook her head, smiling. "Tarkyn, there is nothing to forgive. Even if you were slightly overzealous, you strove tirelessly on our behalf. All of us saw what you were prepared to endure to protect the forest and us."

To cover his embarrassment, he looked down at the large stone flask he was holding. "I suppose we had better drink this then. Is there enough to go around, do you think?"

"As it turns out," replied Running Feet, laughing, "we have a few more of those flagons that we can draw upon if the need arises."

"Oh, good. Because after the last few days, I think we may need them." So saying, Tarkyn headed for the firesite, found himself a comfortable tree to lean against and, assisted by equally enthusiastic woodfolk, began to work his way steadily through what was to be, by the end of the night, several flagons of wine.

Unusually, Tree Wind had followed close behind and sat down next to him. As the evening wore on and the wine made him more expansive, Tarkyn finally raised the issue that had puzzled him ever since he had arrived in the forest

"Tree Wind, even though you are still the person who often asks the hard questions, am I right in saying that you do not feel so antagonistic towards me as you used to?"

The woodwoman nodded and gave a wry smile. "Yes. Despite every intention I had of hating you always, you have managed to creep in under my guard."

Tarkyn studied her, frowning. "I know that no one wanted me to come here, but it has always struck me that your dislike of me was much stronger than other people's. Is that true?" When she nodded again, he asked, "Why?"

She glanced at him then looked fixedly into the fire. "Because I was to marry Falling Rain. And when he gave away our existence and precipitated our subjugation to your father and you, I lost him."

"Oh, Tree Wind. I am so sorry. That must have been very hard for you." He paused and asked gently, "Could you not have followed him into exile?"

Tree Wind shook her head. "It is very rare for anyone to be exiled. If they are, they may take nothing and no one with them."

Tarkyn frowned. "That is very harsh."

"It is to stop the possibility of a rival community being set up that could then lead to conflict within the woodfolk."

"There is wisdom in that, I have to admit." He held out his flagon. "More wine?"

"Thanks." Once her cup was refilled, Tree Wind said, "I know you were not responsible for the loss of Falling Rain, but when you arrived, you were the personification of the injustice done to him and to all of us."

Tarkyn grimaced. "So I gather. Unfortunately, I still am and always will be." He glanced at her. "And this is not just a short-term inconvenience. I'm afraid I'm a way of life everyone has to become used to."

Surprisingly, Tree Wind smiled. "I think we have enough discrimination to be able to separate you from the actions of your father. At least we do now, even if we didn't have to start with." She shrugged. "And as to having to put up with you; in some ways, you're lucky we have had so long to get used to the idea. On the one hand, the fear that had built up in our minds of what it would be like to be subject to someone's wishes meant you had a tough start. But now, the reality is so much less dire than the expectation."

"So. I'm less dire than expectation." Tarkyn took another hearty draught of wine. "Hmm. I don't think I'll actually take that as a compliment."

Tree Wind laughed. "No. I wouldn't if I were you. You'd have to be pretty desperate to think it was."

"Hmm. Well, at least I'm not desperate."

Tree Wind considered him over the rim of her goblet. After a moment, she lowered it and said seriously, "But I will pay you a compliment. It took someone very special to break through the wall of hatred I have nurtured over all these years. Danton is right. You do care about people and even though you say you can't consider yourself as equal with us, you treat each person with respect."

Tarkyn frowned. "Of course I do. Rank and personal value are not at all the same thing."

"I see," said Tree Wind thoughtfully. "I have trouble

understanding rank. The whole concept is so alien to our culture. Do you think your father understood the difference between rank and each individual's value?"

Tarkyn shifted his back against the tree while he thought about it. "I don't know. I can't really remember him in great detail. I know more of him from Waterstone's and your memories than from my own. If I had only seen your memories, I would say no. But Waterstone worked with him as he visited everyone who was sick and he did treat the sick people he visited with respect." He shook his head. "I think he knew the difference but perhaps he gave more weight to rank than personal worth. He was, after all, the king."

Tree Wind raised her eyebrows. "So, does that mean that if you ever became king, you would change your attitude to people?"

Tarkyn gave a short laugh. "Still asking the hard questions, I see. I don't know. I would hope not. But a role like that forces a lot of behaviour onto you. That's another reason I don't want it. You have to have *time* to be able to care for people. If your time is dictated by protocols and ceremonies and other people's expectations, it is harder to find the time you need to understand each person. And when you see people only as a crowd, then your care for them is diminished." He took another swig of his wine and waved his cup around. "You should ask Ancient Oak. He wasn't too impressed with my attitude to crowds."

Tree Wind's eyes narrowed as she thought back to the occasion he might be referring to. She gave a slight smile as she figured it out. "Perhaps it was more that you weren't too impressed with the crowd's attitude to you."

"Very good, Tree Wind. You start from where I finished with Ancient Oak. I had to explain that to him."

Tree Wind shrugged. "In fairness to Ancient Oak, you

might have had to explain that to me at that stage too. Back then I, too, would have assumed the fault was yours, not the crowd's."

"Hmm, now you mention it, there wasn't much I could do right in your eyes at that point in the proceedings." He smiled. "Well, I'm glad you are not so determinedly against me anymore because, wherever you are, you're a power to be reckoned with and I'd rather we were on the same side, both for my sake and for the sake of woodfolk generally."

"Thanks. I'll take that as a compliment."

"It is." He took another sip of his wine and looked at her over the rim of his goblet. "So, are you coming with us to find Falling Rain?"

"Yes." She smiled ruefully. "Yes, I am. I would never have thought two weeks ago that I would be saying that. Even though I badly want to see Falling Rain again, I didn't think I would be able to stand your company."

Tarkyn winced. "Don't feel you have to keep pointing out how much you disliked me. The memories you shared with me when I first arrived were more eloquent than any words could be."

Impulsively, she placed a hand on his arm. "I'm sorry. There is still a small part of me that resents you."

Tarkyn repressed a sigh and nodded. "I'm sure there is. If it's only a small part, you're doing better than most."

"Hi, prince," said Rainstorm, breaking breezily into the conversation as he plonked himself down cross-legged on front of them. "How's your flagon going? Need a re-fill yet?"

Tarkyn waggled his flagon and listened. "Hmm. Not much left in there. I think I might need some more in the very near future. I'll make you a deal. I'll pour you a drink now if you find me another flagon when we run out."

"Deal!" said Rainstorm, holding out his cup.

Just as he was about to pour, Tarkyn frowned and asked, "Just a minute. Aren't you too young to be drinking?"

Rainstorm and Tree Wind both burst into laughter.

"What are you talking about?" asked Rainstorm. "Why don't you ask your niece if she's s too young?"

Tarkyn was shocked. "What? Sparrow? You're not telling me that she is drinking wine? She's only ten."

Tree Wind shrugged. "Old enough to be included in a hunt. Old enough to drink wine."

Tarkyn boggled. "You're joking. She's just a little girl." He frowned. "Does Waterstone know?"

Tree Wind and Rainstorm smiled at each other.

"Waterstone know?" laughed Rainstorm. "Waterstone gives it to her. Now, are you going to give me some of your wine or will I have to go elsewhere?"

Tarkyn thrust the flagon at him. "Here! Far be it from me to impose my expectations." He shook his head in bemusement. "I think we may have hit on a *slight* difference in our cultures here." He held his hands up. "But I'm outnumbered. I retreat." He looked from one to the other of them. "I may have to talk to Waterstone about this, though."

"Oh, good idea, Prince," said Rainstorm as he took a long draught of wine. "I'm sure Waterstone will be keen to hear a younger man's views on how to bring up his daughter."

The prince's eyes narrowed.

"Ooh no," said Rainstorm lugubriously. "Don't tell me I've done it again."

"Done what again?" asked Tree Wind.

"Been rude to Tarkyn." He gave a delicate little hiccough. "I am not very good at behaving well around princes, you know." He smiled rather crookedly. "I try but I haven't had much practice."

Tarkyn was watching him quizzically. "Rainstorm, I was

merely thinking about what you said. As usual, you've said something worth listening to. So, stop carrying on. I'm not angry with you."

Rainstorm rolled his eyes at Tree Wind. "Well, thank heavens for that. Tarkyn is really quite crushing when he's angry, you know." He added in an unintentionally loud undertone, "I think my parents could learn a thing or two from him...but I hope they don't." He peered into his cup. "Hmm. These don't hold much, do they? I'd better find you another flagon so you can fill my cup up again."

"Thanks," said Tarkyn dryly as Rainstorm lifted himself unsteadily to his feet and wandered off.

When the next flagon arrived, it was borne by Waterstone, not Rainstorm.

"Hello," said Tarkyn. "Where's Rainstorm? We haven't frightened him off, have we?"

Waterstone grinned. "Oh, I don't think so. He's subsided into a happy heap against a tree over there. I expect we'll have to carry him to bed in a while."

"And how's Sparrow?" asked Tarkyn in what he hoped was a casual manner.

"She's fine. She's been in bed for a couple of hours now. Can't have her staying up too late. She gets crabby. And if we're heading off tomorrow, she'll need plenty of sleep tonight."

"I see. Oh good. Tarkyn shot a suspicious glance at Tree Wind, but she didn't look as though she had been teasing him. "Well, I hope she's not as legless as Rainstorm. That really would make her crabby tomorrow."

Waterstone frowned. "What are you talking about? Why would she be legless?"

Tarkyn began to feel uncomfortable. "From drinking wine?" he ventured.

The woodman snorted. "I don't think she's going to have a

problem with one little cup of wine. Helps her to sleep well. And if you think that a young girl like Sparrow should be allowed to drink as much as a strapping lad like Rainstorm then I'm afraid I'll be very careful about leaving her in your care."

Now Tree Wind was grinning. "I think you'll find Tarkyn has very different views from you about young people drinking," she said mischievously.

"Hmph." Waterstone frowned at Tarkyn. "Well, I hope you will respect my right to decide what is best for Sparrow. I wouldn't want her tainted by any of your undisciplined sorcerer's ways."

"Help!" said Tarkyn in a small voice, rolling his eyes beseechingly at Tree Wind.

Tree Wind laughed. She placed one hand firmly on Waterstone's shoulder and pushed him around so he was looking at her. "Waterstone, I suspect sorcerers may not be as undisciplined as you think. Tarkyn doesn't think children should drink at all. In fact, he nearly refused to give Rainstorm a glass of wine."

Waterstone raised his eyebrows and turned his gaze to stare at Tarkyn. "Did you? How very odd."

"I can't win with you, can I? You are not impressed when you think I would allow children to drink whatever they want. Then you are equally unimpressed when you discover that I think they shouldn't drink at all."

"Tarkyn, it's a matter of degree. A lot or none are extremes. A little bit won't hurt Sparrow. And Rainstorm? Rainstorm is not even relevant to this conversation. He's sixteen, for heaven's sake." Waterstone glanced over to where Rainstorm was snoozing and smiled. "He's busy learning about his tolerance levels as we speak."

Tarkyn considered the sleeping young woodman for a minute then looked back at Waterstone. "I didn't have my first drink away from my tutors until I was eighteen. I learnt what to drink and when and how much but only under very close supervision. Once I started to drink alcohol, I was very closely monitored."

"What? Even when you were away from the palace?"

Tarkyn smiled. "Oh yes. Young Danton over there was one of the people charged with making sure I maintained my sense of decorum."

Waterstone frowned. "How could he do that? If you decided to get drunk, what could he do about it?"

"Ah, well, you see, that's where caring for people has its drawbacks." Tarkyn took another sip of wine. "If I had disgraced myself, it wouldn't have been me who was disciplined. It would have been Danton."

"I see. What sort of disciplining are we talking about here?"

Tarkyn considered. "It would depend on the level of public notice I had attracted, I suppose. It could vary from a public dressing down to having his pay docked. In an extreme case, it could even lead to a public flogging or dismissal from the service."

"And the consequence to you?"

"That would be the consequence to me. Enduring those things happening to Danton."

Waterstone looked thoughtful. "Did it work?"

Tarkyn looked across at Danton. "Yes, it worked. There was only one time following a drinking session that I had to watch Danton being publicly berated for something I had done. I couldn't allow someone else to be punished for things I was doing."

"If you don't mind me asking, Tarkyn," said Tree Wind, re-entering the conversation, "did it work with your brothers?"

"Not as effectively." He glanced at Tree Wind. "I'm not saying they didn't care for their friends, but there were always two of them to egg each other on. So, they were more likely to get carried away. Whereas there was only one of me surrounded by people with a vested interest in controlling my behaviour."

Waterstone studied Tarkyn as he thought about it.

"What?" asked Tarkyn eventually.

"That first night you drank with us in the forest, the night we discovered you were the Forest Guardian and the night you became a woodman. They must be about the only times you've ever been close to drunk."

Tarkyn smiled. "Yet another reason I drank so much that first night with you. Finding out about the oath and how much you all hated me. Seeing my father in your memories, Tree Wind. And having no one charged with keeping me sober. I haven't had much practice at learning my own limits."

"You had weeks away from your minders on the way to the forest after you were exiled," pointed out Tree Wind.

Tarkyn raised his eyebrows, "I was not so desperate to get drunk that I would risk being out of control when I was on the run. That first night with you people was the first time I had felt even vaguely safe for quite some time."

Waterstone frowned across at Danton. "No wonder you were unsure whether you could trust Danton. Because even though he professed to be your friend, you always knew that he was accountable to someone else."

Tarkyn nodded. "Everyone's first loyalty must be to the King."

"Which, if Danton's friend is the local blacksmith or farmer, wouldn't matter two hoots," said Tree Wind. "But does matter if his friend is the King's younger brother."

Waterstone frowned. "So was there anyone you could trust to keep your secrets?"

Tarkyn thought carefully. The silence drew out. A couple

of times, he nearly spoke but thought better of it. Eventually, he raised his eyes to look at Waterstone. "There have been some people who have overlooked small misdemeanours on my part, like pinching apples from the trees in the orchard or feeding the horses when I was supposed to be studying. Things like that. But had they been asked directly, I would have expected them to give me away." He shook his head. "So, no. The answer to your question is no. There has never been anyone I could trust, including Danton."

"So, it wasn't just the vying for power in court that caused you to mistrust people, was it?"

"No, although it is all part of the same thing. Everything anyone has ever done around me has been with the King in mind, in one way or another." Tarkyn shrugged. "It's not as bad as it sounds. After all, we all understood the rules. I always knew everything I said or did would get back to Kosar. No one was acting without my knowledge. So, I just behaved as I would have if he were there watching all the time."

"You're well out of it, I'd say," said Tree Wind caustically.

"Despite the loss of all those luxuries I was used to, I would have to agree with you." Tarkyn broke off as Waterstone stood up. "Where are you off to so suddenly? I hope you're not taking that flagon with you."

"No. You can have it." Waterstone refilled his cup before handing the flagon to Tarkyn. "Tree Wind, you might have to keep an eye on our young friend here if he is to have any hope of getting up early tomorrow. I'm off to have a chat with Danton. I'll see you later."

9

Waterstone skirted around the fire, gently brushing off several invitations for him to join in various conversations, until he reached the young sorcerer. Danton stood out from everyone around the fire. He was the only person with blond hair and the only person wearing blue robes. Other than Stormaway who wore green, everyone else was clothed in a soft brown that blended into the backdrop of tree trunks and branches.

Waterstone sat down with his back against a recently vacated tree trunk. "I've just been talking to your liege lord over there." The woodman noticed that he still couldn't bring himself to say *our* liege lord. "You lot had a very strange way of getting on with each other, didn't you."

Danton eyed him askance. "You could hardly expect me to think it's strange if it's what we always did and secondly, I have no idea what you're talking about."

"Enjoying the wine then?" Waterstone laughed. "Hmm, I don't think I made myself very clear, now that I think about it." He took a sip from his goblet and frowned. "How could you call it friendship when you were really just an agent for Tarkyn's brother?"

Danton's eyes glittered and his hands balled into fists. "Do you know," he said in a low, shaking voice, "the only thing stopping me from belting the living daylights out of you at this moment is that, whether you accept it or not, I acknowledge you as a prince of the realm."

Waterstone blinked. "Danton, you are really a most unusual person. I find you much more difficult to fathom than Tarkyn." He realised that Danton was still wired up, ready to strike, and so waved a placatory hand. "I apologise, Danton. I didn't really mean to offend you. Although, to be honest, I find *myself* offended by what I hear of your behaviour."

"Just be glad," said Danton through gritted teeth, not surprisingly quite unappeased by this, "that I have had years of discipline as a palace guard or you would be out cold by now."

Waterstone raised his eyebrows but forbore to enter into a game of one-up-manship, asking instead, "So, explain it to me, Danton. How can you be someone's friend and yet report all his actions to the King?"

Danton frowned at him as he let the question sink in. "Because, until recently, we were all on the same side. I saw myself as looking after Tarkyn on the King's behalf. We all saw it as our duty to protect the prince and make sure that protocols were observed by anyone coming into contact with him."

"But didn't you report back to the King on Tarkyn's behaviour?"

"We were quizzed on it from time to time, certainly. Usually by Barnaban, the King's minister for security. But I thought of that as everyone working together to make sure Tarkyn was kept safe." Danton shrugged. "Anyway, there would have been little point in trying to cover anything up because Barnaban had other sources. Saying that, if Tarkyn had ever asked me to cover for him, I would have. He just never asked." A thought struck him. "Anyway, I bet you lot report back to each other on what he's doing. Doesn't mean you're not his friends."

"Hmph. That's different." Waterstone's words didn't carry much conviction.

Danton merely raised his eyebrows and waited.

The woodman waved a hand. "Fine. So it's not all that different."

"No. And as soon as I knew that the King had turned on Tarkyn, I left his service and set out to find Tarkyn."

Waterstone nodded slowly. "You did, too." He smiled apologetically. "Looks like I've jumped to the wrong conclusion about you again. Sorry about that." He took another draught of his wine and said confidingly, "It's the sorcerer thing, you know. I just thought you must have a different concept of friendship."

Danton looked at him for a few moments without speaking. Then he said, "Next time you are offended by my behaviour, make sure you talk to me about it, just as you have now. I really don't want to find myself tied up any more times than I absolutely have to."

Waterstone grinned. "Deal. And if, in return, you can talk to me about any of our behaviour you find offensive, we should be able to navigate our way through our differences without too much conflict." He paused. "Anything on your mind at the moment, now we're on the topic?"

Danton shook his head ruefully. "Nothing in particular but everything in general. But you already know what I think of the way everyone treats Prince Tarkyn. The lack of formal respect constantly offends me, but since the prince has ordered me to accept it, accept it I must."

"Hmm. Not too much we can do about that." Waterstone

looked at Danton over the rim of his cup. "You see, it would offend and embarrass us if we had to follow those protocols of yours."

Danton gave his head a little shake. "How odd!" A thought struck him. "So, does it offend you when *I* follow those protocols, such as bowing to the prince?"

"No." The woodman eyed Danton before offering his next remark. "It astonishes us. We find it very interesting."

"And amusing," finished Danton dryly for him.

"Mmm. Afraid so. Not always, but sometimes. But we are too polite to show it, you know. And I wouldn't have told you except that I have probably drunk too much."

Danton gave a short, embarrassed laugh. "And there I was, thinking I was leading by example."

Waterstone became serious. "How you behave with the prince is none of our business. No one thought it amusing when you knelt before Tarkyn the other morning and told him he was the hope of Eskuzor. I think we were all moved by that. It was an impressive avowal of faith."

Danton smiled with a hint of sadness. "I'm glad that you, at least, took that seriously." He shrugged. "I can't always help it, you know. Tarkyn has asked me to act more like you people do towards him. But I have a lifetime of training in royal etiquette to overcome. Any sign of disrespect would have been severely punished, so it is pretty ingrained. Besides, as you know, I do respect him, and I am proud to be of service to him. When I bow, I am thanking him for the trust he places in me by allowing me to serve him."

"Whoa. We have just spun off on different trajectories here," exclaimed Waterstone, blinking in astonishment.

"Why? What do you mean?"

"You're grateful for being able to serve Tarkyn? I can't even begin to grasp that concept. We all resent it like blazes."

Danton shot upright, spilling his wine, beside himself with outrage. "How dare you? Are you not aware of the honour you have been accorded? To have the opportunity to be this close to the prince and to provide for him? Thousands of sorcerers throughout the country would do anything to have that chance."

Waterstone was scathing. "What? Even now, when he has been exiled?"

"Yes. Even now. Have you no idea how great an honour it is to serve the son of forty-eight generations of kings? His life and wellbeing are beyond value."

A spirit of wickedness engendered by the wine made Waterstone say, "Well, you were pretty quick to slough off Kosar, who is also the son of forty-eight generations of kings, not to mention being the present ki..."

A lightning fast fist to the jaw sent Waterstone flying over sideways. He sat up slowly, rubbing his jaw, and peered into the cup that was still clenched in his other hand. "Blast. Now you've spilt the rest of my wine." He looked up at Danton and said dryly, "Looks like your court training has deserted you. But of course, I'm not the son of all those kings, am I, even if you do recognise me as a prince of the realm."

Waterstone hadn't really thought about what reaction he was expecting from this little gambit, but what he received, astonished him.

Danton bowed his head and clenched his hands together, white faced. In a shaking voice, he said, "Your Highness, I know it is too much to ask, but please forgive me. I throw myself on your mercy. Flog me if you will. I deserve nothing less, but please spare my life and I will serve you and Tarkyn faithfully to end of my days."

Waterstone was horrified. He resisted the impulse to send for Tarkyn, realising that his presence might place him in a position where he would feel obliged to punish Danton. He glanced across the fire and, sure enough, Tarkyn was watching him, frowning. Waterstone shook his head slightly and returned his attention to the distressed sorcerer. "Come with me," he said shortly.

He stood up and waited only long enough for Danton to scramble to his feet before he headed off into the gloom of the forest. Once they were away from prying eyes and ears, Waterstone stopped and turned to face Danton who stood, taut with controlled fear, in front of him.

"Danton," said Waterstone gently, "put your mind at rest. Do not fear for your life and do not fear punishment." He put his hand on the sorcerer's tensed shoulder. "I do not wish to offend you, but I could not accept your service. However, I would be honoured to accept your friendship and to work with you to support Tarkyn."

"But, Your Highness, I have attacked a member of the Royal Family. My life is forfeit. At the very least, I must make reparation."

"Yes, you must," came Tarkyn's voice out of the gloom behind him, stone cold sober.

W aterstone rolled his eyes, as the sorcerer spun around
and sank to his knees. This was exactly what he had
been trying to avoid.

"Your Highness," Waterstone began, realising that even
though they were far from court, this was a time for titles, "I
provoked Danton unfairly. If I had realised that his actions
could lead to a punishment, I would never have done so... and
then I could not have had as free a discussion with him.
Therefore, it would be to all our detriments if he were to be
punished."

"And yet, Waterstone, if I am to honour you as you have
honoured me by accepting me into your family, then I must
uphold your right to be treated as a member of the royal
family."

Waterstone grimaced. "I thought you'd think that. That's
why I brought Danton away from the firesite."

"Hiding a person's crime from me is coming perilously
close to dishonouring the oath. Not worth risking the forest for,
I would have thought." Tarkyn did not sound angry so much as

sympathetic. He transferred his gaze to the kneeling sorcerer. "Stand up, Danton. You have placed me in a dilemma, my friend. Out of everyone around the firesite, only you and Stormaway are punishable for attacking Waterstone or Ancient Oak because it is only in the world of sorcerers and wizards that they should be recognised as princes. Within the woodfolk, there are no ranks with the exception of my own."

The prince began to pace back and forth as he thought about his words. "I could argue that, because we are within the woodland, they need not be recognised as princes and therefore there is no crime. But I will not. It is not a geographical but a cultural distinction. Among sorcerers and wizards, they must be recognised wherever they are."

"Do I get any say in this?" asked Waterstone.

"No," said Tarkyn briefly, not even looking at him. "This involves protocols that have been laid down for centuries. None of us has any say in it."

"Well, what is the least punishment that can be given?" asked the woodman.

"In court? I have never known of anyone to lay a hand in anger on a member of the royal family and survive." Tarkyn regarded him sternly. "They have always, without exception, been killed on the spot or been hanged within a few days."

"But, Tarkyn, I mean, Your Highness." Waterstone ran his hand through his hair. "I remember you saying that if we had been at court, you could not have saved me, and yet I am still here."

"That was for only threatening me. You only actually laid a hand on me the second time when I had already given you permission. You have never actually hit me without my permission. However, Danton here knows that an adopted member of the royal family requires the same treatment as a natural member of the family, don't you, Danton?"

"Yes, my lord."

"And that, therefore, your crime is punishable by death."

"Yes, my lord. I do know that." Danton's tone was resigned. He brought his head up to look at the prince and said proudly, "I am sorry I have let you down, Your Highness. I said I would serve you all my life and I have. I had hoped I could have given you more than this short time. But my will is yours to command, now and always."

Waterstone felt as though his heart was breaking. He couldn't believe that events had moved so quickly. He could feel his heart thumping in his chest and his legs shaking and wondered vaguely whether they would give out beneath him.

"Please, Your Highness. Is there nothing that can be done?" Waterstone's voice sounded nowhere near as calm as Danton's had. It was pitched high with strain.

"The Sovereign may grant clemency," said Stormaway, appearing suddenly in their midst.

"I am aware of that, Stormaway, but I am not sovereign lord of sorcerers and wizards," objected the prince.

"No, my lord. You are not. But in the woodlands, you are sovereign, and although Waterstone's right to be called a prince is not geographical, your sovereignty is."

The prince's eyes narrowed. "But even though I am liege lord of the woodfolk, surely Kosar is sovereign of the forests since they are part of the kingdom of Eskuzor."

"Do you still give him your allegiance?" asked Stormaway.

"No," answered Tarkyn firmly.

"Then neither the forests nor the woodfolk are beholden to King Kosar. Your father made you sovereign of both in your own right." Stormaway shrugged and smiled. "Of course, there is the slight issue that Kosar may not know this, but I have in my possession papers drawn up under your father's seal that verify it, should a dispute ever arise."

During all this debate, Danton stood stolidly at attention, watching Tarkyn, his fate hanging in the balance.

Finally, Tarkyn turned to his liegeman standing so rigidly before him. "Lord Danton. You have heard this discussion. I have now established, rather to my surprise, I must admit, that I am sovereign lord within these forests and so I may grant clemency if I so choose. However, I wish to ensure that Waterstone and Ancient Oak are not just paid lip service. I would not wish to treat a sorcerer's crime against them any differently from a crime against me. Do you understand?"

"Yes, Your Highness. I understood that right from the beginning."

"And yet, Danton, I cannot imagine you ever coming close to hitting me."

Danton looked profoundly shocked, "Of course not, my lord."

"So, you see, Danton, you have in fact *not* understood from the start what Waterstone is due or you would never have hit him."

Danton bowed his head. "I stand corrected, my lord. However, once I realised what I had done, it was I who told Waterstone that my life was forfeit."

"I see. I am pleased you did that. It shows that you respect Waterstone as you should, even if you have attacked him."

"Your Highness, it was only because Waterstone specifically asked me not to that I did not address him as Your Highness right from the start." Despite his predicament, the ghost of a smile appeared on Danton's face. "Although I may not have accorded him the same respect as I give to you, I believe I still wish to pay him more signs of respect than he wishes to receive."

Tarkyn gave a grunt of laughter. "I can imagine that. So, my lord Danton, when I think back to the altercations between Waterstone and myself, the only difference is that I was able to throw up a shield when Waterstone first attacked me that prevented him from touching me, whereas Waterstone could not do that when you attacked him. In fact, I suspect that Waterstone's attack would have been more ferocious and prolonged than your one punch on the chin if I had allowed him to reach me."

"And what punishment did you decree, Your Highness, if you don't mind me asking?"

"None. The oath did it for me. A large tract of forest was damaged."

"And what if he had laid a hand on you before you gave your permission?"

Tarkyn thought carefully. "This is where we come to the crux of the matter. If I had been caught unawares, I may have flung him away from me, but then I would simply have kept him at bay until he calmed down. I would not have exacted the death penalty. But in a woodman's case, whether I like it or not, the oath exacts its revenge on the forest. However, you are not a woodman. You're a sorcerer and should know better." He looked across at Waterstone and added hastily, "... about protocol, I mean. And since the oath will not exact a punishment on you, I must."

Images flashed through the prince's mind of the punishments exacted for disrespect. He thought about his brother holding court and what he would have done. He thought about the incidents with the woodfolk and how he had handled them. Tarkyn ran his hand through his hair. He realised he had reached a point where having no assumptions left him without a foundation for his decision. There were no longer any absolute rights and wrongs. Everything hinged on his judgement. He thought of asking Waterstone or even

Danton to decide the punishment but realised he was just dodging his responsibility.

Finally, the prince drew a breath and said, "Within the forest, my word is law. Having nothing else to guide me, I choose the road with heart. Danton, you have served me well and truly. You have left all your friends and family to search me out and you have risked your life and our good opinion of you in the service of the woodfolk and me. You have also shown that you do honour Waterstone." He paused. "Because of these things, I will waive the death penalty. But there must be some punishment. I have tried to hit upon something that will affect you, at least to some extent, in the same way that damage to the forest affects the woodfolk.... Therefore, I decree that from tomorrow onwards, while you live within the forest, you must wear the same attire as the woodfolk."

Danton blinked. "I beg your pardon, my lord?"

Tarkyn gave a slight smile. "Although you have done wrong by hitting a member of the Royal Family, you do not deserve to be severely punished for a small altercation between friends in a context far removed from the formality of court. I know your clothing and appearance are important to you. So, your punishment is that you will wear woodfolk attire...with pride," he added dryly.

An involuntary shiver of released fear travelled down Danton's spine. He gave a small bow and spoke with heartfelt sincerity, "Thank you, Sire. I am overwhelmed by your generosity." As he straightened up, he glanced at Waterstone. "However, I am not sure how complimentary it is to the woodfolk to decree that their way of dress is a punishment."

Tarkyn laughed. "It would not be a punishment to most people. I myself find their clothing very comfortable, practical and attractive in its way. However, I know it will be a challenge for you to forgo your fine clothes."

Danton gave a little sigh. "Yes, it will be, Sire, but I could be regretting so much more than losing my fine wardrobe. So, I will accept it with equanimity." The blonde sorcerer's eyes narrowed as he gradually focused on the woodman. "Do you know, I think we may be able to improve the cut of these clothes of yours, Waterstone? And some touches of subtle embroidery down each side of the front and perhaps a little on the sleeves could do wonders."

"Danton," said Tarkyn gently. "As long as you understand that in the world of sorcerers, Waterstone is a prince and that even though he does not want that formally recognised, he is worthy of your respect."

Danton immediately became serious. "Waterstone has always been worthy of my respect, regardless of his status."

"Be that as it may," said Waterstone gruffly, entering the conversation, "I understand enough to know that I need to give you permission to hit me if we are to be able to have decent conversations that may get a bit heated at times. I'll be talking to Ancient Oak about that too." He looked across at Stormaway. "And you? You're not the hitting type really, are you? You can have my permission if you want it. I'm not having these shenanigans again. What a nightmare!" He heaved a deep sigh of relief. "I'm sorry, Danton, for what I said...and for what you've just been through. I wouldn't have wished that on you for the world." He clapped his arm across Danton's back. "Come on. I think we all need a drink after that."

As they turned to walk back to the firesite, Tarkyn said, "Waterstone, I would prefer it if this were kept between the four of us. It was after all, a matter of sorcerer's law, not woodfolk's."

Waterstone glanced at him. "I wouldn't dream of demeaning Danton by sharing it with anyone, other than Ancient Oak, of course."

Tarkyn was left feeling that he had once more blotted his copy book in Waterstone's eyes. Sensing this as he came up beside Tarkyn, Stormaway gave the young prince a clap on the shoulder, saying in a quiet but carefully carrying voice, "Well done, Your Highness. I have never seen or heard of such sound judgement combined with such clemency before. You managed to find a way to save Danton from certain death while preserving both your own and Waterstone's honour. I don't know whether your father would have approved. In some ways, you are stronger and kinder than he. Your brother certainly wouldn't approve. You showed great strength of character to go against years of tradition to reach your own judgement."

Waterstone stopped dead ahead of them and turned around. "Sorry, Tarkyn. I was judging you by woodfolk standards. Thanks, Stormaway," he added, not for a moment deceived about the purpose of the wizard's little speech. "You're right. Tarkyn does deserve acknowledgement." For the first time, he took in the lines of strain around Tarkyn's mouth and said slowly, "I guess that was just about as hard for you as it was for all of us, wasn't it, Tarkyn?"

Tarkyn nodded shortly but made no other reply, clearly not comfortable with discussing it in front of Danton.

The woodman gave his head a little shake. "You sorcerers are a scary bunch with your draconian approach to punishment. I can't imagine why anyone would ever want to risk going to court in the first place."

The prince ignored this little jibe and asked, "Waterstone, what did you say, as a matter of interest, that so incensed Danton that he lost control?"

Waterstone eyed Tarkyn. "Danton had just finished telling me what an honour it is to serve the latest generation of forty-eight kings...."

Tarkyn smiled broadly. "With which, I'm sure, you were in full accord."

"Hmph. Then I said that, in that case, he'd been pretty quick to abandon Kosar who, let's face it, has more right than you to his subjects' loyalty."

Danton listened in silence, his face set, rigidly back in control but still obviously unhappy with the conversation.

"Oh my word, Waterstone. You really were playing with fire, weren't you." Tarkyn glanced at Danton. "My friend here has talked very little of his decision to come after me and leave the King's service. But knowing him as I do, I would hazard a guess that it was one of the hardest decisions he ever had to make."

Danton looked up and met Tarkyn's eyes. He shook his head and smiled. "No Tarkyn, it wasn't. I have always been your man. You just never tested me. What was hard was coming to terms with losing my faith in two people whom I had revered all my life. As I was saying, before I so rudely interrupted myself," said Danton with a flash of humour, "even if my loyalty lay with you, I always considered it an honour to be asked to serve any member of the Royal Family. But no longer. Now, I only consider it an honour to serve you."

Tarkyn smiled slowly. "Danton, I fear I have grievously underestimated you."

"No, my lord," said Danton. "You have underestimated yourself. You never gave me or anyone else the chance to stand by you."

"Perhaps not. But I would not have wished to place anyone unnecessarily at risk on my behalf."

Danton gave a proprietal smile. "You see, Waterstone, why it is such an honour to have been asked to serve His Highness?"

"I acknowledge Tarkyn's integrity, but we weren't asked. We were forced," pointed out Waterstone. "And it is your culture not ours that reveres generations of kings. We don't even acknowledge any difference in rank."

"Except mine," put in Tarkyn.

"Yes, but that's force, not belief," said Waterstone conversationally, at which point he became acutely aware that he was in the midst of three people who were finding his words offensive.

Into the stony silence that greeted this remark, Danton said, "I would think very carefully about giving me permission to hit you if you are going to make remarks like that."

"But it is exactly because I don't believe in ranks that I give you my permission."

Danton turned to Tarkyn. "And why did you give your permission to Waterstone, if I may ask?"

Tarkyn smiled at Waterstone while he considered his answer. "Many reasons. More now than at the time. First and foremost, to protect the forest from the consequences of Waterstone's anger. Secondly, and this will sound strange coming from me, Danton, to put us on a more equal footing."

Danton looked bewildered. "I don't understand. Why would you do that?"

Tarkyn ran his hand through his hair. "This is hard to explain. Because Waterstone always treated me as an equal, it somehow seemed only fair to return the compliment"

"But Your Highness! That was an outrageous presumption for Waterstone to treat you as an equal."

Tarkyn smiled. "On the face of it, you would think so. But under the circumstances in which we found ourselves, it was an act of true generosity of spirit for him even to consider getting to know me. But more than that, Waterstone is the first person I ever met who saw me firstly as Tarkyn and secondly, or sometimes not at all, as a prince."

Tarkyn glanced at Waterstone and a look of

understanding passed between them, while Danton mulled this over for some time, clearly struggling in his mind's eye to detach Tarkyn from his role. Eventually, he asked, "You say the first, not the only person. Are there others who treat you in this way?"

"Yes. And more as time goes by. Autumn Leaves was the next after Waterstone. Thunder Storm mostly does, but he gets a bit confused sometimes. Raging Water and Rainstorm do. Ancient Oak does now and, of course, Sparrow. Golden Toad does, surprisingly, and possibly now Rushwind. North Wind and Tree Wind are getting there."

Danton looked pole-axed. "But this is dreadful. All these people seeing you as a mere person. And do all of these people have your permission to attack you?"

"No, Danton, not all of them." Just as Danton was relaxing, Tarkyn added with a little smile, "Only five others."

Danton frowned in consternation. "But, Your Highness, these rules were made to protect the Royal Family. The monarchy must be detached from the people. Otherwise you will have anarchy before you know what is happening."

Much to Tarkyn's surprise, Stormaway rose to his defence. "No, Danton. You need have no fear of that. At first, I too feared for the prince's consequence. But despite my earlier qualms, Tarkyn is, so far, managing to walk the tightrope between maintaining true friendships with these people and maintaining his status. It is not an easy balancing act by any means. Far easier, in my opinion to keep a distance but, largely due to this woodman here, it is not the path Tarkyn has chosen to take."

Waterstone raised his eyebrows. "I think you will find that Tarkyn is quite able to assert his authority if he feels the need."

"The trick is knowing when to do it and how strongly," added Tarkyn with a wry smile. "And I don't think I always judge that correctly." His eyes twinkled. "But I do have a few fail-safes built into my system."

Danton frowned. "Such as?"

"Such as particular people who will tell me if I am being too harsh or too autocratic. Waterstone, Ancient Oak and Autumn Leaves, to be specific. Oh, and Sparrow, now I come to think of it."

"And who will tell you if you are being too lenient?" asked Danton.

The prince smiled. "That's where you and Stormaway come in. You two always have a weather eye out for my consequence. So, you see, in our funny way we have advisors from all viewpoints, just as we would have at court."

III

THE GREAT WEST ROAD

11

By mid-morning, the woodfolk had left the damaged area far behind them and were strung out along the Great West Road through the forest. Crossing the road undetected was always a major undertaking for a large group. Its width made it impossible to cross via overhanging trees, and their ability to flick into hiding was too short-distanced to take them right across its breadth. Consequently, they had to cross where the road surface was rocky and they would leave no footprints. They chose a straight section of road that curved out of sight about one hundred yards away to the east and disappeared over a hill towards the west. Lookouts were placed on the curve and on the brow of the hill to give warning of approaching travellers.

For over an hour, they remained hidden in the bushes near the roadside waiting for a gap in the flow of small, varied groups of walkers, riders, pack animals and carts. Each time they readied themselves to move, a lookout would signal the approach of another group of people.

"This is so tedious," whispered Tarkyn to Waterstone.

Waterstone shrugged. "The price of elusiveness."

"Maybe we'll have to wait until dark."

"Unlikely. There's usually a break, although the traffic is quite constant today." Suddenly Waterstone put up his hand for silence and froze. As he went out of focus, Tarkyn picked up images of intruders among them.

Tarkyn sent Waterstone an image of Stormaway and Danton with a query. In return, he received an image of them further along, deep in a thicket of hawthorn lying beside Running Feet and Falling Branch.

As Tarkyn waited, he became aware of a ragged, rough individual, long, curved blade held in his right hand, who was moving quietly between the trees towards the road not twenty feet from him. The man seemed intent on watching the road and paid little heed to the surrounding woodland. Tarkyn heard a slight sound and realised another ruffian was moving towards the road on the other side of him.

"How many?" mouthed Tarkyn.

Waterstone went of focus for a short time then mouthed "Eight."

As they watched, a small family appeared over the hill, a teenaged son leading their reluctant, bad-tempered packhorse. The mother and father were in the lead while two daughters walked between them and their son.

Within the trees, the brigands tensed and crept closer. Suddenly, brigands further down the road began to loose arrows. Before thought could intervene, a bronze streak of power flashed out and burnt the arrows in mid-flight and a translucent bronze shield slammed into position around the traveller family. Within the shimmering bronze light, the family cowered in fear and the son struggled to control their plunging packhorse.

Beside Tarkyn, Waterstone rolled his eyes and shook his

head. Then he received a clear image of the brigands being struck by slingshots. With a resigned shrug, he transmitted Tarkyn's request to his fellow woodfolk and, along the road, eight brigands fell senseless to the ground.

"So, now what, *Your Highness*?" hissed Waterstone.

"Waterstone, I couldn't let them die."

"They are nothing to do with us," exclaimed Waterstone vehemently.

"They are everything to do with me, however."

Waterstone glowered at him. "You will give us all away. And you will give yourself away and put yourself in danger."

"Waterstone," Tarkyn's voice was calm but firm, "I would never reveal your presence to outsiders. Your oath is my oath. But after the purging the other day, people know I'm somewhere in the area anyway." He grimaced ruefully at the woodman. "And now I will have to reveal myself to this family. They will already know from the colour of my magic that I am here, and I don't want them thinking I'm attacking them. I'm sorry. I know I haven't consulted you properly, but events overtook us. I will give you these choices though. You can disappear and leave the brigands to wake up and wonder what hit them, you can simply kill them, or you can bind them so that we can question them before we kill them."

Waterstone's eyes widened. "Wolves' teeth, Tarkyn. You're pretty cold-blooded about all this. I don't think you understand. We can kill, and will if someone sees us. But it almost never arises. None of us has ever killed in cold blood when someone is bound and helpless."

Tarkyn looked at him quizzically. "Well, let's compromise. You people keep them unconscious until we work out what we want to do – Where are Stormaway and Danton? I think we may need them." He smiled. "Meanwhile I'm going out there to reassure that panic-stricken family"

"Don't take long. Be prepared to cut and run if I relay an image from the lookouts."

"Agreed."

Leaving Waterstone to organise the woodfolk, Tarkyn disentangled himself from the bushes and stepped out onto the road.

As Tarkyn approached, the packhorse was pulling back on her reins and rolling her eyes in fear at the unexpected noise and light that had erupted around her. Without conscious effort, the forest guardian sent a wave of reassurance that quietened her. His focus was on the family who, as one, went down on one knee, hand on heart, and bowed their heads when they saw him.

Tarkyn was not impressed. "Stand up. Don't toy with me. Why are you offering me obeisance if I have been branded as a rogue sorcerer? As I understand it, you no longer owe me your allegiance."

"We would beg for mercy, my lord."

"You do not need my mercy," he said flatly.

"Then why have you have imprisoned us with your shield?" The man glanced fearfully at his wife and then straightened his shoulders and looked directly at the prince. "If you must kill someone, Your Highness, take me and spare my family. We have done you no wrong. Please let us live."

Tarkyn sighed. "You have no need to fear me. I have no intention of hurting any of you. If I remove the shield, do I have your guarantee that you will not try to harm me?"

The man was shocked. "Your Highness, I wouldn't dream of it. Of course, none of us would..." A thought struck him and he turned to his teenage son whose set mouth and narrowed eyes boded ill for the prince. "Markel, do I have your word?"

A long silence greeted this request.

"Or would you rather die at the prince's hand?"

Before the boy could respond, Tarkyn intervened, "Now, just a minute. I did not say I would hurt anyone, let alone kill them if they did not make that guarantee. Fight your own battles with your son. Don't use me."

"I beg your pardon, my lord. I truly thought that would be the consequence of non-compliance."

Tarkyn gave a weary wave of his hand and dissipated his shield. "The shield was never meant to imprison you. It was to protect you from the brigands who were secreted by the side of the road waiting to attack you. Did you not see the arrows?"

The man shook his head and looked uncertainly at his wife before answering, "No, my lord. All I saw was two flashes of bronze light before we were engulfed in your shield."

"I don't believe you," stated the rebellious teenager.

Surprisingly, Tarkyn smiled at him. "Do you know," he said, "one of my best friends is someone like you? I hope you have the perceptiveness that he has. It goes a long way towards excusing his belligerence. Otherwise, I'm afraid I will find your rudeness inexcusable." He looked at the parents. "And do you believe me?"

"Of course we do, Your Highness," said the woman placatingly.

Tarkyn's eyebrows flicked together. "Madam, whatever you do in your dealings with me, do not lie and do not humour me. I know my reputation. I will understand if you fear me or doubt me, but you will get very short shrift should you be dishonest with me." He paused. "Do I make myself clear?" He stared at her for long seconds, giving himself time to transmit a visual message to Waterstone, before saying, "Come. It is unreasonable to expect you to believe me. I will show you."

He led them off the road to a small clearing where the two brigands who had fired the arrows were now lying unconscious, their weapons a short distance away from them.

"I beg your pardon, my lord," said the fat woman, grunting at the effort of bowing low. She had to straighten and catch her breath before she added, "Instead of doubting you, we should be thanking you for saving our lives."

Tarkyn frowned. "I did not show you the brigands to elicit your gratitude. But I knew my shield had given away my presence, and I didn't want you to misinterpret my actions, as in fact you did. My reputation is damaged enough without you assuming that I am out to harm you."

Just as they were about to turn back onto the road, the son placed his hand on his mother's arm to hold her back. "Wait a minute. There is another bandit lying over there," said the teenager, pushing his way around the bushes. Then he spotted the other bandits sprawled unconscious among the trees at regular intervals along the road. His eyes widened. "Oh my stars! Mum, Dad, look at this. He's killed eight of them."

Tarkyn raised his eyebrows. "I think you will find they are only unconscious."

The teenager shrugged. "Dead. Unconscious. That's not the point. The point is you've overcome eight bandits on your own, Your Highness. And they weren't even in a group. I don't know of any magic that can attack in several places at once." He whistled, "That's amazing!"

"Hmph." Tarkyn grimaced, aware that he had trapped himself into taking credit for someone else's efforts but unable to see how to avoid it.

"What are you intending to do with them, Sire, when they wake up? Or are you going to kill them?" asked the father.

Despite what he'd said to Waterstone, Tarkyn felt that being seen as a cold-blooded executioner was not something he wished to add to his already dread reputation. "No. Perhaps if you could assist me in tying them up, we can leave them by the roadside for soldiers to find them."

"Certainly, Sire. I am sure we can find enough twine in our baggage." The man addressed his son. "Markel, you bring all the bandits over here," he said, indicating a shady spot under a tree on the roadside, "and Caris, you get the twine."

With a muttered incantation, Markel levitated the limp bandits one at a time to the place indicated by his father. By the time he had them all in place, his mother and sisters had returned with twine, and between them, the family had the bandits trussed up within a few minutes. The young girls seemed quite phlegmatic about assisting in tying up the unconscious men.

While the family attended to the brigands, Tarkyn walked over to the packhorse and stroked her gently along her neck. He sent her a query and in return received an image of a stone wedged in her hoof. Tarkyn lifted each of her hooves in turn until he discovered the stone dug deeply into her left rear hoof.

"Markel. Come over here for a minute," Tarkyn requested quietly.

Once Markel had straightened up and walked over to the prince, Tarkyn showed him the stone wedged in the horse's hoof. "Next time your horse is unwilling, look for the cause. You have dragged this animal for miles with this stone digging into her hoof. Treat her well and she will serve you well. Treat her badly and she will let you down. Do you have a knife or sharp stick to dig this out with?"

Markel produced the hunting knife he wore on his hip and proceeded to remove the stone without comment. When he had finished, he ran his hand down the horse's leg and said gently to her, "Sorry, old girl. I should have realised something was wrong." Tarkyn received a wave of relief and thanks from the horse while Markel flicked a glance at him. "Thank you, Sire. I'll look after her better. I guess we were all tired, and I just thought she was sick of the journey."

By this time, the rest of the family had finished trussing up the brigands. They stood up, dusted down their hands and faced the waiting prince.

"Your Highness."

Tarkyn nodded. "You may introduce yourself to me."

The father too gave a slight bow before saying, "This is Caris, my wife, Markel my son, Posy and Mayla, my daughters. My name is Tomasett."

If Tarkyn was impatient to be on his way, he hid it well and replied, "I am pleased to make your acquaintance. Where are you travelling to?"

"Sire, I am a miller in the village of South Heading, which lies twenty miles south of Tormadell. We have been visiting some distant relatives and are now returning home."

"I see. And were you aware that this area is renowned for bandit attacks? It would be better for you and your family to be well away from here before dark." He considered Markel and his parents. "Can any of you raise a shield and keep it up?"

They looked at each other.

"We can all do it, but not for long. We tend to get distracted and lose concentration," said Caris.

"Well, do the best you can. Take it in turns. Remind each other to concentrate; whatever works, but keep a shield around your family until you're well away from here. Understood?"

The father bowed deeply. "Yes, my lord. I thank you for your concern for our safety. Your will is our command."

"Excuse me, Your Highness," interrupted Markel. "Is it true that there is a price on your head?"

Tarkyn's eyes narrowed but he answered almost conversationally, "I have heard that there is. However, I think you will find it difficult to overcome me if you're thinking of taking me captive."

The belligerent son frowned and shook his head slightly at

the prince's response. "No, Your Highness, even if I thought I could, I would not. I would not be so churlish as to repay your protection of us by betraying you." He hesitated. "No. I was going to ask what you did that outlawed you."

Tomasett cut across him with a fearful glance at the prince. "Markel. Mind your manners. You are speaking to a prince. You can't just ask whatever you want to."

Tarkyn waved a hand. "Let him speak. I will answer him." He drew a breath. "I am not a rogue sorcerer, even though I have been branded one. I have not lost my senses nor am I out of control." He gave a wry smile. "Of course, I would say that. Truly mad people don't realise they're mad, do they? However, I did kill several palace guards. At least six, I think. I'm not sure." He sighed. "It was not intentional. Something went wrong with my shield and caused it to reflect back the shafts of power they were aiming at me. Then the ricocheting shafts brought down the Great Hall."

Caris frowned. "But, my lord, why were they aiming at you in the first place? Hadn't you already wiped out a whole stand of spectators at the Harvest Tournament?"

Tarkyn went still. After a moment, he shook his head slightly. "No, Caris, I hadn't. A shaft of my power hit the bottom of a stand and made it sag a little. Everyone jumped off, but no one was even hurt, let alone killed."

Caris' eyes narrowed but she said nothing further.

Tarkyn folded his arms. "You may believe me or not as you choose. There is nothing I can do about it. And whether or not I am guilty is of little relevance. My brothers wanted me disarmed and no longer a threat to them as they saw it, in which they have succeeded. I am no longer a factor in the politics at court."

"And were you a threat to the King, Your Highness?" asked the boy.

"No, Markel. I was always loyal to both of my brothers."

"And are you still?"

Tarkyn shook his head regretfully. "No. They have lost me, just as I have lost them."

"So, will you challenge them and bring civil war, Your Highness?" asked Tomasett.

Tarkyn looked around himself. "Do you see me at the head of an army?"

"What is now and what may be are not at all the same, Your Highness," replied the miller with an unexpected flash of acumen. "Begging your pardon, but you have not answered my question."

Tarkyn glanced over at the bandits to check that they were all still unconscious. None of them was yet moving. He brought his gaze back to meet Tomasett's clear blue eyes. "Tomasett, provided the King keeps his people well, there will be no challenge from me. I would only ever feel compelled to act if the people of Eskuzor were suffering. For myself, I am content to be away from Tormadell."

Tomasett raised his eyebrows. "Interesting response, my lord."

The prince gave a slight smile. "Is it?" Suddenly Tarkyn's head went up. Even as he received a warning from the lookouts, Tarkyn heard the first faint sounds of another group of people approaching from the west. "I must go," he said, already moving. "I suggest you also get on your way as quickly as you can. I don't think you will want the little ones around to witness the soldiers arresting those bandits. The soldiers' roughness could well frighten them."

"And will you be all right, my lord?" asked Tomasett. "Do you lack for anything that we could give you?"

Tarkyn hesitated at the edge of the road. "It would be a kindness in you if you did not mention to any soldiers that you have seen me, but I would not ask you to persevere in protecting me, should they threaten you."

"It would be an honour, Your Highness, to protect you in whatever way we can," replied the miller bowing. "If you should ever need somewhere to stay for a while, you will always be welcome at the South Heading Mill."

"Thank you, Tomasett." Tarkyn turned to look at Caris and raised his eyebrows. "However, I'm not sure that your wife would feel too happy with that. Unless I much mistake the case, she does not share your faith in me."

The sturdy woman folded her arms and glowered at him. "Your Highness, it is rare for folks like us to have truck with people like you, and so, I am not good at gauging your merit. But I am not ungrateful. I do know that my family and I owe you our lives, and so you are welcome if you come our way, whatever you may have done in the past."

Tarkyn eyes twinkled. "Thank you, Caris. That is most magnanimous of you." The sounds of approaching horses had become louder. "I must go. Travel safely." With that, he turned and threaded his way lithely between the trees, soon lost to their sight in the density of the undergrowth.

As the little family resumed its journey, Caris said, "Well, that's something to tell our friends. Fancy meeting the Rogue Prince... and living to tell the tale." She turned to her son. "Markel, put your shield around us for the next little while and then I'll take over."

"He didn't seem so bad, did he?" observed her husband.

Caris was thoughtful. "No. No, he didn't. But you have to ask yourself why he is hanging around an area known for its bandits."

"What? You don't think the prince has taken up with brigands, do you? After all, why would he foil their attack on us if that were the case? He's probably on his way to somewhere else, the same as we are."

"Maybe he's keeping himself busy by protecting travellers from bandits. That's what he did for us," suggested Markel. However, unlike Tarkyn, as soon as he began to talk, his shield faded. So, this remark was greeted with urgent reminders to concentrate on maintaining his shield.

As they plodded off around the curve in the road, the first horses appeared over the brow of the hill to the west.

12

─────────

A s soon as Tarkyn was out of sight of the road, Waterstone appeared at his side.

"I think we're too late to question those brigands. A group of soldiers is approaching from the west... probably from the encampment."

Tarkyn grimaced. "Yes, I thought that might happen, but I couldn't really see what else I could do. I was a bit worried the brigands might come round while the family was still there. At least they were neutralised once they were tied up." He looked at the woodman. "Thanks, Waterstone, for your help."

Waterstone clapped him on the back and said philosophically, "I guess it was only fair that we helped you to save some sorcerers. You helped us to save woodfolk from the encampment, after all."

"I don't know how successful I was in improving my reputation. At least they listened." Tarkyn gave a wry grin. "But now they think I can knock out eight people in different locations all at once."

"Yes, I saw that. And I saw you squirming when you took the credit for it too."

Tarkyn gave a short laugh. "Yes, very embarrassing. Especially when I knew the people from whom I was stealing the credit were watching."

Waterstone smiled. "Come on. Let's find ourselves a vantage point so we can watch the soldiers collect the brigands. We can forget about crossing the road until they've gone anyway. So we might as well keep ourselves entertained."

"Where's Sparrow?" asked Tarkyn suddenly.

Waterstone frowned. "With Thunderstorm and Creaking Bough and their two kids. Why do you ask?"

Tarkyn shrugged and looked a little sheepish. "I just remembered telling her I would keep her safe when big men on horseback were around. I don't want her to think I've let her down."

"Well, we can't have Sparrow with us while we're watching the soldiers. It might upset her. So it's one or the other. Either go and be with her, or watch the soldiers taking the bandits away."

"Maybe you can ask her how she is and whether she needs us?" suggested Tarkyn.

Waterstone shook his head a little. "I know how she is. If I thought for a minute she was feeling unsafe with Thunder Storm and Creaking Bough, I'd be with her now."

Tarkyn nodded, but even though he said nothing further, he still looked uncertain.

"All right. Fine." Waterstone rolled his eyes. "Far be it from me to get in the way of a concerned uncle. I'll ask her and tell her you're worrying about her. Good enough?"

Tarkyn's face relaxed into a smile. "Thanks."

Waterstone went out of focus for a couple of minutes. When he returned, he had a wry smile on his face. "You were right. And so was I. She feels perfectly safe but was feeling put out that you hadn't checked. She's fine now. She's in the middle of some complicated game with other two and is quite happy where she is."

Tarkyn sent her an image of himself with a wave of friendship and reassurance and received back a little ripple of thanks. He smiled at Waterstone. "Good. Now that's settled, let's go."

By the time they had joined Autumn Leaves and Tree Wind in a good vantage point in an overhanging pine tree, the soldiers had already dismounted and were bent over the trussed up brigands. As they turned the prostrate men over and saw their faces, the soldiers looked in consternation at each other.

"What are they doing here?" asked a tough, burly sergeant.

The soldier beside him shook his head. "I have no idea, sir. How could they have got themselves tied up like this?"

In the tree above them, Tarkyn and the woodfolk exchanged perplexed glances.

Now that their attention had been drawn to it, they could see that the men's rags covered up uniforms like those of the encampment guards.

A thin, sharp-faced soldier was bending over another brigand. "Sir, here's Consar. It must be his patrol. He's out cold."

The thickset, balding sergeant stood up and frowned as he surveyed the group of trussed men. "This is what happened to the perimeter guards; they've all been knocked out somehow. Very strange. No obvious wounds. And no one has been killed, just temporarily disabled."

"Obviously, it's bandits of some kind, sir. The last lot were after the horses. I don't know what they wanted this time, but I suppose they just stole whatever they could get their hands on."

The sergeant shook his head. "Very strange bandits - to

leave them trussed up like this. Why didn't these bandits just kill them or leave them lying unconscious while they made their escape? Why leave them neatly tied up by the side of the road?"

"Because, my good sir," said Stormaway, appearing unnoticed in their midst, "These men are themselves bandits. Some upright citizens captured them and left them for your justice."

Stormaway was dressed in a heavy padded jerkin and laced leggings with a sumptuous green cloak flung over his shoulders. His hair was mid-brown, shoulder-length, and slicked back. All in all, he had the appearance of a wealthy merchant and was quite unrecognisable as the diffident tailor who had entered the encampment a week ago. This was just as well because, when the officer looked at him, Stormaway realised that he was Sergeant Torgan, the gruff, friendly guard Danton and he had met on their first day in the encampment.

"What utter nonsense!" declared the sergeant. "These men are fellow soldiers."

"And how do you explain their dress then?" asked Stormaway with a superior smirk.

Sergeant Torgan frowned but continued gamely, "I can only presume they have been doing undercover work for us, trying to flush out the brigands who have been hounding travellers along this part of the road."

"Indeed? And does undercover work include attacking a defenceless family?"

The sergeant looked uncertainly at his men then back at Stormaway. He frowned. "What foundation do you have for your accusations, sir?"

Stormaway waved an elegant hand. "Why, I witnessed it with my own eyes. These men were firing arrows at a hapless family as they travelled along the road here."

Sergeant Torgan straightened up and put his hands on his hips. "Sir, if that is the case, where is the injured family? And where are the arrows?"

"The family have continued on their way unharmed after tying up their attackers. The arrows were burned in mid-air." The wizard peered around. "You may find some traces of ash if you look carefully."

One of the soldiers looked up at him and said disdainfully, "You're barking mad, you are. What are you talking about? Who's going to be able to intercept an arrow in mid-flight?"

The wizard rubbed his chin. "Hmm. Let me think. Someone who has very good reflexes. Perhaps the type of person who could win a Harvest Tournament."

In the tree above him, Tarkyn frowned and leaned over to whisper in Autumn Leaves' ear, "What is he up to?"

The heavy woodman shrugged and whispered back, "He didn't bother telling anyone."

Stormaway wandered over to the spot where arrows had sped towards the travellers and bent down. He gestured to the officer. "Come here. You see? Short, thin lines of ash. How do you explain that?"

Despite appearances, Sergeant Torgan was reasonably astute. He frowned at Stormaway. "So, are you telling me that you have seen the Rogue Prince?"

Stormaway hesitated. "Not directly, but I did see streaks of bronze light that intercepted the arrows. Then the traveller family were encased in a bronze shield for a few minutes until the attack ceased."

"But who disarmed the brigands then?"

The wizard straightened up. "I will let you draw your own conclusions."

"Are you telling me that the prince was responsible for

135

disarming these men? All eight of them?" demanded the sergeant.

Stormaway gave a slight smile, reflecting that even if he didn't do it himself, Tarkyn was indeed responsible for it. "Yes. I think you will find that was the case."

"But if he is a rogue sorcerer, why didn't he just kill them... and the family for that matter?"

Stormaway appeared to consider the matter carefully. "Perhaps we may have to conclude that he is not as black as he's been painted." He paused. "Just out of interest, have any of these men had anything stolen from them?"

The sergeant nodded to his men who searched the unconscious prisoners. It soon became clear that the brigands were still carrying their money folders and wearing rings of value and other jewellery. By the end of the search, the soldiers-cum-brigands were beginning to come around. As they shook their heads and wished they hadn't, they caught each other's eyes, and looks of alarm passed between them.

"Ah," said Stormaway congenially, "I believe our friends are waking up. Perhaps you could ask them to explain why they find themselves in this predicament, if you don't believe me."

The brigands scowled at him but held their peace.

"Come on, boys," cajoled Torgan. "I can imagine why you're in those filthy clothes, but I'm struggling to understand how you managed to get yourselves tied up." Not letting them know what Stormaway had said, he asked, "Would one of you like to offer me an explanation? I'm all ears."

The disguised solders pressed their lips firmly together and all looked to the one among them called Consar, who appeared to be their leader. Consar glanced at his companions and shook his head slightly, perhaps warning them to be quiet, perhaps just clearing it. "I have no idea what happened." He took a deep breath and launched into fantasy. "We were shadowing a gang of brigands through the woods on the north side of the road." He shrugged. "That's the last thing I remember." After a moment he added, "Maybe there were more gang members behind us that we weren't aware of. I don't know."

Sergeant Torgan frowned. "I would like to believe you, but surely a gang of brigands would simply kill you if they caught you spying on them. Why would they leave you tied up?"

Consar looked uneasy but shrugged. "Perhaps they figured that if we were captured, our soldiers would think that brigands had been at least partially eradicated from the area and leave them alone. If they'd just killed us and left us in the woods, our soldiers wouldn't have known about the reduced numbers of brigands."

"This, of course, assumes they didn't realise you were really soldiers yourselves." The officer thought for a minute then nodded. "That sounds reasonable." He swung around to confront Stormaway. "Much more likely than arrows being intercepted in mid-air. Give me one good reason why I should believe you above my fellow soldiers."

"If a rival gang wanted it known that these brigands had been eliminated, why wouldn't they just kill them, strip them of their valuables, and leave their bodies to be found by the side of the road?"

"Because," answered Consar triumphantly, "then you'd know there were other brigands who had killed us."

The sergeant shook his head regretfully. "No. That doesn't hold water at all. Because, having been left alive, you've just told us that there are other brigands in the area." He scratched his head then indicated Stormaway with his thumb. "And what does this man hope to gain by coming up with such a bizarre story?"

"What is his story?" asked Consar with a definite sneer.

"That the Rogue Prince intercepted your arrows and shielded the travelling family from your attack."

A look of comprehension appeared on Consar's face before he could stop it. "Oh. Is that what happened? His magic is bronze, isn't it? That must be what the bronze flashes were. And that's how that family suddenly shielded themselves? He was doing it for them." The bound man's face blanched. "Oh my stars! We're lucky to be alive."

The sergeant's eyebrows snapped together. "I'm not sure that you will continue to think so. So, are you confirming what this gentleman has told me?"

The bound soldiers glowered at Consar. There was an appreciable pause during which it was obvious that Consar's mind was working furiously. Finally, he said, "It is true about the bronze magic, but I think this poor addled prince has misinterpreted what we were doing. Obviously, he didn't realise that we were shadowing another gang and mistook our intentions."

Stormaway's face suffused with anger, and he made a sudden movement towards the bound man that was barred by the officer's arm. Sergeant Torgan raised his eyebrows. "Do I detect a certain strength of feeling for this prince, sir?"

Stormaway drew a quick breath and recovered himself. "No. It is not that. I simply object to being treated as a fool. How could anyone have the knowledge of tactics and the speed of reflexes required to win the Harvest Tournament but then mistake their protagonists' intentions? The whole concept is laughable."

Sergeant Torgan looked long and hard at Stormaway then transferred his gaze to look long and hard at his prisoners. Finally, he shook his head and said, "I am not a judge but I think these boys, at the very least, have some explaining to do. I will take them back to the encampment and deliver them to my commanding officer, Captain Guerion. Perhaps their commanding officer will be able to shed some light on their activities. He usually patrols with them but is unwell at the moment. That's why Consar here is in charge."

A glimmer of suspicion that quickly coalesced into certainty crossed Stormaway's face. "And who is their commanding officer?"

"Captain Andoran. Perhaps you know of him. I believe he has quite a reputation in Tormadell."

Stormaway gave a slight smile. "I have heard a little of him. I am sorry to hear he is unwell. Nothing serious, I hope?"

The officer shook his head. "Just some sort of unpleasant irritation. He's covered in a nasty red rash. I'm sure he'll be better in a few days." He thought for a moment. "I'm tempted to retrieve that travelling family and hear their side of the story. But at this stage, there does not seem to be any dispute that the prince acted in good faith to protect them. And they obviously did not see what was happening off the road if they were taken unawares anyway. So, we are left with the dilemma of whether the prince was accurate in his interpretation of what he saw, and obviously, he won't be coming forward to testify." Sergeant Torgan frowned. "Which way did you say the Rogue Prince went? I suppose we should be trying to track him down."

"Yes," responded Stormaway dryly. "That would be a just reward for protecting people, wouldn't it?"

Torgan's eyes narrowed. "I was right. You do have some sympathy for this outlaw. Are you refusing to tell me which way he went?"

Stormaway spread his hands placatingly. "No. Not at all. I'll leave you to live with your own conscience. Since I didn't actually see him, I can't be sure, but all the activity came from the north of the road. So, I'm assuming he headed back up north somewhere."

The sergeant nodded. "Yes. That fits with other reports we've had. I don't know what he's up to, but the centre of his activities does seem to be to the north of here." He looked sternly at the wizard. "He burnt down a whole section of forest, you know. Wanton destruction. I've lived near the forests all my life and it pains me to see the forest damaged like that. So you see, I don't feel a lot of sympathy for him, even if he does do the odd bit of good here and there."

Just as Stormaway was trying to find a way to counter the sergeant's misunderstanding, they were interrupted by a diffident ahem from the side. They looked around to find a diminutive soldier listening earnestly and clearing his throat.

"Yes, Drummock? What is it?"

"I beg your pardon, sir. But I was on the patrol that investigated the reports of the fire in the forest. We couldn't get close enough to see everything because the horses took fright, but I am certain the bronze magic appeared in the sky well after the fire had been started. When we investigated the next day, we found an almost perfect circle of burnt out forest." The small man gave a twinkly smile. "I think you are maligning our Rogue Prince, sir. I don't think he started the fire. I think he put it out."

Although this was not actually what had happened, it was near enough for Stormaway.

The sergeant frowned and said severely, "Drummock, I hope you would not be anything less than zealous in your pursuit of a known criminal."

"I didn't say that, sir. I was merely supplying you with more accurate facts."

Torgan relented, "Thank you, Drummock. If I pursue a man, I like to do it for the right reasons."

Stormaway raised his eyebrows. "And what, may I ask, are the right reasons?"

Torgan frowned. "Where have you been, man? Haven't you heard what happened?"

"I have heard many different versions of the same set of circumstances. So I am interested to hear your version."

"Sir, as a soldier, I go by the official version, of course."

"Which is...?"

"That Prince Tarkyn ran amok in the Harvest Tournament, destroyed a whole stand and killed many of the spectators. Then he ran rampage in the Great Hall, killed every guard he could reach and brought the hall down around them before fleeing."

"Hmm. Have you ever wondered how he could have won the Harvest Festival tournament if he killed off most of the spectators halfway through the competition? A very forgiving judging committee, wouldn't you say?"

Sergeant Torgan's eyes narrowed as he thought about it. "You know, sir, that is very strange, now you mention it. Humph." He turned to the small soldier waiting beside him. "Drummock, have the men lift these lads to their feet. Keep enough men here to guard them as we walk back to the encampment. The rest can remount and continue our patrol. We'll lead our horses." When the soldier was out of earshot, he turned back to Stormaway, "Not proper, you know, discussing the accuracy of official notices in front of the men. No, definitely not. However, sir, I like to think that I am a fair man and I wouldn't like to be hounding a man based on false information." He eyed Stormaway sharply. "I believe my first impressions were correct. For some reason, you are championing the young prince's cause. However, I am willing to listen to you awhile if you are willing to walk with us."

Stormaway bowed his head in acquiescence and fell in beside the sergeant as they walked back along the road to the west. After a short silence, the sergeant spoke again, "So, what is your name and business that I may gauge the value of your words?"

Stormaway glanced at him then looked up the road ahead. "My name is Stormaway Treemaster."

Danton, under whom he was passing at this point, nearly fell out of the tree with shock when Stormaway gave his real name.

"And your business, sir?"

"I am a merchant. I buy and sell goods across the country, specialising in fine wines, preserves and jams. I also buy cloth, tools, and tableware. So you see, I hear many tales as I travel around."

"And your interest in the prince?"

Stormaway shot him another glance. "I'm not sure that I'm ready to tell you that. Suffice it to say that I have had a long association with the royal family, closer at some times than others."

"Are you not concerned that I might drag you back to the encampment to interrogate you on your knowledge of the prince's whereabouts?"

Stormaway smiled. "No. For two reasons; firstly, it would be pointless because I have already told you as much as I know; and secondly, I too can gauge a man and I believe you have more integrity and good judgement than to use unnecessary persuasion."

Rainstorm, under whom the wizard was now passing, was astonished by the ease with which Stormaway wandered back and forth between truth and fiction, at all times sounding totally sincere.

"Hmph." The sergeant was slightly non-plussed by the wizard's vote of confidence. After a moment, he asked, "From your understanding of what you've heard, is the official version correct? I only ask because, if it is incorrect about the tournament, it may well be inaccurate on other ways too."

"I do not like to strain your credulity too much, but I think the real events in the Great Hall bear little resemblance to the official version."

The sergeant frowned. "How would you know that?"

Stormaway shrugged before inventing freely. "I ran into a palace guard up in the north of the country who had been there when it happened. According to him, the prince was fired upon first and he did not actually fire at anyone himself."

"But there were some guards killed, weren't there?"

"Oh yes. Several. The guard I met said the prince had been horrified by the whole series of events. The shafts of magic aimed at him by the guards were reflected back by the prince's shield. That was what killed the guards. That, and the collapse of the building."

Torgan frowned. "This is a very different story from what I've heard. Why would the official version be so wrong?"

"Why would Prince Tarkyn be arraigned on charges of reckless magic when all he had done was slightly damage a spectator stand and hurt no one?" asked Stormaway in return.

Torgan's eyes narrowed as he turned to regard the wizard. "What you are saying is coming perilously close to treason, my good sir. Do you doubt the King?"

Stormaway shrugged. "As you've noted yourself, the facts in the official version do not stand up to scrutiny. I only ask the question. I will leave you to answer it."

They walked for several minutes in silence while Torgan struggled to come to terms with this new perspective. Eventually, he flicked a shy glance at the wizard and then, keeping his eyes on the road ahead, said, "If you should happen to come across the young prince, which I'm inclined to think you may, tell him I am sorry for his plight. I don't really know what else to say or do to help him. But I don't like to think of him running scared if he has done nothing wrong."

"I don't think the prince feels he has done nothing wrong. He feels responsible for those guards' deaths even if he didn't deliberately attack them. But I will convey your message to him, if I should happen to see him." Stormaway looked around and checked that the other soldiers were at a safe distance from them. "If you were interested in helping him, there may be one or two things you could do..."

By this time, Stormaway had passed beneath the last of the woodfolk, and so none of them heard what grand schemes the wizard devised with the stalwart sergeant as they walked out of sight over the hill to the west.

13

S hortly after this, the lookouts signalled the all clear and the woodfolk were able to cross the great west road undetected. For the next few hours, they made good time through woodland sufficiently dense to provide cover, but well-spaced enough for them to thread easily through the undergrowth. Tarkyn was surprised when the woodfolk called a halt in the late afternoon, deep within a dark beech grove, and proceeded to set a fire and prepare the evening meal well before their customary time.

"There are several miles of open grasslands ahead of us," explained Running Feet. "It would not be safe for us to cross it in daylight. So we will rest here for a few hours and then travel on under cover of darkness."

"So, I gather you've been this way before?"

Running Feet raised his eyebrows. "Of course I have. There are many woodfolk living in the foothills of the mountains. There are caves beneath the mountains where we store the wines while they mature."

"So which group of woodfolk are they? And which group do you belong to?" asked Tarkyn.

"They are called the mountainfolk. But I belong to the wanderers usually. People can switch and swap if they want to but we tend to gravitate towards a particular group." He smiled. "Your home guard, as you call them, are all wanderers. I suppose we're the woodfolk most adaptable to new ideas."

Tarkyn grimaced regretfully. "Oh dear. So when you went with the gatherers to avoid me, you were separated from your usual companions, were you?"

Running Feet glanced at the prince and smiled wryly. "Yes. It seemed the lesser of two evils at the time. The gatherers are a friendly enough lot, so I was content to live with them for a while. After all, they do quite a lot of travelling too. Still, Waterstone, Autumn Leaves and Thunder Storm are my closest friends."

"I can see why." Tarkyn thought for a moment. "These woodfolk in the foothills – Where do I stand with them? Will they know that I am accepted as a woodman? And did any of them swear the oath?"

Running Feet shook his head. "None of them is oathbound, but they do know that you are Waterstone's blood brother. There were a few of them at the gathering and your inauguration ceremony but they didn't stay for long."

"Hmm. We may have a problem ahead of us. And I've just realised I need to talk to Falling Branch. He and Rainstorm are the only woodfolk travelling with us who haven't sworn the oath, aren't they?"

"Yes." The woodman sounded puzzled. "Why do you ask?"

"I'll explain it to you later." Seeing Running Feet's face tighten, Tarkyn added hastily, "It's not to do with trust. It's to do with courtesy. You'll understand when I explain it."

Once their early meal was finished, Tarkyn asked

Rainstorm, North Wind and his brothers to meet with him before the woodfolk settled down for a few hours' sleep.

"What's the problem?" asked Rainstorm. He looked around at the selection of woodfolk and said, "No. Don't tell me. Let me guess. It's the spread of the oath, isn't it? We five are the only ones who know that more woodfolk have become bound by your sorcerous oath."

Tarkyn nodded unhappily. "A few issues are rushing up to meet us. We can't just let it drift any longer. For a start, I don't feel happy about you four having to keep information secret from the others. It's not fair to you or to them and it's potentially divisive. Secondly, I gather from Running Feet that we are heading towards a group of woodfolk in the foothills who believe they are not bound by the oath."

Looks of consternation passed between the gathered woodfolk.

"We forgot about that," admitted Waterstone.

"And thirdly," continued Tarkyn, "and most importantly at the moment, we all know that Falling Branch is labouring under a misapprehension and we are not being straight with him. I suddenly realised that he is the only member of this group who is directly affected." He let his gaze travel around them. "We can't talk to the whole group about it until we tell Falling Branch."

"You're right," said Waterstone, "and I feel uncomfortable not talking to Autumn Leaves or Thunder Storm about it too."

"And I have just had to fob off Running Feet by saying I'd tell him later," added Tarkyn.

"Okay. So how do we want to handle it?" asked Waterstone. "Do you want to talk to Falling Branch on your own or with Rainstorm, or do you want one of us to talk to him for you?"

Tarkyn gave a half-smile. "No. I will do it. I owe him his

privacy when he finds out and I feel responsible. So I should be the one to tell him."

Ancient Oak frowned. "But you're not responsible. Your father instigated the oath, not you."

Tarkyn shrugged. "Perhaps it's an inherited responsibility then. Be that as it may, it is between Falling Branch and me that the relationship may change because of the oath, so it is I who must work it out with him."

"You can call on me if you need me," offered Rainstorm. He gave a little smile and looked around at everyone. "I guess you can call on any of us if you need us." And even though this statement could have been a snide shot at the fact that they were all bound to serve Tarkyn, everyone understood that it was not.

"Thanks," said Tarkyn. "Okay. So once I've cleared this hurdle, we'll discuss it with the rest of the group. Everyone happy with that?" When they all nodded, he stood up and headed off to find Falling Branch.

He found the woodman sitting against a tree, skilfully carving a forked branch into a neat, symmetrical slingshot. Tarkyn sat down in front of him. "What happened? Did you break your slingshot?"

Falling Branch glanced up briefly from his work. "No. We forestals specialise in making and repairing weapons. I'm making this for Golden Toad. He lost his when he was captured. When I've finished his, I'll start work on slingshots for Rushwind and Ibis Wings."

"Can't they make their own?"

"Yes, of course they can. They probably wouldn't be as well-crafted but they would do the job." Falling Branch held up the half-finished slingshot to inspect its surface against the light. "But they have lost quite a lot of equipment. So I am making these to help them to recover and to offer them gifts to welcome them back into the fold."

Tarkyn watched in silence for a few minutes, admiring the smooth skill of the forestal's knife strokes. "I've never seen Rainstorm doing anything like this. He's a forestal, isn't he?"

"I don't think Rainstorm has the necessary patience to do this yet." Falling Branch smiled wryly as he continued to carve. "He may never develop it. He's a bit of a handful, young Rainstorm."

Tarkyn gave a short laugh. "He has his moments, I agree. But never underestimate him. He has one of the sharpest minds I've ever come across."

At this, Falling Branch stopped carving and looked up. "Do you think so? You're not just saying that because I'm his father?"

Tarkyn boggled, "You're what?"

Falling Branch smiled broadly. "I gather he didn't tell you, then?"

"No. Neither did you, if it comes to that." Tarkyn shook his head a little. "Is that why you came with us, to keep an eye on him?" he asked, a tinge of disappointment in his voice.

Falling Branch shook his head and laughed. "No. It was more *despite* the fact that Rainstorm came. There are plenty of people here to keep an eye on him, including you. No. I came because I wanted to support you, our forest guardian, in protecting our people." He dropped his eyes back to his carving as he shaved off another sliver of wood. When he had finished, he looked up at Tarkyn and smiled. "Mind you, I wouldn't have come if I hadn't had faith in you, forest guardian or not."

"Thanks, Falling Branch." Tarkyn ran his hand through his hair. "Oh dear. This makes what I'm about to say all the more difficult."

"Why? What is it?" The woodman was all kind concern.

Tarkyn resolutely brought his eyes up to meet those of the woodman. "I think that you and the forestals have become bound by the oath." Tarkyn stopped himself from looking away or wincing. An apologetic wave washed around the woodman. "If this is indeed the case, I am truly sorry."

"Hmph." Falling Branch's eyes narrowed but he kept his gaze locked with Tarkyn's.

The silence lengthened. Several times the woodman nearly spoke but didn't. Suddenly he threw down the half-finished slingshot, leapt to his feet and strode off through the trees.

Tarkyn was left staring at the empty space vacated by the woodman.

"Ooh dear," he said quietly to himself. "That could have gone better."

Just as he was wondering what to do next, Falling Branch returned and stood glaring down at him, hands on hips, eyes sparking with anger. "So. Three questions. How long have you known? Does Rainstorm know? And who else knows?"

"I have known since Rainstorm fought Danton and then turned on me."

When Falling Branch nodded shortly, Tarkyn continued, "Rainstorm knows. North Wind was there when I told Rainstorm my suspicions, which Rainstorm immediately confirmed by attacking me again."

"I can imagine," said Falling Branch dryly. Although the woodman was still clearly angry, Tarkyn took heart in the glimmer of humour in his reply.

"I also told Waterstone and I was obliged to tell Ancient Oak. No one else knows."

"I see. Fine." Falling Branch turned away and took several brisk paces before returning to glower at Tarkyn. "So. Two more questions. Why did you take so long to tell me? And what will this sorcerous oath force me to do to protect the forest?"

Tarkyn waved his hand and let it drop. "I didn't tell you before because I didn't want to upset you and everyone else until we had Golden Toad and his family safe. Since then, we have fought that ghastly infection, and it is only now that things have settled down enough to think about dealing with it."

Falling Branch paced back and forth a few more times. "What if I had done something that triggered damage to the forest because I didn't know?"

Tarkyn shrugged and smiled. "I took a slight chance but I had no reason to think you would attack me and I made sure I didn't give you any orders."

"So now, I presume, you will feel free to order me around?"

Tarkyn shook his head. "What do you think, Falling Branch? You know me well enough by now. You have seen me with the home guard, all of whom have always been under oath. I would not expect too much to change between you and me, would you?"

"Only my sense of freedom and autonomy. Quite negligible really," replied the woodman bitingly.

Tarkyn's mind wandered through a few possible responses, but on balance, he decided to say nothing. In the silence, a thought struck the angry woodman.

"Do you mean to tell me that Rainstorm has known about this for over a week? And he has come to terms with it all on his own?"

Tarkyn nodded. "He did talk to Waterstone and North Wind about it and to me, but he understood the need to keep everyone focused on the rescue. Despite your differences though, I think he found it difficult not being able to talk to you about it. So it has not been easy for him."

Falling Branch grunted. "I must say I didn't think he could exercise so much self-control. The one silver lining in a very black cloud."

It was then that Tarkyn realised with dismay that he was never going to be able to re-enact this scene over and over again as each individual or group was told that they had become subject to the oath. He simply didn't have a thick enough skin. He drew a deep breath and ploughed on, determined at least to settle things between Falling Branch and himself. "You do realise that I did not instigate this?"

Falling Branch waved a hand impatiently. "I told you I trust you and, despite this, I still do. So I don't think you would have doubled-crossed us like that. No, I know when it happened."

Tarkyn raised his eyebrows in surprise. "You do?"

"It was when Raging Water averred that woodfolk were all one people and that the forestals couldn't help their kin to betray their oath." Falling Branch studied Tarkyn through narrowed eyes. "Up until that point, we could have accepted your offer and killed you with impunity. But as soon as Raging Water acknowledged that we were all one people, it was as good as saying, 'Their oath is our oath.'" The woodman let out a long sigh. "I'm sure that's when it happened. Even at the time, the possibility fleetingly crossed my mind and I felt something - I'm not sure what - something like a slight shift in the feel of the forest." He gave a wry smile. "But I blocked it out because I didn't really want to contemplate it."

"It wasn't Raging Water's fault," said Tarkyn gently.

"No." Falling Branch shrugged. "Anyway, he was right. We are all one people and we should never have left only some of us to bear the burden of fulfilling the oath."

"Waterstone did say that it had virtually created a class system of oathbound and oathfree, that they were made to feel like second-class citizens, particularly the home guard who, in fact, showed the greatest courage and bore the greatest burden on behalf of all woodfolk." Although Tarkyn words sounded objective, he was beginning to withdraw into himself. He stood up and dusted down his hands, saying briskly, "So. Now the burden can be shared among many and you can all commiserate with each other on an equal footing. Although I didn't design this new development, I think it will be better for the unity of the woodfolk. But I know it will be difficult for those such as you who must come to terms with losing their autonomy." He gave a wistful smile. "I think you'll find Waterstone and Rainstorm and the others waiting to talk to you, if you want them. I'll leave you all to it for a while."

Tarkyn turned to walk away, but Falling Branch placed a restraining hand on his arm.

"Tarkyn, I will go to them because I need to talk it through, but it will not be a diatribe against you." He paused and took a deep breath. "And thanks for talking to me about it like this. I've seen you upset before and I know you are now." He shrugged. "I guess we both have realities to accept that we don't particularly like."

Tarkyn stared at the woodman for a moment. "You people amaze me. If this were the other way around, I would be gloating over any distress my oppressor was feeling."

Falling Branch gave a short laugh. "But if you were truly an oppressor, so would I."

Suddenly Tarkyn's eyes twinkled. "You know, if this were Tormadell and you were a sorcerer, this would be the proudest day of your life, coming into service with me." His smile faded a little. "But of course, it's not and you're not. And I am sorry that you have been forced into it." Unconsciously, he drew himself upright. "But if it's any consolation, I feel proud to be a woodman and proud that you are my liegeman."

Falling Branch smiled and shook his head. "To be described as anybody's liegeman is no consolation at all, but it does matter that you are proud to be one of us." He gave Tarkyn a little push. "Go on. Go and find Danton and talk to him about us while I go and talk to Waterstone and Rainstorm about you."

Tarkyn laughed. "I don't know that I want to give Danton so much fuel for his fire."

"You can manage him. Go on. He needs you to need him." So saying, Falling Branch turned on his heel and walked off, leaving a thoughtful sorcerer prince in his wake.

14

Tarkyn procured some wine and a couple of goblets before setting off to find Danton. He found the guardsman sleeping a little way off, his head on his pack and his soft brown woodfolk cloak wrapped around him. As Tarkyn approached, Danton's eyes flicked open, and in one swift movement, he rolled up into a crouching position, knife in hand. When he saw who it was, he relaxed and his face lit up in welcome.

"Good evening, Danton," said Tarkyn dryly. "Good to see your reflexes are still working well. I'm sorry I startled you."

Danton waved a dismissive hand, realised he still held the knife in it and sheathed it before giving a slight bow and saying, "I beg your pardon for my poor welcome, my lord."

Tarkyn smiled disarmingly. "I'll make sure I make a lot of noise from a distance next time I approach you." He looked Danton up and down. "The woodfolk clothing suits you. It highlights the purple of your eyes and your blonde hair."

"Thank you, Sire. We aim to please." Danton sketched an ironic bow.

Although Tarkyn realised Danton had been trying to get some sleep, he didn't even consider offering to come back at a more convenient time. He knew Danton would never contemplate placing his own needs above the prince's. Instead, Tarkyn sat down against a convenient log and, placing the two goblets on the ground, asked, "Will you join me in a drink before we settle?"

"It would be my pleasure, Sire." Danton sat down next to the prince and accepted a goblet of wine. He glanced sideways and smiled. "And I don't have to risk Waterstone's disapproval by reporting our activities back to anyone..." he let his eyes rove around the surrounding trees and shook his head slightly when he saw no sign of woodfolk, "although I'm sure we are being monitored."

Tarkyn smiled. "They are uncannily clever at camouflage, aren't they? You'll never see them if they don't want you to." Tarkyn took a sip of wine and sat quietly for a moment, listening to the sounds of the forest; birds chirruping as they settled for the night, the evening breeze whispering through the trees, stirring the sparse golden and brown leaves and, somewhere nearby, the rustle of some creature pushing through a tangle of brushwood. "Hear that? That's a stubborn old badger who is becoming incautious in his old age and has just shoved his way through a thicket instead of sneaking around it."

Danton looked at the man sitting next to him. "You're not guessing, are you?"

"Me? Oh no." Tarkyn gazed into his wine while he let his thoughts wander out into the surrounding woodlands. A gentle smile appeared on his face as he said, "We are surrounded by little creatures bustling through the undergrowth. There's a large owl a few trees away who has just woken up and is deciding which way to go to hunt. Most of the smaller birds are feeling drowsy and have returned to their nesting places ready to sleep. That badger is still grumpy and has just given a younger one a telling off on the way past." He pulled his mind back in. "But enough of their lives. Let's talk about our own. How are you doing, my friend? Do you like living in the woodlands? Have you found people you can feel comfortable with among the woodfolk? Or are you missing home?"

"Amazing." Danton shook his head slightly. "So, to answer your question. The woodlands are cold, damp and inconvenient and there are no servants to iron our clothes and bring our wine. On the other hand, these clothes wouldn't really profit from being ironed. The delicacies prepared by the royal chefs have been replaced by more basic but probably fresher fare. There are no women stalking around us in their brightly coloured gowns and dazzling jewellery, watching us from beneath long, carefully curled lashes and smiling at us with rubied lips. The clusters of covert gossipers are notably lacking and the level of intrigue is disappointingly low." Danton took a sip of wine and held up his goblet. "But their wine is excellent. And they have made me welcome in a way that I doubt that we would have made them welcome if they had appeared at court." He shrugged. "I'm getting used to it. I actually find the woodlands quite beautiful and peaceful. It's just that I'm not really a peaceful sort of person."

"You could hardly call the last few days peaceful."

Danton gave a grunt of laughter. "No, you couldn't. But in the forest, there is always the threat of things becoming too peaceful." He frowned slightly. "Why do you ask? Are you thinking of sending me away?"

"No, Danton." Tarkyn looked at him in concern. "Have I been so remiss in my care of you that I cannot ask after your welfare without another purpose?"

"No, my lord," replied Danton, too quickly to be convincing.

Tarkyn waited.

After a moment, Danton shrugged. "You have been very busy and everything you do has had a purpose. I have not spoken to you alone for days. So I assumed you had a reason for coming to see me."

Tarkyn considered his words carefully before replying, "You are right. I do have a purpose in coming to see you. I came to find you in search of a friend. But caring for your welfare is part of friendship, is it not?"

"I do not wish to sound churlish, sir, but why do you suddenly seek out my friendship when you have Waterstone and all your woodfolk friends?"

Tarkyn raised his eyebrows. "Does my friendship with others preclude me from having a friendship with you?"

Danton raised his eyes and looked resolutely at Tarkyn. "I think you are working so hard to be a woodman that you don't want to be identified with me, a fellow sorcerer. So, at the moment, yes, it does."

Tarkyn stared back at him, anger flickering in his amber eyes before his innate honesty asserted itself. He let out a long sigh. "Oh, Danton, I'm sorry. And the only real contact I've had with you in the last few days is to pass judgement on your behaviour with Waterstone." He spread his hands, spilling a bit of his wine as he did so, "Well, I am here now and I have come to you particularly because you are a sorcerer and can understand where I have come from, in a way that no one else can."

"Is that so? And when this particular issue is past..." Danton waved a hand. "No, never mind. I am happy to help when I can. I will always be here when you need me."

Tarkyn shook his head. "No, Danton. Not 'never mind.' It is not someone I wish to be: a person who uses their friends only when they need them." The prince thought for a moment.

"I think you too have been careful not to present us as a united front against the woodfolk. You have kept away from me and seated yourself elsewhere around the firesite. I didn't ask you to do that."

"No, but equally you didn't call me over to join you." Danton shrugged. "Anyway, you're right. I didn't want an 'us and them' situation to develop. So I have tried to blend in and become one of the crowd."

Tarkyn smiled his appreciation. "You are a strategic courtier, aren't you, attuned to the requirements of diplomacy?"

"Yes and no. I don't seem to be very good at matching my expectations to those of the woodfolk. Waterstone informed me that my behaviour towards you is sometimes a source of amusement among woodfolk."

"I did warn you. That's why I suggested you leave behind the protocols of court."

"That's easy for you to say. You haven't had a lifetime of being under threat of punishment for any step out of line. It doesn't feel right... and anyway, unlike this ungrateful lot, I do wish to honour you as you deserve." Danton glanced around the surrounding trees and frowned. "You realise someone is probably listening to all of this?"

"Hmm. Just a minute." Tarkyn's mind scanned the area and tuned into two hidden woodfolk, nearby but at a discreet distance. "No, it's safe to talk openly. Creaking Bough and Rustling Leaves are close but not too close." The prince picked up the thread of their conversation. "The woodfolk are not ungrateful, but equally they do not accept differences in rank. So my presence among them is uncomfortable for them."

Danton glanced at the prince. "They're a bloody arrogant lot, you know. When I asked Waterstone what gave him the right to warn me about my behaviour around you, he said it was because he was a woodman, when all along he should have told me that he's a prince by right of being your blood brother. He thinks being a woodman matters more than being a prince."

Tarkyn laughed. "Of course he does. He doesn't believe in princes. None of them does. And he carefully didn't use your values instead of his own, just to gain the upper hand."

"Hmph. And I've never met a bunch of commoners before who were so confident and blasé about speaking to members of the nobility."

"Oh my stars!" Tarkyn shook his head. "Danton, get it out of your head that they are commoners. It doesn't work like that here. All of them consider themselves to be equally at the top of their social hierarchy. You heard what Waterstone said. They only acknowledge me as their prince because of the oath. They wouldn't otherwise. They all consider themselves to be my equal....and your equal."

Danton was so agitated that he shot to his feet, slopping his wine, and began to pace back and forth. "I can't help it. I find that absolutely outrageous. How dare they?"

"They dare because they respect people only on merit not on the basis of protocol. They couldn't care less about your title. And they wouldn't want it even if you gave it to them."

Danton stood over Tarkyn, staring down at him. Suddenly he realised what he was doing and hastily moved back with a muttered apology.

Tarkyn waved his hand. "Think nothing of it. The woodfolk do it all the time. Come on. Sit down again and calm down."

Danton reluctantly lowered himself down next to the prince and took a long breath.

"Now, Danton, if you are to give me any support over the next few difficult days, you will have to accept, as I do, woodfolk as they are, not as you would like them to be."

Danton turned his head to look at Tarkyn. "What will be difficult about the new few days?"

Tarkyn ignored his question and persisted. "Danton, can you do that?"

Danton shook his head slowly. "To be honest, I will struggle. I have spent my life protecting your consequence. But if you wish it, I will try."

"Perhaps if you think of them all as nobility, that may make it easier."

"Without the graces, you mean?" said Danton acerbically.

"Do graces create the rank?"

"No, but they usually come with it."

Tarkyn shrugged. "Woodfolk have their own graces. They are kind, honest and perceptive. They accept who you are, and if you earn it, they will respect you. They have as strong a sense of their own consequence as any noble in the land. They just don't express it in the same way."

"You really like them, don't you?"

"Oh yes, I most certainly do. They look me in the eye and see who I, the man, am. And they tell me hard truths when they need to be said." Tarkyn paused and looked at Danton. "You've been doing a bit of that yourself lately. You are more forthright in your comments to me than you ever were in the past. Why is that, do you suppose?"

Danton thought for a moment. "Partly because, even if I fear your wrath, some things need to be said and at least the weight of the court is not standing by, ready to punish me for insolence. And I suppose partly because I have watched you accept the woodfolk speaking to you frankly." He shrugged. "But, as you strongly pointed out over the incident with Waterstone, the rules apply differently to me since I am a sorcerer and they are woodfolk." He drank the last of his wine. "It is as tricky a situation as any I have ever found myself in. I have no idea where the lines are drawn anymore... Maybe that's another reason I sit on the other side of the fire," he laughed humourlessly, "but even that didn't keep me safe."

Tarkyn glanced at him, then looked away. "Do you think I was unfair?"

Danton raised his eyebrows in surprise. "No. It is the way of the world that different people are treated differently. No. I accepted your judgement without question and, to be honest, with a great deal of relief. Within the sorcerers' framework, you were very lenient."

"But," supplied Tarkyn, "from the woodfolk's point of view, the issue would never have arisen."

"Exactly. So, you want me to behave as a woodman, yet I am still under threat of punishment for transgressing as a sorcerer." Danton hurried on, "Don't misunderstand me. I know I shouldn't have hit Waterstone. But I am confused about where the expectations stop and start."

"Danton, my friend, so am I." Tarkyn shook his head. "But that will not do. For your sake, I must be clearer. Give me a minute to think about it. Perhaps you could pour us another wine in the meantime."

In a silence that lengthened into minutes, Danton poured the wine then kept himself entertained by trying, without success, to spot the hidden woodfolk.

Eventually, the prince shifted position and spoke, "Danton, I have tried to consider every possibility. I realise now that my first reaction to you speaking forthrightly has been outrage, and yet it is something I value in the woodfolk as long as it is phrased courteously." He smiled and glanced at his friend. "You may be interested to know that Rainstorm was on the receiving end of my ire the other day for speaking discourteously. I do have expectations of woodfolk also. So, provided you are courteous, which I am sure you would be, you may speak as forthrightly with me as you please. You may have to endure my initial reaction, but I will not continue to be angry."

Tarkyn took a sip of wine before continuing. "Secondly, I would not brook deliberate rudeness but neither do I expect the protocols of court. You may choose how you behave in that respect. However, an excess of obeisance will not do either of us any good in the eyes of the woodfolk." He smiled. "But I must admit, I do like the odd bow here and there. I do it myself at times." He paused. "And I give you permission to be more familiar with me, provided you are also respectful. I know I tense up when you put your hand on my shoulder but I'm pleased that you persevere. I too have a lifetime of training to overcome. I'm afraid you will have to gauge, in each situation, the level of familiarity that is tolerable, but if I think you have transgressed and become too familiar with me, I will tell you but will not punish you."

"Thank you, my lord. That reassurance will make things easier."

Tarkyn nodded acknowledgement before continuing, "And try to use my name at least some of the time. Despite what you may think, I do not consider us to be in a public forum among the woodfolk. So there is no need for the formality of titles. I haven't been using yours, you may notice."

Danton nodded but said nothing, aware that the prince had not yet finished.

"With regard to my woodfolk family, I would suggest even less formality than with me but respect nevertheless, as I would expect you to respect all woodfolk. Has Ancient Oak also given his permission for you to lay hands on him?"

"Yes, Sire." When Tarkyn raised his eyebrows, Danton waved a hand. "I know, but this feels official at the moment. I'll try to use your name later."

Tarkyn smiled. "Fair enough. And lastly, I also give you permission to lay hands on me."

Danton boggled, "I beg your pardon?"

"I trust you, Danton. Among all these people, you are the only one who serves me willingly. I would give you some recognition of that."

Danton bowed his head briefly. "Thank you, my lord. I am honoured by your trust."

"You should have been honoured by it a long time ago, my friend, but I have never really felt able to trust anybody until recently. You can thank Waterstone and the woodfolk for that." The prince took another sip of wine. "So. Is that clear enough?"

Danton breathed a sigh of relief. "Yes. That feels much better. I know where I stand now and don't have to guess so much." He sipped his wine and then asked, "So, why are the next few days going to be so difficult?"

"Because, inadvertently, all the forestals, and possibly all woodfolk, have become subject to the oath... and sooner or later we will have to tell them."

Danton exhaled. "Oh, I see. That's pretty grim, isn't it?"

Tarkyn smiled gently. "Danton, I'm so glad you didn't say, 'Well, so they should be.'"

Danton laughed. "Well, of course they should be, but that is another issue entirely. And I know enough about them to understand that there will be some serious animosity towards you while they come to terms with it." He shrugged. "Almost, I don't blame them. I wouldn't want to be forced to swear my life away to a woodman."

"In fairness, I think they would feel just as bad about having to swear fealty to one of their own, maybe even more so."

Danton shook his head. "Strange bunch. So, who do you have to tell?"

"I've just told Falling Branch."

"I see. No wonder you needed a drink. And what about his son? Rainstorm should be an even greater obstacle."

Tarkyn frowned. "How did you know that Falling Branch was Rainstorm's father?"

"I asked." Danton watched quizzically as the prince mulled over the significance of this response. He didn't comment but asked, "So, what about Rainstorm?"

"Rainstorm has known ever since the day he attacked you."

"Has he? I thought he'd have been upset about being subject to the oath."

"He was," said Tarkyn dryly. "Very. But he kept quiet about it for the good of the woodfolk until the rescue was over."

Danton smiled broadly. "That's absolutely brilliant. He's a real hero to have managed that. He's only young."

"Yes, I have a lot of time for young Rainstorm, despite his hot head." Tarkyn smiled slowly. "So you've forgiven him then, for attacking you?"

"What? Of course I have. I didn't give it a second thought. I even forgave him for attacking you, though that was more difficult."

Tarkyn grinned. "Well, you'll be pleased to know he is one of the people I have given permission to attack me."

Danton frowned. "No. I am not pleased at all. Why on earth did you do that?"

"Think, Danton, think. He's a hothead struggling on his own to come to terms with having to serve me, and the forest pays the penalty if he becomes too distressed."

"I see. And I hope he hasn't taken advantage of it."

Tarkyn laughed. "Not since I gave him permission."

"So, how much forest is going to be damaged while all these other woodfolk vent their spleen on you?"

Tarkyn shook his head. "I don't know. That's what I'm

worried about." He glanced at Danton then looked away. After a moment, he drew a deep breath and once more met Danton's eyes. "Danton, the other thing I'm worried about is how I will handle it. It is very hard to stand by and watch people as they realise with horror that they are under oath of fealty to me. I feel apologetic and reviled. I try not to take it personally but at times like that I completely forget that some people actually feel honoured to serve me." He gave a rueful smile. "I managed to remember when I was with Falling Branch, but that was probably the first time I had thought of it... and it was mainly because you stated it last night."

Danton returned his gaze steadily while he thought about it. Finally, he said, "Tarkyn, I will be by your side when you need a reminder of your heritage. I would prefer not to advocate on your behalf because I think that would be inflammatory, but I will be here for you. Just remember the tribute the woodfolk made to you. They value you for yourself and for your protection of them. With luck, those woodfolk who know you will advocate for you and the storm of ill feeling towards you should be short-lived."

Tarkyn let out a breath. "Thanks, Danton. That's just what I need. I agree that you shouldn't advocate for me. It would only widen the gap. The whole situation is vexed. The trouble is that I agree with the woodfolk that they shouldn't have been forced into this oath, and even more so that the forest shouldn't be forfeit for non-compliance. So, when they talk about the burden of serving me, I can't help but agree that I am an undesirable hardship they have to endure." He gave a wry smile. "It is not very elevating for the spirit."

"But we love him anyway," said Waterstone cheerfully, appearing out of nowhere and patting him on the back.

Tarkyn looked up at him to find himself surrounded by a small group of woodfolk. He regarded Waterstone quizzically. "And how long have you been eavesdropping this time?"

The woodman laughed. "Tarkyn, how could you say that? No. We've just arrived. We knew you needed a private chat, so we announced our presence from the start." He brought Falling Branch to the fore and said, "Falling Branch has almost recovered from the shock, although it has taken nearly a full bottle of wine to reconcile him."

"And not only that," continued Ancient Oak, "but Falling Branch now has a whole new area of mutual interest to discuss with his son."

"Wonderful," replied Tarkyn. "Glad to be of service. Are you lot going to sit down? Otherwise, I'll have to stand up. I'm developing a stiff neck looking up at you all."

As one, they sank down to sit cross-legged in a semi-circle around Tarkyn and Danton.

"So, Danton," said Waterstone spuriously, "here comes your big chance to protect your liege's consequence. What are you proposing?"

Danton eyed him askance. "I have no intention of advocating on Tarkyn's behalf, if that's what you're thinking."

"Disappointing." It was becoming increasingly clear that Waterstone had been drinking too. "I was looking forward to a feisty display of fireworks between sorcerers and woodfolk."

Danton stared coldly at the woodman. "Do not confuse a passionate devotion to service with stupidity. They are not at all the same thing. You, after all, are passionately devoted to the woodfolk, and I would never make the mistake of thinking you stupid. I am well aware of the futility of, in fact, the *harm* I would cause by advocating for Tarkyn."

"So, what will you do to support him?" persisted Waterstone.

Danton considered carefully before replying, "I will be

there as a reminder to Tarkyn that not everyone resents serving him." He spread his hands disarmingly. "Beyond that, I will do whatever you think will be most helpful."

Suddenly Waterstone's belligerence disappeared and he beamed at the sorcerer, "Danton, I always knew you were a fine fellow. I doubted Falling Branch's wisdom in suggesting that Tarkyn should come to see you but obviously some of Rainstorm's acuity comes from his father."

There was an uncomfortable pause.

Danton looked at Tarkyn. "So, it wasn't your idea to come and talk to me?"

Tarkyn sent Waterstone a poisonous glance before replying with incurable honesty, "No. But I didn't have to follow Falling Branch's suggestion."

Everyone held their breath as chagrin warred with amusement on Danton's face. Finally, amusement won, and he shook his head smiling. "Tarkyn is right. You really are kind people. For Falling Branch to have even considered what either of us might need at a time like that was quite remarkable." He took a long draught of wine, then pointed his goblet at Rainstorm. "And you, young Rainstorm. You kept all of us in the dark when you must have been distressed, to protect the welfare of your people – well, as I've already said to Tarkyn, I think you're bloody heroic!" At this point, it was borne upon the others that Danton, too, had imbibed a substantial amount of wine.

Rainstorm blushed while Ancient Oak looked from Waterstone to Danton and said firmly, "We had better get this announcement out of the way before these two become paralytic. Either that or wait another day. We can't arrive at the mountainfolk's firesite with this issue unresolved."

"For the safety of the children, I would rather we were as far away from the encampment as possible," said Tarkyn. "So, I would prefer to press on." Then, seeing himself surrounded by quizzical faces, he threw his hands up in surrender. "Right. Fine. You're used to hiding from soldiers and marauders. Well, as long as you're sure you can keep Danton and me safe, I will go with your decision.

In the way of woodfolk, the most competent at the time took over the organisation. So Ancient Oak replied, "I think we should make the announcement tonight and see what everyone thinks. My feeling is that the more time that the mountainfolk have to think about it before we arrive, the less angry they'll be. So maybe we should mindtell them tonight but leave crossing the grasslands until tomorrow evening. Then they'll have two full days to think about it."

"Agreed. Let's give everyone a chance to have a couple of hours of peaceful sleep, undisturbed by nightmares of the oath," said Tarkyn wryly. "Then we'll gather together before we set off again."

Ancient Oak, Rainstorm and Falling Branch went out of focus to relay the message as they all stood up and walked slowly back to the firesite.

15

Two hours later, Tarkyn steeled himself to stand up and address the gathered woodfolk. "Good evening all. I will keep this short so that there is plenty of time for discussion. About a week ago, when Rainstorm had his run-in with Danton, I noticed when he turned on me that the trees were suddenly blown about. Not long after this, Rainstorm again attacked me briefly after I had shared my suspicions with him, and this time there was no doubt that the forest was in danger. Consequently, I believe that the forestals, and possibly all woodfolk, have become subject to the oath."

Tarkyn forced himself to send his gaze slowly around the circle of faces. Some were aghast as Waterstone had been. Some eyes had narrowed in suspicion. A few woodfolk were exchanging suppressed smiles. Several were simply stunned, and the remainder were clearly angry. He added with a convincing semblance of calm, "I'm assuming you know me well enough to know that I did not engineer this. Feel free to mindtalk for a few minutes. You can discuss your reactions and plans with me when you have had a chance to talk among yourselves. I will be back shortly."

Tarkyn left the intense silence of mindtalking behind him and walked off into the trees. Once out of sight, he let out a long breath of pent up tension and stood with his back leant against a large beech. He tilted his head back and gazed up into the interwoven canopy of the tree. The evening had drawn in and the last of the small, almost circular leaves and the fine branches of the tree were black silhouettes against the darkening sky. A slight rustle to one side drew his attention to a tawny owl staring down at him. He wondered whether this was the same owl he had seen on the night Tree Wind had shown him her memories. After a moment, he decided it couldn't be because they were far from that area at the moment. As he watched, the owl ruffled her feathers and turned her head to stare directly into his eyes. Gradually, the concerns of mankind faded and Tarkyn found himself submerged in the owl's understanding of the forest. He knew where every mouse hole and rabbit warren was and where this grove of beeches gave way to oaks and ashes. He was aware of the slash through the forest that was the Great West Road now miles to the north. To the south, he knew where the woodlands dissipated into grasslands, and he saw, with a frisson of shock, the rooftops of farmhouses nestled in valleys between these woodlands and the foothills of the mountains.

He wasn't flying over the forest as he had before in a bird's mind. This time, as the owl's mind panned further and further out in a radius around him, he felt himself to be a smaller and smaller part of a great entity and yet, despite this, still having a rightful place in the grand scheme of the forest's life. Slowly the owl brought him back to an awareness of himself standing under the beech looking up into her eyes. Then she blinked and looked away, ruffling her feathers, leaving him filled with the peace and strength of the great forest.

For a few minutes, he just stood there breathing deeply, thinking about the forest that he was now a part of. His care for the woodland had become rooted deeply within himself, well beyond the requirements of the oath he had made to protect it. His own life felt entwined within the forest's life and all that lived within it. He knew that if the forest died, so would he.

With an increased sense of resolve, Tarkyn took a deep breath, pushed himself away from the tree and walked back to join the circle of woodfolk. When he arrived, all eyes turned to look at him. He sat down quietly on a log, his elbows resting on his knees. As his long black hair fell forward to partially cover his face, he pulled it back so that it hung down his back.

He waited for someone to speak, but when no one did, he grimaced slightly and said, "I don't think you need to tell me your reactions. I know you are unhappy about your kindred having to accept me as their liege. I also suspect that in some ways it is a relief for you no longer to have the social stigma of being oathbound when others are not."

The woodfolk could feel something was different about Tarkyn but could not discern what it was. He sat up and put his hands on his knees. "We already know that other woodfolk will be angry and resentful when they find out that they are bound by the oath." Tarkyn looked around him, and his gaze was less apologetic than it might have been before his encounter with the owl. "So, since all of those reactions are entirely predictable, we need not concern ourselves with them." When few people frowned, he waved a hand and said, "I'm sorry. That sounded dismissive. I do not for a moment underestimate the strength of your feelings, but I think they are largely unavoidable. And I think you will all agree that our greatest single concern is the welfare of the forest. Our lives and our livelihood depend upon it. The woodlands are a part of us and we are a part of them."

Now the woodfolk really sat up and took notice. Tarkyn had never identified himself so closely with the forest and the woodfolk's connection with it before.

"Although I come from outside, I am also a woodman. I, as much as you, have a rightful place in the unfolding life of the woodlands. And that place, whatever you may feel about it, is as your forest guardian and liege lord. I have given you my strength, my courage, and even offered you my life in making your cause my own." He gave an apologetic smile. "I do not say this in the hope of further gratitude. You have already given me more thanks than I ever expected. I say this in the hope that you may consider that the oath that binds us together is not all bad. There are some advantages to having me as your liege lord." He paused. "For my own part, I feel privileged to have been given the opportunity of getting to know you all and becoming one of you. Without the oath, that would never have happened." He waved his hand. "I am not for a moment suggesting that I approve of the way in which the oath was imposed or of the sting in its tail. I am simply acknowledging that there are some virtues attached to it for all of us."

"That's all very well," objected Creaking Bough, "but that's easier for you to say. You don't have to serve us. It is only we who must serve you."

"There are different types of service. I have obligations to you just as you have obligations to me. I would like to think that the power and dedication that I bring to protecting you and supporting your cause have some value in that equation."

And suddenly, like a tiny candle flame struggling to stay alight in the wind, a glimmer of true acceptance flickered around the faces of the woodfolk.

"I remember saying that your part of the oath committed

you even more than it did us. There are obligations in both directions, aren't there?" asked Autumn Leaves.

Tarkyn nodded. "Yes, of course there are." He paused. "And I would almost go so far as to say that my obligations under the oath are far greater than yours. I have an obligation to hundreds of you while you share your obligations to one person among many. So much so, that many woodfolk have never done anything for me at all. We all know that, in the main, it is the people gathered here who have supported me in order to fulfil the woodfolk's oath."

Autumn Leaves' eyes narrowed while he thought about it. "But you could insist that one or a few particular people devote their entire lives to you, couldn't you? Then it would be unbalanced."

"Yes. I could insist on a great deal more than I am receiving from you at the moment. I could insist that all woodfolk devoted their lives to me. But, as you know, I have never demanded that level of service from you." Tarkyn leant down and picked up a small stick and began to break bits of the end of it as he talked. "After all, Stormaway made sure that I could be trusted before he allowed the oath to be invoked, didn't he?"

"But that is the difficulty for us with the oath," said Autumn Leaves. "The balance of the equation is entirely dependent upon your discretion, not ours."

Tarkyn smiled ruefully as he looked around the gathered woodfolk. "Yes, that is true. And from time to time, I know I take control and fail to consult you as we agreed. And I know that above all, woodfolk value and expect equality in their dealings with each other." Tarkyn spread his hands disarmingly. "What can I say? I am what I am, a prince of the realm. I try my best, well beyond the limits of my upbringing, to negotiate decisions and to allow a freedom of behaviour around me far greater than any I have ever experienced before. But while I may have mitigated my expectations of your role in fulfilling the oath, I have not mitigated my expectations of myself and I intend to give you full measure as your liege."

"And so now the balance swings the other way," stated Autumn Leaves.

"Maybe. Maybe not. Within the freedom I have offered you, you have that choice. Many woodfolk will accept the protection I offer but will avoid their obligations. Even among those of you who have stayed to pay the price on behalf of your kin, your enthusiasm for fulfilling the oath is underwhelming." Tarkyn held up a hand to stall the impending protests he could see in a few faces. "It is understandable. As your liege, I have a role I was bred to. As my liegemen and women, you find yourselves in a role that you find distasteful and alien to your culture. And, as you so rightly point out, I have the upper hand." A small smile curved his mouth. "But you have given me something far more valuable than the requirements of the oath. You have given me true friendship and acceptance... and for me, these are beyond price." He took a long breath and let it out slowly. "And I think, I *hope*, that for your part, you are not too unhappy with the way we work together."

As Tarkyn hesitated, trying to formulate what to say next, Rainstorm stood up and, throwing a defiant glance around the ring of faces, said firmly, "Prince, I'm not unhappy with it. I will support you and stand by you when you have to face the next wave of resentment." The rebellious young woodman folded his arms across his chest. "And if I can handle the authority given to you by the oath, anyone can."

North Wind stood up opposite Rainstorm and added his support, "And I think having you with us, both as protector and friend, outweighs the discomfort of oath."

Waterstone glanced at the two young woodmen standing defiantly before their kin and rose to his feet, saying with a wry smile, "I hate the oath and always will. But Tarkyn, I wouldn't lose you for the world."

"If you can win me over, you can win anyone over." Tree Wind smiled as she stood to join the others. "We will ride any storm that faces us together."

Autumn Leaves lumbered to his feet. "And you have put up with us getting angry with you, which I suspect," he said, looking at Danton for confirmation, "is something you're not used to."

Danton shook his head. "Not at all."

"And," continued Autumn Leaves, "you haven't yet burnt me to a crisp and you have even gone so far as to rescue me. So, I think we have a fair deal."

As each of these people spoke, others in the background were nodding agreement. Then Falling Branch stood up and everyone waited with baited breath for him to speak, knowing he had only just found out that he was subject to the oath. "Among the people gathered here, only Rainstorm and I witnessed the lengths to which you went to placate the forestals and to ensure that the woodfolk were not divided by the oath. I may not like this oath but I have every respect for you and will give you my support."

As Ancient Oak stood up, the remaining woodfolk also stood, "For my part, I am proud to have you in our family." He paused. "And so, little brother, I think you are right. Our virtues and yours have overcome the evil in the oath with only minor disruptions to the woodfolk ways. We can live with the oath... and with you," he added with a quirky grin. He looked around him. "And we are all prepared to support you when we face the mountainfolk."

Then slowly, all eyes turned to look at Danton, still seated far from the prince. Danton stood up, let his eyes travel around the ring of woodfolk and then returned his gaze to Tarkyn.

With a gentle smile, he bowed. "I also will support your cause, my liege."

Waterstone noted with approval that Danton didn't point out that he had been supporting the prince's cause for much longer than any of the woodfolk.

Tarkyn rose slowly to his feet, rising from looking up at them all, to surveying them from a greater height. His eyes were bright with emotion. "Thank you, my friends," he said gravely. "I am truly grateful that I don't have to face this alone."

Waterstone came over and clapped Tarkyn on the back as he addressed the group. "Right everyone. So, let's see if we can find a way to reconcile the mountainfolk so that they don't endanger the forest. We'll have to think carefully about how we will phrase it when we mindtalk to them about the oath, for their sakes and for all our sakes."

"We will," agreed Thunder Storm. He addressed the prince, "Do you mind us mindtalking to confer? We'll get back to you."

Tarkyn waved a hand to indicate acquiescence. As the woodfolk converged, he looked across to Danton, standing discreetly on the other side of the firesite and smiled. Then he pointed at Danton and indicated that he should come over to join him. He mimed drinking and pointed to the large pot of boiling water that was hanging over the fire. Danton's face relaxed into a smile as he stood up and walked around the outside of the ring of quiet, conferring woodfolk. He detoured to make two steaming cups of tea as requested.

"Thanks," said Tarkyn quietly, as he blew on his tea to cool it. "I thought we had better not drink too much until we know whether we're leaving tonight or tomorrow." He frowned. "I already have some doubts about your ability to travel."

"Fear not," replied Danton, waving his cup around. "I'm as fit as a fiddle."

"I wasn't concerned about your fitness. It's your ability to move quietly that concerns me," said Tarkyn, suppressing a smile.

"Oh ye of little faith. I'm an elite guard, remember. I do stealth well. I even made it past the woodfolk's lookouts when I first arrived."

Tarkyn smiled. "You did too. But not after you'd been drinking, I suspect."

At this point, their attention was drawn to Thunder Storm who said, "We're are about to mindtalk to the mountainfolk and tell them that it is probable but not certain that they have come under the oath. Are you happy with that? Depending on their reaction, we'll decide when to leave. Agreed?"

Tarkyn nodded and they went back out of focus. Over the next few minutes, Danton and Tarkyn watched as various woodfolk winced at the reactions they were receiving. Then their faces suffused with anger followed by set mouths and frowns of determination. Danton and Tarkyn exchanged glances but didn't say anything to distract the woodfolk. Time rolled on quietly. A few frowns of uncertainty flitted across some of the faces and when eventually the woodfolk refocused, they looked shaken and worried.

"We will travel on tonight," announced Ancient Oak flatly.

"If their reaction was so unpleasant, as it appears to have been from watching your faces, may I ask why?"

"Because, Tarkyn, the mountainfolk tell us that the weather is closing in over the mountains unusually early. We are running out of time if we want to reach Falling Rain this year." Ancient Oak shrugged. "It will take us a good twenty-four hours to reach them anyway, by the time we cross the grasslands, rest, and then cover the last part of the journey through the forest. That will give them long enough." He glanced at Waterstone before adding, "I think we may find our encounter with them difficult."

"Which is no surprise to anyone," responded Tarkyn dryly. "Very well. Let's press on then."

Once the decision was made, the woodfolk acted quickly. Tarkyn and Danton barely had time to finish their tea before the woodfolk were packed up and ready to go, all signs of their presence, even the firesite, obliterated from the clearing.

Ahead of them lay the grasslands and the uncertain reception of the mountainfolk.

IV

THE GRASSLANDS

16

D arkness had closed in and the moon had not yet risen as Tarkyn and Danton moved gingerly through the woods, each close behind a woodman who seemed to have a much better facility for night vision than they did. As they broke out of the forest into the grasslands, a glow on the eastern horizon heralded the impending rising of the moon.

"This is not ideal," whispered Waterstone, coming up beside the prince. "We really don't want to be silhouetted against the sky by a full moon." He looked up. "Blast it! Stars everywhere," he said, without the slightest thought for the beauty of the firmament above them. "Not a cloud in sight."

"At least we won't get wet."

Waterstone gave a grunt of laughter. "Such an optimist. We will, sooner or later."

"Such a pessimist," retorted Tarkyn.

"We're going to have to skirt around the ridges and keep within the valleys. Unfortunately, that takes us closer to the farmhouses. Their dogs are likely to set up a din and bring their owners out looking for trouble."

"I can quieten them," offered Tarkyn.

"Part of that obligation you were talking about?"

"If you like..." after a pause, he added, "or just part of being a member of the group but with a particular skill. Depends how you want to view it."

"Hmm. The latter appeals more, I must say."

"I think so," said Tarkyn, and Waterstone could hear the smile in his voice.

A couple of minutes later, Tarkyn's voice issued from the darkness, "Waterstone, could you stop and let me place my hand on your shoulder. I need to stand firm while I concentrate."

When he was ready, Tarkyn sent his mind out across the grasslands to the nearest farmstead and nudged against the sheepdog's mind. The dog gave a low growl of uncertainty but then acknowledged the forest guardian's presence with a few sweeps of his tail. Tarkyn sent images of himself and woodfolk, accompanied by waves of friendship and reassurance. Just as the dog hunkered down, ready to jump up and bark an enthusiastic greeting, Tarkyn imagined the dog sitting quietly and wagging his tail. The sheepdog gave a quiet whine of excitement but managed to contain himself. Then Tarkyn sent him an image of the other houses and other dogs sitting quietly as the woodfolk moved past. With a nuance of thanks, Tarkyn withdrew from the dog's mind and returned to the awareness of his hand on Waterstone's shoulder and himself standing under a starlit sky in the darkness of the grasslands.

"Done," he said quietly. He gave Waterstone a clap on the shoulder to thank him before letting his hand drop.

"Just a minute," said Waterstone, "I'll let the others know." After a brief pause, they continued on their way.

They skirted quietly over the lower part of two ridges and around the heads of the valleys in between. Lower down in each valley lay a large stone-built farmhouse surrounded by sheds, barns and outhouses. All was quiet and no light shone from any window.

"They always build their houses low in the valley," whispered Waterstone. "The winds howl across these grasslands, and they need all the protection they can get."

"Why are there no trees here?" asked Tarkyn quietly.

"There were, once." Waterstone stopped to scan the surroundings before beginning the climb up the next ridge. "Then a small group of sorcerers came to settle in this area. They cut down all the trees so they could plant crops and graze stock. But the winds have taken over, with no trees to stop them. Over the years, the topsoil has drifted away and their crops do not prosper. The grasslands still support their sheep and cattle so that is now their main livelihood. Down in the valley, where they are out of the wind, the land can grow enough for their own needs but not enough to market."

"It must have broken your hearts to watch the forest dying at their hands."

Waterstone threw him an amused glance that appeared as a flash of white in the moonlight. "It would have if I had seen it. But they came here well over a century ago. Having destroyed their patch, they now seem content to stay within this tract of grassland."

"What would you do if they decided to expand their holdings?"

"They have tried in the past. Whenever they mount any attack on the trees, odd accidents begin to happen. Sometimes people are killed. Their tools break and twist, their cattle become unmanageable and rampage through their vegetable gardens. Weird sounds are heard at night."

Tarkyn's eyes grew round. "And the forest does all this?" he asked in wonder.

Waterstone made a strangled gurgle that turned out to be a repressed laugh. "No, Tarkyn. We do."

"Oh."

"We were caught unawares when they first arrived and they came in one large group that we couldn't really oppose. But since then, they have only worked as individual farms and we are alert to the danger." A flash of white teeth showed that Waterstone was grinning. "The legend of the curse of the forest has grown over the years. So, we don't have to do much these days to stop them."

"Hmm." Silence ensued for a long period after this as they cut across a valley close to a farmstead. Tarkyn sent out a reassurance to the resident dogs and received a welcoming greeting in return.

Once they were further from the buildings and less concentration was needed, Tarkyn had a chance to mull over Waterstone's words. As he neared the top of the ridge leading into the next valley, he remembered Danton's concern that his prince's commitment to the woodfolk would affect his birth responsibility to his fellow sorcerers. Here was a case in point: he would have to choose his allegiance. *I'm sorry, Danton,* he thought. *I am the forest guardian. I would choose the forest and the woodfolk, at least in this case.*

Danton, walking a few yards to his right, frowned and glanced over at Tarkyn as he picked up the feeling of apology without the cause. Tarkyn, intent on his own thoughts, didn't notice.

Suddenly, Tarkyn was tripped up and slammed to the ground by a hard thump in the back. Nearby the dogs were barking. He lay on the ground, his cheek pushed into the rough grass, his heart beating hard. He could see nothing but blades of grass around him. A heavy weight pressed down on his back, keeping him pinned to the ground. Then an image of a woodman lying on top of him and holding him down firmly with his arm came into Tarkyn's mind.

"Just me," hissed Autumn Leaves in his ear. "There's a group of horsemen riding hard towards that house we've just passed. We're at the top of the ridge. They might be able to see us in the moonlight if they look this way."

Tarkyn mumbled something into the grass but Autumn Leaves missed it.

"What?"

Tarkyn spat out some dirt and a few blades of grass and said quietly but more distinctly, "Why did I have to score the heaviest woodman on my back?"

Autumn Leaves grinned in the gloom. "Just lucky, I guess. Anyway, another woodman mightn't have had enough weight to push you down."

"And were you thinking of getting off me at any stage?"

"Oops. Sorry." Autumn Leaves rolled off the prince and lay beside him in the long grass. He was grinning hugely.

"Or you could have just told me to get down," said Tarkyn dryly.

Autumn Leaves shook his head, still smiling. "Ooh, I don't know. I seem to remember you giving us strict instructions not to order you about."

"Very funny," Tarkyn quipped back but then became thoughtful as he realised that Autumn Leaves was only half joking, and with good reason. The woodfolk might be prepared to risk his ire by ordering him around in a situation such as this but if his automatic outrage caused any hesitation while he quelled it, it could place them all in danger. He looked at Autumn Leaves lying up close to him in the long grass. "Hmm. I might need to do some work on my reactions, mightn't I? And be prepared to hand over command, so to speak, in situations like this."

Autumn Leaves' eyes twinkled in the dark as he shrugged. "Up to you. Depends how much you like being thumped to the ground and manhandled."

Tarkyn grinned. "Except for the dirt and grass in my mouth, I'm all right with it. Makes a change from the monotony of walking."

At this point, muffled sounds of a struggle came to them from nearby. An abrupt movement and a thud were followed by the sight of Danton's back parallel to the top of the grass.

Tarkyn and Autumn Leaves looked at each other and crawled on their bellies over to Danton. They found him kneeling over Rainstorm, a knife to his throat.

"What are you doing, Danton?" hissed the prince angrily.

"This bloody idiot decides to attack me while we're close to the farm house. I don't know what his problem is. He caught me unawares to start with and had me pinned down, but I have sorted that out."

Tarkyn realised that Danton hadn't had the advantage of a transmitted image to reassure him. He looked at Rainstorm and saw that he was lying quite relaxed beneath the point of Danton's blade, with a slight smile playing around his lips. He was obviously enjoying himself.

"I think you could have explained your actions, Rainstorm," said Tarkyn. "It rather defeats the purpose of pushing Danton out of sight if he then rears up the next minute to fight you off."

Rainstorm grinned. "I wanted to see some of this expert training we keep hearing about. He's quite good, isn't he?" The grin dropped from Rainstorm's face, and Tarkyn turned to see Autumn Leaves out of focus and looking very severe. "Sorry, Autumn Leaves and everyone," said Rainstorm contritely after what had clearly been a mental berating. He shrugged and glanced sheepishly at Tarkyn, "Wrong time and place."

Tarkyn shook his head with a slight smile. "Rainstorm,

Danton is right. You really are an idiot sometimes. Never mind. No harm done."

As Danton gave a grunt of acceptance and withdrew his knife, Autumn Leaves froze and his eyes went out of focus. Tarkyn knew better than to interrupt. A minute later, Autumn Leaves reported quietly, "The horsemen have reached the house. Some of them were riding doubled up. Lapping Water thinks that there are at least two riders with injuries of some sort. They are being lifted down and carried into the house."

"Can we creep up closer and see what's going on?" asked Danton. It was unclear whether he was asking the woodfolk or Tarkyn for permission.

Tarkyn looked at Autumn Leaves and said, "I, too, would like to know what's happening but I will bow to your decision."

After a couple of minutes out of focus, Autumn Leaves replied, "Danton can go down, if he wishes. He at least will be able to explain his presence." He glanced at the blonde sorcerer. "I understand you are less dogmatic than your liege here about being creative with the truth. So, are you prepared to say that you are on your way to the mountains to do some trapping, if you are caught?"

Danton nodded, his eyes gleaming in anticipation. "Back soon," he said quietly as he slipped away into the gloom.

"So now we wait," said Tarkyn as he sat up and brushed down the front of his shirt.

"I've asked Lapping Water to intercept him when he's nearer the house so that she can be his link back to us," said Autumn Leaves.

"What about me?" asked Rainstorm plaintively. "I could have gone up closer with him to be the link."

Tarkyn and Autumn Leaves both turned their heads and looked at him with raised eyebrows. After a speaking silence,

Autumn Leaves said mildly, "Lapping Water is already down there."

Rainstorm subsided in a huff.

Lower down the valley, Lapping Water reared up out of the grass just as Danton neared her and startled him. He let out a hiss of breath. "Phew. You take your life in your hands if you do that to me."

Lapping Water gave a low laugh. "I trust your reflexes. You wouldn't kill anyone until you knew who they were."

Danton nodded. "True. So, what are you doing now? Are you coming down to the house with me?"

"No, but I will come down as far as that tree and wait for you there. Then if you need to talk to the others, I will relay your messages to them."

Lapping Water saw the gleam of his smile in the gloom.

"Thanks," he said briefly.

They moved doubled up and silent towards the house. As they neared the tree, a slight sound to Danton's right alerted him to Lapping Water's disappearance. Not a leaf rustled out of place to betray her arrival in the tree. Danton stopped to survey the approaches to the house. A long rectangle of light shone over the trampled earth outside the open back door. Through a window to the right of the door, he could see someone moving around what seemed to be the kitchen, filling a kettle and placing it on the hob. No one else was visible from his present vantage point. As he moved closer, he spotted the black and white, long-coated farm dogs chained near a barn on the right. They were sitting quietly but wagging their tails furiously in welcome, brushing shaggy semicircles in the dirt behind them. Danton deviated from his course to visit them and spent some time stroking them in thanks for their discretion. After a final pat, he moved on.

He crept through the shadow of the barn around to the side

of the house. Towards the front, light was shining from a window. He approached quietly, hugging the side wall, and lifted his head slowly to peer over the lintel into the lounge room.

Inside, he could see a group of nine farmhands, both men and women, standing in a worried cluster to one side. A dark-haired young man had been laid on the floor, his head on a large cushion and a blanket over him. He was conscious but his face was white and pinched with shock, and from time to time he grimaced with the severity of the pain. From where he was, Danton could not see what was wrong with him.

On the couch along the front window lay a young woman, her long, dark brown hair lying matted around her head on the pillow. She appeared to be unconscious. Her breathing was so shallow that Danton was not sure that he could see her chest moving at all. A fleck of blood stained the side of her mouth but again her injuries were covered by a blanket.

A thickset, well-dressed, middle-aged man paced up and down distractedly, from time to time stopping to kneel and brush back the hair of the suffering young man before his feelings overcame him, forcing him to rise to continue his pacing. Then he would cross to the couch and stand looking down at the young woman before stroking her head gently and resuming his pacing. Eventually, one of the older women detached herself from the group and, laying her hand on the man's arm, spoke a few quiet words in his ear. The man heaved a sigh and brushed his hands over his eyes.

As Danton watched, another woman brought a large tray laden with hot drinks and bread rolls from the kitchen. It seemed rather incongruous that food should be served in the midst of all the suffering, but the farmhands accepted it willingly and began to wolf down the rolls.

Suddenly, Danton heard the sounds of two horses,

approaching fast. He looked around wildly for cover but realised that any hiding places required him to cross the open moonlit area at the side of the house. He pressed himself deeper into the shadow of the house and waited.

The riders, two women, threw themselves from the horses and entered the house at a dead run. One of them ran to the distressed older man and threw herself into his arms. After a short, intense embrace, she turned her attention to what were clearly her children. Meanwhile, the other woman had pulled back the blanket on the young woman and was examining her. The front of her gown was soaked in blood. The healer ripped open the front of the gown and found wads of material already in place over a wound in the upper left-hand side of the young woman's chest. She looked around and nodded her approval at the gathered farmhands. She then gave out a series of instructions that led to the arrival of a bowl of steaming hot water and a variety of herbs picked from the front garden by a farmhand. The healer studied the girls' blue, blood-flecked lips with great concern and flicked a worried glance at the parents.

When she had bathed and bound the wound as best she could, she turned her attention to the young man. When she drew back the blanket, she had to repress a cry of distress. The trouser leg was caked in blood and the end of a jagged bone could be seen poking out of a tear in the material over his thigh. Despite tight binding, thick blood was seeping slowly onto the floor below the young man. The healer produced a tight reassuring smile, but when she began work on cutting off his trouser leg, her hands were shaking.

Danton had learnt enough about battle wounds to know that this young man had little hope of survival, and even if he lived, he would be lame for life. He could not bear the distress he saw on the faces inside that room. He pushed himself out from against the wall and melted up into the shadows of the hillside. When he reached the tree, he called quietly, "Lapping Water, are you there?"

In the next instant, Lapping Water was standing beside him. Despite himself, he jumped when he turned and found her there next to him.

"Blast it! You people take a bit of getting used to." He took a breath. "Lapping Water, there are two young people injured and, I think, dying down in that house. I don't know how they were injured, but I can't stand by and let their parents watch them die. Please, will you ask Tarkyn to come down and use his esse on them?"

"Danton, we do not concern ourselves with the affairs of sorcerers and wizards. It is unfortunate, but it is not for us to interfere."

"Lapping Water, I'm not asking you to interfere. I'm asking Tarkyn to."

"He is a woodman," stated Lapping Water flatly.

Danton ran his hand through his hair. "Please. Send him my message. Surely it is up to Tarkyn to decide for himself."

"We must protect him and he must not betray our presence."

"I will go before him and pave the way. I will protect him."

Lapping Water was clearly unhappy. "I will send your request but I will also voice my opinion."

Danton nodded. "Thanks. I'm sure every other woodman and woman will voice their opinion too, but at least they will know what I know."

After a moment, she returned into focus and asked, "How many people are down there? What type of people? What resistance might you expect?"

Danton had already summed up the situation in his head. "There are nine farmhands, a kitchen hand, the healer and the parents. Judging by the way they looked after the wounds, they haven't dealt with much fighting. Saying that, they look quite strong and would probably fight to protect their lord against an attack, even if inexpertly."

After a brief delay, Lapping Water looked at him disapprovingly and said, "Tarkyn is willing to do as you request. He has conferred with everyone. We have come to an agreement that Tarkyn may go down but on three conditions. He must be accompanied by you, Waterstone, and Autumn Leaves. I will stay close by to relay the situation, should anything happen to the two woodmen. Waterstone and Autumn Leaves will not enter the house but will keep watch from outside the windows and be ready to intervene if necessary."

"Agreed."

"Secondly, you must promise to place Tarkyn's welfare above all else."

Danton waved an impatient hand. "Of course. And the third condition?"

Lapping Water looked at him coldly. "If any or all of those people sees one of us or becomes aware of our existence, they will be killed instantly."

Danton exhaled a deep breath. "That seems fair."

"So will you, if you betray our presence," added Lapping Water, not at all pleased.

Danton shrugged, completely unmoved by this snipe. "I would expect nothing less. After all, I swore to conceal your presence on pain of death."

The woodwoman subsided into a disgruntled silence.

It was not long before Tarkyn and the two woodmen appeared out of the gloom. Surprisingly, Summer Rain followed in their wake.

Danton frowned in confusion. "You're not coming in to heal them, are you? They're not allowed to see you, surely?"

"No, young man. Of course I'm not. I have come down close to the house so Tarkyn can relay images to me and I can advise him. I'll have to give my advice in images so that should be quite a challenge for me. If worst comes to worst, you could duck outside and confer with Waterstone and I'll send the words to him."

"You could come and stand outside the house too," suggested Danton.

"No, I could not," replied Summer Rain severely. "We cannot afford to lose our healer on some trumped-up adventure." She poked him in the chest. "And we can't afford to lose our forest guardian, or these boys or even you, for that matter. So be careful."

Danton was so overcome that she had included him in that list that he forgot himself and bowed to her. "Yes ma'am. I promise we will not save their lives at the cost of our own." He straightened to find himself surrounded by suppressed smiles. He gave a slight shrug and grinned. "I know. But old habits die hard."

17

"So, are we going?" asked Tarkyn. "Or shall we stand here chatting while these two sorcerers bleed to death?" As they headed down the ridge towards the farmhouse, he added, "I presume you will precede me to introduce the idea of my presence gently?"

"I think I had better." Danton pointed to the two dogs who were now straining at their chains trying to reach Tarkyn but still managing to restrain their excitement to the odd quiet whine. "Perhaps you could chat to these dogs while I pave the way. They are obviously keen to see you." He shook his head briefly in wonder. "I'll be back shortly. Waterstone and Autumn Leaves, if you come with me, I'll show you where I stood watching."

Once the woodmen were installed outside the window, Danton walked around to the front of the house and calmly knocked on the front door. There was a sudden silence followed by a flurry of activity on the other side of the door. When the door opened, five of the farmhands stood in a semicircle before him, cudgels in hand.

"Good evening. My name is Danton Patronell," said Danton urbanely. "I wish to speak to the master or mistress of the house." He waved a hand around himself. "As you can see, I am alone."

"They're busy right now and not to be disturbed."

"I know they are busy. Perhaps I could speak with the healer, although no doubt she is busier still."

A short wiry individual said, "Here. How do yer know there's a healer in here?"

Danton smiled and replied calmly, "I saw her arrive and watched her activities through the window." He paused. "I'm sorry. I don't know your name.

"Bantram's my name. Yer've got a bloody cheek. Get on yer way before we send yer on it."

Danton leaned in and lowered his voice. "I suppose you realise that, without further help, neither of those young people in there will see the dawn."

"The healer knows what she's doing," came the belligerent reply.

"I agree with you. I think she does. So ask her whether or not I'm right."

The wiry man's eyes narrowed, and after a moment's thought, he started to move away.

Danton put up a hand. "Might I suggest you don't talk to her in front of the parents?"

Bantram paused. "Yer full of good ideas, ain't yer? Keep yer eyes on him," he said to his mates over his shoulder as he disappeared into the lounge room.

A few minutes later, the healer returned with him, shutting the door behind her. She wiped her bloodied hands on her apron. "Yes, young man. What can I do for you?"

Bantram indicated Danton with a grimy thumb and said,

"This bloke says these kids won't see temorrer without other help. He reckons yer know that as well."

Tears sprang to the healer's eyes. She nodded. "I'm afraid he's right. But worse than that, there is no other help." She let a sob escape before she pushed her apron against her mouth to stop herself.

The semi-circle of farmhands looked stricken.

"Madam, there is something else that can be done," said Danton gently. "I have a... friend waiting nearby who can heal them."

The healer shook her head. "They are beyond saving. The girl has internal bleeding and is descending into a fever. The boy's leg would have to come off if there were to be any hope of him surviving, and I don't know how to do that. He would bleed to death."

"I know how desperate it is. Believe me. Otherwise, I would not have offered this assistance." Danton spread his hands. "What do you have to lose? They will die anyway without the help."

The woman looked at him, summing him up, then nodded briskly. "Come inside. Explain yourself to Tol and Juney. I will support you."

Once inside the lounge room, Danton glanced quickly at the injured young sorcerers. The young man had lost consciousness in the intervening period.

Faced with the two distraught parents, Danton bowed and said gently, "My name is Danton Patronell. I happened to see your children's suffering as I passed outside your window. I have come to save their lives, if you will allow it."

Both parents' eyes widened and they looked at the healer, who nodded. "I have done all I know how. I don't know what this young man and his friend can offer, but your children will not live with only the help I have given them. They need more than I can do."

The lord and lady looked at each other and then asked, "Can we trust him?"

The healer shook her head. "I don't know. I've never met him before. But without him, they will surely die so it seems there is nothing to lose."

The lord straightened himself up and stared Danton in the eye. "What payment do you require for your services?"

The surprise on Danton's face was clear for all to see. "I do not think of payment, sir. I think only of your children's lives." He paused. "In fact, I am taking a great risk in coming in to see you, but I could not leave them to die and you to suffer if I, if we could help."

The lord became brusque. "Time is short. Bring in your friend and see what you can do."

Danton bowed. "Thank you, my lord." He hesitated. "There is one more thing before I fetch my friend. I need your guarantee that you and your staff will not harm my friend, no matter what you may think of him."

The lord frowned. "That seems a very odd request. Is he deformed, frightening or violent? Are we under threat from him?"

"No. I do not find him frightening but others may. However, I can assure you that he does not present a threat to you. Do I have your guarantee?"

The lord waved his hand. "Yes. Provided he does not attack us first."

Danton considered for a moment before nodding. "Agreed. I will return shortly."

The parents were conferring quietly with the healer when Danton returned. The farmhands did not recognise Tarkyn as he walked in, but the lord and lady, having travelled more widely, knew him instantly. They blanched and sank into a low bow. The healer and farmhands, seeing their reaction, followed suit.

"Please rise," said Tarkyn quietly. "Would you mind leaving the niceties of introduction until I have attended to your children? I understand their situation is grave."

The lord and lady rose and nodded in dumbstruck agreement. Tarkyn turned to the healer. "Who first?"

"The boy, my lord," said the healer who, not knowing who he was, was less overawed. "He's bleeding to death. It may already be too late."

Tarkyn nodded and knelt down beside the injured boy. He focused on the boy's leg, relaying the details to Summer Rain. After a short, visual conference, Tarkyn closed his eyes and placed his hands on the young man's shoulder. He sent his strength down through the boy's body until he came to the damaged leg. He flowed in and around the torn blood vessels and wove their fabric back together as best as he could with the jagged bone ends still sitting in amongst them. He stayed inside the young man giving him enough strength to renew his blood supply. Then when he was sure the boy was strong enough to survive, he pulled slowly out and came to himself kneeling in the lounge room of the farmhouse.

"The boy will live," he declared flatly, taking a few deep breaths to restore his own strength. "We will mend his leg after I have seen to your daughter."

Without waiting for their response, he moved to the side of the young woman lying on the couch. Her face was now flushed with fever, and when he pulled back the blanket, it was soaked with perspiration. He could see that the wound had already festered. He focused on it and waited for Summer Rain's response. After a few moments, he turned to the healer and asked, "Do you know of an herb that has small yellow and blue flowers in summer and red berries in the autumn?"

The healer nodded. "Yes. It is called the mountain sunrise. I did not know it had any healing properties. The berries on it are poisonous. Are you sure you have the right one?"

"Bring some to me, and I will check."

As the healer hurried out into the front garden, Tarkyn turned his attention to the young woman before him. He placed his hand on her shoulder, well away from the wound, and sent his mind and life force down through his hands into her damaged shoulder. The muscles had been ripped mercilessly apart by the arrow's thrust. The edge of her lung had been nicked, and although she was not drowning in her own blood as Tarkyn once had been, the blood was slowly seeping into the surrounding tissues and clogging her breathing. Within the wound were traces of dirt and some substance that Tarkyn suspected was a poison. He tuned his mind and sent images back to Summer Rain. She merely visualised him repairing the tearing so he followed her instructions and did so. He wove shut the cut on the side of her lung and gradually drew the fibres of her muscles together and provided the healing force for them to knit. Then he flowed through her blood stream searching for the bacteria that were taking her over. He didn't really know what he was looking for so, in the end, he used the techniques he had used on Rushwind's infestation and projected a sharp wave of anger through her. Somewhere outside, she cried out as it burnt through her and for a moment, he was aware of a struggle before the sound faded away. Tarkyn soothed her bloodstream and left her with enough *esse* to repair and recover.

When he withdrew, Tarkyn found himself next to Danton, surrounded by Danton's aqua shield. On the outside of the shield was a ring of angry sorcerers, frustrated in their attempts to attack Tarkyn and rescue the daughter of the house. Tarkyn smiled at Danton and ran his hand through his hair.

"Thank you, my friend, for minding my back. It's a dangerous game, this healing." Tarkyn ignored the sorcerers standing on the outside of the shield. "We'll just sit here quietly until she comes round." He nodded over at the young man. "I think he's beginning to come to already. Not really what I would prefer. We have yet to repair his leg. It will hurt him a lot less if he's out to it." He shrugged and directed a smile at the father. "Still, you can't blame anxious parents for over-reacting. It was a remarkable leap of faith for them to let me anywhere near their children in the first place."

Behind him, the young woman moaned and fluttered her eyelids. Slowly she opened her eyes and gazed up at Tarkyn. A small frown of puzzlement appeared on her forehead and a smile played around the corners of her mouth. "I know you, don't I? But I've never met you. How strange."

"I came into you to repair you. I expect your mind knew I was there, even if you were unconscious."

She gazed around her. "Why are we within someone's shield? Are we under attack?"

Tarkyn gave a short laugh. "No. You are not under attack. I am. Someone did attack you and send an arrow into you earlier today but you are safe now."

In response to a nudge from Danton, Tarkyn turned around and discovered that the pendulum had swung once more and all the sorcerers outside the shield were now on their knees bowing in supplication and apology. Tarkyn sent Danton a dry look and stood up. He put his hands on his hips and made them wait a considerable time before saying, "Provided you do not intend to continue your attack on me, you may rise. However, should any of you lay hand on me, I will have you summarily executed. Do I make myself clear?"

With murmurs of, "Yes, Your Highness," the lord, his lady and their liegemen rose to their feet, shaken and contrite. It did not seem to occur to any of them to query how he might have them executed. His manner brooked no doubt and, as Danton thought to himself, Tarkyn actually meant it or he wouldn't have said it.

"You may remove your shield, Lord Danton. Thank you for your assistance. Now, I believe introductions are in order." Tarkyn paused then said, "I am Tarkyn Tamadil, Prince of Eskuzor and Guardian of these Forests." He indicated Danton. "My friend, Danton Patronell, Lord of Sachmore." He nodded permission for the lord to speak.

The lord and lady bowed very low. "Your Highness, I am Tolward, Lord of Middle Grasslands and this is Lady Juniper, my wife. My daughter, Edelweiss, you have already met, and Winguard, my son."

"And your liegemen?"

The lord barely masked his look of surprise as he went on to introduce all the members of his holding. Lastly, he came to the healer whom he introduced as Karlian.

"So, Karlian, do you have my herb for me?" asked Tarkyn.

Karlian curtsied and held out the prescribed herb. "Yes, my lord."

"Thank you." Tarkyn stood still for a moment and focused on the herb, sending the image to Summer Rain. Then he looked up and smiled. "This is the correct herb. It needs to be boiled until it softens. Then make a paste with it and place it on Edelweiss' wound. It will draw out the poison that was on the arrow tip."

"Certainly, my lord."

As the healer turned to leave, Tarkyn called her back, "Perhaps someone else can boil it up for you. I will need your assistance with young Winguard here."

Tarkyn knelt down next to the young man, ignoring the fact that every set of eyes in the room were trained on his every movement. He watched as the young man gradually became aware of his surroundings and then focused in on the prince.

Winguard frowned and said coldly, "I know who you are. You're the Rogue Prince. Stay away from me." He lifted a feeble hand to push the prince away. Tarkyn leaned away from him until his arm dropped and then leaned back in. Winguard shook his head to clear it but only succeeded in feeling more bewildered. "But you're not a rogue, are you? I know you. You've met with me inside me, haven't you?" He shook his head. "I don't understand. I must be going mad. How can that happen? And if you're who I met inside, you're nothing like you're supposed to be." Winguard looked around at the people gathered there, with a hint of panic in his eyes. "Father, say something. Tell me what's happening."

His father came and knelt next to Tarkyn. "Winguard, my son, this is indeed Prince Tarkyn, but as you have rightly said, he is nothing like his reputation." He shook his head. "I don't know how he did it, but he saved you from bleeding to death and saved your sister from the infection of the arrow."

"Winguard," Tarkyn waited until the young man's eyes had returned to rest on him. "I have a gift for healing. I take my strength inside you and work with you to repair yourself. So, you are right. I was inside you. You are not going mad."

"So, am I better now?"

Tarkyn shook his head regretfully. "No, I'm afraid not. Not yet. We must still repair your leg. And this will hurt. I can give you two choices: either stay awake and bite down hard on something or take a sedative of some kind to send you back to sleep while we put your leg back in place."

Winguard glanced uncertainly at his father. "I think I should stay awake."

Lord Tolward looked at Tarkyn in query, not rushing to accept his son's offer of courage. Tarkyn shook his head and said, "I don't know which is better. I have the power of healing, but I'm a little short on knowledge. Just let me confer with Karlian first. Karlian, what is your opinion? Asleep or awake? And do you have the right herbs or will I find them for you?"

Karlian frowned. "Your highness, you are a strange mixture of knowledge and ignorance if you don't mind me saying so. How can you be so sure about mountain sunrise herb if you don't know something as basic as this?"

Tarkyn glanced over at Danton. "Has something about me changed? Why are people so presumptuous around me these days?"

"I beg your pardon, Your Highness," said Karlian hastily. "I am sorry if I offended you."

"So you should be, Karlian. I may be a combination of skill and ignorance, but I am very clear where my limits are and I would not tell you something were so, unless I knew it to be true." The prince frowned at Karlian. "Now, is it too much to ask that you answer my question?"

"No, no, of course not, Your Highness. There would be a much better chance of putting the bone back in place if Winguard were asleep. I believe I can prepare something, but it will take some time."

Tarkyn screwed his face up as he considered. "No. We cannot stay too long. Just a minute. I'll think about it." He closed his eyes and conferred with Summer Rain who sent back the image of a slingshot. Tarkyn spluttered with laughter. He opened his eyes to find himself the focus of several disapproving looks. "Sorry. It's not a laughing matter, I know. But you will understand better when you see my solution." He stood up and walked to the corner of the room. "A word, Danton."

Danton followed him and Tarkyn whispered Summer Rain's suggestion. "Have you got one with you?" he asked more loudly.

Danton frowned. "Yes, but I'm not as good at this as some."

Tarkyn chortled quietly. "We could ask everyone to leave the room and then open the window."

"Tarkyn, this is getting silly. And Winguard would have to make sure he shut his eyes."

"Fine," said Tarkyn in a louder voice. "You go outside and see what you can find, while I talk to Winguard about what will happen."

Tarkyn returned to kneel on the floor next to the young man. "Winguard, I appreciate your offer of staying awake when you know it will hurt, but I think the accepted wisdom is that we will be able to move your broken leg around better if you are not awake to resist it. Now in a minute, when Danton returns, I will ask everyone to leave the room and you to close your eyes. Then we will put you to sleep using a little magic that will be quicker than waiting for Karlian's concoction. Are you happy with that? Then hopefully when you wake up next time, your leg will on its way to being mended."

Winguard nodded. "Thank you, Your Highness, for all you are doing for me."

Tarkyn looked at him for a moment wondering how he could turn it to his advantage, but in the end, he merely replied, "It is a pleasure. I am glad I happened to be here so that I could help."

Danton returned and ushered everyone out into the hallway. "Won't be long. Whatever you do, don't open this door until I say so. Clear?"

Although they were puzzled, the sorcerers agreed readily enough. Danton closed the door on them and put a chair up against it in case someone became curious. Then he crossed to the window and opened it. "Ready?" he asked.

Tarkyn gazed at Winguard. "Now close your eyes and keep them shut. Your life depends on it. Can you do that?"

As Winguard closed his eyes, Waterstone appeared at the window and shot him neatly in the head. In an instant, the woodman was gone and Danton crossed to the door and opened it.

"Right! Everyone back in who's coming in."

Tarkyn had taken the opportunity to confer with Summer Rain and now knew what to do to repair Winguard's leg. "Karlian, Winguard has been shot with a slingshot and will remain unconscious for perhaps twenty minutes." Tarkyn put up a hand to quell the murmurs that greeted this. "So, we need you and at least two strong men to manoeuvre Winguard's bone into place. Don't be afraid to pull hard. It will take some strength to pull against his muscles, but you will meet less resistance now that he is unconscious. I am going into him to make sure you have it lined up properly. When it is in place, I will raise my hand like this, and then I want you to hold it steady until I say to stop." He glanced around. "Everybody clear?"

Winguard's father and another man came over to assist while Danton remained aloof so that he could keep guard. When everyone was ready, Tarkyn placed his hand on Winguard's shoulder and followed his power into the young man's body. He flowed down into Winguard's leg and watched as the two ends of bone wove back and forth past each other until they finally came to rest more or less in place. Tarkyn struggled to reconnect quickly with his own body in time to hold his hand up. Once he had succeeded, he let go and returned to begin the repair work on Winguard's severed bone. The process of knitting such a large bone was slow and difficult so that, after what seemed a long time, he had only just created a tenuous link between the two edges. He transferred his attention to the stressed, battered muscles and at least made some notable progress with them. He sent a short zap of anger into the knitting bone to ward off infection and closed off the gash that had allowed the bone to poke through. He realised that they needed time to bind up Winguard's leg before he came round. So, then he withdrew and returned to his own body.

Tarkyn took a deep breath and opened his eyes. "You will need to hold his leg in place until someone splints it." He shook his head. "I'm sorry. I tried but I have only just begun the repair work. He will have to put up with a splint and crutches for a few weeks." Tarkyn smiled at his father. "But then he should be back to normal."

"My lord, I cannot thank you enough."

Tarkyn put up his hand. "I think you should thank Danton for his part in this. It was he who saw your need and strove to get help for you. It is not easy to disentangle me from the other demands on my time. And his shield saved your lives. If he had not prevented you from harming me, you would surely have died."

Lord Tolward hung his head. "I am truly sorry, my lord, that I doubted you, especially when I had given my guarantee to Danton that you would not be harmed."

Tarkyn looked away from him towards the window where his woodfolk friends waited for him. "I understand that it is hard to see your daughter in pain at the hands of someone with such a besmirched reputation. I wish I were not seen everywhere in such a terrible light, but" he shrugged, "unfortunately, there is not much I can do about it. I cannot return to court to defend myself. So, it is as it is."

The lord of the manor glanced at him. "Your Highness, will

you tell me what really happened. Then I will undertake to support you and tell people the truth. It is the least I can do after what you have done for me."

Tarkyn's face relaxed into a smile. "Thank you. That would be most kind of you. I accept your offer, provided you do not put yourself at risk on my behalf. All these people depend on you." Tarkyn told him the truth as he remembered it.

When he had finished, Tolward shook his head. "You have really been stitched up, haven't you, my lord?"

Tarkyn gave a short laugh. "I suppose I have but I am not entirely blameless in all this, you know."

Lord Tolward nodded and said gravely, "In civil war, no one is blameless."

"It is not civil war." Tarkyn frowned quizzically. "It is merely two older brothers getting rid of an irritating younger brother."

The older man looked at him. "You really don't know, do you?"

"I know my brothers fight cat and dog all the time and both want to be king, if that's what you're talking about."

"No. Everyone knows that," said Tolward impatiently. "And everyone is sick of it. There was a huge groundswell of support for you to usurp the throne. We were organised and ready to approach you with the idea but then came the Tournament and your exile, and everything we had planned fell apart." He paused and regarded the prince silently for a moment. "But having met you, I now know it would have fallen apart anyway. You would never have betrayed your brothers, would you?"

"No, not then," said Tarkyn quietly. "But then they hadn't betrayed me. I do not acknowledge fealty to anyone anymore. However, I have never had aspirations to be king and still haven't. Only dire circumstances would compel me to consider it." He nodded at his friend waiting patiently beside the lord's daughter and smiled wryly. "Lord Danton also has high expectations of me. He thinks I'm the hope for Eskuzor's future."

"And so you are, my lord. Now that I know that you have not turned rogue and have gauged your calibre, I would agree with him. Your brothers are wreaking havoc. My son and daughter were out herding cattle when a band of cattle thieves shot at them and drove Winguard's horse into a frenzied bolt. Eskuzor is rife with tragedies like this. You saved my son and daughter today from the neglect of your brothers. No one is looking after the populace anymore."

Tarkyn gazed at him. "You have given me food for thought." He paused. "Do you happen to know someone called Davorad, Lord of Stansbeck?"

Lord Tolward snorted with derision. "You mean Jarand's puppet?"

"Oh no! Is he? Are you aware of the gathering of vigilantes in the encampment north of here?"

"Of course. It is not far from here. Only a day's ride. There are strange doings in that encampment. I believe they were even using wolves at one stage, heavens know why. Now the wolves are gone, and it is rumoured that they intend to replace them with bloodhounds."

Tarkyn went still. "Bloodhounds, you say? Why would they do that?"

Lord Tolward shrugged. "They are hunting someone. It might be brigands. It might even be you."

Tarkyn persisted, "And were you aware that it is financed by Davorad?"

The lord looked disgusted. "No, I was not. In that case, we can safely assume that the whole thing is a ploy to show up Kosar's incompetence in maintaining law and order. It may even be a gathering of forces to mount a coup. Constantly there is talk of some secret army they are planning to enlist to their cause." He continued bitterly, "What it is not is a genuine effort to support the people of Eskuzor. We are left to protect ourselves against a mounting wave of outlaws."

"I only hope my brothers realise what is happening before it is too late. Lord Tolward, what you have told me concerns me greatly. I promise you I will think on it. But for now, I must go. I must reach the safety of the mountain foothills before dawn. Please do not attempt to follow me."

"But, Sire, how may we contact you? I don't want to lose you when I have only just found you."

Tarkyn thought hard. At last, he said, "Do you have parchment and a pen I can take with me? There is a tree halfway up the ridge behind your barn. I will leave instructions on how to contact me in that tree. I am travelling south beyond the mountains over the next few months but I will be back. Look for me in the spring."

As Tarkyn stood to go, Winguard stirred and opened his eyes. "Goodbye, Your Highness. And may your friends continue to protect you as well as they have so far."

"What are you talking about, Winguard?" asked his father, crossing to kneel beside his son. "His Highness is only with Lord Danton."

Tarkyn frowned fiercely. "Did you open your eyes?"

Winguard shook his head. "No, my lord. But when you flow through me, I learn things about you. And I know the people you travel with, whoever they are, are your staunch allies. You are lucky to have such friends."

Tarkyn smiled. "Yes, Winguard, I am. And now I must go. Look after yourselves. Make sure that poultice is put on your shoulder, Edelweiss. And you will have to endure crutches for a while, Winguard, but at least you will have a perfectly good leg at the end of it. Come on, Danton. We have a long way to travel before morning."

"Just a moment," said Lady Juniper, returning from the kitchen with a large bulging bag. "We have put together as much food as we could gather for your journey." She smiled in turn at Danton and Tarkyn. "I would thank you for the lives of my children."

As they headed towards the front door, all the farmhands were lined up to bid them farewell and to thank them both. Lord Tolward saw them off at the door. "Thank you, Danton, for your care and your courage. And thank you, my lord, words cannot express our debt to you."

"Goodbye. It was a pleasure to meet you all. Now go back to your children. They need you tonight."

Minutes later, the four of them collected Lapping Water and Summer Rain from the tree and headed back up the ridge.

18

It was an hour before dawn when they reached the forest on the other side of the grasslands. Already the sky had lightened and the first birds were beginning the dawn chorus. The clear sky had let out all the heat of the earth and the early morning air was frosty. People's speech came out in clouds of mist. Everyone was cold and tired and the children were whining with fatigue and hunger.

"This is where life in the forest is undesirable," murmured Danton to Tarkyn.

Tarkyn nodded tiredly. "Still, I wouldn't complain too much, if I were you. We'd have been here nearly two hours ago if we hadn't deviated to Tolward's house. And we could have rested more along the way."

Waterstone strode over, still full of energy. "Come on, you two. Not much further now. There are ready-built shelters just a little further into the woods. We can all collapse there and have a good sleep before the last leg of the journey to the mountainfolk." He peered closely at Tarkyn. "Is it just the dawn light or are you looking pallid? No, I think maybe you've

213

used up too much of your reserves. You might consider sleeping next to a tree or maybe sitting next to one while you have breakfast later. Hmm. I wonder if any of these shelters is big enough for you?" Waterstone went out of focus for a moment. "Some of the others will go ahead to check and build a quick extension if necessary. I think you need rest as soon as possible." The woodman looked across at Danton. "He's a great one for overcooking it, isn't he?"

Tarkyn rolled his eyes at being talked about, then said wryly, "Sometimes trying to respond to the expectations of two societies has its drawbacks."

"Your choice," chorused Waterstone and Danton simultaneously, each sniping at the need for the other's society to be considered.

Tarkyn raised his eyebrows. "I'll leave you two to fight that one out between yourselves. Let me know when you've reached a resolution." So saying, he surged on ahead, leaving the woodman and the sorcerer a little non-plussed in his wake.

"Hmm, something went a little awry there," mused Waterstone. "Are we putting too much pressure on him, do you think?"

Danton shook his head. "You haven't demanded anything of him that he hasn't demanded of himself. No. I think it was just the difficulty of responding to those injured kids while we were on such a tight timeline. No one was forcing him. It was just an unfortunate circumstance that we couldn't be caught in the grasslands." They walked on in silence for a few minutes before Danton said, "But I was listening to the conversation Tarkyn had with Lord Tolward, and I think the demands on Tarkyn are mounting from the sorcerers' side."

"What do you mean?"

"It began with what I said about him being the hope of Eskuzor. Then Stormaway reiterated it, and last night, Tolward told him that they had planned a coup against Kosar and Jarand and had wanted Tarkyn to support them."

Waterstone frowned. "When was this?"

"Just before Tarkyn was arrested." Danton smiled slightly. "He wouldn't have done it, of course. But he might now." Seeing Waterstone's look of consternation, Danton modified his statement. "Not right now. But maybe sometime in the future, if things don't improve. Tarkyn told the lord to look for him in the spring, after we come back from our journey. He gave no undertakings, though."

Waterstone cleared his throat, a sure sign that he was worried. "Tarkyn was right. We will have to reach a resolution, if this is true. How can he be all things to all men? He can't. Our societies are mutually exclusive." He glanced at Danton. "We don't want to lose him, you know. Not now. He is our forest guardian...and he's Tarkyn."

Danton shook his head. "Even though I would like to see him in his brothers' place for the sake of the sorcerers, for Tarkyn's sake I would not." He looked at the woodman. "I have known Tarkyn all his life. He has never been happier than he is now among you people. I would not like that to be taken away from him."

"Is that so? I'm pleased to hear that and pleased that you are prepared to weigh up his welfare against the needs of your sorcerers." Waterstone sent Danton a fleeting smile. "You know, I'm beginning to think that you and I really can work together for all of our causes. In fact, we will have to. Hmm. No wonder Tarkyn is touchy about it. We have some serious thinking to do over the next few months, haven't we?"

V

THE MOUNTAINFOLK

19

Several hours sleep, a good breakfast and an hour with his hand against an old mountain ash went a long way towards restoring Tarkyn's spirits. However, a certain aloofness remained in his dealings with Waterstone and Danton. Although they noticed it, they decided to give him some time and space before addressing it. As they approached the mountainfolk's firesite late in the afternoon, Tarkyn kept company with Rainstorm and North Wind, laughing and joking with the younger woodmen in an effort to forget the pressures of his many roles and the difficult impending meeting.

As it turned out, the mountainfolk were quite friendly when Tarkyn and his home guard arrived. A welcoming feast of spit-roasted venison and baked vegetables was cooking slowly over the fire, all ready to be accompanied by the best possible selection of woodfolk wines. The mountainfolk greeted their fellow woodfolk effusively and, although a little more reticent with the sorcerers, were courteous and friendly enough.

"Good evening, Your Highness," said a white-haired old man, bowing slightly. "My name is Dripping Rock. We have heard a lot about you and it is of great interest to us to finally meet you."

Tarkyn contained his surprise that the old man had bowed and used his title but, following his lead, inclined his head in return, saying, "Good evening. As you may know, my name is Tarkyn Tamadil, and this is my friend, Danton Patronell. It is a pleasure to meet the makers of the fine wines I have been drinking. From personal experience, I can tell you that they are among the best in the land."

"Thank you, my lord. I'm pleased they meet with your approval. I believe you have met my wife," he said, indicating a scrawny old woman who appeared from nowhere to join him.

Tarkyn's face lit up. "Dry Berry! I didn't realise you belonged to the mountainfolk. This is indeed a surprise. How is your wrist?"

"My wrist is well, thank you, young man. I hear you have been busy since we last met, and I am pleased to see Golden Toad and his family once more among us. I understand you had some difficulties in restoring their mindtalking ability. By all accounts, both you and the forest suffered. A little careless, don't you think, young man?"

"A lack of experience, ma'am. I will try not to let it happen again," replied Tarkyn with a smile in his voice. "To be honest, it was not an experience I would choose to repeat."

"So I understand. Would you like some wine?" She poured them each a glass of deep gold wine from a beautiful blue-glazed earthenware jug. Tarkyn noticed that Danton and the woodfolk from his party were being served wine from more mundane earthenware flagons. He frowned in passing at the unusual preferential treatment but then dismissed it from his mind.

Dry Berry smiled at him. "I am glad you saved Autumn Leaves, even if it did put you at odds with your overzealous minders." She patted him on the arm. "You're a good boy, Tarkyn. You take your role very seriously, don't you?"

"I do, but in that case, it was not my role but my friendship that made me rush to Autumn Leaves' aid."

"And I believe you laid down the law, as you see it, to those who protested at you putting yourself at risk," she added in a deceptively friendly tone of voice.

Tarkyn stilled. Although it was not being spoken of openly, he knew they were discussing the implications of the oath. "I wished to curtail their enthusiasm for molly-coddling me," he said carefully. "We must all take risks in life. Otherwise we do not live..." He paused, trying to find a way to say what he wanted to without mentioning the oath, "And without risk, we cannot give to others the full measure of ourselves."

Dry Berry gazed at him through narrowed eyes. "And did you really say to them that you could order them around or not as you choose, but that none of them had the right to tell you what to do?"

Tarkyn, never a great one for subterfuge, gave up on subtlety. "That is the reality of the oath...Besides, other than with my sorcerer brothers, that has always been the underlying premise of my dealings with people... It is just that I do not usually state it so baldly."

"You wouldn't need to, would you, if it is understood," the old woodwoman said dryly. She took a sip of wine but her eyes never left Tarkyn's face. Just as he was tensing himself for the next onslaught, she smiled disarmingly and said, "But I have also heard that despite what you could demand, you usually negotiate."

Some of the tension left Tarkyn's shoulders. "I try, Dry Berry. I do try. It does not come easily to me and I forget to consult sometimes, but I do try." He glanced away from her intense gaze, hoping to catch the eye of one of his woodfolk to back him up.

He frowned as he spotted first one and then another of his woodfolk sprawled out on the ground near the fire. Alarmed, he swept his gaze around the firesite as he realised that all of his home guard were lying asleep, interspersed between mountainfolk who were alert and watching his every move. There was no sign of Sparrow and the other children. Tarkyn's eyebrows snapped together in consternation as he turned to Dry Berry. "What have you done? Where are the children?"

"We have administered a mild sedative in your woodfolk's wine. The children are playing with our children in a shelter not far from here. There are some things they may not wish to see."

Tarkyn's stomach turned over, but he maintained a front of calm which, under the circumstances, was probably not the most sensible ploy. "Such as?"

Even as he spoke, his arms were dragged roughly behind him by two strong mountainmen and bound. Tarkyn glared at Dry Berry. "If you hurt a hair on their heads, you will rue the day you were born."

"I doubt it," she replied calmly. "You have sworn an oath to protect all woodfolk. That includes us. And from what I've seen of you, you don't break oaths."

Tarkyn shook his head, perplexed. "If you think that of me, why are you doing this?"

A hard fist came out of nowhere and caught him on his right cheek. Tarkyn gasped and staggered as the force of the blow knocked him sideways. Blood spurted from a cut beneath his eye.

Dry Berry frowned. "Carefully. Not so hard! Now, just once more, I think, just to make sure."

Another fist slammed into his stomach, making him double over in pain, retching and gasping for breath. Tarkyn's mind screamed outrage, and a cry for help reverberated silently across the treetops, over the cliff faces and up into the crags of the lowering mountains.

"Right, that's enough," said Dry Berry sharply.

But the two woodmen ignored her. Before Tarkyn could recover, an uppercut to his jaw jerked him upright again, followed by another fist slamming into his face from the other side. A haze of blood dripped from a cut on his eyebrow, obscuring his vision on one side.

In the background, he could hear the assembled mountainfolk jeering and heckling. Only Dry Berry's voice demanded that they stop, but heedless, another fist slammed into his side. Rough hands held him up to prevent him from collapsing to the ground as the two thugs alternated between holding him up and hitting him. The pummelling continued, with Dry Berry's voice becoming shriller but still ineffective in the background. Her pleas to get Dripping Rock or anyone else to intervene fell on deaf ears.

Suddenly, out of nowhere, an enormous mountain eagle swooped down on one assailant, raking his back with her talons. Shrieking with anger, she held on and belted him around his head with her wings. As the mountainman cowered with his hands over his head, the eagle launched herself off his back. He screamed in pain as her talons dug in. She flew straight at the other assailant who released his hold on Tarkyn and tried to duck out of her way. Tarkyn, unsupported, collapsed to kneel doubled up. The eagle dug her wicked hooked beak straight into the top of his assailant's head and flapped her black and gold wings around him. She landed on him, her talons digging deep holes into his shoulders, her great weight throwing him over backwards. Then she launched herself off him as he fell, and after flying in a tight circle, came back to land in front of Tarkyn. His two assailants scrambled out of range and stood shocked and battered off to one side. She stalked back and forth in front of the Forest Guardian, shrieking and flapping her wings to keep everyone at bay.

The watching mountainfolk were so stunned that no one made any move to attack either Tarkyn or the eagle. Before they could recover, a dozen more huge birds of prey flew in to join their comrade and landed in the surrounding trees, fixing their fearsome gazes on the mountainfolk below. Utter silence descended. Every now and then, one of the huge birds swooped across the clearing to make sure none of the mountainfolk approached Tarkyn. An attempt by Dry Berry to walk around him to untie his bonds was swiftly discouraged by both the eagle on the ground and another that swooped low over her, shrieking, and catching the end of her hair in its talon, dragging a chunk of it out by its roots.

With an enormous effort Tarkyn, in his own private world of pain, dragged himself up from his knees to stand upright before them. He backed up to lean against a gnarled oak, gasping for breath, unable to hold himself up unaided. All the time, as the mountain eagle patrolled up and down in front of him, the prince fought against the pain and reaction from the beating, holding himself rigidly upright against the oak and drawing a trickle of strength from it as he stood there.

After what felt like an eternity to Tarkyn but was actually only a few minutes, the effects of the drugged wine began to wear off and his home guard slowly opened their eyes to a very strange sight.

As they looked around them, they tuned into the shocked disbelief on the faces of the mountainfolk. Then their eyes were inevitable drawn to their forest guardian – hair matted and hanging half over his face, clothes torn, and face bruised and bloodied, standing with his back against the twisted oak. Stalking back and forth in front of him was a feisty mountain eagle standing almost as tall as Tarkyn's thigh, ruffling its feathers, occasionally flapping its wings and sweeping its golden glare across the surrounding woodfolk. In very short order, the home guard galvanized from drowsiness to outrage.

Waterstone and Rainstorm jumped up, staggering from the after-effects of the drug but propelled by a surge of adrenalin.

"Tarkyn, what have they done to you?" demanded Rainstorm, as he rushed forward.

Waterstone ran unhesitatingly around behind Tarkyn, ignoring the eagle who merely ruffled her feathers, jumped a little to one side and kept her sharp golden eyes trained on him. Waterstone tried to untie Tarkyn's hands, but Tarkyn had strained against the knots so much that the ropes had cut into his wrists and the knots were stuck fast. The woodman drew his knife and sliced through the rope.

"Thanks," croaked Tarkyn and cleared his throat.

Unable to focus clearly enough to heal himself, Tarkyn rubbed his wrists where the ropes had cut in. When his circulation was sufficiently restored, he pushed his matted hair back and wiped the blood out of his eyes with the heels of his hands. Only then was the full extent of the battering to his face revealed. There was a sharp intake of breath from his home guard and a groundswell of angry muttering spread among them.

Tarkyn drew a deep, shuddering breath and, with a visible effort, pulled himself together enough to speak. He raised his hand, and the woodfolk fell silent as he addressed Dry Berry.

"So, this is the honourable way mountainfolk treat their guests, is it?" asked Tarkyn scathingly, his voice starting as little more than a rasp. He glowered at Dry Berry. "You may not remember this, but I am your kin, just as they are." He turned his smouldering gaze upon the stunned mountainfolk. "You would not have allowed any woodfolk to be hurt as you have just hurt me. And don't give me any rubbish about testing out the oath. You could have done that without hurting me. Waterstone damaged the forest just by threatening me. Those two hit me brutally right from the start and none of you came forward to intervene. In fact, you cheered them on. Only Dry Berry tried to stop them." The woodfolk of Tarkyn's home guard glared at their kin in disgust. Tarkyn took another shaky breath. "I had thought woodfolk were above enjoying the spectacle of a public beating, but apparently not."

Feeling Tarkyn's anger, several of the birds of prey in the surrounding trees took off and swept low over the gathered woodfolk, coming to land protectively around him. A black hawk landed on his left shoulder and glowered down on Waterstone, causing Tarkyn to stagger under the unexpected weight. On the other side of Tarkyn, Rainstorm stood firm as fearsome birds of prey strutted around him. A large black kite, a whistling eagle and a tawny owl landed in the oak above Tarkyn's head, ruffled their feathers and proceeded to glare out across the crowd.

Dry Berry had recovered enough from the shock to find her voice. "Tarkyn, I did not realise those men wouldn't stop. I only wanted to check whether we were subject to your oath."

"I know that," said Tarkyn bleakly. "It is the only reason you will live." He pushed his hair back again and looked in distaste at the blood on his fingers. "I also know that you condoned two men, whose calibre you must have known, to have free rein with me. You may have tried to stop them but you allowed them to start." He took a laboured breath. "Raging Water told me that the forestals could not help their kindred to betray the oath because you are all one honourable people.

Clearly there are nuances in woodfolk society that I have yet to learn."

"We are not dishonourable," protested Dry Berry hotly. "We have not sworn your oath, so we were not sworn to protect you. We did not allow your woodfolk to betray their oath. That's why we drugged them. So they could not be held responsible. And we, *I* did not intend to hurt you so grievously. We only wanted to find out where we stood."

"So now you know," said Tarkyn slowly. "You are not under oath. Do I presume that your joy at finding yourselves to be free caused you to indulge in a frenzy of cruelty? Or did your attack on me spring from fellow feeling for the oathbound woodfolk who could not attack me themselves?" He glanced at Waterstone and Rainstorm, standing stalwartly on either side of him. "I'm sure they will be most grateful." Waterstone was relieved to hear sarcasm underlying this last remark.

Dry Berry looked at Dripping Rock and then went out of focus. For long minutes, there was an uneasy silence. Tarkyn stood silently before the mountainfolk, flanked by loyal woodfolk and guarded by deadly birds of prey, never more clearly the guardian of the forest. He could feel waves of fear, shame and anger sweeping back and forth among the mountainfolk that rose to a crescendo and then dissipated, although ripples of resentment still emanated from little hotspots here and there around the firesite.

Dry Berry took a deep breath and addressed Tarkyn, "When we last met, I observed that you could get exactly what you want without the oath, as your mastery over these powerful lords of the sky so clearly proves."

Even through the haze of pain, Tarkyn had time to be glad that the birds of prey could not understand what Dry Berry said. He knew that these fearsome birds would never call anyone their master.

Then Dripping Rock bowed obsequiously and spoke, "Your Highness, we are truly sorry that things have gone so badly awry and would make you reparation." He glanced fearfully at the predatory birds glaring down at them. "We yield before your power. You are indeed Lord of the Forest. And so, we have agreed that we will take your oath."

Tarkyn raised bloodied eyebrows and replied disdainfully, "I do not want your oath. I have never wanted it and I particularly do not want it now. I would not want the safety of our forest dependent on your honour and goodwill."

There was a shocked intake of breath. Shamefaced mountainfolk glanced surreptitiously at each other or lowered their eyes. None of them could meet the eyes of Tarkyn or the home guard.

But Tarkyn did not relent. "In my society, it is an honour to serve a prince. You do not deserve that honour. And for me, it is an honour to have such fine people as these," Tarkyn swept his hand around his home guard, "as my liegefolk. I would not feel honoured to have you as liegefolk."

Beside him, Waterstone let out a long slow breath of consternation.

Still, Tarkyn had not finished. "And you will certainly make me reparation but not on your terms, on mine. Danton," The name came out as a croak. He coughed and tried again, "Danton. Come here, please."

Danton steeled himself to approach the fearsome eagles. As he made his way up to stand beside Tarkyn, a buzz of conjecture spread through the crowd.

Tarkyn, Prince of Eskuzor, pushed himself away from the oak and stood tall. He sent out an imperious order for silence. The mountainfolk blanched, never having experienced his mind-images before. Even his own woodfolk were shocked.

Tarkyn waited until all eyes were turned to him. He

cleared his throat again before pronouncing, "The penalty for attacking a member of the Royal Family of Eskuzor is death." His voice became stronger. "On some occasions, clemency may be granted." Tarkyn let his amber gaze travel across his audience. "This is not one of those times."

To Danton by his side, Tarkyn pointed out his two assailants who had now moved around to the other side of the fire where they stood with their arms folded, clothing ripped and bloodied, but having recovered enough to be looking aggrieved by the eagle's treatment.

"Those two," was all he said.

Before anyone had time to react, two knives flicked fifty feet across the clearing and embedded themselves deep in the mountainmen's chests. The thugs died with looks of surprise on their faces. A horrified silence fell like a curtain on the gathered woodfolk. Then a babble of outrage and anger broke out around the firesite. In the branches above, the gathered birds of prey shifted their positions and ruffled their feathers uneasily.

On one side of Tarkyn, Waterstone was looking a little sick. On the other, Rainstorm looked even sicker. Danton stood impassively beside his liege, having always understood the reality of this edict.

"What right have you to impose punishment?" demanded Dripping Rock hotly. "You have just refused us. We are not under your oath."

"Whether you are subject to the oath or not, you are still subject to the laws of the land as I, in the forest, choose to enforce them."

"And what about *your* oath?" Dripping Rock persisted.

Tarkyn shrugged and said disdainfully, "I would hardly be protecting woodfolk if I allowed vermin like that to continue to pollute your firesite."

"How *dare* you impose your judgement on our kin?" raged the old mountainman.

The eagle at Tarkyn's feet turned its glare on Dripping Rock, stalked a few threatening steps in his direction and flapped its wings. The mountainman shuffled quickly back out of range.

Tarkyn drew himself up against protesting bruising. "I dare because I am a Prince of Eskuzor and Guardian of your Forest. I dare because everything I have seen of woodfolk until now leads me to believe that woodfolk do not condone such cruel, undisciplined behaviour. And I dare because, if you lose me, your guardian of the forest, you may lose everything you hold dear." He turned his gaze to Dry Berry. "Last time we met, you described me as a dangerous young man. You were right. I am dangerous and you have crossed me at your cost."

Dry Berry drew breath. "Tarkyn, we made a mistake, a bad mistake. I did not realise how deeply the resentment ran among some people. I should have remembered that most people here haven't met you before. It does make a difference to one's attitude, you know."

Tarkyn stared at her for a moment, appearing to consider her words. In actual fact, he was wondering how much longer he could stand up. He drew a painful breath. "I presume I have your undertaking that you will not mount another attack on me?"

Dry Berry and Dripping Rock nodded. "Of course, Your Highness," averred Dripping Rock. "We would not dream of trying to outface the lords of the air."

Tarkyn let his gaze rove around the other mountainfolk. "And you?"

There were hurried nods, several people throwing covert glances at the dead woodmen still lying on the other side of the firesite.

Tarkyn nodded over at the corpses and said casually, "You might like to remove those bodies before your food is cooked."

He turned his attention to the gathered birds of prey and sent them feelings of gratitude and release. In response, the huge birds launched themselves off the ground and from his shoulder, flapping their enormous wings ponderously as they rose. For a moment, Tarkyn was completely obscured by the tawny greys, blacks and browns of the great birds of prey and the distinctive gold and black of the mountain eagle. Then they glided low over the clearing, forcing woodfolk to duck before resettling themselves in overhanging branches around the clearing rather than flying away.

He raised his eyebrows in surprise, reopening a cut as he did so. "I see they do not yet feel ready to trust you with my safety. It is a grim day when the forest turns against woodfolk." He looked for his own woodfolk in the faces before him. "Autumn Leaves, is there a stream nearby? Could you come with us please? I need to clean up." As they moved forward, Tarkyn added, "Thunder Storm and Creaking Bough, would you please retrieve our children if the mountainfolk will be so good as to release them?"

Another angry muttering rose among his woodfolk.

Dry Berry held up her hand. "That is not quite fair. The children are playing together quite happily. We have merely ensured they were kept away while we...while we..." Her voice trailed away into an embarrassed silence.

"But without asking any of us," rumbled Thunder Storm, more forcefully than Tarkyn had ever seen him. "We want them back with us immediately."

"I will take you to them," said a woodwoman with a strangely echoey voice. "My name is Cavern."

"And make sure you have cleared away your two

henchmen before we get back," rumbled Thunder Storm peremptorily.

It occurred to Tarkyn that the status of the home guard had just risen with his refusal to accept the oath of the Mountainfolk. Tarkyn ran his hand through his hair and grimaced when he brought it back down, again sticky with blood.

"I think you had better come with us too, Summer Rain, if you don't mind," he said calmly as he turned to follow Autumn Leaves out of the clearing and towards the nearby stream.

20

As soon as they were out of sight of the mountainfolk, Tarkyn asked tightly, "Any lookouts?"

"Not in sight of here," reported Autumn Leaves after a quick scan of the surrounding trees.

"Good." Tarkyn stopped in his tracks. "Waterstone, Danton, your shoulders, if you will."

As Tarkyn allowed himself to sag onto their shoulders, they realised with shock that his whole body was trembling and he was struggling to support his own weight. It was borne upon them the degree of determination that it had taken for him to stand upright for so long.

"Oh, Tarkyn, you poor bugger," said Waterstone sympathetically. "Do you want to rest or get down to the stream?"

"How far is it?"

"Not far. Another forty yards or so. It's just around the bend in the path, past those mountain ashes," replied Waterstone calmly, although his chest felt tight with concern.

"Right then. Let's get there quickly before you both collapse under my weight."

Danton and Waterstone virtually carried Tarkyn the rest of the way to the stream. When they reached the bank of the stream, they lowered him carefully down onto the ground with his back up against a mossy boulder. Beside him, the water tumbled down a steep gully over great boulders, gathering in small deep pools in the shadows of the rocks.

Very little was said over the next ten minutes while Summer Rain removed Tarkyn's shirt and attended to the gashes and bruises that covered his upper body and face, but there were some narrowed eyes and thinned lips among his onlookers. Rainstorm placed a cup under the falling water and brought it to Tarkyn, but his hands were shaking so badly that Rainstorm had to hold it for him while he drank.

Tarkyn lay with his eyes closed while Summer Rain did what she could. When she had finished, she said, "There. That's the best I can do for now. Your wounds have all been cleaned and there are healing and disinfecting herbs on all your abrasions. The bleeding has stopped. Nothing is broken, but you will be very sore for the next few days unless you heal yourself."

Tarkyn opened his eyes and gave a careful smile, wincing as the movement of his mouth pulled on his cut lip. "Thanks. I will, in time. I couldn't concentrate on healing myself while I was still in danger. And I have just tried again but I'm too churned up at the moment. I can't stop thinking about the attack long enough to gather my forces. Maybe later tonight, after we have eaten and settled down; I may be able to concentrate then."

Waterstone squatted down next to him and asked, "So, how did you get yourself into the situation with your hands tied behind your back? Did you allow them to do it as you did with the forestals?"

"No, my friend. I was not planning any heroics this time. They grabbed me just as I noticed that you people had been drugged. I think Dry Berry kept me talking to her so that I wouldn't notice you getting drowsy until it was too late." He couldn't disguise the note of bitterness that had entered his voice. He ran a hand dispiritedly through his hair, and once more it came away sticky. He looked at it in disgust. "Hmm, I can't be having that. Any of these pools big enough to bathe in?"

"You'll die of shock if you go into one of those pools, Prince," said Rainstorm firmly. "That water is melted ice."

Despite his cut lip, Tarkyn achieved an evil grin. "I'm sure we'll manage, Rainstorm."

Rainstorm rolled his eyes. "Someone tell him. It's way too cold."

"I don't know," replied Summer Rain thoughtfully. "Now he's over the shock, it may be helpful. Reduce bruising and stimulate his circulation."

Everyone stared incredulously at the healer, thinking that at last she had cracked a joke. But then they realised she was calmly serious. All heads looked back to Rainstorm.

"Probably be good for you too, Rainstorm," said Danton with a perfectly straight face.

Tarkyn was smiling. "Come on, Rainstorm. Help me over to one of those dark, inviting pools. I can't go around with hair matted with blood. It will start to stink soon, if nothing else. You'll love it once you're in."

It took more than Rainstorm's effort to get Tarkyn up and over the slippery wet rocks and into a dark pool. The pool looked bottomless, but as it turned out, the water was only slightly over waist height.

As Tarkyn was assisted to lower himself into the water, he drew in a long sharp breath. "Whoa, this is so cold it hurts! I don't know which is worse; getting beaten up or this." As they let him go, he drew in a breath and dropped under the water. A second later, he came up gasping, "Oh no. Definitely this. Come on, Rainstorm. You have to come in because I can't move my arms well enough at the moment to clean my hair."

"I can do it from the side," Rainstorm replied flatly.

Tarkyn promptly moved into the centre of the pool. Suddenly there was a splash from the side and Autumn Leaves came up gasping next to Tarkyn.

Tarkyn looked at him in astonishment. "Good heavens, Autumn Leaves. I didn't realise the depths of your heroism."

The big woodman smiled self-deprecatingly. "I owe you one. Besides, maybe I have a bit more covering to keep me warm."

Tarkyn gave a sudden shudder. "Nothing will keep you warm in this."

"Right. That's it. I'm in," said Rainstorm, jumping off the other edge. As soon as his head emerged, he yelled, "Aagh! Tarkyn, you're mad. Why did I let you talk me into this? It's horrendous."

Tarkyn laughed. "I didn't talk you into it. You just didn't want to be shown up by Autumn Leaves."

"Ugh." He shivered and gave a cheeky grin. "You're right. Bad for the image, you know."

It was probably the world's quickest hair wash, but Tarkyn emerged feeling clean and revitalised. As the three of them sat shivering on the grass, with towels wrapped around them, a constrained silence fell on the group.

Finally, Tarkyn said, "Executions aren't common among woodfolk, are they?" He looked around and saw solemn head shakes all around him.

Autumn Leaves cleared his throat. "Actually, I have never known of one before. To be honest, it was really quite shocking. I felt sick for quite a while afterwards."

"You felt sick?" said Rainstorm derisively. "That could have been me. I've hit Tarkyn. I nearly vomited on the spot."

Waterstone kept his own council but his face had become tight and shuttered.

"I knew you people would struggle with it," said Tarkyn. "That's why I asked Danton to do it."

"It was wise not to put the forest at risk." Waterstone's small comment spoke volumes.

Tarkyn looked at him. "One of those times when your principles would be in conflict with the welfare of the forest?"

Waterstone shrugged. "I don't know, to be honest. I felt pretty murderous about the whole thing. If you'd asked, I might have said yes, but I have never had to follow an order to kill. It would feel like handing over the key to my conscience."

"I'll remember that," said Tarkyn thoughtfully. "Actually, I suppose I already knew that, which is why I left you out of it and directed Danton to do it."

"But, Danton, don't you have any qualms about following an order like that?" asked Waterstone.

Danton shook his head decisively. "No, none." He would have said more but after glancing around the woodfolk's faces, he subsided.

"Go on," urged Waterstone. "Say what you were going to say."

Danton shrugged. "I know you find me amusing, but I would always do anything for Tarkyn without question. I willingly entrust him with my conscience." He gave a little smile. "Actually, I would have struggled more if he had *forbidden* me to kill those men."

Autumn Leaves frowned at Danton. "You know, Danton,

I've formed the wrong impression about you. I thought you weren't a good marksman."

Danton looked surprised. "I have never said that."

"Well, why did you get Waterstone to fire the slingshot at that young sorcerer yesterday if you could have done it yourself?"

Danton smiled as realisation dawned. "Oh, I could easily have hit him, but not without killing him. I don't have your amazing delicacy of touch that allows you to judge the power of your shot so well that you can knock someone out without killing them. No," he added casually, "I'm always deadly accurate in every sense of the word."

There was a short silence as everyone digested this information and re-adjusted their views about Danton.

Tarkyn looked in some amusement at the thoughtful woodfolk. "I did explain to you that Danton was an elite guard. He just hasn't had much need until now to use his skills."

Danton frowned. "I don't see why you found the execution so upsetting. Any one of you would have defended Tarkyn if they had still been attacking him when we came round from the drugged wine."

Autumn Leaves waved a hand from under his towel. "Oh, that's different. Then it's in the heat of the moment. I would have killed them without a second thought if I had caught them attacking Tarkyn." He paused as he thought about it. "I would kill to keep someone safe or to protect the woodfolk if someone saw us, but I couldn't do it to protect someone's consequence." He shot an apologetic glance at Tarkyn then dropped his eyes.

After an uncomfortable silence, Tarkyn said gently, "Autumn Leaves, I thank you for your honesty. I would rather we talked about it than have it hanging between us all." He drew his damp towel around himself and shivered. "It is partly about consequence but it is more about protection. Anyone who finds themselves as a ruler of men will face more attacks than other people."

"Unless of course you have an egalitarian society like ours," put in Waterstone dampeningly, "in which case the whole argument should be redundant."

"But obviously, it is not," countered Tarkyn, "with me among you." He shrugged. "I could argue that I, as your forest guardian, am worth protecting unequivocally. But in the end, I think that I would be trying to argue something that is actually a matter of belief. Danton and I, in fact all sorcerers, have grown up with the belief that the Royal Family is sacrosanct. Any attack on a member of the Royal Family is regarded as treason." Finding himself surrounded by closed faces on the four woodfolk, the prince threw his hands up, sending his towel flying off his shoulders. "You see? How can you understand? You don't even have any form of government to commit treason against." Tarkyn dragged his towel back up and pulled it around himself. "Waterstone is probably right. My arguments don't hold water in your society." He smiled wryly. "And you are probably right, Autumn Leaves. It is more about consequence than anything else."

"So why didn't you have Waterstone and Rainstorm summarily executed then?" asked Autumn Leaves, keeping his voice carefully neutral.

"Don't, Autumn Leaves," said Tarkyn gently. "I wouldn't do that to people who have treated me with respect and kindness – not when it's only a matter of a temper outburst. I am not as extreme in my interpretation of the law as I could be. I don't need to be, when no one among you has ever been deliberately cruel. And I don't feel that my consequence is threatened by any of you. Danton may disagree with that...?"

Tarkyn threw a glance at Danton, who gave a minute shake

of his head. "No, Tarkyn. I did think that, but I don't any longer. At least, not in woodfolk terms."

"You all respect me, and I respect you. But, even allowing for different cultures, those dead men back there showed utter contempt for me and subjected me to systematic brutality." He shrugged. "I cannot allow that. Whether you agree with me or not, I simply cannot, and will not, countenance that. Rainstorm and Waterstone have always respected me, maybe not always as a prince, but always as a person. Both of them only attacked me briefly and in anger, not in cold-blooded premeditation. I can dint my expectations enough to allow for that. But, as a prince of the realm, I can't allow the deliberate violation of my person to go unpunished."

"They stepped over one of your boundaries, didn't they, Prince?" said Rainstorm, with some satisfaction.

"They did more than step over it, Rainstorm. They threw themselves over, well beyond any hope of recovery." Tarkyn looked around them. "But surely they crossed over your boundaries too? What would you have done if they had attacked Waterstone, for instance, as they attacked me? It wasn't a fight, you know. They bound my hands behind me, then held me between them and took turns in belting me savagely."

Rainstorm's eyes narrowed. "So how many times did they hit you?"

Tarkyn gave a short laugh. "Too many times." Seeing no change in Rainstorm's intensity, Tarkyn sighed and gave in, "I don't know. I lost count. Maybe sixteen, twenty times, before the eagle arrived and fought them off. It was pretty dreadful, to be honest."

Sickened glances passed between the four woodfolk before Waterstone said slowly, "I concede your point, Tarkyn. You are more of a target than any of us. Maybe you did need to react with such force." He shook his head. "Nothing like this has ever happened before. No one has ever been so brutal, and woodfolk have never stood by and allowed someone to be attacked like that. Even if a fight has broken out, bystanders will only let it go so far before intervening."

"I personally think they deserved to be killed," said Summer Rain, much to everyone's surprise. She spread her hands. "What else could you do with them? To have acted like that, they represent a threat to everyone. If you exiled them, what guarantee would you have that they wouldn't come back and prey on the outskirts of our forest? I would say the same thing whether it were Tarkyn or Rainstorm. We have never had to deal with brutality like that." She nodded her head at the blond sorcerer, "And I would like to thank you for doing our dirty work for us."

Danton gave a tight smile and nodded in response. He quelled his automatic response to say that it had been a pleasure, realising the possible misinterpretation.

Tarkyn broke in at this point, "I would have to admit that when I told Danton to kill them, my decision was not wholly objective. I was outraged and vengeful; however I may have appeared on the outside."

Finally, Waterstone eased up and gave a small smile. "I think just a *little* of your outrage made its way to the surface in your confrontation with the mountainfolk," he said ironically. "I would not say that you came across as calm and objective. But, to be frank, I think we would all have had concerns for your sanity if you had."

After a short companionable silence, Tarkyn asked, "I know we don't share the same values over this, but are you all right with me again?"

"Tarkyn, after what has happened to you, you shouldn't have to be talking us into supporting you. I think the question should be, 'Are you all right with us?'" replied Autumn Leaves caustically. "I feel that we've let you down badly. We should have been much more on our guard than we were."

Tarkyn gave a wry smile. "True. Probably not the best idea for absolutely everyone to start drinking as soon as we arrived, given that we were worried about their reactions." He shrugged. "Still, it's easy to be wise with hindsight, isn't it? I guess we'll know better next time."

His liegemen all noticed that he said 'we' not 'you.'

"Come on," said Summer Rain bracingly. "We have sat here freezing for long enough. These three are going to catch a chill if we stay here much longer. We must go back to the firesite.

As they helped Tarkyn to his feet, Autumn Leaves asked, "So, will you go back to their firesite and pretend all is well with you? What happened to your dislike of creating false impressions?"

Tarkyn subjected the woodman to a long stare as he considered his response. "Maybe we all have limits to our honesty. Once I had managed to drag myself back upright, I was determined to remain standing. I'm afraid my pride wouldn't allow me to give in to them and fall apart before their eyes. I think I was true to myself and honest in showing them who I really am. All I hid was my body's reaction, not the reaction of my spirit."

Autumn Leaves' face broke into a broad smile. "Great answer! I wish I could think of things like that to say."

Tarkyn gave a slight smile and shook his head. "Autumn Leaves, where would I be without you to keep me honest? Having set myself a standard for honesty that you seem to find unacceptably high, I can see that you have now appointed yourself as watchdog to ensure I meet it."

"I just keep checking that you're not a hypocrite. It's hard to believe that anyone can have such implacably high standards."

Tarkyn shook his head, smiling. "So, do I have your permission to put on a brave front or should I wince at every twinge?"

"Oh no. Be brave," said Autumn Leaves without hesitation. His eyes twinkled. "That is, after all, the true reflection of your spirit."

Tarkyn glanced at Autumn Leaves, then looked away hunching his towel up around his shoulders. "Hmph."

Waterstone watched him with some amusement. "You don't know what to say, do you?"

"Can't a man be a little discomforted without having a commentary on it?" asked Tarkyn in some exasperation.

"I'll take that as a no, then, will I?" The woodman smiled across at Danton, his new ally. "How come this prince of yours can live a lifetime surrounded by flattery then be left speechless by a throwaway line from Autumn Leaves?"

Tarkyn gave a short laugh. "You know perfectly well I could never trust a word that was said to me at court. It was everybody's daily business to flatter me. It didn't mean anything; it was just a big game."

Danton looked steadily at the prince before saying, "Actually, some people meant what they said. Just as some people were trustworthy. I am eternally grateful to Waterstone for breaking through your mistrust but a little saddened that during all those years I have been with you, I was unable to do so myself. And I do beg your pardon for wasting your time with comments I have made. Clearly they meant more to me than they did to you." He gave a slight bow. "Excuse me, I think I'll go on ahead and make sure there is somewhere comfortable for you to sit."

Danton turned on his heel and walked off around the bend.

The others all looked at each other. Tarkyn gave his head a little shake. "Unless I mistake the case, Danton is seriously angry with me. Why is it that just when you need someone's support, you manage to offend them?" He frowned. "Rainstorm. No, Summer Rain. Go with him. He may need protection."

"I can do that," protested Rainstorm.

"Very well. Both of you go. We'll follow on behind you."

Just before they emerged into the clearing, Waterstone went out of focus to check on the state of play around the firesite. Then he reported, "Resentment is running high and the mood is beginning to turn ugly. I'm not surprised, after the way you summarily dismissed their efforts at reconciliation. And the executions have given them an excuse to turn their shame into anger. Ancient Oak said to tell you to remember the conversation in the oak tree." Waterstone frowned quizzically. "I don't know whether that means anything to you?"

Tarkyn gave a grunt of laughter. "Yes. He's warning me not to be too arrogant. Perhaps the time has come to be more conciliatory." The prince shrugged. "After all, we don't want a rift among woodfolk, do we?"

"Not any more than we already have," replied Waterstone tightly.

"This is going to be hard," said Autumn Leaves, shaking his head. He took a deep breath and gave Tarkyn a couple of hearty pats on the back. "Come on then, show them what you're made of. We're with you all the way."

Tarkyn flicked him a grateful smile, before squaring his shoulders and walking back into the clearing.

21

As soon as they appeared, Sparrow came running up to greet them. "Tarkyn, are you all right? Everyone's talking about you being hurt. And there are huge eagles everywhere in the trees here. Someone said they're mad at the mountainfolk for hurting you. They look pretty scary. I hope they're not mad at us too." She peered up at him. "Your face has patches of red and purple on it. Are they bruises? That's not very nice of them, is it?"

Tarkyn grinned and, despite his protesting muscles, bent down to pick up the chattering little girl onto his hip.

"Ooh," he groaned quietly, "Waterstone, can you please hand me up your daughter? I don't think I can lift her."

As he delivered Sparrow, Waterstone whispered into her ear, "Careful, young lady. Tarkyn is a bit sore."

Sparrow put her arms around Tarkyn's neck and gave him a kiss on the cheek. "There. That will make it better."

Tarkyn smiled at her. "I think it will. Thanks, Sparrow. I just needed a hug about now."

She gave him a big squeeze that hurt him but was worth it.

Then she leant away from him so she could study him. "Tarkyn, you look terrible. Purple everywhere and nasty cuts. Worse than green, even. Can't you fix yourself?"

"I will soon. I promise. You won't have to put up with me looking like this for long," he said lightly.

Then Sparrow burrowed her head against his neck and whispered in his ear, "Tarkyn, I'm so sorry they hurt you. But *we* love you."

He gave her a big squeeze. "Thanks, Sparrow. I love you too." After a moment he asked, "Shall we find somewhere to sit and have some food? I'm starving."

As she nodded, Tarkyn reflected that the great thing about children was the way the rest of the world seemed to disappear for the time you were talking to them. He let his awareness pan back out to include all the people gathered around the firesite. They were all watching him, either surreptitiously or directly. The air was thick with a strange mixture of resentment, shame, and anger. Danton had made sure there was somewhere for him to sit but was nowhere to be seen. Rainstorm and Summer Rain were also missing. Giving a mental shrug, Tarkyn swung Sparrow down and sat with his back to an enormous log. Sparrow sat snuggled up next to him, with her father on the other side of her and Autumn Leaves on the other side of the prince.

With a sigh, Tarkyn saw that everyone was waiting for him to speak. He realised that nothing could be resolved until he had at least opened the informal proceedings. He looked longingly at the roasted meat and vegetables that were piled in large dishes next to the fire waiting to be served out but knew they would have to wait.

Tarkyn sent his gaze around the gathered woodfolk. "I came here in friendship but expecting you to be resentful. From our own particular points of view we have each offended against the other. You have orchestrated a brutal attack on me. I have killed two of your fellow woodmen. It was the worst of beginnings for our association with each other. We cannot change that. All we can change is the effect that it has on our future relationship." He paused. "The last thing I expected was that you would offer to swear the oath. And the last thing I meant to do was to create a rift between woodfolk."

He took a deep breath. "I am not such a hypocrite that I can suddenly turn around and say that I know I can trust you. I have only known most of you mountainfolk for a couple of hours, and I have very little on which to base my trust. Waterstone can tell you that my trust is hard won at the best of times." He paused. "Except for this one incident which is open to interpretation, you may well be honourable people. All other woodfolk I have met are. But even if I were convinced that you were honourable, I still would not want you to swear that sorcerous oath."

At this, some quiet murmurs broke out within his audience. He held up his hand and waited until they were listening again. "I have always said that this oath with its sorcerous consequence for non-compliance is an insult to the integrity of woodfolk. I would not accept it from you or anyone else. If I had the choice, I would release all woodfolk from its sting. If you really wish to align yourself with me, you may devise an oath of your own making that depends only on your honour. Then time will show us the calibre of your integrity."

Before the murmurings grew too high in volume, Tarkyn added apologetically, "I know it is not my place as your guest to ask, but do you think we could eat while we talk?"

This mundane request released a ripple of quiet laughter through the crowd and went a long way towards clearing the air of constraint. Some of the mountainfolk immediately came forward and set about serving out plates of roasted venison and vegetables.

As Tarkyn began to eat, he realised that it was going to be a painful process. Every time his jaw moved, it hurt and he had to manoeuvre food carefully into his mouth between split lips.

Autumn Leaves glanced at him and commented, "I think your brave face is slipping. You keep wincing as you chew."

Tarkyn grimaced. "There's a particular spot that I hit from time to time that is sorer than the rest. I think the tooth might be a bit loose." He looked down at his plate. "How am I supposed to bite into that great wad of venison? My jaw is too sore."

"I thought you weren't eating meat anymore?" queried Waterstone. "Weren't you worried about chatting with it one minute and eating it the next?"

Tarkyn glanced up into the trees at his bevy of feathered retainers. "My ongoing association with our predatory friends up there has changed my view again. They think nothing of associating with their fellow creatures if they happen to find themselves in the same tree, provided they're not hungry. Then they'll eat them as quick as look at them, when they are." He shrugged. "To be honest, they have been quite derisory about my efforts to be vegetarian."

"Do you communicate with them all the time?"

"Often enough. Mind you, they are so strong-minded, these birds of prey, that it only takes one wave of derision to make me start questioning myself." Tarkyn flopped his piece of venison back down on his plate in disgust. "I think I'll be forced to be vegetarian tonight. I can't bite into that. And I can't cut it up because my hands are still too stiff from those blasted ropes."

"Here," said Autumn Leaves. "Swap plates. I'll cut yours up into little bits then swap back. How's that?"

Tarkyn scowled ungraciously. "Embarrassing. But I'm so hungry I will accept. Just try to be subtle about it."

"Certainly, Your Highness," said Autumn Leaves obsequiously.

Tarkyn eyed him belligerently for a moment. "Sorry," he said shortly.

Waterstone chortled and said quietly to Sparrow, "I think your Uncle Tarkyn is in a bad mood. What do you think?"

For an answer, Sparrow tugged on Tarkyn's sleeve and when she had his attention said, "Don't worry. It won't be for long. Then you can go back to eating like a grown up again."

Splutters of laughter from both sides greeted this remark. Tarkyn blinked at her for a moment, bemused. Gradually, a slow smile spread across his face. "Thanks for that, Sparrow." He looked from one to the other of the laughing woodmen and shook his head smiling. "So much for being subtle. Now everyone's looking at us wondering what the joke is."

Waterstone reached past Sparrow and patted him on the shoulder. "Well, if it's any consolation, I'm sure most of them were watching you anyway."

"True. I don't know why I try to delude myself into thinking I can get away with anything unnoticed."

As Autumn Leaves handed his plate back to him, Dry Berry stomped defiantly over and plopped herself cross-legged in their circle with her plate on her lap. "Young man," she said sharply, "I will not stay here if you would rather I didn't, but if at all possible, I would like to repair our friendship."

Tarkyn considered her silently for a long minute while he nibbled gingerly at a small piece of venison. Finally, he said, "Dry Berry, I would value your friendship but I need one undertaking from you before I can speak easily with you again."

Dry Berry's eyes narrowed. "What is that?"

"That you will never again converse with me for the sole

purpose of distracting my attention. That, more than anything, has undermined my faith in you."

Dry Berry glanced with some discomfort at the other two listening in. Then she brought her green eyes resolutely back to meet Tarkyn's. "I beg your pardon for that, Tarkyn. It was ill done. I do have a genuine interest in you and your doings and I should not have used that to manipulate you. You have my word that it will not happen again." She put her head a little to one side and gave a slight cackle. "Besides, I can't imagine it would work again. No matter what undertaking I give you, I suspect you will be more on your guard with me in the foreseeable future."

"Maybe. Maybe not. Now that you have made your test, there may be no more reason to be disingenuous with me. I hope not, anyway." He nibbled his way through another piece of meat before asking conversationally, "So, do you mountainfolk still want to swear an oath to me?"

Dry Berry frowned. "I thought you said at the ceremony when you became a woodman that you didn't want an oath from us. And you obviously still feel the same way, perhaps even more so."

Tarkyn shook his head. "No. I said I had no intention of *asking* you to swear an oath. But today you offered me your oath. Because I was hurting and angry, I rejected your offer and, by doing so, opened up a rift among the woodfolk." He shrugged. "And so to repair the unity of the woodfolk, I think it is now important that I accept an oath from you. Not the sorcerous one, but an oath, nevertheless."

The surrounding mountainfolk had broken off their own discussions and were now blatantly listening into the conversation between Dry Berry and the Forest Guardian.

Autumn Leaves leaned forward. "What you may not have realised, Dry Berry, is that you cannot alienate Tarkyn without alienating all of us. Regardless of the oath, he is one of us and a member of one of our families. If you insult him, you insult us."

"We all felt grievously offended by your welcome," said Waterstone sternly. "Suffice it to say that unless you people swear some sort of undertaking towards Tarkyn so that we can be sure he is safe and treated with the respect he deserves, at least as a fellow woodman, you will not see any of us again."

Murmurs of consternation rose among the mountainfolk then fell into the silence of mindtalking. While they conferred, Tarkyn leant over and asked Autumn Leaves, "Where are Danton, Rainstorm and Summer Rain?"

Autumn Leaves sent out a query. When he received nothing in return, he tried again. His eyes widened in alarm. "Rainstorm and Summer Rain aren't answering. Waterstone, you try."

Tarkyn didn't wait. He sent an image up to the birds of prey lowering in the trees above. Immediately, six of them took off to scour the surrounding woodlands while two more swooped over the mountainfolk, shrieking just above their heads, their six-foot wingspans blotting out the sky. Before they realised what was happening, the mountainfolk had been effectively herded to the other side of the clearing by two aggressive eagles. Without hesitation, Tarkyn sent a peremptory mind image, ordering his home guard to gather around him. As they arrived, Tarkyn struggled to his feet and raised a translucent bronze dome around his woodfolk and himself.

Ignoring all this activity, Waterstone shook his head. "No. No response. That means they are either unconscious or dead. Blast it! We should have looked after Danton better. I dread to think what they've done to him."

"The eagles and hawks can't see them anywhere," reported Tarkyn.

"They must be out of sight somewhere then, possibly in a shelter or a cave." Waterstone tilted his head to one side. "How are you with bats?"

Tarkyn considered briefly. "I've never tried but I can't imagine I would do very well. Bats use sound not vision, don't they? And I can't send or receive sound."

"No. Bats can see. They just use sound to augment their vision."

"Oh. In that case, which way do the caves lie? I need to know where to direct my mind." Once Tarkyn had the direction clear, he placed his hand on Waterstone's shoulder to steady himself. "This could be quite tricky, maintaining the shield and finding a bat at the same time." He took a deep breath, focused on the shield then carefully placed its maintenance to one side in his mind. Then he sent his mind out towards the mountains in the direction of the caves. He let himself wander into a large cavern before homing in on a little mind, high up on the ceiling. He nudged it and gave it a picture of Danton and the two woodmen. There was a response of willingness, and suddenly, Tarkyn's mind was flitting through inky blackness. He could feel the movement but couldn't see more than vague shadows in the darkness. He felt the cool of the caves and then the chilling breeze as the bat flew out into the open air. For a minute or two, the light dazzled him, and when he felt himself swoop inside out of the breeze, he had no idea where the bat was. While the bat's eyes adjusted to the dim lighting, it used its sonar to discern its surroundings. It was already transmitting excitement and satisfaction even as Tarkyn began to make out three indistinct heaps in the dimness of a shelter. Tarkyn spoke carefully, trying to stay in touch with the bat. "I think it may have found them. They look very still, though. I can't tell whether they are dead or alive... and I don't know where they are."

Waterstone made a slight movement, but before he could say anything, Tarkyn rushed on, "It is not because of my navigational skills... at least not only that. It's because the bat carried on regardless, while its eyes adjusted to changes in light but during those times I couldn't see what was happening."

Waterstone smiled to himself at Tarkyn's defensiveness but responded seriously, "Ask the bat to fly out into the sunlight again but to fly in circles until your eyes adjust. Then, when you have had a clear view of where our friends are being kept, ask it to come here."

Following Waterstone's suggestion, Tarkyn was able to get an image of a shelter and its location as the bat flitted up, into and around the surrounding trees before returning to him. Tarkyn conveyed his thanks to the little creature as it swept over his head with a series of high pitched squeaks and up into the deep shade of a nearby beech tree.

Tarkyn glanced across at the mountainfolk before addressing his own woodfolk, gathered within the dome of his translucent bronze shield. "They're in a shelter, not far away. How are we going to do this? How can woodfolk outwit woodfolk? The lookouts will see any of you who tries to sneak up on the shelter. Quickly! What can we do?"

The woodfolk looked at each other and went out of focus. After a very short conference, they returned their focus to Tarkyn.

"I'm afraid you will have to do it, Tarkyn," said Thunder Storm. "If you don't mind," he added hastily.

"Have to do what?"

"You will have to negotiate with the mountainfolk, using your eagles, your magic and us, as backup." Thunder Storm shrugged. "The only safe way is for you to hold them all to ransom, so to speak."

Tarkyn frowned fiercely. For a moment, Thunder Storm

thought he was going to have to endure another tongue-lashing, but Tarkyn wasn't even thinking about him. He nodded abruptly. "Agreed. Let's move closer to them. I just have to get the order right. I keep the shield up all the time in case lookouts in the trees try to fire on us, use the *Shturrum* spell to immobilise them, then call off the eagles so that we can hear ourselves speak."

Once they were close enough, Tarkyn focused on his shield, placed it firmly in the corner of his mind and then waved his hand, incanting, "*Shturrum!*" With the mountainfolk now motionless before him, he requested the raptors to return to the trees.

He waited until the birds of prey had settled quietly in the branches nearby. Then, carefully holding the two spells in place, he asked, "Can you see where the lookouts are?"

After a moment, Autumn Leaves reported, "We can see three of them. The other one must be around the other side somewhere. There may be others nearer the shelter where Danton, Rainstorm and Summer Rain are being held."

"Right. I'll keep the shield up then." Tarkyn turned to address the stationary mountainfolk. "You should have killed me while you had the chance. Now, I will make this very simple for you. We who stand within this shield cannot be harmed by any of you. I, on the other hand, can ask the raptors to attack you or can attack you myself. To secure your safety, you must send a message to the lookouts to retrieve our friends. None of you will be released until they do this. If any of our friends is dead, the slayer's life will be forfeit. When we have our friends safely back with us, we will consider what to do next."

It seemed an eternity before three woodfolk arrived carrying the inert bodies of Danton, Rainstorm and Summer Rain. The two woodfolk were placed carefully on the ground but Danton was dropped unceremoniously. His hands were tied and his face carried the marks of a beating.

Tarkyn dragged his eyes from them and demanded of the lookouts, "What have you done to them?"

The mountainman shrugged disparagingly. "They have been knocked out by a slingshot." He scowled at the woodfolk within the shield. "You people are a disgrace to the woodfolk nation, allowing a sorcerer to live among you. It is bad enough to have to endure this prince, but at least you had an excuse for that. This man," he said, nudging Danton's still form with his boot, "has killed our kin. We will try him and he will be summarily executed, just as he executed our kin. My name is Blizzard."

"Get over there with your kin," ordered Tarkyn.

"You can't order me around," snarled Blizzard.

"Just watch me," replied Tarkyn. With an effort, he held his two spells as he incanted, "*Liefka*," and lifted the unpleasant woodman into the air. "At least this one deserves it," he said in an aside to Running Feet. He swung his arm until the woodman was hovering above his kin then dropped him from a height of eight feet. The lookout landed on several motionless woodfolk who all toppled to the ground, unable to move to save themselves. The other lookouts decided that discretion was the better part of valour and moved around to join their kin to avoid the same fate. When Tarkyn was sure they were all gathered together, he released his shield, placed it over the mountainfolk instead and released the paralysis spell. As an outpouring of rage issued forth from the mountainfolk, Tarkyn simply incanted, "*Shturrum*," again and immobilised them again.

Then he swept cold eyes over them and spoke in a low voice that was flat with anger. "Let me make one thing clear. Lord Danton is not responsible for the deaths of your kin. I am. I ordered it. He obeyed. The responsibility lies only with me. If you had taken the time to ask your fellow woodfolk, you would know that he placed his life on the line for woodfolk against sorcerers to retrieve Golden Toad and his family. He does not deserve this treatment from you."

As he spoke, Waterstone was kneeling beside Danton, untying his bonds and wiping his face with a damp rag. He looked up at Tarkyn. "I think someone has kicked him in the face. He may have a broken cheekbone."

Tarkyn ran his hand through his hair. "What has it come to, that woodfolk can be so malicious? You have destroyed all my belief in the honour and gentleness of woodfolk." He paused. "No. That is not true. I still believe it of most woodfolk, but it seems the mountains breed a tougher, harsher style of woodfolk." He waved his hand and released the paralysis spell again. "If you can contain yourselves, I will leave you free to move within my shield. Otherwise, I will freeze you again. Either way, you are under my complete control and will remain so until I see fit to release you."

"May I say something?" asked Autumn Leaves.

"Of course."

Autumn Leaves turned to address the mountainfolk. "When Danton appeared in the woodlands seeking out Tarkyn, we were preparing to rescue Golden Toad and his family from a huge sorcerer encampment. We knew some sorcerers had already seen woodfolk, and in view of that, we thought that we might as well ask Danton to help us. He has sworn an oath on pain of death not to reveal our presence to anyone. Since then, he has had many chances to betray us and has not done so. Without his help, we would have found it very difficult to release Golden Toad and his family." Autumn Leaves looked thoughtfully at the captive woodfolk. "I have known most of you for many years. We have shared hard winters and fruitful summers together. Do not follow Blizzard's lead and condemn us out of hand. Surely none of you who knows Waterstone or Thunder Storm could believe for a moment that they would jeopardise the welfare of our people."

"I think you're rather missing the point here," sneered Blizzard from within Tarkyn's shield. "Two of our kin were slain here today... by a sorcerer."

Autumn Leaves shook his head. "No. It is you who are missing the point. The only reason it was a sorcerer who killed your kin was that Tarkyn asked him to do it to save us the dilemma. If we had not been drugged during your kinsmen's attack on Tarkyn, we would have killed them ourselves."

"Of course you would have. You are bound by the oath."

"Yes, we are. But the time has long since passed that our care for Tarkyn sprang solely from the oath." Autumn Leaves frowned impatiently. "Don't you understand? Your people attacked Waterstone's brother, Ancient Oak's brother, Sparrow's uncle. He is one of us."

"But that other sorcerer is not," retaliated Blizzard.

"No, he is not," said Autumn Leaves slowly. "But maybe he should be."

Dry Berry pushed her way to the front. "So, young man, what are you going to do now? You can't keep us in here indefinitely."

Tarkyn looked at her dispiritedly. "I don't know, Dry Berry. What do you suggest?"

Dry Berry raised her eyebrows in surprise. "Hmm. Perhaps you do negotiate. Give us a few moments to confer. I'll get back to you."

Tarkyn waved a hand. "Have as long as you like. I need to heal my friends." So saying, he turned away from the mountainfolk and knelt beside Summer Rain.

"I thought you couldn't concentrate to heal yourself, let alone someone else," said Waterstone.

"I don't have to deal with the memories of the attack that flood up when I'm trying to heal myself. I think I'll be able to focus on them." Tarkyn closed his eyes, made sure he had the shield securely in the corner of his mind and then, ignoring the mountainfolk completely, drew power up from inside himself to flow through his hand into Summer Rain's shoulder. It did not escape the notice of the mountainfolk that Tarkyn healed the woodfolk before the sorcerer. Almost immediately, Summer Rain stirred and opened her eyes. Tarkyn moved straight on to Rainstorm, and soon, he too was sitting up and looking around.

The young woodman frowned. "Prince, what are we doing here? What's happened to Danton?" He looked stricken. "Oh no, Prince. I was supposed to protect him and now look at him."

"It's all right, Rainstorm," said Tarkyn gently. "No one is blaming you. We just set you too hard a task." He turned to

Summer Rain. "Can you look at Danton for me please? Waterstone says he may have a broken cheekbone."

The healer examined his cheek carefully before releasing a long sigh. "No. I think the cheekbone is intact. Perhaps if you go in, I'll direct you where to look. He will need some healing to reduce the bruising in that area anyway. I'm more concerned about this heavy bruising over his temple. I hope he comes around all right."

Tarkyn followed his power into Danton, and using Summer Rain's instructions, sought out Danton's bruised temple. He found signs of trauma both inside and outside Danton's skull. He worked carefully to dissipate the blood that had flowed into the surrounding tissue and made sure the capillaries were repaired. Then he flowed around Danton's bruised cheek and repeated the process there. He flowed back out and returned to himself just as Danton began to come to.

"Hello," said Tarkyn, leaning over him. "How are you feeling?"

Danton's eyes swam into focus. His hand went instinctively to his cheek but, as he discovered only a slight soreness, frowned in confusion. "I thought that would be sorer. The last thing I remember is a booted foot coming towards my face." He glanced up at Tarkyn. "Is that your doing?" When Tarkyn nodded, he thanked him briefly, then sat up and took in the scene around him. "Hmm. Events have moved on a bit, I see. Not going too well, by the look of things."

"No. Rather badly, actually. I'm afraid I had to be quite directive in my requirements to have you, Rainstorm and Summer Rain returned to us," said Tarkyn. "Autumn Leaves has just been extolling your virtues to the mountainfolk, but I suspect it will take more than that to reconcile them to you. I'm sorry, Danton. I should have realised sooner the danger I had placed you in."

"So what's happening now?"

"They are working out what we should all do next." Tarkyn shrugged. "I don't have any bright ideas and I'm sick of employing strong arm tactics. So I've left them to come up with a solution."

"Sire, how far away can you go and still maintain your shield?" asked Danton.

Tarkyn shrugged. "I'm not sure. I would have to stay in sight though."

"So, why don't you and I retreat to the edge of the clearing and leave all the woodfolk to sort it out among themselves? You can keep the shield up around the mountainfolk to protect our woodfolk and us. When our woodfolk feel safe enough, you can remove your shield and I'll place mine around us."

Tarkyn turned to Autumn Leaves and Waterstone. "Did you hear that idea? What do you think? That will give you free rein to say whatever you think to your fellow woodfolk."

"May I suggest one change?" asked Waterstone. "Could you take the kids over with you? I think they've heard enough disturbing information for one day and they're starting to get bored."

So, Tarkyn sat against a tree at the edge of the clearing and watched Danton playing marbles with the children of the home guard, while the woodfolk conferred through Tarkyn's barrier. The last of the autumn sunlight faded and still there was no change. Sparrow and her friends snuggled down against the two sorcerers and gradually fell asleep. Tarkyn had stiffened up and was struggling to maintain his shield after long hours of concentration by the time Waterstone walked over to join them.

He squatted down in front of them. "You can release your shield now. You won't need one over yourselves either... " he smiled and nodded at the sleeping children, "even without the children as a safeguard for you."

Tarkyn frowned, but before he could speak, Waterstone answered, "And no, I didn't send them with you to protect you. I wouldn't do that. You have your shields. You can protect yourselves."

Tarkyn extracted his arm from beneath Rain-on-Water, Thunder Storm's quiet five-year-old son, and waved his hand to dissipate the shield. As the child stirred, Tarkyn stroked his back and murmured quietly to him to settle him down again. He looked up quizzically at Waterstone. "If anyone wants to talk to either of us, they will have to come over here. I don't want to disturb the kids until they are transferred to bed."

"No. I don't think we're quite up to that yet." Waterstone nodded at the children. "Do you want us to organise them into bed now or are you happy to wait?"

Tarkyn glanced a query at Danton before replying, "We're happy enough. They could maybe use a blanket or two and we could use a drink. Hmm. Perhaps just a cup of water would do – straight from a stream." He waved a hand. "No, on second thoughts, it will cause too much controversy. Skip the drink. We'll do without for now."

Once Waterstone had provided them with blankets and returned to the other woodfolk, Tarkyn asked Danton, "Are you all right?" When the sorcerer nodded, Tarkyn smiled at him. "I bet this wasn't the type of work you were expecting to do when you signed on as a palace guard."

Danton smiled briefly in return. "No, not really."

Tarkyn could hear the reserve in Danton's voice and remembered their earlier conversation. "Danton, I am sorry for what I said. I should not have dismissed everyone at court, and everything that was said to me, so sweepingly. I may have been unsure of your loyalties but I have never thought you were sycophantic." He gave a slight smile. "In fact, I always found that at those times when you did not feel free to be openly critical, your speaking silences were remarkably eloquent."

This drew a reluctant, answering smile from Danton but he did not unbend enough to speak.

The prince heaved a mental sigh and, wondering at his own perseverance, tried again, "Danton you, more than anyone, should know that I have never been good at differentiating between people like you and people who prevaricate for their own ends... So I have always held everyone at bay to keep safe. I have not wanted to appear foolish by responding eagerly to a compliment that wasn't really meant. So I have treated compliments with courtesy but, I suppose, scepticism."

Danton looked at his liege. "Tarkyn, what did Waterstone do that I have been unable to do for all these years that inspired your faith in him?"

Tarkyn raised his eyebrows in surprise. "I thought you knew. Where were you before you set fire to the infected trees?"

"Guarding Rushwind, Sire."

Tarkyn's brow cleared. "Oh, I see. So you missed it when I inadvertently told everyone what Waterstone had done?"

"Which was?" asked Danton patiently.

"He shared all his memories with me. Well, not all of them, but he gave me free rein to choose what I wanted to see."

Danton looked down at Trickling Stream's head resting on his thigh and stroked her hair gently. After a few moments, he raised his vibrant purple eyes and glanced at Tarkyn. "He is such a strong man, isn't he? So sure of himself, to be able to do that. And to do it for a stranger in his land who had ultimate power over him." Danton shook his head in wonder. "You were very lucky to find him, Tarkyn. I don't know that I could have done that, even if I knew how to."

"No, very few people would be willing to lay themselves open like that." Tarkyn smiled. "So, with that level of self-assurance, it is less surprising, isn't it, that he sets little store by titles and didn't bother to mention to you that he is my blood brother."

Danton heaved a sigh. "At least now I can understand what he offered you that I haven't been able to. Sorcerers can't open their minds up like that – except for you." He gave a slight smile. "You're a hard nut to crack, aren't you? I never realised how little you trusted anybody."

Tarkyn smiled wryly. "But in the end, trusting nobody is just as pointless as trusting everybody. I still didn't have the discernment to know where the danger would come from."

"And do you now?"

Tarkyn shook his head. "Not always, but I have had Waterstone to guide me so that the circle of people I trust has widened. If Waterstone trusts them, then so can I. And now if anyone in that circle trusts someone, then so can I." He ran his hand through his hair. "I just needed one sure point of reference to start from."

"So it was really Waterstone and not you who decided that I could be trusted, after you dragged me back from the encampment?" Danton almost succeeded in sounding objective.

Tarkyn thought about it then shook his head and smiled. "No. You convinced me. I suppose I would have listened if Waterstone had had any serious misgivings but as he said to you, he was always fairly sure he could trust you."

"He didn't get it right with the mountainfolk, did he?"

"I think he was out cold before he even had time to think about it. But you're right. All of us were much too casual in that instance."

Movements over by the fire distracted them at this point

and they both tensed as two figures approached them through the gloom. The shadows resolved themselves into Creaking Bough and Thunder Storm and two others who each picked up a child and carried them off to bed.

"You might like to join them at the fire now," said Thunder Storm over his shoulder, as he left carrying Rain on Water. "Up to you, of course," came his rumbling voice trailing back out of the gloom as he disappeared towards the shelters.

Tarkyn smiled ruefully at Danton as he stood up carefully and began to walk towards the fire. "I'm never going to live down telling him off for ordering me around."

With difficulty, Danton repressed his reaction and held his peace, realising that he could think of nothing to say that the prince would agree with.

Tarkyn's voice came out of the darkness ahead of him, "Well done, Danton. You are so disciplined."

"Thanks," replied the sorcerer dryly.

As they approached the firesite, each was given a beautiful, hand-blown glass filled with golden wine. With rigid control, Tarkyn repressed the urge to glance in alarm at Danton. Instead, he graciously accepted the wine and took a good-sized sip.

"This is an excellent wine," he said urbanely, scanning within himself for any ill effects. "I believe I have tasted it just once before, on the occasion of the King's twenty-fifth birthday. I believe it is one of your rarer, older wines. Is that correct?"

A thin middle-aged man with tatty hair and a long nose came forward and spoke, "Indeed it is, Your Highness. We have very few bottles of it left and we treasure them. My name is Sighing Wind."

The prince gave a slight bow. "I am honoured that you consider my palate worthy of the sacrifice of such a fine wine."

The thin woodman indicated a comfortable position near

the fire, in a mossy position against an oak tree. "Would you like to sit down and make yourselves comfortable? I believe you have particular preference for oaks. They are very grand trees, aren't they?"

Tarkyn contained a private smile and sat down awkwardly, taking care not to spill his wine. "Thank you. That is very thoughtful of you."

Once the sorcerers were seated, all the woodfolk arranged themselves around the fire. With a slight twinge of trepidation, Tarkyn noticed that Waterstone and most of his home guard were on the other side of the fire from him. He drew a deep breath to steady himself and awaited events.

Firstly, small bowls of nuts were handed around. Then plates of sweet little doughy rolls and dried fruits were brought in and placed around the fire where everyone could reach them and a large pot of water was hung over the flames.

"Might I suggest," said Sighing Wind diffidently, "that you only eat nuts with this wine. The sweetness of the rolls would detract from its flavour."

"I am sure you are right," replied the prince, taking another sip. "I would not dream of desecrating this wine by eating anything but savoury fare with it."

Slowly, as the excruciating minutes ticked by, small pockets of conversation sprang up around the fire. Tarkyn and Danton, although seated together, ignored each other and spoke only to their neighbours on the other side of them. Despite their years at court, neither of them had ever experienced any occasion more formal. The level of courtesy was almost paralysing.

When the precious wine was finished, Sighing Wind removed their glasses and offered them sweet rolls and fruit to be eaten in accompaniment with cups of locally grown tea. Both accepted graciously. Occasionally, Tarkyn would throw a glance over the fire to Waterstone or Autumn Leaves, but they assiduously avoided his gaze. Tarkyn felt that his trust in them was being tested to the limit by the situation in which he found himself, surrounded by uncertain woodfolk and with no protection in place. Over time, he let his gaze travel slowly and inconspicuously around the firesite, checking where Blizzard and Dry Berry were seated and looking for any signs of tension or subterfuge. He took a deep breath and released it, giving himself into the hands of his woodfolk.

"I beg your pardon," he said, returning his attention to Sighing Wind who was standing before him handing him a steaming cup of tea. "I missed what you said. Thank you." He produced a smile and accepted the tea.

And finally, when everyone had a cup of tea in their hands, the business of the evening began. Dripping Rock stood up and cleared his throat. He waved his hand around to encompass everyone seated at the firesite. "I have been asked to speak to Prince Tarkyn on behalf of the woodfolk of the mountains, commonly known as the mountainfolk. We have talked long and hard with the prince's band of woodfolk, as he may have noticed, over several hours. After the provision of a great deal of information previously unknown to many of us and after fierce debate, we have reached the following conclusions."

Tarkyn's stomach tensed up until he again reminded himself to trust his woodfolk.

"We absolve Lord Danton of any responsibility for the deaths of our fellow woodfolk."

Danton, who had been unconscious for the previous discussion, frowned in confusion but wisely kept quiet.

"We also acknowledge that Lord Danton has proved himself to be a friend of the woodfolk and thank him for his part in the rescue of woodfolk from the encampment." There was a slight pause as he went briefly out of focus to receive a prompt from someone. "And for helping to save the forest from the infection."

Danton nodded his head in acknowledgement.

"We accept our community's responsibility for the degree of harm suffered by Prince Tarkyn and, after much debate, acknowledge his right to inflict the death penalty, partly because of the unprecedented savagery of the attack and partly because the laws of the outside world have come to reside in the forest, whether we like it or not."

Tarkyn raised his eyebrows but did not make any acknowledgement, making it clear that from his point of view, there was no debate.

Dripping Rock took a swig of tea with a hand that shook a little. "We also apologise for our own breach of etiquette in not welcoming Prince Tarkyn properly to our firesite."

There is euphemism for heckling and jeering, if ever I heard one, thought Tarkyn.

"We appreciate Prince Tarkyn's concern that there should be no rift among the wood folk and we thank him for allowing all of us to come to an agreement ourselves without the use of force and without imposing his views on any of us."

Waterstone must be hating this part, reflected Tarkyn, thinking of the woodman's loathing of the oath.

Dripping Rock took a deep breath. "And finally, we come to the question of swearing fealty. Before he arrived, news of the prince's efforts to support the woodfolk had preceded him. We had decided that, in the best interests of woodfolk unity, we should join in swearing the oath, both to support our forest guardian and to support our fellow woodfolk who have carried the responsibility ever since the prince arrived in the forest. However, we were curious to see whether, in fact, we had already become bound by the oath."

Suddenly the prince spoke. Everyone was so intent on

Dripping Rock that another voice came as a shock. "Excuse me for interrupting, but how could you all have come to an agreement to take an oath with that level of resentment among you?"

Dripping Rock glanced at Dry Berry uncertainly before replying, "I think some people's concerns were not given sufficient attention."

"And now those people are dead?"

Dripping Rock shook his head. "No, I'm happy to say, not all of them. But I believe we have been more assiduous this time in listening to the dissenters' views and debating with them."

"I see. Go on." Tarkyn stopped himself from glancing across at Blizzard to gauge his reaction.

"So, now that the mayhem of today has died down and we have had a chance to gather all the details of the prince's activities within the forest, and to actually see his affinity with the creatures of the woodlands, we can reiterate our intention of joining our fellow woodfolk in swearing an oath of allegiance to him, if he will accept it. And this time, I believe we will have unanimous agreement." Dripping Rock had a very strange way of addressing Tarkyn in the third person, as if he were talking about someone else.

"I understand you have debated long and hard amongst yourselves but I have not been a party to these discussions. So I would ask, why would such egalitarian people as yourselves choose to swear an oath of allegiance?"

"Because, even if we must concede a degree of autonomy to the prince, we at least will remain equal among ourselves."

"With the exception of Waterstone's and Ancient Oak's brother."

Dripping Rock's eyes widened but he merely said, "Even as you say."

Unexpectedly, Tarkyn turned to Blizzard and asked pleasantly, "And what is this oath that you are prepared to swear to me?"

Blizzard turned red and blinked like a rabbit caught in a bright light. "I, I am not sure, Your Highness. That is, I do not know the exact words. But I am prepared to swear it, on my honour."

"I will not force you to swear it, or harm you if you don't. But I need to know why you would. What has changed your mind?"

"Hearing about all the things that you have done already to help woodfolk. But more than that, watching your family and friends supporting you so vehemently after we heard you give them the right to say what they pleased."

Tarkyn regarded him steadily. "They always have that right. That was a tactical remark, not a permission." After a moment's thought, he asked, "And what of Lord Danton? Has your attitude changed towards him too?"

Blizzard threw a sharp glance at Danton before facing the prince and replying, "I don't know why I am bearing the brunt of your interrogation. The thought that woodfolk might be killed by sorcerers has always been everybody's worst nightmare, not just mine." He cleared his throat and dropped his eyes. "It is difficult to accept strangers among us when we have been brought up to avoid anyone who is not woodfolk. But my mind is no more closed than the next person's." He looked back up. "I was angry and upset. I have known those men who were killed, all my life. They may not have been the best of men but they were not always the worst either. And no one had told me half of what I know now."

"So, can you cope with Danton living among us?"

"Yes. He has proved his worth." Blizzard shrugged. "Besides, now I understand that he did not kill those men.

You did. And if I had been beaten up like that, I would have too."

Although this was a simplistic version of Tarkyn's reasons for having his assailants killed, there was enough truth in it to leave it uncorrected. "I beg your pardon if I seemed to be badgering you. I chose you to question because you seemed the most antagonistic earlier. I felt that if you could justify your change of heart then I could be satisfied that everyone's change of heart was genuine. Thank you for helping me."

Tarkyn turned back to Dripping Rock. "Please accept my apologies for interrupting your flow. Now that I have it clear in my mind why you wish to swear this oath, we come to what. What oath are you planning to swear?"

On the other side of the fire, Thunder Storm and Waterstone stood up and came around to stand before Tarkyn.

"I will say it to you so that they are not swearing something you may not agree to," rumbled Thunder Storm. When Tarkyn nodded, he spoke the words quietly so that only those closest to him could hear.

Tarkyn gave a slight smile and said, "There is just one slight change I would ask to be made. In the last phrase, can we change 'my fellow woodfolk' to 'your fellow woodfolk'. Then it is clearer than I too am woodfolk. Do you agree?"

Waterstone smiled. "Yes, I agree. I will put it to them. I'm sure they won't mind." After a short mind conference, he nodded and said, "If you would please stand, Your Highness, Thunder Storm will orchestrate the oath-taking."

Tarkyn noted the use of his title and followed Waterstone's request.

"Must they kneel? It is so embarrassing," whispered Waterstone.

Tarkyn raised his eyebrows and said quietly, "You had to do

it. So must they. I will begin the proceedings. Then Thunder Storm can dictate the oath for them."

The prince drew himself up and spoke in a strong clear voice, "If you wish me to accept your allegiance, you must kneel before me to swear your fealty."

With discomforted glances between them, the mountainfolk sank down to kneel before their forest guardian.

"Now, repeat the words of the oath after Thunder Storm."

Every member of the mountainfolk incanted, "*On behalf of the forests of Eskuzor, the creatures of the woods, the birds of the air and the fish in the streams, I give my solemn vow to honour, serve and protect you, Tarkyn Tamadil, Prince of Eskuzor, Guardian of the Forest, until the end of my days. I am bound by my honour to fulfil this oath in support of you and your fellow woodfolk.*"

"Thank you. I accept your oath. And now I will re-avow my oath to you." Tarkyn created a bronze flame to shine up from his hand as he intoned, "*I, Tarkyn Tamadil, Prince of the Forests of Eskuzor, Guardian of the Forest, give my solemn vow that I will fulfil my obligations and responsibilities as your liege lord and will protect the woodfolk and the forests of Eskuzor. Your just cause will be my cause and your fate will be my fate. This is the covenant bequeathed to me by my father, Markazon Tamadil, 48th King of Eskuzor.*"

There was no dramatic ending to this oath-taking because it was bound by honour not by sorcery. Tarkyn quietly extinguished his flame and looked around at the kneeling mountainfolk. "You have overcome a disastrous set of events today to come to a resolution between us all. You may rise, secure in the knowledge that the woodfolk style of governance has once more found a way through."

23

Deep in the night, Tarkyn lay sleepless within his shelter. His body was exhausted and hurting, but his mind could not release its hold on consciousness. Every time he began to sink towards sleep, a slight sound or a sudden thought would startle him back into full wakefulness. His mind kept going over and over the attack on him. The same thing happened each time he tried to focus to heal himself. He couldn't let down his guard enough to focus inwardly. He did not feel safe among these woodfolk but placing Danton or a member of the home guard outside his shelter would have insulted the mountainfolk who had so newly sworn their allegiance to him.

Although he had accepted their oath in order to mend the rift between woodfolk, he did not yet have any faith in their honour. He had meant what he said when he had told them that only time would test the calibre of their integrity.

In the darkest hour before dawn, he finally gave up the struggle to sleep and, pulling his cloak around him, slipped out of his shelter to go for a walk. As soon as he straightened up, he heard a quiet rustling in the branches above him and looked up to see a large eagle owl keeping watch over his doorway. Before he had taken two steps, Waterstone appeared at his side from one direction and Autumn Leaves from the other.

His shoulders sagged with relief and he smiled in the darkness. Waterstone took hold of his arm and guided him sure-footedly away from the sleeping woodfolk and down to the stream where they could talk unnoticed.

Tarkyn sent him a picture of lookouts with a query.

"It's all right. Our people are guarding this side of the clearing," replied Waterstone quietly. "What's up?"

Tarkyn gave a rueful grin. "I couldn't sleep. I didn't know you two were keeping watch or I might have been able to."

"Sorry, Tarkyn," said Autumn Leaves. "We couldn't find an opportunity to tell you. I hoped you might realise that we wouldn't leave you unguarded again."

When they found somewhere to sit, Tarkyn groaned with the effort of lowering himself down.

"Haven't you done anything about healing yourself yet?" asked Waterstone.

Tarkyn shook his head. "I didn't feel safe enough to concentrate. I'm sorry. I know you spent hours sorting things out with the mountainfolk, but I can't just turn around and start trusting them after what they did to me."

"So, you were going to take a walk in the dark, in amongst them all, were you, without your shield? That didn't strike you as foolhardy?" asked Autumn Leaves.

Tarkyn shrugged. "I didn't feel safe in the shelter. So I thought I might as well not feel safe outside instead. If I had put up my shield I would have given away the fact that I still didn't trust them, wouldn't I?" He pulled his cloak up around his shoulders, "I think I have thrown enough scorn on their honour for one day."

"So now you know we're here and you know your feathered friend is guarding you too, do you want to go back and try going to sleep again?"

"What about you two?"

Waterstone smiled. "We take turns on watch, remember? Though to be honest, Autumn Leaves and I have stayed vigilant all night tonight. Maybe we'll sleep tomorrow sometime. So, if you want to make our effort worthwhile, you should take advantage of it to get some sleep and repair yourself."

Tarkyn yawned. "Thanks, you two. I will."

He lifted himself up gingerly from the ground taking noticeably more time than usual. Just as he straightened, a slight rustling came from a nearby bush. He jerked around and froze, staring wild-eyed at the source of the sound. A little hedgehog came trundling out and wandered unconcernedly along the edge of the bushes before disappearing into another hole.

"Tarkyn, it's all right now. We're here," said Waterstone firmly.

Tarkyn pushed his hair back with a shaking hand. "Sorry. I know you are. I'm just a little on edge still."

"Hmm, you are, aren't you? No wonder you haven't been able to sleep." Unseen by Tarkyn in the darkness, Autumn Leaves went out of focus for a few seconds.

Before they reached the clearing, Summer Rain arrived and presented Tarkyn with a mixture of herbs stirred into a cup of water. "Here. Drink this. It will ease the pain, relax you and allow you to sleep. Be assured we and your raptors will protect you while you sleep."

Tarkyn threw Autumn Leaves a wry glance before throwing down the draught.

"Ugh. Disgusting as usual, Summer Rain. How do manage

to find such foul-tasting herbs?" He sighed. "Thank you one and all. My life is now truly in your hands if I am about to succumb to a sleeping draught. I'll see you in the morning."

He slipped back into his shelter and lay down. For a few minutes, he lay smiling into the darkness thinking about the care of his friends before the sleeping draught took hold and finally drew him down into oblivion.

24

I t was late in the morning when the prince finally appeared. As he stepped out of his shelter, he nearly fell over Sparrow and the other children playing outside, with Creaking Bough and Thunder Storm apparently supervising them. He glanced up into the tree, but the owl was gone. However, as he scanned the area, he spotted a large black kite up in a distant tree but in full view of Tarkyn's shelter.

"Good morning, all," he said. "You've been playing very quietly. I didn't even hear you."

Sparrow looked up and gasped, "Tarkyn! You look terrible. I thought you were going to fix your face."

The bruising had now come out on his face and the whole right-hand side was mottled dark blue and purple. He had a black eye, and his jaw and one side of his lip were swollen.

Thunder Storm stood up and came to greet him. "What's happened? Why can't you heal yourself?"

Tarkyn glanced at the children and said, "Nothing to worry about. I just might need Summer Rain's help." He shrugged and winced as it pulled on bruising lower down.

"Someone's help, anyway. I don't seem to be able to do it on my own."

"I'll come with you for the walk," said Thunder Storm casually. Once they were out of earshot of the children, he said, "Don't you need to have your hand against a tree?"

"Maybe I do. I thought I would have enough strength to heal myself without it."

Thunder Storm surveyed him. "You're not looking particularly strong at the moment, if you ask me. I think your body may well have used up its reserves, coping with the shock from all of that." He paused, "And you healed Rainstorm, Summer Rain and Danton as well, yesterday."

Tarkyn glanced at him out of his blackened eye. "I don't think it's that simple. Every time I try to channel my strength into an injured part of me, I re-live the damage actually being done to me. Then the shock jolts me out of my concentration." He ran his hand through his hair. "I wish Stormaway were here. He would know what to do."

"Yes. I don't know that Summer Rain will know much about this focusing business you use in your magic."

Tarkyn shook his head despondently, "That's what I'm worried about. But who would know?"

Thunder Storm scratched his head. "Well, the only other person around here who knows about your kind of magic is Danton."

"But he knows nothing about my healing power."

"I don't know about that. He saw you fighting against that hideous infection and healing Rushwind. And he must use the focusing techniques himself."

Tarkyn let out a long sigh. "All right. I'll try with him." He lowered his voice, "I'll need someone else to watch our backs if we're both trying to concentrate."

Thunder Storm raised his eyebrows and rumbled quietly,

"Don't worry. We won't leave you alone again." And in a louder voice, said, "I think you'll find Danton down near the stream competing with Rainstorm in a little slingshot competition they've devised. I'll walk down with you and we'll see what they're up to, shall we?"

Just as they were leaving the clearing, Dry Berry bustled up. "There you are, Tarkyn. You've missed breakfast altogether. It won't be long until lunchtime now. Look. I've brought you a cup of tea and some seed cakes to keep you going until then." She thrust them into his hands and then stepped back, obviously feeling awkward but wanting to be friendly.

Tarkyn looked down at the offerings in his hands and said, "Thank you, Dry Berry. These look very good. I'm just going down to the stream to watch the spectacle of Danton trying to beat a woodman at slingshot. So I'll take them with me, if you don't mind." He waited as she clearly had something more to say.

After a moment, she came out with it, "Just so you know, I was not aware yesterday evening, that some of our men had taken Danton and your two woodfolk captive. I was not leading you on again in our conversation over dinner."

"I see," said Tarkyn. "Thank you for telling me that. I hadn't really thought about it, but now you mention it, perhaps it was niggling at the back of my mind."

She cocked her head to one side. "Young man, you do not seem to be doing much about healing yourself. Are you leaving your injuries as a deliberate reminder to us of our shameful behaviour?"

Tarkyn shook his head. "No, Dry Berry. All that was needed to be said was said yesterday." He paused, summing her up before deciding to continue, "No. The memories of the attack are stopping me from healing myself. I can't focus my will properly."

"Take your own advice, young man. Don't let your past control your future."

When Tarkyn looked a little puzzled, Dry Berry said impatiently, "You said it last night when you came back from your swim. You said, 'We cannot change what has happened. All we can change is the effect that it has on our future relationship.'"

Tarkyn's brow cleared. "Oh yes. So I did."

"So don't let the actions of those bullies control you. Fight them. You couldn't fight them yesterday because you were bound and helpless. But you can fight them today."

Comprehension dawned. "Thank you, Dry Berry. I think I know what to do now." Tarkyn glanced at Thunder Storm. "I still might need that tree first, though. Thanks, Dry Berry. I will tell you how I go."

"You won't need to," she said in her abrupt way. "One look at your face will give me an update." Seeing Tarkyn immediately close up, she added kindly, "I will be interested to hear how you achieve it though."

Appreciating her good intentions but not convinced of her genuine interest, Tarkyn gave a slight smile and replied noncommittally, "Hmm, we'll see. There mightn't be anything worth telling."

Tarkyn was deep in thought as they walked the short distance to the stream. Suddenly he stopped Thunder Storm and said, "Don't say anything to Danton about it yet. I think it is Waterstone I need. So let's leave it for now. It will just have to wait until he wakes up. Let's go and watch these two battling it out with their slingshots."

When they arrived, Tarkyn and Thunder Storm sat themselves off to one side and watched Rainstorm and Danton taking it in turns to hit a series of differently weighted rocks that were balanced on top of a large stump. It soon became clear that it was more of a training session than a competition. Even more intriguing, it was the young woodman who was teaching the experienced guardsman. As they watched, a medium-sized rock was hit by Danton and rolled off the back of the stump. Far from being pleased, Danton scowled in frustration. After a few minutes, they broke off their activities and came over to join Tarkyn.

"Hi, Prince," said Rainstorm cheerily. "You look awful. Just thought I'd mention that. Looking at your face, I can tell you if they weren't dead yesterday, they'd be dead today. Bloody bastards!"

Tarkyn smiled. "Hello, Rainstorm. What are you two up to?"

Rainstorm beamed. "We're trying to take the lethal out of Danton's slingshot style. We're practising hitting rocks without dislodging them. The lighter the rock, the lighter the touch needed to leave it in place."

Tarkyn raised his eyebrows at Danton. "So I presume that last rock you knocked off is another hapless woodman that you've killed instead of knocking out?"

Danton grimaced. "Something like that. I'm getting better though. Actually, I hadn't dislodged one for quite a while. Perhaps I was distracted by you arriving."

"Maybe. If that's the case, I'll have to turn up regularly so that you can learn to deal with being distracted," said Tarkyn lightly.

A slight noise off to their left made Tarkyn's head whip around in sudden alarm.

Rainstorm frowned at him in concern. "Just me throwing a couple of pebbles, Tarkyn. Take it easy."

Tarkyn nodded, let out a held breath, and returned his attention to their conversation. "Sorry. What were we saying?"

"Nothing important," said Danton. "Just about me being

distracted. You seem to be a lot more easily distracted than I am at the moment."

Tarkyn grimaced. "Maybe I just need something to keep me busy." He gave a slight smile. "Let me have a go at your stones."

They walked back over to the target range and Rainstorm offered Tarkyn a slingshot. The sorcerer shook his head with a smile and sent a bronze shaft of light spearing towards the rocks. He then neatly hit each rock one after the other, without dislodging any one of them.

The two woodmen and Danton were wide-eyed in admiration.

Tarkyn laughed. "Marvellous, isn't it?" He waited for a moment, then confessed, "In fact, none of my shafts touched the rocks. I made them all stop just before impact. I don't know if I can actually hit them with the right degree of force or not. Have you tried using your power, Danton?"

Danton shook his head. "I didn't think it would be polite when Rainstorm is specifically teaching me about slingshots."

"Ooh, I'm in trouble now, Rainstorm." Tarkyn smiled. "I think I've been impolite."

Danton frowned. "Your Highness,... " he began.

"Definitely in trouble, Rainstorm. He's come over all formal on me again."

Rainstorm was grinning hugely but Danton looked flustered.

"Your Highness, I beg your pardon. I didn't mean to imply you were rude," he said in a rush before either of them could interrupt him.

Tarkyn clapped him on the shoulder. "I know, Danton. I'm just teasing. Relax." He waited until he felt Danton relax under his hand. "Come on, my friend. I bet Rainstorm and Thunder Storm would love to see some of your magic. Besides, the instructions are probably much the same. Just a different weapon."

"Yes. Come on, Danton. That would really be something if I could instruct a sorcerer in the use of his magic." Rainstorm chortled. "I could be a famous sorcerer trainer. The only one in the woodfolk world."

Thunder Storm shook his head. "You're all mad."

Tarkyn looked at him. "What about you, Thunder Storm? Strut your stuff. Show us how it's done."

Thunder Storm shook his head. "I wouldn't like to show you all up," he said with one of his sudden flashes of humour.

Rainstorm was smiling privately. "Go on, Thunder Storm. Make them rock."

Thunder Storm shrugged, drew his slingshot and, after casually sending forth a barrage of small stones towards the targets, replaced it in his belt. When Tarkyn and Danton looked at the target, every rock on the stump was rocking gently back and forth but remaining in place.

"Oh. Is that what you meant when you said 'Make them rock'?" said Danton, blinking in astonishment. "On my oath, Thunder Storm, you are good! That is amazing."

Thunder Storm gave a slow smile. "Thanks. So now let's see some of your magic."

"Okay, here goes."

A streak of aqua ripped through the air and blasted every rock on the stump to pieces.

Danton blushed. "Oops."

"Not much subtlety there then," said Thunder Storm phlegmatically.

Rainstorm and Tarkyn caught each other's eye and grinned broadly at each other. Then, despite their best efforts not to, they laughed and then kept laughing until the tears rolled down their faces.

When they had recovered the power of speech, Rainstorm commented, "Nice coloured magic, Danton," which promptly set them off again.

Danton stood there with his arms crossed, a reluctant smile playing around his lips until they had recovered themselves.

"Thanks, Danton," said Tarkyn, grinning and gingerly wiping his eyes. "I needed that."

"Always glad to be of service, Sire," said Danton dryly, giving an ironic little bow.

"I think, since we are now lacking a target, it might be good time to break and go back for lunch," suggested Thunder Storm.

The others nodded and headed up the path.

25

As they neared the mountainfolk's firesite, Tarkyn gradually became more distant and withdrawn so that by the time they arrived, he had become carefully courteous with everyone. There was nothing he wanted to do less than sit around with his blatantly battered face, sharing lunch and conversation with the people who had jeered at him yesterday. All the oaths in the world would not wipe their previous behaviour from his mind.

Today they were all apparently friendly towards him and at some pains to make amends. Only the importance of repairing the rift within the woodfolk nation kept him seated at the firesite. When he judged he had spent the minimum time possible there to be polite, he stayed another half an hour to make sure. Then, with his duty done, he smiled, thanked them for the lunch and escaped, pleading a headache which he did in fact have.

He sent a message to Sparrow, asking her to meet him. In less than a minute, she came bounding up. "Hi, Tarkyn. Did you want me?"

"Yes. I was just wondering if you think Waterstone would have had enough sleep yet. What do you think?"

Sparrow looked at him. "Did you want to see him?"

Tarkyn nodded. "But I don't want to wake him up. He was up all night, you know."

Before he could stop her, Sparrow went out of focus. Then she smiled. "He's coming."

Tarkyn frowned. "No Sparrow. I didn't want you to wake him."

"Yes, but he *did* want me to wake him. He said if you needed him, to wake him up. So I did."

"I'm not sure that he meant like this. He probably just meant if I *really* needed him."

Sparrow put her head on one side and looked up at him. "I think you *really* need him or you wouldn't have asked if he's awake yet. You would just have waited."

Tarkyn was still looking at her trying to work out whether or not that was true, when Waterstone walked up, ruffling his hands back and forth through his hair and yawning.

"Sorry, Waterstone. I only asked Sparrow when she thought you'd wake up. I didn't ask her to wake you.

Waterstone smiled at Sparrow. "Good girl." He looked at Tarkyn. "What about a cup of tea then?" Seeing the hesitation on Tarkyn's face, he turned back to Sparrow. "Do you think you could get us cups of tea and bring them down to the stream?"

She smiled and nodded before heading off to the firesite.

As they turned and walked from the clearing, Waterstone asked, "Are you okay?"

Tarkyn glanced around at the surrounding trees and sent Waterstone a query.

After a brief pause, Waterstone reported, "No one in

earshot. One of theirs over to the left. One of ours more towards the stream."

"Who?"

"Ancient Oak, actually."

Tarkyn breathed a sigh of relief. "Good. I can relax then." He sent a wave of greeting up to Ancient Oak in passing.

Waterstone repeated the question, "So, are you all right?"

"Yes and no. Mostly no, I suppose. Thanks for getting up. I should have just waited. I didn't realise Sparrow would get you up on the spot."

Waterstone smiled. "She was under strict instructions to call me for the slightest thing. Anyway, I've had enough sleep. Thunder Storm and Creaking Bough took over just after dawn." He paused. "So, did you want me for anything specific?"

Tarkyn glanced at him. "Yes and no." Then he gave a quick grin. "Hard to get a straight answer out of me, isn't it?"

Waterstone raised his eyebrows. "Yes. I was just wondering how long it would take us to get to whatever point you're aiming for."

Tarkyn heaved a sigh. "There are many points I'm aiming for. I need your help to fix my injuries. I'm still on edge and jumping at shadows. And I can't stand being around the mountainfolk after all their jeering yesterday."

"So, when I asked were you all right and you said 'yes and no,' which bit is yes?"

Tarkyn shrugged. "I don't know. I guess knowing I have all of you supporting and protecting me. I actually had a very funny time with Rainstorm, Thunder Storm and Danton before lunch. I don't feel all bad." He gave a wry smile. "I just need some repair work."

They walked down past the site of the target practice, and Tarkyn pointed out the shattered remains of the rocks and their significance on the way past. When they had rounded the next bend in the stream and were well away from the firesite and lookouts, they found a discreet, mossy hollow under a stand of gnarled old oaks whose roots were partly exposed and hanging entwined out over the stream. Soon after they had sat down, Sparrow arrived with Rain on Water, each carefully carrying a cup of steaming tea. Once she had handed over the tea, Sparrow produced some rolls and fruit from her pocket for her father and Rain on Water shyly offered some fruit to Tarkyn. After thanking them profusely, Waterstone sent them back up to the firesite to play with the others, with a quick mindmessage to Thunder Storm to tell him they were coming.

"So, let's start with the obvious," said Waterstone, as soon as they were gone. "You're looking pretty grim and still haven't been able to heal yourself, even though hopefully, you eventually felt safe in your shelter."

Tarkyn glanced sideways at his friend. "Every time I focus on part of me that's injured, the memory of being injured blasts back up at me and I lose focus." Tarkyn shook his head. "It's not just then, either. All night and even most of this morning, even when I'm talking to people, I'm constantly thinking about what happened."

Waterstone didn't say anything, but simply waited.

"Waterstone, have you ever had anything like that happen to you?" When the woodman shook his head, Tarkyn continued, "Of course you haven't. The only people I can think of who would have endured something like that are condemned criminals on their way to execution. When I was attacked, the jeering of the crowd in the background was the least of my problems. But now! Now, I have to sit with those same people, and make polite conversation with them when I know yesterday they were revelling in my pain." He shook his head. "Waterstone, I am trusting you as I have never trusted you before. Please don't tell anyone how I'm feeling. The unity of the woodfolk is far more important than how I cope with the aftermath of yesterday. But I need you to help me, the private person, so that I, the political person, can support the woodfolk cause. Can you do that?"

Waterstone shook his head and smiled. "Tarkyn, you're not thinking straight at all. To what advantage would it be for me to tell the world how you're feeling? I too have woodfolk unity at heart. I would not wish to jeopardise it any more than you would."

Tarkyn raised a hand and let it drop. "I don't know. Maybe I was worried that you might go forth in some righteous rage and champion me against the mountainfolk."

Waterstone smiled. "Is that what you want?"

Tarkyn grinned. "It has its attractions, I must say... But no. I wouldn't mind you sympathising with me, though, when no one else is around." He put his head on one side and considered his friend. "I remember that soon after we met I made the assumption that your loyalties would always lie with woodfolk above your loyalty to me and you said in no uncertain terms not to make your decisions for you." Tarkyn laughed. "You're such a feisty bastard." He became serious again. "I'm not asking you to support me against them. I'm just asking you not to tell them everything."

"Stop worrying, Tarkyn. There is no conflict of interests here. You and I are on the same side and want the same things. I don't share the contents of all my conversations with everyone. I pick and choose, just as you do. I won't feel that I'm betraying woodfolk if I don't tell them everything about you. It's none of their bloody business, most of the time." Waterstone took a breath. "So, is the interrogation over now? Do you feel safe enough to continue?"

"Sorry. Am I trying your patience?"

"If you hadn't been beaten up within an inch of your life in front of a heckling audience yesterday, I might say yes. But as it stands, no."

Tarkyn gathered his thoughts before saying, "First and foremost, I would like to find a way to heal myself; mostly for myself, but also because my battered face is a constant accusation against the mountainfolk. The sooner that incident becomes past history, the better for everyone."

"So, how can I help?"

"Dry Berry told me that I shouldn't let my past control my future and that now that I'm not bound and helpless as I was yesterday, I can outface my attackers."

Waterstone nodded. "Sensible woman, Dry Berry, at least most of the time."

Tarkyn found himself a stick and began to break it methodically as he spoke, "When she first said it, I thought it was an easy solution. But it's not. It is a solution but it's not easy." He glanced up at Waterstone then looked back down at his stick. "It's not fear I'm battling against. It's worse than that. It's a feeling of, I don't know, horrified inevitability, of being helpless and watching fists coming at me with the full weight of the man behind them and being unable to do anything about it. Andoran and Sargon's treatment of me when they tried to take me for the reward was a total non-event compared to this."

"So, what happens when you try to repair yourself?"

"When I focus on some damaged part of me, the image of the pain coming towards me freezes me. I pull away before I know what I'm doing."

Waterstone placed his hand firmly on the young prince's shoulder. "Tarkyn, you are strong and you are brave, and you have me. Dry Berry is right. You must fight fire with fire. Before you focus on the damage, be prepared to fight against your image of the incoming pain. Don't focus on your damaged flesh.

First focus on your tormentors and defeat them. Then when they are gone, you can look to yourself."

"But they're not real. They're already dead. I have already defeated them."

"No, you haven't. Because the damage to your spirit still lingers. You have to defeat your image of them, what they meant to you. You have to defeat your helplessness."

Tarkyn's spirit wavered. "I don't know that I can. It was ghastly being held there, unable to do anything."

"But, Tarkyn, you did do something. You called on the eagles and they came. You weren't helpless. You only appeared to be for a while."

Tarkyn threw down his stick and looked up at Waterstone. "Yes, that's true, isn't it? But at the time, I didn't know they would come. So I thought I was helpless"

"But now you know you weren't. So you have something to fight those images with."

Tarkyn let out a long sigh. "All right. Shall we try?"

"What do you want me to do?"

"I'm going to tap into the oak and go down deep, as I did when I had the broken rib. I want you to be here to keep me connected to the world and to be my anchor. I need your strength and your faith in me."

"I'll be here."

Tarkyn lay down and placed his palm against the mossy old oak. Waterstone sat beside him and placed his hand firmly on Tarkyn's shoulder. Tarkyn closed his eyes and focused on drawing strength from the old oak. Slowly, he felt himself drifting down and away from his surroundings. Now and again he would come back up a little to reassure himself that Waterstone's hand was still on his shoulder but eventually he placed his trust in Waterstone and drifted far beyond the outside world. For a while, he just lay there gathering strength from the oak, forming it slowly into a kernel of power. When he felt strong enough, he drew on the power and prepared to outface his tormentors. He directed his focus towards his bruised stomach and chest, ready to thrust outward. But although he could feel the origin of the attack, it no longer drove him away from his injured body. He now knew that, ultimately, his aggressor had no power because the eagles were coming. All he needed to do was to place a small barrier along the outside of his body and endure while he repaired the flesh. He let his power flow into his violated tissue and felt himself relax as the pain finally diminished.

Forty minutes later, Tarkyn rose gently back into consciousness to find Waterstone's face looking down at him. Waterstone smiled. "Hello there. You fixed yourself, I see. Well done. Was it hard?"

Tarkyn stayed where he was and shook his head. "Nothing like it had been. Once I took into the battle the knowledge that I wasn't really helpless, there was no battle. Thank heavens for the eagles, is all I can say."

Waterstone shook his head. "You would have found a way, Tarkyn, even if the eagles hadn't come. You are the hope of Eskuzor, remember?"

Tarkyn gave a wry smile. "Hope can flicker out just like a flame in the wind. Do not set too much store by the words of an old wizard and a passionate young sorcerer." He put his hand up to feel his cheek and his jaw, "Hmm, not bad. Still a tiny bit tender in places but good enough." He sat up. "Has all the bruising gone?"

Waterstone inspected him carefully. "Yes, I think so. Sparrow may be able to stand the sight of you again now."

"Good of her." Mention of Sparrow made him look in his cup. "Oh dear. My cup of tea has gone cold and I hardly drank any of it."

"Never mind. I enjoyed mine. Do you want some water?"

Tarkyn shook his head. "No. I'll just drink cold tea."

"So, why didn't you approach Danton to do this? He is a sorcerer and warrior, after all. He understands fighting."

Tarkyn looked assiduously into his cup. "Because you are my anchor." He looked up. "I knew I would have to become vulnerable before I became stronger and I trust you with everything about me." He grimaced. "I know you will find this hard to understand, but Danton comes from a world where the Royal Family is adulated. I don't know how well he would cope with my vulnerability and I don't know how well I would cope with him knowing about it."

"You told him your fears about dealing with reactions to the spread of the oath."

"Yes, I did. And that was a start. But that was on a completely different level from this." Tarkyn grinned. "Danton is loyal and passionate and devoted but we grew up in a society where he is my social inferior. He still thinks of himself like that and so do I." He stared steadily at Waterstone. "But despite my insistence on saying I won't accept equal status with woodfolk, in actual fact, I consider you my equal in all but name."

Waterstone's face lit up in a smile. "Coming from anyone else, I would almost be offended. But coming from you, that is high praise indeed."

Tarkyn smiled. "In some areas, more than my equal."

"Now settle down, Tarkyn, you'll make me blush in a minute." Waterstone eyed him briefly before saying, "Now here is something I don't want you to tell any woodfolk either." When Tarkyn nodded agreement, he continued, "Among woodfolk, to be honest, some woodfolk are more equal than others, if you know what I mean. Well, you're up there with the best of them."

It didn't even cross Tarkyn's mind to be offended that anyone would consider ranking him against other woodfolk. He laughed with pleasure. "Oh, Waterstone, what an admission from you. Thank you. Both for your trust and for saying I'm among the best."

"Hmph. Don't you ever tell anyone that I said that."

Tarkyn just laughed. "Of course I won't. What a political hot potato that would be if it got out."

"Precisely."

"Do you know, that's the first time you've ever told me something that you wanted kept secret from other woodfolk. I assumed you didn't want the memory sharing advertised but you didn't ever say so directly to me."

"It may be the first secret I've told you but that's not because I didn't trust you. It is more because I have nothing to hide."

"Except for this one small, underlying premise of all woodfolk dealings," chortled Tarkyn.

"Stop it. You'll make me wish I hadn't told you."

Tarkyn stopped laughing abruptly. "Sorry. I am not paying your confidence due respect."

"And no, the inherent inequality of woodfolk is not an argument for your feudal style of government. It does not seem to me that rank in your society is based on worth or ability or any other comparative quality I can think of. At least in our society, we give everyone's opinion its due, regardless of ability."

Tarkyn threw his hands up and beat a hasty retreat. "I was not about to mount an attack on woodfolk governance. In actual fact, I am quite impressed with it... although it does seem to have struck a few problems among the mountainfolk. But that's no reason to change it. As far as I can see, it just needs a bit more care taken with the outriders, so to speak. It's just a pity it had to go wrong when I was the issue."

Waterstone's face relaxed into a smile. "I think, since you are the biggest issue that has been around for quite some time, it is almost inevitable that if it's going to go wrong, it will go wrong over you."

"Blast it, Waterstone. That is so unfair."

Waterstone raised his eyebrows. "I don't remember when there was anything fair about this situation."

"True. Point taken." Tarkyn sighed. "So what am I going to do about having to endure the company of these hypocritical rabble-rousers?"

"I don't know. You're the expert on crowds. I remember you telling us all how fickle crowds can be... and that was on a day that they were being nice to you."

The prince's eyes narrowed. "Yes, I have a great wariness of crowds... which yesterday's effort has just strengthened. They exist above and beyond the individuals. They are maverick and dangerous; one minute cheering your victory, the next minute glorying in your defeat. And then they dissolve and all that passion and venom dissipates. A few still maintain it away from the crowd but most just shake themselves and leave it all behind them."

"So that's what happened yesterday. They all gloried in your pain but now they have gone back to being themselves."

"...until the next time." Tarkyn frowned. "And the fact that they are now acting as individuals does not excuse the behaviour they indulged in as part of a crowd."

"Oh no. It most certainly doesn't," said Waterstone severely. "It will be a long time before I can trust the good intention of any of them."

"Will it?" Tarkyn gave a surprised smile. "I'm glad to hear you say that. I thought you had all sorted out your relationship with each other in yesterday's long discussion, and I was the only one left with any doubts."

Waterstone frowned quizzically at him. "Why do you think I would put myself to the trouble of staying up all night if I trusted them?"

"Well, I thought maybe you were just doing it to reassure me."

"Except that I did it regardless of whether you knew or not."

"True. So you did." Tarkyn frowned. "But then, what was gained from your long negotiations?"

Waterstone shrugged. "The semblance of unity among woodfolk. The *intention* of becoming as close as we once were. Their agreement to take an oath when you had just executed two of their kin. A greater understanding and acceptance of you and Danton. And our acceptance of their future good faith." He stood up and took his cup to the stream to wash it out. "All of that took a great deal of work. Still, it is better by far to have a semblance of cooperation than to have out-and-out enmity. It might not be ideal, but the mountainfolk would make tough enemies."

"So I am not the only one who does not feel easy around their firesite?" asked Tarkyn.

"I wouldn't think so." Waterstone shook his cup out and then filled it with water that was pouring in a small waterfall between two rocks. "Sure you don't want some water?"

"Yes, I will. Thanks." Tarkyn tipped out the last of his cold tea and tossed his cup to the woodman.

When he had handed Tarkyn his cup filled with icy water, Waterstone asked, "Will that make it any easier for you to endure, if you know others of us are not yet feeling comfortable with them?"

Tarkyn nodded. "Yes. Much. I thought I was alone in my mistrust."

Waterstone looked at him for a few moments. "I know you caught the brunt of it, but they did drug all of us too, you know. That doesn't do much for trust levels."

"Hmm, I suppose not." Tarkyn thought for a moment. "How would you have felt if they had only hit me twice, as Dry Berry intended?"

"About you or us?"

"I don't know. Both, I suppose."

Waterstone's eyes narrowed as he thought about it. "To be honest, I am loath to tell you until I know what you think."

Tarkyn smiled wryly. "That can only mean you would have condoned it."

"I could have lived with that a lot better than what actually happened."

"Stop pussyfooting around. You think that would have been an acceptable way of finding out whether they were under oath or not, don't you?"

Waterstone looked a little anxious. "All right, yes. I do. I could have accepted being drugged because they had to make sure we couldn't intervene. And I could have accepted you being a little hurt to resolve the question." He eyed Tarkyn. "Of course, then you would probably have felt obliged to kill them for attacking you, if Danton's case is anything to go by. And that would have been unhelpful for future relationships." He took a tense breath. "So what do you think?"

"Much the same as you actually, except that it would have depended on how hard they hit me whether I insisted on the death penalty or not. If it had clearly been only been an experiment, I probably would have overlooked it. If they had hit me as hard as those men did yesterday, that would have been inexcusable."

Waterstone's eyes widened. "So, they were effectively dead even after only two hits yesterday?"

"Absolutely." Tarkyn glowered at him. "Don't start making judgements about something you didn't see, or feel for that matter. They packed everything they had into those first two punches in case the forest was threatened and they had to stop." Suddenly, Tarkyn's voice vibrated with passion, "They were utter bastards, Waterstone, complete and utter bastards."

For a moment, Waterstone saw a flash of the rage that Tarkyn was keeping contained within himself before he closed it off and stood up, shaking out his cup and saying in a completely different voice, "But they didn't stop at two, did they? And so my decision was totally straight forward." He glanced sideways at Waterstone and the woodman could see the rage still smouldering behind his eyes as he added in an unnervingly urbane voice, "I think I restrained myself very well in allowing them such a swift clean death. I could have used the eagles."

As Tarkyn turned to walk back up the stream Waterstone, feeling jarred by the emotion he had just witnessed, called him back. "Tarkyn," He waited until he had the prince's full attention before he said, "Tarkyn, you deserve to feel such rage but no one, other than those two dead men, deserves to be on the other end of it."

Tarkyn drilled him with his amber glare for long seconds. Then suddenly, he let out a long breath and relaxed. Waterstone breathed a quiet sigh of relief.

"Waterstone, your courage never ceases to amaze me. Thank you for saying that. I will remember it."

VI

MIDNIGHT

26

As Tarkyn walked back around the bend in the stream, he found that the target practice had expanded to include several mountainfolk as well as members of his home guard. The minute he appeared, the talking and the laughter faltered, and for a moment, an awkward silence fell over the participants. Then Lapping Water extracted herself from the group and came over to him.

"Hello, Tarkyn," she said, taking his arm and steering him towards the others, "Come and join us. Danton has managed to control his magic at least to the extent that he can leave larger rocks in place." She smiled. "Smaller rocks are still too much of a challenge."

Tarkyn flicked her a grateful glance. "Well, at least that's better than this morning."

"Hi, Prince," said Rainstorm casually. "You're looking better."

Tarkyn nodded shortly, not really wishing to discuss it in front of the mountainfolk.

"And what about you, Waterstone? Going to join us?" asked Rainstorm, quickly moving the conversation on.

Waterstone smiled and shook his head. "Not at the moment. I need to spend a little time with young Sparrow. I'll see you all later."

Rainstorm returned his attention to the prince. "So, are you going to have a go, Tarkyn?"

Tarkyn smiled. "Maybe in a while. A crafty competitor always checks out his opposition first. So I'll just watch for the time being and see if anyone else is as good as Thunder Storm."

"What did Thunder Storm do that was so good?" asked a wiry woodman whom Tarkyn recognised as being one of the lookouts who had taken Danton, Summer Rain and Rainstorm captive yesterday. "My name is Rock Fall."

Tarkyn inclined his head. "Pleased to meet you. Thunder Storm could make every stone rock gently without falling. But perhaps you can all do that? I found it extremely impressive."

Rock Fall thought about it. "I think I could do that."

"Go on then," urged Tarkyn. "Let's see how many people can replicate Thunder Storm's feat."

Rock Fall stepped up to the mark and carefully aimed his slingshot at the first stone. He sent a small pebble flying and, sure enough, the stone rocked gently back and forth but stayed where it was.

Rainstorm chortled. "Nice warm up, Rock Fall. But Thunder Storm can make all the stones rock at the same time."

Rock Fall raised his eyebrows. "Can he? That *is* impressive."

"And quickly. He had his slingshot back in his belt before they had stopped moving," said Tarkyn.

"Right then." Lapping Water stepped up to the mark. "That will give us something to live up to." She sent a series of pebbles flying at the stones. Five out of seven rocked gently, one fell over and one didn't move. "Blast! Nearly."

Tarkyn smiled and shook his head. "Pretty good, but I have to tell you that Thunder Storm was also faster, as well as more accurate."

Lapping Water smiled up at him. "I'll try to get it right at this speed first and then work on becoming faster."

Tarkyn felt his heart miss a beat as he met her eyes but merely said, "Good idea."

For the next hour or so, everyone took it in turns trying, without success, to replicate Thunder Storm's feat. Tarkyn didn't really want to join in because he didn't want to appear better or worse than the people around him. Eventually though, the requests for him to take part could no longer be avoided.

"Magic or slingshot?" he asked.

"Magic," came back the chorus.

"I'm glad you said that," replied Tarkyn, "because I have only been using a slingshot properly since I came into the woods. It is not yet my weapon of choice." He looked thoughtfully at the target. "There is only one sure way I can think of to come even close to Thunder Storm's feat..."

Tarkyn narrowed his eyes as he calculated and then sent a spear of bronze light hurtling towards the stump. The beam of magic hit the stump with a dull thwack and the vibrations of the stump set every stone on top rocking gently. Tarkyn withdrew his magic and waited, his eyes shining with laughter.

Sure enough, cries of protests and outrage, mainly from woodfolk of his home guard, broke out around him. When the mountainfolk saw his own woodfolk taking issue with him, a couple of them quietly lent their voice to the protests.

"That's cheating," roared Rainstorm.

Tarkyn laughed and threw his hands up in mock surrender.

"No one said I had to hit the stones. We were just trying to make them rock ...which I did."

"But we were trying to replicate Thunder Storm's feat," pointed out Lapping Water.

Tarkyn smiled. "Yes, but was it the method or the result that we were trying to replicate? After all, I wasn't even using a slingshot so I couldn't possibly replicate the method."

Lapping Water frowned severely at him, but with a smile in her eyes. "You know perfectly well that wasn't what we expected."

He laughed. "You're just jealous you didn't think of it yourselves."

The attention then turned to the question of whether the woodfolk and Danton could replicate Tarkyn's method of rocking the stones. They soon discovered that it took considerable force to shake the stump, but eventually, after a bit of experimenting, everyone achieved it to their satisfaction.

As they walked up the path towards the firesite, no one appeared to have noticed that Tarkyn had avoided showing them whether he could hit as fast and accurately as Thunder Storm, and the mountainfolk were noticeably more relaxed in his presence. Although he caught the odd person looking at him curiously, no one else mentioned his improved appearance.

But just before they entered the clearing, Tarkyn received an image of himself and the group coming towards the firesite from a viewpoint somewhere behind a clump of trees on the other side of the clearing. The image was accompanied by a sense of loneliness and longing. Tarkyn frowned but before he could wonder at its origin, his attention was claimed by mountainfolk who had been awaiting his return to present him with food and wine as continued proof of their contrition.

27

"Your Highness," said Sighing Wind when Tarkyn had had time to consume the first round of offerings, "would you be interested in seeing the caves under the mountain where we ferment and store our wines? We have a couple of hours before the evening meal is ready."

Tarkyn inclined his head. "I would feel privileged to be shown the source of your fine wines." For the life of him, the prince couldn't relax and be anything less than formal with the larger group of mountainfolk. Sighing Wind, having orchestrated the pre-oath ceremony the night before, was particularly difficult to be casual with.

Sighing Wind took a smouldering branch from the fire and, gesturing for Tarkyn to follow him, set forth with two other mountainfolk from the clearing in the opposite direction from the stream. Before they had even left the clearing, Ancient Oak appeared at the prince's side. Moments later, Tarkyn became aware that Rainstorm and Lapping Water had also appeared and were bringing up the rear.

"Hello, Ancient Oak. Finally got away from guard duty, did you?" asked Tarkyn.

Ancient Oak glanced at the accompanying mountainfolk and gave a slight smile. "More or less, little brother. Thought I might take the opportunity to see their cellars. These fellows are reluctant to let other woodfolk into their cellars as a general rule."

One of the mountainfolk looked around at this remark, "It is hardly surprising that we need to be careful about letting people in. One drunken evening and most of our finest, oldest wines would be scoffed by revellers."

With a slight shock, Tarkyn realised that the speaker was Blizzard.

"I can imagine a party of drunken revellers near your cellars might be hard to contain," replied Tarkyn, even as his mind checked the relative numbers of home guard and mountainfolk in the group and wondered where Danton was and whether he was well enough protected.

Tarkyn jumped as Ancient Oak gave him a pat on the shoulder, leaving his hand there reassuringly for a moment. Luckily, Blizzard had already returned his gaze to the direction of travel. Tarkyn smiled down wryly at Ancient Oak and let his shoulders droop as he released the tension in them.

"We promise we won't scoff all your wine," said Rainstorm cheekily from behind, maintaining the flow of the conversation.

"I don't think that we were planning on letting you scoff any of it," replied Blizzard repressively.

Rainstorm was quite unabashed. "Well, that's a shame. But at least I'll be able to think about where the wine comes from, next time I drink some."

Their way lead them over a series of huge tumbled boulders and down into a crevice at the head of a steep valley. The cave opening was disguised by a dense covering of hawthorn and brambles, but even when these were negotiated, the entry into the caves was oblique; indiscernible until one stood at a particular angle.

As they entered the quiet gloom of the cave, Sighing Wind touched his smouldering stick to two brands hanging in brackets that had formed in the twisted vines clinging to the wall inside the doorway. He handed one brand to Blizzard and kept one for himself as he led them into the gloom beneath the mountain.

Tarkyn took a deep breath, flicked a wry glance at Ancient Oak and then exhaled slowly. He would have felt more relaxed with his shield around him but had to be content with his three woodfolk and his own reflexes. As he moved forward into the depth of the first cave, he felt a wave of reassurance emanating from somewhere ahead of him. Then he received an image looking straight at the mountainfolk in front of him from somewhere deeper in the cave. The mountain folk appeared relaxed and unconcerned, quietly focused on leading the way into their cellars. Tarkyn sent a small wave of thanks with a query about the source of the image but received no further response.

The back of the cave tapered into a tunnel that rounded a corner and then ceased. Tarkyn's eyebrows snapped together in suspicion, but Sighing Wind merely turned around and said, "This is the main entry to the cellars." He pulled on a small outcrop of rock high on his left and a large section of rock wall slid silently sideways, revealing a further passageway.

Blizzard's eyes narrowed as he studied the ground around the doorway. "That little pest has been here again," he said to his fellow mountainfolk. "What's he up to this time?"

Suddenly Tarkyn received an image of an immense cavern, its ceiling emanating a soft light from hundreds of glow worms. A feeling of pride and invitation flowed into his mind.

"Stars above!" breathed Tarkyn. "That's beautiful."

"What is?" asked Rock Fall in confusion.

"Your beautiful, glowing cavern. Is that where you keep the wine?"

Sighing Wind frowned. "How do you know about the cavern? We still have some way to go before we reach it."

Tarkyn shrugged. "I don't know how I know. I just saw an image of it. Are there any animals living in there?"

"Bats? Glow worms?" suggested Blizzard.

Tarkyn thought for a moment then grimaced. "No. I don't think so. It doesn't feel right for a tiny mind like that. Besides, the view is looking up at the glow worms on the ceiling from somewhere lower down."

Rock Fall, Blizzard and Sighing Wind all looked at each other then back at Tarkyn.

"We do not know of any animals inhabiting our caverns except bats and glow worms and perhaps the odd rat from time to time," said Rock Fall. "We would not like to risk taking you into danger if there is some unknown animal in there. Perhaps we should turn back?"

Tarkyn smiled and shook his head. "Thank you for your concern, but I believe the source of the image is friendly, whatever it is."

When the mountainfolk still looked uncertain, Ancient Oak said, "There are seven of us. One of us is a powerful sorcerer and the rest of us are experienced hunters. It will have to be something quite extraordinary to overcome us."

Sighing Wind nodded reluctantly. "Perhaps you should raise your shield, Your Highness?"

Now that he could, Tarkyn realised that he no longer needed to. The concern of the mountainfolk had allayed his fears about them.

"I will be ready to do so, should the need arise," he replied calmly. "I am happy to continue into your cellars and would be disappointed not to, if you feel able to proceed."

"Very well." Sighing Wind turned away and resumed his tour into the depths of the mountain.

After following a convoluted path for another few minutes, the passageway opened into the cavern that Tarkyn had seen in his image. He and his woodfolk stopped dead and, with indrawn breaths, admired the vista before them. The cavern rose far above their heads and was naturally decorated with stalactites. In the areas between them were rows upon rows of shelves laden with huge wooden barrels and dusty bottles of wine.

"Hey, Prince, this place is amazing," said Rainstorm quietly. "I suppose princes are used to grand sights like this, are they?"

Tarkyn smiled abstractedly as he gazed around the cavern. "Yes, princes are used to grand sights. But I have seen nothing grander than this, Rainstorm. This place is magnificent."

The three mountainfolk looked suitably smug.

Suddenly, there was a little scattering of stone in a corner behind a row of kegs within a small enclave created by the stalactites.

As the three mountainfolk rushed at the sound, Sighing Wind ordered over his shoulder, "You three, protect the prince. Your Highness, put up your shield."

Tarkyn raised his eyebrows but stayed as he was while his three woodfolk arrayed themselves before him. After a brief struggle, the three mountainfolk emerged from behind the barrels carrying between them a squirming, angry boy, a few years younger than Sparrow. They dumped him unceremoniously on the floor and Blizzard placed a firm foot on his chest to hold him down. The youth in question glowered at them and, from time to time, struggled to free himself.

Tarkyn could feel waves of anger, resentment and hatred emanating from him towards the mountainfolk. Then, amidst the chaos of the little boy's thoughts, Tarkyn felt a hopeless cry for help.

"Let him go," said Tarkyn quietly.

"No, Your Highness," replied Blizzard, "he may hurt you."

Tarkyn raised his eyebrows. "I will take my chances. Now, let him go."

When Blizzard still looked uncertain and made no move to comply, Tarkyn spoke in a voice edged with displeasure, "I believe you forget yourself. I have ordered you to let him go. I would not like to have to ask you again."

Blizzard cast an unhappy glance at Sighing Wind.

"LET HIM GO." The prince's voice ripped through the cavern, echoing against the walls and rattling wine bottles in their racks. "And don't you *ever* hesitate to do my bidding again. I don't give many orders, but when I do, I expect them to be obeyed."

As though stung, Blizzard whipped his foot from the scruffy little boy who took the opportunity to scrabble up and disappear behind the racks of kegs. But rather than looking chastened, Blizzard appeared stricken and confused. He looked past the irate prince and frowned uncertainly at the Tarkyn's woodfolk. "But I don't know what I'm supposed to do. Am I not supposed to protect the prince?"

Ancient Oak glanced at Tarkyn then gave the mountainman a wry smile and said quietly, "You protect as you may, while Tarkyn does as he chooses. Not always the safest, but Tarkyn's wishes override the requirement to protect."

Blizzard wiped his hand over his forehead and let out a breath. "I didn't realize it was so complicated." He resolutely turned his gaze to meet Tarkyn's forbidding stare. "I beg your pardon, Your Highness. I would not like you to think I was acting dishonourably. I truly did not understand."

With a slight jolt, Tarkyn remembered Waterstone's words about keeping his rage under control and realized that he had just thrown some of it out over Blizzard. He let out a held-in breath and said in a calmer voice, "And I beg your pardon, Blizzard. I should have realized that you were trying to do the right thing. I fear that I am still a little edgy after yesterday... Now, who is that young man and what has he done that causes you to treat him so roughly?"

"I would hardly call him a young man, my lord," replied Sighing Wind shortly. "He is little better than an animal. He lives beyond the boundaries of our clearing and will answer to no one. He causes mischief and comes and goes as he pleases."

Tarkyn frowned. "But surely, if he is woodfolk, he must belong to a family?"

"His father is dead, as far as we know, and his mother is a trapper who spends most of her time in the mountains. She brought him back and left him with us two years ago." Blizzard shrugged. "Even when she returns, his mother doesn't have much to do with him. They seem to hate each other."

"Why? Who looks after him? Surely he does not have to fend for himself completely?"

Blizzard growled. "He knows how to look after himself. He steals other people's food and clothing or we give it to him if he needs it. He never speaks and he never does what anyone asks. He's not supposed to be in here, but here he is again."

"And what is his name?" asked Tarkyn.

"Midnight, my lord. He is named for the darkest, quietest hour because he never speaks."

"I see. Just a moment. I need some time to consider." Tarkyn sent a wave of friendship and reassurance out across the cavern to the corner where the young boy was hiding. He followed it with an image of himself standing where he was with the boy next to him and then a query. A picture of the boy being attacked by the mountainfolk returned to Tarkyn accompanied by fear and uncertainty. Tarkyn sent back an image of himself holding the mountainfolk at bay.

Tarkyn spoke very quietly. "If the boy returns, I want no one to move until I say so." He looked around at everyone and checked that he had their agreement. Then he sent a clear request for the boy to come to him, edged with power but also with comfort.

For a long time, nothing happened. Then in the corner, a shadow detached itself from the wall and resolved itself into the scrawny, tattered little boy. Midnight edged his way closer to Tarkyn, keeping his eye carefully on the mountainfolk. As he came closer, Tarkyn saw that the boy's hair was a darker shade of brown than the other woodfolk's and his eyes were a harsh, brilliant green, different from the soft green of the rest of them.

Tarkyn sent him a wave of reassurance and then slowly sank down onto one knee so that he would not tower over the boy as he approached. As the boy drew closer, Tarkyn sent an image of himself and the boy within his shield with a query. Midnight returned a feeling of relief and safety attached to Tarkyn's image.

"Excuse me," said Tarkyn quietly to the woodfolk. "I do this to reassure our little friend, not out of fear of you." So saying, he waved his hand to create a shimmering bronze shield encasing the two of them, but his sudden movement frightened the child into jumping backwards.

Having been startled, the boy then found himself trapped and panicked, even though he had agreed to the shield in the first place. As Midnight banged his fists against the inside of the shield, Tarkyn sent him waves of reassurance and sat down on the dusty cavern floor. Then he sent an image of removing the shield with a query. The boy was too distressed to reply, so Tarkyn dissolved it. The removal of the shield sent Midnight flying forward. He threw himself into a forward roll and came up facing them, gasping with fright, waiting to fend off an attack and glancing sideways to make sure he had a line of retreat.

"Could you all step back slowly please?" asked Tarkyn very quietly. "Give me a clear space."

Tarkyn sent the boy the image he had received of himself and the woodfolk returning from the slingshot practice and then sent an image of the boy with a query. Midnight nodded. Tarkyn emitted a wave of friendliness and an image of the slingshot practice with a sense of invitation. He received back a cautious acceptance underpinned with strong apprehension. So, Tarkyn showed himself standing with the boy while he kept woodfolk at bay, followed by another request for the boy to approach him. Surprisingly, the boy gave a wry little smile before sending a request for the shield to be re-instated.

This time, Tarkyn gave the boy an image of himself waving his hand to create the shield so Midnight would know what to expect. Once he had nodded, Tarkyn waved his hand and recreated the bronze dome. Midnight looked around himself at the shimmering bronze light that looked so vague but was actually quite impenetrable. He put out his hand and touched it, then ran his hand up and down the shimmering wall. He sent Tarkyn the tingling sensation of touching it, with a feeling of interest and enjoyment.

Tarkyn smiled and waited. After a minute, Midnight turned his eyes towards Tarkyn and considered him. Then he looked across at the woodfolk standing a short distance away. He returned his gaze to Tarkyn, inhaled and, as he made his decision, let his breath out in a gust. As though his life depended on it, Midnight walked slowly towards the prince and came to stand before him, rigid tension in every line of his little body. Slowly, Tarkyn brought his hand up and, after a mental request for permission, placed his hand gently on the boy's shoulder. Tarkyn drew on his life force and sent a gentle wave of strength and calm into the boy. Midnight's eyes widened and for a moment fear flickered through him, but he had made his choice and did not run. Gradually, the rigid lines of his little body relaxed and his stance became less wary. Tarkyn ran his hand down the boy's arm and took his hand in his own. Then he gave it a squeeze and let go.

After a minute, Midnight sent an image of Tarkyn being hurt yesterday with feelings of horror and sadness. He leaned forward and frowned, gently running his finger down Tarkyn's cheek with a query. Tarkyn began to explain in images but then decided to demonstrate instead.

Tarkyn flicked a glance down, not wanting to take his eyes off the boy for more than a split second and found a sharp piece of stone. Keeping his eyes on Midnight, he reached slowly for the stone and brought it up in one hand. He directed Midnight's eyes to the stone and then used it to scratch a shallow cut across his own forearm. As the blood welled up, Midnight frowned in consternation. Tarkyn sent a brief wave of reassurance and then focused on the scratch to heal it. As the skin became smooth, Midnight's brow cleared and he touched Tarkyn's face again and pointed to him. Then he reached down and touched Tarkyn's hand and then touched his own shoulder.

Tarkyn smiled and nodded. A feeling of pleased comprehension from the boy was swiftly followed by an image of the two mountainfolk being killed with an accompanying feeling of intense satisfaction. Tarkyn gave a short laugh that made the boy jump but didn't scare him away.

Tarkyn sent him an image of the oathtaking and a query.

Midnight shook his head and showed an image of himself watching from beyond the clearing. Tarkyn merely nodded slowly in understanding, but Midnight pointed at the prince then at himself and then closed his hands around each other in a gesture of bonding with a plea attached. Tarkyn indicated agreement then slowly rose to his feet. He sent an image to Midnight of the boy kneeling with his hand over his heart still with a query. The prince was not going to insist that this strange boy take the oath. But Midnight immediately dropped to one knee, bowed his head and placed his hand over his heart. Tarkyn tilted the boy's chin up so that the boy could see him and then placed his own hand over his heart and sent an image of himself protecting Midnight.

Midnight's face lit up into a happy smile. A sense of belonging, of being accepted as rightful member of the woodfolk and a strong attachment to the prince flooded into Tarkyn. The prince put his hand under the boy's elbow and indicated that he should rise. Then he firmly placed Midnight's grubby hand in his and kept it there. He indicated the shield with a query and, after Midnight nodded, winked it out of existence.

At last, Tarkyn looked around at the mountain folk. "Thank you for waiting. Why was Midnight not included in the oathtaking?"

Sighing Wind frowned a little. "We did not even consider him, my lord. We would not have been able to make him cooperate, even if we did. And to be frank, I would not have thought, before now, that he would even have understood what was going on. None of us can talk to him."

Tarkyn frowned. "What about using signs or gestures?"

"We always thought he was gone in the head," replied Blizzard, whose harsh voice reflected his usually harsh choice of words. "So we didn't bother unless we really had to. He generally ignored us anyway."

The prince glanced down at Midnight to make sure he was still all right, then said, "I have just had a long conversation with him. And do you know what his main reaction to taking the oath was?" When the mountainmen shook their heads, Tarkyn continued, "Pleasure at being counted as woodfolk."

"It looked more like he wanted to be connected to you, my lord," said Sighing Wind.

Tarkyn shrugged self-deprecatingly. "That too. After all, I am someone he can talk to."

"And how can you talk with him?" asked Rock Fall.

"In the same way I talk to birds and animals. We use images and feelings."

Sighing Wind raised his eyebrows. "As I said, Sire, he is little better than an animal"

"Don't you ever say that about him again." Tarkyn's eyes glittered with anger. As Tarkyn's displeasure made itself felt, Midnight looked up at him uncertainly. The prince smiled down at him. "He is a fine little woodman whose only problem is that he can't hear or speak. That means you need to be more protective of him since he can't hear danger approaching, not relegate him to looking after himself and ignoring him."

Sighing Wind gave a condescending smile. "Of course, Sire, you have only just met him while we have had to put up with his antics for years. I think you will find he is a nasty little piece of work when you come to know him better."

There was a short silence as Tarkyn went still to think. After a moment, he turned to Ancient Oak. "What are the rules about a child staying with their parent?"

"A child stays with their parents unless they are unable to care for them for some reason. With the parent's permission, the child may stay with others. If you are thinking about

Midnight, I would say that his mother's opinion is of little account because she has effectively abandoned him."

Tarkyn turned back to the mountainfolk. "I would like to take Midnight with us when we go. Do you think anyone will object?"

"Hardly, my lord," replied Sighing Wind. "I think we would all be glad to see the back of him."

Tarkyn looked at his three woodfolk. "And you?"

"As long as you can persuade him to have a wash in one of those icy pools, Prince." Rainstorm squatted down and gestured, "Come here, little feller. Come and say hello."

Midnight glanced up at the prince, but when Tarkyn sent a wave of reassurance and a picture of Rainstorm and himself as friends, the little boy let go of Tarkyn's hand and walked over to stand in front of Rainstorm.

The mountainfolk shook their heads in amazement. Rainstorm took Midnight's hand and stroked it as a greeting then gave him a pat on the back.

"He wants to join in with the slingshot practice," supplied Tarkyn.

Rainstorm mimed using a slingshot and raised his eyebrows with a smile. Midnight glanced at Tarkyn, then back at Rainstorm, and nodded with a wavery smile. Then he took a little breath and rushed back to stand next to Tarkyn again, grabbing his hand firmly and holding it with both of his.

"I think you have an appendage, I mean, friend," said Lapping Water with a smile. She looked down at the little boy and smiled and waved at him. Midnight returned her regard solemnly and then released a hand to give a quick little wave in return before grabbing onto Tarkyn again.

Tarkyn smiled ruefully. "I think you're right. I'm not sure what I've just taken on here but there's no going back now.

Shall we continue our tour so we can return in good time for dinner?"

"There is not much more to see, Your Highness," said Sighing Wind. "There is a smaller cavern to the right where we bottle the wines and label the bottles before sending them out."

Tarkyn relayed this to Midnight who sent back an image of two more caverns running off from the rear and the left.

"And the other two caverns?" asked Tarkyn.

Sighing Wind frowned. "They house our most precious, oldest wines. I would prefer not to take you into those caverns with Midnight."

Tarkyn smiled. "Oh, you needn't worry. Midnight goes into them all the time. He knows from watching you that they are important but doesn't know why. So he goes in to look at them."

"Blasted little pest. Going where none of the other children are allowed," growled Blizzard.

Tarkyn raised his eyebrows. "Other than leaving footprints, has he caused other damage?"

"He moves things around and hides things. Sometimes they take months to find."

Ancient Oak laughed. "He's playing. Every kid plays hide-and-seek of some description."

"This is not supposed to be a child's domain in here. He can play outside," snapped Sighing Wind.

"With whom?" asked Tarkyn dryly. "At least in here, you are forced to take notice of him." He gave a short laugh and added, "I think you'll find one of your better corkscrews over in that corner behind that rock."

2 8

Once the tour was finished, the next hurdle was returning to the clearing with Midnight in tow. The boy had gradually become used to Tarkyn's woodfolk, but he had kept up a constant barrage of poisonous looks at the mountainmen. He had a long history of derision and disregard from the mountainfolk in the clearing, and as they neared the firesite, he baulked and pulled back. If Tarkyn hadn't kept a firm grip on his hand, he would have bolted.

Tarkyn stopped walking and knelt down in front of the boy. He put his free hand on his heart and then gave a firm instruction for Midnight to come with him into the clearing. Midnight eyed him askance for long moments, then placed his hand on his heart and bowed his head. With a shuddering, deep breath, he raised his head high, looked Tarkyn in the eye and nodded. Tarkyn smiled and stood up. Together they walked into the clearing, ignoring all the curious and astonished gazes. Everywhere, eyes went out of focus as conjecture raged around the firesite.

Ignoring them all, Tarkyn walked across the clearing with

his little charge in tow and asked, "Danton and Sparrow, would you like to join us for a short slingshot competition before dinner?" He looked around. "And Summer Rain, could you bring a towel and something to scrub up this young man please? He may need some sort of a tonic too. I don't really know about these things. He seems a bit malnourished though, don't you think?"

Once he had things in place, he turned around to the rest of the woodfolk gathered at the firesite. "To those of you who don't know him, this is Midnight. He is a young woodman who has been shamefully neglected. He belongs to the woodfolk and deserves as much consideration as any of you, perhaps even more since he can't hear or speak. He is not stupid or crazy. He has been lonely and reviled but that is now at an end. If you dishonour him, you dishonour me. I have promised him that he will be safe and will be made welcome among you. Please make sure that I keep my word."

"But how have you tamed him?" asked Dry Berry, round-eyed with amazement. "He is a wild thing."

Tarkyn smiled down at Midnight. "I have not tamed him. I have talked with him and reassured him, using images and feelings. As with all of you, he is bound to me as I am to him. Until his mother reappears, I will take responsibility both for his actions and his wellbeing. If you have an issue with him, take it up with me."

Tarkyn watched as an interesting ripple of nearly-voiced complaints considered, but quelled on second thoughts, by their owners. He smiled wryly. "I see you have decided to let bygones be bygones. I agree with your decisions. Let us start from here and let each of you give the other a fresh start."

Once he had overcome his nervousness, Midnight proved to have a high degree of competence with a slingshot for a seven-year-old. He stayed close to Tarkyn the whole time, and if he was more than a few yards away, kept throwing anxious glances at him. When people smiled encouragement at him, he frowned ferociously at them, thinking they were making fun of him. Only Tarkyn's constant reassurance kept him from rushing angrily at people who, for the first time in his small life, were actually trying to be friendly towards him.

Sparrow frowned at Tarkyn. "He's not very easy to get on with, is he?"

"No, he's not, but give him a chance, Sparrow. He's frightened still and he's not used to people being kind to him. He will learn, if we are patient, that we are his friends."

Further difficulties awaited them at the cold deep pools when Summer Rain and Rainstorm tried to persuade the little boy into the water for a bath. Midnight twisted and wriggled until he finally broke free and ran panting to the edge of the treeline where he stood trembling and glowering at them. Tarkyn took him in hand and gave him a severe instruction to cooperate. Midnight sent him a woebegone look full of reproach and, with tears rolling down his cheeks, submitted to the ministrations of Rainstorm and Summer Rain. He cried piteously the whole time sending out waves of betrayal and despair to Tarkyn. Even when Tarkyn wrapped him in a towel and helped to dress him in a fresh set of clothes, an honour unrecognised by Midnight, the little boy wouldn't meet his eyes and turned his shoulder away from the prince as he sniffed and hiccoughed his way through the aftermath of his tears. As soon as he was dressed, he hunched himself up in a small unhappy ball, turned away from everybody and closed himself off.

Tarkyn frowned at the woodfolk. "What am I supposed to do now? He thinks I've betrayed him and won't speak to me."

"You could show him yourself going into the pool yesterday," suggested Rainstorm. "To show him it's not a punishment..." He gave a cheeky little grin. "Though of course it is, both to yourself and those of us around you, *forced* to accompany you."

Tarkyn gave a slow smile. "It's just as well he can't hear you. But I will try your idea." Tarkyn shared his memory of his dip in the icy pool with the distressed child and received a response of flat disbelief.

Tarkyn blinked in confusion and looked at Rainstorm. "He doesn't believe me. I've never had this problem before. How do I show him that I am telling the truth?"

Rainstorm grinned broadly. "Ha. That must be quite a shock for you. You, who are as honest as the day is long."

Rainstorm walked around in front of the sullen little heap and squatted down in front of him. Midnight hunched himself into an even tighter ball. Rainstorm tapped gently on his shoulder and kept on tapping until Midnight lost patience and swatted his hand away. Rainstorm immediately brought his hand back and resumed his tapping. Midnight finally looked up, his eyes filled with venom.

Rainstorm pointed to himself, Tarkyn and then the deep dark pool. He nodded and then grimaced and pretended to shiver. Then he pointed at Tarkyn and wiggled his finger in a circle near his temple indicating that Tarkyn was crazy. Suddenly Rainstorm found himself knocked onto his back with an irate seven-year-old, loyal even when upset, straddled over him ready to belt the living daylights out of him. Rainstorm grinned up at him, pointed to Tarkyn and gave a thumbs up sign then sent a series of gestures to show Midnight firstly that the little boy and Tarkyn were friends and then that he was also Midnight's friend.

Midnight scowled down at him, then sat back on Rainstorm's stomach and folded his arms. After a minute, the child pointed at himself and then Tarkyn, still without looking at him. He wrapped one hand around the other in the sign he had for friendship but then, with a caught sob, threw his hands apart.

Rainstorm still pinned to the ground, frowned and shook his head and reiterated that Midnight and Tarkyn were friends. Midnight pointed at Tarkyn, then put his hands on his hips and frowned furiously.

From the sidelines, Sparrow gave forth a chortle. "He thinks Tarkyn is bossy too." She walked around into Midnight's line of sight and nodded vigorously. Then she too pointed at Tarkyn and wagged her finger as though she were telling someone off.

Tarkyn, watching all this, sighed. "Even when people can't talk, they still talk about me. It is amazing." He came around to stand next to Sparrow. "Right. I've had quite enough of this." He leaned forward and picked Midnight up from on top of Rainstorm and swung him onto his hip. Midnight immediately pulled back and tried to wriggle away but received a very stern instruction to stop. The little boy flicked a shocked glance at Tarkyn, but being a boy of spirit, recovered enough to make another half-hearted attempt to escape. Holding him with one arm, Tarkyn frowned and prodded Midnight and himself in the chest then firmly placed his hand over his own heart. The prince raised his eyebrows and sent a query tinged with disdain.

Midnight's face flushed with chagrin. With both his hands braced against Tarkyn's shoulders to hold himself away, Midnight stared for long moments into Tarkyn's steady amber eyes. Then he slowly placed his hand on his heart and subsided with a sigh to rest his head on Tarkyn's shoulder.

Tarkyn smiled proudly over the little boy's head at everyone watching. "You see? In the end, he is an honourable little woodman."

29

But if Tarkyn thought that simply giving Midnight support and protection would stop his mischievous ways, he was sadly mistaken. Midnight was a playful, wilful seven-year-old who had grown up with little but punishment and abuse. He had a very weak foundation on which to base his trust in anyone, and it gradually became clear that the first task he had set himself was to test out both Tarkyn's limits and tenacity.

The next morning, Tarkyn emerged holding a frog he had found in his shelter. He held it out ruefully to show Lapping Water.

She laughed. "You know why that is, don't you?" When Tarkyn shook his head, she continued, "Because he was angry that you went off into your shelter without him. He's used to being alone but he doesn't want to be. He wants to be with you, especially at night, not with the other children in someone else's shelter."

Tarkyn frowned. "But I thought he would like to be with other children. And will he not become too reliant on me if he is always with me?"

Lapping Water smiled up at him. "He is already too reliant. But he will need to feel safe with you for a long time before he gains enough trust in the world to venture forth without withdrawing completely again. If you hold him close, he may eventually gain enough strength to pull away without running."

"And if I hold him at arm's length?"

"If he chooses to stay and persevere, he will never feel secure and will alternate between trying to come close to you and forcing you to push him away."

"With frogs, for instance," said Tarkyn dryly.

She nodded and took the bright green tree frog out of his hands. "At least he's only using harmless little frogs. He could use stinging nettles or snakes if he were really malicious.

Tarkyn looked much struck. Then he shrugged and smiled. "I don't for a second think he's nasty, just pesky." He looked around. "Where has he got to now?"

Even as he spoke, a soggy wad of moss hit him on the back of the head. As Tarkyn swung around, Midnight's head appeared from behind a rock, laughing uproariously.

"Little sod," whispered Tarkyn. "Watch this." The sorcerer sent a sharp ray of bronze into the tree above Midnight's head and severed a small branch that dropped down on Midnight. The boy jumped in fright and looked around wildly. "Whoops. I've frightened him now."

Tarkyn hurriedly sent out waves of safety and an image of what had happened. Much to Tarkyn's dismay, the little boy sank down and dissolved into tears. "Oh dear. He thinks I'm angry with him and was punishing him. Poor little bugger. No one has ever played with him before."

Tarkyn walked quickly over to Midnight's hiding place, picked the little boy up and held him close, stroking his hair and patting his back. He surrounded him with kindness and played out a mock battle in images to explain to Midnight what he had been doing. Lapping Water brought over the frog and held it out. She pointed to the frog and then to Midnight with a smile. Midnight's eyes flickered in alarm but when it was clear that no one was angry, he grinned sheepishly and held out his hand.

"I'll take that if you don't mind," said Tarkyn, intercepting the frog's return. He sent a series of images indicating no frogs in the shelter and waited. Midnight placed his hand on his heart and then lay his head sideways on Tarkyn's shoulder so he could still see his face. Tarkyn smiled and gave him his frog. Then he pictured Midnight in Tarkyn's shelter at night with a query. Midnight flung his arms around Tarkyn's neck and squeezed so tightly he nearly choked him. Then he wriggled to get off and once down, shot off into the undergrowth.

Lapping Water shook her head. "Strange boy but devoted. He's yours, heart and soul, whether you want him or not."

Tarkyn stood staring at the spot where Midnight had disappeared. "Oh, I want him. I wouldn't dream of abandoning him."

Lapping Water tucked her hand into Tarkyn's arm. "You know, you really are such a kind person. Many people wouldn't bother with him unless they had to, even if they could talk to him."

Tarkyn smiled down at her, feeling a little breathless at her proximity. "They would if he could share his thoughts with them. He, too, is kind."

Lapping Water nodded. "I saw him touching your face and checking out your injuries."

"Hmm. I'm afraid he saw the execution of those men." Tarkyn hesitated before adding, "He was pleased by that but I don't think it was ghoulish. It was more in support of me and justice being done, if you see what I mean."

"That's when you laughed, wasn't it?"

Tarkyn nodded ruefully. "I suppose I shouldn't have but he had such a deep feeling of satisfaction about it that I couldn't help myself. It was such a straightforward emotion. No doubts or debate. Plain, simple, justifiable revenge from his point of view."

Suddenly a shower of leaves, twigs and nuts fell down around them. Tarkyn looked up to see Midnight laughing in the branches above him.

"Ooh dear. I've started something now," he said, as he sent a ray of bronze to dislodge a small dead branch that was hanging above Midnight. The little boy still jumped in fright when the branch hit him unexpectedly but he recovered instantly, grabbed the branch and threw it down on Tarkyn before disappearing further up into the tree. Tarkyn and Lapping Water dodged out of the way, laughing.

"I think I need reinforcements," said Tarkyn as he sent a message to Sparrow and the other children to join him as he waited for Midnight's next move.

When they arrived, he told them about the mock battle and asked whether they would like to join in. Sparrow, who knew him too well, said, "Can't manage on your own, hey? I bet you've run out of ideas already."

Tarkyn grinned ruefully. "I have already used the same idea twice... Out of two times."

Sparrow giggled, then asked, "Can you get him to come here? We need to make two teams. Otherwise it will be all of us against him."

Tarkyn nodded. "Thanks Sparrow. I'll see what I can do." He sent his mind up into the trees and when he found Midnight, gave a clear instruction for him to return. Midnight at first refused, but Tarkyn sent him an image of hand on heart and received reluctant agreement.

When Midnight saw the other children, he sidled up and

stood behind Tarkyn. Tarkyn drew him out, not unkindly, to stand next to him and held his hand reassuringly while they talked. He translated Sparrow's idea into images and waited. A shy smile appeared on the little boy's face and he nodded.

"You sort out the teams, Sparrow. Don't let people choose their teams and leave Midnight until last. Don't forget he can't hear or mindtalk. So you'll have to figure out how to deal with that before you all go off in different directions. You can use me for instructions at the start."

"I can use you to relay messages all the way through," said Sparrow, blithely unconcerned about loading up Tarkyn with an ongoing task. "You can use images to talk to him and to us. It's just that he can't connect to anyone else."

Tarkyn glanced down at the little boy who was nearly quivering with excitement and trepidation beside him. He sighed. "Very well. I will do that for his first time but I can't be on call every time you play. So you will have to figure something else out in the future. Agreed?"

Sparrow nodded and set about organising the teams, firstly taking Midnight to be on her team.

Tarkyn, the anxious guardian, added, "You had better make sure he knows the rules before you start. Otherwise he may do something to annoy you all because he doesn't understand."

Sparrow frowned at him repressively. "I think I can figure that out for myself. The hard bit is explaining it in pictures."

It took less time than they expected to explain the rules and then to develop tactics within Sparrow's group. Even though Tarkyn had told everyone that Midnight wasn't stupid, most of them had had lingering doubts. So, they were agreeably surprised at the speed with which he understood the requirements and sent back images of other workable suggestions. In less than ten minutes, the children had dispersed into the surrounding forest to play out their battle.

For the rest of the morning, Tarkyn sat at the firesite chatting, drinking tea and from time to time, relaying messages from one active little mind to the next. He monitored Midnight occasionally, checking what he was up to and how he was feeling, until Midnight sent him an exasperated message to stop distracting him.

Lapping Water and Falling Branch laughed when he told them.

"I can see my role as guardian of a small urchin is destined to be short-lived," he said ruefully.

Lapping Water shook her head. "Oh, I don't think so."

"No, just be glad of some peace and quiet while you can get it," added Falling Branch. "I think you've gained yourself a full-time job."

Tarkyn gave a grunt of laughter. "Oh good. Because I never have anything else to do."

E ven before he had finished speaking, half a dozen chattering children and one quiet but happy one came running into the clearing and rushed off to get food and drink.

Hard on their heels, Waterstone appeared by the firesite and walked purposefully over to Tarkyn. "We have trouble brewing. Remember how you set up the relays of woodfolk so we could keep in touch with everyone?"

Tarkyn nodded.

"We have just received a mindmessage from some of our woodfolk near the encampment. Stormaway went for a walk in the forest to make contact with them. They have brought in huge hunting dogs..."

"Bloodhounds," supplied Tarkyn.

Waterstone frowned. "How did you know that?"

Tarkyn grimaced. "Lord Tolward mentioned a rumour that they might be bringing them in. I forgot all about it. Sorry. I should have told you."

"Hmm. Anyway, Stormaway says his old apprentice, Journeyman Cloudmaker, has led a group of mounted men to the crossing on the Great West Road where you were last seen and has set these bloodhounds on your trail."

Tarkyn blanched. "Oh my stars! That trail will lead them straight here. When did they leave?"

By this stage, an anxious audience had tuned into the conversation. Glances of trepidation and resentment passed between the mountainfolk. Catching some of these, Waterstone said gruffly, "Don't blame Tarkyn. We are the experts at covering our tracks. We should have been more careful. After all, we knew this sort of thing could happen because we've had the wolves tracking us down before. And then it wasn't Tarkyn they were after."

Tarkyn ignored the strained atmosphere and asked again, "So when did they leave?"

"Sorry. Not long ago. Maybe a couple of hours."

"We left the Great West Road three days ago," rumbled Thunder Storm. "We slept for a couple of hours before crossing the grasslands and then for a few more hours once we were in these woods. And we've now been here for nearly two days. If they come straight here without a break, they could arrive in less than a day."

"I don't think they could travel for that long without a break," put in Danton. "Their horses and the bloodhounds will need rest and food."

"True, but they will travel faster than we did, with horses and without children," Thunder Storm pointed out. "And we also stopped for a couple of hours in the grasslands."

"Oh no!" breathed Tarkyn. "Lord Tolward and his family. My scent will lead straight to his door."

Dry Berry waved a dismissive hand. "That is the least of our worries. We have to make sure they don't find you or any of us."

"Or the cellars," added Sighing Wind.

Tarkyn ran his hand through his hair. "I'm afraid Lord Tolward's family is not the least of my worries. If I can do anything about it, I cannot allow those people to suffer on my account." He looked at Waterstone. "How long do you estimate it will take them to reach his place?"

Waterstone grimaced. "I don't know. If they left a couple of hours ago, maybe four or five hours, perhaps a bit longer."

"And how long would it take Danton or me to travel back to them?"

"Too long, Tarkyn." rumbled Thunder Storm. "Even if you ran all the way, it would take you a good eight or nine hours. Their house is much closer to the other side of the grasslands. And you can't run all the way, so it would take longer."

Tarkyn looked up at the ring of people who had gathered around them. "We need to think this through carefully. Could you all sit down rather than standing over me and we'll work out what to do."

Once everyone was seated, Tarkyn continued, "We have two problems to sort out. Most importantly, we need to make sure we are gone from here leaving no scent before they arrive. Basically, I think that is something you all know much more about than I do. So, I'll leave you to confer about that and let me know what we're doing. Secondly, and more urgently, I have to figure out how to warn those sorcerers that a posse is headed their way. I know sorcerers are not your concern but they are mine. So, could some woodfolk help me with this please, while the rest of you work on the other?"

The woodfolk resolved themselves into two groups, the smaller one containing the two sorcerers. Tarkyn was pleasantly surprised to find a couple of mountainfolk in his group along with several of his own woodfolk.

"The easiest solution would be for us to send a mind message to someone in the vicinity so that they could tell your

Lord Tolward to clear out." Rainstorm enjoyed watching Tarkyn's surprised expression, before adding, "But of course, that's not going to happen."

"They could leave a message for the sorcerers to find," suggested Danton.

"What sort of message?" asked Waterstone.

Danton looked around him and coloured faintly before saying slowly, "A note, a written message..." He ground to a halt and grimaced. "You don't write, do you?"

"No," said Rainstorm, quite unembarrassed about being illiterate. "What for? That's more of a sorcerer-wizard thing."

Tarkyn smiled faintly at Danton's embarrassment and suggested, "What about a drawing?"

Everyone thought about that idea for a few minutes, but although they could think of a series of pictures involving a figure with long black hair running from big dogs, they struggled with trying to show the relevance and the timing of the events.

"Blast Stormaway!" Tarkyn grimaced in annoyance. "If he were closer, he could do it, but he's still at the encampment, from what you were saying."

"It's just as well he is or we may not have realized this was happening," said Danton.

"Possibly," said Autumn Leaves, with a wry smile. "But we have left woodfolk watching that area as per his lordship's instructions."

Tarkyn gave a grunt of laughter. "You know perfectly well we worked those instructions out together and I just delivered them."

At this juncture, Sparrow came over and sat herself down on Waterstone's knee. Tarkyn frowned suddenly, as he realised that Midnight was nowhere in sight. He gave his head a little shake, thinking he would sort out the sorcerers' dilemma first, and then look for his pesky little acquisition.

"Your Highness," said Rock Fall tentatively, "why don't you write a note and order one of your eagles to deliver your message?"

Tarkyn gave a wry smile. "I hate to disillusion you, but Dry Berry overstated the case when she said that I had mastery over the eagles. They protect me as they choose. I struggle to make even owls do my bidding if they are not in the mood. They are certainly not messengers."

"They might accede to a request, mightn't they?" asked Lapping Water.

"They might," conceded Tarkyn, "but I suspect they would have to see the relevance of it to the forest, you woodfolk or me. I think their interest in the welfare of sorcerers is pretty much on a par with yours."

"Virtually non-existent," said Autumn Leaves flatly. "Sensible birds." Then he spotted Danton trying to maintain a neutral face and added, "Present company excepted, of course."

Thunder Storm's quiet older son, Rain on Water, came to sit on his knee while they were talking.

Tarkyn's anxiety levels rose even higher. "I wonder where Midnight is. I haven't seen him since they all came back. I assumed he was off on his own, doing something, but it's beginning to be a long time since I saw him."

A silence filled with unspoken thoughts greeted this statement.

Tarkyn smiled wryly. "So you think I should take a bit of time out to go and find him? I thought we could figure out what we were going to do first and then find him."

Thunder Storm smiled. "Kids don't always work that way.

They don't conveniently run by your timetable. You don't want to lose track of him if there is crisis looming."

"Fine. I'll go and look for him while you people think of ideas. I'll be back soon."

Tarkyn walked to the edge of the clearing and sent his mind out looking for Midnight. Eventually, he homed in on him, but the little boy's mind was closed off and Tarkyn couldn't find a way through the barrier. He could, however, follow its trace to the source. So, he set off through the forest to find his little protégé.

Midnight was curled up inside the hollow of an old dead tree. He had withdrawn into himself and did not respond to Tarkyn's mindmessages. A feeling of stoic resignation emanated from him. As Tarkyn touched his shoulder, Midnight jumped in fright, then raised a tear-stained face that lit up with cautious relief when he saw Tarkyn.

Tarkyn crouched down, scooped the little boy up into his arms and sent him a query. Midnight responded with an image of all the woodfolk gathered around, looking stern and worried while he had stood in their midst frightened that something was happening he didn't understand. He had feared that everyone talking to Tarkyn would be followed by the prince sending Midnight away. Nevertheless, he had waited, still hoping that Tarkyn would come for him, and watching the other children going to their parents. From the little boy's point of view, there had been a wall of people he would have had to breach to reach the prince. Tarkyn could see all too well how impossible it would have been for Midnight to walk through all those uncertain people to reach him. He had fled the clearing long before everyone had sat down.

"Oh, Midnight," he murmured, "I'm so sorry. You are the last person in the world who needs a celebrity looking after you." Tarkyn hugged him close and sent waves of contrition and warmth to the little boy. He replayed Midnight's imagined vision of Tarkyn sending him away and then shook his head and put his hand on his heart.

As they walked back, Midnight's hand held firmly in his, Tarkyn asked about the mock battle and gradually Midnight recovered enough to show him all the ploys they had used against each other. After a few queries from Tarkyn and a few added details from Midnight, they were back on an even keel again.

In response to a query from Midnight, Tarkyn produced an image of the bloodhounds following a trail through the woods. He used a complicated series of imagined and real images to show Midnight what they had been talking about when he left the clearing.

Midnight stopped responding after a while and, when Tarkyn sent him a query, was waved impatiently aside. Tarkyn frowned, not at all pleased at being so casually dismissed. He was just about to berate Midnight when the little boy tugged at his sleeve and looked up at him. When he was sure he had Tarkyn's attention, he reeled off three images in quick succession; water washing away the scent, wolves attacking the bloodhounds and finally Tarkyn scolding the bloodhounds and making them turn away. When he had finished, he tilted his head and raised his eyebrows, requesting Tarkyn's response.

Tarkyn blinked in astonishment. "Inventive little thing, aren't you?" he said and nodded his approval.

Midnight smiled but when Tarkyn indicated that they should share the ideas with the others, the boy's fragile confidence deserted him and his face tightened in trepidation. Waves of reassurance washed around him, but they did little more than stop him from running away. No one had ever taken any notice of him except to shoo him away so the thought of several people focused on him and evaluating his ideas was unnerving, to say the least. Tarkyn gave his hand a friendly squeeze but kept a firm grip on it.

As they entered the clearing, Rainstorm glanced at Midnight, gave him a little wave and patted the ground next to him. Midnight returned the wave half-heartedly and looked from Rainstorm to Tarkyn and back again, clearly not wishing to offend Rainstorm but not wanting to leave Tarkyn's side either.

"Come on, young fellow," said Tarkyn with a wry smile, "I'll squeeze in next to Rainstorm and you can sit on my knee. Move over Rainstorm." Matching actions to words, Tarkyn settled himself in next to Rainstorm and looked around at everyone. "What did I miss? Any ideas?"

"You could spook the horses as you did last time," suggested Rainstorm.

"Yes, I could, although if the trackers are really determined they will abandon the horses and continue on foot."

Rainstorm shrugged. "At the very least, it would slow them down."

"True," Tarkyn pondered a moment. "Last time, some of the riders were quite cruel to the horses. I'll keep it in mind, though." He paused. "I have a few suggestions. I'll just show them to you, shall I, and you can see what you think?" He transmitted Midnight's ideas and waited.

Thunder Storm heaved a sigh. "It would solve all our problems if we had a good solid shower of rain. But it has been inconveniently dry for the last few days." He paused. "I don't suppose Stormaway could conjure up some rain for us, could he?"

Tarkyn shrugged. "Maybe if he was in the right place, but I doubt that he could do it long distance and I don't think he'd have enough power for a widespread storm."

"Water is a good idea though," said Waterstone. "We can

bring water up from the stream to cleanse this firesite, if nothing else. It will take a lot of water though. We might be able to combine that with laying a false trail."

"You could use water to obliterate the trail from the top of the ridge down to the sorcerer's house," Lapping Water narrowed her eyes as she thought, "but I think it would be too hard for the couple of woodfolk in the vicinity to do on their own. If there were more woodfolk there, it would work."

Tarkyn grimaced. "And to be honest, I have reservations about the wolves idea. I think I could persuade them to attack the bloodhounds, but many of them may be killed or mauled, either by the bloodhounds or by arrows from the men on horseback."

"I like the idea of you bossing around the bloodhounds," chortled Sparrow. "Tell Midnight. I bet he'll like it too."

"Thanks, Sparrow," replied Tarkyn dryly. "Actually, Midnight already knows. It was he who thought of these ideas."

There was an arrested silence. Then all eyes turned to Midnight who was studiously keeping himself occupied by tying knots in the ties of Tarkyn's shirt.

"Not bad, for such a little fellow," said Rainstorm. "In fact, pretty bloody impressive. None of us has come up with anything better yet."

Feeling everybody's eyes on him, Midnight flicked a glance around them all. Even though he could feel Rainstorm's approval, he couldn't deal with the intensity of so many people focused on him, sure from experience, that something would go wrong. He made a convulsive attempt to escape but Tarkyn was ready for him and kept a firm arm around him.

"Uh-uh. Stay here, young rascal," said Tarkyn as he surrounded him with reassurance. "No one's going to hurt you."

Midnight looked up at Tarkyn, gauged the determination in his face and subsided.

"So, will you try to control these bloodhounds then?" asked Waterstone.

Tarkyn raised his eyebrows and asked caustically, "What? Break their spirits as I did the wolf pack leader's? I'm surprised you would condone such a course of action."

Waterstone returned Tarkyn's glare steadily. "Unlike wolves, bloodhounds are born into servitude. Their spirits are broken before they are even born."

Having had more experience of domestic dogs than Waterstone, Tarkyn would have liked to challenge this statement, but faced with an undercurrent of tension in the woodfolk that had nothing to do with dogs, he chose to back down.

"Well, good. That will make it so much easier for me to impose my will, won't it?" he said lightly, looking way from Waterstone to glance around the group. "Where's Running Feet? Ah there. I'll need a bit of peace and quiet to work from this distance. Would you come with me to help navigate my mind to those bloodhounds please?"

Tarkyn dislodged Midnight from his knee and but kept hold of his hand as he stood up. He thought of asking whether Midnight would stay with Rainstorm but decided that Midnight wasn't ready to be left alone in a large group yet. As the three of them left the clearing, he smiled at Running Feet. "You see? This is what comes of having in depth discussions with Sparrow over maps. I now think of you as my chief navigator."

"Why not? I'm as good as any at navigating, better than some. And I've already worked with you on sending your mind over long distances. So it saves you having to explain it all over again."

Tarkyn smiled. "True. As long as you don't mind."

Running Feet looked down at Midnight trotting along at Tarkyn's side. "I think you can probably let his hand go now if you want to. He won't run away with just us. It's the crowd that he needs to get away from."

Tarkyn loosened his grip but left it up to Midnight whether to take his hand away or not. Midnight looked up, smiled and left his hand where it was.

As soon as they were out of earshot, they found a comfortable log to lean against and sat down. Midnight left them to it and headed off to play nearby.

"Right. It will be easier this time because you have just travelled this route yourself. Last time you had never even been there."

"True," said Tarkyn, "and if I had any sense of direction at all, I should probably be able to do this on my own." He shrugged and grinned. "But as it is, I haven't a clue which way we came from." He looked around. "Except that I know we didn't come from up there in the mountains."

Running Feet grinned in return and shook his head. "You must have more idea than that."

Tarkyn's eyes twinkled. "Well, the mountains were ahead of us and to the left. So," he swept his arm through a wide arc, "we must have come from somewhere over there."

Running Feet laughed. "Yes, we did. And yes, I can see why that's too vague a guide to follow to retrace our steps."

"I thought so," said Tarkyn with a hint of perverse triumph.

Over the next few minutes, Running Feet led Tarkyn's mind back over their journey until they reached the forest between the Great West Road and the grasslands.

"They should be somewhere in here," he said quietly.

Tarkyn let his mind rove around, feeling for the minds of

the bloodhounds. After a few minutes he frowned. "I can't find them. Just a minute. I'll try to contact a bird to help me."

Tarkyn's mind wandered higher among the treetops until he found a large brown kite. He nudged its mind and asked it to fly across the forest in search of the bloodhounds. Suddenly, Tarkyn was soaring across the treetops scanning the ground far below him. He noticed with interest a small rabbit hopping for cover and a weasel sneaking through a stand of grass. With great forbearance, he left them untouched and continued his search. A pale blue haze attracted his attention and he swooped down for a closer look. Below him he saw men on horses following bloodhounds, all encased in a sorcerer's bluey-grey shield.

"Hmm. That explains it," grunted Tarkyn. He thanked the kite and pulled out to find himself next to Running Feet with Midnight kneeling next to him, peering anxiously into his face.

Running Feet gave a wry smile. "You forgot to tell your young friend what you were doing. I'm glad you weren't gone too long. He's been getting tenser by the minute."

Tarkyn smiled, grabbed Midnight before he could shy away and pulled him down to sit next to him in the circle of his arm. Tarkyn shared the images with both of them. "They must have realised that their animals were being interfered with. And they've taken precautions this time."

"Blast! And that knocks out another idea we had about using slingshots on the bloodhounds." He glanced at Tarkyn. "We didn't particularly want to do that anyway, because the soldiers had already noticed that the brigands and the encampment guards had both been mysteriously knocked out in the same way."

"Yes. It's becoming as much of a trademark as arrows would be. Just no proof."

Tarkyn relayed this conversation to Midnight as they

walked back to the firesite. Then, at Midnight's request, he asked Running Feet, "Are bloodhounds afraid of wolves? And do wolves smell strong?"

Running Feet shrugged. "I don't know anything about bloodhounds but most animals are afraid of wolves. And I think they do have a strong scent. They certainly have a strong taste."

"I can vouch for that." Tarkyn grinned as he passed this on to Midnight.

Just as they sat down, Midnight tugged at Tarkyn's sleeve to gain his attention and sent an image of wolves milling around and running back and forth along the grassland ridge closest to the sorcerer's house.

Tarkyn's face lit up and he nodded his approval. He let Midnight know that he would tell them all in a little while. The advent of the sorcerer's shield into the equation worried all of them and needed discussion. Sorcerer's shields were difficult to deal with.

"That means they could arrive here and we would be unable to attack them to defend ourselves as we did with the wolves," rumbled Thunder Storm.

"But equally, the bloodhounds can't attack you from within a shield, although they could get up very close before the shield was removed," said Tarkyn.

"But you can attack from within your shield," pointed out Rainstorm.

"Yes, I can, but that is using magic." Tarkyn shrugged. "Besides, being able to perform more than one lot of magic at once is a skill I've only recently developed and I don't think other magic users can do it." He smiled reminiscently. "Holding up several branches at once to be repaired taught me that."

"But couldn't one huntsman hold up the shield, and another use magic to attack?"

Tarkyn shook his head decisively. "No one can penetrate another person's shield, from without or from within. Anyway, as long as we have warning of their advent, we can be long gone before they get here."

"We still have the problem of keeping the trackers away from Tolward's house," put in Danton.

Tarkyn smiled. "Yes, we do. But I think our young friend has come up with another idea that might just work."

Rock Fall shook his head in amazement. "Far from being the fool we all thought him, this child's mind is bursting with ideas. No wonder he gets up to so much mischief."

Midnight had lost interest in the proceedings at this stage and had settled down on a patch of dirt, trying to draw the sorcerer's house he had seen in the images.

"So, what's his idea this time?" asked Rainstorm.

"That I ask the wolves to run up and down along the sorcerer's side of the ridge so that their scent frightens the bloodhounds from that side and masks the trail down to the house. No need to endanger the wolves. They can be gone long before the hounds arrive." Tarkyn looked around. "Will that work, do you think?"

Thunder Storm pushed his son off his knee and directed him to go and play with Midnight before saying, "Yes, I think so. The scent of the wolves will make them shy away from heading down the slope, especially since the trail will still continue along the top of the slope."

Despite his intentions of avoiding conflict, Tarkyn could not resist flicking a snaky glance at Waterstone and saying, "Of course, it will require me to capitalize on having broken the wolf's spirit."

Waterstone didn't give an inch. "Having imposed your authority on the wolf as you have on the rest of us, you might as well make use of it."

The air sizzled with tension. Midnight looked up, alarm in his eyes. Tarkyn tried to send reassurance to the little boy but Midnight could feel the tension and glanced at Tarkyn then at Waterstone. He pointed to both of them, then with his head tilted in query, wrapped his hands around each other in his gesture of friendship. Tarkyn nodded firmly.

Midnight looked a query at Waterstone who let out a breath and said, "Of course I am. I just can't stand hierarchies."

Tarkyn grimaced. "You weren't angry at the wolf for imposing its leadership on the rest of the pack. Why pick on me for imposing it on him?"

"I would have thought that was obvious, Tarkyn. The wolf did not impose his leadership on us."

"Neither did I, if you remember," snapped Tarkyn. "My role was imposed on me as much as it was on you. And in case you haven't figured it out, imposing leadership does not necessarily mean breaking someone's spirit."

Before any more could be said, Tarkyn stood up and strode out of the clearing, leaving an uncomfortable silence in his wake. Midnight watched him leave but knew better than to go near an angry adult. So, he returned to playing with Rain on Water to watch and wait.

31

After a short pause, Rainstorm said with spurious cheerfulness, "So, it's great, isn't it, that Tarkyn can depend on our support when he's going through a difficult time."

"There are moments," said Waterstone through gritted teeth, "when you live on borrowed time." He heaved a sigh. "He doesn't let much pass him by, does he? I made one snide remark, must be a week ago now, and he's been fretting over it ever since."

Autumn Leaves shifted position to get more comfortable. "That's because he knew and you knew that it meant something more than was said."

Rock Fall listened to this exchange with some concern. "He hasn't broken anyone's spirit, has he? What have we let ourselves in for?"

Waterstone waved his hand dismissively. "No, of course he hasn't. He hasn't even come close. In fact, he spends more time carefully preserving everyone's autonomy."

Rock Fall grunted. "Can't say that's the impression I've

had. Poor old Blizzard. Threw him around like an empty wine keg, then bellowed at him for disobedience when Blizzard was just trying to protect him. Ordered us all to be nice to Midnight when we've had nothing but grief from him for years." He shrugged. "The prince seemed friendly enough when we were mucking around with the slingshots, but mostly he's pretty distant and formal. Still, I suppose that's what princes must be like. Hopefully, we won't have to have too much to do with him."

The woodfolk around him were so non-plussed by this speech that none of them knew where to start in rectifying Rock Fall's impression. After a stunned silence, in the way of things, they all started talking at once.

Rock Fall held up his hands. "Whoa. Sorry I said anything. I didn't mean to upset you."

"We're not upset," replied Lapping Water. "That is, we're not angry with you. I suppose we are upset that you have the wrong impression of Tarkyn."

"I can see why, though," added Ancient Oak. "He was pretty harsh with Blizzard in the caves, much worse than he has been with any of us."

Rainstorm nodded. "Yep. I must admit he was fearsomely angry for a moment there."

Autumn Leaves and Waterstone looked at each other and had a quick mental conference before Waterstone said, "We are in a bit of a dilemma here. We can explain Tarkyn's behaviour, at least to some extent, but we're worried that it will be a betrayal of his confidence."

After another short conference, Autumn Leaves continued, "Because you and Cavern are the only mountainfolk to make the effort to join this group, we'll tell you. But only if you don't go around telling everyone else."

Rock Fall and Cavern looked intrigued but agreed readily

enough. Autumn Leaves took a deep breath and let it out. "Tarkyn was badly hurt by that attack. As soon as he was out of sight of you all, he virtually collapsed. He has been angry and jumpy ever since. He is very wary of trusting people at the best of times and despite the oath you gave him, he is nowhere near trusting any of you yet. He appears formal because he does not yet feel safe among you. If you think back, he wasn't formal or distant with Dry Berry when he first saw her."

Rock Fall nodded reluctantly. "True."

"Yes, I had forgotten that," said Cavern in her strangely reverberating voice.

"At least reserve your judgement about him," added Waterstone. "What you're seeing now is the aftermath of the attack."

Lapping Water placed her hand on Rock Fall's arm. "If you think about how he behaves with Midnight and how he is with us, that's more like his usual self. Although even with us, a fight between Waterstone and him has blown up out of nowhere."

Waterstone grimaced. "I'm afraid I didn't help matters. I could have backed down and apologised for my previous remark but didn't. I'm pretty rattled at the moment myself. I've always hated the whole business with the oath and I find the degree of magical power that Tarkyn can unleash if he chooses very unnerving. Watching the absolute control Tarkyn exerted over that ferocious animal is what prompted my remark about breaking the wolf's spirit in the first place. And when I see unbridled displays of his power, I can't help thinking that if he chose to behave that way, that could be me or any of us."

"That was us, the other day," Rock Fall pointed out.

"Yes, but quite frankly, you deserved it," said Rainstorm flatly. "Bashing up Tarkyn, jeering at him, beating up Danton, and even more unforgivably, attacking two of your own, Summer Rain and me."

"So, it's acceptable for them to attack Tarkyn and me, is it?" demanded Danton.

"No, it is not," snapped Rainstorm, "but from the point of view of woodfolk unused to sorcerers, it is more understandable."

Just as things were beginning to overheat, a gentle wash of humour swept around them and they turned to find Tarkyn leaning against a tree smiling wryly.

"I'm sorry I was snaky, Waterstone. I just can't seem to exert that total control you're so worried about, over myself. So little bits of anger keep leaking out all over the place."

Waterstone gave a grunt. "I too am sorry, Tarkyn. Rainstorm is right. Now is not the time to fall out with you. I suppose we are all a bit edgy at the moment."

Tarkyn's eyes lit up. "Have you noticed how often Rainstorm is right about things? He is an ornery bastard sometimes, but he's usually right." He sent a little wave of friendship specifically to Rainstorm, as he smiled around the group. "Now, if you could keep yourselves from each other's throats for a little while longer, I'll borrow Running Feet again to see whether I can politely ask the wolf pack leader for assistance."

Waterstone's eyes narrowed, aware that he was being teased. "And if he refuses?"

Tarkyn smiled and gave a little bow. "If you will permit me and if it does not offend your sensibilities too much, I will have to resort to bluff over such a long distance since I am quite unable to exert any real power."

"You outfaced him last time, long before he came anywhere near your magic. So I am sure you can do it again this time."

Tarkyn became quietly serious. "And yet, I truly do hesitate to do that, Waterstone, if it is going to upset you. I do want to protect that sorcerer family but I'm sure we can think of another way, if we have to."

Waterstone's eyes gleamed in appreciation, both at the offer and at the tactics. "No. Time is short. Stick with this plan. The damage, if there is any, has already been done."

Tarkyn considered him for a moment. "Very well, but I will only agree to doing this if you are with me, tuning in to my exchange with the wolf. Then you can satisfy yourself that I am not breaking this animal's spirit or if you think I am, can intervene and stop me. – Agreed?"

Wryly aware that the situation had been reversed so that he was now persuading Tarkyn to do something he had previously disapproved of, Waterstone reluctantly nodded agreement.

As they left the clearing, Tarkyn checked briefly with Midnight but the little boy was happy to stay where he was in the corner with Rain on Water.

With one woodman guiding the direction and another monitoring his intent, Tarkyn sent his mind roving into the western forests searching for the fearsome, feral mind of the wolf. Tarkyn tuned into him just as the pack leader and a group of five other wolves were mounting an attack on a hapless red deer. The three men watched with the lead wolf's fierce intensity as the wolves circled the deer. Then, a brief flicker of command radiated from the pack leader and the wolves sprang at the deer with business-like aggression. The men could feel the sharp teeth of the lead wolf biting into the strong neck muscles of the deer and tasted the dusty, bristly coat and the blood. They saw the close proximity of the other wolves' fangs and yellow eyes and felt the weight of the deer on neck and jaw as the animal was dragged down.

As Tarkyn pulled his mind away from the wolf's, he was left with a faint impression of sneering derision. He looked a little pale. "I'm afraid my lupine associate is now thinking that I am faint-hearted." He gave a wry smile. "There may be some truth in that. I have to admit I did not relish the idea of partaking in a freshly killed, uncooked meal of blood, bone and flesh, complete with fur and gristle."

Tarkyn was pleased to notice that the two woodmen also looked a little unwell.

"No," said Running Feet, "I don't think I could have stood that for too long. Besides, you would have had to exert enormous force to pull him away from his lunch. He has such a harsh, focused mind, doesn't he? You're better off waiting until he's sated."

"Then he'll probably be too full to move," pointed out Waterstone.

Tarkyn grimaced. "True. Bad timing, isn't it? How far is he from Lord Tolward's house on the grasslands, Running Feet?"

"I can't be sure, but I would say a good twenty miles further east. What do you think, Waterstone?"

"Yes, at least that. They have returned to their homelands deep within the western forests."

"Twenty miles!" exclaimed Tarkyn. "They'd never make it to Lord Tolward's with a safe enough margin for disappearing before the bloodhounds arrive, anyway." He ran his hand through his hair. "Blast it! Now what are we going to do?"

"You could send in a horde of rats to drive the sorcerers out of their house before the trackers arrive," said Waterstone, "but young Winguard won't be able to get far with his broken leg."

"And the trackers will still know I have been in the house."

"At the very least, you can alert their farm dogs to make a fuss and give them advance warning of the bloodhounds. After all, your sorcerer friend knew about these bloodhounds, didn't he?" asked Running Feet.

Tarkyn grimaced. "Yes, he did. But I don't think he

expected them to be used so quickly or to bring danger right to his door."

They mulled over possibilities for the next ten minutes. Tarkyn had just decided that the dogs were the best option when intense feelings of satisfaction, relish and, surprisingly, gratitude flooded into his mind. He blinked then closed his eyes and managed to connect the two woodmen as the wolf's mind connected with his. With a glint of sardonic humour, the wolf crunched down on a final piece of gristle as he sent a query to Tarkyn. Before Tarkyn answered, he asked why the gratitude and received back images of the wolf enjoying his dinner and of chains in the encampment being broken and thrown away. Then the query came again.

Using a complicated series of images, Tarkyn managed to convey his visit to Tolward's house and that he wanted to protect the house from the bloodhounds following him. He demonstrated his request but managed to show that distance now made this impossible. The intense yellow eyes of the wolf filled his mind, the mere existence of its fierce personality posing a threat. Tarkyn held quietly firm and waited. Slowly, an image of two lone wolves skirting the edge of the woods to the east of the grasslands filled his mind. As he watched, the wolves halted and lifted their heads sniffing the air, their eyes focused into the distance. Then they wheeled around to their left and loped swiftly out into the open space of the grasslands, up the slope and along the eastern side of the ridge.

With the ease of years of mental co-operation, Running Feet immediately sent directions to Tolward's house through Tarkyn to the two wolves. As they neared the sorcerers' houses, the pace of the wolves slackened. They slunk along lower to the ground and sought out scant cover behind low bushes or tall stands of grass. Tarkyn belatedly realized that the wolves' safety was threatened not only by bloodhounds but also by the very people they were striving to protect. He sent an urgent message to wait. With a wrench, he broke contact with the wolf and then, using Running Feet's guidance, found the farm dogs, showed them the wolves and requested their silence.

Re-connecting with the wolf was not difficult. As soon as Tarkyn released his focus on the dogs' minds, the lead wolf's mind pounced and firmly restored the connection between them. Tarkyn explained what he had done and received a feeling of critical evaluation followed by acknowledgement. Clearly, the wolf was not used to participants in his operations initiating their own actions. Attention reverted to the two wolves, who had now reached the point at the top of the ridge above Tolward's holding. They ran back and forth, crossing and re-crossing the area between the ridge and the house. Now and then, one of them would stop and stare insolently down at the farm dogs who watched them, quiet but rigid with frustration.

Then, surprisingly, they did not skirt back around to return to the forest but continued along the ridge, zigzagging back and forth across Tarkyn's trail where he had rejoined the woodfolk at the top of the ridge. To lend weight to their presence, they chose a few places to urinate before finally retracing their own trail back along the ridge and down into the forest. Tarkyn sent out waves of approbation and appreciation.

Again, Tarkyn's mind was filled with the image of the lead wolf staring at him with frightening intensity. Then, just for an instant, the wolf blinked and looked away in a gesture of submission before returning his fearsome gaze to Tarkyn. Keeping his own eyes trained on the wolf, the prince bowed his head slightly in acknowledgement and sent a final wave of thanks before pulling out of the wolf's mind.

32

F or a few minutes, the three of them just sat there in silence, recovering from the intensity of the wolf. Finally, Waterstone blew out a breath and said, "Fair enough. I take your point. There is no way that wolf's spirit is broken. He exudes strength and domination." He glanced sideways at Tarkyn. "You're a scary bastard, Tarkyn, if you have achieved dominion over his will."

Tarkyn smiled faintly and looked at his friend. "I guess that is something we all have to live with."

"What is?" asked Running Feet from the other side of him.

Tarkyn's smile broadened. "That I'm a scary bastard."

"Oh."

Waterstone chuckled. "You know, when you put it like that, it seems much more straightforward. I can live with that. Meet my friend, the scary bastard. Has a certain ring to it, don't you think?"

Tarkyn smiled but shook his head regretfully. "I'm afraid I have been too much of one lately, especially to Blizzard."

"That's the thing I've noticed about you though," remarked

Running Feet. "You tend to return like with like. If a person is kind or needs your help, they receive your kindness and help but if they are unpleasant or threatening to you, you return their unpleasantness in full measure and then some."

"The trouble is that sometimes I get the wrong end of the stick," said Tarkyn. "For instance, when I first met all of you, I subjected you to my anger because I wrongly thought you were forcing me to stay in the forest, and yesterday I tore into Blizzard for refusing to obey me when he was determinedly risking my ire to protect me."

"Perhaps yesterday his heart was in the right place, but the day before he was downright nasty. So I'm not surprised you were ready to expect the worst of him," said Running Feet.

Waterstone frowned. "Anyway, I don't think it's true that Tarkyn returns unpleasantness in kind as a general rule." He glanced at Tarkyn. "What about Rainstorm? You sidestep his challenges all the time without beating him down."

Tarkyn laughed. "Not all the time, but usually. His churlishness isn't about me though. It's about him. He's not unpleasant, he's entertaining."

Waterstone turned back to Running Feet. "And what about the forestals? They attacked him, were untrusting and unfriendly, shot arrows at him and tied him up." He raised his eyebrows at Tarkyn. "And from what I gather, you just let them do it until they calmed down."

"True, but let's face it. That was tactical," replied Tarkyn with a twinkle in his eyes.

Running Feet frowned and said casually, "So, how do you justify not executing any of them when they actually shot arrows at you?"

Suddenly, the air between them stilled, a clear indication that Running Feet's words had gone beyond the pale.

With a careful effort, the prince took a breath and replied

tightly, "I do not have to justify myself to you." He let out the breath as he controlled his anger and continued, "Having said that, because you are my friends, I will try to. I'm afraid you may not like my answer, though."

Waterstone looked at this man who held so much power and had just resisted his urge to hit them with his inbred disdain. He knew that Tarkyn often had to overcome such feelings and he smiled warmly at him. "You know, Tarkyn, I remember you saying that it was difficult for you to keep a dignified distance from us when you first came here and that, subsequently, you decided not to. But I don't think many people realize how hard you have to work on yourself to keep your friendly lack of distance. Just to let you know I appreciate how hard it is and that you make the effort to do so."

Tarkyn gave a wry smile. "Thanks. I try. But I'm afraid I'm having no success at all with the mountainfolk."

Running Feet who had watched this exchange with some interest, said, "Hardly surprising. You can't go from the verge of outright war through to casual friendship in the space of a couple of days. How long did it take you and the home guard to feel comfortable with each other?"

Tarkyn shrugged. "It depends on whether you count the two weeks I was unconscious or not. After all, in a funny way, my friendship with Waterstone was forged during that time and it gave people a chance to become used to my presence among them even if they weren't talking to me. But after that, I suppose it was at least another week before we began to feel at all comfortable with each other. Then, of course, it all blew up and I left and found the forestals." He grimaced. "Which brings us back to your question, Running Feet. How do I justify not executing the forestals when they fired on me with intent to kill?"

Tarkyn picked up a stick and concentrated on breaking bits

off the end of it as he basically thought out loud. "This is not an easy question to answer. Firstly, I came as a complete surprise to the forestals. They had only vaguely heard of me, had had nothing to do with the oath-taking and knew little about royalty and the world outside the forest. All they really knew about me was that I had thrown my weight around when I first entered the forest and that I was branded a rogue sorcerer. Whereas, by the time we reached the mountainfolk, they had had long conversations with you, and Dry Berry had been to my inauguration into the woodfolk and had had time to report back. Secondly, the forestals were frightened of an unknown outsider and were acting in self-defence. The mountainfolk already knew my reputation within the forest and knew I was no threat to them. Their attack on me was driven by resentment and viciousness. One was self-defence, as they saw it. The other was unprovoked, unjustified attack." He raised his head and looked at them in turn. "I'm sorry. That's the best I can do. In the end, the reality is that my justification is simply a matter of the motivation behind the attack." He gave a slight smile. "Which is not actually very helpful for anyone thinking of attacking me and wondering if they can get away with it."

There was a thoughtful silence. Waterstone picked up a couple of pebbles and started tossing them. "I think that's pretty clear, actually. I just think you hadn't really thought it through until now."

"I hadn't. I'm afraid I basically made my decision in both cases without thinking it through at all." Tarkyn smiled ruefully at them. "You see, what I said at the start is true. I don't have to justify my decisions. I can do as I choose." He threw away the last of his stick. "But luckily for all of us, what I choose to do is to stay true to myself and to you, and at least for the most part, to act in ways that you will approve of." He gave a little shrug of embarrassment. "Because, after all is said and done, I value your good opinion of me." Tarkyn stood up and brushed himself down. "So you see," he said, not looking at them, "that absolute power of mine that you're so worried about is not so unboundaried as you may have thought."

Waterstone threw away the pebbles he had been playing with, stood up and grasped Tarkyn's arm. "Look at me," he said firmly. When Tarkyn reluctantly met his eyes, he continued, "I do not think you would exert your power over me or the others like that. I'm sorry I said that to Rock Fall. That is my gut reaction sometimes, when I see you wielding power, but it is not what I truly think. I trust you, Tarkyn. I always have. I think perhaps I need to discipline my own reactions a little more. You deserve better support from me than you have been receiving."

As they started walking back to the clearing, Waterstone added, "And you're not a scary bastard. You're an impressive bastard. It would be all too easy to turn you into a monster when really, you have used your power and integrity in acts of true heroism on our behalf."

Running Feet cleared his throat and said gruffly, "He's right, you know. At least he is now. He shouldn't have doubted you."

Tarkyn took a deep breath. "Oh yes, he should. Power is very seductive." He eyed Running Feet whom he did not know so well and hesitated. After a moment, he decided to continue, "It is fun and exciting to wield so much power. It is intoxicating and therefore incredibly dangerous. I can feel that it could be quite addictive if I let it be. Never become complacent about my power nor let down your guard on my behalf. I need people I can trust to monitor me. I need you to be my boundaries."

"Tarkyn, it is because you are so honest and recognize the dangers that we can trust you," objected Waterstone.

"Recognising and avoiding danger are two different things."

Tarkyn grimaced. "The problem is that if I became seduced by power, I would be unlikely to listen to your objections anyway."

"Then make sure you remember this conversation. So I can use it in the future if I need to" said Waterstone phlegmatically.

Tarkyn smiled. "You're so practical. I will take care to remember it but let's hope we never need it."

33

W hen they returned to the clearing and Tarkyn had been effusively greeted by Midnight, they filled everyone in on the success of their efforts with the wolves. Once the discussion had run its course, the prince quietly asked Waterstone to request Blizzard to come to see him a little way from the clearing. Even though no one else heard the message, all eyes were on Blizzard as he walked across the clearing like a man condemned, in the direction that Tarkyn had taken.

"Please take a seat." Tarkyn gestured at a tree stump and sat on one himself. He considered the mountainman, noting the tension in his posture and his set face. "Blizzard, I must apologise to you."

Blizzard looked up in surprise.

The prince continued, "I have treated you unkindly on two occasions. On the first occasion, I could argue that you deserved it, as much for the way you spoke to me as anything else. But equally, I know that you felt justified in your actions at the time."

Blizzard nodded uncertainly, not sure where this was going.

"On the second occasion, in the caves yesterday, I'm afraid the fault was entirely mine. I should have made clear my expectations before making you the target for my anger. So, for that, I apologise unconditionally." Tarkyn waited but Blizzard sat there, saying nothing. "Well, if you have nothing you wish to say to me, you may go."

Blizzard looked flustered but didn't move.

Tarkyn frowned and asked gently. "Is something else wrong? I don't know what else I can do but apologise to you."

"No, my lord." Blizzard cleared his throat. "This is much better than I was expecting. I thought you still were angry with me." He twisted his hands in his lap and he raised his eyes anxiously to meet Tarkyn's. "You see, I thought I had betrayed everyone's honour and I have been feeling terrible about it."

"Did you not believe me when I apologised at the time? I said then that I should have realized you were trying to do the right thing."

"I wasn't sure if trying was good enough." Blizzard kept wringing his hands. "I often try to do things, but when they aren't good enough, I still get into trouble about them. Just trying to do something has never kept me out of trouble before. It's only when I succeed that it's all right."

Tarkyn began to realize that part of Blizzard's antagonistic style was bluster to cover his uncertainty. It was becoming apparent that Blizzard struggled to keep up with sharper minds around him. The prince placed a hand over Blizzard's hands to still them. "Listen to me. I made the mistake, not you. You were very brave to stand up to me when you were doing what you thought was right. Are you clear now what I expect?"

Blizzard nodded. "I think so. I protect you, but if you ask me to do something, I do that then go back to protecting you."

"Exactly." The prince took his hand away. "And are you clear about what I think of you?"

Blizzard looked a bit panic-stricken. "Only sort of."

"In the past, we did not agree." Tarkyn waited until the mountainman nodded. "But now that you have sworn the oath, you have been honourable and shown respect to me and I'm sure that will continue. Clear so far?"

Blizzard nodded, at last looking a little relieved.

"And," continued Tarkyn, "if you respect me and abide by your oath, then I also will protect you, treat you with respect and help you in any way I can. Clear?"

Blizzard heaved a sigh of relief. "Yes, Sire. And I'm sorry I was rude to you when we first met." He glanced at the prince and then looked away. "I don't know if you can understand how many nightmares I had when I was young, about meeting a sorcerer when I was alone in the woods or being attacked by an outsider because I hadn't taken enough care."

"I must admit I still have some reservations about your physical roughness with your fellow woodfolk but I do understand why you reacted as you did. It used to scare the life out of me when my mother told me frightening stories about meeting a rogue sorcerer in the woods." Tarkyn gave a wry smile. "And the funny thing is, now I have been branded one myself."

Blizzard's brow wrinkled. "What is a rogue sorcerer as opposed to an ordinary sorcerer?"

"Do not be frightened off by this if I tell you, because it is not true of me. Someone has spread untrue rumours about me." Tarkyn took a breath. "A rogue sorcerer is someone who has a lot of power like me but is evil or deranged in their use of it - not like me."

Blizzard considered him for a long time while he thought through everything Tarkyn had done against them with his power. Finally, he nodded his head and said slowly, "No. I can see that you are not a rogue. Just." For the first time, a glimmer of humour showed through. "Though, to be honest, if I thought you were, the last thing I would do is admit it to you."

"So, we are no further forward." Tarkyn thought for a moment. "Yes, we are because you wouldn't have said the last bit if you really thought I was a rogue. True?"

"True."

"Do I gather from what you said earlier that someone or several people are giving you a hard time about yesterday and saying that you have let them down?" asked Tarkyn.

"Bloody old Sighing Wind came back and told Dry Berry and now they are both getting stuck into me. They're not too happy about what I did with your sorcerer friend either. So, one way and another, I am seriously in the shit."

"Blizzard, you have such a charming turn of phrase."

The woodman rolled his eyes. "Oh no! Sorry. I've stuffed up again, haven't I? Here I am, trying to be polite to you and look what's happened. It's a bloody nightmare."

Tarkyn laughed. "Being polite to me does not mean you can't swear. It means you can't swear at me."

Blizzard breathed a sigh of relief. "Well, that's all right then. Because I swear like a stinking town dweller when I get rattled."

Tarkyn raised his eyebrows. "I presume town dweller is the ultimate insult, is it?"

"Absolutely. It doesn't get much worse than that." Tarkyn watched in amused silence as it dawned on Blizzard what he had said and a dull red crept up over his face. "Oh. I suppose you're one, aren't you?"

Tarkyn grinned. "Don't worry, Blizzard. I know you're not meaning to be offensive to me. Anyway, I may have been a town dweller once, but not anymore." He stood up. "Come on.

Let's return to the others. I'll see what I can do about getting them off your back."

The prince put a friendly arm around Blizzard's shoulder as they turned to walk back. At first Blizzard jumped a mile, but then endured it with rigid compliance.

Tarkyn smiled. "Now come on, Blizzard. Let's have some of that courage. We are going to walk back into that clearing looking like old friends but only if you can get that scared rabbit look off your face."

Blizzard glanced up at him and took a deep breath. "I'll try."

"You know, Blizzard, I am no more dangerous up this close than I am several feet away. In fact, having my arm around you hampers my ability to cast spells. So you are arguably safer up close."

"Like me with a bow and arrow?"

Tarkyn raised his eyebrows and smiled. "Exactly. So, provided neither of us is planning to use a knife, we should both be reasonably safe."

Blizzard relaxed enough to smile back. "You wouldn't feel unsafe anyway, would you?"

"Me? Absolutely I would. Without my shield, I'm as vulnerable as the next man. And I probably trust people a lot less than you do. Didn't you notice me getting bashed up the other day?"

Blizzard actually gave a little laugh, at just the right moment as it turned out, because it meant that as they entered the clearing, he was smiling. "Yes. I did happen to notice that. But I also noticed the eagles and the fact that you recovered quickly."

"Only the body recovered quickly, Blizzard." Tarkyn smiled wryly. "That's why you scored all that anger yesterday."

Light dawned. "Oh, I see. So, when you said you were a little edgy...?"

"I meant I was as jumpy as a wild cat among a pack of wolves."

Blizzard stopped walking and swivelled around so he could see Tarkyn clearly. Tarkyn's arm fell naturally from his shoulder. He looked puzzled. "Are you always this honest and open with people you hardly know?"

Tarkyn smiled wryly. "Yes to the first and no to the second. But I owed you an explanation, my friend." He clapped Blizzard on the back. "Come on. Let's find ourselves a drink, shall we?"

Blizzard leaned in close to him and whispered, "You don't have to keep hanging around with me if you don't want to. Everyone's seen us now."

Tarkyn laughed. "You don't think much of yourself, do you?"

Blizzard was taken aback. "Well, when you put it like that, no, I suppose I don't. Certainly not enough of myself to think that a legend would want to hang around with me."

"A what?"

"You know. A real forest guardian."

Tarkyn gave him a slow smile. "Well, if you can deign to drink with a sorcerer, I guess I can put up with drinking with you."

Blizzard blinked, then hazarded a more daring flash of humour. "When you put it like that, I guess I'm doing you a favour."

By this stage, their assumed friendship was becoming less contrived, and silent word spread like wildfire that Blizzard had managed to restore the mountainfolk's uncertain honour.

34

M idnight watched Tarkyn returning to the clearing with Blizzard and decided to keep clear. He could still remember the feeling of Blizzard's boot on his chest holding him down in the cavern. He was slowly beginning to trust Rainstorm and Lapping Water who had both been in the cave when he had first gone to Tarkyn and had made an effort to take Midnight under their wings when Tarkyn was busy, but he was still wary of all mountainfolk.

Midnight tapped Lapping Water on the arm to gain her attention, then pointed to the plaited leather wristband that she wore. He mimed making one and then pointed at Tarkyn who was standing talking with Blizzard on the other side of the clearing

Lapping Water smiled and looked over Midnight's head to meet Rainstorm's eyes. "Do you have any leather thonging anywhere?" she asked.

"I expect so," replied Rainstorm. He disappeared, to return a few minutes later with an assortment of pieces.

Lapping Water helped Midnight to tie off three long pieces of thonging at one end, attached it with a loose knot to a slim low branch, and then showed him how to weave the three strands back and forth over themselves to create plaiting. Midnight quickly took over and became absorbed in his self-appointed task. He frequently inspected his work critically and redid any part where he spotted twists or unevenness in the plaiting.

Midnight had just been helped to tie off the other end of his creation when he felt a warning tap on his shoulder and looked up to see Blizzard walking towards them. His convulsive flick into hiding was forestalled by Rainstorm who grabbed him firmly around the waist. Midnight thrashed and twisted but Rainstorm held firm. As Blizzard bent down to hand Lapping Water a goblet of blackberry wine, Tarkyn came into view behind him.

"Oh dear. This is not the way I wanted Blizzard to be greeted," he murmured quietly.

Even as Tarkyn sent out a wave of reassurance tinged with disapproval, much to his and everyone else's surprise, Midnight went limp in Rainstorm's arms. The little boy then sat himself up, his cheeks pink with embarrassment and managed to convey that he had made a mistake.

Once he had handed Rainstorm and Midnight their drinks, Tarkyn sat down and swung Midnight onto his knee.

"Thanks for looking after the young one," he said. "Has he been trying to run off all the time?"

Rainstorm shook his head. "He's been quite happy until now. He just got a fright, that's all."

As soon as Blizzard was looking the other way, Rainstorm gave Midnight a friendly nudge. When Midnight looked up at him, he nodded in Blizzard's direction and scowled furiously. Midnight remembered that Rainstorm, too, had experienced a run-in with Blizzard and smiled conspiratorially. Tarkyn glanced at the two of them, took one look at their smiling faces and made sure he kept Blizzard's attention directed elsewhere.

After a minute or two, Rainstorm rejoined the conversation by asking Tarkyn, "So, have you given Midnight a cup of wine?"

"No, I have not. Midnight's drink is fruit juice."

Blizzard looked from one to the other. "I wouldn't be giving Midnight wine either."

Ignoring Tarkyn's triumphant glance, Rainstorm frowned. "Wouldn't you? But you people are the winemakers. I would have thought your children would learn to appreciate good wine from an early age."

"Of course they do, but not until nearer bedtime...and not at all tonight if we are leaving soon."

Tarkyn rolled his eyes. "For a moment there, I thought I had an ally."

"No," smiled Lapping Water. "You're on your own on this one."

As evening fell, plans were finalized for dealing with the impending arrival of the bloodhounds. If the trackers were really keen, they could conceivably arrive before dawn, although it was more likely that they would not risk injury to their horses by travelling through thick forest at night. Once the woodfolk's evening meal was over, the firesite was cleared and false trails were laid, leading away from their planned route over the mountains. The sorcerers and the woodfolk then doubled back either by levitation or through the trees, respectively, and set up camp up in the huge pines in the foothills of the mountains. The mountainfolk had agreed that they should remain with the home guard until the danger had passed. Until the bloodhounds had been and gone, they would all sleep up in the trees, a prospect Tarkyn looked forward to with some trepidation.

As everyone settled down for the night, Tarkyn wedged himself into the crook of a branch with his legs dangling down either side. He leant forward and rested his head on his arms and tried to go to sleep. But he had never tried to sleep in a tree before. Every time he began to drift off, he would jerk awake, sure that he was sliding sideways and about to crash down through the branches onto the forest floor far below him. He wondered whether Danton was managing any better.

After jerking awake for perhaps the seventh time, Tarkyn felt a jab of irritation directed at him from somewhere above. He grunted and returned a sleepy apology. A small wave of exasperation was followed by the appearance of Waterstone who stood casually on the next branch, one hand on his hip and one hand holding the branch above him.

"You're a bloody pest, Tarkyn. Every time you wake up, you send a small judder up the whole tree."

Tarkyn smiled apologetically. "Sorry. I've never done this before. It's harder than I thought it would be and I didn't think it would be easy."

Waterstone stood looking at him for a minute or two, considering what to do. Finally, he asked, "Would it help if we tied you to the trunk?"

Tarkyn's face brightened. "Yes. Good idea. I think it would. I could focus on the rope holding me in place then."

Between them, they secured Tarkyn to the trunk using a slipknot that he could yank on to pull himself quickly free if the need arose. Once he was comfortable again, he asked after Danton.

"Danton is sleeping like a baby," responded Waterstone dryly, with a clear inference that being a sorcerer was not an excuse.

"Be kind, Waterstone," came Lapping Water's voice softly from the side. "Danton didn't fall down twenty feet, out of a tree, with his hands tied behind his back."

"Oh blast it, Tarkyn! I should have thought of that." Waterstone was so chagrined by his lack of thought that he was flustered. "You should have said something. I forgot all about that. No wonder you're having trouble sleeping."

Tarkyn gave a quiet laugh. "To be truthful, I didn't think of it either."

"Didn't you? But I bet the memory comes up as soon as you start drifting off."

Tarkyn shrugged. "Maybe." He thought for a moment. "Yes, maybe it does." He smiled. "But now I should feel safe enough with the rope around me and that will hopefully forestall the memories as I go to sleep. Go on. Go and get yourself some sleep before morning...and thanks." When Waterstone had disappeared up into the boughs above, he added quietly, "And thanks to you too, Lapping Water. I should be able to separate past from present now." Before he settled to sleep again, he glanced across at the spot where Midnight lay curled up in the fork of three branches nearby. Bright green eyes glowed back at him through the gloom. Tarkyn started a little at their intensity but sent a little wave of friendship before closing his eyes.

Next time he opened them, the morning light was well established and there were sounds of activity all around him. Tarkyn sat up and rubbed his eyes to chase away the last of his sleep. He waggled his feet, which were feeling rather leaden after dangling down all night, and then lifted his legs so that he was sitting cross-legged against the trunk of the huge pine. With the rope still fastened stalwartly around his waist, he took great pleasure in being able to sit unconcernedly so high up.

Lapping Water brought him a bowl full of nuts and dried

fruits and sat down near him to eat hers. Seeing Tarkyn awake at last, Midnight clambered over to them and plonked himself down in the nest of Tarkyn's crossed legs.

"Where's your breakfast, young one?" asked Tarkyn, matching images to words.

"He ate his, ages ago," said Lapping Water. "You know kids. Always up at the crack of dawn."

Tarkyn's eyes twinkled. "You know princes. Always keeping everyone waiting."

Lapping Water choked with laughter on a mouthful of fruit. "I didn't say that," she protested.

Tarkyn grinned. "You didn't have to. It's blindingly obvious that everyone else has been awake for hours."

As they talked, Tarkyn did his best to keep Midnight in the conversation. So, at this point, the little boy sent him a picture of Lapping Water keeping everyone quiet and out of the way so that Waterstone and Tarkyn could sleep on.

"Thanks, Lapping Water," said Tarkyn, pointing at Midnight when she frowned a query. "Why didn't I keep disturbing you earlier in the night as I did Waterstone? You could have used more sleep too."

Lapping Water smiled. "No, I'm fine. I was in the next tree along so I didn't feel the tremors when you kept waking. Besides, Waterstone is constantly on guard for your welfare, far more than anyone else. Sometimes he, too, needs a break."

Tarkyn glanced at her. "Do I place too many demands on him, do you think?"

"No, it's not you. It's his own choice. You couldn't shift him from it, even if you wanted to."

Tarkyn smiled. "He's so wonderfully stubborn, isn't he?"

Lapping Water snorted in a truly unlady-like fashion. "Loyal and dedicated might be a kinder way of putting it," she grinned, "but stubborn is also quite accurate. Here, let me take your bowl if you've finished."

As she reached across to take Tarkyn's bowl, her arm crossed Midnight's line of vision and her leather, plaited wristband dangled before his eyes. Even as Lapping Water registered his eye on her wristband, a wave of consternation from the little boy engulfed Tarkyn. But before he had time to react, Midnight was gone.

"Oh no!" exclaimed Lapping Water. "Quick! Someone stop him!" She went out of focus to send out a silent rallying cry.

"Lapping Water! What's going on? Where has he gone?" asked Tarkyn urgently.

The woodwoman looked distressed. "He made you a leather wristband last night and finished it just before you walked over with Blizzard. None of us thought any more about it. I bet he's left it hanging from the tree in the clearing and has gone back to fetch it."

In the blink of an eye, Waterstone, Rainstorm, and Ancient Oak were gathered around them. Tarkyn looked around them. "Have they found him?"

Waterstone shook his head. "No one will be able to catch him if he doesn't want them to. He's fast and he's used to evading people. Try calling him, Tarkyn. You're the only person he can or will listen to."

Tarkyn sent out an urgent demand for Midnight to return but the little boy's mind was closed off. "I can't reach him. His mind seems to shut down when he's upset about something."

"That's kids for you," rumbled Thunder Storm, appearing to one side. "They get an idea in their heads and can't think of anything else. He will have forgotten all about the bloodhounds and sorcerers. We taught our kids years ago to keep part of their mind open enough to notice when we were trying to contact them but Midnight hasn't had that training."

"I'll have to go after him," stated Tarkyn, unequivocally. He stared around at the circle of mutinous faces and said, "Please. I can't leave that little boy out there on his own, with a pack of sorcerers and bloodhounds bearing down on him. I must go. I promise you I will keep my shield up. Danton can come with me to protect my back. You can't go. You can't risk being seen. Anyway, Midnight will probably only come to me."

Rainstorm, who was quicker than the others to recognize the inevitable, asked, "So, does anyone have an object from near the clearing that Tarkyn can use to translocate?" Faced with hostile stares, he merely shrugged and added, "If he is going, the sooner he gets there the better. He has to find Midnight and be out of there before the bloodhounds arrive."

Reluctant nods preceded a mental conference.

"You had better check how far away the sorcerers are," said Waterstone. "You don't want to translocate into the middle of them."

"No, I certainly don't. Just give me a minute." Tarkyn closed his eyes but opened them again almost straight away. "Hang on. Which way are they coming from?"

Five arms pointed simultaneously in a north-easterly direction, behind and to the left of Tarkyn.

Tarkyn grinned. "Fine. Thanks," He closed his eyes again. Almost immediately he tuned into a nearby golden eagle. So quick was the connection that he suspected the raptors were still keeping watch over him. He transmitted his request and found himself soaring above the forest scanning the ground below. To his shock, he spotted the horses and bloodhounds converging on the clearing less than seven miles away. They were moving steadily, and Tarkyn estimated they had less than forty minutes before their arrival. He transmitted the image to the others before opening his eyes and said urgently, "We have no time to lose. They must have ridden through part of the night."

Just then, Dry Berry appeared bearing a sprig of rosemary that she thrust abruptly towards Tarkyn. "Here. This is from a rosemary bush we planted downstream from the clearing." She produced two small pinecones from her other hand. "These are for your return. Don't worry. They are from a branch close to the ground. You look after yourself."

"I will, Dry Berry. Thanks." Tarkyn looked around. "Where's Danton?"

"Here I am," replied his liegeman as he clambered gingerly over from a neighbouring tree. "Some of us are not as nimble as others, up at this height."

Tarkyn looked around at the woodfolk. "I think you will need to stand by, ready to catch Danton in case he doesn't succeed." He turned to the blond sorcerer. "So, Danton, here is your chance to try translocation. Are you willing?"

"Of course. You cannot go alone."

Tarkyn forbore to respond to that remark and handed his liegeman half of the rosemary sprig. "Here. Now focus closely on the rosemary and use the same incantation as I do. Clear?"

When Danton nodded, Tarkyn stared at the leaves in his hand, incanted, *"Maya Mureva Araya,"* and faded from sight.

Danton took a deep breath, focused on his sprig of rosemary and repeated the incantation. For a moment, he became translucent but then he reverted to shocking solidity and vomited down between the branches onto the forest floor far below. Woodfolk hands held him and kept him from falling as he recovered.

He wiped his mouth with the back of his hand and gasped, "Oh dear. I'm still here. And I feel dreadful."

"However," said Ancient Oak dryly, "Tarkyn is not. So, you'd better sort yourself and try again."

"Give him a minute, Ancient Oak. He's obviously not well," said Lapping Water softly. "Do you know what went wrong? Can you do anything about it?"

Danton nodded and glanced sideways at her. "I know what went wrong. I was overwhelmed by fear and pulled out."

Rainstorm chortled. "What? You? An elite guard? You don't get frightened."

Danton looked daggers at him. "I don't know whether to belt you for not taking me seriously or to accept what you've said as a compliment. The fact remains that fear overcame me. I am not afraid of fighting or of people but faced with losing myself... It scared the life out of me."

"Is that what it takes?" asked Waterstone.

"It seems to." Danton shook his head as though to clear it of a bad memory. "It feels as though you have to dissolve completely to find yourself in another place."

"No wonder Tarkyn has no trouble with it," cackled Dry Berry. "I have never met anyone with a stronger sense of their own worth and identity than Tarkyn."

"True," said Waterstone. "Although he does become confused, sometimes,"

"Of course he does. We all do. But he must have such a strong sense of himself to be able to hold out against all of us without being remote." Dry Berry turned her attention to Danton. "Now, young man, you too are strong. You held out against public opinion to stand by Tarkyn. Just focus on yourself; who you are, your heritage and why you are doing this translocation before you begin."

Danton took a deep breath. "Thanks, Dry Berry." He glanced around at everyone. "Wish me luck." Amidst murmurs of support, Danton closed his eyes and drew another deep breath. Then he opened his eyes, gazed intently at the sprig of rosemary and incanted, *"Maya Mureva Araya."*

This time he faded from sight and stayed away. The woodfolk immediately sprang into action; some to head back to the clearing and others to prepare for the journey ahead.

35

Tarkyn found himself lying nauseated beside the tumbling stream not far from where he had talked with Waterstone. He rolled over and retched but managed to keep his breakfast down. True to his word, as soon as he could focus, he raised his shield. He heard the sound of rushing air but when he turned, no one was there.

"Looks like I may be doing this without Danton," he murmured to himself, not particularly perturbed.

After a few moments, he sat up and walked over to the stream to splash his face. He scooped up a handful of icy cold water and slurped it down with less than his usual finesse, happily aware that, for once, no one was watching him. After slurping down another handful, he sat down against a rock preparing to reconnect with the eagle to find Midnight.

Another rush of air this time deposited Danton in an unhappy heap next to the rosemary bush. The blond sorcerer lay curled up for a few moments before heaving and retching. Tarkyn went to him and patted him gently on the back until he began to recover.

"On my oath, Tarkyn. This is a hideous process," groaned Danton. He looked down at himself. "At least I'm still me. So that's something, I suppose."

Tarkyn looked at him quizzically. "Of course you are. It does make you feel pretty terrible though, doesn't it?" He placed his hand under Danton's arm. "Come on. Drag yourself to the stream and splash some cold water on your face. That's it. Now have a drink and you'll soon be feeling better."

A few minutes later, Danton heaved a sigh and pulled himself together. "Well, that was interesting, I suppose. Okay. So, what do you want me to do?"

Tarkyn smiled at his loyal liegeman. "Thanks, Danton, for going through that. Now, will you guard my back while I find out where Midnight is, please?"

Danton nodded and kept watch as Tarkyn sat back against a tree and closed his eyes. He quickly reconnected with the same golden eagle and asked it to check on the progress of the bloodhounds and then to search for Midnight between the place Tarkyn was now and where he had just come from. The eagle rose above the height of the trees and showed Tarkyn the horses and bloodhounds, already noticeably closer, before wheeling southward to scan the trees for Midnight. Just as the imminence of the bloodhounds' arrival was prompting Tarkyn to pull out, the eagle spotted a little figure dashing down a narrow pathway through the trees. Although it had taken the woodfolk hours to reach the hideaway in the trees where they had spent the night, they had travelled above ground, a slow effortful process. Midnight's tumultuous flight was taking him back to the clearing much more quickly than Tarkyn had anticipated. The little boy was further away from the clearing and in another direction from the bloodhounds, but he was travelling faster and looked as if he would arrive at the clearing at more or less the same time as the sorcerers. With brief thanks, Tarkyn pulled out.

"Dog's teeth, Danton!" Tarkyn was shaken. "We have serious trouble. Midnight and the bloodhounds are converging on each other and should both arrive in the clearing in about twenty minutes time."

"Then we have to intercept Midnight before he gets there," said Danton calmly.

In an uncharacteristic fluster, Tarkyn flapped his arms. "But which way is it?"

Danton smothered a smile. "Tarkyn, I thought you just looked at it from above."

"I did, I did. Please, Danton. Don't argue about what I should know. Just tell me which way we should go."

"Come on. It's this way." Danton set off at a dead run up through the clearing and towards the mountains. "You know we are ruining all our efforts at diverting the bloodhounds? Our scent will take them straight from the clearing to us."

Tarkyn jogging at his side, answered between breaths, "I don't care. I would rather we faced them than ran from them anyway. You and I can handle this upstart of a wizard and his pet sorcerers. As long as the woodfolk are well away, we can manage."

Danton raised his eyebrows but said nothing.

A few hundred yards later, Tarkyn gave a short laugh. "Danton, you produce such speaking silences, I don't know why you ever bother to talk."

"Very funny, Your Highness."

"Oh dear. And now we're back to being formal. You think I'm being arrogant and over-confident, don't you?"

"Far be it for me to criti..."

"Oh, put a sock in it, Danton. Speak your mind, for heavens' sake. We don't have time to pussyfoot about." He glanced at his friend as they ran. "And keep your eyes out for Midnight. We don't want him to get past us."

Danton's mouth thinned with annoyance but he was not going to let Tarkyn force him into incivility. Without commenting on Tarkyn's previous pronouncement, he said, "I think we should stop in a minute and either you can try to contact Midnight again or use one of your bird friends to find him. It would be too easy for him to bypass us, particularly if he is instinctively avoiding people."

Tarkyn knew Danton had dodged his challenge but let it rest as they dealt with the more pressing issue. Tarkyn sent his mind wandering through the trees ahead of them searching for Midnight's mind. Remembering the last time Midnight had been upset, he realized that he should be able to locate the boy, even if he couldn't communicate with him. Suddenly, he exclaimed, "He's up ahead over to the right. Quickly. If you veer off and come at him from the other side of him, you can shepherd him towards me."

Danton sped off without another word. A few minutes later, Tarkyn saw the little boy streaking through the undergrowth towards him. As soon as he spotted Tarkyn, Midnight veered away before he had even had time to register who it was. Tarkyn waved a hand and roared, "Shturrum!"

Between one step and the next, Midnight froze and, caught off balance, toppled to the ground. Tarkyn strode over to the motionless boy and made sure he had a good grasp on him before releasing the spell. Midnight stared up at him in shock before remembering his mission and struggling to get away. Tarkyn sent him such a severe command to stay still that the colour drained from Midnight's face. Keeping the boy's arm in a very firm grip, Tarkyn projected images of the approaching sorcerers and bloodhounds and made clear the danger that they were all now in. As it became borne upon him what he had done, Midnight's eyes dilated with fear and he cowered away from Tarkyn, clearly expecting to be hit. Tarkyn loosened his grip slightly and surrounded the little boy in reassurance. Tears welled in Midnight's eyes but with a shuddering breath, he kept himself rigidly under control and sent a query asking what he should do.

Tarkyn eased his grip further and squatted down in front of him. Using images, he told Midnight to climb up into a nearby pine tree and to wait for him away from the clearing. He made it clear that Midnight was not to be seen by the sorcerers or the wizard. Then he placed his hand on his heart and waited until Midnight reluctantly did the same. As Midnight turned to leave, the little boy's face crumpled and he could no longer contain his sobs. Even though time was short, Tarkyn turned him back around, gave him a fierce hug and wrapped a wave of understanding and comfort around him before sending him on his way.

Tarkyn stood up to find Danton watching him from a short distance away.

"So now what do we do?" demanded his liegeman.

"We must go back and confront these sorcerers," replied Tarkyn. "Our trail will lead them straight to us anyway and to Midnight. We must meet them in the clearing and keep them away from Midnight."

Danton stood with hands on his hips. "Right. Now I will say it. I think you're mad. How can you hope to outface a posse of mounted sorcerers and half a dozen bloodhounds?"

Tarkyn turned and began to run back to the clearing, calling over his shoulder, "Danton, don't just stand there. Argue with me as we run. We must be well away from Midnight when they arrive. If we get to the clearing first, I can at least rescue his wristband for him."

"Tarkyn, what are you thinking, worrying about a wristband when you are facing capture?"

Tarkyn smiled unnervingly. "I have my shield. You have yours. How can they touch us?"

Danton shook his head but said nothing more, saving his breath instead for the upcoming confrontation.

By the time they reached the clearing, they could already hear the baying of the hounds. Tarkyn glanced quickly around the clearing, summing up its potential dangers and advantages. He strode over to the place where they had all been sitting on the previous night and found the little plaited wristband hanging from the thin low branch. He untied it and placed it around his wrist. He raised his eyes to meet Danton's and smiled. "Quickly. Can you tie this for me? It's for luck, you know. To remind me of all I have to lose and all I have to fight for."

Danton gave his head a little shake as he tied the wristband and smiled in return. "Whatever happens, we will not let them find our woodfolk."

Even as he finished speaking, the first pair of bloodhounds thrust through the undergrowth. Tarkyn whirled around to confront them, his long black hair swinging out behind him. Within moments, the clearing was filled with horses, men and hounds, all encased in a shimmering greyish blue. Tarkyn stood stock still, watching them from within his bronze haze while Danton stood stoically beside him, surrounded by aqua.

For a few moments, no one spoke. The wizard and the sorcerers were clearly non-plussed to come across their quarry so suddenly; even more so to find him confronting them, rather than running. They controlled their fretting horses and gradually brought them to a standstill with their hounds ranged before them. The wizard sat astride a fine white charger at their head.

"Good morning," said Tarkyn quietly and gave a slight bow, betraying not one whit of fear. "I am Tarkyn Tamadil, Prince of Eskuzor." He indicated Danton. "This is my friend and liegeman, Danton Patronell, Lord of Sachmore." Danton obligingly produced a florid bow. "Perhaps if we are to have a discourse, you might like to introduce yourselves."

The wizard's uncertainty was betrayed by the restiveness of his horse that stamped its hoof and switched its tail. The silence drew out. Tarkyn raised his eyebrows and spoke in an aside to Danton, "Do you think they are unable to speak or is it perhaps that they lack training in etiquette?"

"My name is Journeyman Cloudmaker," said the wizard abruptly. "And I have come to take you back to be tried for the deaths of the guards in the Great Hall."

The prince ignored this last remark and asked, "And your companions?"

Journeyman huffed but decided on balance to respond. Once he had introduced all eight sorcerers, he reiterated, "And now can we put an end to this farce? You are coming back to be tried on multiple counts of murder."

"What about the original charge of damage to public property?" enquired Tarkyn maddeningly. "I suppose that has been overshadowed by later events, hasn't it?" He shrugged. "It was always a trumped-up charge anyway." He folded his arms. "You don't need to try me, you know. I freely confess to causing those deaths although I do not admit to murder. I did not cause them intentionally. I didn't fire on anyone. My shield reflected the guards' power rays when they fired on me."

The wizard glared down at him. "What rubbish! Shields absorb, they don't reflect. Of course you killed them intentionally. You murdered them before fleeing the Great Hall."

"As it turns out," said Tarkyn calmly, "I have no interest in arguing with you about it. You are free to believe as you will."

The wizard's voice hardened. "Regardless of your lack of interest, you must return with us to stand trial."

Tarkyn smiled slightly. "I think not."

The wizard boggled at him and waved his arm around. "Can you not see that you are outnumbered?"

"Certainly."

Journeyman glared at him. "How can you hope to defend yourself against our greater numbers?"

Tarkyn shrugged. "In return, might I ask how you are planning to penetrate my shield?"

"I don't have to. I can just outwait you." As he spoke, the young wizard waved the sorcerers to spread out into a semicircle around the prince. "There are more of us to take it in turns to maintain our shield. Sooner or later you will need to sleep... and then we will have you."

"Oh, I don't know. Danton and I can take shifts for a very long time; the rest of our lives, if need be. I concede that it may become tiresome but it's workable, nonetheless."

"Sooner or later you will let your guard down," replied Journeyman flatly.

"You may well be right," agreed Tarkyn conversationally. "The rest of our lives is such a long time, isn't it?"

"So, are you prepared to wait it out until one or the other of you falters, or will you concede and come quietly now?"

"Do you know, neither particularly appeals. You see, there is just one small factor that you haven't accounted for," said Tarkyn imperturbably. As he spoke, he wandered over to the edge of the clearing and leant comfortably against a tree, much to the further irritation of the wizard. Danton followed to stand beside him.

Journeyman gave up and rolled his eyes. "Which is?"

"Neither of us can penetrate the other's shield. Correct?"

Once the wizard had nodded, Tarkyn continued, "And none of you can penetrate your own shield from within, can you?"

"Obviously," replied the wizard impatiently.

Tarkyn smiled. "Now there, you see, is the difference. I can send forth power from within my own shield and I can perform more than one spell at a time. Quite helpful, wouldn't you say?"

The wizard flicked an uncertain glance at his henchmen before saying, "Not particularly, if you can't penetrate our shield anyway."

"Now, you're not thinking this through carefully, are you?" said Tarkyn in a kindly tone that made the wizard's blood boil. "Look above you. See that enormous tree? What do you think would happen if I felled it on you? Your shield would probably protect you, if you could maintain your focus amidst the mayhem, but you would be pinned to the ground." He shrugged. "Then Danton and I could just leave you to your fate and walk away." He glanced at Danton. "Not that I think we would because, despite the rumours, neither of us is totally heartless."

"I don't believe you," said the wizard flatly. "No one can perform more than one piece of magic at once. You're just bluffing."

Suddenly, Tarkyn's eyes flashed with anger and a spear of bronze power shot out from within his shield to blast a deep hole in the ground just outside the greyish blue shield in front of the wizard. The horses cavorted and snorted in fright and the bloodhounds set up a din of bloodcurdling baying. For several minutes, chaos reigned inside the greyish blue shield until the animals were once more brought under control. The young wizard looked a little shaken but issued sharp orders to his men, nonetheless.

A group of three horsemen encased in a purple shield suddenly broke away from beneath the blue-grey shield and attempted to drive at Danton and Tarkyn from the left. At the same time, three more carrying a large net between them broke through on the right. Suddenly, Tarkyn and Danton had sorcerers bearing down on them from three sides at once, with a tree behind them.

"Up, Danton! Drop your shield. I'll cover you. Straight up. Now!"

The two sorcerers rose into the air inside a bronze haze. The frustrated horsemen milled around beneath them as Tarkyn and Danton landed on a sturdy bough ten feet above their heads.

Tarkyn ignored the sorcerers below them while he talked to Danton, "You hold me steady while I concentrate. I will maintain the shield and continue my attack. Clear?"

Danton nodded, placed one arm around the trunk and the other around Tarkyn's waist.

Once he had steadied himself and placed the maintenance of the shield into the back of his mind, Tarkyn sent forth a bolt of bronze power into the ground at the base of the tree. Immediately, the horsemen were forced back into the centre of the clearing as their horses shied away from the noise and flying dirt.

Another bronze shaft tore into the ground, driving the horsemen back and to the right as the horses plunged away from the blast. Shaft after shaft struck the ground, each time leaving long enough between strikes so that the horses didn't completely panic but rolled their eyes in distress and backed away from the noise and light.

Danton realized that Tarkyn was slowly but surely driving

the sorcerers and bloodhounds towards the mountain stream that plunged over slippery rocks down the steep valley.

"Danton, I'm going to have to change position. We need to move to that next tree. Let me go now while we levitate to that pine over there."

"I have a better idea. Why don't you climb on my back and I will levitate for the two of us? Then you can keep up your attack," suggested Danton.

Tarkyn eyed him uncertainly. "Are you sure? Can you hold us both up?"

Danton grinned. "O ye of little faith! Let's try it here where you can grab a branch if I fail."

Tarkyn grasped the branch above and swung his legs either side of Danton who hovered in the air next to the tree. Gradually, Tarkyn allowed his weight to settle on Danton's hips and, as Danton held firm, let go of the branch altogether.

"This is marvellous, Danton. It's like having an aerial horse."

"Thanks," replied Danton dryly. "I think I've just been demoted."

"Oh, not at all," chortled Tarkyn. "It's well known that aerial horses outrank elite guards."

Danton snorted with laughter, which made them dip alarmingly. "Whoops!" He refocused on the job at hand and bore Tarkyn towards the beleaguered sorcerers who had just managed to calm their animals again.

As soon as he was within easy range, Tarkyn sent down a shower of bronze blasts one after the other, now clearly driving the sorcerers in a particular direction. Even though the wizard and sorcerers realized what was happening, they were powerless to do anything about it. The path to the stream was narrow and any attempt by the sorcerers to deviate from it lead to a bronze shaft of power blasting a hole in the ground of their attempted escape route.

Before long, the sorcerers found themselves backed up on the banks of the tumultuous stream. The rocks were far too slippery and treacherous for any horse to attempt to cross them and a slip would send them plunging over the edge or into one of the deep rockpools. Either would mean the end of the horse and possibly its rider.

Danton hovered near an overhanging oak until Tarkyn had swung himself off his back. Then they both stood on a low bough looking down at the dishevelled men who, once more, were trying to quiet the baying hounds and calm their frightened horses.

Eventually, when order was restored, Tarkyn and Danton floated down to land calmly in front of the wizard.

"So, what are you planning to do with us now?" demanded Journeyman querulously. "Compound your crimes by murdering us as well?"

"I wouldn't do that to the horses," replied Tarkyn sweetly. As one of the sorcerers made a sudden movement to quiet his still skittish horse, he added, "Unless I was forced to."

"I think," said Danton, beginning to enjoy himself, "your mistake was in disbelieving His Highness. He is very particular about honesty, you know."

Journeyman glared at Danton. Then gradually his brain began to work and his eyes narrowed as he asked the prince, "Since you can indeed use more than one spell at once, is it also true that your shield was reflective?"

Tarkyn raised supercilious eyebrows. "I have not told you a single untruth. It is up to you whether you believe me or not. I have no interest in convincing you."

Journeyman Cloudmaker became very thoughtful.

Eventually, he said slowly, "If that is the case, that would mean you are not a rogue sorcerer after all."

"No," replied Tarkyn, "I am not. If I were a rogue sorcerer, I would have driven you and your men onto these rocks to plunge to your deaths down the cataracts. Nevertheless, my shield did kill those men."

"Interesting," mused Journeyman. "This changes everything." He shot a penetrating glance at the prince. "How long have you been in the forest?"

"I'm sorry. I don't remember when I agreed to answer your questions," said Tarkyn, determined not to place himself in a situation where he might have to lie to protect the woodfolk, more because he knew that he would not be able to lie convincingly, rather than from his natural honesty. "And I don't remember when I gave you permission to address me without due courtesy."

The wizard gave a slight bow from the back of his horse. "I beg your pardon, Your Highness. Could I just ask you whether you have met up with anyone? I understood that you had protected a family and captured quite a large group of bandits single-handedly. Quite impressive."

Tarkyn stood up abruptly. "This audience is at an end. I did not come here to answer your questions. I came here to send you on your way back home. Now I suggest you leave."

"Excuse me one moment, Your Highness." Journeyman turned his horse around so that he could confer with his companions. Tarkyn waited patiently until he turned back to face the prince and said, "Your Highness, I acknowledge that you have the advantage over us."

Tarkyn raised his eyebrows and murmured quietly, "How very astute."

Journeyman continued as though Tarkyn had not spoken, "However, before we leave, may I just ask whether there is any way we can keep in contact with you without having to hunt you down?"

Tarkyn frowned in perplexity. "Journeyman, that is a very strange request. Surely you cannot expect a fugitive to leave his forwarding address."

"No, but there may be some things we wish to communicate to you in the future."

Tarkyn's eyes narrowed. "If, having seen my powers and knowing now that I am not a rogue sorcerer, you are seeking to enlist my aid to your cause, I can tell you that I will not support either of my brothers against the other." He sighed. "But I do fear for the future of Eskuzor. So, if you can do anything to protect her people, please do so." He thought for a moment. "As you enter the forests from Tormadell, there is a large old horse chestnut tree with a hollowed-out trunk on the left hand side of the road. If you place any messages in there, I will receive them eventually. It may take several weeks, though, for me to come that way again. Obviously, if I become aware that the tree is being watched, nothing will be picked up." He gave a slight smile. "I should warn you that I have a comprehensive intelligence system. I have known you and your bloodhounds were coming, ever since you left the encampment."

Journeyman looked a little stunned at this information. "And yet you stayed to meet us. You could have been miles away by now."

"Yes, but then that would have been on your terms and I prefer to set my own terms. I do not like to be hunted." Tarkyn was completely in control. "Now that we have met and you have gauged the calibre of my opposition, you may be less keen to waste your time and mine in hunting me down. And I think if you decide that an army will solve your dilemma, you may find me more elusive."

The young wizard knew that he had more than met his

match. He bowed low from the back of his horse. "It was a pleasure to meet you, Your Highness, and you, Your Lordship. I have taken careful note of the fact that you could have harmed us but chose not to and would like to thank you for your forbearance since in similar circumstances, I believe I would not have been so circumspect."

Tarkyn's eyes twinkled. "I appreciate your honesty and will take care not to give you the advantage in the future."

Without another word, the wizard, followed by the sorcerers and bloodhounds, picked their way carefully past the prince and his liegeman to head back towards the clearing, and from there, to begin their long journey to the encampment.

Just before they disappeared from sight around the bend in the path, Tarkyn called quietly after the wizard, "And, Journeyman, I would not be so merciful should you choose to double back on us and try again. Remember, I have eyes everywhere."

As soon as they were out of sight, the two sorcerers looked at each other and grinned.

"That went well then," said Danton jauntily.

"I think so."

"It's a pity you couldn't have asked him what he knows of woodfolk."

"But then you would have had to betray the fact that you knew about us, too," said Waterstone, who had just appeared.

"Precisely," said Danton.

"Exactly," agreed Tarkyn, "so we couldn't."

Waterstone looked from one to the other. "You two seem very pleased with yourselves."

Danton beamed. "It's not every day you outface one wizard, eight sorcerers and six bloodhounds."

"And nine horses," added Tarkyn.

"And nine horses," agreed Danton with a huge smile.

Waterstone smiled broadly in return. "So perhaps now, you two could finish off the rescue you started. There's a certain little boy sitting up in a nearby tree, refusing all attempts to get near him or to bring him down."

"He's a good little fellow, isn't he?" said Tarkyn. He smiled wryly. "I made him swear that he would stay in that tree until I came back for him. I didn't want him either misguidedly trying to help or running away."

Waterstone raised his eyebrows. "I don't know that everyone else thinks he's good, after running off and thrusting you and Danton into danger."

"Oh, come on, Waterstone. Surely you can see what he was doing. He didn't mean to cause trouble."

"Yes, of course I can see. Anyone who still has kids can see. It's the people who've grown out of kids or whose kids have outgrown them who don't make allowances for the way kids' minds work." Waterstone flicked Tarkyn a glance, knowing he would not like what he was about to say. "He will have to learn some discipline though. Had he been just a few years older and betrayed our presence, he would have been be exiled."

Tarkyn let out a low whistle. "What? A little boy? Sent off on his own? Dog's teeth, you people are tough."

Waterstone raised his eyebrows. "Oh. It's you people again, is it?"

"Waterstone, I could never countenance sending a little boy away like that."

The woodman shrugged. "You're tough about people laying hands on royalty. We're tough about having our presence being betrayed. At least in our case, it's for the good of the whole community."

"In our case, it is also for the good of the whole community," retorted Tarkyn hotly. "Without the King and due respect, our society would be thrown into chaos."

"That's simply because you people don't have enough patience and enough respect for each other to be able to reach a consensus. So, your people sacrifice their own authority and allow someone else to tell them what to do."

As Tarkyn stood glaring at Waterstone, a dry cough interrupted the debate that was fast turning into a heated argument.

"Not wishing to distract you from this entertaining interchange, but there is still a boy up a tree," said Danton urbanely.

Without another word, Tarkyn turned on his heel and walked off to collect Midnight.

Danton watched him go but didn't follow him. Instead, he turned to Waterstone and said, "I would like to see how your holier-than-thou attitudes would work in a society ten times the size of your own and with no mindtalking. Each point in a discussion would take months to be communicated around the kingdom. At that rate, even a simple decision could take several years. By then, it might no longer be relevant."

Waterstone went to answer but stopped himself. His eyes narrowed as he tried to imagine the woodfolk without mindtalking. Finally, he said, "You could at least use consensus within each smaller community."

"You could," replied Danton, "and in some villages I expect they do, but I would have to admit that most communities are under the governance of either one liege or a small council of men and women who make the important decisions for them and make representation to the King, should the need arise. Don't forget, we have to stop what we're doing, travel to some central location and confer face to face each time we want reach a communal decision."

"Hmph," grunted Waterstone. "I will have to think about

this. No mindtalking is a serious disability for your society, isn't it."

Danton gave a quizzical smile. "I can't say I had ever viewed it in that way. Since none of us has ever known about, or possessed that ability, we have not realized our lack."

Meanwhile, Tarkyn had reached the pine tree where he had deposited Midnight and was standing beneath it looking up into its branches. Midnight had ensconced himself as high up in the branches as he could, where heavier woodfolk could not venture. He was exuding a disquieting aura of fear, hostility and self-loathing. Rainstorm and Lapping Water were positioned lower in the pine tree but had not wanted to climb any closer, in case Midnight retreated further still up into branches too weak to carry his weight. Tarkyn's attempts to contact the little boy were met with a determined barrier.

"He's not letting me talk to him," said Tarkyn to the two woodfolk. "Can you two stay where you are and be ready to try to catch him if he falls. I'm going to come at him from another direction. I don't want to risk driving him up higher."

Tarkyn strode off through the forest. From high in the tree, Midnight watched him go and huddled down deeper into himself allowing his misery to engulf him, desolated that the prince had given up on him so easily. Suddenly, strong arms grabbed him from behind, pinioning his arms to his side. In his fright, Midnight thrashed about and kicked out but couldn't make contact with the person behind him. Then he looked down and saw the leather wristband he had made, on Tarkyn's wrist where it lay across his chest. He stopped wriggling and slowly moved his pinioned hand enough to touch the wristband. Then the little boy sent out wave after wave of contrition and dissolved into tears. Tarkyn turned him around, swung him onto his hip and held him close until the wracking sobs had subsided.

It was only when Midnight raised his red-rimmed eyes and looked about him that he realized he was being held by Tarkyn as the sorcerer floated in the air beside the tree, far above the forest floor. His first reaction was to grab convulsively onto Tarkyn but after that, he peered down and around with great interest. Slowly, a big smile dawned on his face and he gave a little wave to Rainstorm and Lapping Water who were watching from lower down in the pine tree.

As they slowly drifted down to earth, Tarkyn held up his wrist, nodded at the leather wristband and indicated his appreciation. Nearly bursting with pride that Tarkyn was wearing it, Midnight sent him a long-winded, detailed image of himself making it. Once Tarkyn had conveyed his admiration for the effort and skill, Midnight finally remembered to send a casual enquiry about the sorcerers and bloodhounds.

Tarkyn suppressed a smile as he responded by replaying the sequence of events. Only when Midnight saw the number of sorcerers and bloodhounds facing Tarkyn and Danton did he truly understand the enormity of the danger he had placed Tarkyn in. His eyes grew round, but his horror at the danger was soon replaced by admiration of Tarkyn's actions, which moved quickly into a calm certainty that Tarkyn would always prevail. Tarkyn's efforts to disabuse him of this notion were met with smug disbelief. The best the prince was able to achieve was an undertaking from his little admirer that he would never deliberately place him in danger, even though he did think Tarkyn was indestructible.

Midnight clearly thought that Tarkyn's need for this undertaking was superfluous. He placed his hand over his heart and with his head slightly to one side, raised his eyebrows in a fair imitation of the look of disdain the prince had faced him with two days before. Then, much to Tarkyn's bemusement, Midnight queried whether Tarkyn had forgotten the oath.

VII

THE TRAPPERS

36

Rainstorm and Lapping Water who had joined them on the ground, burst out laughing.

"What are you laughing at?" demanded Tarkyn.

"That was such a perfect copy of your expression," grinned Rainstorm. "The gall of the kid to think you might have forgotten the oath. But best of all, he is obviously unaware that disdain is the prerogative of princes."

This all flowed over Midnight who by this time was engaged in drawing Lapping Water's attention to the fact that Tarkyn was wearing his wristband.

"I am not disdainful and besides, disdain is not the prerogative of princes," objected Tarkyn.

"Yes, you are and yes, it is," replied Rainstorm cheerfully. "You don't see other people around here with that expression on their faces."

"I've seen many disdainful sorcerers," said Tarkyn, frowning. "I'm sure I've seen Danton looking disdainful."

Rainstorm chuckled. "Then he must be on his best behaviour with us because I haven't. The closest expression

I've seen on him is outrage when he was shocked at our treatment of you."

"Hmph," Tarkyn subsided into a small huff.

"I shouldn't worry about it, Tarkyn," said Lapping Water kindly. "You generally use it to good effect. You don't come across as disdainful very often." She smiled. "But I must admit your disdain was truly breath-taking when you rejected the mountainfolk's offer to swear the oath."

"Oh, yes! That was excellent," agreed Rainstorm enthusiastically. "I wish I could pull off something like that."

A reluctant smiled tugged at the corners of Tarkyn's mouth. "Hmph." Then he grinned. "That was quite good, wasn't it?" He glanced around anxiously. "I hope none of them is nearby to hear that."

Lapping Water shook her head. "No. You're safe."

"Mind you, that was exactly how I felt." Tarkyn shook his head a little and frowned. "That they should have had the temerity to think that I would even consider accepting them as liege folk after that, was quite mind-boggling."

Rainstorm laughed. "I love it when you're so supremely arrogant. It's so...so amazing."

"I am not arrogant," protested Tarkyn. He smiled ruefully. "I am merely cognizant of my status which clearly, you are not."

Rainstorm shook his head. "No. The only status you have in my eyes is that of forest guardian but to be fair, that is far more impressive. Princes are born every few years. A forest guardian only comes every four or five hundred years. So it has to be worth more."

"Well, there you are, you see," said Tarkyn. "Why shouldn't I show some discrimination in whom I accept to work with me to protect woodfolk?"

Lapping Water laughed. "When you put it like that, it almost sounds reasonable."

Tarkyn glanced at her but decided, on balance, to say nothing further. Instead he returned his attention to his armful of mischief and, after a firm instruction to stay close, swung Midnight down to walk beside him. They turned their steps to the south once more and began the short trek back to their previous night's campsite.

As they walked, other woodfolk appeared around them and congratulated Tarkyn on facing down the hunting party. As Danton and Waterstone caught up with them, the woodfolk widened their comments to include Danton.

A short distance down the path, Tarkyn asked, "Why are we not up in the trees again, or spread out as before, carefully covering our tracks?"

Thunder Storm pointed upwards. "Look at the sky."

Tarkyn looked up and saw heavy dark clouds lowering over the forest.

"Oh. So, are we just going to walk along getting soaked, or are we going to run for cover somewhere?"

Waterstone grinned. "Don't worry. There's a shallow cave in a rocky outcrop just a few hundred yards ahead and to the right. I think we'll make it before those clouds drop their load."

As he spoke, they could hear the first heavy drops of rain falling on the pine branches far above them. The density of the foliage meant that the water did not at first penetrate to the forest floor. Nevertheless, they all quickened their pace.

A few minutes later, a damp group of woodfolk and sorcerers reached the shelter of the small cave. They ranged themselves around inside so that they could look out and watch the storm now gathering force outside. They could hear the wind sweeping down the mountain from behind them which meant that the cave, although shallow, offered effective protection. Outside, trees thrashed and bent in the wind, lashed by sheets of driving rain. Even though it was midmorning, the world outside was dull and grey, heavy clouds blocking out the sun. The sky flashed with lightning followed almost immediately by the rumbling of thunder.

Tarkyn glanced at Thunder Storm, tempted to joke by asking him if he had spoken, but he had a suspicion that it might be in bad taste. The fact that no one else made the obvious quip went a long way towards confirming his suspicions.

However, Thunder Storm caught his glance and smiled slowly. "I know what you're thinking. And no, we don't comment on each other's voices. But I hope you're enjoying trying to decipher mine against the thunder."

Tarkyn's frown of concentration betrayed the difficulty he was having in hearing what Thunder Storm was saying. As Thunder Storm continued to talk inconsequentially about the storm and the journey ahead, Tarkyn struggled more and more to hear what he was saying. Suddenly he realized that the woodman was deliberately pitching his voice to obscure it in the sounds of the storm.

Tarkyn stopped concentrating, sat back and laughed. "You're a bugger, Thunder Storm. My ears are nearly falling off trying to follow what you're saying."

Thunder Storm grinned broadly, joined by all but Midnight who had no idea what was going on. Tarkyn sent a brief image explaining that he couldn't hear Thunder Storm above the noise outside but it was beyond him to explain why.

As time passed, there was no sign of the storm abating and the temperature had dropped considerably. Since they had left in such a rush, most of them had brought neither cloaks nor provisions with them. Running Feet, Summer Rain and Autumn Leaves had followed more slowly and had brought their packs. So, there were some meagre rations that they could share out amongst everyone.

Tarkyn looked at Danton. "Can you create heat?"

Danton grimaced. "I can, but I don't think I can keep it up for long. What about you?"

Tarkyn shook his head. "Fireballs, yes. Ongoing heat, no. A bit all or nothing with me, I'm afraid."

"What about that bronze flame you had in your hand at the oath taking?" asked Autumn Leaves.

"No. That's just an apparition. There's no heat to it."

Rainstorm brightened. "Don't worry. One or several of us can dash out, grab some wood and even if it's wet, one of you could light it and we can get a fire going. What do you think?"

Tarkyn nodded. "Sounds feasible. Who's going?"

"I will," said Lapping Water immediately.

Tarkyn couldn't repress his frown of consternation in time for it to go unnoticed.

"What's wrong?" asked Rainstorm.

Danton smiled knowingly as Tarkyn waved his hand and said, "Nothing. Just leave it. Anyone else going too?"

Rainstorm looked at him uncertainly, but said, "I'll go."

Tarkyn glanced down to find Midnight tugging at his sleeve, querying what was happening. Once it was explained to him, he pointed to himself and then outside. After a brief exchange of assurances, Tarkyn agreed.

The three of them took a deep breath and dashed out into the driving wind and rain.

"So, what was that all about?" asked Waterstone curiously.

Danton grinned. "Unless I'm much mistaken, Tarkyn is still taken aback sometimes when women offer to do physical or dangerous tasks."

Waterstone raised his eyebrows in astonishment. "Are you?

But surely women in your society do physical work, don't they?"

Tarkyn smiled faintly. "Possibly. But not in the circles I moved in." His smile broadened, as he thought about the women at court in their elaborate, fulsome dresses. "No. I can think of no women in my past who would have conversed with me one minute and dashed off to fight the elements or swing through trees or do anything at all physical or dangerous, the next. They may have taken a gentle stroll or ridden horses, but very decorously."

Waterstone frowned. "So, if they didn't do anything, what did they find to talk about?"

"People, intrigue, rumours, the latest fashions," answered Danton, his eyes sparkling with animation.

"What are fashions?" asked North Wind.

Danton blinked, momentarily taken aback. "Fashions are different ways of wearing clothes that change from time to time. There are also fashions in the types of food you eat, even in some manners and activities. So, if you came to court you would make sure you were wearing the latest fashion and knew how to play the latest games and dance the latest dances."

The woodfolk all exchanged glances.

"I suppose our kids have crazes on playing particular games," said Thunder Storm slowly.

"And what did they do with their old clothes then?" asked Running Feet.

"I don't know. Gave them away to the poor, used them as rags." Danton waved his hand airily. "You would not wish to be seen in the same outfit too often." He smiled wistfully. "I like to think I was quite a leader of fashion."

Waterstone glanced at him then glanced away, beginning to understand the true import for Danton of being required to wear woodfolk garb. He decided to move the conversation on, before Danton had too much time to reflect on what he had lost.

"So, Tarkyn, what would you have thought if any of those women at court rushed out into the rain to fetch the wood?"

Tarkyn glanced sideways at him. "Truthfully? I would have been shocked by their unruly behaviour."

"So, do you disapprove or find it offensive when our woodwomen do more than sit around and talk?"

"No. The context and the expectations are so completely different. No, in fact I find I like it. I am just caught out sometimes." Tarkyn grimaced. "If anything, I am perplexed. In our society, neither of us would stand by and allow a woman to go out into that rain. We would insist on bearing any discomfort. But I am reasonably sure that protectiveness of that nature would be regarded with disdain by woodwomen."

Waterstone scratched his head. "Well, I don't know. Any of us would be grateful if you offered to do something for us."

"Lapping Water wasn't when I offered to carry her water for her one time."

"Probably the prince thing," said Autumn Leaves. "She might accept more readily now she knows you better and we're not all on tenterhooks waiting for you to tell us what to do all the time."

The conversation was curtailed at this point by the noisy, wet return of Rainstorm and Lapping Water as they dodged into the cave and dropped large bundles of sodden wood in the middle of the floor.

"Well done, you two," said Waterstone. "Where's Midnight?"

Rainstorm shrugged unconcernedly. "I don't know. I expect he'll be along in a minute." He shuddered. "I'm freezing. It's nice and warm in here though. Have you been pouring out heat while we've been away?" he asked Danton.

Danton smiled and nodded.

"So you have!" exclaimed Thunder Storm. "I didn't realize I wasn't cold any more. Well done. Thanks."

"A pleasure," replied Danton. "But now, if you organize your wood, Tarkyn can take over and blast a little fireball into it and get a fire started."

By the time they had half the wood piled to one side and the rest in a neat pyramid in the middle, Tarkyn was beginning to worry about the non-appearance of Midnight. Just as he had decided he would have to head out into the rain to look for him, the little boy staggered into sight, dragging an enormous long branch along the ground. Rainstorm dashed back out to help him drag it over the last few yards. They brought one end in so that it could be fed gradually onto the fire and left the other end sticking out in the rain.

Midnight glowed with pride as everyone expressed their admiration at his enormous branch and Tarkyn ruffled his hair. When everything was ready, Tarkyn sent a small but intense fireball into the wet wood. It caught alight instantly and its cheery light and heat filled the cave.

As they settled down to wait out the storm, Tarkyn spotted Autumn Leaves leaning back against the wall of the cave and closing his eyes. He remembered what Dry Berry had said and leaned over to the heavy woodman. "Autumn Leaves, are you all right? Is your head aching?"

Autumn Leaves opened his eyes, screwing them up as the light from the fire struck them. "Yes, it is hurting again, especially after all that running around."

"I'm sorry. Dry Berry did mention it when we first arrived, but with everything that happened, I forgot to seek you out. Would you like me to help now?" When Autumn Leaves nodded, Tarkyn looked around. "Summer Rain, why would Autumn Leaves still be having headaches after all this time?"

The woodwoman shook her head. "I don't know. Perhaps you should go into him and relay information to me. Look for anything that appears swollen or out of place."

Tarkyn looked at Autumn Leaves. "You all right with that? Right, shut your eyes, relax and we'll see what we can do."

Tarkyn placed his hand on the woodman's shoulder and closed his eyes. He let his awareness flow down through his arm into Autumn Leaves and up into the area around the bridge of his nose where he had been struck by the knife hilt. Before long, he spotted a small piece of bone that had been chipped off Autumn Leaves' eye socket and was pressing into inflamed flesh. Tarkyn relayed the information to Summer Rain and, unusually, received a firm instruction to come out.

He flowed out of the woodman, back up his own arm and opened his eyes. Autumn Leaves opened his too and exclaimed, "That's a weird feeling! It feels like a spider running over your hand, soft pattering, but on the inside, instead of on the outside."

Lapping Water crinkled her nose in distaste. "That sounds creepy."

Autumn Leaves smiled. "No, it's all right. It's quite nice actually when you get used to it but I would have died of fright if I hadn't known what was causing it." He looked at Tarkyn. "So, is it fixed?"

Tarkyn shook his head. "Not yet. Summer Rain told me to come out." He turned expectantly to the healer.

"From what I've seen of your healing power, I don't think you can repair that damage. I think we need to remove it rather than try to move it back into place and reconnect it."

"Not wishing to pry, but could you two tell me what Tarkyn found?" There was a definite rebuke in Autumn Leaves voice.

"I'm sorry, Autumn Leaves," said Summer Rain quietly. "A

small piece of bone has been chipped off and is now pushing into the area in your eye socket next to your nose. It's quite dangerous, I think. If it travelled, it could damage your sight or possibly even work its way back into your brain. Either way, it needs to come out."

"What? Now?"

"As soon as possible. Now seems as good a time as any."

Autumn Leaves looked a little frightened and, to Tarkyn's surprise, glanced across at Thunder Storm for reassurance. Before Tarkyn had time to wonder why, Thunder Storm rumbled, "Don't worry, little brother. I'll be here and I'll be the one to knock you out if that's what's needed."

"Why do I never know these family connections?" asked Tarkyn, with a puzzled frown.

"I told you that Autumn Leaves and Thunder Storm would have asked you into their family," said Waterstone quizzically. "Wasn't it obvious from that?"

"I thought you meant into either of their families. I suppose I wasn't listening closely enough."

Waterstone smiled. "You were a little drunk at the time. You were probably past noticing detail by that stage."

"Hmph." Tarkyn couldn't help feeling a little sidelined. He gave himself a mental shake and returned his attention to Autumn Leaves. "Don't worry. We'll look after you. You know you're in good hands with Summer Rain."

"We'll need as much light as we can get. So, can we have some space near the entrance for Autumn Leaves to lie down in, please?" As she spoke, Summer Rain was rummaging through her bag, producing little switches of herbs, tweezers and a needle and thread. "Danton, could we borrow one of your knives please? They strike me as being remarkably sharp."

Almost before she finished speaking, a small dagger appeared in his hand. He offered it to her hilt first.

"Thank you, but if you could hold the blade in the flames for a short time and keep it until I'm ready for it, that would be most helpful."

"Certainly, ma'am," said Danton.

"And the tweezers, if you wouldn't mind."

Tarkyn eyed the needle and thread. "If you can extract the piece of bone, I think I can close up the wound and heal it without needing stitches," he offered.

"That would be better, certainly, but I'll keep them nearby just in case we need them."

A few minutes later, everything and everyone was in place. Summer Rain knelt on one side of Autumn Leaves, Tarkyn on the other with his hand on the woodman's shoulder. Danton was holding the cauterized knife and the tweezers.

"Are you ready, Autumn Leaves?" rumbled Thunder Storm from a little further back in the cave.

Autumn Leaves closed his eyes, grimaced, and took a deep breath. "Go on."

In one fluid motion, Thunder Storm drew his slingshot and fired. Suddenly, Thunder Storm was thrown over backwards from his crouching position, his slingshot ripped from his hand and thrown across the cave. He found himself staring up into bright green eyes, as a protective Midnight sat on top of him and pummelled him.

"Oh no," said Rainstorm, rolling his eyes. "He thinks Thunder Storm has attacked Autumn Leaves." He grabbed Midnight from behind and hauled him off. "Come on, Tarkyn. Explain to him."

Midnight thrashed and kicked out, trying to get back to stop Thunder Storm from rising. Tarkyn sent out a feeling of calm and tried to send images of what was happening but Midnight's mind wasn't receiving again. With a sigh, Tarkyn stood up and came around to crouch in front of Midnight.

Midnight kept looking in alarm at Thunder Storm, panting with the effort of struggling to get free, but Tarkyn grabbed the little boy's shoulders and forced him to look into his eyes. Then he re-sent the images and used hand signs to show that Thunder Storm was friend to both Autumn Leaves and himself. The little boy glanced over at the unconscious Autumn Leaves and frowned in perplexity. Tarkyn sent reassurance and showed him again what they were about to do and why. Midnight took a deep breath and glanced sideways at Thunder Storm who had stayed where he was until Midnight was contained.

A look of consternation dawned on the little boy's face. He sent a plea for Tarkyn to let him go and when Tarkyn's grip loosened, scrabbled across the cave to retrieve the slingshot. He dusted it off and presented it to Thunder Storm. Then he grasped Thunder Storm's shoulder and frantically tried to help him to sit up, all the while sending out waves of contrition.

"He's trying to send you a message to say he's sorry," interpreted Tarkyn.

Thunder Storm sat up, brushing down his dusty sleeves. "I think I can tell that," he said dryly.

Midnight's eyes flickered around everyone else watching him and realised that no clear path lay between him and the mouth of the cave. Wide-eyed and vigilant, he backed himself into the deepest corner of the cave and cowered down trembling, with his hands curled over his head protectively.

There was shocked silence.

"This poor little boy has been badly treated by someone," said Summer Rain sadly.

Without standing, Thunder Storm shuffled over to the cowering child who flinched away and shut his eyes as the woodman neared him. Thunder Storm stroked Midnight's hair and gradually manoeuvred his other arm around behind him.

All the while, Midnight trembled and cowered away, as far into the corner as he could get. Thunder Storm slowly but firmly pulled him into his arms and held him quietly, stroking his hair and rumbling quietly to him until the trembling subsided.

"Tarkyn, could you please thank him for me for risking himself against me to protect Autumn Leaves, even if he mistook the need. After all, the fault is ours that we did not explain beforehand what we would be doing. He was actually very brave."

"I'll try," said Tarkyn. "It's complicated saying things without words." He sent reassurance and an image of Midnight standing over Autumn Leaves protecting him with a sense of approval and thanks.

Midnight raised his tearstained face and looked up at Thunder Storm with his head on one side. He looked across at Tarkyn and then around at everyone else. He let out a shuddering sigh and frowned uncertainly. Tarkyn sent waves of reassurance and Thunder Storm gave him a squeeze and held him close. For a moment, Midnight looked bewildered but then gradually his face relaxed. He gave Thunder Storm a hug in return, to reiterate that he was sorry. Then he sent Tarkyn a clear message that the prince should be helping Autumn Leaves before snuggling down against Thunder Storm's chest.

"Huh, little rascal," laughed Tarkyn. "He's just told me to get on with helping Autumn Leaves!"

"That's rich!" exclaimed Rainstorm. "When he's the one who created the diversion."

"Quite. He is, however, right." Tarkyn re-positioned himself next to Autumn Leaves with his hand on the woodman's shoulder. "So. How do you want to do this, Summer Rain?"

"Can you point to where that piece of bone is located?"

Tarkyn frowned and tried to remember the position of

everything relative to where he had been inside Autumn Leaves. He nearly pointed to a spot on the right-hand side of Autumn Leaves' nose that was in fact correct, but then hesitated and withdrew his hand. He shook his head regretfully. "I'm afraid my hopeless sense of direction is letting me down again. I keep getting confused when I try to see it from another angle."

Summer Rain smiled kindly. "Don't worry. We'll find another way." She thought for a moment. "If you go into him, would you be aware of any pressure from the outside?"

"What do you mean?"

"I could press with the point of the tweezers around the area and you could tell me from inside when I'm over the place where the piece of bone has lodged. You would only need to raise your finger to let me know."

Tarkyn took a breath. "Yes, I can do that. Just. It's hard to stay in contact with my outside body when I am flowing inside someone else."

"Would it help if I squeezed your hand each time Summer Rain presses with the tweezers?" asked Danton. "Then you would feel a sensation near your finger."

Tarkyn nodded. "Yes, I think that may make it easier. Right. Let's go."

He closed his eyes and flowed down through his arm into Autumn Leaves. He made his way to the damaged area and waited beside the embedded piece of bone for pressure from the tweezers to occur above him. From time to time, far away, he felt his hand being squeezed as Summer Rain pressed on various places nearby. Finally, she prodded directly above him. Using the squeeze on his hand as a guide, he reconnected with his body enough to raise his finger. Then he retracted himself, retreated up his own arm and into his own body.

By the time he opened his eyes, Summer Rain was

preparing to make a small incision just under Autumn Leaves' right eyebrow near the bridge of his nose.

"Hold on," he said. "What do you want me to do now?"

Summer Rain glanced up at him. "Nothing for the moment. There is no need for you to be in there to endure the pain of the cut. You might as well wait until we are ready for him to heal."

"Very well." Tarkyn glanced over at Midnight and gave him a smile. Then he looked up at Thunder Storm who was sitting with his arms still around Midnight and a feeling of common understanding passed between them.

"Actually," said Summer Rain, "can you use your Shturrum spell on someone who is unconscious? Because we don't want him to move while we're doing this."

Tarkyn brought his gaze back to the healer. "I don't really know. After all, you wouldn't usually use a spell to freeze someone if they were already unconscious, would you? There wouldn't be any point."

"They don't need to be able to hear you," reasoned Danton. "Remember. You used it on Midnight and he can't hear and wasn't even looking at you."

"True," mused Tarkyn. "Well, I'll give it a try. It can't hurt, can it?" He focused narrowly on Autumn Leaves, waved his hand and murmured, "Shturrum."

"Thanks," said Summer Rain. "Someone had better hold his head still, just in case that doesn't work and he starts coming round."

"I will," offered Waterstone. He came around to kneel beside Tarkyn and firmly grasped Autumn Leaves' head, placing a gentle downward pressure on it.

Summer Rain took a deep breath and let it out slowly. Tarkyn realized with a slight shock that the usually phlegmatic healer was nervous. He sent her a wave of strength and belief in her. She looked up in surprise and smiled warmly at him. Then she turned her attention briskly to her patient and without further hesitation, inserted a small incision below Autumn Leaves' right eyebrow. For several minutes she worked quietly and intently. No one else spoke or moved. Finally, she lifted the tweezers holding a jagged, bloody piece of bone.

"I have it," she said triumphantly. "Tarkyn, if I hold the wound shut, can you go in and repair it?"

Without another word, Tarkyn closed his eyes and sent his essence flowing down his arm and into Autumn Leaves. He found the cut made by Summer Rain and let his power flow into the damaged tissue. He wove together the tears in blood vessels and soothed the violated nerves. Then he simply supplied the power and let Autumn Leaves' body heal itself. Minutes later, he withdrew.

When Tarkyn opened his eyes, everyone was looking more relaxed. The wound had healed right over and only a pink line showed where Summer Rain had made her incision. He waved his hand to release Autumn Leaves from the paralysis spell and looked over at Thunder Storm. "How much longer will he be unconscious, do you think?"

"A little longer. Perhaps another five minutes. Ten at the outside."

Tarkyn smiled. "Good timing then. Luckily our little misguided hero didn't waste too much of the time we needed. Do you want to swap places? I'll take the rascal and you can wait next to Autumn Leaves if you like."

"Thanks."

Shortly afterwards, Autumn Leaves wandered back into consciousness and groaned. He shook his head to clear it and groaned even more. "Blast it, Thunder Storm. How can I tell if my head's better? It's hurting from the slingshot."

"Stop whingeing, Autumn Leaves," said Rainstorm with

mock severity. "I'll have you know Thunder Storm paid dearly for knocking you out."

Thunder Storm smiled. "Yes. You had a little warrior championing your cause."

Autumn Leaves frowned and then put his hand up to feel his newly healed wound. "Hmm. That feels a little tender but not like the earlier pain." He returned his attention to the conversation. "What are you talking about? What warrior?"

Tarkyn answered from the corner of the cave where he had been trying, with indifferent success, to explain to Midnight the need to keep his mind open. "This young menace here threw poor Thunder Storm onto his back then sat on top of him and pounded him until Rainstorm dragged him off."

Autumn Leaves laughed. "What? That little thing? That's pathetic, Thunder Storm!"

"Thanks. Your sympathy is overwhelming." He glanced over and smiled at Midnight. "But I'll tell you this. I would rather have him on my side than against me. He didn't hesitate. He was fast, accurate and aggressive in your defence."

"You're not telling me he really kept you pinned down?" Autumn Leaves looked perplexed.

Thunder Storm grunted with laughter. "No, of course I'm not. I was just caught unawares. Rainstorm had hauled him off before I had time to react. But he had grabbed my slingshot, thrown it away from me and shoved me onto my back before I knew what was happening. If I hadn't been crouching, he couldn't have, of course, but maybe he would have done something different then."

"It's just as well we explained what was happening, before Summer Rain made her incision. He might have knocked her hand with the knife in it when it was close to Autumn Leaves' eye," said Waterstone.

Tarkyn looked at Midnight and shook his head. "Oh dear.

We will have to be very careful that we tell him what's happening."

"Still, he's not the nasty piece of work that Sighing Wind said he was, is he?" Rainstorm smiled across at Midnight who scowled, knowing he was being talked about.

"Which is all credit to him," said Summer Rain, "considering the treatment he has obviously endured."

When Autumn Leaves looked confused, Waterstone went out of focus to explain.

"Perhaps he is a nasty piece of work to the mountainfolk," suggested Lapping Water. "He certainly doesn't like them."

"I'm not surprised," said Summer Rain sternly. "Someone has been beating him. Either they maltreated him or allowed his mother to." She shook her head. "There is some evil loose among these mountainfolk."

There was an arrested silence.

"Do you think so? Do you mean that literally?" asked Tarkyn. "Is it not the general nastiness you find in people everywhere?"

Waterstone's eyes narrowed. "You are coming very close to being offensive, Tarkyn. When have you seen behaviour like that among us?"

Tarkyn threw his hands up in apology. "I beg your pardon. I have not. But don't people everywhere have a dark side?"

"Not that dark," stated Autumn Leaves flatly. "There's a difference between being angry and being malicious. Anyway, even if I concede that we do have a dark side, we do not have to act on it. That's the whole point, isn't it? We keep it in check, just as you do."

"And that's another thing," said Rainstorm in a complete non sequitur, "Why weren't they subject to the oath as the forestals are?"

Tarkyn shrugged. "I don't know. Maybe because they

didn't acknowledge, as your people did, that they were part of one people."

"But they did. Remember? Dry Berry said they carefully didn't help their kin to betray the oath. And once they swore fealty to you, why didn't it convert to the sorcerous oath, in that case?"

"Maybe it has," suggested Running Feet.

Tarkyn shook his head thoughtfully. "No, I don't think so. There was no sorcery in the air at the end of the oathtaking. I certainly hope not, anyway. I really don't want the forest beholden to their honour; even more so if there is something amiss with them."

"Maybe we are too far away from where the spell was first cast," suggested Danton.

"That's possible," conceded Tarkyn.

"Or perhaps the sorcery of the oath does not accept corrupted woodfolk, just as it would not have accepted you, if you were corrupt." Autumn Leaves sat up carefully and dusted himself off. "Does anyone have a drink?"

Several hands offered leather flasks of water.

"I don't know about that," said Waterstone. "I think it was Stormaway who determined Tarkyn's integrity and invoked the oath, not the sorcery in the oath itself."

Tarkyn looked quizzically at Rainstorm. "So, to sum up, we have no idea. Since Stormaway was responsible for casting the spell, he is the only person who really knows." He shrugged. "And he's not here."

37

S uddenly a lightning fast flurry of activity erupted around Tarkyn and Danton. Next thing they knew, they were on their own and Tarkyn's mind was filled with an intense image of himself with his shield around him

"Shield!" Tarkyn ordered peremptorily as he raised his own.

Instantly, Danton surrounded himself with an aqua haze. He glanced at Tarkyn but did nothing more, merely waiting for further instructions.

A few moments later, two very rough, scruffy individuals dodged in through the rain and stood sloughing off the worst of the water. They were dressed in roughly sewn furs plastered with mud and their shoulder-length hair was wet and bedraggled. Their long straggly beards hung in soggy rats' tails. A strong smell of stale sweat and wet animal fur filled the small cave.

"Morning," said the taller one, swinging his rucksack onto the floor. "Don't mind if we share your fire, do you? It's absolutely tipping it down out there."

"Yeah, throwing it down," agreed the shorter one.

Tarkyn waved his arm around the fire and the dry cave. "Please. Help yourselves," he replied urbanely as he wondered where the woodfolk were hiding and if they were getting drenched.

"Thanks very much."

They approached the fire, rubbing their hands together and squatting down in front of it. For a few minutes no one spoke. Gradually, the strangers' wet furs began to steam as the fire warmed them up. Once they had begun to thaw, the two interlopers transferred their attention to Tarkyn and Danton.

The taller one nudged the shorter, fatter one and said in a quiet voice, "Hey, Bean, these two have put their shields up. Are they expecting trouble, do you think? Maybe we should put ours up as well."

The shorter one sighed and flicked up a soft burgundy shield over the two of them. "I hate bloody shields. Means I can't relax properly." He looked across at Tarkyn. "So what's the problem? Wolves? Bears? Marauders?"

Tarkyn and Danton looked at each other before the prince replied with a slight smile. "You. We have our shields up, against you."

"Oh, I see," said the shorter one calmly. Then he caught his companion's eye and spluttered with laughter. The two grinned steadfastly at the fire for a few moments but were unable to repress the whoops of laughter that welled up. As they laughed, the burgundy shield wavered and disappeared.

Tarkyn smiled at their antics but asked Danton in an undertone, "I'll leave it to you to judge. Are they simply trying to put us off our guard or are they genuine?"

"I would say," responded Danton, carefully using neither name nor title, "that if you find it easy to maintain your shield, then you should continue to do so. You have nothing to lose but a slight loss of face for appearing overly cautious. The other way, you stand to lose everything if you are wrong."

So, the two of them just sat there watching until their two uninvited guests had laughed themselves to a standstill. Eventually the taller one wiped his eyes with the back of his hand and took a couple of deep breaths. "That's better. Nothing like a good laugh, I always say." He looked across at the prince and his companion. "Shields still up, I see. Fair enough. You don't know us, after all. Can't be too careful these days, I suppose." He rummaged around in his knapsack and produced a brace of dead rabbits with a flourish. "Here we are. We'll just skin these and we'll have the makings of a good hot lunch. You gentlemen are welcome to join us, if you would like to. We'll be using your lovely fire, after all, so it's the least we can do."

Tarkyn inclined his head. "That would be most kind of you."

The taller one's eyes narrowed. "You're a courtly sort of gent, aren't you? No wonder you get nervous when a couple of rednecks like us thrust ourselves upon you. Not used to being out and about, I shouldn't wonder."

"Actually," replied Tarkyn, "I have become used to being out and about, as you call it, but I am not so used to sharing my firesite with strangers."

"Is that so?" said the taller one slowly. "Your firesite, you say? Now that's an interesting expression, isn't it? Myself, I would say campfire or cooking fire, but not firesite."

The shorter one studied the prince. "He's quite tall, though, isn't he?"

The taller one nodded. "Yes. Too tall, I'd say. Colour's all wrong, too. The other one's closer in height but again, the colouring is wrong."

Tarkyn frowned. "And what would you be talking about?"

The two interlopers looked at each other, then the taller one shrugged disarmingly and replied, "Nothing at all. Just your unusual vocabulary. Must just come from a different area. Local dialect, I expect."

After a fractional pause, Tarkyn asked, "Would you mind introducing yourselves? I would like to know with whom I am sharing my fire."

Danton smiled slightly at the way Tarkyn reverted to being formal when he was unsure of the people he was with and wondered how the prince would introduce himself in return.

The taller man produced a rather crooked-toothed smile. "No problem. Might make you feel easier if we all get to know each other a bit. Not that I'm pressuring you to take your shield down. You leave it up until you're good and ready. Better safe than sorry out in these parts, if you ask me... well, in any parts, if it comes to that." He cleared his throat. "Anyway, my name's String and this is my mate, Bean." He chuckled, "Broadbean, of course."

"Oh really?" said Danton dryly.

String waved his hand dismissively. "Well, we had real names once. Bean's real name is Benson and mine's Stevoran, but we stopped using them a long time ago." He shrugged. "Anyway, as you've probably worked out, we're trappers. Live up in the mountains most of the year. Come down into the lower country about now before the weather really closes over. Stay down until the spring." Before Tarkyn could speak, he put his hand up. "Now, don't go thinking you have to tell us who you are. Obviously, it's a worry for you or you wouldn't be so cautious. If you're on the run or whatever, that's none of our business. You get all manner of strange folk up here. So feel free to keep it to yourselves. As long as you don't hurt us, we won't hurt you."

Tarkyn smiled gently. "You have no idea who I am, do you?"

"No," said String firmly, "don't really care that much either, to be honest."

"What if I were a rogue sorcerer?" asked Tarkyn.

"Well, we'd be stuffed then, wouldn't we?" said Bean calmly, as he held the skinned rabbits out in the rain to wash them down. "Because, between you and me and your quiet mate over there, I'm bloody useless at keeping my shield up for more than two minutes at a time. I lose concentration." He shrugged. "Anyway, the stinking shield warns animals that we're around and they all go to ground. So it does more harm than good most of the time."

Tarkyn smiled and waved his shield away.

Immediately, Bean threw a thin blast of burgundy power at him. Faster than thought, Tarkyn intercepted it head-on with his own power ray and simultaneously re-activated his shield.

Bean relaxed back and smiled. "Very good. You're fast and, unless I'm much mistaken, you performed two spells at once. That is very impressive. Did you see that, String?"

Within his bronze haze, Tarkyn put his hands on his hips. "So, what was that all about?"

"Don't mind Bean here. He's just playing. He wanted to see how wet you really were." String gave a grunt of laughter. "Not very, as it turns out. But not a rogue either. You didn't use more power than you needed to." He nodded at Danton. "Your friend here wasn't much help to you, was he? With his shield up, there wasn't much he could do for you, was there?"

Danton turned red with chagrin and immediately dropped his shield.

"Danton, don't let them wind you up. You will be no use to me dead."

"Interesting, isn't it?" said String to Bean. "This fellow

Danton is prepared to lay down his life for our mystery man here." While he was speaking, String was calmly skewering the rabbits onto a long thin branch and pushing up a couple of wooden forks into the dirt on either end of the fire to hang the rabbits between. "So, young Danton, who could be so special that you would risk your life without question for him? Your master? No. Despite your reticence, you don't strike me as a servant. In fact, you don't look a subservient sort of a character at all. More used to command than being commanded. And earlier on, our mystery man deferred to your judgement. Body guard? Minder? What do you think, Bean?"

Before Bean could reply, Danton said, "I thought you didn't care who we are. If that is the case, why all the conjecture?"

Bean raised his eyebrows. "You're right, String. He is looking after the other one's interests." He took the rabbits from String and placed them carefully over the fire. Then he glanced at Danton and smiled. "Don't worry. We're not interested in who you are, in terms of doing anything about it. But we do like to pass the time working out riddles. So, excuse us if we continue to figure out who you are. Think of it as a pre-dinner game."

"You know," said String suddenly, "our mystery man was surprised we didn't know who he was. That means he is either famous or notorious."

"Or both," said Tarkyn with a smile.

Bean put up his hands. "No, don't tell us. We'll work it out." He screwed up his face in thought. "You know, String, there is something about him that rings a bell but I'm sure I've never met him before."

"How long have you been out of circulation up there in the mountains?" asked Danton.

"Six, eight months," said Bean. "Why? Missed something, have we?"

Danton gave the ghost of a laugh. "Just a bit."

String scratched his head. "Hmm. What could have happened in the last six months?" He snapped his fingers. "I know. The Harvest Tournament." He smiled triumphantly at Tarkyn. "And you're good. So maybe you won the Harvest Tournament. That would explain why you thought we might know who you are."

Bean grimaced. "Trouble is, we don't know who won the Harvest Tournament."

Tarkyn laughed and waved out his shield again. "You're doing well. I don't know how much further you're going to get, though."

"Hmph, I think you might be right," Bean turned to Danton. "Go on then, give us a hint. What's your full name?"

Danton glanced at Tarkyn for approval before saying, "Danton Patronell, Lord of Satchmore."

String threw his hands up. "Blast it! Too easy! That's given the game away entirely."

Bean nodded sagely. "Yes, I'm afraid so. A lord's not going to protect anyone but Royalty. And obviously he's not one of the twins because each wouldn't trust the other one out of his sight for this long... and wrong colouring."

"So, you must be the youngest prince, Prince Tarkyn. That's why he rang a bell. It's his colouring; black hair with golden eyes. I've heard about it," concluded String. He nudged his companion sharply in the ribs and they both rose stiffly to their feet and, rather awkwardly, bowed low.

"Thank you," said Tarkyn quietly. "Please be seated again, if that is your wish."

The trappers promptly sat down but an air of constraint had settled over them and they kept their focus firmly on the cooking rabbits.

After a few minutes of silence, Tarkyn stood up and walked

over to the mouth of the cave to peer out into the driving rain. As the trappers made to stand, he waved a hand. "No. Don't get up. I wouldn't want our lunch burnt because you lost concentration."

They glanced at him and then at each other.

The stockier one leant over and murmured to String, "Is he being funny or is he really worried about his lunch?"

Tarkyn ignored them as he put his hand out into the rain. "Oh dear! Anyone out in that is going to be very wet."

The two trappers glanced at each other again before Bean said kindly, "Don't worry too much about your friends, Your Highness. They are experts at dealing with the elements. I bet they've found somewhere else nice and dry."

The prince spun around with a frown on his face. "I beg your pardon?"

String frowned furiously at Bean. "Bean means that if you happened to have any friends nearby, they would, of course, be skilful or they wouldn't be in the service of a prince. Isn't that right, Bean?"

Bean cleared his throat. "Just exactly what I meant."

Tarkyn looked across at Danton then came in and sat down. He picked a twig off one of the logs in the woodpile and began to break bits off the end. "Your logic wasn't right, you know," he said, carefully diverting the conversation. "I didn't expect to be known for having won the Harvest Tournament."

"No, obviously not," said Bean, thawing a little. "You've been well known all your life, haven't you? Yes, that was a bit of a red herring, wasn't it?" His eyes narrowed as he thought. "Hmm, still a puzzle here, now I come to think of it, isn't there String?"

String nodded. "Yes. No doubt about it. Very interesting." He nudged his companion. "Still, not sure that it's seemly to carry on with our guessing game. Might save it for later."

Tarkyn leant back against the wall of the cave and waved a hand. "No. Please continue, if you would like to. It is most entertaining."

"I think I agree with them that it is not seemly, my lord," said Danton repressively.

"And yet, Danton," Tarkyn spoke lightly but there was no mistaking the underlying edge, "I think I would rather hear whatever they conjecture, than leave them to reach their conclusions behind my back."

Bean and String looked at each other and a small nod passed between them. "Your Highness," said Bean, speaking for them both, "what we said before still holds true. That you are here with only Lord Danton as your retinue is none of our business. Neither are the friends you choose to keep. We keep well away from Tormadell and the affairs of the realm."

String turned the rabbits over and prodded one of them with his hunting knife. Then he looked up and met the prince's amber eyes. "You do not need to hear our conjecture to satisfy yourself that you are safe. We are no threat to you."

Bean shrugged. "I can see why you're worried, though. Price on your head, branded a rogue sorcerer, exiled by your brothers," he said casually. "They really are a pair of bastards, those two."

Danton threw his shield up around Tarkyn and himself. "You lied to us," he hissed. "You've known all along who we are."

Bean waved his hand disparagingly. "Oh, put your shield away, you feisty lad! I just told you; we're not planning to hurt you." He nodded at the prince. "Mind you, not sure that we could, even if we wanted to, but that's bye the bye." He began to rummage through his rucksack. "Go on, String. You explain while I get a plate out."

String settled himself with his hands linked loosely across his knees. "Your Highness, you brought the idea of a rogue sorcerer into the conversation, not us. Pretty rare things, rogues. Not something you'd normally think of. Obviously, you're on the run. So, I would say you've been branded a rogue." He picked up a stick and stirred the coals under the rabbits. "From your little display earlier, we have already established that you are not a rogue."

Bean picked up the thread. "So that can only mean you've been set up." He gave a slow smile. "You know, it was probably a tactical error on your part to win that tournament. We are talking pathologically jealous brothers here." He shrugged. "Still, what is obvious to everyone else isn't always obvious to those involved. Anyway, if you're on the run as a rogue, you're bound to have a price on your head and the only person who could sanction a price on your head would be the King." He swept his hand in a flourish and bowed from where he was sitting. "So, you see, we do not need to have known who you were earlier, at all."

Tarkyn laughed. "I think the mountain air must be good for your brains. You are a fine pair of thinkers."

"Thank you, my lord," said Bean, smiling. "We do have a lot of time to practise, you know. I think that helps."

Tarkyn glanced at Danton. "Enough, I think," he murmured quietly.

Without a word, Danton extinguished his shield.

"And you were saying about my friends?" continued Tarkyn pleasantly.

This time the look that passed between Bean and String was quite blatant. After some hesitation, Bean said, "I like your clothes. They're good for camouflage, aren't they?"

"Yes, they are," replied Tarkyn steadily, his eyes never leaving Bean's face.

"Do you know," said String conversationally, "I have never been able to find a shop that sells clothes exactly like that."

Danton smiled patronisingly. "But then, you have never been to Tormadell, have you?"

Bean raised his eyebrows. "You know, String, that's a very good point. I bet there are shops everywhere in Tormadell selling clothes like that. I understand muted brown tones are all the rage at court."

"No, actually they are not," replied Danton without missing a beat. "These are more for your country wear."

Bean smiled at String. "You have to give it to him; he's good."

Tarkyn smiled appreciatively. "Yes, he is, isn't he?"

Bean and String's attention returned to the rabbits for a few minutes. They pushed each rabbit towards its own end of the long stick. Bean then cut the long stick in half while String held the two cool ends. Once he had lowered the hotter ends onto the plate and they were sure String had a firm grip, Bean wrapped a rather grubby rag around the other hotter end of one stick to hold it and then cut the stick in half again, leaving half a rabbit on each section. He handed the skewered meat over to Tarkyn and Danton before repeating the process with the other rabbit.

Once they were settled with their food, Tarkyn said, "You know, I would be very careful, if I were you, about jumping to any conclusions. Sometimes it can be quite unhealthy to know or see too much."

Bean and String glanced at each other. With a mouth full of rabbit, Bean mumbled to his friend, "We should have shut up. We go all these years without breathing a word. Bloody curiosity. That's the trouble."

"And why has curiosity not led to you into a discussion with other sorcerers before now?" asked Tarkyn.

"You know, Your Highness," replied Bean, pausing to spit a piece of bone into the fire, "I think my answer to that might require me to jump to one of those conclusions you were talking about. So, if you don't mind, I won't answer."

"Personally," said Danton, entering the conversation for the first time in a long while, "I think this has gone too far already to be allowed to drop."

"And how do you propose to resolve it without placing these two gentlemen in danger?"

Danton shrugged. "They are already in danger. It is more whether we can bring them through safely without compromising ourselves."

Bean and String looked at each other and rolled their eyes. "Oh shit!" exclaimed Bean.

"I agree," said String fervently.

"My friend Danton is right, I'm afraid." Tarkyn leant forward and tossed the remains of his rabbit on the fire. He sighed. "In all conscience, I cannot let you walk out of here until I know what you know."

"Blast it! Blast it! Blast it!" exclaimed String, suddenly working himself up into frenzy. "We're stuffed now. We should never have come in here. He's going to kill us. They always do. Why were we so stupid? Oh no! Oh no! Oh no!"

Bean thumped his friend on the back. "Stop it! Calm down. We're not dead yet. We've thought our way out of tight corners before. Just settle down." Bean rolled his eyes at the prince. "Sorry about this. He's a bit of a panic merchant at times."

"String, look at me," Tarkyn's voice was firm and sure, and cut across the tall man's panic. "I have no wish to kill you nor to see you die." He gave a slight smile. "That would be poor thanks for such a tasty lunch. But I very much fear it is already out of my hands."

String stared at the prince and gulped. "If they know we know, we're dead. We've seen it before, you know."

"Who are they that you fear?" asked Tarkyn.

Bean narrowed his eyes. "If you don't know, I'm not about to tell you." He hesitated, and added as an afterthought, "Begging your pardon, my lord."

Tarkyn glanced at his liegeman. "Danton, we seem to be at an impasse."

"Tricky. We are under oath, and these men are in fear of their lives."

Bean's eyes narrowed. "How can you be under oath? Why have they not killed you?"

"Who?" asked Danton.

"Oh, the bloody woodfolk, of course. You know who we're talking about." The stockier trapper hunched his grubby furs around himself. "I can't be bothered with all these shenanigans. You obviously know about them and for some reason, are immune. We, of course, are not." He glanced at his companion who was gobbling at him and said impatiently, "Oh, stop it, String. These men aren't woodfolk themselves. With any luck, they won't feel the necessity to kill us."

Tarkyn grimaced. "You are not quite right in your conjecture there. You are right about Danton, but I'm afraid I am, in fact, woodfolk."

Bean stared at him in astonishment. "Well, shave my head and call me boulder! That's amazing. I've never seen any woodfolk before who didn't have light brown hair and green eyes." He nudged String and added quietly, "I think now might be a good time to panic, if you're going to. We are well and truly stuffed."

3 8

T arkyn couldn't help smiling. "Bean, why don't you come straight out with it and tell us what you know. Then we'll work out what to do about it."

Bean glanced at his friend then took a deep breath and turned resolutely to the prince. "We've been up in these mountains on and off for the last forty years. What we don't know about these mountains isn't worth knowing. They're good, these woodfolk. They're fast and vigilant and they have some trick of blending in that is beyond the ability of wizards and sorcerers. It's not that we're quicker or cleverer than they are. It's just that we have been around so long that sooner or later they were going to be caught out by us." He paused. "String, stop looking like a scared rabbit. Get the billy out and make us some tea." He gave a wry smile. "After all, it might be our last cup."

Tarkyn frowned a little. "If you are so certain we are going to kill you, why are you not planning to try to escape?"

"How do you know we're not?"

The prince shrugged. "You don't feel strung up in the way

a person does before action. You're worried, String more so than you, but you're not tensed up, waiting your chance."

Bean shook his head. "You're right. I'm not planning any heroics. We've been around a long time. We've been in worse situations than this and come through. Besides, your mates are all around us outside. If we rushed out of here, we'd be dead before we made the cover of the first tree."

String steadfastly concentrated on untying a battered old tin can from the side of his pack. When he had it free, he carried it to the mouth of the cave and held it out in the rain to fill it. Tarkyn thought this was likely to keep him occupied for quite some time.

"Did you see them?" asked Tarkyn.

String nodded unhappily from the doorway. "More or less. We just saw a blur of movement, but we knew what it was. Most people wouldn't have even noticed."

Tarkyn considered. "Perhaps we should invite them back in, since you know they are here anyway. What do you think?"

A look passed between String and Bean. Then Bean shrugged. "Yeah. Why not? Might as well be hung for a sheep as for a lamb. If we're going to die for knowing about them anyway, at least we could meet them. I have always wanted to but .... Well, too dangerous, as you know."

String nodded. He seemed to have calmed down completely and be resigned to his fate. "Yeah. Actually, that would be pretty exciting. Takes a bit to get us excited these days but that would be really something."

"I will need your oath that you will not try to harm them."

"Huh, that's rich," snorted Bean. "It's not us who's the threat. It's them,"

"Nevertheless...."

Bean sighed. "Yeah, fine."

String also nodded from the doorway. "It would be a bit

pointless to attack them, anyway. It would just make our deaths even more certain."

"Very well. Just a minute." Tarkyn sent an image of the woodfolk arriving in the cave and sitting with the four sorcerers.

A moment later, three damp woodfolk appeared, brushing themselves down and glaring balefully at the two interlopers.

"Would have been good if you had reached this point sooner. Then we could have been in here next to the fire," scowled Rainstorm. "It's bloody miserable out there."

"Never mind," rumbled Thunder Storm. "We've brought better provisions this time, and Waterstone and Autumn Leaves will be here in a minute with some extra wood. Your little one is with them."

"And what about Lapping Water and Summer Rain?" asked Tarkyn.

"No," replied Rainstorm, "they've headed off to join the others in a bigger cave further up the mountain. North Wind, too."

Tree Wind stared at the trappers. "So, Your Highness, what makes you think we might want to sit around and chat with outsiders rather than kill them off?"

"And how did they come to know we were here?" asked Thunder Storm. "I am assuming you two did not tell them."

Tarkyn raised his eyebrows. "Good of you to assume that."

Rainstorm chortled. "There it is again. That expression."

"Oh, stop it, Rainstorm." Tarkyn relaxed. "I am not being disdainful. Well, not quite. Thunder Storm is trying to wind me up, though." He turned to the trappers who were looking on with great interest. "Let me introduce you to String over there in the doorway collecting water for our tea...at least he was. He seems to have forgotten what he is doing..." String immediately

raised his arm so that the billy was once more catching water...
"and Bean."

Bean nodded his head. "It is a pleasure to meet you after all
this time. I know the cost may be high, but it is still a pleasure."

"You're a calm sort of a character then, if you know the
cost," observed Rainstorm, whose voice had a tendency to
blend in to the noise outside if he walked too close to the mouth
of the cave. "I am Rainstorm."

Bean shrugged. "I only put energy into things I can change.
In this case, my only hope lies in gaining your friendship."

"Well, there is no hope of that," declared Tree Wind flatly.
"We don't mix with outsiders. My name is Tree Wind."

"And yet," replied Bean mildly, "I see at least one outsider
here who obviously knows you."

"Exceptional circumstances," she replied shortly.

String, who seemed to have completely recovered his
equilibrium, said casually, "If you don't mind me saying, there
is something quite exceptional about His Highness being
woodfolk as well. He obviously wasn't born woodfolk and I am
guessing he can't do your disappearing act or he would have, as
you did, when we arrived."

Thunder Storm's eyes narrowed. "Did you see us leave?"

String shrugged. "More or less. Probably less than more,
actually. But we still knew what we had seen."

Thunder Storm nodded shortly as he digested this. "I
gather you have known of us for quite some time."

"Yeah, a little while," said Bean laconically. "What would
you say, String? Maybe twenty, twenty-five years?"

The three woodfolk stared at them.

"So, who else have you told over that time?" demanded
Tree Wind.

Bean shrugged. "No one. We knew what the penalty was
for having seen you. We've seen people killed."

"So, why now do you finally admit to knowing about us?"

Bean considered her for a moment, gauging her intelligence and her mood. Finally, he smiled and said, "I will tell you the one thing you don't know and you work out the rest."

As Tree Wind frowned, Tarkyn put in, "They love riddles."

A slow smile dawned on her face. "Go on."

Bean glanced over at Tarkyn. "His Highness said he wasn't used to having strangers around his firesite."

"And they are dressed as we are and you saw us leave," Rainstorm butted in enthusiastically. "So you knew they knew."

Bean nodded. "Exactly."

"Precisely," agreed String. He peered down into his billy. "This is still only quarter full. We'd never have said anything otherwise but curiosity got the better of us, I'm afraid. Haven't told a soul for twenty-three years.... It's twenty-three years, Bean ... And now look at us. Up to our necks in it."

Thunder Storm held out a water flask. "Here. I can't stand the torture of watching you collect water so slowly. I am Thunder Storm."

String grinned. "Thanks. I don't normally travel around with an empty water flask but it started raining when we were at the stream, so we just made a dash for it." He looked at the flask in his hand. "Nice. Well made. Deer hide. Did you make it?"

Thunder Storm shook his head. "No. The forestals made it. They're good at craft work...with the possible exception of young Rainstorm here."

Rainstorm scowled. "You've been listening to Falling Branch too much. Don't believe everything you hear."

"You people are refreshingly normal," observed Bean dryly, as String took his filled billy over to the fire and settled it in the flames between two burning branches.

Rainstorm frowned. "I don't see how you can be refreshing and normal all at once."

"If you're expecting something complicated and unusual, then the norm becomes exotic," explained String over his shoulder.

"Whoa. You two have been out on your own for too long, with too much time to think." Rainstorm laughed. "Anyway, of course we're normal. I would say your lifestyle is a lot weirder than ours."

"Of course you would," replied Bean. "You're used to yours."

Just then, Waterstone and Autumn Leaves arrived bearing armfuls of wood. Midnight was right behind them sopping wet but happily dragging another large bough. He walked into the cave and shook himself. Then he spotted the trappers and did a double take. Just as Tarkyn was ruing the fact that he hadn't thought to warn the unruly little boy, Midnight astonished them all by breaking into a beaming smile, dashing over to Bean and throwing his arms around his neck. Bean wrapped his arms around him and gave him a big hug.

"Hallo, Midnight. How are you keeping? I haven't seen you for ages."

Midnight leant back and smiled at the trapper, knowing he had spoken but only able to guess what he was saying. He pointed to Tarkyn and himself and then wrapped his hands around each other in his sign for friendship.

Bean raised his thumb and smiled. "I'm glad you have a friend, Midnight. You're a great kid."

Everyone had stopped what they were doing and were staring at Bean and Midnight. Bean ignored them and pointed to String. "Go on. Say hallo to String. He misses you too, you know."

Midnight looked around at String and gave him a wave.

When String beckoned him, Midnight jumped up and went over to hug him, not quite as effusively as he had hugged Bean but warmly, nevertheless. String bent over and swung the little boy up into his arms. He put his hand in his pocket and pulled out a small, carved, wooden animal of indeterminate species. He held it out to Midnight and nodded encouragingly. The little boy accepted the gift and gave him a shy smile. String patted him on the head and let him down.

Midnight ran over to Tarkyn and held out his little wooden animal. The prince smiled and sent a query about the trappers. A short silence ensued while Midnight showed him images of Bean and String walking through the mountains and sitting around a fire with his mother and him.

Bean, who was watching them intently, exclaimed, "You're talking to him! I can't hear you but you are, aren't you?"

Tarkyn smiled and nodded. "More or less. We're sharing images, not words."

"That's great. Poor little bugger. He's been so lonely since his mother left him with the mountainfolk."

Tree Wind frowned. "And what was his mother doing, keeping company with you? She has broken our bond of silence." She did not sound very pleased.

Bean put up his hand hastily. "No, she didn't. We knew about you woodfolk for what...?"

"Fifteen years," supplied String.

"...fifteen years before we met Hail."

Suddenly Thunder Storm loomed over Bean. "You're not the person who's been beating him, are you?" he rumbled threateningly.

"He's hardly going to admit to it if he is, with you standing over him like that," Rainstorm pointed out.

Thunder Storm glared at Rainstorm but remained where he was.

Bean ignored the woodman and asked his friend, "String, is that tea ready yet? A man could die of thirst waiting." When String filled a cup and headed towards him, he hissed, "Not me first. Give His Highness a cup of tea first. Then worry about the rest of us."

"Oh yes, good point." He swung around and gave the steaming cup of tea to Tarkyn instead. "Sorry about that, Your Highness. Not too good at these social niceties."

Rainstorm chortled. "Welcome to the club. The only person around here who has any idea of what to do, or any wish to do it, is Danton.... Besides Tarkyn, of course."

"Interesting, isn't it, Bean?" said String, handing his friend a cup of tea.

"Very. We'll have to think about this." Bean sipped his tea before finally meeting Thunder Storm's eyes. "And no, I did not beat young Midnight. Neither did String. His mother did often enough, though."

"So, if you knew her, why did you do nothing about it?" demanded Thunder Storm.

"We did." Bean stared up at the woodman. "Now, are you going to sit down and relax while we talk to you or would you rather I stood up? It feels very uncomfortable having you standing over me like this. We promised His Highness not to harm any of you and frankly, we'd be mad to try. So, feel free to relax."

Waterstone nodded briefly and sat down. The others followed suit. String pottered around providing cups of tea for everyone before sitting down himself.

"Go on then," said Waterstone. "What did you do about it? I am Waterstone."

"We talked her into giving him to the mountainfolk to mind." Bean scratched his head. "I'm not sure that that was such a great idea, in retrospect. They haven't been very kind to him either."

"We couldn't keep him, you know. She wouldn't let us." String sipped his tea. "Not, mind you, that we were busting to, much as we like him. Big commitment for a couple of confirmed bachelors. But we did offer."

"Woodfolk are not usually so unkind," said Thunderstorm thoughtfully. "I can't believe she would treat her own son like that."

Bean sipped his tea and looked over the rim of his mug at Thunder Storm and said conversationally to his mate, "Should I bother to continue, do you think, String? If we are to be disbelieved, I can see little point."

Thunder Storm gave a slow smile. "I beg your pardon. I did not mean it like that. Perhaps I should have said that I find it hard and distressing to believe."

String frowned at Bean. "Stop being so pedantic, Bean. You knew what he meant."

"Just wanted to set the ground rules, String. We are, after all, in a reasonably sticky situation from our point of view." He returned his attention to Thunder Storm. "Hail hated that kid. From the moment he was born."

"No, Bean. Get it right," interrupted String. "From the moment he was conceived."

"Yeah, true." Bean sighed. "It was all so bloody unfortunate. There was a landslide, you see. Hail was caught in it and swept down the mountainside. She was found, injured and unconscious, by a trapper who went by the name of Pipeless...lost his pipe a long time ago and never made himself another one...Do you remember his real name, String?"

String frowned in effort of memory but shook his head. "No, not at the moment. It may come to me, though."

"Anyway, Pipeless took her back to the little hut he had

built to stay in, up on the mountains when the weather was bad. He looked after her for weeks while she recovered and, unfortunately, fell in love with her."

"As you would," put in String, "looking after a maiden in distress."

"But of course, she was woodfolk and wasn't having any. She was horrified to find herself in close proximity to a wizard in the first place."

"Yeah, Pipeless was a wizard you know. Very learned," supplied String helpfully.

"Not that it matters for the purposes of this story."

"Well, it does."

"String, shut up. I'll never get through this if you keep interrupting me."

String put up his hands and shrugged. "Just trying to help. But no problem. I will leave it to you."

Bean looked at him for a moment before continuing, "One day, when she was nearly recovered, they were out walking near his hut and he just lost it. He'd tried to make her love him in return and when she didn't...well, the long and the short of it is that he raped her."

There was a shocked indrawn breath all around the fire. Midnight looked around at everyone, aware that they were disturbed about something. Tarkyn looked down at him, sent reassurances and placed a steadying arm on his back.

Despite himself, it was String who continued, "We heard her crying out, but by the time we arrived, we were too late. We dragged him off her and as soon as her arms were free, she drew a knife and threw it at him. It hit him in the chest and he dropped like a stone. But as he died, he muttered some words and we're pretty sure it was some kind of a curse."

Bean shrugged. "We don't know much about wizardry. So we don't know what he said. But we've remembered it. We've remembered the syllables even though we don't know what it means because we were worried that it might matter to Hail."

"Anyway, she had put the last of her returning strength into that throw and passed out. We carried her back to the hut, put her to bed and made her comfortable but when she awoke, Hail was mortified," said String, picking up the story. "She hated us, all sorcerers and wizards, with a vengeance after that but she still wasn't well enough to leave or to look after herself. We kept her supplied with food and water but kept well away, other than that."

Bean gave a wry smile. "After all, neither of us wanted a knife in the chest!"

String shook his head sadly. "Poor girl. She had a terrible pregnancy. She threw up all the time and couldn't find the strength to leave. So we looked after her from afar, leaving supplies for her outside the door and then departing as quickly as we could."

Bean sipped his tea. "Then one day, as I was dropping off some food, she came out of the hut and asked me in. She kept a knife in her hand the whole time I was there, but it was a start. I think she wanted to find out how much we knew about woodfolk and whether she could trust us not to say anything."

"And she was lonely. We went there often after that, didn't we, Bean? She always kept her knife close to hand and we didn't ever try to dissuade her from it."

"As she came closer to term, she found it hard even to get out of bed. So one or the other of us came every day to look after her." Bean drank the last of his tea and shook out the mug. "We were there when Midnight was born. We helped her through that too."

String grunted with laughter. "She kept that knife next to her through the whole thing. I don't think she really thought we were any kind of threat by then, but it had become a habit with her." He shrugged. "Still, if that's what she needed to feel safe, then fair enough. Like you blokes with your shield earlier on. We may be trustworthy but you bring your own reasons for mistrusting us to the table. It's no reflection on us if you don't trust us."

"Can be inconvenient though, can't it, String?"

"Yeah, true. Anyway, once she had borne her child, she recovered quickly and left the hut about six weeks later."

"But she always hated that baby, didn't she, String?"

"Yeah. Everything was too hard and too much trouble. She resented him like crazy. Maybe if he'd been a girl, it might have been better."

"No, don't think so, String. Whether he was a boy or a girl, he's still half-sorcerer and conceived by rape."

"Yeah, true. Poor little bugger. Not his fault."

The woodfolk and Tarkyn had all transferred their attention to Midnight who was quietly sitting in the dirt next to the prince and playing with his wooden animal. Feeling their eyes on him, he looked up and confronted them with the brilliant green of his non-woodfolk eyes. For a moment, he panicked, but Tarkyn grabbed him before he could run and held him firmly. After a few seconds, Tarkyn gradually released his hold, checking that Midnight wouldn't run. Tarkyn put his hand on his heart and pointed to himself and then Midnight. The little boy slowly relaxed into a smile, put his own hand on his heart and, reassured, went back to playing with his animal.

"You're a nice prince, aren't you?" said Bean. "I thought princes didn't concern themselves with the affairs of the hoi polloi."

Tarkyn's face reddened slightly and he glanced around the woodfolk. "To be perfectly honest, I haven't, until recently. In retrospect, not something I feel too proud of."

"Sire, you should not be too harsh on yourself. You have

always been meticulous in fulfilling the expectations of your role," said Danton.

"I know I have, Danton. Where I have fallen short is in accepting those expectations without question." The prince smiled around at his woodfolk companions. "Luckily, these people have done my questioning for me."

"But to be fair," said Waterstone, "you did not have to respond to our questioning. It is you who have chosen to change your expectations."

"Speaking of which," responded Tarkyn, slipping in under their guards, "have your own expectations changed in any way after hearing these sorcerers' story?"

Tree Wind huffed. Thunder Storm looked thoughtful. Autumn Leaves smiled wryly at Tarkyn, while Rainstorm chortled at Tree Wind's discomfort. Then surprisingly, all eyes turned to Waterstone. Tarkyn raised his eyebrows and waited.

Waterstone folded his arms. "You could order us to accept them."

"I could."

"Hmph." Waterstone's eyes went out of focus as he communed with the others.

"They are discussing it," explained Tarkyn quietly.

"Interesting," commented String. "What are they doing? Speaking telepathically?"

"Yes, more or less. Images and words," answered Tarkyn.

Bean studied the woodfolk for a few moments. "And what's their range?"

Tarkyn shrugged. "I'm not entirely sure but it is several miles."

"Is it? That's marvellous, isn't it?" mused Bean. After a short pause, he became bored with waiting and said laconically, "Of course, we might have been bullshitting. One of us might have been the rapist."

For a split second a ripple of uncertainty flicked across Tarkyn's face. Then he shook his head. "No one had to know any of this, if you hadn't told us. No one has mentioned it. I don't think Hail has told anyone. So why would you bring it to light if you were the guilty party? Doesn't make sense."

"Well done, Tarkyn," said Danton dryly. "You answered their next little riddle."

Bean laughed. "Have to keep oneself entertained, you know."

String frowned anxiously. "They're taking a long time, aren't they?"

"I expect they are consulting with all the mountainfolk and the other woodfolk as well. After all, it is a fairly momentous decision, isn't it?" replied Tarkyn.

"And begging your pardon, Your Highness, but if you could order them to accept us, why didn't you?" asked String.

"Hmm, tricky question. You explain, Danton."

"The woodfolk were forced to acknowledge Prince Tarkyn as their liege lord by his father. Until the prince arrived in the forest two months ago, they have never had leaders among themselves. So the prince does not wish to assert his authority excessively," replied Danton urbanely.

"I see," said Bean thoughtfully. "Breaking them in slowly, are you?"

Tarkyn glared furiously at the trapper and then glanced at the woodfolk in some trepidation. Sure enough, Waterstone had come back into focus and was watching him, waiting for his reply. "No, I am not," he said vehemently. "I would never do that. These people are my friends and kinsfolk. We have reached an agreement that will stand until we feel the need to change it, at which time we will discuss it together." He could feel himself going red. "Waterstone, you believe me, don't you? This is not the thin end of the wedge."

Waterstone gave a slight smile. "Tarkyn, don't panic. I always believe you." With that, he went back out of focus.

Tarkyn heaved a sigh of relief. "Stars above, Bean, that was a thoughtless comment. They can all hear you while they are mindtalking, you know. Just as you can tune into another conversation when you're talking."

Bean nodded. "Sorry about that, Your Highness. They seem to have great faith in you, though, that woodman in particular."

The prince smiled. "They all do, as I do in them. That woodman in particular is my blood brother, Waterstone."

"I should point out," put in Danton, "that His Highness could not lie to save himself. So, we are all quite safe in trusting his word."

"Precisely," said Waterstone, coming back into the conversation. He smiled at his blood brother. "But we would be safe, even if he could lie." He turned to the trappers. "Did you see Hail again after she left the hut?"

"Yes. We achieved that much at least," responded Bean. "She is a trapper, just as we are; and by choice she spends most of her time in the mountains on her own. But if our paths have crossed over the years, she has always shown herself and we have shared a meal together before she moved on." He chuckled. "Always with the knife. But never mind. So we have watched Midnight grow up. For months at a time she would disappear and return to the outskirts of her people but always the mountains would draw her back."

String grimaced. "She was very harsh with Midnight. She hated him. He was living proof that she had, in her own eyes, betrayed her people and that she had been raped. And she hated the fact that he couldn't hear and didn't understand her. She would beat him when he didn't know what she was asking him to do, out of frustration as much as bitterness. It was dreadful to watch. And it was hard to talk to her about it. She resented anything we had to say. And we knew, if we pushed too hard, she would go away and never let us see her or Midnight again and then we wouldn't be able to help him at all."

Bean looked over and, when he caught Midnight's eye, beckoned to him. The little boy came over and Bean sat him on his knee with his arm around him. "We're not very fatherly types but we were the only people he ever saw who weren't shouting at him or belting him."

"Finally, we talked her into leaving him with his kin when she returned to the mountains. We thought that they, at least, would have no cause to hate him, as his mother did." String grimaced. "But none of them knew how to handle a deaf child."

"They thought he was a fool," put in Tarkyn.

Bean grimaced. "And I suspect his mother must have told them that he was disobedient and wilful." The trapper felt a continual tugging on his beard and looked down. "Which he is sometimes, like all little boys, but he's not bad or evil." He frowned. "And what do you think you're doing?" he asked Midnight.

Midnight grinned and lifted part of Bean's beard up. It was halfway through being neatly plaited. Bean nodded and smiled. "Go on then. Anything to keep you busy."

Waterstone went back out of focus briefly to relay the last piece of the jigsaw. When he returned, he was looking grim.

"There is a strong faction among the mountainfolk that want Midnight killed. They think it is an abomination to have a child who is half-sorcerer and half-woodfolk."

After a shocked silence, Tarkyn said flatly, "They are under oath. Tell them that Midnight's fate is not up for discussion. He will remain with me and it is the responsibility of all woodfolk to keep him safe even as they look after all woodfolk children. Clear enough?"

Waterstone gave a slight smile. "Yes. Thanks."

A few minutes later, they were all back in focus.

"We have some good news and some news that I suspect you may not like," reported Rainstorm.

"Go on," nodded Bean.

"You will be allowed to live," said Rainstorm.

String breathed a sigh of relief and exchanged glances with Bean. "And the uncertain news?"

"You must live with us until we are sure of you. At least six months," said Tree Wind.

"Are you holding us prisoner?" asked Bean.

"Don't be silly," rumbled Thunder Storm. "We don't have jails or the time to stand guard over you. But if you leave us, then the first woodfolk who see you, will kill you."

String looked strained, as though he was on the verge of panic again. "What if I want to go off for a walk on my own or just with Bean? I can't last too long around a lot of people, you know."

"As long as you stay within view of our lookouts, you'll be okay. That gives you a fair degree of latitude," said Thunder Storm. "We'll show you the sort of area that covers. If you look as though you're going too far away, the lookout will send a warning arrow into a tree next to you."

String took a deep breath and then another but failed to calm himself. "Oh no! Oh no! Oh no! I can't manage this. I have to go. Out of my way!" String jumped up and rushed out of the cave into the pouring rain.

Bean sat calmly, watching him go. "Don't worry. He'll be back. It's too wet out there for one thing, and he's left his pack behind." He transferred his gaze to Midnight and tapped him on the head to gain his attention. "Hey, little one, How's the beard going?" He tapped on his beard to explain what he was saying.

With a smile, Midnight held up half of the beard, which had been neatly plaited into four braids. Bean held up a thumb to show he liked it. Midnight smiled and began work on the second half.

"At least we'll see more of Midnight," said Bean. "Though to be honest, he's probably easier to take in small doses." He looked around at the woodfolk. "Thank you for advocating on our behalf. And have you decided which of your groups we will reside with? I gather there is more than one."

"We are the forest guardian's home guard," said Rainstorm with a touch of pride. "We are on the move, whereas the mountainfolk, who are Hail's people, will stay here. Personally, I suspect they would make your life difficult."

"I think you are right," agreed Tree Wind. "They are not used to sorcerers as we are and they will be filled with horror at Hail's fate at the hands of a sorcerer."

"So, we suggest that you throw in your lot with us," rumbled Thunder Storm, adding with a twinkle. "We'll try not to crowd you in too much."

Suddenly Bean beamed. "I think it's marvellous that we can stay with you for a while. We can learn so much from you and, you never know, you may learn a thing or two from us."

"So, you're not worried about needing to be off on your own?" asked Tarkyn.

Bean waved his hand airily. "No, not at the moment. I suspect there may be times further down the track when it grates with me. But worry about that when it happens. Right now, I'm happy to stay alive and to have the pleasure of getting to know you after all these years of carefully avoiding you."

Just then String erupted through the doorway dripping wet, and demanded, "So, do you have lookouts out there already?"

"Always," replied Waterstone.

"And did they already know about the warning shot if we go too far?"

Waterstone nodded.

String breathed a sigh of relief and sat down. "Oh, well, that's all right then. No one shot at me. So it must be a reasonable area to move around in." He looked around expectantly. "So, whose turn is it to make the next cup of tea?"

VIII

THE CURSE

39

By mid-afternoon, the storm had cleared, leaving the forest glistening and damp, mud and puddles underfoot. As they prepared to leave, String asked casually where they were going and was horrified to discover that they were heading up into the mountains.

"We've only just come down from there. What about our furs? We haven't even had time to take them into a settlement and sell them."

"And you're leaving it a bit late, you know," added Bean whose beard was now neatly plaited into eight thin braids. "The weather's starting to close in. If you thought that storm was bad this morning, wait until you're in one full of sleet and snow."

"All the more reason to set off quickly," said Waterstone firmly. "We can organise to sell your furs for you, if you would like us to. Where are they?"

The trappers looked at each other and then at Waterstone. Bean nearly spoke but thought better of it and turned to String again. A strange silent conversation ensued where they nodded and grimaced queries and uncertainties at each other.

Eventually, Waterstone lost patience with them and turned on his heel to walk away. "Let me know what you decide. It makes no difference to me but might make a lot to you, if your furs are spoiled by the time you come back."

Tarkyn strolled up and said to the two trappers. "You've offended him, you know. Waterstone is the most trustworthy person I have ever met." He paused. "And you might like to remember that, as far as you're concerned, both Ancient Oak and he are princes, just as I am."

Faced with that reminder, the two trappers scrambled to their feet and bowed.

"I beg your pardon, Sire," said Bean. "I'm afraid we are rather out of practice with social niceties." As Tarkyn turned to walk away, Bean rolled his eyes at String and said sotto voce, "Being stuck with woodfolk is one thing. Being stuck with court etiquette is quite another. This six months could turn out to be quite a trial."

Tarkyn swung back around and glared at him. "I do not appreciate snide remarks behind my back. You will find that I do not, in fact, expect all the etiquette of court, but I do expect respect, both for myself and for everyone else. I suggest you speak to Danton about my expectations. If, after that, you are still dissatisfied, then speak to me about it. But whatever you do, do not complain about me behind my back. Clear?"

Bean glanced at String then nodded. After a slight pause, he asked, "And will we find that your expectations include us enduring tongue-lashings from you, as the mood takes you?"

Tarkyn put his hands on his hips and shook his head in amazement. "These forests seem to breed an excessively independent attitude, whether you be woodfolk or sorcerer. And to answer your question, yes. If I choose to take you to task, you will have to endure it but I will give you right of reply, which is more than you would be given at court."

The trappers exchanged glances. "Seems fair," said String. "Now, before you go, would you mind telling us who this forest guardian is? Rainstorm mentioned that they were the home guard for him..."

"Could be a her, String."

"Yes, could be... and we can't figure out who or what it is."

Despite his previous displeasure, Tarkyn grinned and gave a slight bow. "Look no further. You see him before you. I am the Guardian of the Forest."

String's brow wrinkled. "So, is it just a courtesy title instead of prince?"

The prince shook his head. "No. It is far more than that." He stopped short as he remembered what Danton's reaction had been – that Tarkyn was either unhinged or conning the woodfolk. He eyed the two trappers. "You don't know much about me, but two things you have hopefully learnt by now; I am honest and straightforward and I am not mad."

String and Bean thought for a moment before nodding.

"I would agree with that," said Bean. "So, your point?"

Tarkyn took a deep breath and smiled self-consciously. "The guardian of the forest is a figure of woodfolk legend who appears among them every four or five hundred years to support them through a time of serious strife. The guardian is a person with magical power who can be recognised because of his or her particular abilities."

"Which are...?" asked String.

"The ability to heal and promote growth, and the ability to communicate with animals."

Bean's eyes grew round. "Can you do that?"

Tarkyn nodded, smiling. "I use that ability to talk to Midnight. That's why only I can talk to him."

Bean frowned repressively. "He is not an animal."

"No, of course he's not. But I can exchange images and feelings with him, just as I can with animals and with all woodfolk, for that matter."

"Not words?" asked String.

"No, not words. I wish I could, but only woodfolk can use words."

"So, it is as we thought," said Bean slowly. "Although you tell us you are woodfolk, you do not have their abilities and do not look like them. And obviously you belong to the highest sorcerer family in the land. So...?"

"So, I have been inaugurated into the woodfolk nation as a member of Waterstone's family because I have demonstrated my dedication to upholding my oath to them." Tarkyn unconsciously drew himself up. "I am very proud to have been accorded that honour. I am the first outsider ever to have been accepted as one of them."

Bean whistled. "That is impressive. And what did you do that impressed them so much?"

Tarkyn waved a dismissive hand. "I think I have done quite enough of blowing my own trumpet. You will have to go elsewhere for that information."

"He gave us the chance to kill him so that our kin could be released from the oath and woodfolk unity could be preserved," said Rainstorm, coming up behind him.

The two trappers stared at Tarkyn who suddenly felt as though he had grown two heads. He couldn't meet their eyes and after an embarrassed moment, muttered, "I had better go and see what Midnight is up to." With that, Tarkyn wheeled around and strode off.

Bean put his hands on his hips as he watched the prince walk off into the middle distance. "He's amazing, isn't he? At the start of this conversation, I was resenting having to put the effort into standing up and bowing to him. But I'm beginning to realise that he is far more impressive than he comes across at first meeting. Compared to his worth, he is quite modest in his demand for recognition, isn't he?"

"And Danton thinks Tarkyn is the only person who provides any hope for the future of Eskuzor," added North Wind entering the conversation at this point. "So, in time, he may become a legend for you sorcerers as well."

"And you haven't heard anything yet," responded Rainstorm with some pride. "Wait 'til I tell you about him rescuing our woodfolk from the sorcerers, saving the forest from the sickness, healing the sorcerer's children and best of all, persuading the mountain eagles to come to his rescue. Tarkyn is already a walking legend for what he has done, as much as for being our forest guardian." The young woodman shrugged and added casually, "Doesn't mean I'd bow to him or do what he says, necessarily. There are limits, but..."

".... in reality, you would cut off your right arm for him," finished North Wind for him. "And so would I," he added before Rainstorm had time to react. "With or without the oath."

After a slight hesitation, Rainstorm grinned and nodded. "True. Yes, I would."

40

A s Tarkyn walked past Sparrow who was using some sticks to build a miniature shelter, he noticed her glance up at him and then look quickly back down at what she was doing. He stopped dead and squatted down beside her on the muddy ground, privately ruing the state of his mud-splattered leggings.

"Hello, young one," he said. "Am I wrong, or are you mad at me?"

"Why would I be mad at you?" said Sparrow aloofly, keeping her attention fixed firmly on what she was doing. "I haven't seen you enough to have anything to get mad about."

"Sparrow, look at me." When the little girl reluctantly raised her eyes, Tarkyn continued, "Have I been neglecting you since Midnight arrived?"

Sparrow shrugged. "You don't have to play with me if you don't want to. You're not my dad."

"I am your friend though, and your uncle. And I like doing things with you. Midnight can't replace you, you know. He's his own person, just as you are."

Sparrow sniffed. "At least I can talk."

For a moment, Tarkyn's eyes narrowed, but he merely said, "Yes, that's handy isn't it? I can talk to you about lots of things that I can't talk to Midnight about. And it makes it so much easier for you to do things with your friends, doesn't it?"

Although nothing in Tarkyn's tone gave away that he didn't like what she had said, Sparrow's face reddened. "I'm sorry. I shouldn't have said that. It was mean."

Tarkyn smiled and ruffled her hair. "It was a bit, wasn't it? But also true. And unlike some of the mountainfolk, you haven't been mean to him. In fact, you have helped me by including him in the mock battle and playing in the slingshot tournament with him." He grinned. "And let's face it, he's not the easiest character in the world to get on with."

A slow smile dawned on Sparrow's face. "No, he's a bit tricky. He's very shy, you know. The only time he's played with more than one person is when you were there." She hesitated. "Dad says Midnight's had a hard life." There was a long pause while she finished off her little shelter. Finally, she looked up at Tarkyn and took a deep breath. "But I have too. I lost my mum. So why is it okay for Midnight to be so naughty and run away all the time? And he put you in danger and I don't want to lose you too."

"I don't want to lose you either, so I promise I will be careful. Come here." He twisted around to sit on a damp log with a mental apology to his leggings and swung Sparrow onto his lap. "You have had a hard time losing your mum. But you know, you have always had Waterstone who must be the best dad in the world." Sparrow nodded briefly as though this was obvious. "And you have Autumn Leaves, and Ancient Oak and Thunder Storm and Creaking Bough and all the other kids... Midnight has had no one. He has never had a dad, his mother hated him and the only people he ever saw in his life who liked him were String and Bean, and he only saw them once every few months." He considered Sparrow for a minute before saying, "His mother used to beat him all the time, you know, when he wouldn't do what he was told, even if it was because he didn't understand."

Sparrow drew in a shocked breath. "That's awful. No wonder he runs away all the time."

Tarkyn nodded. "He gets frightened. We're just lucky he doesn't react by lashing out at everyone."

"He attacked Rainstorm and Thunder Storm, though."

Tarkyn chuckled. "Yes, he's a feisty little thing, isn't he? He attacked Rainstorm for saying something mean about me, and Thunder Storm to protect Autumn Leaves. Both times he was protecting someone. It wasn't rage or fear. When he's scared, he runs."

"Is it true that his dad was a sorcerer?"

"A wizard, no less. That's a sorcerer who has learnt a lot about magic."

Sparrow looked up at Tarkyn. "So, does that mean Midnight can do magic too, like you can?"

Tarkyn raised his eyebrows in surprise. "Do you know, I hadn't even thought of that. That's a very interesting question." He smiled. "I'll have to see whether I can teach him some. He can't say incantations so that will limit him a bit, but maybe thinking them might be enough. I don't really know. You can help me, if you like. What do you think?"

Sparrow nodded enthusiastically. "That would be fun, as long as he doesn't use his magic to run away or to hurt anyone."

"Yes, good point. I'll have to sort that out with him first. I wish Stormaway were here. He's the expert on magic." *And he would know what that curse meant,* Tarkyn added to himself.

"Wish no longer, Sire. I am here."

Tarkyn's head whipped around to find Stormaway

Treemaster, dressed once more in his everyday green forest attire, producing a low florid bow. The old wizard straightened up and smiled. "I am pleased to see you, Your Highness. I hear you have acquitted yourself well, both with Lord Tolward and his family, and with the mountainfolk. Lord of the Eagles, no less. Most impressive."

Ignoring the inaccuracy about the eagles, Tarkyn swung Sparrow off his lap and stood up to grasp Stormaway in a bear hug. After a slight hesitation, Stormaway returned his embrace.

"I am so pleased to see you, Stormaway. There have been times when I sorely needed you. I have missed you on this journey and I thought that we would be going over the mountains without you."

When they drew apart, Stormaway was a little flustered but did his best to cover it up.

"Harrumph. Well, here I am now. I do not like to begin our renewed acquaintance with a rebuke, but I am not at all sure how seemly these public displays of affection are, my lord."

Tarkyn laughed, not at all fazed by the wizard's response. "Stormaway, you told me yourself that, within the forest, my word is law. So, it is up to me, is it not?"

The wizard, having recovered his equilibrium, gave a slight bow. "It is indeed, Sire, and I would thank you for your warm welcome." His eyes dropped to Sparrow, "And how are you, young lady? And how is your dad?"

"We are fine. Dad's off doing something with Danton at the moment but he'll be back soon. Tarkyn has had a very hard time but he is nearly better now."

Tarkyn frowned. "What do you mean, *nearly* better?"

Sparrow giggled. "You still jump at sudden noises sometimes, you know. Rain on Water and I have been watching you. We threw a rock into the bushes yesterday as you walked past, just to see you jump."

"This is the sympathy I get," he said wryly, smiling at Sparrow. Then Tarkyn raised his eyes to meet the wizard's fleetingly before looking away again.

"I begin to realise that I have been away too long," said the wizard gently. "I am sorry for that, my lord. The affairs of the realm are moving fast and I became involved in the intrigue at the encampment." He patted Tarkyn firmly on the back. "Perhaps I need to remember that my first loyalty is to you, not to Eskuzor."

"Is it? I was not sure of that, Stormaway. I thought perhaps your care for me sprang solely from my value to Eskuzor. All the portents you saw were, after all, why my father and you worked to protect me."

Stormaway threw a speaking glance in Sparrow's direction and made no reply. Tarkyn gave the little girl a pat on the head. "Would you mind if we had a chat on our own now, Sparrow?"

Sparrow rolled her eyes. "I know. Adult's business. I'll go and see if I can find Midnight," and skipped off.

"Tarkyn, that is true. I do care about what you may offer Eskuzor in the future and I have worked on your behalf long before I knew you as a grown man. But it is not for me to decide the fate of Eskuzor. Her future is in your hands, not mine. And so, to support Eskuzor, I must support you." The old wizard took a deep breath and met the prince's amber eyes. "But my care for you runs deeper than that. Your father was my dearest friend. We may have fallen out over various issues from time to time but despite it all, our friendship ran strong and true over many years. He loved you as a child and so did I. And there is enough of your father in you that I feel a strong connection with you that you probably do not return. I suspect I feel that I know you better than I actually do." Stormaway shrugged. "So, there it is. I know you find me tiresome and old fashioned at times. And I know I make you angry. But I have pledged my life to you, for your sake and for your father's sake and, last of all, for the sake of Eskuzor."

Tarkyn half raised a hand then let it drop. "I don't know what to say, Stormaway. I'm sorry I doubted your intentions and I am sorry if I have treated you overly harshly in the past." He gave a rueful smile. "Perhaps whatever it was that set you at odds with my father, exists also in me. I have noticed that I get up on my high horse more with you than with anyone else. On the other hand, you try to dictate my behaviour more than anyone else." He shrugged. "But I can tell you this; I value your support and your wisdom and knowledge. And I have never had greater need of them than I do now."

41

W hile Tarkyn filled in Stormaway on the events that he had missed, Danton and Waterstone were slipping quietly through the undergrowth, searching for two missing sorcerers. When Journeyman and his troop of sorcerers had reached the area covered by the next group of woodfolk, there had still been nine horses but two riders had seemed rather stiff and lifeless. Closer inspection had revealed that these riders were, in fact, stuffed dummies. Somewhere along the way, two sorcerers had detached themselves from the main party and disappeared into the forest.

Waterstone kept in constant contact with all lookouts, but it seemed that these sorcerers were skilled at moving unnoticed or had gone to ground. The lookouts could not possibly cover every part of the forest so there were many places where the sorcerers would be able to move undetected. However, they would not know which places these were, so sooner or later they would be spotted. Above Waterstone and Danton, high in the trees, another six woodfolk were fanned out scanning the ground below them for any signs of movement.

Finally, after more than an hour of searching, Ancient Oak sent through a message to say that a sorcerer had been spotted, sitting quietly against a tree, beneath the overhang of a bush, eating some of his provisions. Waterstone and Danton changed their direction of travel to intercept him.

"What do you think?" whispered Waterstone. "Will they be together or will they be trying to come at Tarkyn from different directions?"

Danton considered, "If I were running this operation, I would spread my men out, to give more chance of surprise. I would hope that even if one were found, the other might get through."

"So, you think that this one will be alone?"

"I can't guarantee it, but I think so."

"We'll need to keep looking for the other one then." When Danton nodded, Waterstone continued, "And how do they know where to find Tarkyn?"

Danton shook his head. "I don't think they do. I think they are searching systematically. I suspect they have taken a quarter each and are working their way outward from the clearing where they last saw us in the two most likely directions."

"So, this is probably the only one who is anywhere near Tarkyn. The other is probably more towards the southeast. Do you agree?"

"Yes, I think so. Perhaps the mountainfolk could join the search for that one." Danton crept closer through the trees, all the while keeping his eye on Waterstone for any signals from the woodfolk stationed above. "What are we going to do with them when we find them?"

"What did Tarkyn say to Journeyman?"

"He said he would show less mercy next time." Danton stopped dead and pushed himself flat against the tree. "He's on the move," he hissed.

Waterstone went out of focus to talk to the woodfolk in the trees. When he refocused, he asked quietly, "No shield. Why?"

"Attracts attention. So, while he is trying to be discreet, he is vulnerable."

"Hmm, we don't really know what Tarkyn would want, do we?"

Danton shook his head. "No. I think you had better knock this sorcerer out while we consult him. I don't think we can assume that Tarkyn would want them killed. What do you think?"

Waterstone gave a short nod and went out of focus. A moment later, there was a crash nearby followed by a dull thud, as the hapless sorcerer collapsed into a bush and then fell senseless to the ground. The woodman grinned. "One down. One to go."

Ancient Oak swung nimbly down the tree and tied the man's hands behind his back. He brushed his hands off. "There we are, big brother. All tied up neat and tidy. I'll send a message through to fetch Tarkyn then, shall I?"

Not long afterwards, they received notice that the other sorcerer had met with a similar fate.

"Good," said Waterstone with some satisfaction. "Now, I'll ask the mountainfolk to secure their sorcerer and bring him over here before he wakes. Then we'll clear off and leave you and Tarkyn to decide their fate."

However, when Tarkyn arrived, it was clear that he was not pleased to discover that all this activity had occurred without his knowledge.

"Your Highness," protested Danton, reverting to formality in the face of the prince's displeasure, "our job is to guard you and that is what we have done. You cannot be involved in every aspect of everyone's lives."

"I don't wish to be, but I do wish to be kept informed of any danger that threatens either the woodfolk or myself. I don't think that is unreasonable. I have no intention of rushing off and dealing with every incident but I would like to know and to have an oversight of events."

"But, Sire, I am informing you now."

"Not good enough, Danton," said Tarkyn shortly, firmly closing the discussion. He turned to consider the two sorcerers lying trussed up on the ground. "So, Wizard Journeyman didn't take his defeat lying down. I can't say I'm surprised. It was a long way to come, to turn back so easily." He frowned down at the unconscious men. "So, I must keep my word that I will show less mercy but at the same time, I do not wish to add to my already dire reputation."

"Waterstone and I thought that you might not want them killed outright, Sire."

"Good of you to consider my wishes," replied the prince acerbically. "Hmm, I think we need do no more than send them on their way with a note in their pocket to the effect that our intelligence network is everywhere and that next time, a surreptitious attempt to approach me will mean their deaths."

Danton looked confused. "And how is that showing less mercy, my lord?"

Tarkyn gave an unsettling smile. "Just wait. You will see."

As he spoke, the sorcerers showed the first signs of regaining consciousness. When they were sufficiently recovered, Tarkyn asked Danton to sit them up and give them both a drink of water.

Tarkyn sat himself on a nearby log and waited until he had their attention. "Good afternoon, gentlemen. As I recall, your names are Rorlan and Mandron. I believe you have come seeking an audience with me?"

The two sorcerers looked at each other, obviously wondering at the prince's credulity.

Tarkyn leaned forward. "No, obviously that was not your intention. If not for my extensive intelligence system, your ploy to catch me unawares might possibly have succeeded." He shrugged. "But, unfortunately for you, your chances of catching me unaware are almost non-existent. More water?" he asked urbanely.

Tarkyn's courtly courtesy was unnerving the sorcerers. Despite the cool weather, a faint sweat had broken out on each of them. They nodded for more water, but clearly more to humour Tarkyn than because they needed it. The prince waited until they had finished and then said pleasantly, "And does either of you have anything you would like to say to me before I reveal your fates?"

Danton watched in fascination as Tarkyn's urbane manner slowly destroyed the two men's defences.

"No, Your Highness," muttered Rorlan, "I can think of nothing to say. You know why we are here. You have already said you would show no mercy if we were caught. So..."

Tarkyn shook his head regretfully and said with a gentleness that froze their blood, "No, Rorlan. I can see that your memory is deficient. I didn't say that I would show no mercy. I said I would show *less* mercy."

"And what is that supposed to mean?" growled Mandron, almost quivering with trepidation. "That you will torture us or maim us but not kill us? I think I would rather die."

Tarkyn smiled sweetly. "And yet I don't recall asking you your opinion." He paused, the silence even more intimidating as his words. "So, to give me some idea of how to proceed, what fate did you envisage for me, had you succeeded in capturing me?"

The sorcerers stared wild-eyed at each other, the sweat standing out in beads on their foreheads now.

"Imprisonment, my lord," said Mandron tightly.

"Really? And yet, I am sure I have been told that it is now the death sentence that I'm facing." Tarkyn crossed his legs and made himself comfortable. "Do you know, Mandron, there is one quality above all that will raise my ire."

"Yes, my lord?"

"Deceit, Mandron. Deceit." Tarkyn's voice hardened, "Never, whatever you do, lie to me or humour me, or your fate will be considerably worse than the one I have mapped out for you." His voice softened again. "Now, are we clear on that, Mandron?"

"Yes, my lord. I beg your pardon, my lord."

"Now, to whose service are you two sworn?" asked Tarkyn in a slightly more business-like manner.

"No one's, Your Highness. We are mercenaries, Sire," replied Rorlan.

"And how did that come about? When I left, everyone was sworn to a lord's house."

Rorlan shook his head. "Not everyone, Sire. Not merchants and townspeople. Only the people on the land. Now, merchants and tradesmen go in fear of their lives and their livelihoods because of the rampant gangs. So, many of us have turned to soldiering to keep safe and to make some money."

"So, with all of that to contend with, why do you waste your energy on coming after me?" asked Tarkyn, for the moment forgetting to maintain his fearsomely smooth courtesy.

"For the reward, of course. You are worth more than I would make in ten years of soldiering."

Tarkyn stood up abruptly, causing Rorlan to flinch away. The prince glanced at his reaction but other than that, ignored it. He paced up and down a few times before turning to confront the two bound men.

"So, have you no care for the future of Eskuzor? Is money your only motivation?"

There was an uneasy silence as the men glanced at each other then dropped their eyes. After a few moments, Rorlan looked up and said, "There is no one worth following. There is no future for Eskuzor. The king plays games with his brother, using people as pawns. Soon they will be encamped on opposite sides of the kingdom, preparing their forces to fight each other in futile battles that will leave hundreds maimed or dead, and farmlands destroyed. While Jarand is alive, Kosar cannot rule." He gave a bitter laugh. "I doubt whether Kosar knows how to rule anyway. His mind has no concept or care for the needs of the people."

Tarkyn began to pace back and forth again, sweeping his hand distractedly through his long black hair. He stopped again before the two men and sat down as abruptly as he had stood. "I am more sorry than I can say to hear of the state of Eskuzor and to know that my brothers are bringing such despair and ruin to her. I am also sorry to find people like you with nothing left to believe in. I do not take that as a fault in you but more as a failure in my brother to protect the nation as he should." He shook his head despondently. "Danton, I don't think I will be able to stand by and let this continue. I don't yet know what I can do to stop it but I cannot allow them to destroy Eskuzor." He heaved a sigh and focused once more on the two men before him. "And as for you two..."

Although the men tensed waiting to hear their fate, they could deal better with the prince's natural manner than his previous dreadful, silky courtesy.

"We will leave your hands tied but other than that, you are free to go. You must not attempt to free yourselves until you reach the encampment. You will be monitored all the way back. If you attempt to untie your hands, you will be knocked out again and re-bound. We will not allow you to reunite with the rest of your party or with your horses. I will send a short letter with you to reiterate my position."

The two sorcerers frowned. "Is that it?" asked Mandron. "No whippings? No beating? No breaking of bones?"

Tarkyn gave a slight smile. "I did think vaguely of breaking your right arms to incapacitate you for a month or so, but I think you will find this difficult enough. It is a long way back to the encampment and walking with your hands tied behind your back is not easy, especially through thick forest. Then there are the logistics of eating and hygiene to consider." He shook his head. "No, I don't think you will find this easy at all but you will be whole and alive when you reach the other end."

The two men's faces lit up. "Thank you, my lord," they said in chorus.

Tarkyn gave a grunt of laughter. "I don't think you'll be thanking me by this time tomorrow. Danton, give them another drink while I organise this letter. Then they and we can be on our way."

"Where is Midnight?"

Everyone was packed and on the move, tracks and signs of the firesite removed, an operation considerably trickier in muddy conditions. They were travelling at ground level once more, having decided that the threat of Journeyman and his sorcerers had been contained. But still there was no sign of Midnight.

Tarkyn's question hung in the late afternoon air, charged with the beginnings of real alarm. Everyone stopped what they were doing and looked around. A silent conference provided no new information.

Tarkyn threw his hands up. "We can't leave without him. Where has that little rascal got to? Who saw him last?"

"I last saw him when he plaited my beard," offered Bean.

"That was hours ago, well, at least three hours ago," replied Tarkyn. "Anyone else?"

Danton walked up to Tarkyn and put a steadying hand on the prince's arm. "Use your mind. Look for his mind. Even if he doesn't respond to your call, you should be able to find him."

Tarkyn pulled himself together, took a deep breath and centred himself. He placed his hand on Danton's shoulder before closing his eyes and sending his mind roaming out through the forest. Nothing. He sent his mind higher, up into the mountains until he was sure he was further than Midnight could have run, but still he detected no sign of the little boy's mind. He jerked back into his present surroundings.

"Stormaway, Danton, Waterstone, Autumn Leaves, String and Bean and anyone else who can spare the time, we have to work this out. Help me. Why can't I find his mind?"

They pulled off into a fall of rocks beside the path to sit and talk.

"He's either unconscious or asleep," replied Waterstone shortly.

Tarkyn's eyes widened with shock. He glanced around to see who might be listening. "You don't think... How can we tell if the mountainfolk are holding to their oath?"

"It's difficult." Autumn Leaves pulled out a long stem of grass and began to suck on the end of it as he thought. After a few moments, he said, "If we ask them where Midnight is, we might be able to work out who is not responding and keeping their minds closed off. What do you think, Waterstone?"

"Possibly. But I don't think we know them well enough to remember everyone. We would need to enlist some help."

"I think I trust Dry Berry," said Tarkyn. "What do you think?"

"First tell me about this curse," said Stormaway. "It may have a bearing on what is happening."

String and Bean looked at each other before Bean replied, "As Midnight's father died, he muttered some words." He shrugged. "Neither of us understood them but we have tried our best to remember them."

Stormaway nodded his head impatiently. "Yes, yes, I know all that. Come on. Out with it man! What were the words?"

Bean glanced at String, took a deep breath and recited, "*Choidayarorshara. Rorsharatayahagarztayadorisolzormatara.*"

Stormaway looked grim but made no immediate response.

After a minute or two, String asked, "So, do you know what it means?"

The wizard waved his hand impatiently. "Yes, of course I do. Give me time to think!"

After a couple of minutes, Stormaway stood up abruptly and turned to walk away, muttering, "It's no good. I will need to confer with my books."

"Stormaway," said Tarkyn more sharply than he intended, "before you go, tell us what it means."

"Tarkyn, time is of the essence for your little Midnight and the mountainfolk." He sighed. "But I can see you cannot contain yourselves. The words mean, 'This child will breed resentment. From resentment will spring hatred. And hatred will slowly destroy the souls, integrity, spirit something like that, of the people of this child's mother.'" He glanced around at the stunned faces. "Do nothing until I return." With that, he whirled around and strode off to consult his books.

"Summer Rain was right," said Autumn Leaves slowly. "There is an evil loose among the mountainfolk."

"And it has been festering slowly for seven years," added Waterstone.

"I wonder if the process sped up once Midnight was forced to reside with them fulltime?" mused Danton.

Tarkyn groaned. "On my life, I hope killing Midnight is not the way to lift the curse. I don't think I could bear that."

"What if his one death would save hundreds of mountainfolk?" asked Waterstone.

Tarkyn stared at him, then slowly shook his head. "No. No,

I couldn't do it. I know a prince should make hard decisions to preserve the welfare of his people, but I couldn't do it to him. I would have to find another way, even if it meant taking Midnight far away."

"Even if it meant abandoning your oath to protect us?"

Tarkyn stood up and began to pace up and down. "I begin to see how invidious this curse is. Whatever I answer, I stand condemned. Either I would betray my oath to you and sanction the destruction of hundreds of your, *our* kin, or I would be prepared to kill an innocent, abused child." He shook his head slowly. "Don't do this to me, Waterstone."

"I think we had better just sit tight without any further discussion until Stormaway comes back," said Bean.

"Yeah, true. I think that's the best idea," put in String. "You never know, maybe this curse becomes stronger once it is revealed. Maybe it's already affecting you."

"Anyway, Sire," added Bean, "I don't see why you have to be stuck with the hard decisions. From what we saw before, you woodfolk make most of your own decisions. Why dump this one on His Highness?"

"Because from what Tarkyn just said, he would override our decision on this. And we couldn't allow any mountainfolk to decide," said Waterstone firmly. "They already want Midnight dead because he's half sorcerer."

"Yeah, but that's probably the curse talking, don't you think?" asked String.

"Possibly," Waterstone paused. "In fact, probably, now I come to think of it. All the more reason not to consult them. Judging by their recent actions against Tarkyn and the rest of us, I would say they are well on the way to being corrupted, some more than others."

Danton followed Autumn Leaves' suit and pulled up a tall stem of grass to suck on. "I wonder if the damage can be reversed or only halted?" He turned his gaze on Waterstone. "Then you would be faced with the dilemma of whether to kill off your corrupt kin if they continued to pose a threat to everyone else. And how would you decide who was so corrupted that they should die and who was tainted but manageable? Interesting, don't you think?"

Much to everyone's surprise, a smile dawned slowly on Waterstone's face. "Danton, you are so loyal I can't imagine how we ever doubted you. And clever. You have placed me beautifully on the horns of a hypothetical dilemma just like the one facing Tarkyn. Well done! I can only sit back and admire your cunning and devotion, and concede that we are all in a difficult position." He leant over to Tarkyn and patted him on the knee. "In future, no more forcing people to make impossible choices. We will work through this together and support each other to protect what matters to them as best we can."

Tarkyn breathed a sigh of relief and gave a slight smile. "Thanks." Suddenly, the prince was just a nineteen-year-old with too much on his shoulders.

String and Bean looked at each other. Then Bean said, "Must be my turn to make the tea, if we're going to be here for a little while. Any chance of a small fire?"

Before anyone could answer, Tarkyn and the woodfolk's minds were assailed by an overwhelming cry for help. But not from Midnight. From Blizzard. As one, despite Stormaway's stricture, they jumped to their feet and headed off towards its source.

"Follow us," said Waterstone briefly over his shoulder to the other three sorcerers. Even as he ran, the woodman went briefly out of focus to send a message via other woodfolk to Stormaway.

They raced up the mountain path, all thought of covering their tracks forgotten. As they neared a copse off to the left-hand side, they could hear the sounds of angry shouting emanating from among the trees. They swung off the path and came to an abrupt halt at the edge of a small clearing within the copse.

A shocking sight met their eyes.

At one end of the clearing, lashed upright to a thin sycamore was Midnight, head lolling forward, hands dragged behind him and secured at the back of the tree. At first glance, it was impossible to tell whether he was dead or unconscious. Ranged in front of him, were twenty or thirty angry woodfolk, yelling at each other. A furious debate was raging among them. Now and again, one of them would break from the pack towards Midnight, only to be restrained by others. Blizzard was in the midst of it, shouting with the others, but a look of relief passed over his face when he spotted Tarkyn and his group at the edge of the clearing.

Before Tarkyn could act, a strong message came through from Stormaway to refrain from interfering. When Waterstone relayed this, the prince's face tightened.

"How can I leave him there?" he demanded hotly. "They might kill him if they haven't already."

"Think straight," said Waterstone firmly. "If he were dead, they wouldn't still be trying to attack him. Just be ready to protect him if any of them breaks away from that group."

Suddenly, a tattered, wild-eyed woodwoman, clothed in an assortment of furs, sprang into the clearing and threw herself in front of Midnight. She whirled to confront the raging woodfolk, and stood braced for action, knives in both hands, sending forth such a torrent of mental abuse and derision that everyone was shocked into silence.

Then she broke into audible speech, "How dare you attack my son? I left him with you to look after him, secure in the belief that woodfolk look after their own. What has happened to you? What has he done that is so terrible that you would do this to him?"

After an uncomfortable silence, a voice spoke up from within the pack, "He is an abomination. He is half-sorcerer."

For a moment, Hail faltered, but then she lifted her head high and looked the speaker straight in the eye. "Yes, for my shame, he is. And I have punished him for it often enough myself. But that was why I left him with you. To protect him from me. I couldn't see him without seeing the cruelty of his father, but you people didn't have to bear that burden. I trusted you with him and look what you have done."

"And how does it happen that you suddenly turn up out of the blue now, so full of concern, having abandoned your son for months without seeing him?" sneered another voice.

"Dry Berry called for me," she replied shortly. After a moment she added more gently, "And now that you all know, I have come to face my past and your judgement."

At that, murmuring broke out, which quickly swelled into another heated altercation. Waterstone threw a restraining glance at Tarkyn but saw that he was standing arms crossed, a forbidding expression on his face but with no obvious intention of interceding.

The shouting grew louder. Suddenly, punches were thrown and a brawl broke out among the mountainfolk.

Still, Tarkyn stood there unmoving. But slowly, the air inside the clearing seemed to soften and people threw their punches with less vigour. Gradually they fell apart from each other and straightened up, raising their heads high and falling silent. Then they turned to face the prince, some shame-faced at first, but all squaring their shoulders and looking him straight in the eye. For a moment, Waterstone thought they meant to attack him. But Tarkyn met their gaze unflinchingly. Then very slowly, without uncrossing his arms, he lifted one hand to place it on his heart.

Almost as though waking from a trance, people blinked and gave their heads a slight shake. A few placed their hands on their hearts in response but gestures like that were not natural to woodfolk, so most just set about making amends with their neighbours and apologizing to Hail. When she felt sufficiently safe, she asked String and Bean to come forward to cut Midnight free, continuing to keep her eye on the uncertain mountainfolk.

Bean walked around behind her and used a thin streak of burgundy magic to cut through ropes binding the little boy. Still, Midnight did not stir, and when the ropes fell from him, only String's hands around his chest kept him from falling forward on to the ground. The scruffy old trappers lowered him gently and String felt anxiously for a pulse in his neck. After a moment, he nodded and breathed a sigh of relief.

Tarkyn's party looked at each other in confusion, unclear about what had just happened right before their eyes. Waterstone glanced a query at the prince who merely responded, "I'll explain later. Right now, I need to help Midnight."

But Hail did not know him and certainly did not trust him so, as he approached, she thrust her knives in his direction. Without a second thought, he murmured "*Shturrum*," and froze her.

"I gather you are Midnight's mother," said Tarkyn coolly, "I will not waste time on convincing you that you can trust me when time may be of the essence. I will release you from this spell on the condition that you do not interfere with what I am doing. If you make any move to attack me, Danton will imprison you within his shield until I have finished checking Midnight. Clear? I will talk to you later." He nodded at his liegeman. "Danton, keep your eye on her. Use your shield without hesitation."

Tarkyn waved his hand to release the spell and moved on past her without waiting to see her reaction. He knelt down next to Midnight and placed his hand on the unconscious boy's shoulder. After a moment, he looked over his shoulder at the gathered mountainfolk and asked matter-of-factly, "What has happened to him? Was it a slingshot? Why is he not regaining consciousness? Someone, fetch Summer Rain or Stormaway. I may need help."

"Your Highness," came the soft voice of Sighing Wind, "I am afraid he has partaken of drugged wine. I fear that the dose may have been too strong for such a small body."

The forest guardian returned his attention to the little bundle of mischief lying so still beneath his hand. For a moment, his rage threatened to well up and overpower him but he took a deep breath and firmly pushed it down so that he could concentrate on helping Midnight. Tarkyn gathered his *esse* to send it slowly and gently through the inert child. For several fraught minutes, nothing happened. Then suddenly, Midnight coughed convulsively and threw up all over Tarkyn.

Tarkyn whipped his arm away but far too late to save his shirt sleeve. His face wrinkled in disgust. "Blast you, Midnight! Look what you've done to me." He shook his arm and frowned at his wet, stinking shirt sleeve. With a resigned sigh, he pulled his sodden shirt over his head, used a clean part of it to wipe Midnight's mouth and his own arm before throwing it, with a certain malice, behind him into the gathered crowd. With his eyes twinkling, Tarkyn frowned ferociously. "Yuck, Midnight. That was revolting." Even though his eyes were red rimmed and he was still feeling queasy, the little boy grinned up at him. The prince smiled back at him and ran his hand through the little boy's hair. "You okay now, little one?" Midnight knew what he was asking, nodded and tried to sit up.

Tarkyn scooped the little boy into his arms and stood up. When he turned around, he found himself face to face with an angry wizard.

"I told you, *asked* you not to do anything," exclaimed Stormaway.

Tarkyn gave a Midnight a squeeze. "I didn't rescue him, although it nearly broke my heart not to," he replied. His gaze swept around his fellow sorcerers and woodmen. "I didn't, did I?"

Waterstone put his hands on his hips and frowned suspiciously. "No, you didn't. At least not directly. But you did something, didn't you, even though I didn't see you move."

Tarkyn smiled proudly, not for himself but for the mountainfolk. "Yes, I sent forth waves of belief in the integrity of the mountainfolk. I figured that, underneath, they were the same as the home guard. So, I gave them my trust." He smiled ruefully. "It was possibly the hardest thing I have ever done, but they vindicated my faith in them and pulled themselves out of the force of the curse."

Stormaway stared at him through narrowed eyes. "Are you sure you haven't studied the art of magic?"

"No. Why?"

"There are two ways to counter a curse; one is to revoke the curse, the other is to strengthen the victims' resistance to it." Stormaway smiled with satisfaction. "You managed to strengthen the mountainfolk's belief in themselves and consequently their resistance to the curse. If you had interfered and rescued Midnight, you would have left them with an irreparable belief in their own maliciousness and destroyed their self-belief, possibly beyond hope of recovery. Instead, you strengthened it. As it is, they have repaired the damage themselves and redeemed themselves."

Tarkyn smiled. "There you are, you see. No need to stay angry with me, is there?"

Stormaway shook his head. "You dice with forces of which you have no knowledge. I just hope your instinct continues to guide you truly."

"But the curse has not yet been destroyed, has it?" asked Tarkyn. "Will it not continue to eat away underneath and make life difficult for Midnight and for all of these people?"

"Yes, it will. You have stemmed its force for now, but it will re-emerge over time. We must find a way to destroy it." Stormaway turned to the people gathered there and began to speak, "Be aware that you are being affected by the curse of which the trappers spoke, placed on you by Midnight's father as he died."

"And before we listen to another word you have to say, who on earth are you?" asked one of the mountainfolk belligerently. "Every time we turn around, there is another sorcerer. How many of you are there now? Five! This is beginning to feel like an invasion."

Tarkyn raised his hand. "I apologise. I should have introduced Stormaway to you, but I think we were all a little pre-occupied." A ripple of dry laughter flowed through his audience. When it subsided, he continued, "This is Stormaway Treemaster, Wizard of the Forest. I think many of you know of him by reputation since he trades your wines on your behalf with the outside world."

"He's the creator of that dreadful oath, isn't he?" demanded another aggressively.

Angry murmurs greeted this remark. Tarkyn put both hands up for silence. "Yes, he is but under my father's direction. He is also the wizard who fought off the storm with me to save the woodfolk from the sorcerers and wolves who were hunting them."

Someone near the front shrugged. "Fair enough then. Some good, some bad. Just like the rest of us." She nodded. "Go on then. Tell us about this curse."

"Thank you," said Stormaway gravely. "As you heard earlier from String and Bean, a curse was uttered by Midnight's father as he died from Hail's knife attack. This is the curse you have all been living with since then – that the child of that union, young Midnight here, would breed resentment among you, his mother's people. That resentment would gradually turn into hatred, which in turn would slowly but surely undermine your integrity and destroy you. As you may now realise, that curse has affected your attitudes and behaviour. It has so far led to the deaths of two of your own and nearly killed Tarkyn, Danton, and two of the home guard. Thanks to Tarkyn's faith in you, the effects of the curse have been halted for the time being. But the entire curse pivots on Midnight."

There was a mass intake of breath and all eyes turned to Midnight. Unconsciously, Tarkyn's arm closed more tightly around the little boy. He felt a tug on the bare skin of his arm and looked down to see Midnight grimacing.

"Oops, sorry," whispered Tarkyn with a smile, relaxing his grip and swinging Midnight around onto his hip so that he could see what was going on. Midnight took one look at everyone staring at him and turned his head away to bury it into Tarkyn's bare shoulder. Tarkyn transferred his gaze to Stormaway. "In light of recent events, to save everyone the embarrassment of asking, I will ask the question that is on everyone's and my mind." He took a tight breath. "If Midnight is pivotal to this curse, what must happen to him to revoke it?" He paused and looked down at Midnight. "Please don't tell me that the destruction of the curse depends on his death."

As Stormaway shook his head, Tarkyn breathed a long sigh of relief. "No. Quite the opposite. If Midnight had been killed, the curse would have been irreversible."

The gathered mountainfolk looked horrified at how close they had come to their own destruction.

"And more than that, the only person who can revoke the curse on the mountainfolk is Midnight himself." After a moment, Stormaway continued, "Only the curser can revoke a curse. If he or she is dead, it becomes very difficult to revoke their curse but it may be done by their direct descendant, in this case, Midnight." He looked at the little boy huddled against Tarkyn's shoulder. "I can foresee grave difficulties here. Firstly, Tarkyn will have to try to explain to him, without words, what we want him to do and why. Secondly, the task is complex. Not only will it be distressing for him, but he will have to delegate part of it because words must be spoken that he cannot speak. Thirdly, he must choose to do it. Tarkyn cannot order him to do it. It must be of his own free will. So that means that he will have to be prepared to endure a torrid experience for your sakes." The wizard's eyes swept around the mountainfolk. "And from what I gather, he is not likely to have your best interests at heart."

"So, what can we do? Are we facing our own inevitable destruction?" asked a voice in the crowd.

"I will not give you hollow reassurances. Possibly. You have your belief in yourselves restored for the time being. Be vigilant with yourselves and each other. Question your motives for everything and strive to defeat the force of this curse. Knowing that it exists will dilute its insidiousness, but your fear of it will give it strength. Make sure everyone knows about it. Work openly with each other. If you have any doubts, I suggest you consult with your fellow woodfolk who have not been cursed. Meanwhile, Tarkyn and I will work with the support of others on revoking it." He turned to Midnight's mother who was standing quietly between String and Bean, a knife still in each hand. "Hail, I believe we will need your assistance... and you two." Stormaway looked once more around his audience. "Do not despair. Difficult is not impossible. We will try our best. If it looks as though we can revoke the curse, all of you will need to come up onto the mountain to the place where Midnight's father died. That is where the curse was created and where it must be destroyed."

"Since we woodfolk are heading up that way anyway," said Tarkyn, "I suggest you mountainfolk accompany us. Whatever the outcome, we can part ways there, you to return to your cellars and we to continue over the mountain." He glanced around to check that he had everyone's approval. "Hail, String and Bean will be our guides."

Hail stared back at him. "I have made no undertakings to you. So, do not assume that I will act as a guide."

Tarkyn returned her stare for a moment before giving a slight bow. "I beg your pardon, ma'am. I had assumed you would want to help your people and rid yourself of this curse."

"As it happens, I do wish to help my people and myself but not because you, a sorcerer, have decided it."

Tarkyn took a slow breath in and managed to contain his irritation. "You must not let appearances deceive you. Like your son, I am also woodfolk."

Hail's eyes narrowed, intrigued that Tarkyn had allied himself so clearly with her maligned son, but she merely said, "That still does not give you the right to dictate to me."

"I have no interest in arguing with you, but I will leave you to consider that I am also the guardian of the forest so you may perhaps have a vested interest in supporting me." Tarkyn shrugged but his mouth was set in a tight line. "However, I will not assume I have your support and will look only to String and Bean to guide us."

Hail still holding knives in each hand locked stares with him for several long seconds. Finally, she said, "And now I must accept the judgement of my people on my past actions."

Tarkyn raised his eyebrows. "If you say you must, that is entirely between you and the mountainfolk. It is no concern of mine."

"And I would like my son back," she said firmly.

There was a stilled hush. Tarkyn looked down at the top of Midnight's head still burrowed into his bare shoulder. He wondered if Midnight realised his mother was standing right behind him and what his reaction would be. He considered how autocratic he would look if he didn't give this abused but unpleasant woodwoman back her child. Then he thought about Midnight cowering in the corner of the cave.

He raised his head and met her eyes. "I will not keep him from you but neither will I allow you to take him away. I have vowed to protect him, and protect him I shall. You may have done your best by this child under the aegis of the curse but your best was not good enough." He nodded at String and Bean. "Had it not been for the kindness of these two, your son could have been damaged beyond hope of reprieve. When you have sorted your affairs with your people, come and see me and we will talk further." He turned to leave but a sudden movement by Hail made him turn back again. "If you make any attempt to attack me with knives while I am holding your son, you will not be allowed near him again," he said calmly, flicking a warning glance at Danton before turning once more to stride out of the clearing.

43

The wind high on the mountain whistled through the crags, swept across the sparse vegetation and found its way in through any slight gaps in clothing to chill the people within. Over two hundred mountainfolk were gathered on the bleak mountain slope, from every firesite in the foothills. Word had gone out and even the trappers, usually a solitary breed, had joined them, all wanting to make sure that, if they were at all related to Hail, they would be cleansed of the curse. The black sky above them was littered with stars but few had any thought to admire them. They were used to such sights and their attention was dominated by two figures seated a little apart, who were staring at each other and gesticulating but making no sound. One was their acknowledged liege lord, long black hair falling down over his wolfskin cloak, intense amber eyes glowing in the reflected firelight as he concentrated on forming images to explain difficult concepts. The other was the small boy they had reviled, who now held their future in his hands.

Tarkyn broke off and looked around. "Where's Hail?"

Midnight's mother disengaged herself from her conversation and walked around the fire to stand before Tarkyn. She glanced at Midnight before turning her attention to the prince.

"Hail, I need your help and I'm afraid this may not be too comfortable for you. You did say you wanted to help yourself and your people. So, could you please give me an image of Midnight's father? It's too hard trying to do this with a shadowy unclear figure. It's hard enough anyway." Seeing Hail's face tighten, he added, "I would ask String or Bean but sorcerers can't transmit images. You are the only person who can show me what he looked like."

Her eyes narrowed and suddenly Tarkyn was assailed with a feeling of terror enmeshed in an image of a harsh, tormented face, bright blue eyes wild with rage, inches from him. He reeled back, his heart thumping, before closing off the image with a snap and righting himself. He took a deep breath and ran his hand through his hair before realising that there was an anxious hand tapping on his knee.

He patted it reassuringly before saying dryly to Hail, "That is exactly why you are not ready to look after Midnight. How could you imagine I would want him to see that?"

"That is his father," she said flatly.

"Yes, it is and I am sorry for what he has done to you. I am not denying that, but it is not all that his father was.... or am I mistaken?"

Hail reluctantly shook her head.

"I know you are angry and hate this man but for the sake of your people, can you cast your mind back to better days so I can show Midnight his father? When he is older, we can explain to him what happened but he is too young to bear such a burden now and he wouldn't understand it anyway." As she still hesitated, Tarkyn continued, "A child does not need to know everything about their parents. Would you want me to show him an image of you throwing the knife into his father's chest? I don't think so. Hail, I will have to show Midnight an image of his father becoming angry and hurting your people so he understands what he needs to do. I can't whitewash his father completely even if I wanted to but I can save the worst of it for when Midnight is older."

For several moments, Hail just stared at him. Then she heaved a sigh, sat down and projected images of slowly waking to find herself inside a sorcerer's hut and being cared for as she recovered, of conversations that became less wary and more friendly over time and even of small kindnesses such as sprigs of wildflowers placed in a chipped old cup beside her bed. The man in these images was gruff and shy, a bit rough around the edges and awkward, lacking the casual social grace of either the woodfolk or the other trappers but he was concerned and caring in his own limited way. When the images faded, Tarkyn saw that Hail's face was wet with tears.

"Thank you," said Tarkyn quietly. He reached out to put his hand on her knee but even in that split second, found his way barred by a knife. He looked up to see Hail's face closed off and angry once more. "Hail, knowing how much he meant to you makes what happened later so much worse. But until you mourn for him, you will never be free of him and the damage he's done to you." He withdrew his hand. "Knowing your way of life, I can't imagine that you would want to mourn in public; but just remember, there are many people, woodfolk and sorcerer alike, who are here to turn to when you need us."

In answer, Hail threw him a look of pure loathing before standing up and stomping off into the night. Tarkyn drew a deep breath and let it out slowly, then turned when he heard a low chuckle emerging from the shadows on his right.

"I don't think she's ready to thank you yet, for making her face her nightmares," came a creaky voice out of the darkness.

"And what are you doing here, Ancient Oak?" demanded Tarkyn, frowning.

Ancient Oak came forward out of the gloom to sit himself on the ground closer to Tarkyn and Midnight to make up the third point of a triangle. "Hi, Midnight." He waved at Midnight who responded in kind. "Hi, little brother. I'm just here keeping an eye on the proceedings." He gave a gentle smile. "Waterstone is busy with Sparrow. So I'm here instead."

Tarkyn put his head on one side as he considered his adopted brother. "Now I think about it, it is often you who is the closest lookout, isn't it? You just quietly get on with it in the background usually, don't you?"

Ancient Oak looked a little embarrassed and shrugged.

A warm smile dawned on Tarkyn's face. "Thanks, Ancient Oak. I'm glad you're here. Now, I'll just get on with trying to explain all of this to Midnight. If I include you in the images, you might have some ideas."

Tarkyn began by showing images of Thunder Storm and Creaking Bough with their children and then showed Midnight between Hail and Pipeless, followed by some of the happy images Hail had given him of her time with Pipeless. Midnight's eyes widened with excitement and he looked around the firesite, searching for the wizard in the image. Tarkyn grimaced, shook his head and projected an image of Pipeless lying down, very white with his eyes closed. Midnight's face fell and he looked close to tears.

Tarkyn threw up his hands. "Oh, this is hopeless. Come here, little one. You need a hug already," said Tarkyn, matching gestures to words. Midnight clambered onto his lap and, with Tarkyn's arms around him, sniffed and let his tears of disappointment fall. The sorcerer looked over Midnight's head at the woodman. "I can't rush this. I will overwhelm him entirely if I do. He's just gained and lost a father all in a few minutes as it is."

Ancient Oak leaned forward and gave Midnight a couple of strokes on the back. "Do you think he'd like a cup of milk or tea?"

Once Tarkyn had checked and nodded, Ancient Oak went out of focus to relay the request. While they drank their cups of tea, Tarkyn sat Midnight on the ground in front of him again so that he could use gestures as well as images.

He showed Midnight that Pipeless had been a trapper like String and Bean. Inevitably, Midnight wanted to know how he had died. Using gestures, Tarkyn made it clear that he would tell him a little bit about it but not all. Then he showed Pipeless becoming angry and striking out and being struck down in return. He did not show Hail or any part of the rape or stabbing. When Midnight wanted to know what had started the fight, Tarkyn showed Midnight getting older and being told when he was bigger. The little boy huffed and eyed Tarkyn belligerently for a few moments but then accepted the inevitable.

After a few minutes' thought, Tarkyn showed Pipeless standing next to a group of sorcerers. Then he showed Pipeless next to Rainstorm and Waterstone and shook his head. Midnight frowned ferociously until he figured out what Tarkyn meant and then his brow cleared and waving his arm, he produced a soft, deep green haze around himself.

Tarkyn raised his eyebrows in amazement. "Well done, little one. No instruction at all."

Midnight grinned, pointed at Tarkyn and waved his hand.

"He learnt it from watching you," said Ancient Oak. "I suppose he didn't think of trying it before."

Midnight gestured for Ancient Oak to come at him and,

when Ancient Oak good-naturedly complied, laughed uproariously when the woodman couldn't penetrate the barrier. Then he waved his hand suddenly, causing Ancient Oak to land in a heap in his lap as the barrier dissolved. The usually reserved woodman grabbed him and tickled him until Midnight was gasping for breath with laughter.

"Well, that seems to have cheered him up. I can see hours of torment and fun coming up from our fledgling sorcerer," said Tarkyn, smiling at them.

When they had recovered, Ancient Oak once more sat quietly to one side. Tarkyn showed the unhappiness caused by Pipeless' anger at the mountainfolk as a precursor for saying that Pipeless should now be kind to them. This plan fell at the first hurdle as Midnight nodded firm approval of his sire's malevolent attitude and re-iterated his satisfaction at the deaths of the mountainfolk who had attacked Tarkyn.

After some careful thought and a good deal of imagination, Tarkyn projected an image of Pipeless sending forth a stream of red magic that turned Rainstorm and Lapping Water into angry, nasty woodfolk. He didn't know what colour Pipeless' magic was but decided on red because it was an angry colour. Then he gestured around all of the assembled mountainfolk and repeated the image with a large group of mountainfolk being transformed from friendly to unkind.

Midnight looked sceptical. In return, he showed Tarkyn image after image of being shouted at and chased away, of creeping up close and having things thrown at him as he dived back into the bushes. He showed himself cold and hungry watching from beyond the firesite as mountainfolk sat around in warmth, enjoying their dinners, and occasionally throwing the odd scrap up into the darkness. He showed himself huddled into the scant shelter of scratchy bushes, curled up against the icy wind as the mountainfolk retired for the night into their well-constructed, draughtless shelters. He showed children playing who would turn and sneer at him if he came close or chase after him to scare him away. At the end of this, he sat with his arms crossed, his mouth tight, anger and resentment in every line of his body.

"Oh, for pity's sake!" breathed Tarkyn. "How can we ask this child to help these people after all they have done to him?" He wiped his hand across his brow. "I think they deserve everything that's coming to them."

Ancient Oak leaned forward and put his hand on Tarkyn's arm. "You don't really. You know it's the curse that has done this. Remember how your faith in them changed them. Show Midnight some of that... Not what they were fighting about, obviously, but the effect of your belief in them."

Tarkyn sighed. "Okay, I will in a minute. I'm glad I don't have to summon that belief up right now. I would be struggling, I can tell you."

He wanted nothing more than to pick Midnight up and hold him close but the strength it had taken Midnight not to despair was holding him together now as he relived the horrors of his past life, making himself inviolate for the time being.

So, Tarkyn took a deep breath and showed Pipeless sending forth his red magic followed by the mountainfolk becoming more and more angry. Then he showed Midnight the scene from a few days before, from his point of view, angled so that it did not show the little boy tied to the tree, but did include the waves of belief emanating forth from the prince and the gradual change in the mountainfolk.

Midnight stared at him, his eyes glittering with hurt and anger. He pointed to Tarkyn's head and then at the mountainfolk, then again to Tarkyn's head then at himself and shook his head. In a woodfolk flick, he was gone.

"Oh no! He thinks that if I believe in them then I don't

believe in him." Tarkyn turned to ask Ancient Oak for help but found that he too had gone. Moments later, he received an image from Ancient Oak of him holding a struggling young Midnight off in the darkness nearby. He leapt to his feet and moved as quickly as he could towards the imprint of Midnight's mind. In a short time, the sounds of scuffling reached him and directed his feet for the last few yards. He waved his hand and intoned, "*Lumaya,*" creating a gentle corona of light to float in the air beside him. Seeing that Midnight was on the verge of breaking away again, the sorcerer glanced apologetically at Ancient Oak who was actually too fully occupied to notice, waved his hand quickly and murmured, "*Shturrum.*" He extricated the now quiescent Midnight from Ancient Oak's still arms and when he was sure he had the little boy firmly in his grasp, waved the spell away.

Immediately he had his arms full of squirming, vengeful anger. Midnight seemed to have grown extra arms and legs, all of which were flailing at Tarkyn. Tarkyn held him tight but when there was no sign that the little boy was either going to relent or tire, the prince sent him a peremptory demand to stop. Midnight did indeed stop, shocked at the strength of the message, but then he threw look of pure venom at Tarkyn before twisting in one final all-out attempt to escape. Ancient Oak stepped in and grabbed him just as he twisted out of Tarkyn's arms. This time, Tarkyn sent a full-blown command laced with anger, hauteur and power. Midnight went still and waited until Ancient Oak had lowered him carefully to the ground, standing ready to grab him if he tried to escape again. Then Midnight faced Tarkyn, his face shuttered and rigid with fury, and stood stiffly, hand on heart.

The prince inclined his head in a courtly response. "Ooh dear," he breathed to Ancient Oak, not taking his eyes off Midnight. "It's a long way back from here. At least even in the extremes of his rage, he has kept to his oath even if he hates me for it. It's more than I can say for some of the mountainfolk." He glanced at his brother. "What am I going to do now? Any suggestions?"

"Wait. Just wait," said Ancient Oak between breaths. "He needs time to calm down. We all do."

"What? Just stand here?"

Ancient Oak nodded slowly, keeping his eye on his little charge. "It may take twenty or thirty minutes but you won't be able to talk to him until he's calmer."

Tarkyn gave a wry smile. "You're better at this than I am. Thirty minutes of just standing here seems like a lifetime to me. I suppose you stand longer than that all the time on lookout duty, don't you?"

Ancient Oak's eyes crinkled with silent laughter. "Just a bit longer." After a pause he added quietly, "I think he will calm down more quickly if we are not talking around him."

"Oh."

It was nowhere near thirty minutes later when Tarkyn had had enough. He decided, mainly due to his own inability to stand still, that a change of tactics was required. So gradually, he sent forth a little trickle of warmth, understanding and acceptance. After building up its intensity for a few minutes, he added his belief not only in Midnight's integrity but also in everything he had told him. Midnight scowled and crossed his arms. Tarkyn put his hand on his heart and steadily met Midnight's brilliant green eyes.

Then Tarkyn sent him a request to come to him. Midnight immediately sent back a query on whether it was a command or whether he could choose not to. Tarkyn let out a little sigh and told him he could choose but that he would like him to. Tarkyn realised that he was towering over the boy so sank down to sit cross-legged on the stony ground and waited. And waited. And waited. Finally, after several minutes of inspecting a mark on his sleeve, peering with great interest at Tarkyn's suspended corona of light and looking around to see if the quiet woodman was still there behind him, Midnight took the two steps to bring himself within reach of Tarkyn's arms. With no further ceremony, Tarkyn grasped him firmly around the waist, pulled him down onto his lap and wrapped his arms around him. Midnight offered no resistance and, in fact, heaved a huge sigh of relief as he leaned in against Tarkyn.

"Oh, the poor little bugger. He's had such a hard time, hasn't he?"

Ancient Oak nodded. "Yes, he has. Not too many people in the world have to cope with being the focal point for a curse."

Tarkyn smiled. "No. Even worse than being the focal point for an oath. At least that has some advantages." He looked down at the brown-haired head and sighed, "So, what are we going to do now?"

Midnight looked up at him and touched his cheek with his hand. Then he pointed to Tarkyn's mouth and then to himself with his fingers moving everywhere with a query.

"He wants to know what I want him to do."

Ancient Oak gave a grunt of laughter. "Well, that's cutting to the chase. You can tell him, can't you, as long as you don't order him to do it? Does he need to understand any more than that?"

Tarkyn shrugged. "I don't know. Can you relay what we've done so far to Stormaway and see what he says?"

The message came back that Midnight had to know what he would be required to do and that his actions would be helping the mountainfolk, even if his reason for doing them was to please Tarkyn. Tarkyn began by making it clear that this was a request not a command. Then he showed Midnight's actions bringing the mountainfolk from being unhappy and angry, to being happy. He waited while the little boy thought about it. Then Midnight used hand gestures to ask whether Tarkyn would remain his friend if he said no. Tarkyn nodded. Then Midnight looked him in the eye and shook his head in an emphatic refusal.

Tarkyn heaved a sigh and smiled wryly at Ancient Oak. "Well, we tried. I can't push it any further because then I'd be coercing him. Maybe when he's older and been away from them for longer, he may consider it. They will just have to depend on their self-belief until then." He gave Midnight a squeeze. "I don't blame him. I don't know that I'd do it to help people who had been so cruel to me, no matter who asked me."

"We might be wiser not to go back to the firesite just yet, though," suggested Ancient Oak. "I'll get some wine and a drink for young one brought out here instead. What do you think?"

Tarkyn nodded and checked whether Midnight would like a drink. Midnight nodded then asked whether Tarkyn was upset at him. Tarkyn smiled at him and sent him reassurances. Midnight asked if he was sad. Tarkyn shrugged to show he was a little sad but okay. Drinks arrived borne by Rainstorm, and Midnight broke off the discussion to slug down a big mug of fruit juice.

"So, no go, I gather," said Rainstorm. "It was a long shot at best. How did you go trying to explain it all to him?"

"Pretty poorly, all in all," replied Tarkyn, grimacing. "I nearly lost him altogether when he thought I was telling him that I believed in the mountainfolk so therefore not in him."

"Oh, whoops!" Rainstorm looked across at Ancient Oak. "Is that how you come to be sporting a swollen cheek?"

Ancient Oak merely grinned and raised his eyebrows.

"Go on, what else?" asked Rainstorm who had come to know Ancient Oak well over the last few weeks.

"Ooh, just the odd bruise and abrasion here and there. He's a savage little fighter, once he gets going." He glanced at Tarkyn. "And one doesn't like to knock him out. After all, we were trying to have a conversation with him. Can't do that if he's unconscious. Tarkyn ended up having to do his *shturrum* thing. Always interesting to be stopped dead in one's tracks, I find."

"Did you cop it too?" chortled Rainstorm.

"I was holding Midnight at the time."

Tarkyn laughed. "Sorry, Ancient Oak. I did try to catch your eye but you were rather busy, as I recall."

Tarkyn was interrupted at this point by an insistent tugging on his sleeve. He looked down to see Midnight smiling up at him and nodding.

Tarkyn frowned his puzzlement. "Yes, what?"

Midnight sent him an image of himself helping the mountainfolk at Tarkyn's request. Tarkyn eyes bugged out of his head. "What? Are you sure?" He gestured to ask why he was saying 'yes' now when he had said 'no' before.

Midnight shook his head, then pointed to Tarkyn and himself and then wrapped his hands around each other in his gesture for friends. This was followed by rapid series of gestures at the end of which everyone understood that because Tarkyn had stayed his friend when he said 'no,' he had decided to do what the prince wanted.

"Checking you out, in other words," said Rainstorm dryly. "Waiting to see whether you would be true to your word about remaining his friend."

"Doesn't know you very well yet then, does he?" observed Ancient Oak.

Tarkyn just grinned. "He hasn't had much to base trust on in his little life. He is wise to make sure." He tousled Midnight's hair. "Aren't you, rascal?"

44

Stormaway paced up and down, running his hand distractedly through his hair and looking more upset than Tarkyn had ever seen him. He stopped his pacing and turned to the prince.

"Tarkyn, I have struck a problem." The prince said nothing, simply waiting for the wizard to continue, "Only the direct descendant of the curser can lift the curse."

Tarkyn nodded. "Yes, that's what you told us before."

"But no one can lift a curse from themselves."

"Oh, I see. So, Midnight is the only person who can lift the curse but also the person from which it needs to be lifted. Yes, that is a bit of a problem, isn't it?" Tarkyn folded his arms. "Pity you didn't think of this a while ago, before we went through all the drama of talking the poor little kid into it

"Oh, don't worry. We still need him. Once Midnight is free of the curse, he in turn must release the mountainfolk from the damage it's done."

"Except that we can't release him from it."

It was a sign of the stress that Stormaway was under, that

497

he waved the prince's remark impatiently aside and returned to his pacing.

After several minutes, a long time in the young prince's life, Tarkyn asked, "Is there not, perhaps, a hierarchy of wizards so that a higher ranked wizard can overturn the spell of a lower ranked one?"

Stormaway shook his head. "No. There are greater and lesser wizards, of course, but they do not hold jurisdiction over each other. A wizard is subject to the laws of the land, the same as everyone else. So, they should obey their liege lord to overturn a spell if requested. But no guarantee, of course."

"But that is still the wizard himself who would overturn the spell, isn't it?"

"I'm afraid so."

Tarkyn frowned. "So, once a person is dead, their spell can live on forever, and if it's destructive like this one, it can cause misery until all the people it affects have died."

Stormaway stopped pacing and looked hard at Tarkyn. "Worse than that, in this case. It will be passed down the generations through Hail's bloodline, turning the mountainfolk into a malicious, evil force within the forest. If they interbreed, the curse will spread throughout the woodfolk and create monsters of them all."

Suddenly Waterstone, Rainstorm, Ancient Oak, Dry Berry, Blizzard and Lapping Water were standing around them.

"We cannot allow that to happen," stated Waterstone unequivocally, quite unconcerned that it was clear that they had all been listening in.

Dry Berry stood with her hands on her hips. "Young man," she said severely to Tarkyn, "I am expecting you to sort this out. A sorcerer caused it and a sorcerer must repair it. You have vowed to protect us. You must find a way."

Tarkyn threw his hands up, feeling beset on all sides. "I am trying. Don't attack me. Help me. Help Stormaway to come up with ideas."

"We are not attacking you, Tarkyn. We are very worried, though," came Lapping Water's gentle voice. "We can't leave the mountainfolk until they are released from the curse. Their trouble is our trouble. We are, in the end, all one people."

Despite his wish to help them, Tarkyn resented being told, with no consultation, that the home guard wouldn't leave. Somewhere in the back of his mind, he wondered what would happen if he ordered them to continue their journey.

Part of this must have showed on his face because Rainstorm placed his hand on Tarkyn's arm and said, "From what Stormaway has said, you too know that we couldn't leave this behind unresolved. It's too dangerous, isn't it?"

Tarkyn's eyes crinkled in appreciation of Rainstorm's support. He let out a breath. "Yes. I do know that. We must find a way to revoke it."

Rainstorm hesitated for a moment while he marshalled his thoughts. Then he lifted his eyes to hold Tarkyn's gaze. "Tarkyn, you are a guardian of the forest. The guardian of the forest has always appeared to help us through a time of great need. I can think of no greater need than this; to prevent the perversion of our whole nation. So..." He took a slow breath. "So, what can a guardian of the forest do, above and beyond other people, that will save us?"

Stormaway's eyebrows snapped together. "You are right, young man. I think your question may hold the key to the answer." He waved a hand and wheeled around to resume his pacing. "Let me think."

After several minutes, during which Tarkyn and the woodfolk stood and watched in silence, Stormaway snapped his fingers and whirled around to face them. "I think I have the answer." He grimaced. "When I say I have the answer, it is fairly radical. I need to check through my books. I think it has been done once before but the outcome in that instance was not ideal."

"When you say, 'not ideal,' what exactly do you mean?" asked Tarkyn.

"Hmm. A score of woodfolk were killed before they realised the danger."

"Oh, come on, Stormaway!" exclaimed Tarkyn impatiently. "We can't have woodfolk being killed. You'll have to think of something else."

Waterstone intervened. "You said, 'before they realised the danger.' Does that mean that if we are forewarned, we may be able to protect ourselves?"

Stormaway thought for a moment. "Yes, I think so. But we are dealing with forces beyond the normal realm so I can't guarantee it."

"Old man, why don't you just tell us what you've thought of and let us decide for ourselves?" snapped Dry Berry.

Stormaway huffed. "You are all so impatient. I would prefer to look up my books first and be more sure of my facts."

"Live with it," said Rainstorm shortly.

Stormaway sighed and gave in. "Very well. To be honest, there's not much more in my books anyway. It's more that I'm nervous about the idea."

"You are not reassuring me," murmured Tarkyn.

"I didn't say this would be easy." The old wizard drew a breath. "So, let me give you a bit of background first. When a person dies, their whole being, body and soul, gradually dissipates into their surroundings. You agree?" When everyone nodded, Stormaway continued, "Over time, natural forces, heat, cold, wind, water, spread the elements that were once a person into the soil, down streams and rivers to distant places and even to the sea. From the soil and water, parts of a person move into trees and plants and from there into animals and people." They nodded again, keeping their eyes on Stormaway. "So, after seven years, there will be a lot of Pipeless still within the forest, in fact most of him. Quite a bit may have dissipated into the soil and the trees but very little will have made its way beyond the forest's borders."

Tarkyn frowned. "I'm not sure that I like where this is going."

Stormaway ignored him and kept speaking, "So. The forest guardian has a unique connection with the forest and can draw power from it." Now, he looked at Tarkyn. "He can also draw forth from the forest all the elements that were once a person and bring them back together into one place. For a short time, you can resurrect Pipeless. Long enough for him to revoke his curse."

There was a horrified silence. Slowly all eyes turned to a white-faced Tarkyn. "But that is necromancy, Stormaway," he breathed. "I have always been told that necromancy is evil and produces excessive, ungovernable power."

Stormaway chuckled. "Don't believe everything you're told, Tarkyn. No one can actually use necromancy although many have tried. It's just a wizard's tale spread to raise wizards' mystique among sorcerers."

"Oh." The young sorcerer looked a little embarrassed, but after a moment his brow furrowed. "But you just finished telling us that this had been done before."

"Yes, but only by a forest guardian, not by your run-of-the mill wizards or sorcerers who would have been the ones spreading the dire tales of necromancy."

Tarkyn glanced around the faces of the woodfolk before asking, "And if I agree to attempt this, what control will I have over Pipeless when he appears? And what powers will he have? Will he be more powerful than he was in life?"

"You will have no control over him, except to release your hold on his elements and dissipate him again. He will have the same powers he had in life, possibly less because not all of him will be there."

"So, he could strike out at us," said Waterstone.

Stormaway nodded. "Yes, he could. That is what happened last time this was attempted. So, we will need to make sure that everyone is shielded."

Dry Berry huffed. "How do you know your shields will work against the powers of a shade?"

Tarkyn raised his eyebrows. "Stormaway?"

The old wizard grimaced. "We have so little knowledge about this, but I don't think his power will have changed. He will still be who he was. And I can't see how he could gather more power when he has been quiescent for so long. He hasn't been an entity for seven years. How, then, could he have become more powerful?"

"What if his parts bring some of the forest's power with them when he reassembles?" asked Rainstorm.

Stormaway glanced at him. "That's possible, I suppose. I hadn't thought of that."

Tarkyn considered it and shook his head. "I *know* the forest." Interestingly, this statement was true even though in many ways the woodfolk knew it much better than he did. "It has great power but it is not available to just anyone. As you know, the forest protects its own. I don't think it would allow its power to leech into someone so uncertain."

"And what mood will this shade be in?" asked Dry Berry. "Will he still be as vengeful as he was at the end of his life? Or will he have mellowed over time?"

Stormaway shook his head. "I don't know. I can't see that he would have had time to reflect and mellow because he has been dead, not lying around thinking. My best guess is that he will return as he left, angry and vengeful."

"Oh good," said Tarkyn in a small voice. "So, that's something to look forward to."

Ancient Oak smiled at him and patted him on the arm. "Never mind. You've had practice in dealing with his son. Maybe that will hold you in good stead."

Tarkyn sent him a wry glance. "Slight difference in size, power and experience."

"But you'll do it though, won't you?" Ancient Oak grinned at him, confident of the answer.

A slow smile dawned on Tarkyn's tense face as he let out a long sigh. "If that is what you all wish me to do, then I will."

45

The moon was riding high in the black sky, occasional thin
clouds scudding over its face. The wind had died down
but a restless breeze wafted across the side of the mountain
sending icy threads of air winding among the gathered
woodfolk. An aqua haze surrounded the main body of the
woodfolk emanating from Danton who was sitting a little to
one side, with Sparrow next to him, to make sure he stayed
focussed.

In front of the assembled woodfolk stood Midnight, within
a horseshoe of String and Bean, Waterstone, Ancient Oak,
Rainstorm and Lapping Water. Stormaway stood with them,
keeping them safe within his bright green shield.

Everyone was faced towards Tarkyn, watching as he sat
with his eyes closed and his hand pressed against the trunk of a
gnarled old yew tree that had been bent over and twisted by
years of withstanding prevailing winds and gales. Because he
was drawing the essence of Pipeless up through the tree, he
couldn't break contact with it by raising his shield. So, he alone

was unprotected and because of this, despite emphatic protests, he had refused all offers of support and assistance.

Tarkyn sent his senses travelling down into the gravesite at his feet. He kept in his mind the kinder pictures of Pipeless that Hail had given him. His mind baulked at the images of Pipeless attacking the woodwoman and he could not use them to focus his attention on summoning the dead sorcerer. He merged Hail's memories of Pipeless with the remaining bones that were still buried in the ground. When he had created a sense of the wizard, body and soul, he merged himself slowly with the forest.

He wished desperately for Waterstone's hand on his shoulder as he began to lose his sense of self, but now he had to deal with his decision to work alone. He took a deep breath to fight down the panic and let himself flow through the yew into the mountain and from there, into the grasses and shrubs on the side of the mountain, and then on down into the woodlands and streams in the foothills below. He lost all sense of the cold night or the people watching him. As he flowed through the woodlands, he kept the image of Pipeless strongly in his mind, using it as a magnet to draw any particles of the dead wizard back towards him. Slowly he gathered together everything he could find and drew it gradually back up the mountainside.

As he approached his point of departure, the sense of Pipeless became stronger and more palpable. Tarkyn could feel the tight, withdrawn personality of the man, laced with yearning, hurt and anger all around him. The closer he came to his own body, the more concentrated became the sense of Pipeless, entwined with his own ranging spirit. Before he returned, Tarkyn knew he had to separate himself from what was left of the wizard. He tried to draw on his own sense of himself but he was too dissipated to have a centre left to focus on.

Suddenly, far away, he felt a hand on his shoulder. He vaguely wondered who had overridden his order and whether the forest was endangered. But with the external contact on his body, he was able to find his own essence and disentangle himself from Pipeless. With a sudden rush, Tarkyn catapulted out of the old yew to land in his body in the cold night air, throwing his hands forward as he did so, to thrust Pipeless out of him.

Dropping his arms to his sides, he opened his eyes to find himself confronting a ten-foot-high wizard, opaque but misty, as though he were slightly out of focus. Below the giant's ribcage was a horizontal slit where Hail's knife had driven home. The huge man's face was contorted with rage and pain. Tarkyn's heart thumped so much, it felt as if it might jump out of his throat. He scrambled to his feet, keeping his focus on holding the elements of Pipeless together in front of him. With another part of his mind, he threw up his shield, glancing sideways to see whose hand had guided him back. His eyes met those of Bean's.

"I guess I can endure another tongue-lashing if I have to," whispered the trapper.

Tarkyn was too dazed to even understand the inference. He returned his attention to the spectre in front of him. The huge wizard's burning blue eyes glowered down at him, blinking as he tried to work out what had happened. Then his rage reasserted itself and the fearsome wizard flicked his arm, albeit a little clumsily and roared, "*Fierspa!*" A blast of fiery power speared towards Tarkyn.

Despite his shield, Tarkyn flinched and ducked, but the fireball spread harmlessly around the outside of the shield before burning out, leaving the two of them unscathed.

Tarkyn straightened and tried to speak but only produced a dry squeak. He cleared his throat and managed to get out,

"Pipeless, I am Tarkyn Tamadil, third son of King Markazon, and your liege lord within the forest."

The wizard took no notice of what he had said, frowned down at him and roared, "Where did you suddenly spring from? And where is Hail?" His voice sounded deep and breathy, but a clear note of panic underlay his anger. His questions came out slowly as though it was an effort to form the words.

Tarkyn squared his shoulders and spoke more loudly, with a firm assurance that he did not feel, "Pipeless, I tell you again, I am your liege lord. I await your obeisance."

The wizard scowled furiously, but his bewilderment was dissipating his anger. A frown of confusion appeared on his brow. "Who did you say you were?"

"I am Tarkyn Tamadil, third son of King Markazon."

Pipeless looked him up and down. "You're well-grown for twelve years old."

Despite the gravity of the situation, Tarkyn couldn't help smiling. "Nevertheless, I am who I say I am." He paused then added with a deliberate note of hauteur, "And I am still waiting."

Then to everyone's amazement, the enormous, frightening wizard bowed low. "I beg your pardon, Your Highness, for attacking you. The last few minutes have been rather confusing." When he straightened, his fearsome blue eyes swept around the gathered woodfolk and narrowed. "And who are all these people?"

"Hi, Pipeless, you know me," said Bean casually. "Do you like my beard? Your son did that, you know."

The wizard's eyes swivelled down to stare at the trapper. "My son? I have no son."

"Yes, you do," said Tarkyn. "The world has moved on. Your son is seven years old."

The deep breathy voice sounded uncertain, "Why has the world moved on? What has happened? Why is everyone so short?"

The prince grimaced. "I'm afraid I have some bad news for you. The pain in your chest comes from a lethal knife blow dealt you by Hail. You are dead and have been for seven years. I drew you back from within the earth and the woodlands. I can only hold you together for a short time. When I let go, you will flow back into the earth and the trees."

"And we are not short," added Stormaway. "I think Tarkyn has not managed to concentrate you completely back to what you were. So, you are taking up more space."

The huge, misty wizard frowned as he tried to remember and to work out what had happened. Slowly, as they watched, his face suffused, not with anger but with shame. He lifted his hands and buried his face in them.

"Why have you brought me back?" came his voice, muffled by his hands. "To stand in judgement on me?"

"No, Hail passed judgement on you long ago," said Tarkyn calmly. "But if you remember, as you died, you uttered a curse on your son and on all of his mother's people."

Pipeless dropped his hands and stared at the prince. After a long unnerving pause, he said, "I did not think. I was hurt and angry. I realise, now you say that I have a son, that I have condemned my own child." He wiped his hand across his brow. "It was a terrible curse, wasn't it?" He let out a slow wheezy breath. "And I would not have wanted Hail's people hurt either. But I died, didn't I? So, I didn't have time to calm down and retract it." He looked around. "Are these all Hail's people?" When Tarkyn nodded, he asked, "And where is my son? Has he suffered?"

Tarkyn pointed to Midnight who was standing between Rainstorm and Lapping Water within Stormaway's shield.

"Yes, he has suffered a great deal. But your friends, String and Bean have stood by him over the years and done what they could and recently, I have met him and will look after him from now on. He is a fine young woodman and a fine young sorcerer. He is deaf but I can exchange mental images with him so he is no longer isolated." He turned back to the dead wizard. "He is a son to be proud of. And he is willing, despite all they have done to him, to help Hail's people to break free of your curse." Tarkyn paused. "But only you can free your son."

Pipeless stared at Midnight, drinking in every detail of him. Lapping Water's and Rainstorm's hands tightened on the little boy's shoulders as he tensed up under scrutiny. Tarkyn sent him waves of reassurance and smiled at him.

Pipeless glanced uncertainly at Stormaway. "You know you will have to drop your shield if I am to revoke the curse?"

Stormaway in turn glanced at Tarkyn. "Your Highness?"

Tarkyn faced the huge wizard. "Pipeless, look at me." When he had the dead man's attention, he continued, "Do I have your word that you will hurt none of these people?"

"Yes, Your Highness. I have nothing left to give you as surety, since my life and honour are already lost, but only at the very end was I a violent man. I am glad that you have given me the chance to repair the damage I have wrought."

As Tarkyn nodded his approval, Stormaway waved away his shield. Immediately, Midnight ran towards the shade with his arms out in front of him. Stormaway moved to intervene but Tarkyn stopped him with a gesture. The huge, misty wizard squatted down. When Midnight reached him and threw his arms around his waist, his father put an awkward arm around the little boy and patted him gingerly on the back. Then he placed his other hand on the boy's head and intoned, "*Choidayarorsharanualla. Rorsharatayahagarznuallatayadorisolnuallazormatara.*" A soft deep blue flowed from beneath the wizard's hand, not the red that

Tarkyn had imagined, and slowly swirled around Midnight. Then the blue spiral gathered force and spun upwards before flowing through the night air towards the gathered mountainfolk.

"Danton, remove your shield!" ordered Tarkyn.

As the aqua shield winked out, the flow of deep blue power spiralled above the mountainfolk, slowly spreading out until it covered all of them. Then it whirled gradually down into their midst, almost obscuring them from view.

Pipeless looked at Tarkyn. "I can only remove the curse from here forwards. My son must repair the damage it has already caused."

"I know. I have explained to Midnight what he must do. Since he is with you, you must support him. It will not be easy for him."

Then Tarkyn instructed Midnight to let his father go and to turn around, so that he was facing the mountainfolk. Reluctantly, the little woodman sorcerer let go of his newly found father and, drawing in a deep breath, turned around. He glanced at Tarkyn and put his hand over his heart. Tarkyn returned the gesture and for a moment they just looked at each other.

Then Midnight exhaled and, with his father's arm around his waist holding him from behind, he flung his arms wide and sent forth, through Tarkyn, all his memories of his time with his mother and the mountainfolk. As each memory hit the people involved, the blue haze around them sizzled and crackled as their own warped memory of the event was challenged and destroyed. The blue around Hail was constantly fizzing and popping as memory after memory of Midnight's hit her. By the time the fizzing and crackling had slowed down and stopped, Midnight was quivering all over and only his father's arm kept his knees from buckling under him.

Then slowly, the soft, deep blue swirls lifted lazily from amongst the mountainfolk and curled up and over them to stream back towards Midnight. Gradually he was bathed in a strong, deep blue light and as it warmed him, he began to really understand what the curse had done, both to him and to the mountainfolk. And once he understood, with his heart and his head, some of the tension left his body, his eyes lost their haunted look and he could see the mountainfolk more as he saw the home guard. But despite understanding, he could not fully forgive them for what they had done to him. And then, as he realised that the true source of his suffering was the strange misty wizard holding him, Midnight twisted out of his grip and ran to Tarkyn who swung him up into his arms and hugged him tight.

Pipeless straightened up and towered once more above them. "I see he has worked it out," he said sadly. "I thank you for looking after him, and you too, String and Bean. I am glad that woodfolk and sorcerers are beginning to live together. It was too soon for Hail and me." He glanced speakingly at Lapping Water, the nearest woodwoman. "Perhaps you will do better in the future, Your Highness?"

Tarkyn promptly turned brick red.

The huge, misty wizard gave a grunt of amusement and turned to Hail who was standing far from him on the other side of the gathering. "And to you, Hail, nothing will repair what I have done but I am truly sorry."

Hail glared back at him, saying nothing.

He shrugged. "She is wise not to trust me. I would no longer trust myself. But as I am not staying..." He turned to Tarkyn. "How much longer do I have?"

"It is straining me to keep you here now. Midnight, say goodbye." Tarkyn matched images to words but with a hint of compulsion. He did not want Midnight to regret missing his last chance.

Midnight looked up at his huge looming father and waved half-heartedly. As the wizard waved back, he began to melt into the ground starting at the feet and moving upwards. Before their eyes, he sank and dissipated, flowing outward into the earth around him until he was lost from sight.

For a long time, no one spoke. The mountainfolk were coming to terms with their past treatment of Midnight and everyone was still stunned by the apparition they had all witnessed and survived.

For a while there was silence but gradually, far in the distance could be heard the sound of the wind brushing through the trees. As they listened, it drew closer until it rushed up through the pines on the mountainside and blasted across the clearing through the people gathered there. It was so strong that it nearly blew out the great fire in the middle of the gathering. Then it was gone as suddenly as it came and a silent detonation shook the ground beneath their feet. Everyone exchanged glances.

"Was that the aftermath of Pipeless returning to the forest?" asked Rainstorm quietly.

Stormaway shook his head. "No. I'm afraid not." He grimaced and unconsciously drew his cloak around him. "That was the sound of the oath binding the honour of you people gathered here to the welfare of the forest."

"Oh no, not again. Not more resentment," murmured Rainstorm, glancing at the prince. "Don't worry, Tarkyn, we are here to support you."

Tarkyn met his eyes briefly but his face, already white with fatigue, was stiff with tension. He stood holding Midnight, rigidly awaiting the reactions of the mountainfolk and the independently minded trappers.

Dry Berry stomped up and stood, arms on hips, in front of Tarkyn. "Young man, stop looking so worried. I don't think there is a man, woman or child among us who doesn't owe their future to you. You have looked a dead man in the face and bent him to your will to save us all. Most of us have already sworn an oath to you on our honour. We will keep our word. Despite having to fight against the curse we, as a group of mountainfolk, have managed to hold true, even if some amongst us struggled. The forest's welfare is safe with us and so are you." Suddenly, she smiled. "In fact it is an honour that the sorcery in the oath now includes us. We must now be a reasonably safe bet."

Tarkyn managed a tired smile.

Dry Berry cackled. "Come one. Come and sit down and have something to drink before you drop. Your little wood sorcerer has gone to sleep so I won't offer him anything but I think we all have a lot to make up to him, if he'll let us."

IX

THE REST DAY

46

Early the next morning, at that time when children wake up full of energy and adults yearn to sleep on, Midnight landed with a thump on top of a sleeping, weary Tarkyn. Tarkyn opened one eye and raised enough energy to suggest that Midnight head off to find Thunder Storm, Lapping Water or Rainstorm. By the time Midnight looked hesitant, Tarkyn was already asleep again. Midnight eyed him for a few minutes, deciding whether to jump up and down on him again. Then he thought about it and realised that Tarkyn didn't usually fob him off onto other people. He peered closer and realised that the prince was very soundly asleep. On balance, he decided to leave Tarkyn and venture outside on his own.

When he pulled back the brush screening and crawled outside, the little wood sorcerer found himself surrounded by an array of dishes full of carefully chosen berries, dried fruits, cheeses, bite-size pieces of venison, soft, freshly baked bread rolls and a variety of fruit juices. His eyes widened and he looked longingly at them all, but he was not about to start a new day by being accused of stealing a special feast prepared for

517

Tarkyn. So, he repressed his hunger and threaded his way past the dishes out into the clearing.

Despite the early hour, the mountainfolk, young and old, were waiting for him. Finding himself surrounded, Midnight panicked and tried to flick into hiding, but a firm grip on each of his shoulders prevented him. He thrashed wildly from side to side only to find Lapping Water and Rainstorm smiling reassuringly at him. When he pulled himself together and turned back to the mountainfolk, he realised that everyone was smiling and welcoming him.

The diminutive figure of Dry Berry came forward and led Midnight back to the plates of food, pointing at him and then at the food. In response, Midnight pointed at the food and then at Tarkyn's shelter with a look of query. Dry Berry shook her head and reiterated that the special foods were all for him.

In a daze, he sat down within the ring of platters and looked around at everyone, frowning uncertainly. Rainstorm and Lapping Water sat on either side of him to keep him feeling safe. After a minute, he tentatively reached for a soft, doughy roll, expecting at any moment to have his hand slapped away. When he was sure that he really could help himself to whatever he liked, he reached for more rolls and offered them with a hesitant smile to Rainstorm and Lapping Water. Then he gestured for all the watching mountainfolk to help themselves before burying his face self-consciously in Lapping Waters' shoulder.

Dry Berry smiled down at him. "He really is such a kind little boy." She shook her head. "That curse was so cruel."

Lapping Water gently pulled Midnight's head away from her shoulder and handed him a strawberry to give him something to look at, other than the ring of faces around him. During the next half-hour, as he sat eating with Rainstorm and Lapping Water, every member of the mountainfolk walked up to him and tousled his hair, patted him on the arm or simply caught his eye to signal their friendship. No sorcerers were in sight. It was purely a woodfolk gesture to welcome Midnight back into the fold and to thank him for his part in dismantling the curse. Only Hail was conspicuous by her absence but if Midnight noticed, he gave no indication.

47

The dawn gave way to a bright, clear morning; a morning deserved by the celebration of the mountainfolk's release from the curse. The atmosphere around the firesite was relaxed and cheerful. No longer was there any sense of distance between the mountainfolk and the home guard. The woodfolk were once more a united people.

Only now were they enjoying each other's company as they would normally expect to, and because of this, the home guard had decided to postpone their departure until early the following day.

At eight o'clock, Rainstorm popped his head into Tarkyn's shelter to let him know who the next lookouts would be and where they would be stationed. Tarkyn barely registered the information, and merely grunted, before rolling over and going back to sleep.

In the middle of the morning, Tarkyn finally emerged, feeling drained. As soon as he appeared, Midnight dropped what he was doing and rushed over, full of excited images of his special breakfast and of him playing with the other kids. He launched himself up into Tarkyn's arms, flung his arms around his neck and gave him a big hug. Tarkyn hugged him in return, but moments later Midnight pulled away, jumped down and rushed off again. Tarkyn smiled after him for a few moments before ambling down to splash his face at the small stream that ran through the coarse grass of the hillside. The water did little to revive him, and he was soon snoozing again, this time on a grassy spot next to the stream. He dozed away, occasionally stirring himself enough to prop himself up on one elbow to watch the kids playing with Midnight before drifting off again. Interestingly no one, not even Midnight, came near him for the rest of the morning.

Midnight and the other children were having a marvellous time playing with the little wood sorcerer's new shield. He would raise the glowing dark green haze around himself and they would run and throw themselves against it. Then he placed the shield around all of them and they would try to crawl out from underneath. The children were fascinated by it and spent a long time, inside and out, running their hands along its surface and peering through it to see how everything looked with a dark green tinge to it.

Further away, a group of young woodfolk including Rainstorm, Lapping Water and North Wind were gathered, chatting and laughing. Tarkyn would have liked to join them but couldn't raise the energy. So he lay back and just watched them from where he was.

The attack, when it came, was two-pronged and carefully orchestrated by Ancient Oak and Rainstorm.

At noon, Ancient Oak wandered past Tarkyn, told him the names of the new set of lookouts who were taking over the watch and mentioned that two of them would be changing position so that they wouldn't be looking directly into the sun. A faint frown flickered across Tarkyn's face, but he was too tired to concentrate properly. He nodded and closed his eyes again.

A short time later, Ancient Oak returned bearing one of Summer Rain's hideous tasting tonics, two steaming cups of tea and some soft rolls filled with meat and cheese. He sat down next to Tarkyn and having placed their lunch carefully on the lumpy grassy bank, prodded his adoptive brother firmly in the ribs.

"Come on, Sleepy Head. We've left you alone for long enough. If you're still tired now, I'm afraid I'm going to have to force this tonic down you."

Tarkyn groaned and sat up, rubbing his eyes and pushing his hair back off his face. "Oh no! How to ruin a perfect morning." He yawned. "Oh stars! I can't believe how tired I am." He gave a wry smile. "Go on then. Give it to me." He took the proffered drink and slugged it down. "Aagh, that's awful!" he said with a grimace and a shudder. "How does she do it?"

Ancient Oak grinned. "Years of practice." He frowned as he studied Tarkyn. "Are you all right? You don't look too good."

For an answer, Tarkyn flopped back down and then propped himself up on one elbow. "I'm fine, I think. I'm just bone weary."

"It's been a taxing few days, one way and another." Ancient Oak handed Tarkyn his cup of tea and a roll. He considered him for a few moments before saying, "I'm proud of you, little brother. Do you know that? What you did last night took enormous courage. I'm not surprised you're tired."

Tarkyn looked at him curiously and frowned in thought as he sipped his tea. Eventually he smiled.

"What?" asked Ancient Oak.

"It's such a proprietal emotion, to be proud of someone." His smile broadened. "It feels nice, to belong to someone enough that they feel proud of me. Thanks."

Ancient Oak gave his head a little shake. "Waterstone was right about you. You are a strange mixture."

"Of what?"

"Vulnerability and strength."

Tarkyn looked at him quizzically. "Isn't everyone?"

Ancient Oak laughed. "I suppose so." After a moment, he added, "I'm not sure about Waterstone though. He seems as solid as a rock, through and through."

Tarkyn raised his eyebrows, leaned in closer and said in a conspiratorial undertone, "Afraid of horses, you know." Then he rocked back and laughed at Ancient Oak's look of amazement.

"I never knew that! How did you find that out?"

"He objected too much to my proposal that we use horses for the rescue at the encampment. I dragged it out of him then."

"Oh," said Ancient Oak innocently, "I thought you must have found out from his memories." Then he sat back and watched with great enjoyment as outrage, anger, realization and then amusement flitted in quick succession across Tarkyn's face.

"You thought no such thing."

Ancient Oak grinned. "No. But I loved watching you think I had besmirched your honour. I was actually hoping for one of those disdainful looks but never mind! I'll keep working on it."

Tarkyn's eyes twinkled at him over the rim of the teacup. "You have a wicked side to you that I am only just coming to appreciate. You take a long time to come out of your shell, don't you?" He thought back, "Hmm, but now I think about it, you were winding me up about being able to trust people even before the sickness episode, weren't you?" He grinned. "I can see I'm going to have to keep my eyes wide open when I'm around you."

For a while they sat in companionable silence eating their

rolls in the soft autumn sunlight, listening to the chattering stream and the distant laughter and voices of the woodfolk.

Tarkyn stretched and let out a long, contented breath. "You know, I've just realised. I don't feel on edge any more. At last I feel safe again. Today is the first time I have really been able to relax since we arrived in the mountains."

"No wonder you're tired then." The woodman looked around at the various groups of mixed home guard and mountainfolk that were dotted across the clearing. "I think everyone has been feeling the strain. That's why it's so good to have this day to spend truly relaxing with the mountainfolk before we move on." He sipped his tea and smiled. "Young Midnight is having a great time playing with his magic shield, isn't he? He seems to have talents from both sides of his heritage." He thought for a moment, "I wonder whether he'll keep flicking into hiding if an outsider approaches or whether he'll gradually identify with sorcerers, especially if you're looking after him?"

"Hmm, interesting one, isn't it?" Tarkyn lay back down with his hands behind his head and swivelled his eyes to look at Ancient Oak. "Now we are moving into the realms of a woodfolk consensus decision. Is our little wood sorcerer over there bound by the woodfolk code or by the code of sorcerers? Should he be treating Waterstone and you as princes because he's a sorcerer or as an equal because he's a woodman? Should he stay hidden as a woodman or walk the world as a sorcerer, if he so chooses?"

"We do not seem to have had the opportunity to make that decision in relation to the other wood sorcerer in our midst," replied Ancient Oak dryly. "What makes you think we will be given the choice with Midnight?"

Tarkyn looked puzzled for a moment. Then he smiled. "Oh. You mean me. Yes. Good point." His smile faded. "Oh, I see. Yes, I haven't revealed to outsiders the presence of any woodfolk but myself. But I forgot to count myself as woodfolk in that equation, didn't I? Blast! That means I've broken my oath to you, doesn't it?" Tarkyn was seriously upset with himself. "No wonder Waterstone was angry with me when we were at the roadside and I betrayed my presence to that family. By the time we reached Lord Tolward's, he must have resigned himself to my own convenient interpretation of my bond of secrecy because he didn't oppose me in that at all."

Tarkyn rolled onto his front and propped himself on his elbows next to the woodman. He cupped his chin in his hands and looked up at the clear blue sky while he thought about it. "You know, I have never broken my word before, over anything. I can't believe I so casually interpreted it to suit myself." He sighed, "And yet, when I look back over all the situations where I revealed myself to sorcerers, I don't know that I could have endured not to. I couldn't have let that family on the Great Western Road be killed, or Lord Tolward's children; and I had to deflect that hunting party away from Midnight. I suppose I could possibly have avoided confronting the two solo sorcerers who returned later. I could have left Danton to deal with that." He slid his eyes sideways to meet Ancient Oak's. "So, do you all think I'm completely fickle?"

Ancient Oak shook his head, smiling. "No. Don't be silly. It's just that you're not only a woodman. Neither is Midnight. So maybe the rules need to apply differently. Rules always apply differently around you, anyway."

Tarkyn frowned. "What do you mean?"

"Well, since your word is law, you can pretty much make rules up as you go along, can't you? And you do. You pick and choose which rules you feel like following."

"I don't."

Ancient Oak threw back his head and laughed. "Oh yes

you do. What about lookout duty, cooking, making shelters, hunting, gathering wood, herbs and fruits? You never do any of those things unless you're bored and feel like it for something to do."

The prince raised his eyebrows and with a suppressed grin, said sanctimoniously, "Waterstone told Sparrow that I have special jobs to do that others can't. So it's fair that I don't have to do cooking and other tasks that I might find distasteful."

"Trying to explain your behaviour to her, was he?"

Tarkyn chortled, quite unrepentant. "Something like that."

They both knew the line was drawn there. Tarkyn would not move any closer towards equality and took it for granted that his status exempted him from performing any tasks that he chose to avoid.

Deciding to change the subject, Ancient Oak nodded at the group of younger woodfolk further along the stream. "I think we may have a few extra members when we leave. You seem to have won Blizzard over entirely, and a couple of woodwomen, Cavern and Melting Snow, would like to join us." He gave a little smile. "I've always been rather keen on Melting Snow when I've come across her in the past. So I'm pleased she's coming with us."

"What about Cavern?"

Ancient Oak shrugged. "She's nice enough too. Just not quite as special as Melting Snow, if you know what I mean." He paused for a moment and then asked casually, closing in for the kill, "So what about you? Are you keen on anyone? Did you go red last night because Pipeless looked particularly at Lapping Water or because of the inference in general?"

Tarkyn coloured faintly. "I was embarrassed at having my potential love life discussed in front of everyone like that," he answered, not meeting Ancient Oak's eyes.

Ancient Oak smiled gently but persisted. "You haven't answered my question."

Tarkyn looked up resolutely and replied, "All right. Both. The inference in general and Lapping Water in particular." He sighed. "But I spend my life looking green, or black and blue around her and throwing my weight around. At least I haven't been throwing my weight around at her. So that's something, I suppose. Thunder Storm thought it didn't matter whether I was green or not, because I look so different anyway. I can't say I found that very encouraging." He shrugged and gave a wry smile. "And now, every time I look, Lapping Water is with Rainstorm. So, I have more or less given up on the whole idea. Besides..."

"Besides, what?"

"Well, many things. First and foremost, you heard what Pipeless said. Maybe it is still too soon for a sorcerer to woo a woodwoman. I don't know. What do you think?"

Ancient Oak didn't rush in with reassurances. He thought carefully before replying, "I think a union between woodfolk and sorcerer is no longer beyond the realms of possibility. But I don't think it is as simple as that. I could brush aside that objection by saying that you are a woodman. But it's not just that you're a sorcerer. The issues would be very different if this were Danton I was talking to. But you? You carry with you the weight of our nation and to some extent, the weight of the sorcerer nation."

The prince sighed. "You're right, of course. I guess I should stop pretending that I can fit in and just act like everyone else. I'm not everyone else." He gave a sad smile. "So, basically, you are warning me off, aren't you?"

Ancient Oak leaned forward and patted Tarkyn on the shoulder. "No, little brother. I'm not warning you off. I mention it because I know the affairs of sorcerers weigh heavily on you and you are not a man to turn your back on people in need. And I suspect that if you're worried about what may happen, it may stop you from making any approaches to Lapping Water. So I thought you might like to talk about it."

"Hmph. I suppose that's a good idea." Tarkyn smiled ruefully. "Thanks. I'm afraid I am not one of those people who could indulge a passing fancy. So, before I made any approach to Lapping Water, I would have to know that a future together was realistic."

"And how would you feel about aligning yourself with someone below your social status?"

The prince's eyes twinkled. "I don't need to worry about that. I accept Waterstone's premise that all woodfolk are equivalent to nobility. And every female in Eskuzor, noble or otherwise, is of a lower rank – even my mother, ever since she became the Dowager Queen. I could only marry a social equal if I were to wed someone of royal blood from another country. And I can't see that happening. My stakes on the international marriage market will have dipped alarmingly after recent events."

Ancient Oak gave a grunt of laughter. "Yes, I imagine they would have. But what about Lapping Water's behaviour? I hear you were quite shocked by the way our woodwomen deport themselves."

Tarkyn rolled over and sat up, linking his arms across his raised knees. He glanced sideways at his woodfolk brother and said tightly, "I suppose everyone knows about that now, do they? That will be the end of any chance I have with any of your women, won't it?"

"I don't think so. Everyone knows that you came into the forest with different expectations from those you hold now. But the question remains: Could you come to terms with a different style of behaviour in your partner? It's one thing to overlook it in other people but quite another to overlook it in someone who is identified with you."

Tarkyn frowned at him. "I feel as though I'm being interrogated by the father of the bride-to-be. Are you sure you're not warning me off?"

When Ancient Oak shook his head smiling, the prince reverted to considering the question and tried to imagine himself in the position of feeling proprietal about Lapping Water. Eventually he replied, "In the context of the woodlands, there would be no issue. I may be taken aback from time to time but that doesn't mean I disapprove. If ever I took her into the society of sorcerers which, for a plethora of reasons, is unlikely to happen, I would like to think that I could endure with equanimity the raised eyebrows and shocked expressions of my fellow sorcerers." He smiled wryly. "In fact, I think I would be perversely proud of her greater physical prowess."

Tarkyn drank down the rest of his tea and shook out the cup. "But the issue still remains: What if I had to leave the forest? If there's any chance I might have to return to the world of sorcerers, I couldn't even consider becoming involved with Lapping Water."

"I'm afraid it's too late to worry about that. You are already involved – with all of us," said Ancient Oak dryly. "And what about your oath? Our fate is your fate. Our cause is your cause. How could you possibly justify turning your back on the forest and all of us?"

Tarkyn looked at the woodman and gave a gentle smile. "You're right. I couldn't. I couldn't because of the oath and I couldn't because I couldn't bear to lose you all." He sighed. "But my own feelings in the matter would be insufficient to keep me from following my conscience back into the world of sorcerers if that was where it led me."

"Just as well we have the oath then, isn't it?" said Ancient

Oak flippantly. The woodman rolled over onto his side and propped himself on one elbow so he was facing Tarkyn. His voice developed a note of strain. "So, otherwise, would your conscience place the affairs of sorcerers above the affairs of woodfolk?"

The prince stared at him. "No. No, that is not what I meant. After all, what I have heard of sorcerers' plights has not deflected me from my mission to find Falling Rain and to redress the wrong done to him. But if sorcerers are suffering and I can help them at no risk or detriment to woodfolk, then I will. Even if my fate is bound to yours, I have neither forfeited my free will nor my right to care for other people." He passed a hand over his face and sighed. "I cannot, and do not wish to, turn my back on all of you. But nevertheless, I think the day is coming when I must find a way to help the sorcerers of Eskuzor."

Ancient Oak studied the prince's drawn face for a moment and then reached over and grasped Tarkyn's arm. "Don't worry, little brother. We will find a way to stand by you, whatever you need to do." He smiled. "Anyway, out of all of this, we have established one sure fact. Even if you must venture forth for your sorcerers one day, you cannot just leave us all behind you. So, if you would like to take your chances with Lapping Water, why don't you explain it all to her and let her decide." He gave a wry smile. "You do have a tendency to make people's decision for them sometimes, you know. She too has the right to decide her own fate."

Not if she's under oath to me, she doesn't, was Tarkyn's immediate but ignoble reaction, quelled at its inception. Then he smiled wryly to himself. Because of the way he had chosen to behave, most woodfolk had never really understood the total loss of freedom that the oath could impose on them, Waterstone being the notable exception.

Seeing Tarkyn's smile, Ancient Oak asked, "So, will you approach her and see how you go?"

Tarkyn shook his head. "No. Because, after all that, there is still Rainstorm."

Ancient Oak smiled. "Oh, did I forget to mention that? To start with, Rainstorm is Lapping Water's cousin and they have grown up together. They're just used to being in each other's company, but it's very much a brother-sister type of friendship. Secondly, he's two years younger than she is and she wouldn't be interested anyway."

"Oh."

"Run out of excuses now, haven't you?"

"Hmm." Tarkyn tried for one last-ditch stand. "Now might not be the best time, so soon after everyone finding out about Pipeless' behaviour. She might be too nervous of me."

"Tarkyn, you are nothing like Pipeless." Ancient Oak squinted at him and then grinned in realisation. "It's not Lapping Water who will be nervous of you. It's you who are nervous of her." He laughed. "I love it. Our fearsome, brave forest guardian scared of a lone woodwoman."

"Stop it," pleaded Tarkyn, his face reddening. He swept his hands across his face then turned to look at his tormenting brother. "You may not realise this, but before I came into the woods, I had never been left alone with a woman."

"What, to sleep with?"

"No. Even to talk to. Women in my circles were always carefully chaperoned. I met them only in formal situations or as part of a larger group. I never had to issue them with an invitation or risk rejection. All arrangements were made by my retainers."

Ancient Oak frowned. "What about your nanny or serving girls?"

Tarkyn looked embarrassed. "I wasn't thinking about them. I didn't, you see. They just fulfilled their roles. I fulfilled mine."

"But I'm sure I have heard that some of your lords have offspring all over the country to various serving girls. And are there not houses where men pay to be with women?"

"I am neither those lords nor those men. I would never abuse my position even to consider serving women in that light and I would never demean myself by visiting a whorehouse." The prince gave a rueful smile. "On reflection, I do not see it as a virtue in me that I didn't consider servants in that light. It was more that I didn't consider them at all, really."

"So, how can Danton say that you care about people if you didn't even think about some of them?"

Tarkyn shrugged. "Best of a bad lot, I suppose. If any of my servants had been distressed, I would have helped them but while they performed their duties unremarkably, I did not usually notice them. If it's any consolation, they too would have looked upon me as a duty more than a person." He glanced at the woodman, waiting for his reaction.

For a long while, Ancient Oak said nothing, and Tarkyn began to worry that the woodman had withdrawn from him. Finally, Ancient Oak looked up and, recognising the prince's anxiety, smiled reassuringly. "Don't look so worried, little brother. I know you care about people. You have proved it to us over and over again since you have been with us. I'm just trying to work out a parallel in our society so I can understand. Maybe it's similar to when we're all working together to hunt down a deer. We are business-like and our role in the hunt is more important than who we are, at those times. But unlike your previous situation, we revert to our camaraderie after the hunt is over whereas for you, the job was never done, was it? You lived it, all day and all night."

Tarkyn let out a sigh of relief. "Yes. That's probably as close as you'll get. Once I had learned what was expected of me, I tried never to allow myself to step out of role before family, peers or servants."

"So how did you know who you really were?"

The prince shrugged. "I don't know. I suppose part of who I am is that role. And for the rest, sometimes I was alone."

48

W hile this torturous discussion was taking place, further along the stream, the second prong of the two-pronged attack was underway.

"So, did you notice Tarkyn's reaction last night when Pipeless looked at you and said the prince might do better in the future?" asked Rainstorm casually.

"Don't be silly, Rainstorm. Tarkyn was just embarrassed. That's all. I would have been too." Lapping Water trailed her hand in the icy water of the stream for a while before adding, "Anyway, he's never shown any sign that he likes me."

"Well, he doesn't dislike you, does he?" persisted Rainstorm.

Lapping Water smiled. "No. I don't mean that. I just mean that he doesn't like me better than anyone else."

"Do you wish he did?" asked North Wind.

Lapping Water gazed down at the water washing around her hand. After a moment she looked up and said, "I'm not sure that that's any of your business."

A general uproar greeted this remark.

"*Of course* it's our business," said Rainstorm over the top of the noise. "We're your friends. And Tarkyn's friends. Anyway, if you think it mightn't be our business, then that must mean you *do* like him, mustn't it?"

A reluctant smile was drawn from the woodwoman. "All right. Yes, I do." She frowned forbiddingly. "But you're not to tell him I said that."

"Gosh, you're brave," said Melting Snow, wide-eyed. "Don't you find him a bit scary?"

"I mean, he's huge, isn't he?" came Cavern's echoey voice. "And he gets angry all the time. And he *kills* people."

"And such weird eyes!" added Melting Snow with an artistic shudder.

Lapping Water laughed. "Will you two stop it? I knew I shouldn't have told you."

"But seriously," said Cavern, "he is a sorcerer." She threw her hands up before they could shout her down. "I know he's a woodman as well but he is still a sorcerer. It's a big decision; to break with tradition like that."

"And he's a prince," said Blizzard, slowly winding up. "And more than that, he's the forest guardian. He's a bloody legend, woman. What do you think you're doing, lusting after a legend?"

By this time, Lapping Water's cheeks were burning. She threw a venomous look at Rainstorm before snapping, "I didn't say I was going to do anything about it. I just said I liked him. Okay? Now leave me alone. I've had enough."

Rainstorm in turn, rounded on Blizzard. "Blizzard, you are the rock bottom. Your way of phrasing things drops us down to a whole new level."

Blizzard threw his hands up in contrition. "Sorry. I didn't mean to upset anyone. Lust after him all you like, Lapping

Water, for all I care. I admire your guts, even to consider it. I felt honoured just to have a drink with him."

Lapping Water relaxed into a smile. "Oh, Blizzard, you're such a funny one. I suppose you're not used to being around him, as we are."

"But you know, Lapping Water, say you did team up with Tarkyn," said North Wind carefully. "How could you have an equal partnership if one is under oath to the other?"

A thoughtful silence greeted this.

"You know, that is quite tricky, isn't it?" mused Rainstorm. "You couldn't have an unequal commitment. It wouldn't work, would it? And if you became equal with Tarkyn, where would that leave the rest of us?"

Lapping Water frowned at them. "You don't think you're jumping ahead of yourselves just a bit, do you? I have no intention of telling him how I feel and as far as we know he couldn't care less about me. So, don't you think it's a bit soon to be worrying about how the relationship is going to work?"

"No, not really," replied North Wind. "You don't want even to consider setting out on a journey if you know you can't get there. Better to work out what's possible first."

"All right, all right," said Lapping Water, giving in. "I personally think that if Tarkyn continues to use the oath as he does now, it wouldn't present a problem. The oath doesn't say that he has to consult, but he generally does and that's the main imbalance."

Rainstorm chortled. "You've thought this through already, haven't you?"

"That's it. I've had enough. I'm going." Lapping Water went to stand up but Rainstorm grabbed her arm and pulled her back down.

"Sorry, sorry, sorry. I'll stop teasing now, I promise." He looked at her seriously. "You really do like him, don't you?"

Lapping Water nodded but kept her eyes fixed on the ground.

Rainstorm's tone was thoughtful, all teasing gone. "Hmm, in that case, North Wind is right. We'd better make sure this is possible." He looked up. "Blizzard, do you think you could get us all some of your precious wine? I think we need a good long chat."

The sum effect of Rainstorm's and Ancient Oak's separate but synchronised attacks was that Tarkyn and Lapping Water avoided each other like the plague for the rest of the day. And whereas previously, Tarkyn would happily have joined the group of young woodfolk when he had recovered, Lapping Water's presence amongst them meant that he now felt too self-conscious to approach them.

Instead, he wandered over to where Midnight was playing with some of the mountainfolk children using his marvellous deep green shield. Tarkyn sat down next to Sparrow and murmured quietly, "Watch this."

He waited for a time when the other children were not too close to Midnight then muttered, "*Fierspa,*" and sent a gentle shaft of bronze flame towards the deep green shield. The little boy started in fright but held his shield firm and the bronze magic spread harmlessly around him. Tarkyn nodded his approval and smiled. Midnight beamed from inside his shield. The mountainfolk children shied away but stood at a safe distance watching, wide-eyed. After a short query, Tarkyn sent another slightly stronger bronze beam, but still Midnight's shield held and the watching children all cheered.

Sparrow tugged at his sleeve. "Tarkyn, what would happen if you put your shield up and then bumped up against Midnight's?"

Tarkyn grinned. "Let's find out, shall we? Do you want to come inside my shield?"

Sparrow nodded, eyes shining with excitement. Tarkyn raised his shield around them and slowly walked towards Midnight, sending him an image to explain what he was doing. When the shield met, there was a slight fizzing but neither shield gave way. When Tarkyn pushed to get closer, his own shield bent out of shape to accommodate his movement but Midnight's stayed rounded. Within his shield, Tarkyn applauded.

"He's pretty good, you know, Sparrow. I don't think Bean could concentrate on keeping his shield up for as long as this. In fact, I'm sure he couldn't. He's quite hopeless at it."

Sparrow giggled. Tarkyn grinned, backed slowly away and released his shield. "I'd better stop before he falters. I don't want him to lose face in front of the other kids. They wouldn't understand how hard it is to keep focussed, especially when you first start."

Immediately, Midnight's shield also winked out. He blinked and wiped his hand across his forehead. Tarkyn sent an image to tell Midnight to stop for a while and to get himself a drink. After checking with Sparrow, he asked Midnight to get one for her too. The little wood sorcerer smiled happily and headed off with a couple of children.

"It's amazing, isn't it?" said Tarkyn, smiling down at Sparrow. "It's only now, watching Midnight, that I can really see how much trouble that curse was causing."

Sparrow lost focus for a moment and then stared at Tarkyn. She blinked a couple of times then said, "Guess what? That was Midnight asking if I wanted berry or apple juice!"

Tarkyn boggled, *"Really?* In words? How does he know words?"

Sparrow shook her head. "No. Not in words, in images. But it's better than nothing, isn't it?"

"It's fantastic. He won't be so cut off now." Tarkyn thought for a moment. "I suppose that was part of the curse, cutting him off from everyone like that. I wonder if he'll regain his hearing or whether he'll be able to transmit words like you do, once he gets the hang of it." He smiled. "Interesting, isn't it? You'll have to experiment and tell me what happens."

"He won't know any words, will he?"

Tarkyn shook his head. "Not many. You can try teaching him some with your mind talking. You can pair a word with an image. Then just send the words. See if he can pick them up."

"It will be easy enough to check if he's still deaf, won't it?" said Sparrow. "I'll just sneak up behind him and clap."

"Yes. But don't do it while the other kids are around. The curse may be gone, but kids are still kids. I don't want them making fun of him."

49

W hile Tarkyn was playing with Midnight, Rainstorm had taken the opportunity to wander over to Ancient Oak and exchange notes on their progress. All in all, they were quite pleased with their work so far. But they had another little project underway and in pursuit of this, Rainstorm waited with Ancient Oak until Tarkyn rejoined them.

"Hi, Prince. Having fun with our little wood sorcerer, I see." He peered at Tarkyn. "You still look tired. Maybe you need a tree. Just thought you'd like to know that the lookouts are changing over, as we speak. I think they've moved back into their original positions now that the sun is lower in the sky. Do you think that's right, Ancient Oak?"

"Yes, I would think so," the woodman replied seriously. "Now, you'd better tell Tarkyn who's on for the next shift."

Tarkyn watched this discussion in some bemusement. Just as Rainstorm was about to launch into a recital of the names of the people on duty, Tarkyn waved him to silence. "Actually, Rainstorm, I don't really want to know."

Ancient Oak leaned towards his fellow woodman and said

sotto voce, "Once they are in role, he loses interest in who they are. Told me so himself earlier."

"No, I don't. Not anymore," said Tarkyn hotly. "I wave up at you when you're on duty, Ancient Oak." He frowned. "Just what are you two playing at?"

Rainstorm feigned surprise. "Why, nothing at all, Your Highness. We are just making sure you're kept informed of matters concerning our safety. I believe that was what you required."

"Rainstorm, when you start calling me Your Highness, I know you are up to tricks." The prince couldn't help a smile from playing across his face. "You know perfectly well that I don't want the name of every person on lookout duty or where they're standing."

"But, Tarkyn," protested Ancient Oak. He had thought of addressing Tarkyn by his title but decided it would be laying it on too thick. He was about to lay it on quite thickly, as it was. "You clearly have no faith in anyone else's judgement. So we must bow to the superior knowledge and experience that you have gained in your two months in the woodlands. Sadly, this will mean that you have to put a little effort into overseeing duty arrangements but at least we'll all feel safer for knowing that you, the only competent person among us, have things well in hand. Danton, with his notable lack of experience and training, will also be pleased to know you have taken over. Waterstone will be particularly relieved that he does not have to use his judgement and knowledge since it is well known that they are quite unreliable."

Tarkyn folded his arms and stared at them. There was fraught silence for a minute or two while he decided how to respond. Finally, he said mildly, "I gather I have offended a few people. Have I?"

"Far be it from us to question your judgement..." began Rainstorm.

"I think you have made your point," cut in Tarkyn dryly. "You can stop now. Instead you can advise me on how to repair the damage."

"Oh." Rainstorm was clearly nonplussed at this development.

Before Rainstorm could gather his thoughts, Ancient Oak said firmly, "I think you owe an apology to all of us who sought out those two sorcerers from the hunting party, especially Waterstone and Danton who were coordinating it. Rather than telling us off, you should have thanked us for our efforts and shown more faith in our judgement."

Tarkyn inclined his head courteously. "Thank you, you two, for bringing this to my attention. You could perhaps have done it less theatrically but I suppose that would have been less fun. Since I have you here, Ancient Oak, I can tell you now that I am sorry if I have upset you and thank you for your efforts in apprehending the two bounty hunters. I also acknowledge your superior knowledge and skill within the woodland. You may convey that to everyone else involved if you like, although I will re-address it with them when I see them."

This handsome speech left the two conspirators with absolutely nothing to say. After a few moments, Rainstorm said rather lamely, "Well, that's sorted then."

Just as they were about to turn the conversation to other things, Tarkyn added, "But just bear in mind when you're making your judgements that neither the other sorcerers nor I can join in with your mind talking and are prone to being isolated. Furthermore, I may have less bushcraft than you, but I have vastly more power and experience of sorcerers than you woodfolk and I want it used for everyone's safety, especially if there are outside sorcerers involved."

"Blast it, Tarkyn!" exclaimed Rainstorm in annoyance. "How come you always have the last say?"

Tarkyn laughed. "Years of court training." He looked from one to the other of the woodmen, "I think you two must have spent a lot of last night in each other's company under the influence of a great deal of wine. The air today seems to be thick with your intrigue." After a few moments' thought, his eyes narrowed. "Rainstorm, what have you been saying to Lapping Water?"

Rainstorm glanced at Ancient Oak then gave Tarkyn a cheeky little grin. "Why? What did you think I might have been saying to her?"

Tarkyn waved his hand. "Don't worry. Nothing. Sorry I asked. I'll leave you two to plot away on your own. I'm off to follow your advice and find a drink and a tree." Looking thoroughly discomforted, he stood up and strode off leaving two satisfied conspirators grinning in his wake.

50

U naware of the machinations about to take place among the younger woodfolk, Stormaway sat back with a freshly brewed cup of tea and blew on it to cool it.

"So, is your forest guardian living up to your expectations?" he asked of the group of sorcerers and woodfolk around him.

Waterstone gave a short laugh. "You're just fishing for compliments. You know he is. But we must also thank you for your part in it. In fact, I think you are an essential part of the forest guardian's power. Both with Pipeless and the storm, Tarkyn could not have assisted us without you." He tilted his head as he considered the wizard. "I can understand that your interest in the affairs of sorcerers takes precedence over our welfare. But remembering how you told me that your loyalty to Tarkyn overrode any feelings of compunction you might have had for instigating the oath, I am surprised how rarely you are at the prince's side when he is facing difficult situations."

Stormaway sipped his tea slowly, keeping his eyes on Waterstone. "I have already apologised to His Highness for staying away too long this time. As to the other occasions when you might have expected me to be standing by his side...I have deliberately kept away."

Autumn leaves frowned at him. "But I thought your job was to stand by him and advise him."

"Think back to when you were nineteen and first making your way in the world of adults. Would you have wanted an old man at your elbow guiding your every move? I think not." He gave a gentle smile. "The Tamadils are hard enough to handle, without deliberately antagonising them."

"He's not so bad," protested Running Feet. "He just loses his temper occasionally."

"He's not bad, provided you don't try to tell him what to do," rumbled Thunder Storm.

"Exactly," said Stormaway. "So, I save my advice for when it really matters." He shrugged. "Besides, how much respect would you have accorded a young lord, wet behind the ears in the ways of the forest, who was always reliant on his advisor?"

Waterstone looked at him with dawning respect. "So you forfeited your place at his side in his cause? Didn't you fear that he would not meet your expectations? I remember you saying that one man against a nation was uneven odds, even with the oath. Didn't you feel the need to protect him against us all?"

Stormaway studied his cup of tea. "Yes, I feared for his consequence and I didn't agree with some of his decisions." He looked up. "I'm sure you can remember a few occasions when I expressed my opposition, but I suspect you didn't realise that, on several of those occasions, His Highness used his power to direct private tidal waves of anger at me. He saved me the public humiliation of the full extent of his displeasure but still made his position abundantly clear." He shrugged. "But in the end, people must make their own mistakes and find their own ways to repair them if they can. I would find it very difficult to stand beside him without trying to interfere, while he made those mistakes. Besides, all I can ever do is state my opinion and provide knowledge and advice."

"I would have thought you were more controlling than that," mused Danton, used as he was to the deviousness of the politics around the royal family.

The wizard flashed a smile at him. "You are very astute, my lord. I am as controlling as I know how to be. Everything I do, particularly my recent sojourn at the encampment, is carefully considered to gain the greatest possible benefit for His Highness. Even when I oppose him, aware that I may have to endure a public berating for it, I know that fighting me will either challenge or strengthen his own decisions and make him stronger." Stormaway glanced around the woodfolk in the group deciding how much he could trust them before adding, "And sometimes his opposition to me has improved his image in your eyes."

Thunder Storm let out a sigh. "I don't know how you can risk inciting his anger like that. It makes me want to shrivel up and hide in a corner. I'm not used to anyone speaking to me as he does when he's angry."

Danton patted him on the back with a friendly smile. "That's royalty for you. It's the price you pay for the privilege of being near them."

"That's why we've never gone near Tormadell," put in Bean.

"Yeah, true," agreed String, "and look at us now. Stuck right in it."

"Bean, you may say that, but I remember last night you were prepared to risk Tarkyn's ire to protect him," said Waterstone with a smile.

Bean put down his empty cup and gave a wry smile. "You have to keep things in perspective. I mightn't like being on the end of a tongue lashing but it doesn't bother me enough to risk someone's life to avoid it." He shrugged. "Anyway, he seems to have forgotten all about it. So I think I got away with it."

Stormaway frowned. "He should have thanked you for it. I'm surprised at his lapse in manners."

String snorted. "As you say, that's royalty for you. Angry at you when you don't perform to expectation, ignore you when you do."

"I don't think that is fair, young man," snapped Dry Berry. "Tarkyn went through a very taxing experience on our behalf last night. He could barely stand up by the end of it, let alone address your social niceties." She waved her hand in the direction of the stream. "And look at him this morning. It's late morning and he still couldn't hold a conversation together, I suspect."

Bean nodded. "She's right, you know, String. Anyway, why should he thank us? We owe him one for allowing us to put our case to you woodfolk. And besides, we're just doing the same as all of you, serving our sovereign lord, whether we like it or not. Mightn't have been something we'd have chosen to do, but now that we're here and he's here...well, it's just part of the deal, isn't it?"

Despite his words, they all knew that the potential tongue lashing had been the least of the dangers he had faced when he gone to the support of his prince and that, in view of Tarkyn's clear instructions, he could easily have justified avoiding it.

"Bean, as his older brother, I would like to thank you," said Waterstone solemnly. "If you hadn't been there, I might have had to endanger the forest to be by his side myself. He needed you. He had begun to look very insubstantial and I am not sure that he could have returned to himself without your help." The woodman gave a bitter laugh. "There are times when the oath prevents us from helping him, serving him, whatever you want to call it, as much as we would like to. He told us in no uncertain terms that he would endanger himself to protect us as he saw fit, but yesterday he removed our right to endanger ourselves to protect him." Waterstone shook his head. "I'm going to have to talk to him about this. It's not good enough."

Thunder Storm smiled at him. "Go for it, Waterstone. You tell the prince what we'll put up with. He needs a firm hand like yours to keep him in line."

Danton's purple eyes surveyed them in some amusement. "So, you're going to bring him into line, are you, by insisting that you be allowed to serve him better? That's really telling him then, isn't it?"

A ripple of laughter greeted this sally.

"He's a feisty bastard," chuckled Running Feet, "but we wouldn't be without him. So, we want to be able to protect him, even if we don't have to."

Autumn Leaves turned to Stormaway and asked, "Are they all like that? Harsh at times but inspiring loyalty? What are his brothers like? And what was his father like, compared with him? Usually, I mean, not when we saw him in the forest."

"Danton will know better than I about Tarkyn's brothers now," replied Stormaway. "I haven't seen them for over ten years. When I last saw them, they were fifteen years old and competing in everything. They would never have roused your displeasure by preventing you from taking risks on their behalf. They would have assumed that you would be glad to die for them. They spent more time vying with each other than taking any notice of the people around them. They saw everyone as a tool or an audience to gain points in their ongoing competition with each other." A shadow crossed the wizard's face. "While Markazon was king, it was just friendly sport between brothers. But as soon as he died, the jackals gathered."

"Wouldn't there have been factions around the brothers before that?" asked Autumn Leaves.

Stormaway shook his head. "Not really. No one expected Markazon to die. The twins were still young and their father should have reigned for another twenty years or more. When Kosar ascended the throne, many people who had been friends with both of them, abandoned Jarand to work on gaining favour with the new king. Those who couldn't find a way in with Kosar, turned their attention to Jarand by sympathising with his loss and fuelling his understandable chagrin. To support their own interests, the lords of the land used the twins' rivalry to drive a wedge between them, and the brothers were too young to understand what was being done to them."

"And are Tarkyn's brothers any different now?" asked Bean. "It doesn't sound like it from all that I have heard."

Danton shook his head. "They are far worse. A childhood rivalry has been manipulated into an ongoing dangerous feud. They now hate each other, and with just cause. Each has worked against the other to destroy him. In public, they assume an icy courtesy towards each other that chills the blood to witness. Their betrayal of Tarkyn was one of only a handful of occasions when they have worked in concert."

"And how are they with their liegemen?" asked String.

Danton thought carefully before replying, "They are very similar to each other. Kosar is perhaps more authoritative, Jarand more silky and devious. But I suspect each would act as the other does, if their positions were reversed. They both anger easily and humiliate people at will, particularly if it will throw their brother's decisions or actions into a poor light. Because of their exalted status, the slightest smile or gesture of approval is received with fervent gratitude by their retainers. Everyone at court knows that their future life and prosperity depends on the whim of these two men. More than that, the prosperity and safety of courtiers' families depends on them as well." Danton shook his head. "No, I was not sorry to leave there. But many people thrive on that sort of treatment. They would lay down their lives willingly for the slightest sign of favour."

Waterstone smiled wryly. "You would lay down your life for Tarkyn. I know you."

Danton gave a gentle smile. "Yes, I would. Without a moment's hesitation. But not because Tarkyn threatens me or throws me the odd favour. In fact, by supporting him, I have placed my family at risk and I hope they don't pay a price for my loyalty to him."

"So, what has he done to inspire this degree of loyalty in you?" asked Bean. "I know he is a forest guardian and a legend for the woodfolk but as I understand it, your loyalty to him predates all of this and has lost you any influence you may have had at court and has effectively exiled you."

"Not to mention making me a figure of ridicule for the woodfolk," added Danton. He raised his hand as a wave of protest broke forth and shook his head, smiling. "It's no good denying it. You know perfectly well that it's true." He shrugged. "Anyway, to answer your question..."

"No, wait," intervened String. "Let me work it out." He waved his hand around the circle of woodfolk. "If this lot who were recently forced into his service are trying to make him accept more from them, one can reasonably assume that a lifetime of knowing him would inspire even greater dedication."

"Something like that. But there have been particular things he has done for me for which I could never repay him." Seeing them all waiting for further information, Danton sighed and dropped his eyes to stare steadfastly into his teacup as he remembered, "When I was first sent away from my family to the palace to go into Tarkyn's service, I was eight years old and he was six. I cried every day for a week." At the audible intake of breath that greeted this revelation, Danton glanced up in time to see shocked sympathy on the faces of his audience. He smiled wryly but didn't comment. "Every day, Tarkyn would bring me a new toy or a game to try to cheer me up. Eventually when none of this worked, he disappeared for half a morning and when he came back with his nanny in tow, he had a little fluffy puppy in his arms. He thrust it at me, stood back and smiled hopefully. Actually, to be honest, I didn't like dogs very much then, but I couldn't refuse his gift both because he had tried so hard and because of his position. We named that little puppy Rollabout. We named it together and played with it together and gradually I came to terms with losing my family." He shrugged. "And I suppose I transferred all the affection I would have given them onto Tarkyn. He was my staunch ally. He wouldn't let me take the blame for anything he had done."

"Obviously not," interrupted Autumn Leaves. "Not with his code of ethics."

"No, you don't understand. That was part of my role, to take his punishments. When he did something wrong, I was supposed to be held responsible, and berated or whipped for it."

There was another shocked intake of breath but Waterstone, who had discussed this with Tarkyn before, protested, "But Tarkyn told me himself that you were publicly berated when he had drunk excessively on one occasion. He let you take the blame then."

"We were older then and it was in court in front of the King and his courtiers. If Tarkyn had stood up to his brother in that forum, I would have been whipped or even imprisoned for his insubordination. There was nothing he could do. But he never let it happen again."

Dry Berry frowned. "So what happened when you were younger?"

Danton laughed at the memory, "Even as a chubby little

six-year-old, he was pretty feisty. When I was to be punished, he would stand in front of me, with his arms folded and a forbidding expression on his face. When his nanny or manservant tried to pull him aside, he would demand that they unhand him on pain of severe punishment. They were no more allowed to treat him disrespectfully as a six-year-old than they were as an adult, you see. Their only option was then to fetch his father, mother or brother who would remonstrate with him and would themselves remove him from in front of me."

"Then what would happen?"

Danton smiled. "Then I would be berated or flogged while Tarkyn stood by, yelling and crying and struggling to get away to protect me. He couldn't stand to see me suffer on his behalf. He would be absolutely beside himself."

"All a bit pointless though, I would have thought," remarked Autumn Leaves astutely. "You still ended up with the punishment and, I suspect, probably more for his unruly behaviour."

"True. I did. It took me a long time to get that through his stubborn little six-year-old head. But when he finally did understand what his actions were doing, he changed his tactics." He glanced at Waterstone. "I suspect you won't like what he chose to do next."

Danton stood up and poured himself another cup of tea from the big kettle hanging over the fire. Sitting down he blew on his tea before saying, "One day, soon after Tarkyn's seventh birthday, we were playing with Rollabout and, between the three of us, a precious antique vase was broken. Needless to say, it was I who stood to be punished for it. The dog was shooed outside, and Tarkyn and I were lined up in front of Old Laramar, Tarkyn's tutor, to be disciplined. I was told to take my shirt off and to stand facing the wall. Obviously, I was about to be flogged. Behind me, I heard Tarkyn grab the whip out of the old tutor's hand and order him away. I must admit I sighed to myself, knowing this would mean an even more severe punishment. Old Laramar left in high dudgeon and predictably, returned with a family member, this time King Markazon. I glanced at Tarkyn and shook my head slightly, hoping he would back down.

"And did he?" asked String.

Danton gave a short laugh. "Far from it. For a while he appeared to back down. He stood quietly to one side, which was unusual, and waited until Old Laramar was standing ready to whip me with the King supervising. Then Tarkyn threw up his shield and held out his arm to show the King that he was holding a razor-sharp piece of the vase pressed onto the skin of his forearm. He said that for every stroke of the whip, he would cut his arm once. His father glared at him for several long moments. The King ordered him to remove his shield and to behave, but Tarkyn met his stare and refused to comply. Markazon then turned away decisively and ordered Old Laramar to flog me.

"Even as the first stroke of the whip came down, I heard Tarkyn's voice, calm and strong, saying, "As you choose, father." The King whipped his head back around to see blood welling up from a cut on his son's forearm. Old Laramar had not been ordered to stop. So, as the second stroke hit me, Tarkyn cut himself again. Blood began to drip from his arm onto the polished parquetry floor but Tarkyn paid no heed. His intense amber eyes did not leave those of his father's. As Old Laramar raised his arm again, the King ordered him to stop and waved his hand in dismissal.

"The King yelled furiously at his little seven-year-old son, standing in his shield defying him. He roared that he could order Tarkyn's and, of course, my death as well, for such defiance. When Tarkyn realised that I could be put to death for his actions, he looked uncertain for the first time, but still he did not drop his shield. After a long silence, Tarkyn bowed low and when he straightened, trembling slightly, he finally replied, "Sire, we only broke a vase. And I have only tried to protect my friend. I have tried to be perfect so that he is never punished but I can't do it. I don't remember all the rules all the time, you see. I have tried and tried but I can't do it." Then he started crying but still he kept his shield up and kept the sharp piece of vase in his hand. And all this time, his blood was dripping onto the floor, beginning to pool at his feet. Markazon was clearly at a loss. He saw me watching and snapped at me to put my shirt back on and leave."

Danton took a sip of his tea.

"Well go on, what happened then?" asked Dry Berry impatiently.

Danton shrugged and smiled. "I don't know. I wasn't there, you see, and Tarkyn never told me. But from then on, I was not punished for Tarkyn's wrong doings. We were both just told off together."

"What about when Markazon died and Kosar took over?" asked Stormaway.

"No. Not until we were much older and there was that one incident that came to public notice. I think the brothers were too busy with their own affairs to concern themselves with events in the nursery. Besides, once Tarkyn had his own way, there were no more scenes and disputes, and fetching the family to override his misbehaviour. So there was no need to revise Markazon's decision."

Autumn Leaves was smiling hugely. "You have to hand it to Tarkyn. What a brave, loyal little fellow, to stand up to his father like that. Markazon was terrifying when he was angry. And no wonder the King had faith in his son when he came to us in the forest." He frowned. "But why, after all you had been through together and everything he had done for you, didn't Tarkyn realise he could trust you?"

Danton shrugged unhappily. "I don't know."

"I don't think he understands the effect he has on people; how much you and we are willing to do for him," suggested Waterstone. "And nothing in his behaviour has changed. He was willing to give everything to help you and now it is the same with us. But he never asked or expected you or anyone else to take risks by covering for him then, and he still won't allow us to do it now."

"There is a certain sublime arrogance about all that;" mused Bean, "insisting that he needs no one's help."

Waterstone shook his head. "No. I don't think it's that. He will accept help, provided it does not place anyone at risk. From what Danton has just told us, I think Tarkyn has spent his life making sure people don't suffer because of him. And he's still doing it now."

"If that's true, he must have hated the fact that we had been forced into the oath because of him," said Autumn Leaves. "No wonder he tried so hard to be accommodating."

"Yes, it all fits, doesn't it?" said Running Feet thoughtfully. "Well, I wish you luck, Waterstone, in trying to change it."

Waterstone grunted. "Hmm, could be a challenge, I agree. Still, he's changed other preconceptions, so I hold out some hope."

At this juncture, Tarkyn's message of apology came through from Ancient Oak. Waterstone's eyes gleamed with laughter as he relayed it faithfully to Danton, "Tarkyn says, and I quote, 'I am sorry if I have upset you and thank you for your efforts in apprehending the two bounty hunters. I also acknowledge your superior knowledge and skill within the woodland."

"What is Ancient Oak doing, demanding an apology from Tarkyn after all he did for us last night?" scowled Dry Berry.

"Different issue all together," said Danton with a smile. "I think Rainstorm and Ancient Oak had a lovely little plan to hand over the administration of lookout duty to Tarkyn if he didn't allow other people to take some responsibility."

Dry Berry shook her head disapprovingly. "You're pretty tough on him, you lot."

Waterstone suddenly roared with laughter. "Sorry, Dry Berry. But I think when you hear this, you will realise that it takes more than that to cow our forest guardian. Danton, Tarkyn added a small rider to his apology and I quote, 'Just bear in mind when you're making your judgements that neither the other sorcerers nor I can join in with your mind talking and are prone to being isolated. Furthermore, I may have less bushcraft than you, but I have vastly more power and experience of sorcerers than you woodfolk and I want it used for everyone's safety, especially if there are outside sorcerers involved.'"

Stormaway smiled fondly. "That's my boy. Takes the wind out of their sails but doesn't actually budge an inch."

Hard upon this remark, the man in question arrived in person, helped himself to a cup of tea and sat down next to a scruffy old mountain ash. Holding his cup in one hand, Tarkyn placed the palm of his other hand against the tree and took a deep breath to settle himself in. He looked around at them all. "You're all very quiet this morning. Don't tell me you're plotting too. I've been surrounded by plots for the last couple of hours."

"That wouldn't have been about lookouts at all, would it?" asked Autumn Leaves with a grin.

Tarkyn smiled. "Yes, and the rest." He waved a hand. "But

I won't bore you with the rest of it. Did you receive my apology, Waterstone and Danton?"

"Yes, thank you, and the rider," replied Waterstone evenly.

"Good. So that's settled then, isn't it?" asked Tarkyn, grinning. When neither Waterstone nor Danton replied, the prince's smile faded. "I really am sorry if I made you feel that I didn't trust your judgement." He took a sip of tea, "To be honest, I added the rider mainly to wind up Ancient Oak and Rainstorm. I must have caused quite a bit of discontent if they spent so much time planning today's little gambit. So I apologise." After this, he lapsed into silence and leant against the tree quietly sipping his tea.

Dry Berry peered at him. "You don't look too well, young man. Even after a quiet morning, you still look white and drawn. Perhaps you need another tonic."

"No, one in a day is as much as I can bear," said Tarkyn firmly. "The tree will sort me out." He looked around the group and spotted Bean. "Bean, I remember now. We have some unfinished business, you and I."

Murmurs of protest on Bean's behalf wafted around the group. Tarkyn frowned and they fell quiet. "I seem to be getting it from all sides today," he said, the last of his good humour evaporating. He addressed himself exclusively to Bean, "Sometime this morning, I remembered your remark about enduring another tongue lashing. I am sorry that you are finding it so difficult having to remain in close proximity with me. I will endeavour to keep out of your way as much as possible. I would like to thank you for your support last night. Without your hand on my shoulder, I might not have been able to pull myself apart from Pipeless. Clearly, I made a serious mistake in not accepting the support I was offered. I jeopardised the future of all woodfolk by refusing to allow anyone but myself to put themselves at risk. So, I thank you for the independent spirit that allowed you to risk my ire by coming to my rescue and I also acknowledge that many others of you would have done the same, were it not for the consequences of the oath." Tarkyn took a deep breath, put down his cup and stood up. "And now, I think I will go elsewhere for a while, where I don't have to keep apologising for every move I have made in the last forty-eight hours."

Before anyone could say anything, the prince strode off across the clearing and climbed up a steep path before being lost from sight behind a fall of boulders.

There was a strained silence. Finally, Running Feet said, "Looks like your point has already been taken before you even made it, Waterstone."

"Hmm, I think I was a bit severe about the rider to the apology," he replied thoughtfully.

"Oh, do you think so?" said Autumn Leaves sarcastically. "Forcing him to apologise all over again?"

Danton grimaced. "And perhaps we should have waited until we heard what he was going to say before we all jumped to Bean's defence."

"Definitely, I would say," agreed Bean.

"Absolutely," said String dolefully.

"I told you that you were being too tough on him," said Dry Berry acerbically. "He's worn out. Don't you realise that he's just become the greatest hero of our time and all you can do is complain about the things he hasn't done exactly as you would like? Where's that Rainstorm and Ancient Oak? I think I'll give them a piece of my mind too." She went out of focus to deliver a mental dressing down to the two hapless young woodmen.

"So now what are we going to do?" asked Autumn Leaves. "We can't leave him up there on his own, feeling that everyone is down on him. After all, if we're planning to have a proper celebration tonight to mark his achievement and the reunification of the woodfolk, it will be fairly pointless if he's not there."

"Who hasn't rubbed him up the wrong way today?" asked Running Feet. "Whoever that is, we can send them."

After a mental conference they worked out that for some reason, Rainstorm had reservations about everyone in the group of young woodfolk, that everyone in their own group had blotted their copy book and that children shouldn't be sent to do adults' work.

"Hmm," said Running Feet, "we really have side-lined him today if, between all of us, there is no one to approach him."

"What about Golden Toad or Falling Branch or Tree Wind?" suggested Danton.

"Any of them would be fine but leave it. I'll go after him," said Waterstone. "I'll just give him a few minutes to cool down first."

While this consultation was going on around the firesite, Tarkyn stumbled wearily up the rocky path, the spurt of anger that had propelled his footsteps out of the clearing long since dissipated. Now, with his tiredness threatening to overwhelm him, he smiled wryly at his over-reaction. But as he reflected on whether to stay away for a while or to return, he caught his foot and, with fatigue dulling his reflexes, fell heavily. He rolled to the right down a steep shale-covered slope and before he could gather his dulled wits, flipped over the edge of a rocky gully and plummeted to land heavily on a small ledge fifteen feet below the path. As he fell, his mind sent a brief cry of alarm before closing down on impact.

The first anyone knew of it was Midnight, running up to Waterstone and tugging anxiously on his sleeve. Being preoccupied with trying to sort out their plan of action to make amends with Tarkyn, Waterstone was inclined to be impatient but one look at the little boy's face caught his attention.

Midnight looked into his eyes and when he was sure Waterstone was focused on him, carefully sent an image of Tarkyn calling out.

Waterstone was so alarmed that he didn't even register that Midnight had communicated with him, "Where?"

Midnight watched Waterstone's lips and knew what he had asked but not the answer. He shrugged and waved vaguely in the direction Tarkyn had taken. Waterstone sent his mind out to see whether he could contact Tarkyn, all thought of a careful conciliatory approach forgotten. He checked with the lookouts but they had been scanning in another direction when Tarkyn fell. They were able to confirm that they could no longer see him, however.

Waterstone patted Midnight on the head to thank him then sprang into action, "Autumn Leaves, Running Feet, all of you sorcerers, gather as many people as you can find. Tarkyn has disappeared. He sent out a brief wave of distress or alarm, I'm not sure which, that only Midnight seems to have picked up. The lookouts have lost sight of him but can show us where they last saw him. I can't contact him so I think he's unconscious."

"Probably fallen. Unless a mountain lion has got him but he would have fought back, if it had been one of them," said Bean phlegmatically.

"Of course, if he's unconscious, one of them could get him now," added String ruminatively, sending frissons of fear down the spines of his listeners.

51

Down on the rocky ledge, Tarkyn gradually became aware of something soft and damp rhythmically stroking his face. He slowly opened his eyes and found himself gazing into the grey eyes of a silver fox. The fox froze. Tarkyn sent him a wave of reassurance and after a moment, the fox resumed his licking. Tarkyn closed his eyes and let the fox's gentle tongue soothe his aching face while he tried to figure out where he was.

At first, he thought he had fallen asleep again and wondered why his head and body were hurting and where the fox had come from. He wasn't in his shelter or beside the stream. Then he remembered heading up the rocky path. He frowned in bewilderment. He must have fallen over and hit his head. Slowly he opened his eyes and pushed himself up onto one elbow. The fox stopped licking and sat down beside him, staring into his eyes. After sending him a query, Tarkyn began to stroke him, as he thought about where he was. The path seemed different. He didn't remember the cliff on his left that towered above him and the tumble of rocks on his right also seemed unfamiliar. He shrugged, deciding that he had probably just not noticed, lost as he had been in his thoughts.

He lay down again while he decided what to do. Should he keep heading on up the path or should he return to the woodfolk? Realising that he was now feeling worse than ever, aching all over and still desperately tired, he decided that he had better return. Tarkyn was no longer angry with them. He realised now that his reaction had stemmed mainly from fatigue. He felt himself drifting off again but as the hand stroking the fox gradually stilled, the silver fox licked him a couple of times and then nudged him gently with his muzzle. Tarkyn tried pushing him away but the fox was insistent. Tarkyn sighed, dragged himself back to consciousness and sat up. The fox sat expectantly beside him. With a wry smile, Tarkyn resumed his stroking.

After a while, he gave the fox a final pat and stood up. He was surprised to find that he was still feeling quite shaken. Tarkyn brushed down the front of his shirt and leggings, noting a few rubbed patches and a couple of small tears but his mind couldn't be bothered with trying to figure out these anomalies. Instead, he straightened and turned to head back down the path. Again, he was surprised, this time to find that the path was less distinct than he remembered it and actually involved climbing over a succession of boulders to make his way back down. He shook his head slightly to clear it, which hurt. He was too groggy to remember that he could heal himself. Even if he had, it was uncertain whether he would have had sufficient energy to focus properly anyway.

Tarkyn carefully negotiated his way over a succession of boulders that rapidly carried him lower down the mountain, with the fox leaping from boulder to boulder at his side. After a few minutes, he stopped for a rest. His breath was coming in gasps and his head was spinning unpleasantly. The fox sat next to him, whined and licked his hand. Tarkyn summoned a smile and gave him a couple of perfunctory pats. He looked back up to where he had come from and realised that he had made considerable progress in a short time. It hadn't taken him long to walk up the path and felt that he should be back in sight of the woodfolk in another couple of minutes. He took a deep breath and pushed himself off onto the next boulder and on down the mountain on what he expected to be the final leg.

Several minutes later, Tarkyn stopped again, the rocks having led him deep into a gully and down to a steep mossy mountain stream. The fox sat down quietly beside him and waited. Tarkyn wondered whether this was the same stream that he had laid beside this morning. It didn't look like it but it might be different further along. He felt sure he should have reached the firesite by now. He decided to follow the stream down, carefully quelling his growing sense of panic, ruing his terrible sense of direction.

Before long, he was far enough down the mountain to be back in the thick of the pine forest. At last he heard voices and was just about to emerge from the trees, when he realised that the people in the clearing were sorcerers, not woodfolk.

Tarkyn drew back and stood quietly in the shadows studying them, just feet away. He looked around and realised the silver fox had disappeared. A sturdy middle-aged man was sitting against a tree sharpening his sword. His face was lined with sorrow, and his hands were rough from heavy toil. When he raised vivid blue eyes to respond to someone's question, it was clear that he was the group's leader. Two other men, both slightly younger but with a distinctive family resemblance, were moving about the clearing setting up bedding for the night. A woman sat beside the fire stirring a large pot while another sat against a tree, babe in arms. Two young teenagers, a boy and a girl, chased each other in between and around everyone, their laughter clearly trying the adults' patience. Their clothing was well made and of good, but not exceptional, quality. Tarkyn judged that they were probably reasonably well-to-do farmers or artisans.

Just as Tarkyn was pondering this unexpected development, the teenage girl catapulted out of the clearing, hotly pursued by the boy, and cannoned straight into the prince. The girl shrieked in fright and the boy skidded to a halt and shouted at the prince to unhand her.

Tarkyn spread his arms wide disarmingly and said quietly, "I am not holding her. If anything, she attacked me."

Hearing the commotion, all but the woman holding the baby rushed out to defend their young. Confronted by a bevy of belligerent sorcerers and mindful of his promise to Waterstone, Tarkyn flicked up his shield.

As soon as the leader saw the shield's colour, he leant in closer and stared, frowning, at Tarkyn.

"Stars above!" he exclaimed. "It's the prince. Come on, you lot! Show some respect. On your knees before His Royal Highness."

Without hesitation, every last one of them dropped to their knees and bowed their heads, hands on hearts. Tarkyn stood gazing down on them, a smile playing around his lips. It was a pleasant change to be given his due without question. With a sigh, he acknowledged to himself that it was probably based on a misapprehension.

After a moment, he said, "Before we go any further, may I ask whether you are aware of the events that occurred during and immediately after this year's Harvest Tournament?"

Without presuming to look up, the group's leader replied, "Yes, Your Highness."

"And yet I feel no fear emanating from you. Are you not

concerned for your safety to be in such close proximity to a rogue sorcerer?"

Eyes still firmly on the ground, the sorcerer replied, "No, Sire. I admit I am a little nervous but that is solely because I am unaccustomed to being in the presence of royalty, Your Highness."

"I see." Tarkyn shrugged and smiled, although none but the mother left in the clearing saw it. "Actually, I don't see at all but we will discuss this further. You may rise."

The seven sorcerers straightened up and stood waiting silently.

"I would like to know with whom I am dealing. So, you may introduce yourselves to me," said the prince formally.

Their leader inclined his head briefly. "I am Trey, Your Highness." He waved his hand in the direction of each person as he introduced them, "This is my wife Raitei, my son Lokley and daughter, Lorin. These are my twin brothers, Varga and Vaska. And over there with Baby Bo is Varga's wife and Raitei's sister, Raikel."

"Thank you. I gather you know who I am."

The teenaged boy began to shake his head but received a surreptitious cuff from one of his uncles. Tarkyn raised his hand slightly to quell Varga and spoke to the boy, "I beg your pardon, young man. I obviously assumed too much. I am Prince Tarkyn, youngest brother of the King and Lord of these Forests."

Lokley's eyes dilated and he sank back down onto one knee.

The prince smiled. "No, Lokley. You do not need to bow to me again. Once is enough for the time being. But thank you for the gesture." Feeling that he could not just walk away and that anyway, he didn't know where to go, Tarkyn waved his hand towards the clearing. "May I join you around your fire?"

Trey gave a shallow bow and replied, "It would be an honour, my lord."

There was some confusion as the sorcerers realised they were between Tarkyn and the clearing and didn't like to precede him. After a bit of manoeuvring, they fell back to either side to let him through first.

As he thanked them and walked between them into the clearing, still within his shield, the woman with the babe in arms began to gather her feet under her to stand up. "No, please stay where you are. Your baby looks settled and we would not like to disturb him, both for his sake and ours." The prince gave a slight smile before turning to speak to the others. "Shall we be seated?"

"Would you like some refreshment, Your Highness?" asked Trey. "We can offer you a cup of tea or a bowl of our stew if you are willing to wait awhile."

"A cup of tea would be most welcome," replied Tarkyn, sitting himself carefully against a log. Despite his care, his head still jolted and he frowned in pain. For a moment, his shield wavered, but he took a steadying breath and refocused enough to reinforce it.

Lokley peered at him. "You have hurt yourself, my lord. You have blood down the side of your face and a bruise on your temple."

Tarkyn raised his hand to his temple and gingerly felt the lump that had formed there. He brought his fingers down, sticky with blood and wiped them on the grass. "Not too bad, I think. I fell over," he explained shortly.

"That's quite a bump from just falling over," commented Varga slowly.

Varga, a thick-set stolid character, found himself being drilled by a pair of intense amber eyes.

"Do you doubt me?" asked Tarkyn quietly.

Varga replied, choosing his words carefully, "Your Highness, from your reaction, I do not doubt that is what you believe. However, from my experience, I would say you were either hit hard or fell from some high place. It is hard to imagine that bruising to be the result of a simple fall."

Tarkyn looked thoughtful. "Is that so?" When Varga went to speak again, the prince waved him to silence. "Just a moment. Let me think." After a few minutes, he said slowly, "I was walking along a path up the mountain. I was very tired from events yesterday and deep in thought. I missed my footing and fell... I remember now. I rolled down a slope..." He looked up. "Oh. That's why I couldn't find my way back. I slid over a drop and landed on the rocky ledge below. I'd forgotten that." He waved a hand. "I'm a bit foggy at the moment, to be honest."

"How big a drop, my lord?" asked Varga.

"Hmm, hard to say. Maybe fifteen, twenty feet. Quite a way, now I think about it. No wonder my head is hurting." He smiled ruefully. "I didn't realise until now that I wasn't still on the same path." He ran his hand through his hair. "How am I ever going to find my way back to them? I am completely lost."

"Perhaps they will find you," suggested Vaska, from the other side of the clearing.

Unexpectedly, Tarkyn grinned. "They will certainly be trying to. I came down the mountain over tumbled rocks, though. So, I think even they will have trouble following my trail."

"Perhaps when you have recovered, we can help you to retrace your steps," suggested Trey.

Suddenly, Tarkyn was viewing the campsite from above, through the boughs of a pine tree. His mind swooped into the clearing then climbed steeply until it was clear of the trees and viewing the forest from above. He could see the side of the mountain towering above him as he winged his way up towards its higher slopes.

Then the connection was cut and he found himself back in the clearing leaning against the log, his shield gone and Vaska leaning over him, staring into his face. Before thought, Tarkyn flicked his shield back up and watched Vaska's face tighten as he withdrew, clearly discomforted by Tarkyn's mistrust.

"Your pardon for coming too close to you, Your Highness," said the sorcerer stiffly. "For a moment, you seemed to lose consciousness and I was checking whether you were all right. I did not mean to alarm you."

"Thank you for your concern, Vaska. I was merely pre-occupied for a few moments."

Vaska frowned. "How do you know I'm Vaska? I was on the other side of the clearing when you closed your eyes."

Tarkyn smiled. "You forget. I have twin brothers myself. I am used to seeing the differences." Without even looking at Varga, Tarkyn said, "You are a little slighter, your hair is more bleached by the sun and the laughter lines are more noticeable around your eyes than Varga's."

"Very good, Your Highness. Not many people can tell us apart." Vaska exchanged a grin with Varga. "We won't be able to play tricks on this one, will we Varga?"

"Vaska, you forget yourself," came Trey's voice in reproof.

Tarkyn glanced over at the older man. "I only wish my brothers were as friendly to each other as these two seem to be."

Lorin brought over a cup of tea but stood holding it, not knowing how to give it to the prince while he maintained his shield.

Tarkyn thanked her and asked her to place it on the ground next to him. "Hmm, this presents a small problem, doesn't it? I can't get at my cup of tea without removing my shield. Perhaps now would be a good time to finish our previous conversation before my tea gets too cold."

Trey frowned. "In what way, my lord?"

"Why do you not fear me as a rogue sorcerer if you know about my exile? And why are you prepared to show me due respect?" Tarkyn narrowed his eyes. "I can feel no cunning or antipathy emanating from you but I am loath to trust my own judgement and lower my shield. Too many people depend on me."

"We do not trade in people, my lord," said Trey with an edge of anger in his voice. "No matter who you were, we would not trade a person in for a reward."

Tarkyn raised his eyebrows. "Indeed? And what if the fugitive had ransacked your holdings, raped your women and killed your children? What then?"

Trey shrugged. "Then if we caught him, we would kill him out of hand."

"And what if he had killed others but not those known to you?"

Trey met Tarkyn's gaze levelly. "Sire, I would not presume to exact revenge for someone else's loss. I am no vigilante. But I would protect and avenge my own."

Tarkyn became more specific, "And what if it transpired that you had kin among the palace guards who died?"

Trey gave this some thought before replying, "It would depend on the manner of their death, Your Highness. After all, a palace guard is paid to take risks. But I understand you acted in self-defence and did not actually fire on anyone. Is that correct, Your Highness?"

Tarkyn nodded and frowned. "And now we are back to where we began. How do you know this and how do you know that I am not a rogue? Only two weeks ago, I had a family cowering in front of me expecting me to kill them. What has changed?"

Before Trey could reply, Lorin broke into the conversation to say, "My lord, you could place your shield over us instead of yourself and then you could feel safe and reach your cup of tea." She smiled timorously as she waited for his response.

Tarkyn blinked as he adjusted his train of thought. He smiled, flicked a shield up around the family while maintaining his own. Then he released his own shield, retrieved his cup of tea, and then replaced his own shield before releasing the family.

It took only a matter of seconds for the whole operation, by the end of which he was grinning hugely. "Now there's caution for you. You're a clever young lady, aren't you, to think of that?"

Varga and Vaska were wide-eyed. "That was amazing. You used two shields at once," said Vaska.

Tarkyn beamed. "Yes, I was quite pleased with that too. I haven't done that particular trick before."

"But I've never seen anyone perform two spells of any sort simultaneously before," said Varga.

"No, neither have I," replied Tarkyn, smiling. "I managed to hold off a whole party of nine sorcerers sent to track me down because I could do more than one spell at once. Look, I'll show you."

He sent a bronze ray through his shield and blasted a small hole in the ground, well to one side of the sorcerers.

"Wow, that's great!" Vaska's enthusiasm finally began to override the air of constraint that had pervaded the clearing since the prince's arrival. "We heard about them. We feared for your safety. So tell us how you held off so many...if you don't mind."

By the time Tarkyn had finished telling them the story and everyone had laughed at the image of Tarkyn riding Danton in the air, the sorcerer family had relaxed and were talking naturally to him as though he were one of their own. Tarkyn noted this with mixed feelings, reflecting that the princely air of aloofness that he had nurtured all his life seemed to have deserted him with sorcerers as much as with woodfolk. A thought struck him. "How did you know about that hunting party? It's less than a week since I faced them."

Trey replied, "There are many people keeping an eye on your affairs, my lord. As you probably know, the rumours about you were dire when you were first exiled. I'm actually surprised you survived unscathed. Everyone was out for your blood." The big man walked to the fire and poured himself a cup of tea. "But recently, a new version of events has washed across the countryside. Rumours of you saving a family from bandits at the Great West Road have spread and questions about what actually happened at the Harvest Tournament were raised. Suddenly everyone was asking how you could win a tournament you had already destroyed. That just didn't make sense. Then word spread of your visit to Lord Tolward and a new version of the events in the Great Hall was on everyone's lips. Nothing else has been talked of in taverns across the country for the last fortnight."

"I see." A smile played around the prince's mouth as he recognised the work of Stormaway Treemaster and Lord Tolward. He casually waved away his shield, stood up and stretched, feeling his muscles protest. "Don't get up," he said. "I am merely changing position." Tarkyn moved to a spot further along the log where he could reach a large fir tree at the edge of the clearing. He settled back against the log and placed his palm firmly against the trunk of the tree. After a moment while he focused on connecting himself to the fir tree's strength, he said, "This, of course, changes nothing in terms of my value if I am turned in. No doubt a reward is still posted for my capture."

Trey looked uncomfortable. "I believe that is so, my lord. However, a huge groundswell of support for you is spreading across the land. People are outraged at the treatment dealt you by your brothers. There is little love for Kosar and Jarand as it is, but now their betrayal of you has provided a focus for everyone's discontent."

"Oh dear," said Tarkyn with a sigh.

Trey frowned. "But Your Highness, are you not pleased? Everywhere people are preparing to back you to wrest the throne from King Kosar. We want you to be our king."

"Hmm." There was a long pause while Tarkyn thought out what to say. Finally, he said, "I am honoured that people, and you in particular, would accept me as your king. However, if the people have turned their opinions so radically in a fortnight, no doubt they could just as easily turn them back again." He shrugged. "After all, they have just spent two months crying out for my blood." Tarkyn shook his head. "I think I will wait to see how long their latest stance endures. Will their sudden-found faith in me survive a new set of rumours if my brothers devise some new story? They were quick to believe my brothers the first time. Why not again?"

A gentle woman's voice addressed him. He turned to see Raitei speaking. "I can see you have been hurt, Your Highness. And perhaps you are angry that no one stood by you. But you cannot blame people for supporting and trusting their king. That is how things should be. It is a mark of the esteem in which you are held that anyone was prepared to give consideration to the possibility that the king had given out false information."

"And that the facts about the tournament didn't add up," returned the prince acerbically. "If not for that, it is quite possible that no one would have believed Lord Tolward's story."

Raitei shook her head. "No. The official version only ever held water on the premise that you had undergone some sort of breakdown. Once Lord Tolward bore witness that you were not a rogue sorcerer, the King's story lost all credibility."

"Hmm. This is all very flattering but no one thought to ask me my intentions in all of this." Tarkyn ran his hand through his hair. "Lorin, could I have another cup of tea please?" He smiled as she dropped him a little curtsy and took his cup to refill it. He returned his attention to the adults. "I have no wish to be king. Why should I usurp my brother, assuming that I could?"

The sorcerers looked at each other in confusion.

"But surely, Your Highness, you would want to avenge the wrong done to you?" asked Trey.

Tarkyn shook his head. "No. Not at the cost of countless lives. I have no intention of making my supporters pay with their lives by seeking out revenge on my behalf. And my being slighted does not require a kingdom as recompense."

"You are very generous, my lord," said Raikel from where she was sitting with her baby.

"No, it is not generous to regard other people's lives as having value beyond their relationship with me and my family. If I decide to take issue with my brothers for the wrong, they have done me, it will be between them and me only."

Lorin returned with Tarkyn's cup of tea and handed it to him. He was slightly surprised when she sat down against the log right next to him but smiled down at her, nevertheless. "Thank you for the tea."

She smiled up at him but said nothing.

"How old are you, Lorin?"

"I am thirteen years old, Your Highness. So is Lokley. We are also twins."

"Is that right? Twins run in your family, do they?"

Lorin nodded. "But Trey's twin was killed."

Tarkyn turned his gaze to Trey. "I am sorry to hear that. You carry your sorrow on your face. I wondered what had caused it."

"Prince Jarand's bullies are what caused it," said Trey bitterly. "First, brigands swept through our village looting from us at knife point. Then, just as we had mustered ourselves to drive them out, along came Prince Jarand's vigilantes. They finished what we had started and chased the brigands out of the village but then they returned and demanded that we join their ranks. When we refused, they became angry and threatening." He sighed. "Trask was always hot-headed and provocative. He abused and taunted them until one young officer cracked and drove him through with his sword. It all happened so fast. As soon as Trask fell, the older officer roared at his men and ordered them out of the village. As he left, he gave us twenty-four hours to make up our minds and as an afterthought, flung an apology over his shoulder ... But that didn't bring back Trask."

"And that is why you are now here in the forest?"

Trey nodded. "We do not want to become vigilantes like them. They said they would destroy our houses and our stores if we did not join them. We could not risk our children's lives. And so we fled."

"So, Your Highness, what about the misery your brothers' rivalry is wreaking on sorcerers across the country?" demanded Varga. "If you do not want to challenge the king on your own behalf, do you not care for the people of Eskuzor?"

Tarkyn took a deep breath. "I do care about the suffering that is being caused by my brothers. Most deeply. But if I throw myself in front of a poorly organised makeshift army of supporters, Eskuzor will have civil war, not between two factions, but between three. I am not so vain that I think the entire nation would flock to my standard. They would not. Many powerful lords have vested interests in supporting either Kosar or Jarand."

"I think you would make a very good king, Your Highness," said Lorin softly.

Tarkyn glanced down to find her gazing up at him, her eyes shining. His eyebrows twitched and he resisted the impulse to pull away. "Thank you, Lorin," he said dryly. He looked up to see Varga and Vaska smiling sympathetically and Trey's cheeks tinged red with embarrassment at his daughter's behaviour.

Tarkyn cleared his throat. "As I was saying, I cannot see an easy solution to this."

"Then, you will not help us?" said Raitei sadly.

"I did not say that." Tarkyn's voice held an edge of annoyance. "I said I do not wish to be king and that civil war will cause more damage than good. But I will not abandon you. I just do not yet know what to do." As he was speaking, he put his hand up to feel his temple. "Ah, that's better," he said, pulling his hand away from the tree. "And I think at last I have regained my strength."

Lokley leaned forward and stared at him. "Your bruising has gone!"

"Not green, am I?" asked Tarkyn anxiously.

Lokley frowned. "No. Why would you be?"

Tarkyn shrugged and smiled. "Just a little tendency I have; to turn green when I have taken too much power from the trees."

"You may not be a rogue, Your Highness," remarked Vaska, "but you are a little unusual."

Suddenly an image appeared in Tarkyn's mind of the clearing surrounded by woodfolk. Without turning his head, he could see where each of them was waiting for him, stationed in the fir trees and behind bushes. His face relaxed into a wide smile.

"My friends, I must leave you shortly. But before I do, I would like to know that you will be safe. Do you have enough food? Where are you going? What will you do?"

Trey shook his head. "We have a few provisions with us but they will not last us long." He shrugged. "As to what we will do or where we will go, we do not know. We are running from, not running to." He gave a tight smile. "When I saw you, I had hoped that you would take us into your service and fight with us against the troubles that beset us."

Tarkyn stood up and waited until they too were standing. "I will take you into my service but not to stand by my side. And I will fight for you, but not now and not by main force. I will provide you with directions to Lord Tolward's house and a letter of introduction. I will also ensure that you have sufficient provisions for your journey to the grasslands. Just a moment." He closed his eyes and sent a request for Danton to come to him. When he opened them, he found that the whole sorcerer family had sunk to their knees.

"Thank you, Your Highness," said Trey. "We are truly honoured to be accepted into your service and will do all we can to further your cause."

Tarkyn received an image of woodfolk grinning with mirth all around him. He gave his head a little shake and returned his attention to the people kneeling before him.

"Please rise. Thank you for your loyalty but please remember that you will not further my cause by plotting to make me king. You will further my cause by looking after yourselves and working to protect all sorcerers."

As he finished speaking, Danton walked into the clearing and bowed. "You asked for me, Your Highness?"

Vaska frowned. "You are certainly most magical, Your

Highness, much more so than any other sorcerer I have met. How did you summon your retainer?"

Ignoring the question, Tarkyn smiled. "Allow me to introduce Lord Danton. He is more skilled than I with directions and will hopefully be able to explain to you how to reach Lord Tolward's holding. Danton?"

"Yes, my lord. I believe I can do that."

As Danton explained the route they would need to take, Stormaway arrived rather breathlessly and grumbled at Tarkyn, "Your Highness, these climbs up and down mountains are not good for a man of my advanced years. I am to tell you that if these sorcerers remain here for the night, provisions will be delivered to them before morning."

"Thank you, Stormaway. I apologise for your inconvenience."

"Hmph. I think you have done enough apologising for one day."

Before long, all arrangements had been made and it was time to leave.

"Thank you for your tea and for the news of support that you have brought me. Please do not try to follow me. I promise I will visit you at Lord Tolward's in the spring."

Just as the prince was leaving the clearing, Lorin ran up to him with a small brooch in her hand. She curtsied and offered it to him. "Please accept this as something to remember me, us, by."

Trey frowned furiously in the background, but Tarkyn's eyes twinkled as he accepted it solemnly. "Thank you, Lorin. I will keep it to remind me of my promise to protect the sorcerers of Eskuzor."

52

As soon as Tarkyn, Danton and Stormaway were out of sight and earshot of the sorcerer family, String, Bean and woodfolk appeared all around them.

Tarkyn beamed. "Hello everyone. I am so glad to see you all. I'm sorry if I worried you. I got lost, you see. I fell over a ledge and when I came to, I didn't realise I wasn't on the same path." He looked around. "Where's Waterstone? Waterstone, I know I didn't have my shield up when you arrived but I promise you I had it up for a long time until I was completely sure they were safe." He told them about his machinations with the two shields just to reach his cup of tea. He laughed. "You see, I didn't take any chances, even though it meant making an absolute idiot of myself."

Waterstone smiled and thumped him on the back. "I'm glad to see you too. You frightened the life out of us, disappearing like that. String had us all worried you would be eaten by a mountain lion while you were lying unconscious."

"I wouldn't worry too much if I were you. I had a helpful

little silver fox who licked me back to consciousness and stayed with me until I was near people."

"I don't think a fox would beat a mountain lion," said Ancient Oak doubtfully.

Tarkyn smiled. "No, but there are always the eagles. I suspect the forest is looking after me, don't you?"

Waterstone regained his attention. "Tarkyn, we're all sorry we were too hard on you back there."

Tarkyn waved his hand. "Don't give it a second thought. I just had a short fuse because I was so tired. Once I woke up from my fall, I was trying to come down the path to rejoin you. That's why I'm down the mountain, not up. Anyway, I've been sitting with my hand against a fir tree for the last hour or so, so I have finally recovered." A few minutes later he frowned. "This seems to be taking a long time."

"You were miles away, Tarkyn, and in a completely unexpected direction. Way off to the west and nearly off the mountain altogether," said Running Feet with a smile.

"So how did you find me? I was worried you wouldn't be able to track me across those boulders that I climbed over."

"We were struggling, to be honest," said Autumn Leaves. "For the first part, you had left a few drops of blood here and there but when that stopped, we couldn't trace you." He glanced sideways at Danton. "Even our elite guard had no more success than we did." He shrugged. "We spread out and were just organising a methodical hunt when a large crow swooped down and sat near us on a rock. To begin with, we didn't take much notice but it cawed and ruffled its feathers until it had our attention. As soon as we were watching, it flew a short distance and landed on another rock just out of reach. Then it cawed and ruffled its feathers again until we moved in its direction. It waited until we were much closer than most birds would allow, before taking off and flying a short distance away to repeat the performance all over again. Eventually, it led us to you."

Tarkyn thought back. "I saw that crow. It gave me its view of the clearing and flew above the trees to show me where we were but as you can imagine, it meant nothing to me. I had no idea where I was. When I didn't respond, it must have flown off to fetch you." He gave a grunt of laughter. "Hmm. There you are, you see, the forest looking after me. That's a new one, isn't it? It's the first time an animal has tried to communicate with you on my behalf, without my direct input. Interesting."

"And did you hurt yourself badly?" came Lapping Water's soft voice from the side and slightly behind him.

Tarkyn's stomach turned over and he felt his cheeks redden. He hoped the early evening gloom would cover him. He caught his breath, looked around and said in what he hoped would be a casual tone of voice, "I did a bit of damage to myself." His voice seemed quite scratchy all of a sudden. He cleared his throat and tried again. "I had quite a hefty bruise on my temple and some blood on my face. I thought I had just fallen over but Varga, one of the sorcerers back there, was sure that I must have fallen a long way or been hit. That's when I remembered I had fallen over that little cliff." He cleared his throat again. "I fixed myself up using the fir tree. I hope I'm not green again. Am I?"

Lapping Water smiled and shook her head. "You look fine to me."

"Do I?" he asked hopefully. Tarkyn gave his head a little shake and chastised himself for reading things into simple remarks. "Oh good," he said in a more prosaic tone of voice, "then I didn't overdo it."

As they neared the firesite, Rainstorm appeared on the path ahead, with Sparrow on one side of him and Midnight on the other. Rainstorm smiled and mouthed, "Hi, Prince," from a distance while the children dragged themselves away from him and ran down the path to throw themselves simultaneously into Tarkyn's arms. Tarkyn staggered backwards under the impetus but with the assistance of several hands, managed to keep his feet and settle Midnight and Sparrow onto a hip each. He grinned and hugged them as they both threw their arms around his neck and nearly strangled him.

"Hi, Sparrow. Hi, Midnight. Aagh. Did you miss me?" he managed to squawk out of his squashed throat as he sent an accompanying image to Midnight. This resulted in an even tighter stranglehold on his neck as they both laughed and gave him an even bigger hug. "Oh stop. I'm dying," he gasped, sending them both an image of himself with crossed eyes struggling for breath. He gradually infused a genuine plea into his image that made them release their stranglehold on him. "Hurumph. Thanks." By this time, he had drawn level with Rainstorm. "Hi, Rainstorm. Have you been on babysitting fatigue? Well done. I'm glad these little treasures were left in good hands," he said, successfully overriding any chagrin Rainstorm may have felt at being left behind.

As they reached the firesite, a cheer went up from the assembled woodfolk and many came over to clap him on the back. Tarkyn looked around and realised there were plaited garlands of flowers and foliage strewn around the clearing.

He swung Sparrow and Midnight down and raised his eyebrows. "Well, this is a surprise. What's all of this in aid of, then?"

Dry Berry stepped forward and proclaimed in a loud voice, "Tonight we celebrate the lifting of the curse," she waited for the cheers to subside before continuing, "and the restoration of the mountainfolk into the woodfolk fold." After more cheering, she finished with a flourish, "And above all, we celebrate the courage, skills and good will of Prince Tarkyn, Stormaway

Treemaster and Midnight, to whom we owe the future of our woodfolk nation." Such a resounding uproar greeted this last statement that Tarkyn feared the mountains would be ringing with woodfolk cheers. He glanced sideways at Stormaway who placed his finger surreptitiously beside his nose, so as not to interrupt the revelry. Reassured that the sound was being masked, Tarkyn gave himself over to the enjoyment of the evening.

X

ACROSS THE MOUNTAINS

53

W aterstone took a good draught of his wine. "Now Tarkyn, there is something we have all been wondering about..." he said, glancing at Danton.

Tarkyn eyes twinkled as they moved from one to the other. "Go on. This has sprung from yet another gossip session, no doubt."

It was that mellow time of night when reminiscences are exchanged and people's defences are a little more malleable.

"Pretty much." Waterstone waved his mug around. "So what we were wondering was: After you went to such extremes as a young lad to protect Danton, why would you have any doubts about his loyalty?"

The woodman immediately received a hard jab in the ribs and looked around to see a red-faced Danton beside him, grimacing for him to be quiet. Waterstone gave a little chuckle. "Too late now," he whispered.

Tarkyn watched this interchange with some amusement before turning his attention to the question. He glanced at Danton. "I don't know how much Danton has told you but, just to provide me with companionship, he was dragged away from his family to live in the palace among strangers. Worse than that, when he got there, he became my whipping boy."

"But you stood up to Markazon as a little seven-year-old and even hurt yourself to save Danton from being flogged." Waterstone frowned quizzically. "Didn't you think Danton might have been grateful for that?"

Tarkyn shook his head and, with a little smile, stood up to look for another flagon of wine. When he returned, he poured everyone another drink and handed out some hazelnuts he had found on the way back.

Waterstone persisted, "Why not?"

"Why should anyone be grateful for only having to face the consequences of their own actions just as anyone else in the population does?" countered the prince. "Danton didn't owe me anything for that. I could hardly profess to be his friend and allow that to continue. The way I saw it, I was still in his debt for the misery he had endured because of me." His smile broadened. "Sorry, Danton, I realise now I should have trusted you all the way along. When we were younger, I did trust you unquestioningly. But as we grew older, you became more involved in the machinations of the royal court and became answerable more to the king than to me." He shrugged. "After all, when I last saw you in Tormadell, we were both loyal to the king. How could I assume that you would foreswear your allegiance to the king to come after me?"

"The trouble with you, Tarkyn Tamadil," said Danton emphatically, "is that you had no idea how much it meant to me, that you were willing to undergo such pain on my behalf."

Tarkyn was unimpressed. "You did it for me often enough."

"But I didn't choose to. My father forced me to the palace and your retainers forced the pain on me. But you did have a choice. So, when you put yourself on the line for me against your father who, as far as I was concerned, was the most fearsome person in the world, holding life and death in his hands, well...words fail me." Danton's voice had become husky and he took a hefty draught of wine. After a moment he said, "And, Tarkyn, I had to become involved in court intrigue to protect you, as best I could, from schemers. Not saying I didn't enjoy it. You know I love the intricacies of political and social manoeuvring. But it was always with your welfare in mind."

Tarkyn clapped Danton on the back. "Oh my poor friend, we have both been misused by our families in their quests for power. You, I suppose, at least gained a life in the royal household from it, whereas I lost one." He considered the young sorcerer. "And now you have thrown it all away." He took his hand from Danton's back and holding his wine cup in both hands, gazed sombrely into the dark liquid. After a while, he said quietly, "You know, I really do thank you for doing that, Danton. And when I think how much you love the gaiety and glitter of court..." He lifted his eyes and brought them to bear on Waterstone. "It would be like you never being able to see your forests again."

Waterstone raised his eyebrows and let out a low whistle, "That is impressive. I hadn't thought about it like that. I don't know whether I could do that – leave the forest behind to follow you, assuming I had the choice."

"You couldn't," said Tarkyn flatly. "Not if you couldn't return. You have Sparrow and Ancient Oak and everyone else. You couldn't leave them." He paused. "But Danton has left behind more than the glitter of court life. He too has left behind friends and family." The prince turned to regard his sorcerer friend. "Danton, I fear I have been far too harsh with you. If you don't mind, Waterstone, I will revoke the requirement that Danton must wear woodfolk clothing. It is all you have left to you to remind you of home. I think I have been too cruel in removing that as well."

Danton bowed his head in acknowledgement. "Thank you. But I do not think you cruel, Tarkyn. You were very lenient in the circumstances at the time. I feared much worse retribution." His voice cracked and he rose unsteadily to his feet. "And now, if you'll excuse me for a few moments."

Danton walked off into the gloom beyond the firelight. On his return, Tarkyn and Waterstone fully expected him to be dressed in one of his own colourful outfits. But such was not the case. When they expressed their surprise, he smiled at them. "No, I would not be so quick to insult your woodfolk clothing. Besides, now that I can choose not to wear them, I realise I have grown to like them."

As he sat down, Waterstone handed him a filled cup of wine and raised an eyebrow in query. Danton shrugged and gave a wry smile. "My feelings overcame me."

"Is it so lonely living among us?" asked Waterstone in some concern.

Suddenly Danton grinned. "No. Not at all."

"So, what were you upset about?"

"I was overcome by Tarkyn's acknowledgement." Danton chuckled, even as new tears sprang to his eyes. "And I knew you would think I was an idiot. So I went away."

Waterstone blinked at him and shook his head.

Danton laughed. "But now I think about it, I quite like being made fun of by you lot. I think it's developed into a bit of a game. So maybe next time, I'll stay and wear it."

5 4

Despite the late hour, children were still running joyously around the outskirts of the adults, playing hide and seek, and chasey. Creaking Bough detached herself from the main party and rounded up Trickling Stream and Rain on Water, ready to put them to bed. When she raised her eyebrows at Midnight to ask whether he too was ready for bed, he beamed at her and shook his head. But a few minutes later, when Sparrow wandered over to sit on her father's knee, Midnight's mood suddenly flipped, as moods sometimes do near the end of parties, from happiness to loneliness. After a few moments, he drew a breath to steady himself and followed Sparrow to sit himself quietly in Tarkyn's lap between Waterstone and Danton.

Tarkyn was chatting and absent-mindedly gave the little boy a hug as he arrived. Midnight lay his head against Tarkyn's broad chest and felt it vibrating as the prince talked with his friends. He felt safe and knew that Tarkyn cared for him and yet, as he thought back over his father's curse and what he had endured because of it and his mother's ill treatment, he was overwhelmed with self-doubt as he failed to find any justification for Hail's continued absence. He came aware that Tarkyn was looking down at him anxiously. He felt his hair being stroked and a query appeared in his mind. With a little sigh, he sent Tarkyn an image of Pipeless' blue magic destroying people's warped memories followed by an image of Hail with his feeling of expectancy. Then he sent an image accompanied by a query, of Hail fading away until she disappeared. His breath hitched as he strove to keep in his tears.

He tensed himself to run off into the darkness, but Tarkyn's arms tightened around him. Filled with self-dislike and disappointment, Midnight struggled to get away so that he could lick his wounds in solitude. As he encountered an uncompromisingly firm strength holding him, a red mist of rage enveloped him, and he strained and twisted against Tarkyn's arms, jabbing Tarkyn's chest with his elbows and kicking out at his folded legs, thrusting all the pent up resentment at the people who had hurt him into every vicious movement. Despite his continued savagery, no peremptory command came down to stop him and his attack was not met with any reprisal, but the firm hold on him did not slacken.

Gradually, his anguished mind became aware of a soft stream of understanding, warmth and comfort washing into its turmoil. And then, since he couldn't get away and could no longer hold in his distress, he collapsed like a burst balloon and sobbed out his years of misuse against the one sure rock in his universe. The strong safe arms stayed circled around him and Tarkyn's head bent to rest on top of his. He felt the firm rhythm of a hand stroking his back and slowly his misery played itself out. He felt Tarkyn's chest vibrating again but did not know that Tarkyn was explaining Midnight's reactions and requesting a search for Hail to be instigated.

"Why didn't you use your *Shturrum* spell on him?" asked Ancient Oak who had come to join them when he saw Midnight lashing out. "You'll have bruises all over you now."

Tarkyn looked down for a moment at the little boy who now lay sleeping in his arms and stroked his hair. He gave a wry smile. "I felt the odds were stacked far enough in my favour, without having to resort to magic or rank. I wanted to use the least force possible to keep him contained." He met his wood brother's eyes. "I don't really want it to become a battle of wills. He is a strong little character and he's needed every last bit of his strength to survive until now. I wouldn't want that strength turned against me, I mean, truly against me and I wouldn't want to squash it into submission either."

Waterstone watched this exchange through narrowed eyes. Tarkyn glanced at him and knew he was thinking that this was the same attitude the prince brought to his dominion over the woodfolk. Tarkyn gave a little shrug and was rewarded with a derisive grunt.

"Any better suggestions, Waterstone?" he asked quietly.

"No. But it's unnerving to discover how calculated you are in your dealings with people," said Waterstone.

Tarkyn gave a grunt of laughter. "Huh. I have two things to say to that. To start with, when you first watched me talking to Stormaway, you realised I knew how to deal with people and secondly, most of the time I go by instinct, not by careful calculation. It is only when someone asks me a question as Ancient Oak just did, that I formulate what I'm doing."

Waterstone's face relaxed. "Fair enough, my young friend. I think you handled Midnight very well just then. I was wondering when all that ill-treatment was going to surface in him. The fact that there's a reason for it doesn't remove all his years of misery, does it?"

"No, but at least it makes their memory more bearable,"

said Tarkyn. "It is a shame that Hail has not stayed to be with her son. He feels she must hate him anyway if lifting the curse has not brought her closer to him."

Danton grimaced. "He might be right. After all, in her mind, he is irretrievably linked with Pipeless' rape of her, isn't he?"

Tarkyn nodded. "Yes, but since he doesn't know about that, he thinks that it must be him."

"It's tricky." Waterstone shook his head. "And I don't know how much use it will be to insist that she comes back and faces him."

"Well, you know Waterstone," replied Tarkyn grinning. "in that manipulative little way I have, I wasn't going to let her loose with Midnight until someone, not necessarily me, had talked to her first. But I think we should try, for Midnight's sake."

Just then String, Bean and a group of mountainfolk trappers joined them. Tarkyn noticed that the trappers wore an assortment of furs like String and Bean rather than the standard woodfolk attire. Bean waved his hand. "There are so many places she could have gone, it will be difficult to find her, particularly if she wishes to remain hidden."

"Yeah, true. Not hard to hide up in these mountains, if you want to," added String dolefully.

Tarkyn looked at the mountainfolk trappers. "Can any of you contact her at the moment?"

The mountainfolk trappers went out of focus for a few minutes, letting their minds range through the nearby mountains but then shook their heads.

Tarkyn looked Waterstone. "So, does that means she's unconscious or sleeping?"

"Not necessarily. It did when we tried to contact Rainstorm and Summer Rain because we knew they would want to reply, but in her case, she may have shielded her mind if she doesn't want to be contacted."

Tarkyn looked around the group. "So, what can we do? Just wait until morning and then go looking for her?"

A gnarled old mountainfolk trapper growled, "Not much point, even then. If she doesn't want to be found, she won't be. I am Growling Bear." He handed Tarkyn a stone flask. "Here. Try a bit of that. It's a bit rough but keeps you warm. You seem a little tied up at the moment to get your own."

Tarkyn grinned. "Thanks." He slugged down a good mouthful from the flask before spluttering and coughing. "Oh my stars! A *bit* rough! My throat's on fire."

Growling Bear smiled evilly. "Yeah, but you're warm all the way down your chest now, aren't you?"

Tarkyn nodded, tears starting from his eyes as he struggled to regain control of his voice. "Aagh. Yes, I am but I'm not sure it was worth it."

"Aw, go on!" exclaimed another trapper. "After facing that shade yesterday, you won't convince any of us that you can't take a little drink. Here! Have another swig. I am Sliding Shale."

Tarkyn took a more judicious sip this time and managed not to cough.

"There you are, you see," said Sliding Shale with some satisfaction. "You're getting used to it already. Much longer up in these cold mountains and you wouldn't be able to live without it."

Tarkyn smiled weakly. "Thanks. That might be enough for now." He handed back the stone flask. "I wouldn't want to deprive you boys." A beatific little smile appeared on his face. "Hmm, I do feel warmer, I must say. Perhaps I could have just one more..." He stopped mid-sentence and went very still.

"What is it?" asked Waterstone.

"The brew has knocked him out," whispered someone, followed by a couple of guffaws.

Tarkyn shook his head and blinked. "Whoa! I've just been deluged by a huge wave of self-loathing and despair." He frowned as he thought about it. "Something else too. I don't know, some sort of desperate determination."

"Any images?" asked Waterstone.

"Wait. Let me tune in." Tarkyn closed his eyes and let his mind drift towards the source of the emotions. He found himself looking out across a deep valley, from the edge of a high cliff. In the distance he could see lights of houses winking in the darkness and the moon shining on a ribbon of river that snaked its way across the valley floor. His view swung in across the treeline towards the base of the cliff until he was looking directly downward over stubborn small shrubs that clung to the cliff face. Far below, he could see white foaming water glistening in the moonlight as it raged across jagged rocks and swept around the base of the cliff before churning its way through a narrow chasm around to his left. As he watched, he felt it drawing him towards it, pulling him towards the cliff edge.

Using all the authority of his heritage and his right, Tarkyn hurled an urgent, powerful command into that distant mind to stay still and wait for him to come. Then his eyes snapped open. "It's Hail," he stated baldly as he relayed to his audience what he had seen and done.

Ignoring Waterstone's tightened mouth, Tarkyn reeled off a set of instructions, "I need Ancient Oak, Rainstorm and Lapping Water to come with us to look after Midnight so I can move freely when we get there. I need Dry Berry, String, Bean and whoever else has some relationship with Hail. Waterstone, can you come if someone looks after Sparrow? And Autumn

Leaves? He's good at pouring oil on troubled waters. Anyone else?"

"We may need Stormaway and Danton's magic," suggested Waterstone tightly.

"Yes, good idea. Right. Who knows where to go? It will be quicker to follow you than for me to follow the trace. We have no time to lose." Tarkyn lifted himself to his feet, carefully cradling Midnight so that he didn't waken him.

The trappers didn't hesitate. They knew at once where the image placed Hail. As one, they headed off up the path that Tarkyn had taken earlier in the day with a trail of woodfolk and sorcerers in their wake. They passed the place where Tarkyn had fallen and continued up for another quarter of a mile before turning along a narrow path that wound upward between boulders until it emerged on a plateau above. With Hail standing poised on the cliff edge, it felt like hours since they had left the firesite. Once they could spread out, the trappers stopped and waited for Tarkyn to catch up. They pointed ahead to their right.

"Up there. Probably another hundred yards, I'd say," growled Growling Bear. "You can just see the beginning of the cliff edge from here."

"Thanks. Lapping Water and Rainstorm, can you hold Midnight, please? I'm going up there alone first..." He smiled gently in the darkness. "On second thoughts, no, I'm not. I'll take Waterstone, Autumn Leaves and Danton with me, if you agree. Give us five or ten minutes then Waterstone can send through a message for String, Bean, Dry Berry, whoever she will consider to be her friends, to come up and join us. We'll send a message to you, Lapping Water and Rainstorm, when or if to bring up Midnight. Ancient Oak, can you please stand by in case Midnight wakes up and tries to get away?" He took a deep breath and looked around. "Ready?"

"Come on. Let's just go, for heaven's sake. Our lives and the forest are teetering at the top of that cliff," hissed Waterstone.

Tarkyn glanced at his friend with a slight frown but set off a dead run, saying over his shoulder, "Don't worry. We're all right so far. No wind." Even as he spoke, a sharp gust of wind struck them. His eyes widened, "Oh no. She's faltering. Waterstone, if you can flick the last few yards and grab her, do it."

They ran up the slope and curved around to follow the edge of the cliff. As they crested the top of the rise, Hail glanced at Tarkyn and then, standing with her arms wide, slowly, very slowly, fell forward over the space beneath her.

"*Ka Liefka,*" bellowed Tarkyn. A bronze shaft of power shot forth, and held her horizontal, above the yawning darkness. The sorcerer's bronze beam lifted her and swung her body upright, away from the cliff's edge and back over solid ground. The shaft retracted slowly until she was deposited safely in front of them. She made to scramble to her feet but Tarkyn said gently, "Don't make me stop you."

She glowered up at him but subsided.

Tarkyn squatted down in front of her. "Thank you for waiting for me," he said quietly.

"You tricked me, you bastard! I didn't know you could do that," she snarled. "I thought I could follow your order and protect the forest but still jump in time as soon as you came into sight."

Tarkyn shook his head. "I didn't trick you. You knew I wanted you to stay long enough for me to reach you. You just failed to trick me, that's all."

"Bloody sorcerers." She spat at him. "Destroyed my life. Turned me into a monster. And now, when I finally find a way out, you take that from me as well. But you won't. You can't stand guard over me forever. As soon as you falter, I'll be gone."

"Hail, we don't want to lose you," said Waterstone, squatting down beside Tarkyn. "You are one of us. Your child is one of us."

Hail hammered the ground with her fist. "But don't you see? Don't you realise? You are all better off if I'm gone. How could anyone want to live with someone who has been so cruel? How can I live with myself?" Hail dropped her face into her hands. "I can't." she sobbed. "I can't live with myself for what I've done to that poor little boy." Suddenly she whipped her head up and grabbed Tarkyn's hand, throwing him off balance but not quite knocking him over. "You have to let me go," she sobbed. "Can't you see that? You have to let me go. I can't stand it."

Tarkyn caught Waterstone's eye and jerked his head briefly in the direction of the others. As soon as he saw Waterstone go out of focus, he returned his attention to the distraught woodwoman.

Autumn Leaves was saying, "Hail, you are not to blame for the effects of the curse."

"Maybe not. But your high and mighty prince there told me himself that my best was not good enough, even knowing about the curse." She sobbed and sniffed before she could continue. "And he was right. All I could do was get rid of Midnight, hide him from my sight so I didn't destroy him." She blew her nose on a handkerchief that Danton had produced. "What a pitiful effort! And I didn't even check to see how they were treating him. Just breathed a sigh of relief and left him to their mercy." She broke down again. "Poor little Midnight. And to find him tied to that tree, with my kin fighting each other to stay one another's hands..."

Suddenly she launched herself up and made a rush for the edge.

"Danton. Your shield! Over us all!"

597

Long before she reached the edge of the cliff, she was imprisoned with Tarkyn, Danton, Autumn Leaves and Waterstone within the aqua of Danton's shield. She ran headlong into it and beat her hands futilely against its wall. Behind her back, Tarkyn looked uncertainly at the other three. After a moment, he took a deep breath and sent waves of compassion and calm to her.

As String, Bean and Dry Berry arrived, Tarkyn murmured to Danton, "I will place my shield over her until you expand yours to let Bean and String in. Then I'll release mine."

Once the two trappers and Dry Berry were within Danton's shield, they moved to stand near the woodwoman. Bean placed his hand gently on her shoulder but she shrugged it off violently and sent a smouldering glare over her shoulder at him.

"Leave me alone, Bean. You have no more right than *he* does, to stop me."

"Hail, listen to me, we have always been your friend and Midnight's. Is that true?"

Hail's eyes narrowed but after looking for a trap in these words, she nodded reluctantly.

"And do you remember that we have always tried to stand up for Midnight?"

Again, she looked at the question from every angle before nodding.

"So, Hail," came in String, "if we said something was good for Midnight, would you believe us?"

"You two told me to leave him with my kin. That was a terrible idea. Look what they ended up doing to him."

String winced. "Lesser of two evils at that time, I'm afraid, Hail." He looked at Bean helplessly. "This isn't going too well."

Bean took over. "Listen Hail. Let's come from another

angle. You know we have Midnight's welfare at heart, don't you? We always have."

She looked at him through narrowed eyes before conceding the point.

"And if we told you something about Midnight, you would believe us?"

She swivelled around and stood belligerently with her hands on her hips. "Oh for heaven's sake, just spit it out, whatever you're wanting to say. I'll judge what I think of it when I've heard it."

Bean threw up his hands. "Right. Fine. Midnight is desperately unhappy that you haven't been near him since the curse was lifted. He thought you would want to see him."

Hail blinked in astonishment. "What utter rot! I thought you two could come up with something better than that. How could he possibly want to have anything to do with me after I treated him so badly?"

String shrugged. "Search me. I don't understand kids at all. But he does."

"It's true, Hail," said Tarkyn quietly. "I've just spent the last hour holding him while he sobbed his heart out because you weren't there. He needs you, Hail. He thinks that you must still hate him. He thinks there's something fundamentally wrong with him if you still don't want him. Midnight needs to know that you would have loved him if it weren't for the curse."

"I *do* love him. And I did," she replied hotly. Her voice caught on a sob, "But I hated him too. I hated everything he represented and he just drove me crazy. I'm not maternal. I was never going to have children. And how could I know what the curse was doing? Last night, when I saw his life, our life, from his point of view, it broke my heart. How can I live with that?"

"How can you die," countered Tarkyn, "and leave him

believing that the past is his fault? If you have any care for him, you will find the courage to live."

"What right have you to pass judgement on my courage, you sanctimonious bastard?" snapped Hail. "When have you ever had to face someone you've hurt?"

Tarkyn threw a wry smile at Waterstone. "I once hurt Waterstone badly, didn't I? And I faced up to him, but I admit it wasn't easy." He stared at the woodwoman. "And Hail, I had to face everyone that my father bound to the oath, knowing they would hate me and that my very presence would hurt them and forever be a blight on their freedom."

Tarkyn felt a hand on his shoulder and glanced around to see Autumn Leaves standing quietly beside him before continuing, "I wasn't guardian of the forest then." He shrugged. "Well, I was, but none of us knew it. So everyone simply thought of me as an unwelcome outsider who had arrived to throw his weight around as his father had." He smiled wryly at Autumn Leaves. "Would that be about right?"

Autumn Leaves gave a small nod and a warm smile. "Yes, I'm afraid it would."

Tarkyn grunted. "Anyway Hail, none of that gives me the right to question your courage. But I *have* had to face people who were hurting because of me. And I do understand, because sometimes it has been almost more than I could bear." He gazed unflinchingly into her eyes. "All I can say is that I have tried to diminish the hurt as much as I could. And I would like you to do the same for Midnight."

Hail looked from Autumn Leaves to Waterstone. "Is this true? Has he, who seems so strong, struggled so much?"

"If Tarkyn says it, then it is true," said Autumn Leaves, self-appointed watchdog of Tarkyn's integrity. "But I know it to be true myself."

"Yes, it is true," affirmed Waterstone. "We nearly lost him a couple of times because of it, just as we have nearly lost you. And if we'd lost Tarkyn back then, all woodfolk would have been destroyed by the curse that only he could reverse."

Hail stared at them for a moment before snorting in derision. "I think my loss would be barely noticeable in the wider scheme of things."

"We would all be diminished by your loss, Hail, your son most of all," said Bean quietly. "And whether you wanted to or not, you have created a link between sorcerers and woodfolk that your death will not remove. If it had not been for you, String and I would never have met all these marvellous people. In fact, I think we would be dead by now, because only our association with you saved us when we gave away our knowledge of woodfolk to the prince."

"You see, Hail. You can't predict the effect your life will have on the lives of others," said String.

"Or my death," she retorted.

"No, I suppose not," conceded String glumly.

Suddenly Dry Berry stomped up to Hail and jabbed her repeatedly in the chest with her index finger. "Now listen here, young lady. You have not cornered the market on feeling lousy about how you behaved under that wretched curse. I despise the way I manipulated Tarkyn and set him up for that beating. You weren't there so you don't know. After all, none of us is talking about it because it was too shameful for words."

Hail frowned and looked bewildered. "What beating?"

Tarkyn waved his hand. "Please, no. Unless we must, I would rather not talk about it. You can tell Hail about it later." He grimaced. "Suffice it to say, there are many mountainfolk who behaved regrettably that day." A thought struck him. "You didn't swear the oath that day, did you?"

A malicious little smile played around Hail's mouth. "No, but the meaning of that howling wind that blasted across the clearing last night was transmitted amongst everyone gathered there." She gave a little sigh. "I do understand that I am under oath to you and that you placed the future of our people and the forests into my care when you ordered me to wait." She studied him. "So will you now risk them again by ordering me to stay alive?"

"No."

"No? Just No? And yet you are still holding me within this shield against my will."

Tarkyn raised a hand then let it drop. "Hail, I do not want to own your life. It is yours to keep or throw away as you choose. All I wanted was the chance to talk to you, to show you that there are people who care about you and that there may be reasons to keep living. What Pipeless did to you and the legacy he left you, have been hard to bear I know, nearly as hard to bear as the legacy he left his son. But at least you had a life beforehand to give you some perspective. Midnight's whole life has been mutilated by that curse." He nodded almost imperceptibly to Waterstone as he said, "Hail, if you choose to die, I will do my best to explain to Midnight that you loved him. Whether or not you choose to die, I will still look after him and love him as my own. You can care for him as much as you can manage but you do not have to take the full burden of him."

Hail frowned. "Why are you, a young man of only nineteen, prepared to take on such an enormous responsibility when I struggle with it?"

Tarkyn smiled and shrugged. "My life has never been my own. I was bred to take responsibility. Besides, I love that little rascal to death and back. He's just pummelled me black and blue but I can only sit back and admire that fighting spirit of his that has brought him through all those years of being reviled. Whatever you did right or wrong, you produced a son to be proud of."

The first gentle smile Tarkyn had seen lit Hail's face. "Do you think so?"

"He is a great kid, Hail," answered Autumn Leaves quietly.

"And you haven't watched him since the curse was lifted," added Waterstone, "but he has been playing with all the kids using his sorcerer's shield and they're loving it."

She gazed wonderingly around them all. "I was always so ashamed of him because he was half sorcerer." Tears welled in her eyes and rolled slowly down her cheeks as Lapping Water arrived carrying Midnight with Rainstorm and Ancient Oak bringing up the rear. After a glance at Tarkyn, Danton waved away his shield.

"We all love him, Hail," said Lapping Water as she handed him gently over to his mother.

Hail sat down on the ground and rocked herself back and forth as she cradled him in her arms. "You don't think he'll end up like his father, do you?"

Waterstone sat down beside her. "It doesn't matter if he does ... as long as he doesn't make that same bad mistake. From what I saw of Pipeless, even though he was towering above us, he didn't seem a bad sort of chap."

"He wasn't," said Bean. "He was a very clever but reclusive wizard. He just wasn't very good with people. Midnight is much better company than his father ever was and Midnight can't speak!"

The laughter that greeted this remark roused Midnight slightly and he gazed blearily up into his mother's eyes. When he realised, he shot upright and flung his arms around her neck. As she hugged him to her, Hail's mind was filled with pictures of Midnight playing with the other children, of him dragging in the huge tree branch for the fire in the cave, of him making the wristband with Lapping Water and drifting out of the tall pine in Tarkyn's arms. The image returned to the wristband with a picture of Hail wearing one with a query. Hail was laughing as she said to Tarkyn, "You don't need to send me all these images. You can tell me what he's been up to later."

Tarkyn grinned. "I'm not. Your son is sending them to you. *He's* telling you all about it. You can send images back to him, you know. Just not words, at least not so far."

She looked down as Midnight tugged insistently on her sleeve. When he had her attention, he replayed the image of the wristband with the query. She nodded, laughing and crying all at once.

Dry Berry looked on with an approving smile. "Hail, you know, a wise man once said, 'We can't change the past. We can only change the effect the past has on our future.'" She glanced at Tarkyn and cleared her throat self-consciously. "Something like that, anyway."

Hail just nodded and smiled.

5 5

As they headed back towards the firesite, it became apparent that Waterstone was displeased. He kept his eyes forward and did not join in any of the laughing and joking that was going on around him. His mouth was set in a grim thin line and when they arrived, he left immediately to retrieve Sparrow and retire.

Tarkyn watched him leave but knew that the woodman was deliberately using Sparrow as a barrier to any discussion. When he brought his eyes back to the group around him, he found Stormaway's gaze upon him. He gave a little shrug and returned his attention to the people around him.

The home guard moved out at crack of dawn the next morning. They headed up the same narrow path but swung away to the left when they reached the wider space at the top. At this altitude, the pines had begun to thin and other trees, stumpy and windblown, had been driven into gnarled shapes by years of weathering. The cover was sparser and the wind that blew around the home guard was iced with the first breath of winter. They travelled for half the morning, pushing uphill on legs that became tireder and sorer until finally Autumn Leaves said firmly, "Time for a halt. We are nearly at the top of the range. One more push after breakfast should do it."

Everyone sat down on patches of moss, on rocks or on rucksacks while a fire was lit. After the children had scoffed down bowls of porridge, they shot off to play wolves in the long coarse grass while the adults sat around resting and talking quietly. Waterstone had walked a little distance away with his breakfast and sat, hunched into himself and aloof.

Tarkyn procured two cups of tea and headed over to join him. Waterstone barely glanced at him as he accepted his tea. After sitting in stony silence through half the cup, Tarkyn finally asked gently, "What is wrong, my friend?"

Waterstone turned eyes on him filled with such bitterness and scorn that Tarkyn swayed backwards. "I think the fact that you don't know makes it worse, if that's possible."

Tarkyn's hands whitened around his cup but he said nothing and simply waited.

Eventually Waterstone began to talk, his voice vibrating with hurt and anger. "How could you risk our lives; Sparrow's life, my life, Ancient Oak's life, everyone's lives on the whim of a half-crazed woman?" He took a deep breath to fuel his speech. "With no consultation, not even an apology. Nothing. Do we count for so little that you can stake all of us in one grandiose gesture to save one life?"

"Waterstone, I didn't think..."

"Didn't think?!" Waterstone spluttered. "If that's your best effort, that you didn't even consider us, then I think it would be better if we just kept our relationship formal from here on in. You are the lord. We are your vassals, nothing more. You can do with us as you will and there is nothing we can do to stop you." Then he shook out his empty tea cup before turning to confront Tarkyn. "How could you know that she would have enough clarity of mind to even understand what she was forfeiting if she jumped? You threw our whole welfare into the chance that she would obey you. *You*, a hated sorcerer."

Tarkyn's mouth thinned and he turned his head to look at the tumbling white clouds forming on the horizon. After a moment, even though his eyes were glittering with anger, he said quietly, "I was not going to say that I didn't think of you. I was going to say that I didn't think one refused command would affect the forest too much. If she had disobeyed my command, we would not have lost all the forests."

"How do you work that out?" demanded Waterstone.

Tarkyn leaned forward and placed his elbows on his knees. "Do you remember the time I told you that the oath had spread and you asked whether I was ordering you not to tell anyone?"

The woodman frowned. "Yes."

"And when I tried to walk away, you kept doing your woodfolk flick to bar my way? Well, I ordered you to get out of the way then and you just blatantly said, 'No,' and stood your ground." Tarkyn looked sideways to meet Waterstone's gaze. "Remember? There was a turbulent gust of wind after that, maybe a few leaves drifted down but not much more. No trees nearby were even damaged."

"So why did you look so aghast last night, when that gust of wind hit us as we were trying to reach her?"

"I was worried she wouldn't last until we got there. I wasn't worried about the forest."

Still Waterstone was not satisfied. "But why didn't you say anything when I said that our lives and the forest were teetering at the top of the cliff?"

Tarkyn frowned at him. "I just thought you were being facetious. I must admit I did think it was a little discordant with the gravity of the situation but on the other hand..."

"On the other hand, what?"

Suddenly Tarkyn found that his throat had closed over and he was struggling to speak. He swallowed and said tightly, "On the other hand, until now, it would never have occurred to me that you might think me such a monster." With a supreme effort, he achieved what he thought was a smile but was actually a grimace. "Still, you never can tell with us hated sorcerers, can you?"

With a sense of inevitability, Tarkyn spotted Autumn Leaves heading over to join them. He smiled sadly at the solid woodman as he arrived. "Too little too late, my friend. I doubt that there is much you can retrieve from the fragments of the friendship that just died here this morning." Tarkyn was too dispirited to be bothered getting up to walk away. He just sat there on the rock next to Waterstone, his arms linked across his drawn-up knees encircling the dark pit in his stomach, staring at the clouds building on the horizon.

Autumn Leaves pointed at Tarkyn, Waterstone and then himself. Correctly interpreting this, Tarkyn nodded his agreement for Waterstone to transmit their conversation.

When Autumn Leaves' eyes cleared, he watched Tarkyn speculatively for a few minutes while he tried to work out how to say what he needed to. Finally, he said, "Now, if I begin this conversation, will you contract to stay until the end of it?"

Tarkyn brought dulled eyes around to focus on the woodman. "That can only mean that you concur with Waterstone but yes, I will." He heaved a sigh that did not release any of the tension in him. "If we are to move forward as a people, I will have to confront and deal with what you think of me." Autumn Leaves went to place his hand on Tarkyn's shoulder but the prince held up his hand to keep him at bay. "I agree with Waterstone. Let's just keep this formal for the time being. We may be able to revert afterwards. I don't know."

Autumn Leaves looked uncertain. "Does that mean I have to bow, Your Highness?"

The ghost of a smile wafted across Tarkyn's face. "No. And you don't have to use my title either. It just means that you keep your distance and focus solely on the matter at hand. Don't try to be my friend until I know where I stand."

Autumn Leaves let out a silent whistle and glanced apprehensively at Waterstone.

"Come on. Out with it!" Tarkyn's voice cracked with tension. "It cannot be worse than what has gone before."

Autumn Leaves cleared his throat. "Tarkyn, the rest of us didn't even know that there had been an occasion when your command had been refused with minimal damage to the forest."

"Obviously, Waterstone didn't remember it either," said Tarkyn shortly. He grunted. "So, you all feel as Waterstone does, that I am a heartless monster who would throw your lives away on a gamble? Have you spent the night in mental huddles talking about it? Have you all closed your hearts off to me but not dared to show it?"

"Just be glad that Waterstone's reaction is to show his qualms."

"I'm not feeling glad about anything just at the moment." Tarkyn stood up and began to pace back and forth. By now everyone in the home guard was aware that a tense situation had developed but were keeping well away, watching from a distance. Tarkyn swept his gaze across them. None of them met his eyes. He rounded on Autumn Leaves. "Well, you can tell them this from me; out of all of you, only Waterstone has had the decency to raise it with me and even then I had to begin the exchange. The rest of you were content to let this fester behind my back and destroy everything we had built up without even giving me a chance to explain my actions."

"Your Highness," began Autumn Leaves, using Tarkyn's title despite himself, "it is not as bad as you think. None of us thought that you had deliberately made that decision. It is more that we thought that you had panicked when faced with Hail on the edge of that cliff."

Tarkyn folded his arms and nodded sharply. "And so didn't think of you at all, which, as Waterstone so clearly stated, is even worse."

"Just as you reacted without thinking when you saw that family under attack on the Great West Road," added Waterstone tightly.

Tarkyn looked from one to the other of them, "Reacting fast and forcefully does not necessarily constitute panicking." He paused. "I admit that at the Great West Road, I didn't remember that I should not, as a woodman, have revealed myself, but since it took me all the time until yesterday to figure that out, it was more a lack of understanding than a failure to consider all the angles at the time. I did not place you or the forests in danger through my actions either then or yesterday. And I believed until now that you understood that I had your welfare and the welfare of the forest at heart, above all else." He dropped his arms and said coldly, "After all, I am obliged under the terms of the oath to consider your welfare. So you may be assured that I will continue to do so whether you have faith in me or not."

"It is only that you are young and inexperienced," protested Autumn Leaves anxiously.

"And hold our lives in your hands," added Waterstone tightly, not looking at either of them.

Tarkyn turned and took a few agitated paces before swivelling on his heel to face them. When he spoke, his voice was sharp with annoyance, "Now let's get this straight, once and for all. I am only inexperienced in the ways of living in the wilds. I am not inexperienced in dealing with critical, fast decision-making. Being a successful tournament fighter requires split-second decisions and fast reflexes. And I have spent most of my life being trained in fighting and strategy and have spent years practising it under contrived pressure. They may have neglected my magical training but they did not neglect the basic requirements needed to lead men. When I sent that command to Hail, it was powered by a lifetime and generations of being obeyed without question. I didn't need the oath to keep her on the top of that cliff. She only let go when she saw me because she had already obeyed my command and resented the fact that she had complied. The threat to the forest had nothing to do with it. She would have complied anyway."

"Stars above, you're arrogant sometimes!" exclaimed Waterstone angrily.

Suddenly, the prince smiled. "I know I am. And what's worse, it's because I have reason to be. You know it's true. You're the one who keeps saying I don't need the oath to keep everyone in line. Well, you're absolutely right. The order I gave that you refused was little more than an emphatic request. I sent out a peremptory order for silence after the attack on me but the only person, other than Hail and Midnight, who has ever experienced one of my full-blown commands is Autumn Leaves... and that was only a demonstration."

Tarkyn raised his eyebrows at the heavy woodman who gave a wry smile in return and nodded reluctantly. "Yes, it was quite persuasive, as I recall." Autumn Leaves frowned. "But you let Hail go on thinking that you had entrusted her with the forest's welfare, didn't you?"

"What did you expect me to do? Take time out to explain that I hadn't given her that trust while she was still so vulnerable? I don't think so." Tarkyn waved a hand. "You can go and explain it to her any time you like."

Waterstone, who was not interested in this angle on things, suddenly asked, "Are you now saying that we are effectively free to ignore your commands if we so wish?"

Tarkyn shook his head. "No, I am saying that I don't think the forest will suffer much if you do." When Waterstone looked puzzled, the prince added gently, "Your honour will still be at stake."

The woodman digested this and grunted. After a short silence, he mused, "So the main threat to the forest seems to be caused by direct threats against you. Is that right?"

"So it would seem," agreed Tarkyn. "And the less blatant aggression of the harvesters' sedition caused insidious damage, didn't it? Blackened leaves and mouldering just like the nature of the attack on me. And I suspect that a mass refusal to bend to my will might also elicit severe damage to the forest." He shrugged. "But how can we know?" A thought struck him and Tarkyn turned away to walk off among the nearby scraggy trees, studying their leaves and bark. He gestured for the other two to join him and pointed to dark grey, soft, furry growths that were rotting into the branches and trunks of the trees. "Hmm. I suspect we are looking at the cost of dishonouring me."

"We didn't dishonour you," exclaimed Autumn Leaves hotly.

The prince straightened up and stared down at the two woodmen. "It may surprise you to know that I do not feel honoured by your belief that I might chance your lives on a whim and I do not feel honoured by clandestine gossip about my perceived shortcomings." His eyes narrowed. "However, I am becoming very tired of the sorcery in this oath making my judgements for me."

Tarkyn stared over their heads, thinking through all he knew about the oath while a part of his mind watched the children playing in the long grass and saw the other woodfolk and sorcerers chatting quietly and keeping their eyes on the progress of his discussions. His eyes swung around to alight on Stormaway who was seated slightly apart, watching him intently. Tarkyn murmured a request for the wizard to be summoned.

Waterstone obliged by sending a mental request to Thunder Storm who walked over to deliver the message. But even in that short time, Stormaway had already stood up and taken the first few steps towards Tarkyn. The wizard nodded a brief acknowledgement to Thunder Storm as he continued on his way.

When he arrived, Stormaway bowed low, saying quietly once he had straightened, "You requested me, Your Highness?"

The two woodmen frowned at the unexpected degree of the wizard's deference but Tarkyn accepted it without comment. "Stormaway, among us here, there are at least two people I know of, who have no qualms about lying when it suits them. Danton is one, and you are the other. As you probably know, I am not particularly good at discerning prevarication and I do not expect it to be used against me by those loyal to me."

"May I say that it is one of your more endearing traits, my lord?" said Stormaway gravely but with a twinkle in his eye.

Tarkyn gave a small grunt of laughter. "I myself do not find it particularly convenient. However..." He paused and said with no heat at all, "However, Stormaway, I now realise you have lied to me from beginning to end."

"Indeed, my lord." The wizard gave another slight bow as though he had just been complimented. "But surely this comes as no surprise. After all, I told you when I first met you that I was devious."

Tarkyn couldn't suppress a smile. After a moment, he

folded his arms and said quietly, "Stormaway Treemaster, I command you to remove the oath's bond to the forest."

Stormaway beamed and bowed low. "Certainly Your Highness. It would be a pleasure. Your command is my will." He tapped his long, gnarled staff twice on the ground. The first tap gave a faint echo within the earth, but the second resounded with a great boom that sent shock waves beneath the surface and rippled off across the grasslands, through the windswept trees, out across the mountains and down into the forest below. A streak of green light shot skywards from the top of his staff and spread across the underside of the gathering clouds, leaving a strange dimmed light in its wake until gradually, it dissipated and daylight re-asserted itself.

The woodfolk froze into stunned silence as Waterstone relayed what had just occurred. Even the children didn't move. Waterstone and Autumn Leaves stood with mouths agape. Only Tarkyn and Stormaway looked at one another in satisfaction and smiled.

As a wave of release spread forth from the prince, the woodfolk suddenly came to life and rushed in to cluster around him.

"You really did it," said Tree Wind wonderingly. "I wondered whether you really would when you finally worked out how to."

Tarkyn raised his eyebrows at her. "Of course I did. I always said I would."

"But you lose so much power," she protested.

"No, I don't. I have always said the oath should only depend upon the honour of the woodfolk. All that changes is our fear about the forest."

After a moment, Waterstone recovered enough to say, "Please explain."

Tarkyn grinned. "A long time ago, I asked Stormaway what

would happen if I ordered him to remove the sorcery in the oath. You were there. Do you remember?" Waterstone nodded shortly. "He said 'I'm so glad you phrased it like that because I would refuse.'" Tarkyn shrugged and smiled. "He lied. And he made me think that he would see the forest destroyed sooner than follow any order I gave to defuse the oath. Until today, I didn't realise how significant it was that Waterstone's refusal to obey my order had inflicted only minimal damage on the forest. But today, I put the pieces together and realised that Stormaway had been bluffing. Even if he had refused, the forest would have suffered only minor damage. But he would never have refused."

The prince glanced at his retainer. "Stormaway swore the oath with the rest of you but he is happy to use any deception at hand to further my cause, as he sees it. In the end, he is a man of honour who has always done his utmost to protect me, even to the extent of lying to me. But faced with a direct order, he will always uphold his oath to obey me." Tarkyn gave a gentle smile. "Correct?"

Stormaway inclined his head. "Yes, my lord. And had you ordered me back then, I would have tried to dissuade you but had that not worked, I would have obeyed your command. It was a close call. Rather than ordering me, you asked me, would I not defuse the oath. You gave me the upper hand and I took it to keep you safe."

Waterstone stared at the wizard through narrowed eyes. "And what about your oath to Tarkyn's father? You said you had promised Markazon that you would not destroy the sorcery in the oath."

Stormaway gave an apologetic smile. "Only partly true, I'm afraid. Markazon made me promise that I would not destroy the oath's power for as long as I could, without refusing a direct order. So I could never have told Tarkyn how to defuse the oath but on the other hand, Markazon would never have countenanced me disobeying his son."

"But he didn't mind you lying to his son?" asked Autumn Leaves.

The old wizard shrugged. "Markazon and I worked closely together for years. He knew how I achieved my ends. He, of course, could see straight through me and knew I would never work against Tarkyn. So he left me to follow my own style. He knew that, over time, Tarkyn would see through me too and give me a direct order. We both hoped that by then, he would have gained enough authority in his own right to be safe among you woodfolk."

"Given that we could not be trusted to uphold an oath," said Waterstone tersely.

"Given that we were entrusting the future of Eskuzor to you and you were an unknown quantity," retorted Stormaway.

Tarkyn held up a hand to stop their bickering and addressed the gathered woodfolk, "And so my friends, the long-awaited day has, rather surprisingly, arrived. Our forest is safe from the retribution of the oath." A cheer went up and Tarkyn was inundated with calls of thanks. Everywhere shoulders were straighter and more relaxed, and faces became smoother as lines of tension disappeared. "Today, everything changes even though most things will stay the same. The oath you swore in return for your people being saved from the epidemic is now based purely on trust and your honour, just as it always should have been."

Tarkyn would have said more but he suddenly realised that many woodfolk had actually dissolved into tears and were embracing each other.

"You have no idea what a strain it has been for us trying to emulate a foreign culture; trying to follow foreign requirements with the sword of retribution hanging constantly over us and

our beloved woodlands," sniffed Tree Wind as she clung to
Summer Rain.

Creaking Bough and Thunder Storm stood with their arms
around each other and their children. "And now, at last, we can
be sure our children will have a home to grow up in," rumbled
Thunder Storm, his face wet with tears.

As Waterstone hugged Autumn Leaves, Sparrow and
Ancient Oak came over to join them. Waterstone wiped his
eyes and gave a damp chuckle. "And now I will hold the
dubious honour of being the person who caused the most
damage to the forest."

"What about Rushwind?" asked Sparrow.

"No. That was really the infection, not her," said Ancient
Oak, completely dry-eyed. He patted Waterstone on the
shoulder. "No, I'm afraid there is no doubt that that honour
goes to your father. But so does a lot of the credit for helping
Tarkyn to trust us enough to release the forest from the oath."
He looked around at Tarkyn. "Come on little brother, what are
you doing standing over there by yourself? I know you and
Waterstone are fighting at the moment but it will pass. It
always does. Come and be part of the celebration." When
Tarkyn hesitated, Ancient Oak walked over, grabbed him by
the arm and dragged him back. "Come on. You can continue
your fight with him later, if you must. Now is the time to
celebrate. After all, you must be relieved too."

As Sparrow, Autumn Leaves and Waterstone enclosed him
in their embrace Tarkyn nodded, feeling tears well up more
because Ancient Oak had made the effort to pull him in, than
because of the oath.

Ancient Oak rolled his eyes. "No wonder you two fight so
much. You're both so bloody emotional."

Tarkyn and Waterstone frowned at each other. "We don't
fight that much," they chorused.

Ancient Oak laughed. "I never fight with either of you." He looked down at Sparrow, "Do I?"

Sparrow shook her head. "No," she said seriously, "you are the steady one in the family."

"Thanks very much," exclaimed her father. "I am not unsteady."

Tarkyn shook his head. "No, you are not unsteady." He smiled, remembering a conversation with Raging Water about his own volatility. "Perhaps passionate is a better way of putting it."

"There's a lot to be passionate about, around you," he retorted without thinking. Sensing Tarkyn's immediate withdrawal, Waterstone said, hastily, "No, no, no. I didn't mean it like that. I'm sorry for what I said and for underestimating you, yet again." He gave a cheeky grin. "I told you it would be a struggle to live with a legend. How can one get one's head around the true measure of you?"

Tarkyn frowned and smiled, not sure how to take him.

Suddenly Waterstone grabbed him in a bear hug. "Oh, you big galoot! How can one hope to keep up with you? You look like a lost puppy one minute and the next you're laying down the law and mounting hopeless rescues that actually succeed. Once more, I've cut you to the quick but all I can do is say I'm sorry."

Tarkyn returned his embrace but said with a wry smile. "I wonder how many lifetimes it will take for woodfolk to really, deep down trust any sorcerer?"

"Oh stop it," exclaimed Waterstone impatiently. "Now you're being melodramatic. I trust you. That's why I was so shocked and angry. What I thought you had done undermined my whole faith in my ability to judge people. Turns out I was wrong. Bad news for you is that I'm bound to be wrong some time again in the future. You're too hard to predict and I'm too quick to jump to conclusions. In the interests of family harmony, next time I will give you the benefit of the doubt before ripping your head off. Agreed?"

A reluctant smile spread across Tarkyn's face. "Agreed." He drew back. "I'd better go. I have a bit more to say before we head off. Could you get everyone's attention again to save me shouting please?"

When all eyes were once more turned his way, Tarkyn continued, "Before anything goes wrong, I need to make sure we all understand the new rules of engagement. It is not all good news for you, I'm afraid. After all, the oath still stands, upheld by your commitment to repay my father." He gave a little smile. "And now I have no need to fear endangering the forest if I issue an order.

"Since the forest is no longer your whipping boy for your transgressions," he continued, "from now on, you will have to face your own consequences for your own misdemeanours, should they occur. In general, I would expect consequences to go no further than you struggling with your own conscience and honour. However, if a serious transgression occurred I, in consultation with you folk, would decide upon the retribution. The final say is mine."

Tarkyn raised his eyebrows. "Any objections so far?" Other than a couple of closed faces, there was no indication that this was causing any distress.

He let his vivid eyes travel across them all. "Today, I realised that I have been too diffident." With some amusement, Tarkyn noted stunned expressions at this pronouncement. "Because I am inexperienced in the way of the woodlands and because I did not wish to intimidate you, I have downplayed my training and my heritage. However, when you all assume that I could panic to the extent of endangering you all, enough is enough. To save myself from appearing even more arrogant than usual, I will leave Waterstone and Autumn Leaves to fill you in on our previous discussion in due course." He paused. "However, one thing I will say before we move off; there seems to be a pattern developing of discussing my shortcomings behind my back. I don't know what I have done to make you feel unable to talk to me when an issue arises but I will say two things about it. Firstly, it shows little respect for me and so contravenes the oath, but secondly, and for me more importantly, it isolates me."

"Sorry, Tarkyn," Rainstorm piped up. "We were just having a bit of fun."

"You may have been, but there were a lot of discontented people who didn't come to see me about it or stand up to me at the time."

"Perhaps you should consider your personal style," suggested Running Feet tentatively.

Tarkyn turned to glare at the woodman and snapped, "Perhaps you should consider my personal style and not be so cowed by it." Seeing Running Feet's stricken face, he waved a hand and relaxed into a rueful smile. "Sorry, Running Feet. You are right, and I am right. I need to remember you are not used to being ordered around or snapped at or being told off. I'm afraid my upbringing was a poor training ground for showing respect to people beyond my family. I am trying, but obviously not with total success. On the other hand, you people should know by now that I do care about you and that I will listen, if not at first, at least when you persist." He shrugged. "And without wishing to undermine myself completely, perhaps you should bear in mind that a rebuke from me is far more commonplace than, say, a rebuke from Waterstone or Autumn Leaves or Thunder Storm."

"It still tears your guts out," responded Rainstorm.

"And makes me want to crawl into a corner and hide," rumbled Thunder Storm.

"And makes you feel like you've been hit in the face," said Bean.

"And tends to belittle one, although of course it is up to you," added Stormaway suavely with a slight bow.

The prince ran his hands back through his hair and locked them behind his head. "Ooh dear! I've opened a can of worms here, haven't I?"

"You did ask people to tell you," said Lapping Water gently.

Tarkyn looked at her, his heart giving an enormous thump that he felt everyone must be able to hear. He dropped his arms to his sides. "And what have I done wrong to you then?"

"Nothing. I was just saying, that's all."

"Oh. Oh, I see. Well, that's good then, isn't it, that there's at least one person I haven't upset?" Tarkyn felt a little flustered and tried to stare down Ancient Oak and Rainstorm who were both grinning at him. After a moment, he regained his own attention and asked, "Anyone else want to say something while we're clearing the air?"

Melting Snow took a little breath, said timorously in her tinkling little voice, "I find you thoroughly intimidating in every way," and promptly blushed.

Amidst a ripple of giggles and chuckles, Tarkyn blinked. "Oh dear. Well, I'm sorry about that." He thought back over the events that had occurred since he met the mountainfolk and added, "Perhaps now that things have calmed down, I won't be quite so, I don't know..."

"Irritable?"

"Forceful?"

"Autocratic?"

"Arrogant?"

"Fearsome?"

"Bossy?" said a little voice.

Tarkyn laughed as he turned to Sparrow and ruffled her hair. "And that will be quite enough from you, young lady. No, I was going to say 'busy.' 'Preoccupied' was another possibility but thanks everyone for your suggestions." He turned back to Melting Snow. "I was going to say that I won't be so *busy* now, so you may be able to get to know me better."

Suddenly Hail stomped up to stand in front of him, dragging Midnight by the hand, "Well, I just want to say that you're an interfering, stubborn bastard and thank heavens you are, for my sake and for Midnight's." She thrust Midnight forward, giving him a hearty thump on the back and ruffling his hair as he went, "Here! You can have him. I've had quite enough of him for one day." She glanced sideways at Bean and whispered gruffly, "Actually, I think they're missing each other."

Midnight ran and jumped into Tarkyn's arms. As Tarkyn hugged him, he said, "I heard that and yes, I was missing him." He smiled down into Midnight's brilliant green eyes beaming up at him from beneath his thatch of dark brown hair. "Hello, rascal."

He looked up at the woodfolk and sorcerers around him. "Right, so now that you have all completely assassinated my character, do you think you can come and see me next time I upset you instead of uniting against me?"

They all assured him they would and every one of them made sure they slapped him on the back or patted him on the arm on their way past, as they headed up the last leg of the mountain.

56

Three days later, five sorcerers and the woodfolk of the prince's home guard were ranged along the top of a rocky ridge studying the panorama before them. The descent to the south was much steeper and consisted of a series of sheer drops interspersed with wide sloping ledges of grasslands or forest, rather like giant terracing. Beyond the base of the mountain, the forest gradually gave way to wide chequered plains of farmland, dotted with farm dwellings and from time to time, villages. In the far distance, almost on the horizon, slightly to their right, they could see the silhouette of a large walled city.

"What is that place?" asked Rainstorm, shading his eyes against the glare.

"That, my friends, is the mighty fortress town of Montraya," said Danton. His eyes lit up. "Many a magnificent ball has been held there and we have had weeks of fun and entertainment in the castle and its grounds. The streets are lined with shops and market stalls of every kind. And because it is so close to the southern border, there are exotic wares from

Farenz and other more distant lands. It is the seat of Prince Jarand, Tarkyn's brother."

Rainstorm looked at the sorcerer quizzically. "Would I be right in thinking that holding a ball there is not the same as holding a ball here?" With that, he drew a small padded leather ball from his pocket, threw it up and caught it. "Or do they specialise in decorating balls?"

Danton grinned. "You're only half joking, aren't you?"

Rainstorm nodded and smiled back, quite happy to be made fun of. "Yep. I suspect I have no idea what you're talking about."

When Danton had finished waxing lyrical about balls, Rainstorm then asked, his eyes shining with mischief, "And I presume Jarand's seat is not an enormous chair?"

Danton frowned and asked with just a hint of disdain. "Surely you know what that means?" He was just about to launch into an explanation when he realised that Rainstorm was winding him up. He laughed. "You *do* know what that means."

"Yes, of course I do, but I have finally succeeded in getting you to betray some of your disdain. I love it," chortled the young woodman. "Tarkyn said you could be disdainful but you've managed to hide it until now."

"I am not disdainful," responded Danton hotly.

"Huh. That's what Tarkyn said about himself, too."

"Well, he is quite mistaken," said Danton promptly. "He is often disdainful."

Rainstorm laughed. "No, not often. Just sometimes. But I must admit, you show it very rarely. I suspect it is because you are such a skilful courtier rather than because you don't *feel* disdainful."

Danton regarded him thoughtfully for a moment. "You are a perceptive character, aren't you? Tarkyn said you were. And if you are aware that I have sometimes felt disdainful about you, are you offended by it? I would be."

The young woodman shook his head, smiling. "No. You have only felt like that because you are seeing our actions through your own values. If you can put up with our amusement at you, we can put up with your disdain. It's just different ways of showing the same thing, after all."

Danton gave a wry smile. "Well, after this conversation, I will think twice before thinking of you with disdain in the future. I beg your pardon for underestimating you."

Rainstorm beamed. "That's all right. I'm used to it. Everyone underestimates me... except Tarkyn."

Tarkyn, the two trappers, Summer Rain and Tree Wind walked past them, deep in discussion. Rainstorm nodded at their retreating figures and asked Danton, "Did you know that Falling Rain is Summer Rain's brother? And Tree Wind was going to marry him, you know, before he was exiled." He watched them moving further along the ridge. "I think Tarkyn should be consulting with Waterstone, Running Feet and Autumn Leaves too, if they are trying to work out where he'll be. They all knew him pretty well."

"Why don't you suggest it?" asked Danton.

Rainstorm shrugged. "They'll tell him if they have any ideas. We're in no tearing hurry."

Danton glanced up at the dark, billowing purpley-grey clouds that had gathered overhead. "I don't know about that. I think we might need to seek cover very shortly."

Even as they watched, Blizzard and Hail detached themselves from the main group and ran to join Tarkyn. Danton and Rainstorm could see them gesturing at the sky and consulting with String and Bean.

Suddenly Rainstorm said, "Right. We're off. String and Bean are going to lead us straight down a steep, narrow path to the next level, hopefully in time to find shelter in a cave down there before the deluge. We're not going to stop here for lunch after all." The young woodman groaned. "And I'm starving."

Danton smiled at him and scrabbled around inside his pack until he produced a couple of apples. "Here," he said, tossing one to Rainstorm. "That should keep you going for a little while."

The young woodman gave a quick smile. "You can still underestimate me when it comes to patience, if you like. I don't seem to have that down to a fine art yet. I ate mine just after breakfast."

With String, Bean and Hail leading the way, Tarkyn's home guard threaded their way carefully along a steep narrow path that clung to the face of the cliff before beginning a winding climb down between tumbled boulders. Before they were half way down, tiny white flakes began to drift down out of the heavy clouds and swirl gently around them before settling on their hair and clothing or wandering on down to the ground. The flakes became larger and denser as the snowstorm gathered force and soon the woodfolk were enclosed in a swirling quiet world of whiteness. They loved it. Some of them had never seen snow before. The children were dazzled by it and looked around wide-eyed with wonder at the transforming world around them.

By the time the home guard emerged onto the lower plateau, trees, grass, rocks, logs, everything in sight was covered in a thin layer of white. String and Bean were not even slightly fazed by the change wrought in the appearance of their surroundings and led everyone unerringly to a depression in the ground which, when the gathering snow was pushed away, turned out to be a downwardly sloping entrance to a large cavern.

As they congregated inside the cave, within the corona of

sorcerers' light, Tarkyn leant over and said quietly to Waterstone, "It's lucky this is such a large cave. Our numbers have swollen since we first set out on our journey to find Falling Rain."

Waterstone looked around at the people gathered there. "Yes, they have, haven't they? Golden Toad and his family, Running Feet, North Wind and Tree Wind from the harvesters, Falling Branch and Rainstorm from the forestals and the four new arrivals from the mountainfolk."

"Not to mention String, Bean and Danton," added Tarkyn.

Waterstone nodded. "And Midnight. So, we started out with twenty woodfolk, you and Stormaway and we now have thirty-three woodfolk and five sorcerers, counting both of us. That's nearly double." He smiled. "You can't be too bad after all, to have accumulated all these people. We were scratching around to get anybody at all, to start with."

As they were speaking, the woodfolk were settling themselves in, some to set up bedding, some to venture out to collect wood, others to prepare lunch. The children settled themselves to play near the back of the cave out of everyone's way. String and Bean came over to join Waterstone and Tarkyn.

"This is an excellent cave you have found us," said Tarkyn.

String grimaced. "It does have one slight problem though"

"What? That we are going to be snowed into it?" asked Waterstone.

"Actually, that too," said Bean. "We'll have to make sure we keep clearing the entrance. No, the other problem, and possibly more significant, is that I think there has been a mountain lion in here recently. Come and look at this." He led them over to an area near the front entrance off to the side where the woodfolk had not yet walked. There, clear in the dusty floor of the cave, were the spoors of a large animal.

Waterstone squatted down to examine them. After a couple of minutes, he looked up. "Hard to say how old they are. They look quite new but they could be up to a couple of days old. There's no wind or rain in this cave to weather them." He looked at Hail and Blizzard as they arrived in answer to his mind call. "You two will be better at this. You have more experience of caves. How old do you think these tracks are?"

Blizzard squatted down beside Waterstone and studied the imprints in the dust. He ran his fingers gently over the surrounding dirt to gain a feel for its consistency. Finally, he stood up and brushing off his hands, reported, "I would say they are less than a day old. Although there is no direct weathering, there will be a slight draft and there are tiny insects, rats and other animals that scurry across the floor of caves. Over time, they will blur old prints."

"I don't come down this side of the mountain. None of us woodfolk does. Top of the ridge is the end of our territory," said Hail. "But I know there are mountain lions all through this area. From the size of these spoors, we are dealing with an old, large one here, almost certainly male. And if he's grown to be this old and big, he will be fearsome." She glanced up at Tarkyn. "So I hear you're pretty good with birds of prey. How are you with mountain lions?"

"I've never met one."

Waterstone stood up. "He can manage wolves."

Tarkyn shrugged. "Well, I can manage one wolf and then he manages the rest."

"Mountain lions don't roam in packs," said Hail. "If it's a male, he'll be on his own."

Tarkyn smiled and said casually, "Then I wouldn't worry too much, if I were you. We have five sorcerers here. As long as we are forewarned, we can easily keep him at bay and keep everyone safe." He thought for a moment and added, "But I might just see if I can connect with him before he decides to return. It might save him and all of us a nasty shock."

Suddenly a deep-throated roar issued from the darkness at the rear of the cave. Before anyone could move, two streaks of gold resolved themselves into the eyes of a fast-moving black mountain lion that leapt, teeth bared, at the children playing in the dirt at the back of the cave. Even as the huge cat flew through the air, Midnight's arm swept up and a dark green dome slammed into place around the screaming children. As Midnight stood his ground defiantly, the mountain lion lunged straight at him, hitting the barrier above him with a dull thwack, only feet in front of him, before sliding to the floor, momentarily confused.

Before the lion could gather itself for another attack, Tarkyn threw a dome of shimmering bronze around the dazed animal. Following an instruction from Tarkyn, Midnight slowly moved back from the mountain lion, still with his shield around the other children, until they stood safely among the adults. As Midnight flicked out his shield, the children ran crying to their parents to be comforted. Amid thanks and admiration Midnight, without even a smile, came over to Tarkyn and quietly took his hand. Tarkyn looked down quizzically at him and suddenly realised that the little boy was quivering with fright.

Tarkyn bent down and scooped him up. "Oh Midnight. You were so brave, weren't you? But I should have realised; just because you reacted so decisively didn't mean you weren't frightened, did it?" He hugged him tightly, stroking his back and sending him waves of comfort and praise until the trembling subsided.

Summer Rain arrived with a sweet drink laced with laudanum.

Tarkyn sniffed it and took a little sip before handing it on to

Midnight. "How come he gets a palatable drink and I'm given ones that taste totally foul?"

"Yours require a greater concentration of herbs because you are larger. So, the sweetness would not easily mask the taste." Summer Rain gave a slight shrug. "Besides, you are not a child. You do not need to be pandered to in the same way."

Although he was quite happy to be pandered to, Tarkyn did not feel equal to the task of convincing Summer Rain. Instead he said, "Thanks for the tonic. Midnight will be all right soon." He beamed with pride. "Wasn't he clever though? I had better revise my previous statement. We have six sorcerers here, not five."

Bean cleared his throat. "Hmm. For all the good it nearly did us. We made a fundamental error there, assuming the mountain lion was out of his den. We should have checked the cavern thoroughly before we let anyone into it." He glanced uncertainly at Tarkyn. "I'm sorry about that."

"Yeah, I suppose the storm made us rush people in." String shrugged, not meeting his eyes. "Still, no excuse. Bad mistake."

Tarkyn tilted his head to one side as he looked at them. "You can't possibly imagine that, after this morning's salutary discussion, I am about to tell you off, can you? Anyway, we are all to blame." He smiled wryly. "Perhaps Danton and I less than everyone else, as we are least experienced in the ways of the wild. But still..."

"Blizzard and I should have raised the alarm the moment we saw how fresh those prints were," said Hail, reaching up to give her son a couple of awkward pats on the back. "Hmph. Maybe it's not so bad that he has sorcerer in him, after all." She spoke gruffly but the pride shone in her eyes.

Midnight twisted around to send her a slight smile but made no attempt to get down.

Tarkyn smiled at her too and said quietly, "I told you he

was a son to be proud of, didn't I?" After a moment, he turned his attention back to the black mountain lion that was glowering at them from within the bronze haze. "Well, it's too late to save the nasty shock but I will still try to connect with him. I would rather not kill him unless we must. Are you in agreement with that?"

Waterstone eyed the beast as it raised itself to its feet and paced back and forth, snarling and clawing at the glowing bronze wall in front of it. "I'm assuming you will keep your shield around it?"

Tarkyn gave a slight smile. "Yes. And Danton can raise his shield around all of you if that will make you feel safer. But I will keep my shield around him. If I removed it, there would be nothing to stop him from leaving and I think we need to know where he is until either he is under control or dead, don't you?"

"And the good thing is, if you can render him harmless somehow," said Bean, "no other mountain lion will come near this cave while he is here."

"You could just stun him," suggested String. He shrugged. "Of course, you'd have to have someone keeping an eye on him to make sure he didn't come round or keep a shield over him. So, it would tie up one person, however you did it."

"Let me try first. We'll keep that in mind as a fall-back position." Tarkyn turned to Blizzard. "If I can get him safely out of the cave, how likely is it that he will come back and attack us again?"

Blizzard scratched his head as he thought about it. "If you can scare him enough to make him turn tail and run, he won't come back to face a crowd of people in a confined space. But what he might do is lie in wait further down the track to pick off a straggler."

"Still, saying that," put in String. "There could be any number of them out there lying in wait to pick off a straggler."

"No, I don't think so. Not in this neck of the woods," said Bean. "Around here is this bloke's territory."

"Yeah, but his range won't extend all the way down the mountain," objected String. "As soon as we're out of his range, we'll be fair game for the next one."

"Hmm. These mountain lions aren't as easy as wolves or horses, are they?" mused Tarkyn. "More like the raptors, I would say. Well, let's deal with this one first and worry about the rest later. Hail, can you take Midnight? Now Danton, raise your shield around all but me and the mountain lion." He waved a hand. "You can all carry on with getting things ready, if you like. You'll be perfectly safe within Danton's shield. If you need to go outside, perhaps Stormaway or one of the others could shield you for the time being. But with my shield keeping the mountain lion contained, you should be safe anyway."

He realised that Autumn Leaves and Waterstone were grinning sympathetically at him as everyone ignored his suggestion and sat down expectantly to watch. He rolled his eyes at his friends. "Too much to hope for, I suppose, a little privacy in which to concentrate."

"I'd say so," said Autumn Leaves.

"Do you want me to use my shield to contain the animal," asked Stormaway, "so that you can concentrate on communicating with him?"

"No, thanks. I don't think I will be able to reach him through someone else's shield. I couldn't reach the hounds of the hunting party through Journeyman's shield."

Stormaway frowned. "But you just contacted Midnight through his shield."

Tarkyn raised his eyebrows in surprise. "So I did. And I did yesterday, when I told him to get a drink." He threw a smile at Bean. "Still, I always did contend that Midnight was not just an animal. So obviously, it must work differently with him. After all, woodfolk can talk to each other but not to animals. Hmm, interesting." He shrugged. "However, I don't think I can reach an animal through your shield. So, I'll use mine."

That settled, Tarkyn carefully turned his back on everyone and sat down to concentrate. Firstly, he parked the maintenance of his shield carefully to one side of his mind. Then he sent waves of calming reassurance towards the caged mountain lion. In response, a deluge of pure aggression and disdain rocked him backwards. The sounds of snarling grew louder and the animal let out a great roar of challenge.

In the background, he heard Stormaway saying, "Stand up. Show him you're strong.

Tarkyn realised then, that in his first mental encounter with the wolf, they had not actually been in sight of one another. Slowly, keeping his shield intact, he opened his eyes and stood up. Amber eyes glared at gold. The mountain lion lashed its tail and roared out another challenge. And suddenly Tarkyn knew that if he subjugated this proud animal, the lion would lose his territory and would have to leave and fight for another's range.

He turned away. "I can't do it."

A sigh of disappointment rose from his audience. Their forest guardian was admitting defeat. Tarkyn flicked them a glance of irritation and addressed himself solely to Hail and the trappers. "Do you get wolves around here?"

"Sometimes," said Bean.

"And what is their relationship with these mountain lions?"

"They seem to have some sort of a stand-off. The mountain lion is stronger than a lone wolf. On the other hand, a pack of wolves could bring down a mountain lion but at great cost to the pack. So they seem to have an unspoken agreement that they leave each other alone."

"I see. I'll try to use that then."

Ignoring his disappointed audience, the forest guardian turned back and locked gazes once more with the monstrous black beast. He developed a picture in his mind of the wolves' pack leader and showed the mountain lion an image of the wolf acknowledging Tarkyn's dominion over him. Then he superimposed images of wolves over images of woodfolk and himself. Within Tarkyn's shield, the mountain lion paced back and forth, lashing his tail and snarling, his eyes never leaving Tarkyn's. Suddenly in both their minds, the leader of the wolves appeared and quite beyond Tarkyn's volition, snarled and growled at the mountain lion. Tarkyn merely watched as the minds of the two animals circled each other, testing each other's strength and intention. In the background of the image, Tarkyn became aware of the shadowy figures of the wolf pack standing still and silent, presenting a clear threat to the solitary mountain lion. After several circuits and changes of direction, the pace of the protagonists slowed until eventually, they stood facing each other, growling softly. Then with a wry glance at Tarkyn, the wolf and his pack faded away, leaving him facing the lion alone, eyes locked, in front of his own pack of woodfolk.

The mountain lion stared at him for a few moments longer before turning away in insolent disinterest to lie down and start cleaning himself. Tarkyn grinned and flicked away the shield, confident enough to leave himself exposed.

As he turned towards the woodfolk, Blizzard said, "I thought you said you couldn't do it."

"I meant I couldn't bring myself to subjugate him. He would have lost too much."

"But you didn't subjugate him, did you?" asked Waterstone, with a private smile.

Tarkyn smiled and shook his head. "No." He glanced back over his shoulder at the large, disdainful cat that was completely engrossed in its ablutions. "We have reached an armed truce. He thinks we're a pack of strange wolves, if you must know. Will I show you?"

Once the woodfolk had been shown and the sorcerers had had it described to them, Rainstorm asked, "Where did that wolf come from, the one that took over your image?"

Tarkyn smiled wryly. "You remember him. Waterstone thought I had broken his will. I think he was drawn into the interplay because I was envisaging him so strongly. I didn't ask him. He just arrived. Animals can hijack my thoughts too, you know, just as I hijack theirs."

XI

FALLING RAIN

57

"So why don't woodfolk usually come down this side of the mountain?" asked Tarkyn between mouthfuls of doughy bread that had been baked in the coals of the fire and wrapped around dried meat and hazelnut paste. Ancient Oak and Rainstorm, on the other side of the fire were looking very pleased with themselves because they had managed to manoeuvre Lapping Water into sitting next to Tarkyn on the pretext of helping Midnight to plait a wristband for his mother. Tarkyn and Lapping Water were carefully ignoring each other and the two conspirators.

"Too steep, too little cover and too close to the bloody sorcerers," replied Blizzard trenchantly. In response to a couple of warning glances, he grimaced. "Blast it! Sorry. No offence intended."

Tarkyn's eyes twinkled at the woodman's discomfort but turned to Hail. "So, when you said that the mountain ridge is the end of your territory, does that mean that Falling Rain could be anywhere from now on, on or off the mountain?"

Hail shrugged. "Yeah, he could be. But he'd be mad to be

still on the mountain now that the snow has come. It's windy and horrible on this side of the mountain at the best of times. And he'd be struggling to keep out of sight for a long period of time, if one of these trappers," she indicated String and Bean with a nod, "stayed in the area for a while."

"Now, let me get this straight," said Danton leaning forward, with his arms on his knees. "Falling Rain won't reveal himself to any of us sorcerers because of your woodfolk bond of secrecy." He paused until someone nodded. "And he won't reveal himself to any of you because he has been exiled. Is that right?"

"Yes. Even if we come near him, he should not make contact with us," said Tree Wind. She smiled wistfully. "In the normal course of events, we would never have come anywhere near him anyway."

Danton frowned. "So, when you send someone into exile, you seem to depend on their sense of honour to keep them there. Isn't that a little optimistic?" He waved a hand as he saw Tree Wind about to protest. "Not in Falling Rain's case perhaps, but surely in some cases. If a person has wronged woodfolk enough to be exiled, surely they might be deemed to be untrustworthy?"

Judging by the blank expressions on the faces around him, this had obviously not been an issue before. Eventually Waterstone said, "I think the shame would be enough to keep them away. And even if they did venture back into our territory, sooner or later they would be spotted and shot."

"And if they were untrustworthy, what would stop them from revealing themselves to sorcerers and going to live among them?" asked Danton.

Looks of profound shock confronted him.

"No woodfolk would ever choose to live among sorcerers," stated Summer Rain flatly. "Far better, a life of solitude."

640

A fraught silence ensued. Tarkyn and Danton, even String and Bean, suddenly felt like ugly horny toads, sitting unwelcome amongst a gathering of gentle tree frogs. Only Stormaway seemed unaffected.

Lapping Water reached around Midnight to put her hand impulsively on Tarkyn's knee and said gently. "Don't look like that. We are happy with you among us. But think how long it has taken us to get used to you when there are few of you and many of us. We would be much too fearful to become one woodfolk among many sorcerers, especially in their world, with rules we don't understand and with all that power they have that we don't."

Tarkyn nodded and started to breathe again, not aware until then that he had stopped. His taut face relaxed and without thinking, he placed his hand over Lapping Water's, gave it a squeeze and left it there. "Thank you for explaining that." He took another deep breath to fully recover himself. "So, the likelihood is that Falling Rain is somewhere at the bottom of the mountain, living in one of those patches of forest. And he won't reveal his presence to anyone, woodfolk or sorcerer, even if you or I try to contact him directly. Is that right?"

"Yes. He will have closed his mind off. And even if we can figure out where he is, he will still conceal himself when we come looking for him," added Tree Wind.

"What if I could get close enough to him to order him to reveal himself? Did he swear the oath?"

Waterstone, Tree Wind and Autumn Leaves exchanged glances. After a moment, Waterstone said, "I'm not sure. He was so ill, you see. He may not have." The woodman shrugged and grinned wickedly. "It doesn't make much difference anyway. You have just finished telling me that you don't need the oath to make people comply."

Tarkyn had the grace to look a little embarrassed. "Hmm, yes. In general, I would say that was true but in the case of someone who has lived alone for twelve years and is just possibly feeling resentful towards the Tamadil family in general, I may not have quite the same level of success."

String and Bean's eyes lit up. "Then we're going to have to trap him, aren't we?" said String with some enthusiasm.

"Ooh. That will be a good start to our renewed acquaintance with him, won't it?" Tarkyn grimaced. "But other than me standing in the middle of a forest making an idiot of myself by trying to order him around, I can't see any alternative. Can anyone else?"

After a moment, several heads shook reluctantly.

"As long as you don't hurt him though," said Tree Wind, staring a challenge at Tarkyn.

Tarkyn face split into a grin. "Couldn't help yourself, could you, Tree Wind? You just had to say that."

Tree Wind folded her arms and tried to repress an answering grin. "You just be careful, that's all."

"Tree Wind, I am not going to run this operation. I am just trying to clarify what the situation is, so that I can help. Among you, you can choose who is coordinating it and the rest of us will give you whatever help you require."

Waterstone smiled. "Don't tell me you are handing over the reins, Tarkyn,"

"Probably not, knowing me. But I am trying to, for the time being. So, let me know when you've decided and we'll go from there."

After a very short mind conference, it was agreed that Tree Wind would oversee the task of making contact with Falling Rain. Tarkyn suddenly realised he was still holding Lapping Water's hand but while he was wondering how and when to extricate himself, he was saved from his dilemma by

Midnight who impatiently retrieved Lapping Water's hand to help him with his plaiting. Lapping Water smiled at Midnight and kept very firmly focused on helping him with his wristband.

"Before we trap him, we have to find him," Tree Wind was saying. "We can't just set random traps all over the foothills. So, how are we going to do that?"

"Can you people detect the presence of each other, if one is trying to hide?" asked Bean.

Thunder Storm shook his head. "Very rarely. Only if someone has made a mistake. That's how we train our young, you see. They have to practise hiding and covering their tracks until they can't be found by us."

"Will he have become careless over time, do you think?" asked String.

Tree Wind and Summer Rain looked at each other before Tree Wind answered, "I would say, almost certainly not. Not when he is so close to sorcerers' dwellings."

"So basically, conventional tracking can be ruled out," concluded Bean.

"Tarkyn, you could use an animal to look for him," suggested Running Feet. "Just as you did when you used the eagle owl to find Danton."

Tarkyn smiled at the woodman, still aware that he had snapped his head off earlier. "I could if we knew the general area but I couldn't ask any animal to scour the whole of the foothills. It is too large a task. We need a way to focus upon a smaller area first."

String scratched his head. "Interesting challenge, this one, Bean." He thought for a minute. "So, none of you can trace where his mind is, if he has it closed off? Is that right? That's what you said about Hail."

"True enough," replied Waterstone.

"And yet Tarkyn found Hail, didn't he?" said String. "He traced her through her emotions."

"So, we just have to find a way to make Falling Rain react strongly to something and Tarkyn will be able to pinpoint him." Tree Wind smiled at Tarkyn. "I knew you wouldn't be side-lined for long. Do you think that will work?"

"As long as we're close enough." Tarkyn thought for a minute. "Saying that, I picked up Autumn Leaves' distress when he was being struck by the knife hilt from what? ... about four miles away."

"And it will be easy to elicit a strong reaction in Falling Rain," said Autumn Leaves.

Tree Wind frowned. "How? You're not to frighten him."

Autumn Leaves smiled gently. "As soon as he sees any of us, he will be swamped with emotion, I would think." He tilted his head. "I'm not sure what; anger, resentment, longing, regret, could be fear, but whatever it is, it will be strong. And Tree Wind, I can't see us being able to immobilise him long enough to talk to him without frightening him to some degree. He won't know what our intentions are until we explain them to him."

Tears sprang to Tree Wind's eyes. "Poor Falling Rain. All this time." Then she wiped her hand briskly over her eyes and sniffed before asking String and Bean, "You two must know this area better than anyone. What are the woodlands like at the base of the mountain? Where is the most likely place that a woodman might choose to live?"

String scratched his head. "I don't know. What's most likely to attract a woodman to a particular area?"

"Safety," replied Bean promptly. "He doesn't have the luxury of a lookout roster like the rest of you. So he needs somewhere that he won't have sorcerers sneaking up on him when he's dropped his guard." Seeing Tree Wind frown, he continued, "No matter how well trained or meticulous he is, the man has to sleep and he can't be looking in every direction at once. If he wanted to have a fire or do anything in the open, he would need warning of people coming."

"Or be in a place that was inhospitable to sorcerers," mused String.

"But was all right for woodfolk," finished Bean.

"So, is there anywhere like that?" asked Tree Wind patiently.

Bean shrugged. "I can't imagine anywhere that you folk would want to be that we wouldn't."

"Perhaps there are some things about us that we know and you don't," suggested Tree Wind with a touch of acerbity. "Are there any places in the foothills you can think of that sorcerers don't like visiting?"

There was a long pause while String and Bean let their minds range around their memory of the foothills. Suddenly they looked at each other, clicked their fingers and chorused, "The swamp."

The woodfolk waited patiently until Bean expanded, "There is a large swamp off to the east a little. It's full of old trees and small shrubs that somehow seem happy to grow in waterlogged conditions. Dwelling in the murky waters there are biting fish and large carnivorous creatures which are extremely off-putting."

"Crocodiles or alligators?" suggested Tarkyn.

Bean shook his head. "Don't know. Never seen them... And the air is filled with nasty stinging insects; gnats and mosquitoes and who knows what else. I've never been in there and very few have."

"Couldn't you just levitate your way over the waters if you wanted to go there?" asked Autumn Leaves.

Bean glanced at String before replying, "Not many sorcerers could. I know Tarkyn and Danton are good at it and so is Stormaway if he wants to, but we're not. It's a huge effort for us and we couldn't keep it up for long, certainly not long enough to navigate that swamp." He shrugged. "Even if we could, there are still those dreadful insects to contend with."

"You know, I think this may well be where Falling Rain is living," said Summer Rain, thinking aloud. "It is not difficult to fend off insects. We have several herbs that will do that. And he could move around the swamp from tree to tree, couldn't he?"

"It will make it easier if he's there, won't it?" Tree Wind looked at Bean. "Just how big is this swamp? I suppose it would be too big for us to surround it?"

"Oh yes, much too big. It would cover several square miles. What do you think, String? How big would you say it was?"

String scratched his chin. "I would say it's at least four or five miles long." Amid sighs of disappointment, he added, "But it's not very wide, is it Bean? No, I would say it's less than a mile wide in most places. It follows the path of a river, you see. And there's just this one section of the river as it comes out of the foothills where it has spread itself out into the forest on either side."

"Hmm. Excuse us a minute," said Tree Wind. Without intending to be funny, she added, "We think better thinking than talking."

With that, the quiet of a mind conference descended on the cave. In the background, Tarkyn could hear the sounds of the black mountain lion tearing the last of the flesh and skin off a large snow hare he had brought in earlier. Tarkyn looked around at him and received a warning growl in response. Tarkyn met his eyes steadily for a few moments to maintain the status quo before turning back.

In response to a tug on his sleeve, Tarkyn looked down to see Midnight wave his hand to indicate everyone sitting around the fire and then move his finger from his lips outwards to indicate talking with a query on the end of it. Tarkyn smiled apologetically and did his best, using images, to fill Midnight in on the contents of the discussion.

After a minute, Midnight sent an image of sorcerers lined up along either side of the length of the swamp with the woodman running up and down the length of the swamp but always next to the path of the river so that he was as far from the sides at all times as possible.

Tarkyn smiled and nodded in acknowledgement and then cleared his throat to get the woodfolk's attention. "Excuse me, everyone. I have another little factor to throw into the mix."

When he had finished explaining Midnight's idea, String exclaimed, "Now that he's pointed it out, it's blindingly obvious, isn't it? Of course, Falling Rain will keep to the centre of the swamp, close to the river."

A thought struck Danton. "But what about boats? If it's a river course, couldn't sorcerers navigate into the swamp in boats? Then the river would be the least safe place."

Bean considered this objection for a moment. "They would have to be keen. The swamp narrows at the southern end and then channels into a fast flowing, narrow set of rapids that spreads back out into a calmer, wide river further down. They couldn't climb that steep part carrying a boat. In fact, I think they would have to skirt around and come into the swamp from the west side if they were going to. They would need a very flat-bottomed boat and quite an expedition to achieve even that. Falling Rain would hear them hours before they were anywhere near him."

"No, I think our little friend is right," said String, sending Midnight a smile. "Falling Rain will be near the river."

"So, Tarkyn, is that a small enough area for you?" asked Running Feet.

Tarkyn nodded. "I would say so. How far are we from this

swamp? Do you want me to look for him now or wait until we get closer?"

"Now," said Tree Wind impulsively. When Tarkyn raised an eyebrow at her, she thought again and with a slight smile at her own response, said more slowly, "Yes, now if you can. Because there is no point in us travelling to the swamp if he's not there."

"Very well. What's the weather like outside? Any better?"

Running Feet, who had a fair idea where this was heading, stood up and walked to the entrance of the cave. He wandered out far enough to put his head above ground level, looked around and came back inside. "It's not too bad. The wind has dropped. A few clouds around still, but I think the worst of it has passed." He smiled at Tarkyn. "So I expect we can brave the cold if that's what you'd like to do."

Tarkyn grinned. "Yes. That is what I would like to do. And you'll come with me, will you? Thanks. And we'll need String and Bean. Please, the rest of you stay here so I can concentrate. I won't be long. Meanwhile, Danton and Stormaway, can one of you place your shield over everyone until I return. I don't think we should trust that cat too far."

A fter careful discussions with String and Bean, Running Feet understood enough about the position of the swamp to guide Tarkyn's mind to the general vicinity. With String and Bean keeping guard, Tarkyn closed his eyes and, maintaining his link with Running Feet, scoured through the trees looking for a heron's mind to tune into. He remembered the heron who had taken his mind soaring above the forests and who had treated his attempts at intimidation with such disdain. He searched for a similar stately, aloof mentality and finally zoned in on a female egret, not quite so aloof as the grey heron, perched high in a weeping willow overhanging the bank of a small lake.

The guardian of the forest sent waves of friendship and then a picture of the swamp with a woodman in it and a request to find him. In return, he received a wave of protective hostility.

"This bird knows where he is," murmured Tarkyn, "and she is protecting him. Interesting." Tarkyn sent a wave of reassurance and an image of other woodfolk approaching and chatting with Falling Rain. The egret, who would never have seen Falling Rain talking to anyone, was unconvinced. Tarkyn thought for a moment before sending an image of the woodman looking unhappy, followed by an image of Falling Rain surrounded by other woodfolk, smiling. Tarkyn wondered whether the egret had spent long enough in Falling Rain's company to recognise the meaning of his facial expressions.

Apparently, she had, because she took off ponderously and flapped her way above the trees and across the lake. The south eastern shore of the lake was cut by a river that flowed between loamy banks before broadening into the shapeless waters of the swampland. Unerringly, the egret followed the vague course of the submerged river as it wound its way through the inundated forest below. After a mile or so, she gradually lost height until she glided down between the treetops and landed with a final swoop on a platform of reeds, high above the murky waters of the swamp. Then she looked calmly, straight into the face of Falling Rain.

"Wow. There he is," squawked Running Feet. "He looks fine. His hair's a bit longer than I remember it." At that moment, Falling Rain turned side on to pick up a small fish that he then offered to the egret. "Oh no, Look at that. His hair's a lot longer. It's halfway down his back. I thought it was just long enough to be caught in a bit of thronging, but it's very long, isn't it? He looks a bit more lined. Well, he would be, wouldn't he? It's twelve years since I last saw him. Other than that, he looks much the same. Oh my stars! How exciting! Can we go back and tell the others?"

Tarkyn carefully maintained his link with the heron as he asked, "Can you navigate us to there from what we've seen? Don't forget, you're the only one who knows where to go from this. String and Bean haven't seen it and I won't have a clue."

"Yes. No problem at all. Perfectly straight forward."

Tarkyn was smiling but persisted. "And do you know

enough about the area to plan our approach or should I send the egret up for another look around?"

With an effort, Running Feet calmed himself down. "I think I know enough. You may need to make contact again when we're closer but I know as much as I need to for the time being."

Tarkyn transmitted his gratitude to the egret and pulled out.

"See you," said Running Feet cheerily, giving Tarkyn a few enthusiastic pats on the back before running back to the cave to share the news, the two trappers close behind him.

59

For a long time after the others had returned to the cave, Tarkyn sat in the snow under a tree, wrapped in his wolf skin cloak, wondering about how Falling Rain would react to their advent. The prince was particularly concerned about Falling Rain's reaction to Stormaway when he found out that the wizard had used mind control to force him to betray the whereabouts of the other woodfolk and thus earn himself exile. He heard crunching footsteps in the snow behind him before Waterstone came into sight around the side of the tree. Tarkyn glanced up and smiled as the woodman sat down beside him. "Hello. Come to see whether I'm all right, have you?"

"What you? A hated sorcerer?" Waterstone said lightly, throwing a sideways glance to check that it was taken in good part. "Yes, I have actually."

"Don't worry. I knew you were talking about Hail's perceptions, not your own when you called me that." Tarkyn picked up a long stick and began to break bits off the end of it, "I'm fine. A bit concerned about Stormaway, though. Do you think Falling Rain might attack him when he realises what happened?"

Waterstone blinked at him. "I can't see why you're worried. Stormaway's a wizard. He can just put up his shield. He's hardly under any real threat."

"But maybe I should insist that Stormaway accepts whatever Falling Rain dishes out. After all, his actions caused Falling Rain to be unjustly exiled for twelve years." He glanced uncertainly at Waterstone. "On the other hand, I don't think he should be punished for simply serving my father. What do you think?"

"If Stormaway had known Falling Rain had been exiled for betraying us, he would have told us that he'd used mind control on him, wouldn't he?"

After a moment's hesitation, the prince nodded.

"So it was just unfortunate that we kept him at arm's length and didn't tell him more about our affairs more than we had to." Waterstone shrugged. "It's going to be difficult for many of us. We all feel sorry that we exiled Falling Rain unjustly. He may never forgive us. Who knows?"

"So, have you decided how you're going to trap him yet?"

"More or less." Suddenly Waterstone grinned. "Is it taking you a lot of effort to stay out of it?"

Tarkyn laughed. "No. It would if I were inside listening to it all, but not out here. I don't need to be involved in this at all, if you people want to meet Falling Rain on your own."

"I think that he is so hard to access, hidden up in the trees above the swamp, that we were thinking of making use of Danton, Stormaway and you to levitate people to reach him."

"Oh, were you indeed?" Tarkyn raised his eyebrows. "Falling Rain is going to get the fright of his life having three sorcerers descend on him from on high."

Waterstone smiled. "Maybe, but we figured he probably

has sound traps set up that you can't hear in your image. So, if we try to climb through the trees to get to him, he'll hear us coming long before we reach him."

"You're probably right. He's bound to have some sort of warning system, isn't he? So we float in at him from three sides. How can you stop him flicking into hiding?"

"Hmm. I think we have your work cut out for you. You can throw your shield around him before he can disappear." Waterstone stole another glance at Tarkyn to make sure he wasn't feeling put upon.

"I think we should get Danton to do that," said Tarkyn decisively.

"Why?"

"Well, Falling Rain is going to hate me because of my father and he's going to hate Stormaway because he dragged the information out of him. So Danton is the least threatening of us who can maintain a shield."

Waterstone thought for moment. "On the other hand, you could throw your shield over Falling Rain, Danton and one of us so we could talk."

"Why don't I just immobilise Falling Rain until you three woodfolk disembark. Then we sorcerers will retreat. That way he doesn't have to deal with us close up until he's used to the idea."

"Yes, that seems like a good idea. And it would be better still, if you then put up your shield. Otherwise we'll have to stand there holding him, to stop him from flicking into hiding. And you're the only one who can use your shield while keeping him immobilised," Waterstone gave a knowing little smile, "because Danton would have to place his shield around you and us, wouldn't he?"

Tarkyn gave a wry smile. "You're getting better at understanding our magic. Yes, you're right. Danton couldn't place a shield between Falling Rain and me while Falling Rain is under one of my spells." He stood up and brushed the snow off the back of his wolfskin cloak. "Very well. Let's do it that way. I suppose I can maintain my shield from a distance. You people will just have to calm him down. He's going to get a fright however we do it."

60

The entire company stayed overnight in the cave and set off early the next morning. There had been a suggestion that only the rescue party needed to go, while the rest could stay in the warm cave and await their return. But without either Tarkyn there as pack leader or a constant shield over the woodfolk, the mountain lion presented too great a threat.

The sky was a cloudless blue overhead as they set out and it was not long before the snow turned to slush underfoot. Because they were in unknown territory, the woodfolk kept close together, with lookouts scanning each side, ahead and behind them. There were always two or three at the rear of the group modifying the woodfolk's tracks when they had passed. In the slushy conditions, their tracks couldn't be obliterated completely but any clear footprints were blurred beyond recognition. Anyone coming afterwards would be able to see that a number of people or animals had passed through but would not be able to identify them.

On a clear day, the journey along the narrow path that led them down the next cliff face presented a grave threat. There were certain places where anyone looking up from the valley below would be able to see them. The woodfolk decided that from a distance, no one would know they weren't sorcerers, but they passed through these exposed sections in groups of two or three, with breaks of several minutes between them, so that the casual observer would not realise that a large group was moving down the mountainside.

Still, by the time they had reached the cover of the forests at the bottom of the mountain, the woodfolk were feeling that they had taken many unaccustomed risks in an area far too close to sorcerers for comfort. It was an anxious, muted group who finally set up camp deep in the forest, to the west of the swamp and south of the lake, just as the late afternoon sun was dipping below the trees. Despite the lateness of the hour, it was decided to try to make contact with Falling Rain straight away, in case he became aware of their presence so close to him. According to Running Feet and the trappers' calculations, Falling Rain was only a mile away.

A huge debate had raged over who should be the first three woodfolk to go in with the sorcerers and talk to Falling Rain. It did not take long to decide that Summer Rain, his sister and Tree Wind, his erstwhile fiancée, should go. But there was considerable debate about the third person. It had to be someone who had clearly supported Falling Rain's exile so that the woodman could be sure that it was a full revocation of his exile and not just his supporters trying to persuade him to return. In the end Waterstone was chosen because, at the time, he had been so angry and so adamant that Falling Rain should be exiled.

Summer Rain climbed onto Stormaway's back, Tree Wind onto Danton's and Waterstone onto Tarkyn's. When everyone was secure, the three sorcerers rose gracefully from the ground with their woodfolk cargo. As they levitated straight up above the tree line, the woodfolk's grips around the sorcerer's necks and hips tightened.

"Oh my stars," breathed Waterstone, peering down at the forest floor far below them. "I don't know what made us think this was a good idea. This is terrifying. Are you sure you can keep holding us up? It's an awfully long way down."

Danton smiled across at him. "Don't worry. We can keep this up for a while yet."

"Speak for yourself!" exclaimed Stormaway. "I really am getting too old for this. I struggle to do this on my own without providing the power for two."

Tarkyn eyed him for a minute, trying to gauge the seriousness of his remark. Eventually, he said, "Stormaway, either I can give you some strength or Summer Rain can give you one of her restorative tonics, if you are struggling. Just tell me and it shall be done."

The old wizard gave a gusty sigh. "I wasn't looking for a remedy. I was looking for sympathy and encouragement."

"Stop whingeing, you old windbag!" laughed Tree Wind. "I bet you're loving this. You always like any sort of intrigue and adventure."

"Yes, Stormaway," said Danton firmly. "Stop whingeing or you'll make Summer Rain feel unwelcome."

Stormaway gave Summer Rain's leg a little pat. "What nonsense! Summer Rain knows me better than that. But I do beg your pardon, Summer Rain. I would not like to give you the wrong impression. It is a pleasure to be of assistance to you."

"Hmph. You just make sure, old man, that you can hold me up." The humourless healer paused before adding gruffly, "And thank you for doing this. It means a lot to me."

Sorcerers and woodfolk glided silently between the highest branches of the trees. As the inundated forest spread out before them, they could smell a soft dankness in the air, not unpleasant but quite different from the usual odours of the forest. Occasionally, they saw eddies or a little splash disturb the silky surface and once they saw the rippling V of a snake gliding through the water. Around them in the branches, they passed the odd grey heron perched in stately aloofness. Groups of white egrets clustered in the trees in increasing numbers as they moved further into the swamp. Now and then, a mosquito whined past their ears but the emanation from Summer Rain's herbal ointments would make it shy off.

As the sorcerers and woodfolk drew nearer, they lapsed into silence, aware that their voices might betray their presence too soon. The three woodfolk had all seen the image of the egret's journey and, with their ability to discern and remember minute differences in the forest vegetation, directed the sorcerers unerringly to Falling Rain's hideout.

Leaving Danton, Stormaway and their passengers to wait a short distance from their destination, Tarkyn glided slowly above the trees, carefully keeping his levitation spell firmly to one side of his mind and watching intently for the instant that Falling Rain came into sight. Tarkyn had to immobilise the woodman first before Falling Rain saw him and flicked into hiding. Gradually, Tarkyn and Waterstone became aware of the sound of soft, rhythmic beating and an egret flew slowly past them, eyeing Tarkyn suspiciously as she passed. The egret who, at her slowest, still travelled through the air much faster than Tarkyn, glided in a large circle in front of them before coming back to circle around them in a large figure of eight. Tarkyn's mind was filled with a sharp query and a view of Falling Rain moving around his reed platform, intent on his preparations for his evening meal. A clear warning echoed through Tarkyn's mind before he sent her a wave of reassurance. In response, she showed him other egrets gathered in nearby trees, watching.

Tarkyn transmitted this to the three woodfolk. Suggestions ranged back and forth amongst them but eventually Tarkyn sent the egret a message that, as soon as the sorcerers had dropped off the woodfolk, he would wait among the egrets to show them his good faith. The egret flapped past them once more but this time she flew further ahead, and then swooped back around to fly straight at Tarkyn, her long, sharp beak aimed right at his forehead. The forest guardian stared directly at her, sending out waves of friendship and keeping his course steady, although Waterstone could feel Tarkyn's muscles tensing as she came nearer. At the last possible moment, she gave her wings a strong flap and lifted herself just high enough to skid over their heads, the feathers of her underbelly and the tips of her feet just brushing the top of Tarkyn and Waterstone's hair.

"Whew," breathed Tarkyn. "We have been warned. Your friend seems to have developed a following."

61

Falling Rain had cleaned a fish ready for his dinner. He had a particular area further up in the tree for cleaning and scaling so that the fishy mess did not spread around his small domain. Now he was cutting up a selection of marsh plants that he knew would complement the flavour of his bream. On the other side of the platform, hanging from the branch above, was a large iron pan that he used to contain his fire so that the reed platform did not catch alight. It was already set with dry reeds and twigs. An assortment of branches, broken into tidy lengths, was stacked neatly against the trunk of the tree.

The lone woodman let his gaze wander through the surrounding branches, watching the egrets settling for the night, ruffling their white feathers and sometimes swooping out to land in another tree. Tonight, they seemed more restless than usual and many of them had congregated in one particular tree. Sometimes this happened when a large hawk or eagle was soaring high in the air above them. Falling Rain tilted his head casually to survey the skies for an airborne predator. A wave of horror ran through him as his eyes met the intense amber eyes of a sorcerer who had suddenly come into view above his hideout. Never before had anyone breached the security of his isolated home. Before he could react, the sorcerer murmured something, and Falling Rain found himself unable to move. He felt his heart hammering in his chest and, with a sense of déjà vu, saw the sorcerer advancing on him.

Oh no, he thought, *not again. At least this time, I will know nothing to betray them with.*

Unable to move anything but his eyes, he watched the sorcerer draw ever closer until he landed next to him on the platform. Only then did Falling Rain notice the woodman clinging to the sorcerer's back. Without a word, the woodman climbed down and the sorcerer took off, gliding to the nearest tree to sit among the egrets who were watching the proceedings balefully. *No wonder the egrets have been restless*, thought Falling Rain as, unbeknownst to him, Tarkyn sent greetings to the egrets around him, which were received with a stiff acknowledgement.

A true sense of panic now gripped Falling Rain. He couldn't move to escape and so was unable to fulfil his requirement to avoid woodfolk. Now he would be condemned of betraying what little honour was left to him. Worse still, the woodman who had arrived was Waterstone, one of the strongest protectors of woodfolk values. The exiled woodman watched, helpless, as two more sorcerers descended, deposited woodfolk and left without speaking. He saw that as each sorcerer landed in a tree, the egrets around them rose into the air and flapped their way slowly over to land in the branches around the sorcerer with the amber eyes.

Just when Falling Rain thought it couldn't get any worse, the air around him seemed to erupt into a golden-brown haze. Suddenly he realised he could move again and immediately tried to flick into hiding. But instead of reappearing behind his shelter, Falling Rain thumped against the wall of the barrier and slid to the floor of the platform, still in view of the other woodfolk.

The sounds of ruffling feathers grew louder around the amber eyed sorcerer and Falling Rain saw him glance nervously sideways at a large white egret, only feet away from him.

Inside the shimmering dome, Tree Wind ran over to the fallen woodman and knelt down beside him. "Don't, Falling Rain. You don't have to avoid us." She waved her arm. "And while this shield is in place, you can't."

Falling Rain sat up, his face suffused with chagrin and anger, and pushed her firmly away. "I have tried to leave but can't. So, keep away from me. All three of you, stay over there."

For a moment, Tree Wind's face tightened and it looked as though she might protest but on balance, she decided to do as he asked, and retreated to stand beside Waterstone. Falling Rain stood up and ignoring them completely, gazed around the bronze dome that surrounded him. Once he had taken that in, he stared through the slanting shafts of late afternoon sunlight into the surrounding trees until he had spotted the three waiting sorcerers, before finally bringing his gaze to bear on the three woodfolk before him.

He crossed his arms and said quietly. "So, is it not enough that I am exiled? Do I now have to be imprisoned as well? What has changed that you feel you must do this to me?" As they all began to speak at once, he held up a hand to stop them. "And when did sorcerers become servants of the woodfolk? Last I heard, woodfolk treated everyone as equals."

This last question so stunned his audience that they looked in shock at each other and for a moment, couldn't answer. Eventually, Waterstone cleared his throat and said, "It is not as it seems. These sorcerers are working with us, not for us. They would be here by our sides talking with you too, but we did not want to alarm you any more than we had to." He turned and pointed at the source of the shield. "I don't know if you recognise him, but that is Prince Tarkyn over there, grown to manhood and returned to claim our allegiance." He indicated the other two in turn. "Over there is his friend Lord Danton, who is..." Waterstone broke off with a little smile. "Well, you will meet him later and decide for yourself, but I like him. And over there is Stormaway Treemaster, creator of the oath and, ever since the death of King Markazon eleven years ago, Prince Tarkyn's loyal retainer."

"I see. So it is they who would have me imprisoned?" A self-deprecatory sneer appeared on the woodman's face. "I would have thought they would be grateful to me for betraying you."

"No, Falling Rain," said Tree Wind impulsively, "you are not imprisoned."

The woodman waved a hand over his head at the glowing bronze dome. "So what is this thing, then, that is stopping me from leaving?"

"It is Tarkyn's shield, Falling Rain." Summer Rain spoke in a steady, calming voice. "And if you are imprisoned, so too are we. Do not fear it. Tarkyn will release it at our request when we are sure you will not run."

"We must talk with you, Falling Rain. If you give your word that you will stay, we can ask Tarkyn to remove his shield, if it is unnerving you," said Waterstone.

"I'm surprised you would accept my word," Falling Rain said bitterly.

Waterstone did not make the mistake of thinking that his remark was directed at all three of them. "I will, Falling Rain, without a moment's hesitation."

The woodman folded his arms again. "I will stay with you

until the first star appears. Beyond that, I will make no guarantee."

Waterstone nodded and after a few moments, the shield flicked out of existence. In the nearby tree, several egrets ruffled their feathers and a couple of them flapped from one branch to the next. One egret took off and came gliding in to land on the edge of the platform, tilting her head to eye the group of woodfolk.

"Just a minute." Falling Rain disappeared around the side of his little shelter and returned with a tiny fish that he threw to her. The egret accepted the offering but did not move.

"She is waiting to see whether you smile," Waterstone explained.

Falling Rain frowned. "What rot! How would an egret know what my expression was?"

Waterstone shrugged. "I guess she has spent enough time around you to know your moods."

"And how would you know all this?" demanded the woodman.

"Our prince over there. He persuaded the egrets to guide us to you by showing them an image of you smiling when we came to you." Waterstone grimaced. "So far, that hasn't happened. Until it does, Tarkyn is in a rather awkward position. He offered himself as surety to underwrite his word. It is he who is imprisoned and in danger at the moment, not you."

Falling Rain snorted, totally unimpressed. "You have changed, Waterstone. You never used to talk drivel before. How could those birds hurt a sorcerer? He can just flick up that shield of his."

"He could, but he won't. He gave them his word that we wouldn't harm you." Waterstone squatted down near the waiting heron. "One of them, possibly this one, flew straight at us. Missed us by a hair's breadth." He glanced up. "Your relationship with these birds is most impressive. They are united in protecting you. I have never seen anything like it among woodfolk."

And finally, Falling Rain did smile. "I didn't realise they were protecting me like that." His smile broadened until his whole face was beaming. "That is so marvellous, that they are looking after me." He looked across at the willow, full of egrets. "I was wondering why they had all congregated in one tree. They usually spread out over several." He laughed. "Your precious prince is safe after all."

Waterstone shook his head, smiling. "The risk was small because we had no intention of hurting you. If it had been greater, we wouldn't have let him do it."

"You mean, we would have tried to dissuade him," added Tree Wind dryly.

Falling Rain looked from one to the other. "So, why are you here?"

"To bring you back, Falling Rain," said Tree Wind softly. She took a breath. "You didn't betray us after all, at least not by your own weakness or volition. Stormaway used mind control on you."

The woodman went very still. Only his eyes moved, swivelling to focus in on Stormaway sitting in his green robes high in the branches of a willow. As they watched, his eyes grew dark with anger. "How could he let you think, let me think that I had betrayed everyone? All these years, I have hated myself for betraying you all. I thought the sickness must have weakened my resistance and I have cursed my feebleness and lack of will power."

"There is no way you could have resisted a strong wizard's mind control, especially in your weakened state," stated Summer Rain flatly.

"And so, knowing this, we absolve you of responsibility for

the sorcerers finding us," said Waterstone. "Your honour and your place among woodfolk is restored."

Falling Rain glanced at Waterstone, his mind a turmoil of anger and regret. "I should hate you for the way you treated me and doubted me. And yet I can't, because I did the same to myself." He turned his frustrated anger to stare at Stormaway. "How could he stand by, watch me be sent into exile and do nothing?"

Tree Wind walked to him and put her hand on his arm. "He didn't know, Falling Rain. No one included him in any woodfolk business. We endured his presence because of the oath but it took us a long while even to speak to him, and nearly two years before we started using him to trade goods for us with outsiders."

Falling Rain stared at her. "You trade goods with outsiders? What is the world coming to?" He shook his head. "Why don't you just shout your presence from the treetops?"

Waterstone and Summer Rain glanced at each other but made no comment. Tree Wind kept her hand on the exiled woodman's arm and said quietly, "No one in the outside world knows from where the goods originate. Outsiders think the goods come from the other end of the kingdom or from over the seas."

Falling Rain digested this, clearly still not satisfied. After a moment, he changed the subject, "And so how do you come to have three sorcerers with you? Two, I can understand. You are forced to endure Stormaway Treemaster and Prince Tarkyn. But what about the third one? That Lord Anton or whatever you called him."

Waterstone smiled. "Hmm. Interesting question. Even more interesting answer. You might suspect that Prince Tarkyn had ordered us to accept his friend, but that would be far from the truth. In fact, the prince is officially a woodman now and is bound by the same oath of secrecy as you or I...more or less. Although he doesn't seem to include himself in that, I notice."

Falling Rain scowled. "Well, that's a contradiction straight away. He can't be a woodman and reveal himself to the outside world." He shrugged. "Anyway, you're all talking nonsense. It's as clear as the nose on my face that he's a sorcerer. Looks like one. Comes from a sorcerer family. Can't be both. It's mutually exclusive. End of discussion."

"Anyway, as I was saying, Danton is here because we reached a community decision to allow him to stay with us."

"Why?" demanded the woodman belligerently.

"To help us to rescue three woodfolk who had been captured by sorcerers," explained Tree Wind patiently. She sighed. "Falling Rain, it's a long, complicated story. We have a lot to tell you. Do you think we could leave it 'til later? Right now, all we want to do is ask you to return with us. We have travelled for many weeks to find you and we just want to take you home." She sniffed, determined not to cry while Falling Rain kept her at arm's length.

Suddenly, Falling Rain focused in on her and studied her face, the bright intelligent eyes and the determined mouth that transformed her face when she smiled. He lifted his hand and gently brushed a wisp of hair off her face.

"Hello, Tree Wind," he said, as though seeing her for the first time. All the anger fell from him and he smiled gently. "You don't know how much I've missed you."

Tree Wind nodded vigorously, the tears now falling. "Oh yes, I do."

The woodman pulled her towards him and wrapped his arms around her. He kissed the top of her head and then as she raised her face, their lips met. As they kissed, all the world and all the years disappeared. When they broke apart, they were smiling and Tree Wind was misty eyed. Falling Rain pulled gently away from her and walked over to encase his sister in a great bear hug.

"Summer Rain, I have missed you too." He pulled back and looked her in the face with a little smile. "And there have been times when I have sorely missed your potions, vile though they are."

Summer Rain studied him critically. "You look healthy enough now. You must have been looking after yourself. I am glad to see you, my brother. I fought long and hard to have you restored to us." She waved her hand. "But in the end, when everyone realised what had happened, there was no opposition at all. Everyone wants you to come back." She hugged him again. "I am so glad you are safe." Then she pushed herself away with a final pat on his back.

Waterstone straightened up from watching the egret, came over to him and looked him straight in the eye. Falling Rain's face was tight, knowing he was facing his severest critic but also one of his closest friends. "Falling Rain, I too want you to come back with us. I am so sorry that you were forced unjustly to spend all these years alone. Whatever we can do to make reparation, we will." He clapped his hand awkwardly on Falling Rain's shoulder. "It is good to see you, my friend." A moment later, he grabbed Falling Rain and dragged him into a hug. "Oh, Falling Rain, I am so glad you are all right."

When they separated, Falling Rain was looking puzzled. "It's very strange," he said slowly. "I keep getting these feelings, almost in waves, of relief and warmth and friendliness and welcome. One after the other. It is more or less how I am feeling but not quite. It's very strange."

Waterstone laughed. "That sounds like Tarkyn up to tricks, if you ask me. He is not like other sorcerers. He can communicate mentally. But he uses feelings and images, not words like us. And sometimes he doesn't even know he's doing it. He's a funny character."

"He sounds a bit lightweight to be a prince after what I learned to expect from that fearsome Markazon," said Falling Rain uncertainly.

Summer Rain frowned sternly. "Never make the mistake of underestimating that young man. He may say some odd things at times..."

Tree Wind whispered, "Summer Rain means that he has a sense of humour."

"*But* he is possibly the most powerful sorcerer in Eskuzor and without a doubt, the bravest, when courage is needed to protect us." She stared at her brother, daring him to contradict her. "He is also a forest guardian, the first of his kind for over four hundred years."

"Is he? That's interesting." Falling Rain stared across the stretch of water at the distant figure of Tarkyn sitting among the herons. "So that's why the egret did as he asked and that's how he could talk with them. I was wondering about that. And even though he's a forest guardian, they still made sure I was protected." He gave a little smile. "I feel even more honoured to have been protected by them, in that case. I must say I will miss them... and the little bats that flit past at dusk. And there's a small tree mouse that comes in and shares snacks with me from time to time. I shall miss them all." He brought his gaze back to bear on the three woodfolk. "But not as much as I have missed all of you."

62

"I think you should be very careful, my lord," said Stormaway quietly as he poked around the reed platform until he spotted the small stump that had been used by Falling Rain as a table. He brought it around to the front of the shelter, wiped it off and offered it to the prince first, waiting for a refusal before sitting down on it himself. "The pendulum is swinging too far the other way."

"I'm inclined to agree, Tarkyn," said Danton, lounging against the trunk of the huge river gum in which Falling Rain had made his home. The woodfolk had waved a cheery farewell and had flitted off through the trees back towards the campsite, full of interest at the sights and improvisations that Falling Rain was showing them along the way.

Tarkyn sat with his legs dangling over the side of the platform, the white egret still standing near him. The prince swivelled his head to look at them over his shoulder. "Why?"

"Could you hear what they were saying?" asked Danton.

Tarkyn shook his head. "Not in amongst all those egrets."

"Well I could. Their voices carried clearly across the

water." Danton raised his eyebrows in derision. "Do you realise that Falling Rain thought we were the woodfolk's servants at the start?"

A jab of outrage hit the two sorcerers. "And how did our woodfolk respond?" Tarkyn asked tightly.

Danton shrugged. "In fairness, Waterstone was quick to explain that we were working with them not for them."

"But perhaps that is the impression you are giving, Your Highness. Otherwise, it would not have crossed his mind." Stormaway leaned forward to press his point. "If an outsider views you in that way, it provides you with an objective view of the situation."

"Hmm." Tarkyn stared down into the dark, murky waters that flowed, glinting in the early starlight, beneath the platform. "Anything else?"

Danton glanced at the prince. "Waterstone said you were a funny character – he was talking about your style of communication at the time... and Falling Rain said you sounded like a bit of a lightweight."

Tarkyn drew his long legs up and swivelled around to sit cross-legged facing the other two. "And was this allowed to pass unchallenged?"

Danton smiled and shook his head. "Oh no, not at all. Summer Rain waded in boots and all, to give you a glowing testimonial."

"So it is only Falling Rain's impressions that are the issue here. Is that right?"

"Not entirely," said Stormaway. "He gained his impressions from the way you and the woodfolk behaved towards each other and the way the woodfolk spoke about you. And consider this, Your Highness. They left without even introducing Falling Rain to you, even though he was no longer afraid. I personally do not find that acceptable."

"And you, Danton? What do you think?"

Danton shrugged. "I can understand why it happened. They were excited and keen to explore Falling Rain's domain before it got too dark – And they wanted to rush back to the others. But to be honest, I felt a little chagrin on my own account, let alone yours. So, even making allowances for differences in culture, I think it was disrespectful." He gave a rueful smile. "Well, to be perfectly honest, I thought it was outrageous."

"And it comes hard on the heels of releasing the forest's tie to the oath," said Stormaway ruminatively.

"I trust their honour," said Tarkyn tightly.

"Maybe so." Danton pushed himself upright and came to sit near the prince. "But you allowed them a lot of leeway the other morning to comment on your demeanour and they used it in full measure to criticise you. If you are not careful, you will have no weapons left at your disposal to maintain your status." He shrugged. "Perhaps that is what you want, but you have never given me the impression that you wanted to lose all your authority."

Tarkyn gazed thoughtfully at him. "No. I do not."

"I think the tightrope you walk by maintaining friendships with your subjects is fraying, Your Highness." As Tarkyn frowned, Stormaway put up his hand. "It hasn't broken yet, but it needs attention."

It was an indication of Tarkyn's own level of misgiving that he had not taken umbrage at anything his advisers had said.

"Blast it!" he exclaimed quietly, angry as much at himself as at the woodfolk. "Blast! Blast! Blast! This is going to be so hard to pull back together. You're right. I've almost given away my right to be angry or to remonstrate with people." He stood up and started to pace around the edge of the platform. "I have been far too placatory." He waved a hand. "The trouble was that they so feared and disliked me at the beginning. But now, I've bent over too far. I should never have set myself up to be criticised like that."

"I thought it was quite courageous, actually," said Tree Wind, with a smile.

Tarkyn spun around to find the four woodfolk had suddenly appeared among them, as only woodfolk can. He put his hands on his hips and frowned furiously. "And how long have you been here?" he snapped.

Falling Rain's first close view of the prince was burning amber eyes glaring from beneath drawn black brows, in a face too much like the dreaded Markazon, framed by long black hair. The exiled woodman froze and his breath caught in his throat.

"Not long, Your Highness," Waterstone was saying, unusually respectful. "But long enough to know that you're not happy with us." Without his usual smile, he added, "There have been eddies of discontent whirling through these flooded forests and the odd ripple of anger. I believe we have been remiss." He swept his arm around to indicate Falling Rain. "Your Highness, I would like you to meet our long-exiled kinsman and Summer Rain's brother, Falling Rain."

Falling Rain, his heart hammering in his chest, bowed low.

Waterstone waved his arm grandly at the prince. "And this is my brother and fellow woodman, Tarkyn Tamadil, Prince of Eskuzor and Guardian of the Forest."

Falling Rain's eyes widened and he glanced at Waterstone, wondering at his courage. "I didn't realise he was your brother." He bowed again. "I beg your pardon, Your Highness. I was taken aback. I meant to say that I'm honoured to meet you. But now that I know that you're Waterstone's brother, I am even more honoured than I was before." He glanced uncertainly at Waterstone and gave a little frown, worried that he had said the wrong thing. Waterstone gestured surreptitiously to indicate that he could straighten up.

"I am pleased to meet you, Falling Rain." Tarkyn's voice held a note of reserve, making it clear to the woodfolk who knew him that all was not yet forgiven. To Falling Rain, he sounded detached and chillingly formal. "We have travelled a long time to find you. As soon as I became aware of the inadvertent injustice that had been done to you, I made every effort to see it put right." Despite his best intentions to remain aloof, the prince couldn't help a dash of pique. "I am sure we sorcerers all feel honoured that you found the time to be introduced to us." He took a quick breath to rein in his temper and indicated the other two sorcerers in turn. "You have met Stormaway Treemaster, I believe, under rather unfortunate circumstances. But you have not yet met my loyal friend, Danton Patronell, Lord of Sachmore."

After they had exchanged minimal greetings, a strained silence fell.

After a long minute, the prince said coldly, "Now that you have done your duty, no doubt you would like to see your friends after all this time. Please feel free to leave us. We will follow on behind, at our own pace."

Just as Falling Rain was thinking that their encounter with the prince would be mercifully short, Tree Wind glanced at Waterstone and Summer Rain before saying firmly, "No. I think we would rather go back alongside you. We do not want to start celebrating Falling Rain's return to the fold without you there. You are one of us, don't forget."

"I hadn't forgotten," said Tarkyn, "but I thought you might have." He turned his unnerving gaze on the hapless Falling Rain. "And never again make the mistake of confusing my status. As liege lord, I provide support and protection as I see fit but I answer to no one, not even to the king."

Falling Rain glanced at the woodfolk around him, a slow burn of anger igniting deep inside him, before bowing again. "I beg your pardon, Your Highness, for misunderstanding. I think it was because no one spoke to you or included you. I realise now that all those actions were pre-arranged to keep me from panicking, for which I thank you. I think I would have been truly overwhelmed if I had had six people, three of them sorcerers, on my reed platform. And to be honest," he added tightly, "I do not have the best memories of sorcerers and have spent the years of my exile avoiding them. I am sorry if my uninformed remarks offended you."

For a long moment, Tarkyn just stood there, staring at him. Then he glanced first at Danton and then at Stormaway before bringing his eyes back to bear on the woodman. He dropped his arms to his sides. "Falling Rain, I did not wish to be so harsh at our first meeting. I accept your apology. And it is up to you, but please don't feel you have to bow to me, every time you address me. I know it is an uncomfortable action for woodfolk." With a visible effort, the prince relaxed his stance and walked over to squat next to the egret. He glanced up at Falling Rain. "This particular bird seems very loyal to you. She has not moved from here since you left."

Falling Rain let out a long, slow breath of relief and, grabbing a bit of dried fish from a little bag he had hanging beside his shelter, he came over and, feeling very daring, held it out to the prince. "Would you like to feed her?"

For the first time since the woodfolk had returned, Tarkyn smiled. "Thank you. I would."

The woodman squatted down next to the prince as he held out the fish in his fingers. The egret eyed him for a moment before extending her neck and snapping the offering out of his fingers. Woodman and sorcerer smiled at each other.

"I found her as a fledgling," explained Falling Rain in his

quiet voice. "I don't know what happened to her parents but for some reason they abandoned her. Perhaps they were killed, I don't know. But I rescued her from her nest in one of those trees over there. She was making an incredible noise as she became hungrier and hungrier. So I went to investigate." He smiled sadly. "I suppose she will have to fend for herself now. She can, but she still likes getting little titbits from me."

For a moment, Tarkyn said nothing but then he turned to the woodman. "She would like to come with you, if you would allow it."

Falling Rain blinked. "Did you just ask her that?"

Tarkyn nodded. "In so many pictures, yes."

A smiled spread slowly across Falling Rain's face. "Yes. I would like that very much. It will take her away from her friends and her hunting ground, though."

"She'll be all right," said Tree Wind. "We can all help to find her food if there are places where other birds won't allow her to fish."

Falling Rain put his hand out slowly and gently stroked the top of the egret's head. "Did you hear that, Elsie? You're coming with me."

Waterstone raised an eyebrow. "*Elsie*? You've given her a name?"

Falling Rain nodded happily, at last beginning to relax. "Yes, Elsie the egret. Has a certain ring to it, don't you think?"

Amidst the smiles that greeted this, Summer Rain said firmly, "Shall we go? I am feeling hungry and it will take us half an hour to find our way back in the darkness. We can return tomorrow to collect any things you want to take with you."

Receiving assent from the prince, the woodfolk headed off through the trees while the sorcerers took to the air beside them. A short time later, a loud rattling shattered the quiet of the evening.

"Hear that, Tarkyn?" called Waterstone. "That's one of Falling Rain's sound traps."

"Yes, very noisy. Just as well we approached by air, wasn't it?"

"I think so," said Waterstone. But what they were really saying was that all was well between them again.

63

F alling Rain sat quietly with his back against a tree watching his kinsmen in the flickering firelight. He had been inundated for the first couple of hours but just as he had begun to feel almost panicky at the unaccustomed bevy of people around him, they had all casually melted away to do other things. After a little while, a small darker haired woodchild walked over purposefully and sat himself calmly on Falling Rain's knee. Midnight looked up at him and pointed firstly at Falling Rain, then at himself followed by clasping his hands in his gesture for friendship. When Falling Rain nodded a little uncertainly, Midnight showed him images of Falling Rain standing away from the main group of woodfolk followed by images of himself living alone outside the circle of the mountainfolk.

Falling Rain frowned a little. "What happened to you? What did you do? You are too young to be exiled."

Midnight put his head on one side as he tried to work out what Falling Rain was saying. He pointed to one ear and shook his head. Falling Rain tried mind speaking to him and received

JENNY EALEY

no response. Eventually, Falling Rain pointed at Midnight, pointed away into the darkness and looked puzzled.

The little boy beamed up at him and sent him images of Pipeless with his blue magic swirling over the woodfolk embittering their attitude to Midnight. Then he showed the whole episode of Tarkyn facing the resurrected Sorcerer and the swirling blue magic reversing the woodfolk's attitude to him. Falling Rain was not sure that he completely understood but he knew enough to realise that Midnight was offering friendship based on shared experiences. The woodman nodded and repeated Midnight's first set of gestures.

Falling Rain looked up to see Tarkyn bearing down on them. He tried to hide his immediate fearful response but his dilated eyes gave him away. The sorcerer stopped short, giving him time to recover, before approaching more slowly and sitting down near him, with his knees drawn up and his arms linked loosely across them.

Falling Rain rubbed his hand over his face. "I beg your pardon, Your Highness," he said. "I know you mean me no harm but I am not yet used to the sight of sorcerers around me."

Tarkyn smiled gently. "I too am sorry for startling you. I have come to retrieve this little rascal who knows that everyone is supposed to be giving you a break." He delivered a mock frown at Midnight. "Don't you, rascal?"

Midnight beamed at him and indicated that Falling Rain and he were now friends.

Falling Rain thought through what Waterstone had said about Tarkyn. "Did you ask them to leave me alone for a while?"

"Not exactly. I could feel your panic beginning to mount and relayed your feelings to them. What they did about it was their choice. I hope you don't mind." He smiled suddenly. "I'm afraid I have a tendency to orchestrate events."

"Why wouldn't you? You are their liege lord, after all. I thought that was the whole point of the oath," said Falling Rain trenchantly. He glanced at Tarkyn before letting his eyes travel slowly over the woodfolk and sorcerers chatting in relaxed groups around the firesite. He took a quick breath and then blurted out, "I am just glad that everyone has not suffered too badly under it."

Tarkyn raised his eyebrows. "You do have courage, my friend, don't you? To say that to me, so early in our acquaintance." Falling Rain swallowed nervously but the prince merely said, "I am not the person who can reassure you that they have not. For that, you must ask Tree Wind or Waterstone or one of the others. My hope is that they have not suffered too much. I have tried to fulfil my part of the bargain as their liege lord well enough so that they do not feel too hard done by." He shrugged. "But nothing replaces freedom, does it?"

Tarkyn found himself being scrutinised by the man who had spent long enough alone to pay less heed to social niceties. He endured it without comment until Falling Rain answered, "No. Nothing replaces freedom." Staring Tarkyn straight in the eye, he said, "I did not swear your oath. Must I do so now, to live once more among my kin?"

Tarkyn didn't rush his response. He thought carefully but decided that, if his leadership depended on the oath of one woodman among many, he did not deserve it anyway. "No. I have never intentionally forced woodfolk to make that vow. I would like some reassurance that you will not harm me but you do not have to swear the oath. Perhaps that can be some recompense for your unjust exile."

Falling Rain's eyes narrowed. "If I am the only woodman free to do as he chooses, will that not continue to isolate me?"

"That is your choice. Talk it through with the others, if you like. Perhaps wait for a while before you decide. I personally doubt that it will make much difference either way, but it is not I who stands to lose my freedom. I lost mine a long time ago." In answer to Falling Rain's frown of confusion, Tarkyn said, "I too swore an oath and my commitment is much heavier than any woodfolk's."

When Falling Rain looked sceptical, Tarkyn waved his hand. "I'm not going to argue with you over it. If you don't believe me, ask the others. And now I am going to relieve you of our presence." He transferred his gaze to Midnight. "Come on, Rascal. Bedtime."

He stood up and smiled broadly as Midnight ran and launched himself into his arms.

"What happened to him?" asked Falling Rain quietly. "I know he was isolated and something about a sorcerer with blue magic but I didn't properly understand his images."

"His father put a curse on him so that everyone would revile him. He has had a very hard life. The curse was only lifted a few days ago."

Falling Rain's face tightened with shock. "Isn't he a woodman?"

"Yes and no. He's a woodman with a sorcerer father."

"That's a disgrace!" exclaimed the woodman hotly. "How can this have been allowed to happen?"

Tarkyn hugged Midnight to him. "Might I suggest," he said coldly, "that you make sure you get your facts straight before throwing your opinions around? I would do a lot of listening before I started passing judgements, if I were you. You will hurt people who have already been hurt too much, if you are not careful."

Falling Rain glared at him belligerently for a moment, clearly questioning his right to comment on woodfolk affairs. Then the tension drained out of him. "You are right, of course. I have a lot to catch up on. After all, I have never in my life seen woodfolk and sorcerers talking amicably together."

"If you want to take it slowly getting to know sorcerers, might I suggest you start with String and Bean? They are trappers, used to an isolated existence. None of us has a vested interest in harming or frightening woodfolk. In fact, String and Bean consider it a privilege to be allowed to reside with you for a while, as do I." He turned to walk away but stopped and looked back over his shoulder. "But whatever you do or say, please don't hurt Midnight. He came to you as your friend because he could see that you have suffered as he has. He is not responsible for his parents. However, you end up judging them, don't confuse who you are condemning."

Falling Rain stood up. "Wait." He came over and tapped Midnight to get his attention. Then he pointed at the little boy and himself and made the sign for friendship. Midnight smiled and nodded, giving a little wave over Tarkyn's shoulder as he was borne off to bed.

As it turned out, String and Bean were not the next sorcerers that Falling Rain talked to. Within minutes of Tarkyn leaving, Stormaway Treemaster strolled over and presented himself with a small bow. Falling Rain ignored him and stared straight past him.

Undeterred, Stormaway began, "Falling Rain, we find ourselves in an awkward situation. I would like to apologise wholeheartedly for what I did to you, but unfortunately I can't." Stormaway glanced at the woodman but saw only his profile. "I am and always have been devoutly loyal to Markazon and Tarkyn. Their welfare has always come before all else. So, because the woodfolk are now obliged to protect the prince, I cannot regret my actions. On the other hand, I know Prince Tarkyn was very unimpressed when he found out how I had gained the information from you and I can say that I am wholeheartedly sorry that you were exiled because of it. Had I known, and it had not been to Tarkyn's detriment, I would have told the woodfolk that I had used mind control on you."

Finally Falling Rain turned to look at the wizard. "You are remarkably honest even if I do not necessarily share your opinions."

Stormaway smiled and shook his head. "Never make the mistake of thinking that. I lie, even to Tarkyn when I think it suits his cause. However, at the moment, I think it suits his cause for us to find a way to tolerate each other."

"I, however, have no vested interest in Prince Tarkyn's cause."

Stormaway considered him for a moment. "I think you will find that his cause and the woodfolk's cause are one."

Falling Rain shrugged. "I am not yet sure that I even care about the woodfolk cause. It will depend on what it turns out to be. A lot has changed since I last stood among my kin. No one has had any care for me for a long time. I do not feel that I owe them much."

"What about Tree Wind?"

"Hmm. We'll see. We are both remembering the other person as we were, twelve years ago. I have spent more of my adult life apart from her than with her. A lot changes in twelve years."

"Tree Wind gave Tarkyn such a hard time when he first arrived. She began by physically attacking him...I think she would have killed him then and there, if the swirling wind hadn't shown her that the forest was truly under threat. So, then she showed him how the oath was instigated and made sure he knew how unwelcome he was. She followed this with ongoing agitation against him until he pointed out that her hostility was damaging the forest. She fought him every inch of the way. Eventually she acknowledged that woodfolk would be able to live with him. But only when his actions demonstrated how much he was willing to suffer to protect the forest and woodfolk, did she finally give him her true support and explain to him why she had been so antagonistic."

Falling Rain stared at the wizard. "Why are you telling me this?"

"To show you that some people at least have cared about you the whole time you were away. Summer Rain has advocated for you unstintingly."

"Hmph. Maybe so. But I walk back into a society that suddenly accepts our sworn enemies as friends, where a sorcerer has become a woodman and where a woodchild has a sorcerer father." Falling Rain shook his head back and forth. "I am shocked by what I see. It goes against my whole upbringing, my entire heritage. After what you and your cronies did to me, I will not be so quick to accept sorcerers as my friends."

"What do you mean me and my cronies? Don't spread the blame too widely. It was only King Markazon and I who were responsible for what happened to you."

Falling Rain snorted. "And what about the others?" He began to push Stormaway in the chest almost as punctuation for his phrases, forcing him to take a step backwards with every jab. "Those sorcerers who woke me every half-hour and interrogated me, who removed the food you gave me before I could eat more than a few mouthfuls? – And I withstood all of that and gave nothing away, despite my hunger and illness and lack of sleep. Then suddenly," –Here, an extra hard shove drove Stormaway back against a tree— "after a blank in my memory, I find myself on the road into the forest on the way to betraying my kin."

As he was speaking, a group of woodfolk had quietly gathered to listen to his story, outrage at his treatment clear on their faces. Stormaway was aware that he was surrounded by growing hostility but kept his eyes unwaveringly on Falling Rain.

"Stormaway, you have been dishonest with us," rumbled Thunder Storm's deep voice. "Even after you told Tarkyn about the mind control, you still didn't confess the extent of the torture you subjected Falling Rain to, or that other people were involved." Thunder Storm stood scowling at the wizard. "I know you are devious but I thought you had always been straight with us about keeping our existence secret."

"Waterstone, could you ask Tarkyn to come over here please?" asked Stormaway quietly, his eyes still not leaving Falling Rain.

"Why?" sneered Falling Rain. "Do you need him to protect you from us now that everyone knows the extent of your infamy?"

"No. I am quite capable of protecting myself, should the need arise." The wizard, back against the tree, let his eyes survey the bevy of woodfolk who surrounded him before returning his regard to Falling Rain. "But what you have said concerns me deeply. I did not orchestrate your ill treatment. Someone else knew of your existence without my knowledge."

"Don't be pathetic, old man," spat out Falling Rain. "The game is up and you know it."

"No," Waterstone intervened. "I don't think it is that simple. I'm beginning to wish it were. Stormaway knew you would tell people everything, once you had returned. If he had something to hide, why did he just stay here waiting to be found out? He may be devious but he is not a fool."

"Thank you for those kind words," said Stormaway dryly.

The dark mood of the woodfolk did not lighten. As Tarkyn appeared at the rear of the throng, people moved aside with ill grace, to let him into the group. He glanced around at the angry faces and asked Stormaway, "Why did you send for me?"

More clearly than anything else Tarkyn could have done, that question in the face of seeing Stormaway surrounded by angry woodfolk, told them that he assumed the wizard was in no danger, though whether it was because of the woodfolk's inherent goodwill or the wizard's power wasn't clear.

Tree Wind faced Tarkyn, hands on hips, and said belligerently, "We have just found out that Falling Rain was starved and kept almost constantly awake the whole time he was captive, in spite of the fact that he was desperately ill. We are not very impressed. I hope you feel your welfare is worth that sort of disregard for humanity."

"I think you know I do not," replied Tarkyn evenly. "I do not know what is common practice in interrogating prisoners since I have never been directly involved in it myself. However, I must confess that I suspect some prisoners have met with far worse fates than sleep deprivation and starvation." When an angry babble of voices greeted this, the prince put up his hands. "I'm not saying I condone it. I'm just saying I suspect it happens. However, in Falling Rain's case I was unaware of anything other than the mind control. Saying that, all my information emanates from Stormaway." He transferred his gaze to the wizard. "Stormaway, I am giving you a direct order to answer truthfully. Were you aware of the starvation and sleep deprivation that Falling Rain says that he suffered?"

"No, Sire, I was not."

The dangerous air of displeasure among the woodfolk changed to confusion then consternation.

Falling Rain waved his hand in exasperation. "Why would you believe a wizard above me, a woodman?"

"We don't," explained Waterstone. "We believe both of you. Stormaway would not disobey a direct order from Tarkyn and so we know he is telling the truth. But equally, we have no reason to doubt you."

"...which leaves us with the uncomfortable knowledge that other people knew about you," said Autumn Leaves, "and were working independently of the king and Stormaway in trying to extract information from you."

"But who? I don't know who these people were," said Falling Rain.

Waterstone glanced from Stormaway to Tarkyn before returning his gaze to Falling Rain. "We can hypothesize but only you can really tell us that. It will be in your memories. If you share them with Tarkyn, who is the only sorcerer who can receive images, he may recognise them."

Falling Rain's eyes flared in alarm. He made a sudden move as though to flick into hiding, but Tree Wind reached out and grasped him firmly on his shoulder before he could disappear.

"Let me go," he snapped, twisting his shoulder out of her grasp. "I am not going to open my mind up to some stinking sorcerer. You may all have fallen under his spell but I have no reason to trust him."

"You don't have to show him directly," said Tree Wind, after a moment's thought. "You can show your memories to one of us and we can transmit the images to Tarkyn."

"I don't want to trust him with my memories even indirectly. I don't want to expose my suffering and weakness to a complete stranger, particularly *that* stranger."

Tree Wind was about to say something further, but Tarkyn waved his hand to curtail her. "No. Don't push him. He's quite right. I wouldn't want to begin my relationship with a stranger by showing him what I went through with the virus or the mountainfolk, for instance. Leave the poor man alone. He has enough to contend with, coming back amongst you all. When he feels easier among us and has caught up with everything that has happened, he may feel differently." Just when everyone was thinking how understanding Tarkyn was being, he added firmly, "However, Falling Rain, I do not wish to be referred to again as a stinking sorcerer. I expect my respectful treatment of you to be reciprocated. Even if you do not trust me, I do not think that is too much to ask. Do you?"

Falling Rain's eyes narrowed as he tried to gauge the measure of the man before him. "No. That is not too much. I will agree to an armed truce, so to speak. I beg your pardon for speaking offensively."

Tarkyn nodded shortly, saying as he left, "For those of you who wish to, we will discuss the implications of Falling Rain's revelations on the other side of the firesite when you are ready. You may or may not join us as you see fit, Falling Rain."

Even as he left, Waterstone and Rainstorm peeled off to follow him. When Tarkyn turned to plonk himself despondently against a log, he found them hard on his heels.

"Falling Rain is really angry, isn't he?" said Rainstorm, as they sat down on either side of him.

"Understandably... and Tree Wind has reverted to type again." Tarkyn sighed. "After all these weeks of looking forward to meeting Falling Rain, now that we've found him, he absolutely detests me."

"Hardly surprising. He hates what was done to him," said Rainstorm. "And let's face it, any of us would, especially when it led to his long exile."

"And he must see Markazon and you as the cause of all his misfortune." Waterstone glanced sideways at Tarkyn. "I think he may be your biggest challenge yet. He has more reason to be resentful of you than the rest of us put together."

"Well, at least he's not resentful about the oath. He didn't swear it." Tarkyn suddenly gave a wry grin. "It's great, isn't it? A new reason for being hated."

"I don't think he's too keen on anybody right now," said Stormaway, joining them. "It is only hours since he found out that twelve years of his life were wasted because of miscommunication. He needs time to come to terms with it." He handed around a wine flask and some stoneware cups. "I am shocked by what he told us, though. I've been racking my brains to work out who it could have been." He glanced around the group. "Falling Rain wasn't kept in the dungeons, you know. Because we knew we had found someone extraordinary, I kept him hidden in my private rooms. So I suspect my apprentice, Journeyman Cloudmaker, must have been one of the conspirators because he knew how to enter my rooms and where keys were kept."

"And he's been at the centre of the efforts to hunt us down," added Waterstone.

Other woodfolk began to drift over to join them. Lapping Water handed Tarkyn a soft doughy roll with honey in it before sitting down. "Here you are. To cheer you up."

Tarkyn smiled at her. "Thanks. Did I look upset?"

She put her head on one side as she considered. "Not exactly. But you seem to sort out one episode of ill feeling just in time for another to pop up and take its place. It must wear you down sometimes."

Tarkyn nodded but said nothing further because too many people were now listening. He noticed that Falling Rain and Tree Wind had stayed on their own on the other side of the firesite. He scanned the perimeter of the clearing and spotted the egret perched high in a tree beyond the firelight, neck retracted as she waited faithfully. Sending up waves of reassurance and an invitation, he showed her Falling Rain sitting with Tree Wind away from the crowd. He was rewarded with the sight of her taking off and gliding down in a wide spiral to land beside Falling Rain. He watched Falling Rain break off from his discussion with Tree Wind and, with a gentle smile, stroke Elsie. After a moment, Falling Rain raised his head and looked directly across at Tarkyn who smiled slightly in return before having his attention claimed by Rainstorm.

"Did you see that? That egret just flew down into the middle of our firesite, calm as you like, and landed right next to Falling Rain."

Tarkyn grinned broadly. "Yes, I did see that. That is Elsie, Falling Rain's pet egret. He reared her from a chick. She's coming with us. So don't go shooting her for dinner by mistake."

Rainstorm and North Wind looked at each other and went out of focus for a minute or two. North Wind smiled. "There. Done. We just told everyone so that no one makes a mistake. We'll have to make sure the kids know in the morning. They'll probably love finding things for her to eat. I wonder if she'll let them near her?"

"I think you'd better have that discussion with Falling Rain later," answered Waterstone. He looked quizzically at Tarkyn. "Now, do you think we can drag our minds back to the issue of other sorcerers knowing about us?"

"Sorry, big brother," said Tarkyn meekly, with a smile in his eyes. He hesitated and then said, "Can I just sort out a couple of things that I've been wondering about?" After a rhetorical pause for permission, he continued, "Firstly, how could Falling Rain have led Markazon and Stormaway to you in the first place? Why didn't you just get warning from your lookouts and flick into hiding as you usually do? And secondly, why didn't someone try to use mind control on Golden Toad and Rushwind when they were held captive?"

"It was one of the few times in woodfolk history that we couldn't flick into hiding," answered Summer Rain. "There were too many sick people who were unable to move themselves and we couldn't leave them unprotected. A casual passer-by still would not have found us because of our camouflage, but Falling Rain knew where we were."

"And that young upstart, Journeyman, did try to use mind control on us," replied Golden Toad, "but generally, woodfolk can resist it since we use it effectively ourselves. Falling Rain would only have succumbed because of his weakened state which we've just discovered was even more weakened by hunger and lack of sleep. And secondly, Journeyman didn't really know what he was doing."

"Whereas, I can assure you, I did. Mind control is not a natural skill for sorcerers," explained Stormaway. "And even with training, not all wizards are able to pick it up. Unfortunately, or so I thought at the time – now I think, fortunately – Journeyman was not a particularly adept apprentice. Good at weather, as you've witnessed. Not bad at shielding. Had a way with training animals but used the stick more than the carrot. Never got the hang of mind control. Couldn't remember herbs and potions. Altogether, a bit of a dead loss, really."

"Do you remember with whom he spent his free time?" asked Danton.

Stormaway took a sip of wine as he thought about it, then shrugged. "I took very little interest in his antics outside the confines of my office. He did strike me as a little toadeater though. I think he spent quite a bit of his time fostering powerful connections; ensuring he had a position to move into after he finished his training. I must say I didn't expect it to be my position he moved into. But after Markazon died, I was ousted and Journeyman took my place as court wizard. Pure idiocy on the twins' part. Journeyman was far less skilled than I." He shrugged. "But there you are. I should have paid more attention to what he was doing *between* lessons, not in lessons."

Tarkyn frowned in frustration. "We really need to know from Falling Rain, don't we?"

"And I don't think we can leave it too long. It is important to our safety that we know who knows about us," added Autumn Leaves.

Lapping Water smiled at him. "It can't be that urgent. We have done without the knowledge for twelve years."

"But something has changed." Autumn Leaves helped himself to some wine from the flask as he talked. "We have had three woodfolk captured, and a pack of wolves trained up to look for us. Suddenly, whoever knows about us wants to find us."

"Hmm, I think Tarkyn is what has changed," said Lapping Water, glancing at the prince. "That same Journeyman who controlled the wolves also led the hunting party that tracked down Tarkyn."

"But the first time, the wolves didn't follow Tarkyn's scent. They stopped searching when they couldn't follow our scent up into the trees even though Tarkyn's scent was on the ground leading to the road," objected Waterstone.

Lapping Water threw her hands up. "I don't know. Maybe they weren't looking for Tarkyn then. When the next hunt set out, they knew Tarkyn had been in the area because of the fire."

They were interrupted at this point by the appearance of Falling Rain at the edge of the group. He stood there, hands on hips and looked around the woodfolk. "Because it is important to the safety of woodfolk, I will release my memories to you." He raised his hand to quell the murmurs of thanks. "On two conditions." The woodman brought his hard gaze to bear on Tarkyn. "That you, Tarkyn Tamadil, will agree to receive *all* the memories I wish you to see and that you, in exchange, will expose your memories of suffering to me."

Tarkyn stared back at him, knowing that Falling Rain was planning to wreak his revenge on him by forcing him to confront the extent of the pain inflicted on the woodman both in captivity and in exile. He also believed that Falling Rain would revel in any pain the prince had endured and consider it to be due punishment for what the woodman had been through. But more than this, Tarkyn knew he had no choice if he was to fulfil his commitment to the woodfolk to protect them. As he drew breath to reply, Lapping Water, Waterstone, Rainstorm and several others rose hotly to his defence.

Falling Rain glared at them. "You people are pathetic. This man should face what was done on his behalf. If you want my knowledge, those are my conditions. Take them or leave them."

Amid another round of protests, Tarkyn said quietly, "I will take them."

"No, Tarkyn," exclaimed Lapping Water. "You shouldn't have to endure this."

Tarkyn raised a hand, as others joined their voices to hers. "After what has happened to him, Falling Rain deserves his pound of flesh. And he is right. Since it was done for my sake, I should be the one to give it to him. Waterstone told him that we would make him reparation in any way we could. So here is an opportunity to do so, at least in part." Tarkyn locked gazes with Falling Rain and, ignoring the burning hatred he saw in the woodman's eyes, asked mildly, "Would you like someone with you while you do this?"

Falling Rain glanced at Tree Wind but then said firmly, "No. This is between you and me only."

Tarkyn shrugged apologetically. "I am afraid I will have to insist that at least one person stands guard over us during the proceedings. I have undertaken not to place myself in unnecessary danger and I'm afraid that, since I have had no undertaking from you not to harm me, I must insure my safety while I am concentrating. If, however, you feel you can give me that assurance, lookouts can be deployed simply to ensure that we are not disturbed."

Falling Rain's eyes narrowed as he considered his options. "And who will ensure that you do not harm me?"

Tarkyn raised his eyebrows slightly. "My oath to protect all woodfolk will ensure that."

Falling Rain realised that everyone around him, whether he agreed with them or not, had complete faith in Tarkyn's word and would not see the need for further protection for him.

Surprisingly, Waterstone spoke up, "I will undertake to offer you protection above and beyond Tarkyn's word. I would not see you feeling isolated and unsupported." He gave a wry smile. "There is not much I could do against Tarkyn's power if he chose to use it, but I could throw myself between you, I suppose." His smile broadened. "And I could argue with him."

Falling Rain's stance relaxed slightly. "Thank you, Waterstone," he said warmly. "That means a great deal to me." He looked back at Tarkyn, "I will give you my word not to harm you until the sunrise. Then I will review it. If you are willing to accept my word, then I will accept your assurance that you will not harm me," he glanced at Waterstone, "and so will not draw on Waterstone's offer of protection."

Tarkyn nodded and stood up. He took a deep breath. "Lead the way. I am sure you will know somewhere near here that will suit our purpose." Without meeting the eyes of any of the gathered woodfolk, their prince walked resolutely out of the clearing in the wake of the vengeful woodman, to accept his punishment for deeds done by others at a time when he was only a small boy.

Falling Rain led them into the depths of nearby pine forest. Once they had pushed their way through the outer skirts of the pine trees, they found themselves in another world of damp mosses and soft pine needles.

Tarkyn murmured, "*Lumaya*," and raised a soft ball of white light. "I hope you don't mind," he said. "Sorcerers aren't as adept in the dark as woodfolk." He gazed around at the closely woven canopy above them and the soft yellow and green mosses that grew in such profusion between and up the trees. A narrow trickle of water gurgled gently as it pushed its way through the moss and pine needles. "This is beautiful in here, isn't it?"

Falling Rain eyed him but didn't reply, simply showing him to a dry spot where they could sit cross-legged opposite each other on a soft bed of dry pine needles. "You can put that out now," he said. "There are luminous fungi on many of these trees. They will give us enough light to be able to discern each other in the darkness."

When Tarkyn extinguished his light, he gradually became

aware of a soft, pale yellow light that was emanating from the trunks of nearby trees. He walked over and peered up closely at the fungi. "What do these look like in daylight?"

Falling Rain shrugged. "Just plain brown, uninteresting fungi. Look. There are similar toadstools over there. Exactly the same. Magical at night. Unexceptional during the day."

"Hmm, amazing." Tarkyn took a sharp breath and became business-like as he returned to take up his position sitting opposite Falling Rain. "Right. I suppose we had better get on with it. You realise I can only send you images and feelings, don't you. But I think that is what you want really, isn't it? The feelings?"

Falling Rain nodded shortly. "And what about you? Can you pick up the words in my memories or only images?"

Tarkyn raised his eyebrow in surprise. "Now you mention it, I realise I can pick up words if they are direct memories but I can't if they are images or mind talking." He settled his elbows into his knees and looked straight into Falling Rain's eyes. "Right. You're calling the shots. So how do you want to do this?"

"You will show me what I ask, then I will show you what I choose. In the end I will show you all you want to know. Agreed?" he asked rhetorically. Falling Rain was clearly enjoying wielding his power. "I understand you were also exiled. Let me see that."

Tarkyn took a deep breath to control his anger. "I think I should remind you that we agreed to be civil to one another. You may not be aware of this but I have a very short temper that I can only partially control. I would not push your advantage too far, if I were you." He took another deep breath, "When you are ready, look into my eyes."

Palace guards stream into my room. Feelings of incomprehension turn to embarrassment and chagrin. I am

marched out into the Great Hall where I stand before all the
guards facing the bench. The king speaks. I am flooded with fear,
horror, anger then desperation. My shield goes up. Assailed on
all sides by beams of light that bounce back and drop the guards
standing around me. Cracks in the walls, great chunks of plaster
raining down around me. I crawl under the table, release my
shield, hold coat button. After a blur, I am suddenly in a quiet
factory with no one around. Shock and sadness.

Tarkyn cut the connection to find Falling Rain staring at
him, wild-eyed. "Did you wreak all that destruction?"

Tarkyn nodded. "More or less. My shield went wrong
because I was upset and reflected the guards' rays instead of
just blocking them. I didn't mean it to happen."

"And what did you do to be brought before the court in the
first place?"

Tarkyn showed him the events of the tournament, adding,
"The charges were completely unjust."

"And who are those two men passing judgement on you?"

"I thought you knew. They are my brothers." Tarkyn's
throat tightened and he looked away into the soft light of the
forest. After a few moments, he cleared his throat and brought
his eyes back to meet Falling Rain's. "What now?" he asked, a
hard edge to his voice.

"I want to see what happened after Tree Wind told you
about the oath when you first came to the forest a few months
ago."

Tarkyn stared at him, feeling a knot of anger in the pit of
his stomach. "I have shown no one this before. Not even
Waterstone. At most, I have made a glancing reference to it.
Remember when you watch it, that besides the instigation of
the oath, I had just seen images of my father who had died
when I was eight years old. You all may have hated him, and
possibly with just cause, but I didn't."

I stumble away from Tree Wind, horrified, and seek sanctuary within a large pine. Feelings of sadness, despair, isolation. Visions of resentful, vengeful woodfolk surrounding me. I feel trapped within the forest. Waves of anger at my father then sorrow. I see an owl looking down at me. Comfort. I pull myself together and steel myself to go out and face the woodfolk.

Tarkyn cut back to the present to find Falling Rain watching him thoughtfully. Tarkyn returned his regard defiantly, refusing to be cowed by having exposed his vulnerability. Eventually, Falling Rain commented, "And I believe you must remain in exile and endure living among us?"

The prince nodded. "Yes to the first and no to the second. I must remain in exile but not alone as you were forced to do. And it is no endurance to live with woodfolk. In fact, I would no longer choose to leave."

"How lucky for us," commented Falling Rain sarcastically. "Hmm. So, before I show you any of the events that I have endured, I need to know that you are capable of feeling for someone other than yourself who is suffering. Can you give me an example of that?"

With those few well-chosen words, Falling Rain diminished the value of everything Tarkyn had so far shown him. Before Tarkyn could stop himself, a huge wave of outrage burst from him and threw Falling Rain against the tree behind him. The woodman hit the tree with a dull thump and slid, senseless, to the ground.

"Oh no! Oh blast! What have I done?" Tarkyn scrambled to his feet and gathered the fallen woodman in his arms. The forest guardian drew on his power and sent a wave of healing gently through his hand into the woodman. After a few agonising minutes, Falling Rain stirred. He opened his eyes and found himself looking up into the anxious eyes of the sorcerer.

He could still feel the soft stream of Tarkyn's healing power flowing through him.

A malicious little smile flittered around Falling Rain's lips. "So much for your oath, Your Highness."

Chagrined, Tarkyn replied tightly, "I apologise. I did warn you not to push me too far. And if I hurt you, I have also healed you. But perhaps we had better curtail this enterprise. No doubt you do not feel safe enough to continue."

Falling Rain sat up and felt around the back of his head. "No bump? Disappointing. Nothing to show the others of your treachery. And no doubt they won't believe me above you."

"I will tell them myself," said Tarkyn calmly. "And I will also show them the memories I have shown you and the lack of respect you accorded them."

"I did not realise that you would be willing to expose your weaknesses like that to everyone," said Falling Rain in surprise, clearly wrong-footed.

"I do not consider my feelings to be weaknesses. I consider my inability to control them to be a weakness at times, such as now. But I trust those woodfolk, as I have never trusted anyone before in my life. And so I am quite happy to reveal my transgression to them. They know who I am and that I would not have meant to hurt you."

"Just like all the guards in the Great Hall?"

Tarkyn narrowed his eyes. "If I didn't know better, I would think you were deliberately goading me. Have you any idea how much danger that places you in?"

Falling Rain shrugged. "If you kill or maim me, you will lose their faith in you and that can only be good for woodfolk. They have become too complacent and have accepted you without enough of a fight."

Tarkyn thought through all the things he had done to gain woodfolk's support, but, in the end, he knew that Falling Rain wanted to see woodfolk resistance. "I will show you one memory to refute that. There are complications attached to it that mean the actions are not just pure woodfolk reactions... but I think you will enjoy it," he added snakily. He paused. "You must undertake to stay to the end of it. Agreed?"

When Falling Rain nodded, Tarkyn opened his memory and brought forth all the horror, helplessness and pain of his beating at the hands of the mountainfolk. Even as a memory, it was hard to endure but he persevered until the last blow had landed and the eagles had come to his rescue. As he cut the connection, he took a short juddering breath to recover and spat out scathingly, "There. Of course, yet again I was only suffering on my own account in that image but I'm afraid no one else was hurt in that instance." He glowered at Falling Rain who was actually looking a little ill. Then, abandoning any hope he might have had for the woodman's good opinion, Tarkyn added spitefully, "Except of course, for my two attackers. Naturally, I had them killed."

As Falling Rain's face tightened, Tarkyn pressed home his advantage. "While I'm at it, why don't I show you what happened to me when Rushwind infected me with the parasites after I tried to heal her? I'm sure you'll get a kick out of that."

Before Falling Rain could recover, he was immersed in images of the invasion of Tarkyn by the grey globules of the infection and the wave of woodfolk anger joining with his own rage to send a searing wave of destruction through the sorcerer's blood veins. Then Falling Rain was engulfed in the blinding pain of the burning aftermath. As he experienced for himself the prince's body going into shock, Falling Rain wrenched his eyes away and broke contact.

Breathing hard, the woodman managed to get out between

clenched teeth, "You have still not shown me any instance where you have felt pain for someone else."

Tarkyn glared at him, his own breath coming in gasps. "Actually, you misunderstood. The source of that horror when I first found out about the oath was on behalf of woodfolk's plight, not my own, but I will be happy to show you other examples." He sneered at Falling Rain. "Try not to pull out this time until it's finished."

With that, he blasted Falling Rain with episode after episode of Danton being punished while the young Tarkyn, beside himself with guilt, helplessness and misery for his friend, looked on screaming and struggling to break away from whoever was holding him. Finally, he came to the time when, desperate and determined, he had outfaced his father and cut himself to stop Danton being whipped. Staring white-faced at Falling Rain, he gasped, "So, now you have your proof. I will suffer when I see what you go through. So, having revelled in watching me endure my own pain again, you can now force me to endure yours."

Unexpectedly, the silence went on and on. Falling Rain met his gaze unswervingly but said nothing. Eventually he cleared his throat and said quietly, "When I saw you standing up to King Markazon, I realised I was punishing the wrong person."

"What? Even after I had those mountainfolk killed?"

"Having lived through that attack with you, I think I would have done the same if I could have. If I looked shocked, that was why. I was dealing with that knowledge about myself." Ignoring Tarkyn's surprise, he asked quietly, "How old were you when the oath was first sworn?"

"Seven," said Tarkyn shortly. After a moment, he sighed. "But although I did not engineer it, it was done for my sake. And so you are justified in laying your suffering at my door."

Falling Rain stood up and walked away a few paces before turning to face the prince. He stood a little distance away, hands on his hips, studying Tarkyn, thinking about the similarities and the differences between Markazon and the prince. After a while, Tarkyn found himself a long stick and began to break bits of the end of it. Falling Rain returned and sat down again.

"Your Highness, I am ashamed of what I have just put you through. You knew, didn't you, that I would subject you to this and how much it would hurt you? And yet you were willing to endure it for the sake of our woodfolk. Having seen how much you suffered watching Danton, I know I could easily put you through further torment that again you would accept, to gain the information we all need to stay safe." A little smile played around Falling Rain's lips. "Power can be seductive, can't it? I don't think I have handled it very well."

Tarkyn said nothing and after a few moments, the woodman continued, "And now I think about it, you could just as easily have forced the information out of me. After all, it is not a betrayal of my people to give it to you and so my resolve for withholding it would not have been all that strong. In the service of protecting the woodfolk, you could have justified all manner of ill treatment to force it out of me."

Tarkyn glanced up at him before returning his attention to a second stick he had found. When he had meticulously destroyed it, piece by piece, he looked up and brushed his hands off. "Falling Rain, I am not in the business of justifying ill treatment. I did not travel halfway across the country to find you, just to alienate you further. If you needed to wreak your revenge on me, so be it. I'm sorry I wasn't quite strong enough to endure it without my anger sending you flying, but ..." Tarkyn shrugged. After a moment, he said ruminatively, "I liked you when I first met you and you let me feed your egret.

You seemed to be a reflective, gentle type of person. But perhaps your bitterness had not yet worked its way to the surface. Has it warped you beyond repair? I hope not."

"You were very harsh with me, Sire, when we first met. I was fearful of you and you did nothing to reassure me in the first few minutes. By the time you had taken me to task for mistaking your status, all my fears of Markazon's son had been confirmed."

Tarkyn inclined his head. "I'm sorry. You were caught in the middle of my uncertainty. I was disappointed and offended that you had been borne off without being introduced to me." He gave a rueful smile. "I am a difficult character for you woodfolk to contend with. Despite our friendships and the absence of court protocols, I still require recognition of my status. It can be confusing for all of us, at times."

"You look just like him, you know."

"Do I?" Tarkyn couldn't help smiling. "I'm sorry. I know you hated my father but I didn't, even though as you saw, I didn't always accept his judgement."

Falling Rain regarded the prince quizzically. "If you don't mind me asking, what happened after you stood up to the king like that?"

"Firstly, he threatened to have Danton and me put to death as punishment for defying him." Seeing Falling Rain's shocked expression, he grimaced. "My actions did amount to treason, you know."

The woodman shook his head. "What? Even though you were his son?"

"Yes, even so." Tarkyn glanced at Falling Rain then looked away. "When I realised I was risking Danton's life, it shook me up badly. So I apologised and explained I had only been trying to protect my friend." He shook his head. "I was a stubborn bugger though. Even though I was shaking and crying, I still kept my shield up."

Falling Rain frowned. "So did the flogging continue?"

"No. My father accepted my explanation enough to send Danton out of the room and deal with me privately."

"I see." Clearly Falling Rain would have liked to know more but after his previous intrusions on Tarkyn's privacy, forbore to ask.

Tarkyn gave a little smile. "After all I have shown you, I might as well show you this. You never know, you may think better of him afterwards. I will tell you what is said as it happens."

I am still encased in my shield. My knees are shaking so much they can barely hold me up and I am beginning to feel frightened about all my blood that is dripping into a big pool at my feet. My father walks away from me. He turns and stands by the long drawing room window, silhouetted against the light, with his hands on his hips, just staring at me. After what seems like an age, he finally asks quietly, "And will you remove your shield now, my son?"

I nod and drop my shield. Still he doesn't move. "In the quiet of that big gloomy room, I could hear my blood dripping onto the floor." *I can't do anything about wrapping my arm or stopping the bleeding. Now that Danton's danger has passed, I am rooted to the spot with fear, tears trickling down my face. My father walks over to me and pulls out his handkerchief. Without a word, he takes the piece of vase out of my hand and throws it away across the room. Then he raises my arm and binds it. When he has finished, he lifts me up and swings me onto his knee as he sits down in a big padded armchair. As soon as he is holding me, my tears redouble and I let go completely. He just holds me and lets me cry myself out.*

Tarkyn cut the image to say to the woodman, "And then, do you know what he said to me?"

Falling Rain shook his head.

He looks down at me, his amber eyes glowing in the late afternoon light. "You put us all to shame, my son." *He smiles at me and I try to understand what he means as he keeps speaking.* "You are the best of us but you will suffer for it. And in the end, you must be the one to bring hope to our nation and save us from ourselves." *For a while, he sits there in silence, holding me and thinking. Then suddenly, he swings me off his knee and stands up. He glowers down at me.* "Now, I want no more scenes and disobedience." *When I nod unconvincingly, he smiles slightly and gives his head a little shake.* "I will ensure that your friend no longer suffers in your stead. In future, you will both be brought to book together." *He frowns.* "Now, will you undertake to do as I ask?"

I nod. "I told him I was sorry," Tarkyn explained.

My father shakes his head. "No, you're not. You would do it again, wouldn't you?"

I stare up at him for a moment before replying, "No, sir. Not if Danton might lose his life over it. I would have to find another way."

My father smiles broadly at that and shaking his head, gives me a big final hug before striding off, leaving me standing alone in the gloomy drawing room next to the pool of my own blood.

Falling Rain let out a long breath. "Whew. I begin to see why you might like him but he's still scary."

"Oh yes," agreed Tarkyn. "He was always scary. Even when he was being kind, you never knew when he might turn. Having so much power is very hard to manage and he was volatile anyway."

"But you allowed me to have so much power over you. And now I have let myself and, I suppose, you down by misusing it."

Tarkyn looked at him and smiled. "If you are worrying about having let me down, then you must be starting to care about what I think of you. So that's something, I suppose. However, you did not let me down because I didn't entrust you with that power, in the expectation that you wouldn't misuse it. When you made your proposal, I assumed you would abuse it to its fullest extent and hurt me as much as you could. I suppose I feel responsible enough for what happened to you, to allow you to do that to me." He gave a short laugh. "As it turns out, you've stopped halfway."

"But you didn't take into account how I would feel about myself for abusing someone like that," objected Falling Rain.

"No, you're right. I didn't. On the other hand, it was your choice not mine, what you did with that power."

"Wow," exclaimed Falling Rain. "You're tough, aren't you? Making me take all the blame for how I acted with it."

Tarkyn raised his eyebrows. "It may not have occurred to you, but like my father, I have enormous power at my command all the time. Only I am responsible for how I use it. I could abuse it and force all manner of unkindness on the people around me, but I don't. As you pointed out, woodfolk could be suffering under the oath but they are not, beyond the loss of their autonomy which was, after all, their choice a long time ago, not mine."

Falling Rain mulled this over in silence, gradually becoming more and more solemn.

After a little while, Tarkyn said, "I think I was right in my first assessment of your character. You are gentle. Perhaps I was unkind in giving you that power. I didn't mean to be. But if your bitterness has played itself out, it will be worth it."

Falling Rain raised his eyes from his contemplation of the moss at his feet. "But what will everyone think of me when you tell them how I behaved?"

707

"Everyone was expecting you to behave like that. That's why there were so many protests. But I am not going to run back and tell them what has passed privately between you and me. I only said that before, because you were threatening me. Besides, I turned a lot of it back on you, in case you hadn't noticed. Since I was forced to show you my memories, I threw them at you. I am not the only one who has been upset by this process, am I?"

Falling Rain's eyes narrowed and he shook his head. "No, I felt every blow that landed on you, every burn and every raw emotion. I have never experienced mind images like yours before. And you threw them at me in such a fury. Was that because you were forced to endure the pain again?"

Tarkyn's eyes lit with laughter. "No. I didn't particularly like having to re-experience the pain, but more than that, I hated submitting to your demands. I'm an ornery bastard. Remember I told you when we first met, I answer to no one. I submitted my will to you for the welfare of our people but it enraged me. I felt like a caged lion."

"Whew! I think I was taking a bigger risk than I realised," said Falling Rain ruminatively.

"I did warn you. In fact, I thought I controlled myself very well."

"Except for the little matter of throwing me against the tree," put in the woodman dryly.

"Hmm, yes. That was a bit of an error. But that wasn't deliberate. That was a spurt of outrage beyond my control. You can tell them about that if you like and I won't say explicitly why I did it." Tarkyn chuckled. "They all know I'm a well-meaning loose cannon."

"You know," said Falling Rain sadly, "I could have been your friend, if I'd behaved better. We have a lot in common; closeness with animals, both being exiled, being turned away by our own kin," he flicked a quick glance at Tarkyn and looked away again, "even though you are a sorcerer... and Markazon's son."

"Falling Rain, I know you haven't been here to see our friendship develop, but Waterstone and I are the best of friends. And yet we often fight. He says some horrible things to me and hurts me really badly at times. But we are still friends. I would be pleased and honoured, especially in view of your attitude to sorcerers, if you could consider me your friend... and I would like to count you as one of mine." He gave a quirky smile. "Besides, now you know more about some of the things I've experienced, than most other people do."

A slow smile dawned on Falling Rain's face. "Of all the things I ever imagined about returning home, the last would have been that I made friends with the tyrant sent to rule over us."

"Be nice. I'm not a tyrant."

Falling Rain laughed. "Obviously not, but that's what I expected." He looked at Tarkyn for a few moments. "So. Shall we do it? Look at my memories and see who these people were? I won't show you all of it, as I was going to. I'll just show you what you need. Pull out any time if you want to."

Tarkyn smiled at him. "Now we may have swung too far the other way. Without ramming it down my throat, there may be some things you want to share with me as a fellow exile. What do you think?"

Falling Rain gave his head a little shake. "I'm getting a bit confused. Why would you want to experience it, if you don't have to?"

"So, I know something of what you have been through." Tarkyn shrugged. "You don't have to, but I have shown you a lot about myself that I wouldn't normally have done."

"And in friendship, one reciprocates." Falling Rain smiled.

"But now, it will be our choice, not me forcing you to watch my memories to punish you."

"You see? It will feel different, even though the same thing is happening," said Tarkyn.

"I will show you when I was exiled," offered Falling Rain, his voice suddenly tight.

I am still weak from the illness but I can no longer stay. The king left two days ago and the controversy which erupted in his wake is still raging.

"Our whole way of life has been overturned," says Thunder Storm. "Nothing will ever be the same again. One false move and we may lose our forests."

"And this is because you led them to our door, knowing that we would be unable to leave. You are a disgrace to our nation," proclaims Running Feet.

My stomach turns over and my knees feel as though they may not be able to support me.

Waterstone, grim-faced, raises his arm and points into the distance. "And so, since you have broken our code of secrecy, with such disastrous consequences, you must remove yourself from the lands of the woodfolk and live where no woodfolk or sorcerer will find you."

"Do you understand?" asks Creaking Bough. When I nod mutely, she says, "Now go."

I turn away from them and start walking, holding in the tears, without looking back.

"Oh, Falling Rain! I can't imagine how bad that must have felt. At least when I was exiled, I knew I had been wrongly accused. So, I felt hard done by, but not guilty as you felt. But I still felt so jarred and shocked by it all. And it took my exile to bring me into the woods and discover that Stormaway had used mind control on you." Suddenly, Tarkyn eyes twinkled. "Just as well I was exiled then, wasn't it?"

Falling Rain laughed. "Yes, it was. I can't believe how good it feels to have someone who has been through the same thing as I have. You can't explain it to someone who hasn't been through it. Not really."

"No. I don't think they would begin to understand that degree of isolation. Saying that, I only had to experience it for a few weeks until I came to know woodfolk. You've had it unremittingly for twelve years."

"Yes, but now at last I'm back with my kin and you may never be."

Tarkyn shrugged. "Now that I'm used to basic food and hard floors for beds, I don't think I care. I feel happier and safer here than I ever did in Tormadell. After all, if my brothers can betray me like that, what is there to go back for?"

Falling Rain considered him. "Yes, that is a difference, isn't it? Because even though it nearly broke my heart, at least I knew they were acting in good faith, not as an act of betrayal. In essence I agreed with their judgement. I had the guilt to deal with. You had betrayal."

"And betrayal like that destroys the whole foundations of your faith in people," added Tarkyn sombrely. After a moment, he chuckled, "Poor old Waterstone; sat beside me for two weeks as I recovered from injury and then had to endure my suspicion of him when I awoke. I couldn't believe he would offer friendship without wanting something in return." He smiled. "You see? You are gaining from all that hard work that Waterstone put in. It didn't even cross my mind that you might want my friendship to use me."

Falling Rain frowned a little. "What could I hope to gain that I couldn't just get by asking?"

Tarkyn grinned. "Thus the woodfolk mind. Straight as a die. I love it. Sorcerers at court develop friendships to gain favours and to get closer to other people of influence. You see, if you just went to my brother's court, and asked for something, chances are you wouldn't get it. So you have to manoeuvre people instead."

Falling Rain shook his head. "Sounds unnecessarily complicated to me. Let's get on and do this bit of memory when I'm being held captive by Stormaway. Look into my eyes."

I feel terribly sick and afraid. I am in a strange, solid, enormous building. There are no plants anywhere, only flat hard walls with pictures and tapestries hanging on them. King Markazon and Stormaway are leaning over me, studying me. A knock comes on the door. Stormaway opens it slightly and takes a plate of food and a cup of water from someone out of sight. He brings it back and leaves it on the table next to my bed, indicating that it is for me. Then the king and he both leave. As soon as the door closes behind them, a scrawny lad appears from behind a curtain at the other end of the room and takes away the food. I don't really care. I am too ill to be hungry.

"That's Journeyman, I think," breathed Tarkyn. "Keep going. Was there anyone else?"

I am just settling down to sleep and the curtain pulls aside again and a slightly older youth come in and sits beside me. After looking surreptitiously at the door, he begins to whisper demands to know what Stormaway wants with me. When I close my eyes, he shakes me awake again.

"And that's Jarand," said Tarkyn quietly.

"I think that's it," replied Falling Rain.

"Could you just show me a bit more to be certain, please?"

The night wears on into a blur of the youth and the scrawny boy alternating their visits. Each time, the person sits on the bed and whispers to me asking where I'm from and what I'm doing here. I get tireder and tireder but I refuse to answer. At dawn, Stormaway enters once more, clears away the empty plate and brings me breakfast.

Falling Rain broke contact. "Enough?"

"Wait. Can you just go back and show me the second last visit by the youth again?"

The young man walks in, glances at the door and sits down on the edge of the bed...

"Okay. You can stop. That is not the same youth as before. That is Kosar. You saw the wizard's apprentice and my twin brothers, Jarand and Kosar. And that curtain at the end of the room... I wonder if they were able to stay concealed behind it while Markazon and Stormaway were talking?" Tarkyn shook his head. "I wonder how much my brothers knew of all this? Of woodfolk, the oath, my legacy of the forest?" He smiled at Falling Rain. "Do you want to show me anything else? Did you see any other sorcerers at any time?"

Falling Rain shook his head. "No to both. I think we've both had enough for tonight." He hesitated. "And, Tarkyn, I am sorry that I treated you so badly."

When they re-entered the clearing, it was clear even from a distance that things had changed between them.

"I think Tarkyn has wrought some more of that magic he used on you," said Waterstone dryly to Running Feet.

Running Feet shook his head, smiling. "I don't know how he does it."

Waterstone grunted with laughter. "I don't think he does either. He just stays true to himself and resistance melts around him."

"Eventually," added Tree Wind. "It doesn't always happen straight away."

"No," agreed Rainstorm. "He said you'd reverted to type."

"I haven't. I only said one mean thing," replied Tree Wind hotly. "And you can't blame me. I was upset about Falling Rain's treatment while he was held captive."

"You mean, when Tarkyn was seven?" Rainstorm said sarcastically. "No wonder you thought you should pick on him. Obviously the one responsible."

Tree Wind threw her hands up. "All right, all right. I'm sorry." As Tarkyn walked up, she turned to him and said, "I apologise for what I said to you. Now, do you think you can get your young champion off my back? He's hounding me to death."

Tarkyn grinned. "What a fine young man he is." A thought struck him and he turned to Falling Rain. "Falling Rain, I don't suppose you really know young Rainstorm here. He would only have been four years old when you left. And over here is North Wind. He too would have been quite young."

Falling Rain smiled and nodded at them before turning to Waterstone. "And I believe you have a daughter, Waterstone... and that you lost Skylark. I was sorry to hear that."

"Yes." Waterstone cleared his throat. "Skylark survived the sickness, only to die six years later in a hunting accident. But despite that, I am grateful that the sickness was cured, even at the cost of the oath, because otherwise I wouldn't have had my little Sparrow."

"And Sparrow is worth her weight in gold..." Tarkyn grinned. "Not that I'm a prejudiced uncle or anything."

Rainstorm frowned suspiciously. "So, Tarkyn, what are you so happy about, all of a sudden? You looked pretty bleak when you left with Falling Rain two hours ago."

The prince beamed. "I have found a new friend in my fellow exile, Falling Rain. After a fairly long-winded exchange of ... hmm, what would we call it?... unpleasantries?... we realised that we had quite a bit in common, not least of which is that we have both been exiled. And I have just realised, we both wear our hair extremely long. Another similarity. Marvellous!"

Falling Rain smiled, a little less exuberantly, and said, "Yes, and we both have an affinity with egrets. So there you are. I didn't annihilate your prince after all, though I did put him through the wringer for a while."

"And I didn't annihilate Falling Rain, although in a moment of lapsed control, I did slam him against a tree and knock him out."

Waterstone frowned. "You did what?"

Tarkyn smiled apologetically. "Well, not me exactly. My outrage did it." The sorcerer glanced at Falling Rain. "He was being rather provocative, you know, and I'm afraid for a split second, I lost it."

"Did you hit him?" demanded Rainstorm, eyes shining with excitement.

"No, of course I didn't. It was just one of those waves of spontaneous emotion, well, a small tidal wave of outrage, if you must know."

"Like the one that rocked us backwards when you were happy at becoming a woodman?" asked Rainstorm.

"Something like that but rather stronger." Tarkyn grimaced. "To be honest, I think Falling Rain was thrown through the air by it."

"Stars above, Tarkyn!" exclaimed Waterstone, not at all pleased. "You could have killed him. You are going to have get these emotions of yours under control. You can't just say your anger did it."

Falling Rain's eyes twinkled as he watched Tarkyn meekly accepting a woodman's censure. Nevertheless, he rose to the prince's defence. "He did warn me not to push too hard and I ignored him. He healed me, so there's no harm done. And quite frankly, I more or less deserved it. I was quite poisonous for a while there," he glanced at Tarkyn with a smile, "wasn't I?"

"Absolutely putrid," agreed Tarkyn, smiling in return. "I wasn't much better myself. Autumn Leaves, if you thought I behaved badly when I pushed Waterstone for his memories...

THE WIZARD'S CURSE

well, suffice it to say...that was chicken feed compared to what we have just been through."

"So, who were the other sorcerers, Tarkyn? Or did you forget to find that out?" asked Stormaway dryly.

Tarkyn waved his hand airily. "No, no. We found out." Suddenly he became serious. "They were Journeymen, Jarand... and Kosar."

"What! All three of them?" asked Stormaway in consternation. "I thought it would be Journeyman and I thought it would possibly be Jarand because Journeyman is based at the campsite run by Jarand's crony. But it didn't occur to me that Kosar would also be involved. Hmm, this requires some thinking."

"It is even worse than that," said Tarkyn. "Up one end of your room was a curtain through which they left and entered. I suspect they could have been hiding behind it at any time during your discussions with Markazon about devising the oath."

Stormaway frowned with the effort of memory. "That curtain hid the entrance to a secret passageway. The palace was riddled with them. But I didn't realise Journeyman knew about it. I had placed a glamour on it from my side of the wall so it couldn't be seen if you moved the curtain."

"Stormaway, didn't you think a curtain over a blank wall was likely to arouse his suspicions?" demanded Rainstorm dryly.

The wizard looked at him in some irritation. "Give me some credit, Rainstorm. There was an alcove behind the curtain with shelves full of herbs and equipment along one side of it. The curtain hid my mess when important people such as the King visited my rooms. The entrance to the passage was along the opposite wall of the alcove. But because it was so disorganised, there wasn't room to hide behind that curtain unless the door to the passage was open. So Journeyman must somehow have figured out that it was there and traced it from the other side. Blast it! Maybe he was smarter than I gave him credit for."

"Considering he managed to oust you from your own post," said Rainstorm dryly, "I would say that he almost certainly was."

"Yes, well, quite," huffed Stormaway.

"If Kosar and Jarand were listening while you planned with Markazon to hand over the sovereignty of all the woodlands of Eskuzor to me, I am hardly surprised that neither of them felt they would be able to trust you as their advisor." Tarkyn ran his hand through his hair as he sat down. "You're lucky to have come away with your life."

Stormaway went pale. "Oh my stars! This is a disastrous development. I will have to think through everything I ever said or did that may have been overheard."

"And we don't know who overheard what, and whether they would have shared it with the others!" exclaimed Danton.

Tarkyn raised his eyebrows at Falling Rain. "And thus the sorcerer mind. Crooked as a dog's hind leg, present company excepted... Hmm, except for Stormaway...Hmm, and Danton, now I come to think of it." He smiled. "Well, String and Bean are pretty straight forward, I think."

"So is Tarkyn, for your information," said Danton, wandering over to an earthen ware jug and pouring out two cups of wine. Over his shoulder, he continued, "He tries to be discerning of other people's motives but in reality, he's totally gullible and can only stay safe from sorcerer intrigue by holding himself aloof." He smiled at Tarkyn. "True?"

"True, I'm afraid." Tarkyn shook his head ruefully. "That's why I could never be king."

Stormaway was clearly unconvinced by this remark but didn't take issue with it.

Instead, he said sternly, "Tarkyn, it may no longer be your choice whether to become involved in sorcerer affairs. Someone is obviously hunting for you and for the woodfolk. And you realise now that it is highly likely that at least one of your brothers knows about the oath and its tie to the destruction of the forest."

"Stormaway's right, Tarkyn," said Danton as he walked back over and handed the prince and Falling Rain a cup of wine each. "Remember, when Journeyman realised you weren't a rogue sorcerer, he said, 'This changes everything.'"

Tarkyn stared at him. "So he knew that the oath would be galvanised by my integrity." Unconsciously, he let his eyes rest on Lapping Water, who was seated a short distance away talking to Ancient Oak. He gave a sad smile. "Maybe I will have to leave you all, to keep you safe."

Waterstone walked over to him and put his hand on the prince's shoulder. "No, Tarkyn. The opposite is true. It is more important than ever that we stick together and keep each other from capture. Because they will know that one of us will lead to the others, because of the oath."

Tarkyn rubbed his hand across his forehead. "And what if I find that I can no longer stand by and endure the sorcerers' suffering? What then?"

Surprisingly, Falling Rain spoke, "I am sure you will not be able to. You could not let yourself, your father or the kingdom down like that."

There was a stunned silence.

"What are you talking about?" asked Waterstone tightly.

Falling Rain glanced at Tarkyn for permission to share his private knowledge. After receiving the faintest of nods, he went on, "It is what King Markazon said to Tarkyn after he stood up for Danton." He looked around. "Do you know about this incident?"

"Yes, Danton told us," replied Autumn Leaves, "but no one knows what happened afterwards."

Falling Rain sent a gentle smile to Danton and then to Tarkyn. "That fearsome Markazon, whom we all love to hate, cradled his determined little son in his arms and said, 'Tarkyn, you put us all to shame. You are the best of us but you will suffer for it. And in the end, you must be the one to bring hope to our nation and save us from ourselves.'"

Stormaway grunted. "You see? Just as I told you. I agree with you completely, Falling Rain. Tarkyn will not be able to stand by for much longer and watch sorcerers suffer."

Falling Rain shook his head decisively. "No. Having felt how hard it was for him to endure Danton's suffering, there is no way he will be able to endure the suffering of an entire nation."

"Well," said Tree Wind philosophically, looking around the group, "we all agreed after we rescued Golden Toad and Rushwind, that we would find Falling Rain first and then reconsider our position. And Tarkyn has worked unremittingly for us since then. So I guess it's time to help him."

Autumn Leaves, too, walked over and placed his hand on Tarkyn's other shoulder. "If we have to work with you to help your sorcerers, we will find a way." Coming from Autumn Leaves, sorcerer-hater extraordinaire, this was quite a concession.

Watching them, Falling Rain could see that the oath had no part to play in the support they were offering Tarkyn.

Waterstone's eyes met Danton's. "So, my friend. It looks as though we won't tear your prince in two, after all. We will all stand behind him and, as the woodfolk nation, help him to resolve the affairs of sorcerers."

As they spoke, they could see the tension leeching out of Tarkyn as he understood that he no longer had to manage the burden of the sorcerers' affairs alone. He gave a wry smile. "Of course, I have no idea how we're going to do it."

String and Bean looked at each other.

"If it's a conundrum you're facing, Your Highness," said Bean, with a smile. "We may have to stick around and help you too... beyond the six months, that is. If you'll all allow us to stay."

"Yeah," agreed String. "Politics, we don't like. Puzzles, we do." He shrugged. "Anyway, once you get over first impressions, you're not such a political person yourself, are you, Your Highness?"

This was such an exquisite contradiction in terms that everyone was bereft of speech.

Then slowly, a huge grin dawned on the prince's face. "I think you have hit on the crux of my difficulties. By birth, I am about as political as you can get. By nature, I am not. Naivety and politics are a very unwieldy combination."

"They are a very dangerous combination, my lord," said Stormaway sternly. "But thankfully, you will also have Danton and me beside you every step of the way and both of us are masters of politics and intrigue. So, with any luck, between us all, we will prevail."

"And at least now, no matter what happens, the forest is no longer endangered," said Tarkyn with some satisfaction.

"Isn't it?" asked Falling Rain.

"No," replied Tree Wind, smiling. "True to his word, Tarkyn had the sorcery in the oath removed as soon as he knew how, and it now relies solely on our honour."

"Did you?" Falling Rain smiled. "Well, that's a relief." He frowned slightly. "Why didn't you just waive the whole thing?"

A ripple of tension flowed through the woodfolk until

Waterstone cleared his throat and said firmly, "If you remember, we made that vow as a debt of gratitude to Markazon. Regardless of Tarkyn's wishes, we feel honour-bound to uphold it."

"I see. And your view on it?" asked Falling Rain with the temerity that only someone not steeped in the culture of the group could bring to a conversation.

Tarkyn looked around at everyone and gave a little smile. "When I first found out about the oath and how it was imposed, I would have done anything to destroy it completely. But now? Now I feel I have done enough to earn everyone's allegiance. Besides, I am a Prince of Eskuzor, which matters to me if not to you, and I am the guardian of the forest, which matters to all of us. So, if the choice were solely mine, I would not wish to waive it, now that the forest is safe."

"Anyway," said Rainstorm, "Tarkyn's in no position to release the oath because his commitment is greater than ours and he'd be doing himself more of a favour than us," He smiled evilly at Tarkyn and crossed his arms, "You can't release yourself from an onerous oath. It would be dishonourable."

"Besides," said Waterstone dryly, "our young prince here is nowhere near ready for equality." He smiled at Tarkyn. "Are you?"

Tarkyn eyes twinkled. "No. And never will be. And have no intention of trying to be."

The woodfolk shook their heads and smiled at him, clearly humouring his odd outlook.

Falling Rain let his eyes rove around the group, watching everyone's reactions. "Things have certainly changed since the wrought, raw days following Markazon's visit." He paused for a moment before deciding to add, knowing he would betray some more of his recently gained knowledge. "And since Tarkyn's return into the forest. I applaud you all, sorcerers and woodfolk alike. I never expected to walk back into such harmony."

This pronouncement was met with laughter and several people at once explaining that things weren't always so easy. As he listened to the history of the last few months, Falling Rain looked up and met Tarkyn's amber eyes watching him across the sea of people between them. A smile passed between them before Falling Rain was once more submerged in the enthusiasm around him.

———

Thank you for reading my book. If you enjoyed it, won't you please take a moment to leave me a review at your favorite retailer?
Thanks!

Jennifer Ealey

Dear reader,

We hope you enjoyed reading *The Wizard's Curse*. Please take a moment to leave a review in Amazon, even if it's a short one. Your opinion is important to us.

The story continues in *The Lost Forest*.

To read the first chapter for free, head to https://www.nextchapter.pub/books/the-lost-forest

Discover more books by Jennifer Ealey at https://www.nextchapter.pub/authors/jennifer-ealey

Want to know when one of our books is free or discounted for Kindle? Join the newsletter at http://eepurl.com/bqqB3H

Best regards,

Jennifer Ealey and the Next Chapter Team

THE SORCERER'S OATH SERIES

The Sorcerer's Oath Series Book 3: The Lost Forest

The raging wind threw sharp snowflakes into their eyes and faces. Visibility was reduced to a few feet and although it was almost noon, the day was as dark as dawn. And in the swirling stinging whiteness, stumbling through knee-deep snow, some fell and lost their hold. By the time the travellers reached the relative shelter of the forest edge, the gale was lashing the tops of the pine trees, bending them almost horizontal. The roar of the wind through the pines was deafening. The branches above the woodfolk provided scant cover and only standing in the lee of the trees reduced the force of the icy wind.

But when the woodfolk and sorcerers, frozen and wet, took stock, they realised that nearly a quarter of their number was missing. String and Bean gathered them together, urging them to stay within the tress and wait for the others. They peered out around the trees but the storm was at its height and only a haze of driven snow greeted their eyes.

String shook his head and shouted above the noise of the

storm, "There is no point in going back out into that. Look! Our tracks are almost gone already. You won't find them and you will become lost yourselves."

"Let's hope they are all together and will find their way to shelter," yelled Bean. He looked around. "Who's missing?"

Tree Wind replied but her voice blended in too well with the wind to be heard. When String shook his head and put his hand to his ear, Thunder Storm repeated what she had said, his voice rumbling loudly against the noise of the storm.

"Tarkyn's missing. Midnight, Waterstone, Lapping Water, Melting Snow, Running Feet, Falling Rain... What about Sparrow?"

"I'm here," came a small voice from the back. When everyone looked around, they saw her clinging determinedly to Creaking Bough's hand.

"Anyone else?" yelled String.

"Harkell," bellowed Danton. Falling Branch pushed to the front. "Rainstorm's not here either. Neither is Autumn Leaves."

"What are we going to do?" demanded Danton. "We can't just sit here letting them freeze out there." He turned to the old wizard. "Stormaway, can you do anything to get rid of this storm?"

The wizard shook his head. "This storm is huge. It would take me over an hour to have any effect on it...even then I'm not sure that I would have enough power."

"Tree Wind, Thunder Storm, can you contact them? Can you direct them towards us?"

The woodfolk went out of focus, sending their minds out to find the others. After a few minutes, Thunder Storm breathed a sigh of relief and reported, "It's all right. A couple of them lost their footing and the others stopped to help them up and lost contact with the rest of us. They are all together and just approaching the tree line now."

But the minutes ticked by and still there was no sign of them. Another round of mind talking produced the information that the lost group had reached the tree line. But still they were not in sight.

"They must have veered off slightly and have entered the forest either above or below us," shouted Bean.

Suddenly, an image of huge, twisted, deciduous trees, untouched by the raging wind, came through to the woodfolk from Melting Snow. The images meant nothing to most of them but galvanised Hail and Blizzard.

Blizzard shouted at String and Bean, "They're lost. They are nowhere near us. Somehow, they have entered the Lost Forest"

String stared at them. "I didn't know that was real. I thought it was a myth."

Hail glared back. "It is a myth. But so is Tarkyn."

"So, what do we do?" shouted Bean.

"We seek shelter." Hail's voice brooked no argument. "There is nothing we can do for them."

ABOUT THE AUTHOR

Jennifer Jane Ealey was born in outback Western Australia where her father was studying kangaroos on a research station, one hundred miles from the nearest town. Her arrival into the world was watched, unexpectedly, by their pet kangaroo who had hopped into the hospital. Having survived the excitement of her birth, she moved firstly to Perth and then Melbourne where she spent most of her formative years. She took a year off from studying to ride a motorbike around Australia before working as a mathematics teacher and school psychologist in England and Australia, a bicycle courier in London and running a pub in outback New South Wales.

She now lives in Melton, a country town just outside Melbourne, working by day as a psychologist and beavering away by night as a novelist. She has written two detective novels and has just completed *The Sorcerer's Oath,* a series of four fantasy novels, of which *The Wizard's Curse* is the second.

THE SORCERERS' OATH SERIES
Bronze Magic
Wizard's Curse
The Lost Forest
The Sorceress

I really appreciate you reading my book! Here are my social media coordinates:

Friend me on Facebook:
http://facebook.com/jenny.ealey

Follow me on Twitter:
http://twitter.com/jenniferealey

Visit my website:
http://www.jennyealey.com

The Wizard's Curse
ISBN: 978-4-86747-170-8

Published by
Next Chapter
1-60-20 Minami-Otsuka
170-0005 Toshima-Ku, Tokyo
+818035793528

13th May 2021

Lightning Source UK Ltd.
Milton Keynes UK
UKHW011833090223
416682UK00004B/257